RAVES FOR NELSON DeMILLE AND
THE TALBOT ODYSSEY

"DeMILLE'S PLOTTING IS SOPHISTICATED."
—*New York Daily News*

"DeMILLE DEFTLY HANDLES ALL THE ELEMENTS OF A QUICKLY PACED STORY."   —*Philadelphia Inquirer*

"A STORY IN THE GRAND TRADITION OF ACTION ROMANCE...MR. DeMILLE IS THE ESTABLISHED MASTER OF THE TICKING-BOMB STORY...At the end the reader will be drained—perhaps still frightened."   —Andrew M. Greeley

"WILL KEEP THE READER'S ADRENALINE FLOWING FULL BLAST FROM BEGINNING TO END...[DeMille] has taken an imaginative and complicated plot and very skillfully made it sound plausible—and chilling."   —*Richmond Times-Dispatch*

"DeMILLE KNOWS HOW TO BUILD SUSPENSE TO A NAIL-BITING CLIMAX."   —*Newark Star-Ledger*

"A PREMIER STORYTELLER, AND HIS PLOTS ARE AS FRESH AS TODAY'S HEADLINES...DeMILLE MAY BE THE FIRST WRITER IN THE FIELD OF TERRORISM."
—*Jackson Sun (TN)*

NOVELS BY NELSON DeMILLE

By the Rivers of Babylon
Cathedral
The Talbot Odyssey
Word of Honor
The Charm School
The Gold Coast
The General's Daughter
Spencerville
Plum Island
The Lion's Game
Up Country
Night Fall
Wild Fire
The Gate House
The Lion
The Panther
The Quest
Radiant Angel

With Thomas Block

Mayday

For more information please visit:
www.nelsondemille.net

Nelson DeMille

The Talbot Odyssey

GC

GRAND CENTRAL
PUBLISHING

NEW YORK   BOSTON

Grand Central Publishing
Hachette Book Group
1290 Avenue of the Americas
New York, NY 10104

www.HachetteBookGroup.com

Printed in the United States of America

RRD-C

First trade edition: August 2015
10 9 8 7 6 5 4 3 2 1

Grand Central Publishing is a division of Hachette Book Group, Inc.
The Grand Central Publishing name and logo are trademarks of Hachette Book Group, Inc.

The Hachette Speakers Bureau provides a wide range of authors for speaking events. To find out more, go to www.hachettespeakersbureau.com or call (866) 376-6591.

The publisher is not responsible for websites (or their content) that are not owned by the publisher.

ISBN 978-1-4555-8183-2 (pbk.)

33614080531964

In memory of Clark DeMille
and Morris Wasserman

Acknowledgments

Very special gratitude is due Judith Shafran for her patient and inspired editing.

I'd also like to thank Joseph E. Persico for sharing with me his knowledge of the Office of Strategic Services, Daniel Starer for his careful research, and Herbert F. Gallagher and Michael P. Stafford for their insights into the fraternity of the law.

Thanks to Daniel Barbiero, Bernard Geis, and the late great Reverend D.P. Noonan for their encouragement while I was working on this book.

Regarding Persons and Places

The major characters in this novel are entirely fictional. Actual persons of public prominence have been included within the story in appropriate settings.

Men and women of the Office of Strategic Services, living and dead, have been mentioned en passant for purposes of verisimilitude only. Those men and women shown in the story to be alive were so at this writing. The Veterans of the Office of Strategic Services have in no way helped with or endorsed this novel. The organization of OSS Veterans represented in this novel is not meant to represent in any way the actual above-mentioned veterans' organization.

The weekend home of the Russian Mission to the United Nations in Glen Cove, Long Island, has been described with care and accuracy, though some literary license has been taken. The city of Glen Cove and environs are likewise described with a modicum of literary license.

Author Note

For forty years Western intelligence agents have known a terrible secret: the Russians have a mole—code-named Talbot—inside the CIA. At first Talbot is suspected of killing European agents. Then a street–smart ex-cop uncovers a storm of espionage and murder on the streets of New York, while in a Long Island suburb a civic demonstration against the Russian mission masks a desperate duel of nerves and wits. Engineered by Talbot, a shadow world of suspicion and deceit is spilling onto the streets—leading to a new Soviet weapon and a first—strike war plan threatening the foundations of American government. For the U.S., time is running out. For Talbot, the time is now.

BOOK I

The First of May

PROLOGUE

This is the way the world will end," said Viktor Androv, "not with a bang, not with a whimper...but with a bleep, bleep, bleep...." His wide face broke into a grin and he made a gesture toward the electronic consoles that lined the walls of the long, dimly lit garret.

The tall, aging American standing beside him remarked, "Not really end, Androv. Change. And it will, at least, be bloodless."

Androv walked toward the stairs, his footsteps echoing loudly in the attic room. "Yes, of course," he said. He turned and studied the American in the half-light. He was still rather handsome for his age, with clear blue eyes and a full head of white hair. His manner and bearing, though, were a bit too aristocratic for Androv's own tastes. He said, "Come. I have a surprise for you. An old friend of yours. Someone you have not seen in forty years."

"Who?"

"The grocer. Did you ever wonder what happened to him? He is a capitalist now." He nodded his head toward the staircase. "Follow me. The steps are badly lit. Careful."

The thickset, middle-aged Russian led the way down the narrow staircase and into a small wood-paneled room, barely illuminated by a single wall sconce. He said, "It's unfortunate that you cannot join us at our May Day celebration. But, as we do each year, we have invited Americans who are friendly to us. And who knows? Even after so many years, one of them may recognize you."

The American did not reply.

Androv went on, "This year, we have invited the Veterans of the Abraham Lincoln Brigade. They will bore everyone with stories of how many Fascists they killed in Spain a half century ago."

"I'll be fine in my room."

"Good. We will send up some wine. And food. The food is good here."

"So I see."

Androv patted his paunch good-naturedly. He said, "Well, *next* May Day, Moscow will be importing much American food under very favorable trade conditions." He smiled in the dim light, then pushed open a panel on the wall. "Come." They stepped into a large Elizabethan-style chapel. "This way, please."

The American crossed the chapel, converted now into an office, and sat in an armchair. He looked around. "Your office?"

"Yes."

The American nodded to himself. Since he couldn't imagine a bigger or more elegant office in the mansion, he assumed that the Soviet ambassador to the United Nations had lesser accommodations. Viktor Androv, the chief KGB resident in New York, was obviously top dog.

Androv said, "Your old friend will be here shortly. He lives close by. But there is time for us to have a small drink first."

The American looked toward the far end of the chapel. Above what had once been the altar hung portraits of Marx, Engels, and Lenin, the Red Trinity. He looked back at Androv. "Do you know when the Stroke will occur?"

Androv poured sherry into two glasses. "Yes." He passed a crystal glass to the American. "The end will come on the same day it began—" he raised his glass "—the Fourth of July. *Na zdorovie.*"

The American responded, *"Na zdorovie."*

CHAPTER ONE

Patrick O'Brien stood on the sixty-ninth floor observation roof of the RCA Building in Rockefeller Center and looked off to the south. The skyscrapers fell away like a mountain range into the valley of the shorter buildings downtown, then climbed again into the towering cliffs of Wall Street. O'Brien spoke to the man beside him without turning. "When I was a boy, the Anarchists and Communists used to throw bombs on Wall Street. They killed a few people, mostly workers, clerks, and messengers—people of their own class, basically. I don't believe they ever got one capitalist in a top hat, or interrupted five minutes of trading on the floor."

The man beside him, Tony Abrams, whose late mother and father had been Communists, smiled wryly. "They were making a symbolic statement."

"I suppose you would call it that today." O'Brien looked up at the Empire State Building three quarters of a mile in the distance. He said, "It's very quiet up here. That's the first thing anyone used to New York notices. The stillness." He looked at Abrams. "I like to come up here in the evening after work. Have you been up here before?"

"No." Abrams had been with O'Brien's law firm, O'Brien, Kimberly and Rose, located on the forty-fourth floor of the RCA Building, for over a year. He looked around the nearly deserted roof. It ran in a horseshoe shape around the south, west, and north sides of the smaller top-floor structure that held the elevator. It was paved with red terra-cotta tile, and there were a few potted pine trees planted around. A scattering of tourists, mostly Oriental, stood at the gray iron railings and snapped pictures of the lighted city below. Abrams added, "And I confess I've never been to the Statue of Liberty, or the Empire State Building either."

O'Brien smiled. "Ah, a real New Yorker."

Both men stayed silent for some time. Abrams wondered why O'Brien had asked him to share his twilight vigil. As a process server, pursuing a law degree at night, he had not even seen the old man's office, much less had more than a dozen words at one time with him.

O'Brien seemed engrossed in the view out toward the upper bay. He fished around in his pocket, then said to Abrams, "Do you have a quarter?"

Abrams gave him a quarter.

O'Brien approached an electronic viewer mounted on a stanchion and deposited the quarter. The machine hummed. O'Brien consulted a card on the viewer. "Number ninety-seven." He swiveled the viewer so that a pointer indicated the number 97. "There it is." He stared for a full minute, then said, "That lady in the harbor still gives me the chills." He straightened up and looked at Abrams. "Are you a patriot?"

Abrams thought that a personal and loaded question. He replied, "The occasion hasn't arisen to really find out."

O'Brien's expression registered neither approval nor disapproval of the answer. "Here, you want a look?"

The viewer made a grating noise and stopped humming. Abrams said, "I'm afraid the time has run out."

O'Brien looked at the machine sharply. "That wasn't three full minutes. Send a letter to the *Times*, Abrams."

"Yes, sir."

O'Brien put his hands in his pockets. "Gets cold up here."

"Perhaps we should go inside."

O'Brien ignored the suggestion and said, "Do you speak Russian, Abrams?"

Abrams glanced at the older man. This was not the sort of question one asked unless one already knew the answer. "Yes. My parents—"

"Right." O'Brien nodded. "I thought someone told me you spoke it. We have some Russian-speaking clients. Jewish emigrés down in Brooklyn. Near your neighborhood. I believe."

Abrams nodded. "I'm rusty, but I'm sure I could communicate with them."

"Good. Would it be too much of an imposition if I asked you to sharpen your Russian? I can get you State Department language tapes."

Abrams glanced at him. "All right."

O'Brien stared off into the west for several seconds, then said, "When you were a detective, you sometimes had duty protecting the Russian Mission to the UN on East Sixty-seventh."

Abrams looked at O'Brien for a second, then said, "As a condition of my severance from the force, I signed an oath not to speak of my past duties."

"Did you? Oh, yes, you were in police intelligence, weren't you? The Red Squad."

"They don't call it that anymore. That sounds too—"

"Too much like what it is. By God, we live in an age of euphemism, don't we? What did you call it in the squad room when the bosses weren't around?"

"The Red Squad." He smiled.

O'Brien smiled too, then went on. "Actually, you weren't protecting the Russian Mission at all, but spying on it....You pretty much knew the principal characters in the Soviet delegation to the UN."

"Possibly."

"How about Viktor Androv?"

"How about him?"

"Indeed. Have you ever been out to Glen Cove?"

Abrams turned and stared into the sun setting out over New Jersey. At length he answered, "I was only a city cop, Mr. O'Brien. Not James Bond. My authority ended at the city line. Glen Cove is Nassau County."

"But you've been out there, certainly."

"Possibly."

"Did you keep any private notes on these people?"

Abrams replied with a touch of impatience, "My job was not to watch them the way the FBI watches them. My areas of responsibility were strictly limited to observing the contacts they made with groups and individuals who might be a danger to the City of New York and its people."

"Who might that be?"

"The usual crew. Puerto Rican liberation groups, Black Panthers, Weather Underground. That's all I was interested in. Look, if the Soviets wanted to steal chemical formulas from a midtown research lab, or steal Ratner's recipe for cheese blintzes, I could not have cared less. That's all I can say on that subject."

"But as a citizen you would care, and you'd report that to the FBI, which you did on a few occasions."

Abrams looked at O'Brien in the subdued light. The man knew entirely too much. Or possibly he was speculating. O'Brien was a superb trial attorney, and this was his style. Abrams did not respond.

O'Brien said, "Are you prepared for the July bar?"

"Were you?"

O'Brien smiled. "That was so long ago, I think I took the test in a log cabin."

Abrams had heard that Patrick O'Brien had a disconcerting habit of shifting subjects, seemingly at random, the way a card-shark shuffles a deck before he deals himself a straight flush. Abrams said, "Were you going to make a point about bombings on Wall Street?"

O'Brien looked at him. "Oh...no. It's just that today is the first of May. May Day. That reminded me of the May Day celebrations I used to see down in Union Square. Have you ever been to one?"

"Many. My parents used to take me. I used to go when I was on the force. A few times in uniform. The last few years undercover."

O'Brien didn't speak for some time, then said, "Look out there. The financial center of America. Of the world, really. What would be the effect of a low-yield nuclear weapon on Wall Street?"

"It might interrupt five minutes of trading."

"I'd like a serious answer."

Abrams lit a cigarette, then said, "Hundreds of thousands dead."

O'Brien nodded. "The best financial minds in the nation vaporized. There would be economic ruin for millions, national chaos, and panic."

"Possibly."

"Leading to social disorder, street violence, political instability."

"Why are we talking about low-yield nuclear weapons on Wall Street, Mr. O'Brien?"

"Just a happy May Day thought. An extrapolation of a swarthy little black-clad Anarchist or Communist tossing one of those bowling ball-shaped bombs with a lighted fuse." O'Brien pulled out a pewter flask and poured a shot into the cap. He drank. "I have a cold."

"You look fine."

He laughed. "I'm supposed to be at George Van Dorn's place out on Long Island. If it should ever come up, I have a cold."

Abrams nodded. To be an accomplice to small deceptions, especially one involving O'Brien's partner, George Van Dorn, he knew, could lead to bigger deceptions.

O'Brien poured another shot and passed it to Abrams. "Cognac. Decent stuff."

Abrams drank it and passed back the cap.

O'Brien had another, then put it away. He seemed lost in thought, then said, "Information. This is a civilization which rests almost entirely on information—its manufacture, storage, retrieval, and dissemination. We have gotten ourselves to a point in our development where we could not function as a society without those billions of bits of information. Think of all the stock and bond transactions, the commodities exchange, metals exchange, checking- and savings-account balances, credit card transactions, international transfers of funds, corporate records.... Much of that is handled down there." He nodded off into the distance. "Imagine millions of people trying to prove what they lost. We would be reduced to a nation of paupers."

Abrams said, "Are we talking about low-yield nuclear weapons on Wall Street again?"

"Perhaps." O'Brien walked along the roof and stopped at the

railing at the eastern end of the observation deck. He looked down at the Rockefeller Center complex. "Incredible place. Did you know that there are over four acres of rooftop gardens on these buildings?"

Abrams came up beside him. "I don't think I knew that."

"Well, it's a fact. And that will cost you another quarter." O'Brien took the quarter from Abrams and deposited it in another electronic viewer. He bent over and peered through the lenses, swiveled the viewer, and adjusted the focus. O'Brien said, "Glen Cove is about twenty-five miles and a world away from here. I'm trying to see if I can pick out Van Dorn's pyrotechnics."

"Pyrotechnics?"

"It's a long story, Abrams. But in a nutshell, Van Dorn, who lives next door to the Russians, allegedly harasses them. You may have read about it."

"I may have."

O'Brien swiveled and focused again. "They are going to sue him, in Nassau County Court. They've been obliged to retain local attorneys, of course. Have a look."

"At the local attorneys?"

"No, Mr. Abrams, Glen Cove."

Abrams bent his tall frame over the viewer and adjusted the focus. The Hempstead Plains rose toward the Island's hilly North Shore, an area of wealth, privilege, and privacy. Although he could see very little detail at this distance, he knew, as O'Brien suggested, that he was looking at another world. "I don't see the rocket's red glare," he commented.

"Nor the bombs bursting in air, I'm sure. Neither can you see that our flag is still there—above Van Dorn's fort. But I assure you it is."

Abrams stood straight and glanced at his watch.

O'Brien said, "Well, even Dracula needed a good lawyer. Poor Jonathan Harker. He learned that after you are invited into a sinister castle, you sometimes have difficulty getting out."

Abrams knew he should have been thrilled at the opportunity to stand on this roof with the boss, but he was becoming a bit impatient with O'Brien's musings. He said, "I'm not sure I'm following you."

O'Brien smiled. "There are very few employees in the firm who would admit that to me. They usually smile and nod until I get to the point."

Abrams leaned back against the railed enclosure. A few tourists were still walking around. The sky was pink and the view was pleasant.

O'Brien went back to his scanning, then the viewer went black. "Damn it. Do you have another quarter, Abrams?"

"No, I don't."

O'Brien began walking back the way they'd come, and Abrams walked beside him. O'Brien said, "Well, the point is that I may fire you, at the end of the month. You will be hired by Edwards and Styler, who are attorneys in Nassau County. Garden City. They're representing the Russians in their suit against Van Dorn."

"That sounds rather unethical, since I'm working for you and Mr. Van Dorn now. Don't you think so?"

"Eventually the Russians will abide by Edwards and Styler's request to visit the estate on a day they are being harassed by Van Dorn. They didn't grant Huntington Styler's request to visit today, but probably will the next time Van Dorn plans to have a party. Probably Memorial Day. You'll accompany the Edwards and Styler attorneys, then report back to me on the substance of what was discussed."

"Look, if George Van Dorn is in fact harassing the Russians, then he deserves to be sued, and to lose. In the meantime, the Russians should get an injunction against him to cease and desist."

"They're working on that through Edwards and Styler. But Judge Barshian, a friend of mine, incidentally, is having difficulty making up his mind. There is a fine line between harassment and Mr. Van Dorn's constitutional and God-given right to throw a party now and then."

"I'm sorry, but from what I've read, Mr. Van Dorn appears to me as though he's not a good neighbor. He's acting out of pettiness, spite, or some misdirected patriotism."

O'Brien smiled slightly. "Well, that's the way it's supposed to appear, Abrams. But there's more to it than a civil case."

Abrams stopped walking and looked out over the north end

of Manhattan toward Central Park. Of course there was more to it than a civil case. The questions about his speaking Russian, his patriotism, his days on the Red Squad, and all the other seemingly disjointed and irrelevant conversation were not irrelevant at all. It was how O'Brien played cards. "Well," he said, "what am I supposed to do once I'm in their house?"

"Pretty much what Jonathan Harker did in Dracula's castle. Get nosy."

"Jonathan Harker died."

"Worse. He lost his immortal soul. But since you're going to be a lawyer, like Mr. Harker, that may be a distinct advantage in your career."

Abrams smiled in spite of himself. "What else can you tell me about this?"

"At the time, nothing further. It may be a while before I discuss it with you again. *You* will discuss it with no one. If we proceed, you will report directly to me and no one else, regardless of what claims anyone may make that they are acting on my behalf. Understood?"

"Understood."

"Fine. In the meantime, I'll get you those language tapes. If nothing comes of this, at least you will have sharpened your Russian."

"For your Jewish emigré clients?"

"I have no such clients."

Abrams nodded, then said, "I do have to study for the bar."

O'Brien's tone was unexpectedly sharp. "Mr. Abrams, there may not be any bar exam in July."

Abrams stared at O'Brien in the subdued light. The man seemed serious, but Abrams knew there was no point in asking for a clarification of that startling statement. Abrams said, "In that case, perhaps I *should* study Russian. I may need it."

O'Brien smiled grimly. "It could very well come in handy by August. Good night, Mr. Abrams." He turned and walked toward the elevators.

Abrams watched him for a second, then said, "Good night, Mr. O'Brien."

CHAPTER TWO

Peter Thorpe looked down from the hired helicopter. Below, the three-hundred-year-old village of Glen Cove lay nestled on the Long Island Sound.

The weekend retreat of the Russian Mission to the United Nations came into view, an Elizabethan mansion of granite walls, slate roofs, mullioned windows, gables, and chimney pots. It was laid out in two great wings to form a T, with the addition of a third, smaller wing attached to the end of the T's southern cross. Formerly called Killenworth, the estate had been built by the arch-capitalist Charles Pratt, founder of what later became Standard Oil, for one of his sons. The house had over fifty rooms and was set on a small hill surrounded by thirty-seven acres of woodland. A few other surviving estates of Long Island's Gold Coast sat amid the encroaching suburbs, including five or six other Pratt estates, one used as a nursing home. Peter Thorpe had been at the nursing home several times, but not to visit the elderly.

Also visible below, in what had once been Gatsby country, was a large group of protestors gathered in front of the gates to the Russian estate.

Thorpe looked back at the skyscrapers of Manhattan Island and stared for a while at the United Nations building. He asked the pilot, "Have you ever flown any Russians out?"

The pilot nodded. "Once. Last summer. Do you believe that place? Jesus. Hey, where's *your* castle?"

Thorpe smiled. "The one directly north of the Russians'."

"Okay...I see it—" A star cluster suddenly burst off the port side of the helicopter and the startled pilot shouted, "What the hell—?" and yanked on the collective pitch stick. The helicopter veered sharply to starboard.

Thorpe laughed. "Just some fireworks. My host must be starting his annual counter–May Day celebration. Swing out and come in from the north."

"Right." The helicopter took a new heading.

Thorpe looked down at the traffic along Dosoris Lane. The local mayor, Thorpe knew, was violently anti-Russian and was leading his constituents in a battle against their unwelcome neighbors.

In fact, Glen Cove had a long history of doing battle with the Russians ever since they'd bought the estate after World War II. Red-baiting village cops in the 1950s used to stop everyone coming or going through the gates and write tickets for any minor infraction, though the tickets were never paid. There had been a period of detente, roughly corresponding to the period of Soviet-American detente, but the Red-baiting fifties had clearly returned, not only in Glen Cove but in the nation.

Recently, in retaliation against the mayor's summary banning of Russians from all village recreational facilities, Moscow had banned American diplomats from the Moskva River or something equally inane. *Pravda* carried a long feature article condemning Glen Cove as a bastion of "anti-Soviet delirium." The article, which Thorpe had read in translation at CIA headquarters in Langley, Virginia, had been as idiotic as Mayor Dominic Parioli's ramblings that precipitated it.

Thorpe reflected smilingly that Glen Cove also had given the State Department a headache. But finally, last summer, the federal government agreed to pay the village the $100,000 or so in annual property taxes that they lost because of the tax-exempt status of the Russian estate. In return, Mayor Parioli had agreed to lay off. But from where Thorpe sat now, twelve hundred feet above the village, it didn't appear that Glen Cove was living up to its end of the treaty. Thorpe laughed again.

The pilot said, "What the hell's going on down there?"

Thorpe replied, "The populace is exercising its rights of freedom of speech and freedom of assembly."

"Looks like a fucking free-for-all from here."

"Same thing." But to be fair to the village, Thorpe thought, circumstances had changed since the Glen Cove–Washington accord. There were persistent reports in the national press of sophisticated electronic spying equipment in the Russian estate house. Local residents complained of TV interference, which was to them as alarming as the electronic spying that caused it.

The purpose of the electronics, though, was not to wipe out Monday-night football. The real target of the electronic spying was Long Island's defense industry: Sperry-Rand, Grumman Aircraft, Republic Aviation, and the dozens of high-tech electronic and microchip companies. Thorpe knew that the Russians were also eavesdropping on Manhattan's and Long Island's large diplomatic communities.

The question was always raised, "Where did the Russians get all this high-technology spying equipment?" And the official State Department answer was always the same: through their diplomatic pouches, which were not always "pouches" but often large crates protected from search and seizure by the protocols of diplomacy. Yet, Thorpe knew this was not true. Nearly all the equipment they used to spy on the local defense industry had come from that industry itself. It had been bought through a series of dummy corporations and delivered by helicopter right into the Russians' backyard. Some of the very, very sensitive stuff that couldn't be bought had been stolen and transported around in a purposely confusing manner, which included trucks, boats, and finally helicopter. Thorpe said to the pilot, "When you flew the Russians out here, did they have crates with them?"

The pilot shrugged, then replied, "Yeah, and enough luggage to take a two-year cruise. Boxes of food, too. But I didn't know they were Russians and neither did the dispatcher. I was just supposed to pick up a party at the East Side Heliport and take them out to a Long Island estate. Anyway, they had these boxes and steamer trunks all over. So they dump this shit onboard and tell me to fly to Kings Point, which I do. Then, before I land, they say go on to Glen

Cove, so I go. Then they point out this place below and I land. This van was waiting—some kind of deli catering van. A bunch of guys unload real quick and wave me off. Christ, I still didn't know they were Russians until about a month later I see an aerial picture of the place in the *Times*. There was some flap over taxes and beach passes or something. Never got a tip, either."

Thorpe nodded. "What was written on that deli van?"

The pilot looked quickly at Thorpe. "I don't know. Can't remember."

"Did anyone speak to you about that trip?"

"No."

Thorpe rubbed his chin. The man was suddenly less communicative, which could mean several things. Thorpe said, "You didn't contact the FBI? They didn't contact you?"

The pilot snapped, "Hey, enough questions. Okay?"

Thorpe pulled out his wallet. "CIA."

The pilot glanced at the ID. "Yeah. So what? I used to fly lots of CIA in 'Nam. They weren't as nosy as you."

Thorpe smiled. "What did they tell you? The FBI, I mean."

"They told me not to talk to you guys. Hey, I don't want to get in the middle of some shit. Okay? I said too much already."

"I'll keep it quiet."

"Okay...clear it with them if you want to know anything else. Don't tell them I spoke to you, though. I didn't know you were CIA. Jesus Christ, what a bunch of characters."

"Take it easy. Just fly."

"Yeah. Christ, I feel like a cabbie picking up muggers all the time. Russkies, FBI, CIA. What next?"

"You never know." Thorpe sat back as the helicopter began its vertical descent. This mini-war between the village and the Russian estate had a comic-opera quality to it. More comical perhaps was the open hostility of another local land baron, George Van Dorn, Thorpe's weekend host. Peter Thorpe looked down at the adjoining estates, two small fiefdoms, sharing a common, semi-fortified border, worlds apart in political philosophy and engaged in some sort of bizarre medieval siege warfare. Some of it was amusing, he thought, some of it was not.

A fountain of colored balls from a Roman candle rose into the sky over the helicopter bubble. Thorpe said, "No evasive action necessary, chief."

The pilot swore. "This could get dangerous."

Thorpe pointed out to the pilot Van Dorn's illuminated landing pad, formerly the tennis court. Van Dorn had proclaimed tennis to be a sport of sissies and women. Thorpe, who played tennis, had suggested to Van Dorn that the sissies and women should be accommodated if they were his houseguests, but to no avail.

There was a radio frequency painted on the court in luminescent numerals. The pilot asked increduously, "Am I supposed to radio for permission to land?"

"You'd better, chief."

"Oh, for Christ's sake...." He switched frequencies and spoke into his helmet microphone as he hovered, "This is AH 113, overhead. Landing instructions. Over."

A voice crackled back and Thorpe heard it from the open speaker. "This is Van Dorn station below. Have you in sight. Who is your passenger?"

The pilot looked annoyed as he turned to Thorpe.

Thorpe smiled. "Tell them it's Peter, alone and unarmed."

The pilot repeated Thorpe's words in a surly tone.

The radio operator replied, "Proceed to landing pad. Over."

"Roger, out." The pilot switched back to his company frequency, then said to Thorpe, "Now I know two houses to avoid."

"Me too." Thorpe could see the Van Dorn house clearly now, a long white clapboard colonial, very stately, but not quite as grand as his enemy's castle. Thorpe felt the warmer air from the ground entering the cockpit, and smelled the early-blooming flowers. From the empty but lighted swimming pool, two men were firing skyrockets, like a mortar crew, thought Thorpe, dug in against possible counterfire. "If the Russians could get a fireworks permit," he said to the pilot, "they might shoot back."

"Yeah," growled the uneasy pilot, "and if I had my old Cobra gunship again, I'd waste the fuckers, and these assholes too."

"Amen, brother."

The helicopter came to rest on the tennis court.

CHAPTER THREE

Stanley Kuchik felt the sweat collecting under his shirt. He wondered what the Russians would do to him if they caught him here on their property. For decades the students at Glen Cove High, down Dosoris Lane from the Russian estate, had passed those forbidding walls and portals on their way to and from school. There had been stories of students penetrating into that foreign land, but they were always students in some distant misty past. There was, some speculated, a sense of inadequacy based on the knowledge that none of them, boy or girl, had found the courage or enterprise to redress the insult of those mocking walls.

But now came Stanley Kuchik, with the right stuff. Tonight he was going to prove that even if he wasn't exactly the biggest kid in the class, he was the bravest. Ten of his buddies had seen him scale the fence between the YMCA grounds and the Russian property, and watched him disappear into the trees. His mission was clear: Obtain irrefutable proof of his deep penetration into enemy territory and rendezvous at Sal's Pizza any time before 10:00 P.M. He knew that if he blew it, he might as well apply for his working papers, because he'd never again set foot in Glen Cove High.

Stanley raised his binoculars and focused on the big mansion about two hundred yards off. Purple shadows darkened the broad north terrace, but he could see some activity around the house. A few men and women sat in lawn chairs and someone was serving drinks. He wished they would all go inside.

He checked his Marine K-Bar knife to make sure it hadn't slipped from its sheath, then ran his fingers over his camouflage paint—actually his mother's green eye shadow, supplemented by a few swirls of brown eye pencil. The stuff held up pretty good in all kinds of weather, even when it was real hot and he sweated a lot. He wore his Uncle Steve's tiger fatigues from 'Nam and his own black Converse sneakers.

He finished the Milky Way, stuffed the candy wrapper into his pouch pocket, and retrieved a Snickers. He froze. Two men were coming toward him on a gravel path ten yards off. He listened for dogs, but there weren't any and he breathed a little easier. Even if the men spotted him, he could outrun them. He did the hundred-yard dash in ten flat pretty consistently, which he knew he could improve if he had a few Russkies behind him.

Stanley lay perfectly still as the two figures emerged between the plantings on the path. He recognized the short fat one with buggy eyes: Froggy. He'd seen Froggy in town a few times and on the beach once. Froggy had even spoken to Stanley's freshman class a couple of years back. He was a cultural-affairs guy or something and spoke pretty good English. When the Russians used to be allowed to play tennis on the village courts, most of them hardly ever threw the ball back when you asked. But Froggy would waddle all over to get your ball, grin, and toss it back. Froggy was okay. Stanley tried to remember his name. Anzoff or Androv or something. Yeah. Androv. Viktor Androv.

The other man was one of those slicky boys: swept-back hair, a suit that looked like Stanley's old First Holy Communion out-fit, and dark glasses. The guy looked tough, though. Probably a killer, Stanley thought. A man from SMERSH.

The two men were babbling on in Russian, and Stanley could make out the word *Amerikanski* over and over again. He shifted his body slightly, pulled open his field bag and brought out a Minolta Pocket Autopak 470 camera. He framed his subjects and got off three quick shots. He returned his equipment to the bag and waited until they were a full minute out of sight before he got into a sprint-ing position. He listened. Everything was quiet.

Stanley dashed across an open piece of ground, covering about fifty yards in less than six seconds. He dove into a small, weed-clogged depression and lay still. He felt very exposed, but there was no other concealment around. He looked for listening bugs but couldn't see any, although he thought this should be an obvious place for one. As his respect for the Russians' security lessened, his cockiness grew. Well, he thought, maybe their security *was* good. They just hadn't reckoned on Stanley Kuchik.

Stanley had been awed by his Uncle Steve's stories about his escape-and-evasion course in Panama, and he had given Stanley his old field manuals on infiltration, recon patrols, and outdoor survival. Stanley had taken to it very naturally, when he'd practiced in the woods near his house, as though some feral instinct had been awakened by the pictures of men creeping through the bush.

He peered over the rim of the depression. The Russkies showed no signs of going inside yet. He didn't think they would. It was still warm and pleasant. He'd have to proceed right under their noses.

Stanley knew that today was a Russian holiday. The Russians from the UN would be all over the place soon. He'd already spotted about a dozen walking around the gardens, plus the ones on the terrace. He'd planned this for some time...M-day minus six, M-day minus five... but now he thought he might have been foolhardy. Nuts, actually.

At least he hadn't spotted any kids. Sometimes the Russkies brought their kids with them. The kids could be a pain because they ran wild in the woods and fields. When they weren't around, he'd heard, they went to some kind of camp a few miles away, called Pioneer Camp, which was like a Boy Scout or Girl Scout camp. But he bet that instead of doing camp things, they learned how to spy.

Stanley thought about that for a while, then remembered his mission. He crept forward toward the open end of a drainage culvert where it stuck out below the steep drop in the lawn. The earth stank here and was covered with swamp grass and bulrushes. This was the farthest he'd ever come on the Russian property.

Stanley hesitated, then raised himself up to the open culvert. He squeezed headfirst into the slimy clay and began crawling upgrade. He knew none of the other kids in the junior class could fit in the pipe. Being small had a lot of advantages.

As he got closer to the house, he saw that some weeping willow roots had found their way between the pipe joints. He used them to pull his way through at first, but at one point the roots were so thick he had to cut them away with his K-Bar. He heard chirping ahead and saw little red eyes looking back at him. He struck the pipe with the knife's pommel and growled, "Beat it! Go away!" His heart was pounding and his mouth was sticky.

Stanley remained motionless and took stock. He had less than three inches on either side of his shoulders, and although he was not claustrophobic, he was beginning to get nervous. What if he got stuck? The fetid air was making him nauseous, and the total darkness was giving him the creeps. He felt oppressively confined and had the sudden urge to stand, break free, run in the open air. Sweat covered his body and he began shaking. He thought about going back but didn't think he could get through those roots feet-first. "Well, jerk, you can't stay here."

He resumed his crawl until he reached a juncture of several pipes. The air was better here and he took a long breath. He looked up into a vertical shaft that ran about twenty feet to the surface. There was a metal grating at the top, and he could see the first evening stars twinkling in the sky. "Piece of cake."

He knelt on one knee and unclipped his flashlight from his web belt, turned it on, and pointed it up the shaft. He saw the first iron rung leading to the surface. He replaced his flashlight, took a long breath, and began the ascent, hand over hand, until he reached the metal grate. He pushed up on it and it scraped noisily across the concrete rim. He listened for a few seconds, then stuck his head up and looked around. A white flagpole rose up from the ground not ten feet away. There he spotted what he was after: the dark red flag of the USSR.

The flagpole was surrounded by a circular hedgerow about four feet high. He was concealed within the plantings, unless someone was looking down from an upstairs window. He scanned the second-story windows and the third-story gables, but could see nothing. He hoisted himself out of the shaft and low-crawled through the trailing pachysandra until he reached the base of the flagpole, then rolled over on his back. He drew his K-Bar knife and took a long breath. He listened.

He heard music coming through the partly opened French doors leading out to the terrace. Pretty bad music, he thought irrelevantly. The night was fairly still, though, and he wondered if they would hear the flag falling as the rope slipped through the pulleys. He put the knife to the halyard, but hesitated. Maybe he would just get the hell out of there. But then he looked up at the red flag with the yellow hammer and sickle, and the five-pointed star, snapping in a brief gust of wind, and he knew he couldn't go back without it.

Suddenly there was a noise like a rifle shot, and he almost lost control of his bladder. He lay in the damp pachysandra, waiting. Overhead there was another loud report, and a shower of sparks—red, white, and blue—rained down. More rockets began bursting overhead, and Stanley laughed softly. Crazy old Van Dorn, giving it to the Russkies again. And he had no doubt where all the Russian eyes were turned. He sliced easily through the halyard and the weight of the flag pulled the severed rope through its pulleys.

The flag floated down slowly at first, then grew larger as he stared up at it. It settled over his entire body. It was made of some sort of lightweight bunting. He'd expected something heavier. The flag also smelled funny. Still, he had it.

Stanley lost no time. He cut the flag loose, twisted it tightly into a rope and tied it securely around his waist. He slipped through a space on the blind side of the hedge, away from the terrace, then raised himself into a sprinting stance, ready to run like hell across the lawn. Then the floodlights came on. "Oh, Christ!"

Even though the first rule of patrolling was *never* to go back the same way you came in, Stanley turned and slowly crawled back to the open storm drain. He quickly lowered himself down, pulling the grate cover back into place. "Okay...okay...you got lucky...."

Halfway down the vertical shaft he heard a voice yell down to him, "Stop! Halt! We shoot." A powerful light beam shone down the shaft. Stanley dropped the last ten feet and hit the muddy bottom of the shaft. He ducked quickly into a culvert opening headfirst as he heard the grate being lifted. "Holy Mary..." He realized he was in the culvert that led toward the mansion. He had no choice but to keep moving.

CHAPTER FOUR

The traffic on Dosoris Lane was snarled, and with good reason, thought Karl Roth. There was an international incident brewing and everyone wanted to see it, or take part in it. He edged his old panel truck up a few feet, then spoke with a trace of a Middle-European accent. "We will be late."

Maggie Roth, his wife, glanced into the back of the van. "I hope the food doesn't spoil." She too had an accent, which her American neighbors found charmingly British, but which to Londoners was identifiable as Wapping Lane Jewish.

Karl Roth nodded. "It is hot for May the first." The panel truck's engine-temperature gauge began to climb. "Damn it. Where do all these cars come from?"

Maggie Roth replied, "They are the cars of the exploited working class, Karl. Coming from the tennis courts, the golf club, and the yacht club." She laughed. "Also, Van Dorn is having another spite party."

Karl Roth frowned, then said, "Androv sent word that he has a surprise for us."

She laughed again, but without humor. "He could surprise us by paying his bloody bills on time, couldn't he?"

Roth smiled nervously. "Please be civil to him. He has asked us to stay for a drink. This is a big celebration for them."

She grumbled, "He could have asked us to stay for the whole party. Instead, we go through the servants' entrance like beggars and stand in the kitchen helping with the food. Classless society my foot."

Roth let out a breath of exasperation. "It would be noted by the FBI if we stayed too long."

"They've already noted *your* comings and goings. They're bloody well on to something, I'll tell you."

He snapped, "Don't say that! Do not mention anything to Androv."

"Don't worry on that account. Do you think I want to end up like Carpins—?"

"Quiet!"

The van moved up a few more feet. Suddenly a rocket arched into the gathering dusk and exploded in a red, white, and blue shower of sparks that lit up the purple sky. Several people along the road cheered and auto horns began honking.

Roth sneered. "More provocation. That came from Van Dorn's estate—that reactionary swine."

"*He* pays his bills," remarked Maggie Roth. "And why didn't we get the job on his party, Karl? We could have handled both. Van Dorn likes you. You're so bloody obsequious toward him. Yes, Mr. Von Dorn, no, Mr. Von Dorn. It's *Van* Dorn anyway, Karl. Maybe he's wise to the fact that you snoop around when you go there. Or maybe he just thinks you're popping one of the maids." She laughed. "If he knew what you really were . . ."

Karl Roth let out another sigh of exasperation. *Maggie must watch herself,* he thought. The van moved ahead a few more feet. Angry shouting could be heard now up the road. Police cars were parked on the right shoulder, and on the left he could see the huge ornate wrought-iron gates of the Russian estate. People with picket signs were blocking the entrance and the police were trying to keep order.

From his high vantage point Roth could see several limousines trying to get into the gate entrance. The police were stopping each one and checking licenses and registrations. Roth said, "More harassment."

"Where's our registration? I don't want a bloody ticket. *We* don't have diplomatic immunity."

"There. In the glove compartment. My God, what a mess!"

Another rocket arched high into the air and exploded with a loud report. Maggie Roth tittered. "Mr. Van Dorn is aiming them to explode over the Russians."

"Why do you find that amusing?"

"But it is. Don't you think so?"

"No."

She stayed silent for some time, then said, "Do you realize we've delivered them enough food over the past six months to last out a long siege?"

He didn't reply.

She added, "And all that canned stuff and dried stuff. Those bastards only buy the best—the freshest—now they want tins, dry foods. . . . Well, Karl, what's it all about, then?"

Again he didn't reply.

Her tone was sharp. "Bloody beggars are planning World War Three, that's what they're about. Well, Glen Cove is safe, isn't it, Karl? They wouldn't drop a bomb on their own people, would they—"

"Shut up!"

She retreated into a moody silence, then mumbled, "I hope the damned mayonnaise has spoiled and they all get food poisoning."

CHAPTER FIVE

Stanley Kuchik lay on his back in the upward-curving culvert, his arms above his head and his head bowed under an immovable metal grate. Tears formed in his eyes. "Stupid...moron... Stanley, you asshole..."

He looked up at the grate, all that separated him from the cellar of the mansion. He thought about trying to go back, but if he got caught somewhere below, he'd die there and rot and his stink would be awful and they'd call a plumber who would use a Roto-Rooter and... *ugh!*

He knew that the Russians would be waiting for him where the culvert opened into the bulrushes, but after a while they'd figure out that he'd gone this way instead. They'd be down here soon and yank him out and shoot him. "Jesus, Mary, and Joseph...." In anger and frustration he balled his hands into fists and beat against the grate, tears running freely down his face as he sobbed.

He heard something that sounded like a sharp clink, and stopped. Tentatively he pushed against the grate and it lifted. He cocked his arms and pushed up like a shot-putter, throwing the heavy grate into the air with a strength he didn't know he had. The grate crashed to the concrete floor a few feet away.

Before the adrenaline gave way to the paralyzing muscle fatigue he felt, Stanley grabbed the sides of the opening, pulling and kicking at the same time, heaving himself up and out of the hole, then tumbling onto the floor.

He lay there on the cold concrete for several seconds, breathing heavily, feeling his muscles flutter and his body shake. He drew a deep breath and stood unsteadily. "Well, that wasn't so bad."

Stanley brushed himself, straightened his clothes, and checked his gear. Everything was in place including the tightly girthed flag.

He looked quickly around. He was in the boiler room. Three huge furnaces stood across the room along with three hot-water tanks and oil tanks.

He opened a crudely made wooden door and passed into an unlit room. He found an overhead pull chain and turned on a single light bulb. He looked around. Stacks and stacks of boxes filled with canned foods lined the walls and formed aisles in the immense space. "Christ, they could feed an army."

He turned on his flashlight and walked through the storage space, reading the familiar brand names until he came to a door. He listened, but could hear nothing. He opened the door and entered a room filled top to bottom with steel file cabinets. He selected one at random and pulled open a drawer, shining his light on the file tabs marked with Cyrillic lettering. He extracted a sheaf of papers and stared at the top one. "Crazy goddamned language..." He stuffed the entire sheaf into his field bag and continued walking.

He could see basement windows, opening out to window wells, but there were bars over all of them. He knew he had to find a cellar door that led outside. He could faintly hear music, talking, and laughing in the room above. He continued prowling around the cluttered area.

His flashlight picked out something on the wall, and he steadied the beam on it, then walked toward it. He played the beam around the area and counted three large electrical panels. He opened one of them. Inside were two rows of modern circuit breakers. They were all marked in Russian, leading Stanley to believe that it had not been an American electrician who installed the new system. Stanley retrieved his Minolta and slid the close-up lens into place. He stood directly in front of the electrical panel and held the camera cord straight out to measure fifty centimeters. He framed the panel, stood perfectly still, closed his eyes, and hit the shutter button. The camera flashed. He moved to the next two panels and shot two more pictures. Now he had proof that he'd been in the mansion itself.

Stanley played his flashlight around and spotted something on the floor to the right of the electrical panels. He quickly moved closer to it and knelt. It was a big brute of a generator, American-made, bolted to the concrete above another floor drain. It wasn't running and Stanley suspected that it kicked on automatically when there was an interruption in electrical service. He shined his light farther down the wall. There was a huge oil tank in the corner, probably diesel oil, he thought, to run the generator. "Christ, these guys don't take any chances."

He stood and played the light around, then moved across the room. Rising from the floor was an electric water-well pump, connected by a two-inch pipe to the water main overhead. The pump wasn't running either, and Stanley guessed that it turned on if the generator did, or if the village water was shut off. Stanley scratched his head thoughtfully. "Food...fuel...electricity...water....Real shitheads....Ready for anything." He began walking again.

He passed through an opening in a wooden wall and came to a room full of lawn furniture and gardening tools. He scanned the walls with his flashlight and finally spotted a set of stone steps leading up to an overhead door. "Okay, Stanley, time to go home."

He unlatched the doors and pushed on the left-hand one. It opened with a squeak and he stepped up into the cool night air behind a stand of hemlock.

He found his last candy bar, an almond Cadbury, very expensive but his favorite. He chewed thoughtfully on the chocolate as he surveyed the hundred yards of brightly lit lawn. Beyond the lawn was a thick tree-line. He finished the chocolate, licked and wiped his mouth and fingers, and got into a four-point sprinter's crouch. He waited, looked, listened, took a deep breath, and mumbled, "Okay, feet, do your thing." He shot out of his stance, tearing at top speed across the open lawn toward the trees. He was less than five yards from the edge of the woods when he heard a dog bark, followed by a growl.

"Halt! Stop!"

"Sure—yeah—right." He crashed through the undergrowth, into the woods. He came to a nearly vertical rise in the ground and took it in three long strides.

As he continued to run, the low-hanging branches of the maples whipped at his face and arms, and he felt a gash open above his right eye. A pine bough raked him across the mouth and he stifled a cry of pain. "Oh, screw this! Jesus Christ, never again...never...."

One of Van Dorn's Roman candles shot into the air and Stanley could see where it was fired from, so he changed course slightly and guided toward it.

There were easier ways out of the Russian estate, but Van Dorn's place was his closest, and therefore best, chance. His only chance, really.

As he maneuvered through the woods, the maple and oak gave way to laurel and rhododendrons, and he knew he was approaching the borders of Russian territory. He ran into a coil of barbed wire and sliced his hand. "Jesus H. Christ!" He took his wire cutters and snipped out an opening, then passed carefully through. In the distance he thought he saw lights from the Van Dorn estate.

He could hear the Russians calling out behind him. And the dogs barking. A low stone wall suddenly rose up and he jumped it on the run, then slowed to catch his breath. He had technically crossed into neutral territory, an unused right-of-way that separated the two estates. No-man's-land. He took a few steps toward Van Dorn's place, but he found he was very shaky. A cold sweat covered his body and he was nauseous. He heaved and brought up some chocolate and acid. "Aaahh!" He took a few long breaths and began moving, half running, half walking.

Behind him he heard a sound like a shot and he ducked. Then the sky was lit with a parachute flare. The Russians had tripped one of their own flares, by accident or on purpose, but he was out of the circle of light and kept moving. He wondered if the flare would attract any friendly attention. But he didn't want any attention, he just wanted to make it on his own and keep his rendezvous at Sal's Pizza.

He came to a wooden stockade fence, with pointed pickets at the top, over ten feet high. The boundary of Van Dorn's property.

Stanley slapped at the fence. "Fucking Berlin Wall...." About three inches of cedar separated him from freedom.

He began trotting east along the wall. He saw a rise in the land near the fence. From the top of the rise to the top of the fence was not the impossible ten feet but a more manageable seven or eight feet. He cut back toward the Russian estate to give himself a running start, then swung back toward the small mound of earth. A half-moon had risen above the distant trees and cast a pale light over the long and narrow right-of-way. Stanley looked to his left and saw six Russians and two dogs approach at an angle to his intended path. He knew he had only one shot, if that.

One of the Russians shouted, "Stop! Halt! Surrender!"

Stanley yelled back in a steady voice, "Up yours!"

The Russians released the dogs, and Stanley turned on his last burst of energy and speed. Both dogs lunged, but overshot him, reeled, and came back. Stanley hit the mound running, then jumped. His momentum took him up and forward, and he smashed into the fence but got his arms around the top of the pickets. The dogs leaped at him and one of them got hold of his sneaker. He kicked free. A Russian shouted, "Stop! Stop! We shoot!"

Stanley yelled back, "Sit on it, schmucko!" He pulled himself up and over the pointed pickets, hung for a moment, then dropped to the ground below, tumbling onto the rocky soil. American soil. End of game.

Stanley stood, turned, and began trotting away from the fence, laughing then crying, and finally howling in the moonlight and dancing. "I made it! I made it!" He jumped into the air and clapped his hands. "Stanley, you are *the best!*"

He tightened the flag around his waist and began trotting, then something impelled him to turn back toward the fence. The jagged pickets were silhouetted against the evening sky, and atop the ones he'd just scaled, he could see the moonlit shape of a large man coming over the top. "Oh, no! You can't do that! Back! Stop! Halt! *Nyet! Nyet!* Private property! America!" Stanley turned and began moving as fast as his leaden legs would carry him.

The terrain was fairly open here except for a few white birches and boxwoods. Elongated moon shadows lay over the fields of wild flowers and Stanley tried to stay in those shadows. The ground rose, gently at first, then more steeply, then it became almost a cliff. "What the hell...?" He started slipping in some sort of goo. Clay. White clay. The Long Island terrain was mostly flat and benign, but there were parts of the island on the North Shore that had been formed by the Ice Age glaciers' terminal moraine, some fifteen thousand years ago, and this was one of those areas. And it was screwing him up. There were loose rocks, gravel, and this strange, slippery white clay, which, thought Stanley, was like dog turd. He realized very soon that he had picked the wrong spot to reach Van Dorn's broad lawn.

He heard them again, but without the dogs. He guessed they had helped one another over the fence; at least five of them anyway. The biggest lard-ass stayed behind with the dogs. He wondered what was driving them on. He was running for his life. How much could they pay these guys?

They weren't calling to him anymore, but he could hear them walking, not behind him but off to the west about forty yards. "Bastards."

Stanley summoned up the last of his strength and began kicking toeholds in the resilient white clay, clawing at it with his fingertips. "I'll sue them. I'll tell Van Dorn...they're trespassing on American property. Fucking *nerve*..."

He heard footsteps pattering on the side of the cliff to his left. They had found a path and were moving rapidly up on it. "Oh..." Directly below, about fifteen feet down the cliff, he heard something, and looked back. In the moonlight he saw a Russian who had been placed there to stop him from escaping by sliding back down. The man was holding what looked like a gun, and he was smiling up at Stanley; a very ugly smile, Stanley thought.

Stanley hung on the side of the nearly vertical rise and felt tears forming in his eyes as he realized that, after all this crap, he wasn't going to make it.

CHAPTER SIX

Afew cars behind Karl Roth's deli van, a gray chauffeur-driven limousine also edged through the traffic on Dosoris Lane.

Katherine Kimberly, sitting in the rear, regarded the young Englishman at the opposite end of the long seat. Marc Pembroke was undeniably good-looking, though in a slightly sinister way. He possessed all the charm and breeding of his class, but also its cynicism and affected indifference. She remarked, "It ought to open up a bit once we get past the Russian place."

Pembroke replied politely, "It's just as well Mr. O'Brien didn't come with us. At his age the flu *can* lead to complications."

"He has a cold." Katherine thought she detected a tone suggesting that Patrick O'Brien, senior partner in the law firm in which she was a partner, had simply begged off. She studied Pembroke for a moment. He was dressed in a white flannel pinstripe suit, a straw slouch hat, white silk shirt, and red silk tie with matching pocket handkerchief. He wore black-and-white saddle shoes. He might, thought Katherine, have been on his way to one of the surrounding mansions to play a role in a 1920s movie. She didn't think George Van Dorn would appreciate such foppishness. Yet, in some indefinable way, Pembroke still radiated a hard masculinity. She said, "Mr. O'Brien is usually in excellent health. Last May Day he parachuted from a helicopter and landed on George's tennis court." She smiled.

Pembroke stared at the blond-haired woman. She *was* extremely pretty. She wore a finely cut simple mauve dress that complemented her pale complexion. Her sandals were on the floor, and he noticed her feet were callused, and he remembered that she was an amateur marathon runner.

Pembroke glanced at her profile. She had what they called in the army a command presence. He had heard she was rather good in the courtroom, and he could easily believe it.

She looked up and their eyes met. She did not turn demurely away, as women are taught to do, but stared at him in the same way he was staring at her. Finally he said, "May I give you a drink?"

"Please."

Pembroke looked at the attractive young couple in the facing jump seats. Joan Grenville was dressed in white slacks with a navy blue boat-neck top. Her husband, Tom, wore a blue business suit of the type favored by his law firm, O'Brien, Kimberly and Rose, for its employees. Pembroke, who was not an employee, wondered if Tom Grenville intended to make points with Van Dorn, a senior partner in the firm, and wear the depressing thing the entire weekend. Pembroke said, "May I give either of you a drink?"

Joan Grenville replied, "If you're giving, I'm taking."

Tom Grenville forced a smile and said to Pembroke, "My wife only understands Manhattan idiom."

"Really?"

Grenville said, "I'll make the drinks. Scotch all around?" He busied himself at the small bar.

Joan Grenville addressed Katherine in a petulant voice. "We should have gone in the helicopter with Peter."

Katherine replied, "Even by helicopter, Peter will undoubtedly manage to arrive late."

Marc Pembroke smiled at her. "That's no way to speak of your betrothed."

Katherine realized she had been a bit too candid, and that Pembroke was baiting her. She replied, "Actually I usually arrive too early, then accuse him of being late."

"The Theory of Time's Relativity," said Pembroke, "was first discovered by watching men and women waiting for each other."

No, thought Katherine, *not baited, but led,* and she wasn't going to be led by this charmingly cunning man. She said, "Temperature, too, is relative. Men are usually too warm when a woman feels comfortable. Why don't you take off your jacket?"

"I prefer to leave it on."

And with good reason, she thought. She had spotted the pistol.

The limousine moved up a few feet. Grenville handed the drinks around. "We may be the only people in the country celebrating— what is it called?—Loyalty Day. It's also International Law Day, or something." He sucked on an ice cube. "Well, most of us at Van Dorn's will be lawyers, and most of us are loyal, so I suppose it's fitting." He bit into his ice cube.

Joan winced. "Don't *do* that. God, what a horrid weekend this is going to be. Why does Van Dorn make such a spectacle of himself?" She looked at Marc Pembroke.

Pembroke smiled. "I understand that Mr. Van Dorn never misses an opportunity to make his next-door neighbors uncomfortable."

Joan Grenville finished her Scotch in a long swallow, then said to no one in particular, "Is he going to blare those speakers toward their estate again? God, what a headache I get."

Tom Grenville laughed. "You can imagine the headache *they* get."

Katherine said, "It's all rather petty. George lowers himself by doing this."

Joan Grenville nodded in agreement. "He's going to do it again, isn't he? Memorial Day, I mean. Then *again* on July Fourth. Oh, Tom, let's be out of town. I can't stand all this flag-waving, martial music, fireworks, and whatnot. It's not fun, really." She turned to Marc Pembroke again. "The English wouldn't behave like this, would they? I mean, you're civilized."

Pembroke crossed his legs and looked closely at Joan Grenville. She stared back at him and the first smile of the evening broke across her face. They held eye contact for several seconds, then Joan reiterated, "I mean, are you civilized or not?"

Pembroke rubbed his lower lip, then replied, "Only recently, I think. Are you staying the weekend?"

The sudden shift in subject caught her off guard. "No...I mean, yes. We may. And you?"

He nodded.

Tom Grenville seemed not to notice the currents passing between his wife and the Englishman as he made himself another drink. There was a sharp knock on the window of the stopped vehicle and Grenville lowered it. A helmeted policeman peered in and asked, "Van Dorn's or the Russians'?"

"Van Dorn's," answered Grenville. "Don't we look like capitalists?"

"You all look the same to me, buddy. Pull out on the shoulder and go around this mess."

Grenville instructed the driver through the intercom and the limousine pulled out of the line of traffic and moved slowly on the shoulder.

Before they came to the main entrance of the Russian estate, they passed the YMCA, whose enclosed tennis courts as well as a few other buildings had once been part of Killenworth. Grenville said to his wife, "That's where the FBI headquarter themselves. The CIA uses the Glengariff Nursing Home up the road."

"Who cares?" replied Joan.

Marc Pembroke said, "How do you know that?"

Grenville shrugged. "Local lore."

The limousine drew abreast of the main gates to the Russian estate, moving very slowly through the police cars and motorcycles. Katherine thought there must be at least a hundred people picketing, led by the mayor of Glen Cove, Dominic Parioli, holding a huge bullhorn and wearing an Uncle Sam top hat.

Tom Grenville inclined his head toward the demonstrators. "About a fourth of them are FBI agents, with a few CIA, plus some county and state undercover police. Not to mention a KGB spy or two. If it weren't for all the double agents, Parioli couldn't muster ten people." He chuckled softly.

The demonstrators started singing "America," the police were trying to get the vehicles through the crowd, and rockets were bursting overhead. In the distance, Van Dorn's speakers could be heard now, also blaring out "America."

A separate group of demonstrators, made up of members of the Jewish Defense League and Soviet Jewish emigrés, was shouting anti-Soviet slogans, in Russian, through a loudspeaker aimed at the estate house. A group from the local high school was baiting a few grim-looking uniformed Russian guards through the fence.

Joan Grenville finally spoke. "I wish to God everyone would just calm down. This makes me nervous."

Her husband replied, "We'll be past here in a minute."

Katherine responded, "I think Joan was speaking in a larger sense. This makes me nervous too."

Pembroke nodded and put his drink on the bar. He said, "I think I hear war drums."

CHAPTER SEVEN

Stanley Kuchik hung on to the side of the rising cliff. He didn't think he could climb another inch, yet he refused to let himself slide down into the arms of the Russian below. Overhead, he heard people walking. He took a long breath and continued up the slippery incline, hardly conscious of what he was doing.

Suddenly, he tumbled onto the narrow footpath. It was several seconds before he realized where he was and was able to take in his surroundings. The first thing he saw was feet and legs. Legs coming up the path toward him, and legs coming down the path toward him. He was trapped. He wondered what they would do to him.

A voice said, "What the hell are you doing here? This is private property."

Stanley started to reply, then realized the man had spoken in good American English. A man down the path responded breathlessly, "We chase this thief. He steals from us."

The American said, "What the hell did he steal?"

Stanley raised himself into a sitting position. Two men, Americans, were standing about five feet off to his left on the narrow footpath. Four Russians stood in Indian file about ten feet to his right down the sloping path. The first, a young, hard-looking man dressed in a brown uniform, spoke in an angry voice. "He steals flag. He spies on diplomatic property."

"Oh, bullshit. Spies, my ass. All you people think about is spies."

"He has flag. You see?"

Stanley instinctively moved one hand to the knotted flag around his waist. His other hand moved toward his knife.

The American who was speaking answered brusquely, "I don't see any flag."

Stanley looked at the American. He was dressed in a suit and was kind of old, with white hair and heavy jowls. Stanley thought it might be Van Dorn himself. No one spoke or moved for a while. Stanley got his fingers around the handle of his knife.

The second American, a young man with blond hair and dressed in a white suit, squeezed around the older man and knelt beside Stanley. He spoke. "Hello. My name is Marc. What's yours?"

Stanley stared up at him. He wasn't American after all. Maybe English. He answered, "Stanley."

"Stanley, that's quite an outfit you're wearing."

Stanley looked the Englishman up and down and wanted to say *Look who's talking,* but replied, "Camouflage."

"So I see. Your face is not naturally green, is it? Are you all right?"

"I guess so."

"Well, don't be frightened. You're safe now."

Stanley looked at the larger Russian force and nodded dubiously. He said very softly, "They have guns."

Marc Pembroke nodded and whispered, "I'm sure they do. So just take your hand off that knife. It won't do any good, you know. We'll have to talk our way out of this one."

Stanley did as he was told.

Pembroke said in a normal voice, "Is that a Russian flag around your waist?" He smiled slightly.

The boy nodded.

"Where did you get it, Stanley?"

"From their flagpole."

Pembroke's smile widened. "You don't say."

The older man moved closer and said gruffly, "You stole that from their flagpole?"

"Yes, sir."

"Are you old enough to drink, kid? I'll buy you a drink."

"No, sir. Thank you."

The lead Russian spoke impatiently. "We take flag. We call FBI. This is federal offense."

Van Dorn reached his hand down and helped Stanley to his feet. "It's up to you, kid. You want to keep the flag?"

Stanley seemed surprised that he had any say in the matter. "Well...I..."

Pembroke spoke softly to Van Dorn. "He really can't keep it, George."

"Why not?" bellowed Van Dorn. "He stole it. It's his. That's what American capitalism is all about." Van Dorn laughed at his own inanity.

Pembroke looked annoyed. "Don't be an ass, George. Enough is enough. Be a good neighbor, now."

"Fuck them." He rubbed his heavy jowls in thought, then said, "Tell you what, though. I'll show you all how Communism works. Give me your knife, kid. We'll cut the goddamned flag into seven pieces and give everyone a piece to wipe their ass with." He laughed.

Stanley knew better than to go for his knife. Old Van Dorn, he thought, was a weird dude. Stanley looked at the group of Russians, who appeared a little closer now. Stanley thought they looked pretty mad, like they were going to do something. Stanley wished that Van Dorn would shut up and let the Englishman do the talking.

Van Dorn said to the Russians, "You're trespassing on my property. You understand that we have private property in this country? Beat it."

The tall Russian out front took a step forward and shook his head. "We take flag. Hold boy here. Call FBI."

"Try it," said Van Dorn.

There was a long silence, then Marc Pembroke unknotted the flag and pulled it from Stanley's waist. "Sorry, lad, it is theirs." Pembroke made a movement to throw it up to them, then held it out. The tall Russian in uniform came up the narrow trail and stopped a few feet from Stanley and stared at the boy.

Stanley stared back and noticed that the Russian's uniform was tattered, dirty, and covered with burrs. Stanley smiled.

The Russian snatched the flag from Pembroke's hand and yanked it past Stanley's face, brushing him. Pembroke pulled the boy away. "All right, incident closed. It was only a prank. We'll take care of punishing the boy."

The tall Russian seemed to grow bolder. "We wait here. Boy stays here. We call FBI."

Pembroke shook his head. "We go, chaps. With boy. I apologize on behalf of the citizens of Glen Cove, the American people, and Her Majesty's government. Now leave."

Van Dorn, who had stayed uncharacteristically silent, added in a low, threatening tone. "Get off my property." He raised both arms and leveled a huge, long-barreled revolver at the tall Russian. He cocked the hammer. "Next time...if you cross that fence again... bring pallbearers along. You have ten seconds to turn around. Nine, eight..."

No one moved. Then the tall Russian said to Van Dorn, "Capitalist swine!"

"Seven, six..." Van Dorn fired. Everyone fell to the ground except Van Dorn. The echo of the gun's blast died away and the night was still.

Pembroke got up into a kneeling position, a pistol in his hand, the other hand pressing Stanley to the ground.

Van Dorn said, "Just a warning. Get moving."

The four Russians stood and quickly did an about-face. They began picking their way down the dark narrow trail. Van Dorn lowered his pistol, then slid it into a big holster under his jacket. "You can't let those goons push you around."

Pembroke holstered his own revolver and helped Stanley to his feet. The boy was visibly shaken but seemed to be nodding in agreement with Van Dorn.

Pembroke looked a bit exasperated. He said sharply to Stanley, "What are you supposed to be, then? A commando?"

Stanley mumbled something that sounded surly. The shock was wearing off and already he felt cheated and angry.

Van Dorn rubbed his hanging jowls, then said brightly, "Hey, I've got a Russian flag. Want it?"

Stanley's eyes widened. "Sure." He paused, then said, "Where'd you get it?"

Van Dorn laughed. "At the Elbe, Germany, 1945. It was a gift. I didn't do anything crazy to get it. I think you deserve it. Come on, I'll buy you a Coke or something, and get you cleaned up before you go home."

They began climbing the path. Van Dorn said, "You live around here?"

"Yes, sir."

"Do you know your way around in there?"

"Sure." Stanley was feeling much better. He remembered his pictures, and the Russian file in his field bag. And if Van Dorn gave him the flag, he could show it around... but maybe what really happened would make a better story. He had to think about that.

Pembroke said, "Do you do this often? I mean, go into their estate?"

Stanley replied, cautiously, "I've jumped the fence a few times, but never got close to the house before."

Van Dorn commented, "If we hadn't heard a lot of commotion—dogs and shouting—you'd be *in* their house right now."

Stanley didn't believe they could hear anything from so far off, especially with that damned music blaring.

They reached the top of the path and began walking across a flat, open lawn that had a set of rising bleacher seats at one end. Van Dorn said, "This is a polo field. But I guess you know that, don't you? You're not the guy who steals my tomatoes, are you?"

"No, sir." Stanley looked across the polo field. On either side of the bleachers were two high poles, each supporting a loudspeaker. The speakers were silent now, and Stanley wondered if they hid directional microphones aimed at the Russian estate. Maybe that's how they knew what was happening. On the far side of the lawn he saw the big white-lighted house.

Van Dorn was pulling at his jowls again, then asked, "Hey, how'd you like to do some work on my place? Saturdays. After school. Good pay."

"Sure."

"We can talk a little about your adventures."

Stanley hesitated, then said, "I guess that's okay."

Van Dorn put his arm awkwardly around Stanley's shoulders. "How'd you get so close? To the house, I mean?"

"Drainage culvert."

Van Dorn nodded thoughtfully. He said with a smile, "You didn't get in the house, did you?"

Stanley didn't respond at first, then said, "I think I could."

Van Dorn's eyebrows lifted.

Pembroke said, "What's in that bag you're carrying?"

"Things."

They walked for a while, drawing near the big house, where Stanley could see that a party was going on.

Pembroke asked, "What kinds of things?"

"You know, patrol things."

"What are patrol things, lad?"

"You know. Camouflage paint, flashlight, camera, candy bars, patrol maps. Like that."

Van Dorn stopped walking. He looked at Marc Pembroke, who was looking back at him. Van Dorn nodded slightly.

Pembroke shook his head.

Van Dorn nodded again, very firmly.

Stanley watched them. He had a funny feeling he had not seen the last of the Russian estate.

BOOK II

The Wingate Letter

CHAPTER EIGHT

Katherine Kimberly read:

Dear Miss Kimberly,
A curious and perhaps fateful incident has occurred which prompts me to write you. As you may know, your late father, Henry, was billeted here at Brompton Hall during the war. After his death, an American officer came round for his personal effects. The officer was most insistent on recovering everything that belonged to your father. This was done, I presumed, not so much out of a sentimental regard for Major Kimberly's family but for security reasons, as your father, I'm sure you're aware, was involved with intelligence work of a sensitive nature.

Colonel Randolph Carbury stroked his white mustache pensively as he regarded the attractive woman sitting at her desk. She was, he thought, a remarkable American specimen; nearly forty, as he knew, but looking closer to thirty. Her long hair was a light blond color, her pale skin slightly freckled with a spring tan. He was told she was a runner and he could believe it from the looks of her trim body and well-shaped legs.

She looked up from the letter and met the eyes of the Englishman sitting across from her.

He inclined his head toward the letter. "Please continue."

Katherine stared down at the gold-embossed letterhead: Lady Eleanor Wingate, Brompton Hall, Tongate, Kent. The letter was handwritten with black ink in what Katherine thought was a script so perfect it could have been copperplate. She looked up at Carbury. His face was taut, almost grim, she thought. "Would you like a drink?" She indicated a sideboard and Carbury rose wordlessly and walked toward it. She continued to read.

We were as helpful as possible under the circumstances, but Brompton Hall is rather a large house, and there was almost no staff available to make a thorough search of the places where a man in your father's line of work might choose to secure sensitive documents.

You can see, perhaps, where this is leading. A few days ago we were clearing out Brompton Hall in preparation for its transfer to new owners. In one of the storage closets in the muniment room—a sort of family archive room—was a parcel wrapped in oilcloth which turned out to contain a U.S. Army dispatch case. My nephew, Charles, who was supervising the work, brought it to me straightaway.

Inside the case were well-preserved papers, mostly ciphers and that sort of thing, of no importance by now, I should think. There were also letters bundled and tied. They appear to be a few rather touching notes from your sister, Ann, who was then about five years of age. There was also an item of immediate concern: a locked diary.

After some deliberation, I decided to open the lock to be certain it was your father's diary and, if it was, to determine if there was anything inside that might be painful for you to read. As it turns out, there are references to me and to your mother. But I've decided to delete none of them. You're quite old enough to understand love, loneliness, and war.

Most of the diary, however, is not of a personal nature. There are pages of notes of which I believe you and your government should be made aware.

Katherine paused in her reading. This was really too much to assimilate, she thought. Yet, it was not entirely unexpected. Eleanor Wingate was a name dimly remembered from her childhood, though she couldn't recall the context. Now the memory and the context were clearer. And Randolph Carbury's visit was not unexpected either, though he had been totally unknown to her fifteen minutes ago. She had known that some day Carbury, or someone like him, would appear out of the blue. It was inevitable that the ghost of her father would reach out to her. She read on:

The circumstances involving your father's death in Berlin were, I think, quite mysterious, dying as he did some days after the end of the war. I never had much faith in the official version of what happened. Also, your father said to me once, "Eleanor, if I should die without at least a dozen reliable witnesses to testify that it was from completely natural causes, you'll know the Russians finally got me."

I replied, "Henry, you mean the Germans." To which he responded, "No, I mean our sneaking, cutthroat allies."

And there was something else. The American officer who came for Henry's effects—I didn't like his conduct or the looks of him. Why did he come alone to search this big house and recruit my small staff in this tiring business? Why did another officer come the next day on the same mission? This second officer seemed incredulous that someone had come before him. He said the Army had learned of Henry's death only hours before.

At the time, I was too overcome with grief to make much sense of any of this, but some weeks later I tried to make enquiries. Wartime security, however, was still in effect, and it was quite hopeless.

Well, your father's diary clears up a great many things.

Katherine looked at Carbury and said softly, "Talbot?"

Carbury's eyes widened slightly. "Yes. Talbot and Wolfbane. I didn't realize you knew. How much *do* you know?"

"Not enough." She turned the page of the letter and continued.

Seeing Henry's things in that dispatch case has brought back many memories and rekindled an old sense of guilt—not of our relationship, which was guiltless (my husband had died in Malta early in the war, and your mother was in the process of divorcing your father for some Washington bureaucrat), but guilt at not having contacted you at some point and telling you some of the good things about your father, who was a remarkable man.

Well, there's little more to say. I'm going up to London to live with my nephew, Charles Brook.

These last few weeks have been rather strange—rather sad, too—closing up Brompton Hall, your father's papers, the awakened memories of "the best of times and the worst of times."

But the point of this letter is to advise you of the dispatch case and, more specifically, the diary, which names people who may still be with your government or who are highly placed in American society, and names them in a way that forebodes, I'm afraid, the gravest consequences for your country and for all of us. At least one of those named is a well-known man who is close to your President.

This letter is to be delivered by a trusted friend, Randolph Carbury. He will, I hope, locate you at the law firm with which he tells me you are associated. Colonel Carbury is an old military intelligence man and an excellent judge of situations and people. If in his opinion you are the one who ought to receive the diary, he will arrange with you for the delivery of same.

My first thought was to make these papers available to my government or yours, or both simultaneously, in photostat form. But Randolph seems to think, and I agree, that the material might well fall into the very hands of those it exposes.

O'Brien, Kimberly and Rose was, of course, your father's firm, and many of the OSS intelligence officers who stayed at Brompton Hall were also associated with the firm. If I'm not being indiscreet, Colonel Carbury indicates that the firm still has ties with the intelligence community here and in America. Also, he mentioned that your sister, Ann, is somehow connected with American intelligence. Perhaps you ought to show the diary

to her—or to trusted people in your firm—for critical evalua-
tion. I pray that it is not as grave and foreboding as it appears to
be—though I'm fairly certain and afraid that it is.

My best wishes
(signed) Eleanor Wingate

Katherine stayed silent for some time, then said, "Why didn't you go directly to my sister?"

"She's not easy to locate, is she?"

"No, she's not."

"Given the choice, I'd still prefer dealing with you."

"Why?"

"Because, as Lady Wingate indicated, and as we both know, your firm takes more than a nostalgic interest in affairs such as this. It's in your hands now. Distribute the information as you see fit. But please be cautious."

"Should I ask Mr. O'Brien to join us?"

"I'd rather you didn't."

"Why not?"

"Nearly all of us from that time and that profession are automatically suspect. Including myself, of course."

Katherine stood and looked out from the forty-fourth-floor window of her office. Across Fifth Avenue, the intricate gray masonry of St. Patrick's Cathedral spread out in the shape of a Latin cross. In the café below, the two dozen or so tables were empty. It was an unusually raw and overcast May afternoon, a day of gray vapor plumes and long gray shadows.

Colonel Carbury stood also and followed her gaze. "This view has changed considerably since these were the offices of British Security Coordination. I last stood at this very window in 1945. Yet, you know, the major landmarks are still standing—the Waldorf, Saks, St. Patrick's, the St. Regis—and I fancy it is 1945 again, and I see myself down there, a younger man dashing across the avenue...."

He turned from the window. "I see myself in this office again with my American associates—General Donovan, the Dulleses, Clare Boothe Luce, and your employer, Patrick O'Brien, who never arrived at a meeting without a few bottles of liberated spirits. Algerian wine in the beginning, then some Corvo from Sicily, and, finally, champagne....I met your father here one Sunday. He had a little girl with him, but that must have been your sister, Ann. You would have been an infant."

"Yes, my sister," Katherine said.

Carbury nodded. His eyes passed over a wall where vintage black-and-white photographs hung. "What brave and pure lads and lasses we were. What a war it was. What a time it was." He glanced at her. "It was, Miss Kimberly, perhaps the one moment in history when all the best and the brightest were within the government, unified in purpose, with no distinctions of class or politics...or so we thought."

Katherine listened as Carbury reminisced, knowing he was not deviating from his point or his purpose, only taking the longer route to get there.

Carbury looked directly at her. "The past comes back to haunt us because it was an imperfect past, a shaky foundation upon which we've built so much."

Katherine moved away from the window. "You have my father's diary?"

Colonel Carbury walked to the center of the room. "Not with me. I only brought the letter for now." He nodded toward the three sheets of cream-colored vellum stationery on Katherine's desk. His eyes met hers and he seemed to appreciate her wariness. He spoke softly. "It is not pure chance, as you know, that the law firm of O'Brien, Kimberly and Rose occupies the same offices my people occupied during the war. It was Patrick O'Brien's decision, I believe, to move his firm here. Nostalgia, continuity...karma, if you will." He smiled. "I spent some time in India."

Carbury seemed suddenly tired and sat back down in the chair beside her desk. "Do you mind?" He lit a cigarette and watched the smoke drift upward. "It's difficult to explain to someone so young what a marvel these buildings were in 1940. Futuristic design, air conditioning, high-speed elevators, restaurants with decent food. We English treated ourselves rather well, I can tell you. But it was not much fun, really, for we were all painfully aware of what our island was going through."

"I think I can appreciate what you're saying."

Carbury nodded absently. "Yet, we knew that our mission in America was the single most important contribution to the war effort. We came to New York, over a thousand strong, to fight a different kind of war." He looked around the large office as though trying to recall how it looked then. "To get America into the war, actually. To raise money and arms, to collect intelligence, to lobby, to plead, to beg. . . . We were in a rather bad way. Whisky warriors, some called us. And I suppose we did drink a bit much. . . ." He shrugged.

Katherine said, "History has recorded your contribution."

"Yes, only recently. I've lived long enough to see that. Most didn't. That's the nature of clandestine work." He stubbed out his cigarette. "It is a lonely and frustrating way to serve one's country. Don't you find that so?"

"I'm a lawyer. My sister, Ann, is the one in intelligence."

"Yes, of course." Carbury stared off into space for some time, and Katherine could see that beneath the composed exterior was a man burning with emotion.

"When will I see the contents of the dispatch case?" she said.

"This evening."

"I have an appointment this evening."

"Yes, I know. The Seventh Regiment Armory. Table fourteen. I'm at table thirty-one with some compatriots of mine."

She nodded.

"I'll arrange the details of the transfer with you at that time."

"Where are you staying, Colonel?"

"My old hotel—the Ritz-Carlton."

"The Ritz-Carlton has been torn down."

"Has it?" He rose. "I'll have to find another place." He extended his hand, and she took it. Carbury said, "I've read the diary, of course, and this is most serious. We'll discuss how to proceed tonight."

"Thank you for coming."

"It was my pleasure. You're as beautiful as your mother"—he nodded toward a picture on the wall—"and I suspect as intelligent as your father. Thank you for the drink, and again please forgive me for not making an appointment. I came from the airport straightaway."

As she walked toward the door, Katherine wondered what he had done with his luggage. "How can I reach you between now and this evening?"

"I'm afraid you can't. Sounds a bit paranoid, but I'm being rather cautious."

"So am I."

"Good." He turned and stepped up to the window again, focusing on the scene below. He spoke quietly, almost to himself. "Things may not always be as they appear, but there is a logical explanation for everything. Not always a reassuring explanation, but always logical. We should keep that in mind over the coming days."

Katherine opened the door, and Carbury stepped up to it. He said, "Please consider yourself operational now. Security, discretion, and extreme personal caution."

Katherine replied, "If you are who you say you are, and the letter is what it purports to be, then thank you, Colonel. If you are not who you seem, then be extremely careful yourself."

Carbury smiled. "Good day." He left.

Katherine walked to her desk and pressed her intercom. "Mr. Abrams, will you come in here? Immediately, please."

She folded the Wingate letter and slid it into the pocket of her wool blazer.

Tony Abrams opened the door between her office and the library. Katherine looked at him, framed in the doorway against the brighter lights of the library. He was a tall man, with dusky skin, black hair, and deep-set dark eyes. He did not affect what she called the Brooks Brothers–attorney costume. He seemed to own only dark suits and white shirts, all of which were remarkably alike. The ties—and there were a good number of them—were always colorful, as though he were trying to avoid being taken for a funeral director. His movements were slow and easy, and his manner was taciturn.

They exchanged barely a dozen words at a time, but somehow they had developed a good working relationship.

She nodded toward the door. "An Englishman, name of Carbury." She handed Carbury's card to Abrams. "Just left. Tall, thin, white mustache, about seventy years old. He'll be asking the receptionist for his coat. Follow him, please, to find out where he's staying. Call me."

Abrams handed back the card and without a word turned and left.

Katherine walked slowly to the sideboard. She looked at a picture framed in old silver: Major Henry Kimberly, dressed in officer's tans, without a cap, so that his light hair fell boyishly over his forehead. It was an outdoor shot, in sepia tones. In the background was the blurry suggestion of a stone wall, which as a child she had imagined to be a fort. Now she wondered if it was Brompton Hall.

She picked up the picture and held it closer. Her father's eyes, like her own, were large and very clear. She remembered the only nice thing her mother ever said about him: "He had eyes that sparkled across a room."

She looked at the inscription: *To my Little Kate, I love you, Daddy.* She placed the photograph back on the sideboard. Lifting the decanter of Scotch, she poured some into a half glass of water. The neck of the decanter rattled against the lip of the glass as her hand shook.

She took the drink to the window and held it pressed against her chest. She looked out across the city and took a long, deep breath, feeling the tears forming in her eyes. The cityscape dissolved into a watery blur, and she wiped her eyes with the back of her hand. *Yes,* she thought, *a day of long gray shadows.*

CHAPTER NINE

Tony Abrams crossed the large, beige-toned reception area and saw Randolph Carbury approaching the elevator bank, pulling on a tan raincoat.

Abrams took his own coat from the closet, descended the sweeping circular staircase in the center of the reception floor, and walked to the elevators on the lower floor of the law offices. He pushed the button and waited. The elevator doors opened, and Abrams stepped in beside Carbury. They rode down to the street level.

He followed Carbury through the long, shop-lined concourse and exited with him from the east end of the RCA Building, into the damp, chilly air.

Abrams established an interval of ten yards and followed Carbury around the skating rink, through the promenade, and onto Fifth Avenue, where Carbury turned north.

As he walked, Abrams considered that he was following a man he didn't know for a purpose he couldn't begin to fathom. At forty-three years of age he was doing what he'd done at thirty-three as a New York City undercover cop. At least then he knew the whys and wherefores of his assignments. Now he knew very little about the tasks he was asked to perform for the firm of O'Brien, Kimberly and Rose. Such as agreeing to go to the Russian estate on Monday, Memorial Day. But Patrick O'Brien had assured him he'd be fully briefed before he went. O'Brien's idea of fully briefed, he suspected, did not coincide with his own.

Carbury stopped now and then, ostensibly to take in the sights. Abrams' instincts told him that the man was a pro, a fact Katherine Kimberly had failed to mention.

Abrams stopped and looked into a bookstore window as Carbury waited for a light. Whenever he followed someone, Abrams was reminded of his mother's sage advice: "Get an inside job." In the Bensonhurst section of Brooklyn where he'd grown up, the world was neatly divided into outside and inside jobs. Outside jobs meant pneumonia, heat stroke, and unspeakable accidents. Inside jobs of the tie-and-jacket variety were safe. Notwithstanding that admonition, he became a cop. A little inside, a little outside, once in a while a tie. His mother wasn't altogether pleased. She'd tell her friends, "He's a detective. An inside job. He wears a suit."

He had graduated at the top of his class from John Jay College of Criminal Justice, then entered Fordham Law School. It was then that he'd had an occasion to see the O'Brien firm in action. He had been observing a stock-fraud case for a law class, and it seemed that the defendant had more lawyers than the district attorney had pages in his indictment. The assistant DA trying the case had been dazzled—intimidated, actually. Abrams had been impressed, both as a cop and as a law student, and some weeks later he had applied for and gotten a part-time process server job with the O'Brien firm. Then, a year ago, Patrick O'Brien offered him a full-time position and full tuition reimbursement. At the time, it seemed apparent that they wanted a house dick, someone with special police knowledge and without the encumbrances of being a sworn peace officer. Since his May Day conversation with O'Brien, he wasn't certain anymore of what they wanted of him.

Randolph Carbury crossed the street and stopped again to watch a well-attended sidewalk game of three-card monte. Abrams suspected that Carbury was trying to determine if he had a tail. If so, he'd try to shake the tail. And in a one-on-one situation, that wouldn't be difficult. Abrams considered the unhappy prospect of going back to Katherine Kimberly empty-handed. But he also considered that he was unhappy with the way he was usually kept guessing about these assignments.

There was something decidedly non-kosher about the prestigious firm of O'Brien, Kimberly and Rose, and Abrams had one clue: Like the law firm of the late General William Donovan, which was located a few floors below, O'Brien's firm had national intelligence connections going back to World War II. Not only was Patrick O'Brien an ex-intelligence officer, but so had been the late Henry Kimberly. The late Jonathan Rose had been an Allen Dulles aide in Bern during the war and a John Foster Dulles aide in the State Department during the Eisenhower administration. Also, Abrams had seen a good number of intelligence men and women, who had somehow run afoul of the law, pass through the office. If there was anything irregular about this law practice, it was those connections and associations. Tonight at the dinner he might learn more.

Carbury continued north. Abrams followed. His thoughts turned back to Katherine Kimberly. There was a woman who personified sangfroid. He imagined she took cold showers in the winter and stood in front of an open window to dry off. The Ice Queen, he called her, though certainly not to her face.

Yet when she had summoned him into her office, he had been almost shocked at her appearance. She was ghostly white, very upset, and she'd barely made an effort at hiding it. There was still that ice wall between them, but it had clearly cracked, and she seemed more human and more vulnerable in those brief seconds than he could have imagined.

Obviously the interview with Carbury had precipitated some strong emotion in her. Carbury was British, a colonel, World War II vintage. His card said retired and gave no branch, but the man was decidedly not a quartermaster officer. He was more likely in intelligence or police work of some sort. Abrams, after more than twenty years, could spot the signs. This did not explain what had caused so startling a transformation in Katherine Kimberly, but it was a clue.

He thought perhaps he should have asked her if she was all right. But then she might have borne a grudge against him for noticing and commenting on it; though he wondered why he felt it mattered.

Carbury passed the Plaza Hotel and headed west on Central Park South, then turned into the St. Moritz Hotel. Abrams waited a full minute, then entered the lobby.

Carbury was at the news counter buying a copy of the *Times*. He walked to the desk, spoke briefly with the clerk, then walked to the elevator and took the first car up.

Abrams paused at the news counter. The *Times* headlined: PRESIDENT SPEAKS TONIGHT IN CITY. A subline announced: *Addresses World War II Intelligence Service.* The *Post* read simply: PRES SPEAKS TO EX-SPOOKS TONIGHT. The *News* reported: POSH BASH FOR CLOAK AND DAGGER BOYS. Which reminded Abrams that he hadn't picked up his tuxedo yet. "Damn it."

He walked across the lobby and approached the desk clerk. "Do you have a Colonel Randolph Carbury registered?"

"Yes, sir. Room 1415."

Abrams walked toward the front doors. That was easier than he thought. Too easy? He turned and walked to the house phone. "Colonel Randolph Carbury, room 1415."

After a pause, the operator answered, "I'm sorry, sir. Room 1415 is unoccupied."

"Do you have a Randolph Carbury registered?"

"Hold on.... No, sir, there is no one by that name here."

Abrams' impulse was to go back to the desk clerk and have a talk with him, but it would be better if Carbury thought he'd pulled it off.

Abrams went out and stood on the sidewalk. It was getting late, and he was becoming annoyed. The assignment was better accomplished from a telephone. If Carbury was registered anywhere in the city under his own name, Abrams could discover where within a few hours. Katherine Kimberly made easy use of his time and shoe leather.

He crossed Central Park South and entered a phone booth from which he could see the St. Moritz. A light rain began to fall.

He called a friend in the Nineteenth Precinct and gave him the information, then placed a call to Katherine Kimberly. "I'm across from the St. Moritz—"

"Is he staying there?"

"That's what he wants me to think—"

"You mean he suspects he's being followed?"

"If he's trying to lose me, then he knows, doesn't he?"

"I thought you were good at this."

Abrams gave himself a few seconds to control his voice. "You are supposed to tell me if the man is a pro."

"Oh . . . sorry." She paused. "Does he think he lost you?"

"Maybe. Look, I can't follow him indefinitely. I've got someone working on hotel registrations. I'm leaving."

"No. Stay with him. I want you to see that he's safely in his hotel, or wherever it is he's staying—"

"Safely? Safely implies that someone is trying to do something unsafe to him. You've got a lot to learn about briefing—"

"I'm sorry. I had no time. He left me with the impression that someone may want to harm him."

Abrams looked across the street, then scanned the park behind him. He slipped his .38 "police special" out of his shoulder holster and dropped it into his coat pocket. "He probably thinks I'm gunning for him. Christ, he's probably called the cops. That's all I need, to get busted for harassment—"

"We'll represent you. No charge."

He started to reply, then laughed.

Unexpectedly, she laughed too, a genuine laugh, light and almost girlish, and it surprised him. "Be careful," she said. "Stay with it. All right, Mr. Abrams?"

He lit a cigarette. "All right, Miss Kimberly. But listen, I've decided to skip this thing tonight."

She snapped, "You've got to be there," then softened her tone. "I'm afraid that it's a command performance."

Abrams drew on his cigarette and stared through the rain toward the hotel. "My tux is at the cleaners. Can't get it while I'm doing this."

"I'll have it picked up and delivered to you."

"Good. I'll change in a phone booth."

"Listen to me. Colonel Carbury is going where we are going

tonight, so he also has to dress. Eventually he must go to his hotel—"

"You should have told me that, too. It makes a difference."

"Now you know. So stay with him until then."

"Do you know I live in Brooklyn?"

"Yes, and I sympathize. So you will go to the firm's town house at 184 East Thirty-sixth Street, where your dinner jacket will be delivered. You can dress there, unless you'd prefer a telephone booth. What cleaner do you use?"

He hesitated, then mentioned a formal-wear rental shop, cursing her silently for making him reveal the fact that his wardrobe didn't include such a thing.

She made him repeat the name of the place, and he wondered if she was enjoying herself. She said, "I've called the Burke Agency, and they've got two detectives with a radio car ready to assist you. Can they rendezvous with you now?"

"They could have if you'd mentioned it sooner. Unfortunately, Carbury has just left the hotel. I'll call Burke's office later."

"Call me, too. I'll be here until five fifteen. Then I'll be at the Lombardy Hotel. Ask for the Thorpe suite."

He hung up and crossed the street. Carbury headed south on Sixth Avenue. It was after 5:00 P.M. now, and rush hour traffic was getting heavier. Shop windows cast oblongs of light onto the wet sidewalks. Carbury was barely visible crossing 58th Street.

Abrams hurried to catch up. The telephone conversation had somehow taken the edge off his bad mood. He was interested again. The Lombardy Hotel. Only it wasn't actually a hotel. Every suite above the lobby was owned by somebody who paid more money for it than it would cost to buy the entire block in his old Brooklyn neighborhood. "You travel in the right circles, Ice Queen." The Thorpe suite. Peter Thorpe—Abrams had been introduced to him once in the office. He'd check that out too, though it was none of his business.

Carbury turned abruptly into 54th Street. Abrams followed. Carbury was moving quickly beside the long garden wall of the Museum of Modern Art. Abrams kept well behind on the opposite side of the street. Ahead, at the intersection of Fifth Avenue, he saw Carbury cross to his side of the street, look up and down the crowded block, then mount the steps of a stately old granite building with a long gray awning. The University Club.

Abrams waited, giving it fifteen minutes, then proceeded to the intersection and entered a telephone booth. He called his contact at the Nineteenth Precinct. "Phil, what do you have?"

The detective told him, "Your man checked through customs at Kennedy two days ago. Gave the St. Moritz as his address, but he's not registered there. It's going to take time to phone every hotel in town. Besides, he could be using an alias or be staying in an apartment, a private club, or a place that isn't required to keep registration records. If it's urgent—"

"No. Thanks, Phil."

"You owe me one. I want you to follow my wife."

"She asked me to follow you."

The man laughed. "How's life treating you, Abrams? Got your Esquire yet?"

"Not yet."

"What's this all about?"

"Nothing criminal"—Abrams kept his eye on the doors of the building that Carbury had entered—"matrimonial . . . horseshit."

"Well, you catch that sucker with his pants off and squeeze his nuts. Who'd travel across the Atlantic for a piece of ass these days? Christ, I wouldn't cross the street for it."

"Sure you would."

"Why don't you come around anymore? Never see you at P.J.'s."

"Buy you one."

"Not tonight. The President is going to be at the Seventh Armory. Secret Service and Bureau all over the fucking place. They got me on a goddamned roof. Jesus. Have to go."

"Right. Look, don't bother with the calls. I think I've got him."

Abrams hung up and called Katherine Kimberly. He was told by her secretary that she was not available but that she expected him to call her later at the Lombardy. He called the Burke Detective

Agency and told them to send the car to the northeast corner of 54th and Fifth.

Abrams crossed Fifth Avenue and stood at the appointed corner, where he had a good view of the building across the street. It had been a job well done, and he congratulated himself. He supposed that mounted police on punishment duty also congratulated themselves when they did a good job of shoveling the shit out of the stables.

He leaned against a lamppost and turned up his collar. He realized that Katherine Kimberly, if she was walking tonight, would most probably pass this way to get to the Lombardy. Why, he wondered, would he think of that?

Rush hour traffic flowed around him. He looked through the lighted windows in the building across the street. *Someone may want to harm him.* Very heavy stuff. Carbury thought so too. Yet apparently no one had notified the police, which was suggestive of all sorts of things.

Patrick O'Brien, Katherine Kimberly, tuxedos and town houses, tax write-offs and investment tax credits. Money, power, and status. He had discovered that lawyers almost never took the law too seriously. There was hardly a law on the books, including first-degree murder, that wasn't open to interpretation. They understood the complex society in which they lived and manipulated it from every seat of power in the land. The rest of the nation had to get by as best they could. Or, as a police captain once said to him, "A single lawyer is a shyster, two lawyers are a law firm, three or more are a legislative body."

Abrams' father, a great egalitarian—a Communist, actually— used to instruct him, "We are all pilgrims on the same journey." True, thought Abrams, but some pilgrims have better road maps.

CHAPTER TEN

Katherine Kimberly walked down a deserted corridor on the forty-fourth floor, some distance from her office. The corridor ended at a steel door marked DEAD FILES.

She pressed a buzzer. A peephole cover slid open, then the door itself opened slowly on squeaking hinges. She entered a room that was badly lit and musty.

The room was stacked high with oak file cabinets of a type not seen in many years. At the end of an aisle of cabinets there was a single window, which was grimy, as windows tend to become when they are crisscrossed with steel bars. Raindrops beat against the window of the overheated room. She heard the door close behind her and turned.

"Hello, miss."

"Good afternoon, Arnold." She regarded the elderly Englishman as her eyes became accustomed to the bad light.

"Just making tea, miss."

"Fine." Not to accept tea was to get off on the wrong foot with Arnold, as she had discovered.

Arnold busied himself with the china tea service that was laid on a khaki-painted camp table.

"Do you know a Colonel Randolph Carbury?"

Arnold nodded. He switched on an electric hot plate on which sat a copper kettle. He motioned to a shelf lined with colored tins of Twining's. "What's your pleasure? I've got a bit of Earl Grey left."

"Fine. Is there a file on him?"

"The Earl?" He laughed at his own joke. "Oh, Carbury. Indeed there is." He pulled up a chair, and she sat.

She watched as he spooned the loose tea into the china pot. No, she thought, it was no accident that the firm of O'Brien, Kimberly and Rose had moved from Wall Street to this building in Rockefeller Center after the war. The wartime American intelligence organization where Patrick O'Brien had worked, the Office of Strategic Services, had kept offices in this building. And, as Carbury had reminisced, so had British Security Coordination, which had been headquartered in what was now the suite of the O'Brien firm. Nostalgia, karma, perhaps something else.

When the British had vacated their space on the forty-fourth floor, they had retained the lease on this one room. They had also left behind a good number of files and a caretaker staff, including their archivist, Sergeant Arnold Brin, who was now the sole remaining person. This room, and Arnold himself, were part of the flotsam and jetsam of a once farflung empire, left aground in the ebb tide of the realm.

Katherine once remarked to O'Brien about the expenditure for an intelligence facility that had seemingly been defunct for nearly forty years. He had replied, "It was a gift from them to us."

"But who *pays* for it?"

"The monarch is given a discretionary fund by Parliament for royal functions. Some of this money finds its way into other types of functions."

"Intelligence functions?"

"Yes." O'Brien had smiled. "If you want to know a secret, Congress, during the Second War, set a similar precedent. They voted tens of millions of dollars in unvouchered funds to be used by General Donovan at his discretion. I'll tell you about that some day."

The copper kettle whistled, and Arnold poured the boiling water into the china pot. "Like it strong, do you? Give it a good five minutes."

Katherine looked down the center aisle of the file cabinets. According to O'Brien, British intelligence occasionally paid a visit to the archives. But General Donovan's Office of Strategic Services, with whom it was intended to be shared, had been unexpectedly disbanded after the war. Nearly two years later the OSS was reborn as the Central Intelligence Agency; but lacking the continuity of the British intelligence services, the CIA had apparently overlooked this facility, or asset, as they termed it. Patrick O'Brien and his OSS veteran friends, however, had not forgotten the British legacy and had inherited it by default—or by design. She was not certain which.

She also knew that many of the OSS's own files had never passed to the CIA but were still in this building some floors below.

Arnold set a large teacup on the camp table. He produced a napkin and a teaspoon. "No sugar, no cream." He poured the tea through a strainer.

"Thank you."

Arnold disappeared into the gloom of the file stacks and returned shortly with a buff-colored folder. "Carbury, Randolph, Major. Same man, new rank, I should think." He switched on a dusty green-shaded reading lamp, then extracted from the folder a small ID photograph. "Is that the man?"

Katherine stared at the old photograph. "I have no way of identifying him." Why, she thought, would he assume she could, unless he also assumed that she had met Carbury? She looked at Arnold, and he seemed somewhat embarrassed.

"What I meant, miss, is have you ever seen a picture of him?"

"No." She began to wonder if Carbury had been in this room before his meeting with her. But even if that were so, there was nothing inherently suspicious about that. He could have access to the files, assuming his credentials were in order. That, according to O'Brien, was a stipulation of the legacy.

Katherine leafed through the loose pages of the thin file. It was basically a personal file, very informally arranged, unlike the thick brown dossiers on Fascist agents who had worked in America. There were no details of operations, but there were code-numbered references to those operations on which Carbury had worked. Randolph Carbury, it appeared, was no whisky warrior; he had been highly regarded and highly decorated.

Katherine came upon an encoded Western Union telegram with the decoded text written in pencil below. The decoded signature caught her eye, and she read the message, dated 12 February 1945.

To Major R. Carbury: Again, I must press you for more specifics regarding the light shed by the Hunter's Moon. It is due to rise this year on 16 October, by which time Mars will have set, decreasing the favourable conditions which now obtain for the hunt. A martini is needed quickly. Churchill.

Katherine reread the message. Even en clair it was obtuse, a further guard against unauthorized eyes. Hunter's Moon, she assumed, was the name of an operation. After reading enough oblique wartime communications, one got the hang of it. She looked back at the wrinkled telegram. *Light shed*—a status report was required. *Mars will have set*—the war will have ended. *Decreasing the favourable conditions*—wartime powers will also end, making the hunt more difficult, or something like that. So far, so good.

A martini is needed quickly. Katherine ran her hand through her long hair and thought. The leitmotif was hunting and therefore followed throughout. Hunting and moon, with a mythological reference to Mars. Vintage Churchill.

She thought back to the Wingate letter, to Colonel Carbury's acknowledgment that the letter had something to do with Wolfbane—the American wartime intelligence operation to expose a Soviet double agent highly placed in the OSS. It was just possible that Hunter's Moon was the British code name for the American operation Wolfbane.

If this was true, then the last line became clearer. *A martini is needed quickly* was not an offhand cry of frustration, which in any case Mr. Churchill handled with brandy. It was Churchill changing metaphors based on the word *Wolfbane*. American slang for a martini was a silver bullet. Who was to be the recipient of the quickly needed silver bullet? It was the mythological werewolf.

Katherine took it to the next logical step: The most infamous werewolf, portrayed by Lon Chaney, Jr., in the wartime classic motion picture, was Lawrence Talbot. And Talbot was the code name for the unknown Soviet double agent who was the object of the hunt named Operation Wolfbane, or Hunter's Moon. She nodded.

So, assuming the last line was meant literally, Churchill was giving the order to kill Talbot—if he could be found. They were not to arrest him, not to attempt to turn him, not to bring him to trial, but to kill him outright, as you would kill a wild creature. And she thought she knew why. It wasn't petty revenge. It was because Talbot was believed to be so highly placed that his open exposure would cause irreparable damage to public confidence and morale. It was also because espionage trials of Soviet agents were not politically or diplomatically prudent in those days of the war-time alliance with Russia.

Katherine sat back and sipped her tea. Talbot had never received that silver bullet. For years after the war he had prowled the collective memories and psyches of American and British intelligence; occasionally his bloody work had been discovered: a fresh kill lying at the bottom of a ravine. Then silence. There were theories: He had died a natural death, he'd finally been killed, or perhaps he'd simply retired. Or a more unsettling theory: He had ceased taking the normal risks of the double agent and become a sleeper agent, in order to insure his continued rise in whatever career he had chosen for himself. *A well-known man who is close to your President.* A man who controlled his appetite for treason until he was in a position to satiate that appetite to the fullest. *Grave and foreboding.*

Katherine turned her attention back to the file. She leafed quickly through the thin sheaf of memos, telegrams, and notes. She saw a long memo to Carbury from William Stephenson, the head of British Security Coordination in America, the man known as Intrepid and Carbury's wartime boss. The memo seemed pertinent, and she made a mental note to read it later.

She scanned the remainder of the file, then looked at her watch. There was more here, much more, and she'd have to spend several days with it. She finished her tea and looked at Arnold over the rim of her cup. Arnold was reading a week-old copy of the London

Daily Mirror. She closed the file. "Did you know Randolph Carbury personally?"

Arnold put down his newspaper. "Knew them all. Carbury stands out because he was more interested in Reds than Nazis. Had a different sort of job, if you know what I mean." He winked in a way meant to underscore that meaning.

Katherine regarded Arnold in the dim light. The man was more than a vestige, more than an anachronism; he was a specimen forever imprisoned in the amber of the records room. Despite forty years in America, he retained an accent and manner that she imagined was that of a British noncommissioned officer of the war years. In the past he had spoken of a wife and grown child living in New York, but he hadn't mentioned them in some time.

The man seemed relatively simple and open on the surface, but there was a complexity and furtiveness about him. And there were moments, she thought, when he revealed a presence, a bearing, and a refinement of speech that were more the officer than the sergeant. She remembered a line spoken by an actor in an old British spy movie: "My name is Sergeant Williams. Sergeant is not my rank, Williams is not my name."

She said, "Is there anything against Carbury?"

"Not that I know of." His tone was suddenly sharp. "Then again, we've been taken in by a good damned lot of bloody traitors, haven't we?" He pulled the folder toward him and spoke apropos of nothing. "We won't microfilm these—or computerize them. At least not while I'm alive. Do you know why? Well, miss, there is a special sort of feeling to old dossiers—odd scraps of paper, notes scribbled here and there, underlinings and dog-ears, even coffee stains. That sort of thing. The file develops a character of its own. It tells you things that aren't plainly written. You understand."

Katherine nodded. "The shadow outline on some of these pages, for instance, indicating where a smaller slip of paper lay for many years—yet the paper that made the shadow is missing...."

Arnold nodded enthusiastically. "That's just it. You do see what I mean."

There was a silence, and Katherine realized that nothing further was forthcoming.

Arnold picked up the folder. "Is that it, then?"

"No. Wingate. Eleanor Wingate."

Arnold concentrated on the name.

"Brompton Hall?"

"Ah! Yes, yes...Lady Eleanor Wingate—wife...widow of a Major Lesley Wingate. Brompton Hall...American intelligence billet..." He stood and carried the file into the murkiness of the far aisles, then returned with another folder and laid it on the table.

Katherine said, "How would it be possible for someone to remove something from a folder?"

"Someone would have to authorize that."

"Who?"

Arnold sat down and poured himself more tea. "Well, that's very complex, miss. Very complex. You see, these are not active files, as you know. These are only historical archives, kept for purposes of scholarly research—such as you do. But on occasion a bit of something becomes of interest again, and it's whisked off to London. Mine is not to reason why...."

"I see. And are you certain no one could actually steal something from these files?"

"Oh, I'd be a liar if I said that. It's just not humanly possible to avoid that here. I'm all alone, and my senses are not what they used to be."

Katherine opened the folder marked *Brompton Hall*. There was a brief description of the hall and the grounds, including a reproduction of an old print. Someone had put a tick mark beside a sentence that read, "The south tower holds an unusual and interesting muniment room."

There was also a short biography of the Wingates and the cabled result of a security check on them that seemed to consist mainly of statements of good character from their peers. Very much, Katherine thought, like the letters one needs to join a good suburban country club. And in fact, she noticed, there was a listing of the clubs to which Major Wingate had belonged.

The British system of vetting was, she reflected, still rather quixotic to most American intelligence people. She looked up. "It's simply not possible, is it, Arnold, for a man to be concurrently a member of Boodle's and the Communist party?"

Arnold laughed. "Ah, miss, now you're having a bit of fun with us."

Katherine turned the page of the file and came upon a typed list of American intelligence officers billeted at Brompton Hall. Among the names, some of them familiar, she found her father's. A handwritten annotation read: *KIA—5/?/4.5. REF: Alsos Mission; REF: Hunter's Moon.*

She had heard of the Alsos mission—the joint American and British mission to recover German atomic scientists. Hunter's Moon, she was certain now, was Wolfbane. She closed the file and looked at Arnold. "Do you have anything on Alsos or Hunter's Moon?"

"Not anymore, miss. That's long gone."

"Where would I find information on those subjects?"

Arnold looked around the room as though trying to recall if he had a file lying about. "Don't know. Moscow, I suspect."

Katherine studied Arnold's face but could not tell if he was being facetious. She stood. "Can you be here tomorrow and Sunday?"

Arnold stood also. "If you require it."

"Fine."

"What will you be needing, miss?"

"I don't know yet. One thing seems to lead to another, doesn't it?"

"It's always that way with archives, miss. You can read a file a dozen times and nothing signifies. These files have been read a hundred times each. But then a month later you read another file—or someone says something innocentlike and"—he held out his hands and brought his fingers together dovetail fashion—"it fits."

She stared at him for some time but didn't speak.

Arnold raised his teacup and looked thoughtfully into the dark liquid. He spoke as though to himself. "It's the sequence of the thing more often than not. Dates, especially. Always look at dates. A man can't be in two places at the same time, can he? And background. Pay very special attention to a man's background. I mean his youth. A person reveals himself early on. People seem to have these conversions from one kind of politics to another, but that's a bit of nonsense, because the boy is father to the man, if you know what I mean."

Katherine moved toward the door. "You understand generally what I'm looking for. Gather what you can."

Arnold stood and followed her, carrying a large black book. "Miss?"

Katherine turned and faced the open book, a blind register with strips of paper covering the preceding names. Arnold's fingers were positioned to prevent an accidental uncovering of the signatures. She noticed that two loops of the previous signature extended onto her line and could have been the loops of the signature of Randolph Carbury. She signed the open line without making the same mistake, then added the date and time.

Arnold closed the book. "Have a good evening, miss. Bring me the guest list, if you think of it. I always enjoy reading the old names."

He unbolted the door and opened it. "The list gets shorter each year. That's a bit sad. Heroes shouldn't die a natural death, should they? In hospital and all that. Nurses and doctors, and no one knowing they're watching a hero die."

He blinked in the brighter light of the hallway, and Katherine noticed for the first time how incredibly aged he was. Arnold was lost in thought, then said, softly, "But they weren't all heroes, were they? A good number of traitors there were, who died natural deaths and got a good piece in the *Times,* military funerals, and all that. Those men and women should have ended their days on the gallows forty years ago." He rubbed his thin hair. "There's no statute of limitations for treason, is there?"

Katherine realized the question was rhetorical. "I'll see you tomorrow." She turned and walked down the corridor. After what seemed a long time, she heard the door shut behind her. Arnold's cryptic musings, his metaphors, and his philosophy of life were a bit heavy at times. Yet, she supposed, they came with the territory. Also, they were not entirely beside the point.

She strode down the long, empty corridor. She was more concerned, she told herself, with an ongoing act of treason than with something that had happened forty years ago. On the other hand, from what O'Brien had told her about Talbot, it was known that Talbot had sent dozens of agents to their deaths. One of those agents may have been her father.

She reached an unmarked door, the rear entrance to Patrick O'Brien's suite, which opened directly into his private office. She stopped and raised her hand to knock, but hesitated. *Security, discretion, and extreme personal caution....Everyone from that time is suspect....Distribute the information as you see fit. But be cautious.* She turned and kept walking.

The seeds of distrust, sown even before she was born, grew and bore the tainted fruit of suspicion, and the fruit fell rotten to the earth and reseeded itself again and again.

She halted abruptly. "No, damn it!" She retraced her steps, knocked on O'Brien's door, and entered.

CHAPTER ELEVEN

Tony Abrams stood in the alcove of the Gucci shop on the corner of 54th Street and watched Katherine Kimberly make her way through the crowds on Fifth Avenue, holding her handbag and briefcase in one hand and her umbrella in the other. Her chin was tilted upward, and her stride was purposeful. It was, he thought a bearing that was both regal and slightly arrogant. She didn't see him; he didn't think she saw anyone. As she passed, he stepped out of the alcove. "Miss Kimberly."

She turned, and it took her a second to recognize him. "Oh, Mr. Abrams." A faint frown crossed her brow. "Where's Carbury?"

Abrams nodded toward the building across the street.

She turned and looked at the squat granite mansion. "The University Club."

"I think they have overnight accommodations."

"Yes, they do." She looked back at him. Rain glistened on his black hair, and rivulets of water ran over his face. She moved closer to him and raised her umbrella to bring them both under it. "Are the private detectives here?"

"They're watching the only two doors," he said. "Carbury's safely tucked in. They'll follow him to the armory."

"Why are you still here?"

"Where should I be?"

"On Thirty-sixth Street, getting dressed for dinner. Well, it's early yet, and as long as you're still here...why don't you take a look inside the club and see what you can discover?"

Abrams made an expression he hoped conveyed annoyance.

"You don't have to.... You're probably wet and tired...."

"Why would you think that?"

"Well, do what you think best."

Her voice, he thought, was about as cool as the weather. She was always somewhat friendlier on the telephone. "I don't think I'd pass for a university graduate with money and connections."

"Bluff it."

He didn't reply.

"Or take the direct approach and flash your badge."

"I like to be a little careful with the badge act."

"I understand. But you know if anything goes wrong, we'll take care of it."

"So you said. I'll think about it."

"Fine." She turned and took a step. "Oh, Mr. Abrams, Carbury has something important to deliver tonight. Other people may want what he has."

"Swell."

"Call me before seven thirty if anything comes up. See you at eight, Mr. Abrams."

Abrams watched her continue up the block. He turned and walked across the street and into the marble-columned lobby of the University Club. He could see into an enormous high-ceilinged lounge where men sat in leather armchairs, their faces hidden by *Wall Street Journals*. In the rear, by the fireplace, Carbury sat, reading the London *Times*.

Abrams walked through a passageway in the far rear corner that led to the elevators. In an alcove sat a stock printer, long sheets of its printouts pinned to a bulletin board above it. A group of men stood silently staring at the price quotations and looking, Abrams thought, very staid. But occasionally an eye would twitch or knuckles would whiten around the handle of an attaché case. He imagined that this was how it had looked in 1929, except then the men would ride up in the elevators and come down through the windows.

Abrams explored the area, noticing a staircase and the chlorine smell from a basement swimming pool. Another flight of stairs led up to a bar and dining room. He had determined from the directory that there were seven floors, and each had a function, such as a library, squash court, or billiards room. Most floors also had guest rooms, and the only access was by these stairs and elevators.

A club employee who had tagged after him now approached. "Excuse me, sir. May I be of assistance?"

"No." Abrams reentered the lobby. He knew he should leave before he was shown out, yet he decided he wanted to take something with him, a piece of hard information that he could carry to Katherine Kimberly later, like a good retriever laying a fat quail before its mistress. He smiled at the analogy.

"Sir, unless you're waiting for a member, you must leave." The employee's voice was growing insistent.

Abrams showed his badge. "I need some information."

The man shook his head. "You'll have to see the club manager. Sorry, officer. Rules."

Abrams held a twenty-dollar bill folded between his fingers. "Okay, just show me out the service entrance."

The man hesitated, then snatched the bill in a deft movement and motioned him to follow. Abrams noticed his name tag. "Lead on, Frank."

They passed through the corridor near the elevators and descended a half flight of stairs toward the side service entrance.

Abrams spoke as he walked. "I used to belong to a club, too. The Red Devils. We had a clubhouse in the basement of the Bari Pork Store on Eighteenth Avenue in Bensonhurst. There was a gigantic pig in the window of this store, wearing a gold crown."

The man indicated a door that led into the alley. "Good evening, officer."

Abrams lit a cigarette. "Are you Italian, Frank? I'm Jewish, but I had fun growing up there. Anyway, one day my mother saw me go into this pork store. She stood in front of the fat pig in the window and cried."

The man almost smiled, then said, "Look, officer, I have to get back. What's this all about?"

"Actually, it was a very exclusive club—like this one. No *femminas,* no *melanzane,* no Ricans. *Capice?* They tolerated Jews and Protestants the way we might tolerate a few Martians in the neighborhood. I learned a lot in the cellar of the pig store, Frank. I learned the difference between tough and bluff."

The man sensed some danger and looked quickly up and down the deserted corridor. "Hey...are you a cop?"

Abrams slipped his .38 out of his pocket and pointed it at the man's stomach. "No."

The man's face went pale, and he swallowed. "Hey...hey..." He stared at the muzzle of the pistol. "Hey."

"I learned that when you want something reasonable from a man, something that is no skin off his nose, and that man is being *obstinato*—a stubborn jackass—then you have to take a direct approach. Look at me, Frank, don't look at the gun. That's right. Tell me about Colonel Randolph Carbury."

Frank was nodding in agreement. "Sure...sure...he's registered under Edwards...room 403...two days ago...from London... checking out Monday....That's all I know. Okay?"

"Visitors? Women?"

The man kept nodding but answered, "Don't think so."

"Anything in the safe?"

"Safe...? Oh, I think there is....Yeah, I saw a briefcase that had his name on the tag...."

"Phone calls?"

"I don't know...one long-distance...from London."

"Stay in much? Go out a lot?"

"Mostly goes out, I think...." The man knew he was talking to a professional. "Okay?"

"What's the staff verdict?"

"Oh...nice guy. Quiet. Polite. No trouble. Likes his drink, though. Okay?"

"Okay. Let's go to his room."

"Hey...come on...what's this all about?"

"I'm doing a credit check on him. Move."

Frank turned toward the elevator. "I don't have a key. Honest to God."

"Sure you do." Abrams put his revolver in his pocket. "No funny stuff, Frank, and it's going to be all right." They entered the elevator and rode up to the library floor, then passed through a door into a small corridor with five numbered doors.

Frank found his master key and approached 403. Abrams took his arm and held him back. There was a DO NOT DISTURB sign on the door, and he could hear a radio playing. Abrams took the key, unlocked the door, and pushed it open a few inches. The room was lit, and a security chain was draped across the small crack.

Frank whispered urgently, "He's inside."

Abrams reached through the crack and knocked away the chain, which was held to the lock stud track by a piece of tape. "Old trick, Frank. Calm down." He nudged the man inside and closed the door.

The room was furnished with good solid mahogany pieces, though rather old and scarred. Abrams said, "Stand right here." He made a quick but thorough examination of the bedroom, closets, and bathroom, not expecting to find anything that a man like Carbury would want to conceal. The fact that Carbury had taken the trouble to make it appear someone was in the room did not mean he was hiding something. It only meant he was trying to discourage anyone from entering the room to wait for him. Standard procedure, but it showed the man was taking personal precautions. Abrams turned to Frank. "Has he ever taken that briefcase out of the safe?"

"Not that I know of."

Abrams looked at the open closet. The tuxedo suggested that Carbury did intend to show up at the armory tonight.

Frank was becoming edgy. "Please...look...if he catches us up here, it's my job—"

"Now you're worried about your job. Before it was your life. Worry about your life again."

"Right."

Abrams looked at his watch. Carbury would be thinking about a shower by now. "Okay, Frank, let's beat it."

They left the room, and Abrams reached around the door and retaped the security chain. Frank relocked the door, and they took the elevator back to the ground floor.

Abrams stood at the service exit. "Thanks, Frank. Listen, do you think this will affect the committee's decision on my membership application?"

Frank smiled gamely. "No, sir."

"Good. Good. Don't tell them about the basement of the pork store, okay? Or the illegal entry, or me pulling a gun on you. *Capice?*" He put his finger to the man's lips. *"Omerta."*

Frank nodded enthusiastically and moved off as quickly as he could without actually running.

Abrams left by the service door, and found himself in an areaway filled with trash bins. He walked down a dark alley toward the front of the building and came out through a stone arch onto 54th Street. He crossed the street and approached an unmarked van. A private detective sat in the driver's seat. Abrams said, "Anything new?"

The detective, an ex-policeman like himself, named Walter, squinted in the bad light. "Nah. But it sounds to me like somebody wants to grease this guy Carbury, right? That could get hairy."

Abrams lit a cigarette. "He'll be carrying a briefcase. Keep an eye on that briefcase."

"What's this all about, Abrams?"

"I don't know. But be prepared to do whatever you have to do to protect him and whatever he's carrying. The firm is solidly behind you."

"Yippee."

Abrams moved away from the van and crossed Fifth Avenue, making his way through the hurrying pedestrians. He wondered if he'd overstepped himself on this assignment. It seemed, though, that Katherine Kimberly was very anxious about this, and he had only reacted accordingly. He realized that he too was anxious, not about Carbury but about Katherine Kimberly's evaluation of his work.

But what the hell did she know about this type of work? She sat in her forty-fourth-floor ivory tower and gave him assignments with as much self-assurance as his old captain had. . . . It never occurred to her that she should confide in him. Yet, instead of feeling resentful, he played her game and helped her understand the investigative end of the business, even covered for her a few times. This was a type of loyalty that he'd given to only a few of the very best commanders he'd worked for.

He thought perhaps he was interested in her, but he knew he couldn't be, because nothing could come of it but pain. And no rational man wanted pain. Therefore, he was curious but not interested.

After a time he looked up and was surprised to find he had covered almost twenty blocks and was approaching the street where the town house was located. He walked up to a pay phone, thinking as he dialed the Lombardy that he had never been a guest in a town house before, and certainly never had a tuxedo delivered to one. He remembered a favorite line from Thoreau: "Beware of all enterprises that require new clothes."

CHAPTER TWELVE

Katherine Kimberly entered the lobby of the Lombardy Hotel. The concierge, Maurice, rushed forward with words of greeting, adding, "Monsieur Thorpe is in, madame." Maurice took her umbrella, then escorted her to a back corner of the lobby, opened an elevator with a key, and ushered her in.

As she rode up she reflected, not for the first time, that *she* did not have a key to the elevator or to the apartment. Peter's explanation had been simple and rather direct, yet whimsical, as was his manner: "My heart is yours, my possessions are yours, but the suite belongs to my father and is leased to the government for a dollar a year, as is my father himself. No one but Company people may have a key."

The elevator stopped at the twenty-second floor, which was the first floor of the penthouse triplex. She stepped into a small mint-green hallway.

A voice boomed out over a speaker. "Stand in front of the television camera, and put your hands on your head!"

Katherine's face showed a mixture of impatience and amusement. "Open the damned door."

The door buzzed and Katherine opened it, entering a large anteroom. She passed into a very long two-story-high sitting room. On opposite sides were balconies that served as hallways to the second-story rooms. The balconies were connected by a catwalk that spanned the length of the spacious room. She looked around as she dropped her bag and briefcase on the sofa, then removed her rain-coat. Hidden stereo speakers were playing a medley of theme songs from James Bond movies. She smiled. "Peter! Idiot!"

She walked to the bar, where a pitcher of martinis stood along-side two chilled glasses, and poured a full glass for herself. The French doors that led to the terrace suddenly opened and a gust of cool air blew in. Through the billowing curtains walked Peter Thorpe, clad only in a pair of threadbare jeans.

She stared for some time at his muscular body silhouetted against the towering lighted buildings beyond. "Are you *crazy?*"

Thorpe's blue eyes narrowed in a malevolent glare. "Sloppy trade-craft, Miss Kimberly. If you were a Red agent, you'd be dead." He shut the French doors, then advanced toward her. "See this?" He held up a partly peeled lemon. "This is an anthrax grenade. Catch!" He threw it underhand at her. She fielded it with one hand and, in a swift motion, shot it back at him.

The lemon thumped against his bare chest. She laughed in spite of her annoyance. She said, "Why were you standing in the rain half-naked?"

"I didn't want to get my suit wet." He smiled and embraced her.

"You're very strange, Peter. Must be the red hair." She tousled his long damp hair.

Thorpe worked his hands down the back of her shirt. "Did you have a good day?"

"An interesting day."

They kissed, then Thorpe buried his face in her neck. "Do we have time for a quick dance?"

She smiled. "No. But we'll make time for a slow dance."

"Good." He kissed her neck, then took the martini tray from the sideboard.

She picked up her bag and followed him up the spiral stair-case. Thorpe looked back over his shoulder. "What made the day interesting?"

She started to reply, then thought better of it. Peter was alto-gether too curious about what went on at O'Brien, Kimberly and

Rose. She said, "Just a lot of activity over the reunion tonight. A good number of out-of-towners and foreigners dropping by."

They reached the balcony overlooking the sitting room. Thorpe said, "There's nothing more insufferable than ex-spies."

"They're interesting people. You'll enjoy the evening."

"Perhaps. But I get a little weary of hearing how great the OSS was, and how screwed up the CIA is."

"No one ever said that."

"Your nose is getting longer, Kate." He smiled. "Maybe I'm just sensitive. My father used to bore me for hours with stories of how the OSS won the war."

She took his arm.

He added, "My boss is an old OSS man and he's recruited dozens of others." He stood in front of his bedroom door. "The dining rooms at Langley serve prunes and Geritol now." He laughed.

She said, "Experienced men and women can be useful." She opened the door and he entered first, setting the tray on the bureau.

He said, "It's not the experience that concerns me...some of those old OSS characters were very weird. Very strange backgrounds...."

She looked at him. "Meaning?"

He hesitated, then said, "You know...security risks." He sipped on a martini. "There was a radical fringe in the OSS...they wouldn't pass a normal security check by today's standards. Yet they're being brought back in on a special basis...that bothers me."

"No more shoptalk."

"Right." He set his glass down and pulled off his jeans, throwing them on a chair.

Katherine began to undress.

Thorpe turned down the sheets of his double bed, then watched her hang her clothes in his closet. "We should get married."

She turned and smiled. "You're right. But who'd have us?"

He smiled back and lay down on the bed. "Come here. I want to show you my new decoding device."

"I see it. Does it work well?" She approached the bed.

"It has to be turned on."

"It looks like it just turned itself on." She laughed and came into the bed beside him.

Katherine heard a phone ringing insistently somewhere, but she could not have cared less. There was a protracted silence, then the phone rang again. She felt the dreamy fog lifting, and her senses awakened as Peter sat up next to her in the bed. The yellow light on the telephone was blinking, indicating it was not his private number. "Switchboard call—the hell with it," he said.

"It could be for me."

He looked at her. "Then you answer it."

Katherine raised herself onto her elbow and reached for the receiver. The switchboard operator said, "Mr. Abrams for Miss Kimberly."

"All right." There was a click, and she spoke. "Katherine Kimberly..." Her voice was husky, and she cleared her throat. "Yes?" She looked around the spacious second-floor bedroom. On the outside wall was a fireplace. The mantel clock showed they'd been asleep almost an hour.

Abrams hesitated, then said, "I took your advice and dropped in at the club."

"Is he registered there?"

"Yes. But not officially. He's been there since Wednesday...leaving Monday."

Katherine watched as Thorpe got out of bed and began doing sit-ups, apparently with no interest in her conversation. But she knew him well enough to know he was listening. She spoke in a quieter voice. "All right, instruct the detectives to stay close to him until he reaches the armory."

"I've done that, obviously."

She took a few seconds to control her annoyance, then said, "Of course. See you at the armory, then."

"Right." He hung up.

She sat back in the bed, her long bare legs crossed.

Thorpe finished his sit-ups. "Who was that?"

"Tony Abrams."

"Oh, super sleuth." He rolled into a push-up position. "I met him once. Remember?"

"You were rude to him."

"Was I?" He began his push-ups. "I'll apologize next time I see him."

"Good. That will be this evening."

Thorpe stopped in mid push-up. "Oh, Christ, Kate, you didn't invite him, did you?"

"Why not?"

"He doesn't fit. You'll just make him unhappy to be there."

She didn't respond.

Thorpe balanced himself back on his shoulder blades and began a series of leg exercises.

She watched him. He had an exhibitionist streak in him, and probably a voyeuristic bent as well. Peter, she thought, was pure animal energy: his presence in a room was sometimes like that of a tame tiger cub, clawing and gnawing at a bone, threatening and potentially dangerous. Yet at other times he could be gentle and loving. He was a complex man, an intriguing man. But spies, like actors, were capable of personality metamorphoses. There were Peter Thorpes that she liked and Peter Thorpes that she didn't like. But, she thought, he... or they...were never boring.

She drew the sheet up over her. "Are you still a member of the University Club?"

Thorpe sat on his haunches and scratched his head as though trying to remember. "I was...up until about four nights ago— Monday—you were out of town, I think...."

"Drunk or disorderly?"

"I'm not sure. I remember trying to brush something off my face, but it was the floor."

She smiled and glanced at the mantel clock again. "We should get moving." She began to rise.

Thorpe stood and walked to the bed. He put his hands on either side of her and leaned over. "What's going on, Kate?"

She ducked under his arm and got out of bed. "None of your business."

"Can I help?"

She knelt beside the fireplace and ignited the gas jets. Blue flames curled around a log made of volcanic rock. "There's too much light in here. Why are the lights always so bright?"

"Better to see you, my dear." He went to the wall and turned down a rheostat. The room grew dark except for the glow of the fireplace. He changed the music on the stereo to a Willie Nelson tape, then poured two martinis and crouched beside her in front of the fire. The flame warmed their exposed skin and highlighted Katherine's breasts and high cheekbones. Neither spoke for some time, then Katherine said, "Do you know a Colonel Carbury?"

Thorpe turned to her. "Carbury?"

Her eyes met his. "You know him?"

"Well...slightly. Friend of my father's, Englishman, right? What *is* this about, Kate?"

She finished her drink, stood, and walked to the dresser. She extracted Eleanor Wingate's letter from her bag and came back to the fireplace. She held the letter toward him but did not give it to him. "I'll let you read this with the understanding that you are not to discuss it with *anyone*. Not your people, and not even your father. You'll see why if you agree."

He held out his hand, and she passed him the letter. Thorpe unfolded the pages and began reading by the light of the fire. He sipped his martini, but his eyes never left the letter.

He looked up and passed the pages back to her. "Where is the diary?"

"To be delivered," she said softly. "What do you think, Peter?"

Thorpe shrugged as he got to his feet. He found a pack of cigarettes on the mantel and removed one, keeping his back to her as he spoke. "It's worth following up."

She moved beside him and stared at his handsome features. She thought he looked more agitated than his words revealed.

He said, "Poor Kate. This must be distressing after all these years."

"Yes...as a personal matter, but I'm more distressed about the other implications."

"Are you? I suppose that's normal. You didn't know your father."

She put her hand on his cheek and turned his face so she could see him. "Do you know anything about this?"

"No. But did I understand from your conversation with Abrams that Carbury is to be at the armory tonight? Is that when he's going to give you the diary?"

"Yes. He came to my office this afternoon without an appointment. Said he'd just gotten off the plane. But I guess he's been here since Wednesday. Anyway, we spoke, and he gave me that letter. He said he'd produce the diary tonight."

Thorpe nodded slowly. "Strange...I mean that Carbury should come to New York to see my father receive an award, and to the best of my knowledge my father doesn't know he's in town."

"He may know. You two don't exactly confide in each other."

Thorpe seemed not to hear. He sat on the sofa and lit the cigarette, drawing on it thoughtfully.

His mood had changed markedly. Katherine would have liked to think it was because of his concern for her, but that was not characteristic of Peter Thorpe.

Thorpe said, "You did well to have him followed. Good instincts."

Katherine accepted the rare compliment without reply. She said, "Do you feel this is serious? How did the letter go—'grave and foreboding'?"

Thorpe walked toward the dresser. "Very possibly." He poured another martini. "I'd like to see that diary."

She gathered her clothing from the closet, and walked toward the door. "Did my things arrive?"

Thorpe nodded absently. "Yes...yes. Eva laid everything out in the beige room."

Katherine stopped at the door. "Where is she?"

"Who...? Oh, Eva..." He shrugged. "Someplace. Out."

Thorpe seemed to snap out of his inattentiveness. "By the way, I don't like the blue dress. Icy."

"Who asked you?" She walked out on the balcony that surrounded the living room and turned onto the connecting catwalk that was suspended above the room. Thorpe followed, carrying his drink. She stopped in the center of the walk and looked out a huge picture window that had been recently cut into the north wall. She held her clothes in front of her and watched the rain fall gently in the breezeless night. Thorpe stood beside her. He said, "Hell of a view. You like it?"

She replied, "It fascinates me—not the view, but the fact that you could talk your father into spending a small fortune to put a window into the twenty-third floor of a high-rise, contrary to the building code and over the objections of the management. That's what fascinates me—the fact that you get what you want, no matter how trivial your whims and regardless of what it costs other people in time, money, or bother."

"I like the view. Don't make more of it than it is. I can see Harlem from here. See? I wonder what the poor people are doing tonight. Probably the same thing we did."

"That's crude, insensitive, and boorish."

"Yes, it is . . . Still, I wonder. . . ." He sipped his drink.

"Sometimes you have no . . . no heart, Peter, no social conscience, no sense of propriety, no—"

"Hold on! I'm not going to be lectured to. I'm self-centered and I'm a snob. I know it. I like myself this way."

She shrugged and headed for her room.

Thorpe called out, "Listen, I'm going to dress quickly and leave you here. I've got to meet someone. I'll see you at the armory."

She replied without turning, in a voice that was tinged with disappointment if not anger. "Don't be late."

"It won't take long. You know where everything is. Let yourself out."

She entered the guest room and closed the door behind her. There was, she reflected, nothing of hers permanently left in this huge apartment. Another woman might be suspicious of that, but this was not an apartment in the normal sense—it was a CIA safe house and domestic station, and what went on here could only be appreciated in that context.

Agents in transit sometimes slept here, as did other men and women whose status was not clear to her. On one occasion they'd debriefed a defector here, and the place had been off limits to her for over a month.

And although the decor was old-fashioned, there were high-technology refinements such as the security system and, she knew, a complete recording system. She wondered about cameras. Upstairs, on the third floor, was a great deal of electronics. She'd never seen that floor, but there were times when she could hear the humming of the machines and actually feel the vibrations.

She didn't like it here. But this is where Peter lived when he was in New York, which was most of the time these days. And, for now, she wanted to be wherever he was.

CHAPTER THIRTEEN

Tony Abrams came to an old red-brick house on 36th Street in a block of elegant brownstones. To New Yorkers who had an appreciation of the value of midtown property, this block of private residences, sitting on some of the most valuable land in America, announced: Money. Set in Abrams' section of Brooklyn, the narrow row houses might seem drab, he thought.

Unlike the brownstones, whose front doors were at the tops of high steps for privacy and to allow for servants' quarters below, the door of this house was at sidewalk level. A gas lamp flickered on either side of the door, and to the left was a large multipaned window with scrolled wrought-iron bars. It was a house more reminiscent of old Philadelphia or Boston than old New York.

Abrams peered through a clear spot in the mist-covered window into a small sitting room. Logs were blazing in the fireplace, and two men and two women sat with drinks. The men were dressed in black tie, and he recognized them as George Van Dorn, a senior partner in O'Brien, Kimberly and Rose, and Tom Grenville, a soon-to-be partner. The women, wearing evening dresses, were probably their wives. Suburbanites, using the company digs for a night on the town. The O'Brien firm strongly believed in taxpayer-supported perquisites.

Abrams lifted a brass knocker and brought it down on the black door three times.

An attractive young woman of about twenty-five, dressed in a black jumper and a white turtleneck sweater, opened the door. "Mr. Abrams?"

"Mr. Abrams."

She smiled. "Please come in. You look wet. My name is Claudia."

He stepped inside the foyer. She had, he noticed, an accent. Central European, perhaps. He handed her his coat.

"Where is your hat?"

"On the bureau of my uncle."

She seemed uncertain, then said, "Your things are upstairs. Have you been here before?"

"In my last life."

She laughed. "The second door on the left. . . . Well, come, I will show you." She draped his coat on a hook over a hissing radiator and led the way.

He passed the sitting room and followed her through the narrow low-ceilinged hallway. The stairs were tilted, as was the whole house, but in a nation of straight new houses, the tilt was somehow chic.

She opened a door off the small upper hallway and led him into a miniature room furnished in what might have been real Chippendale. His tuxedo sat in a box on a high four-poster bed. The box was marked *Murray's Formal Wear, Sales and Rentals.*

The young woman said, "There is a robe on the bed. The bathroom is across the hall, and here on the dresser is all you will need for shaving and bathing. When you are dressed, you may wish to join the Van Dorns and Grenvilles for a cocktail. Is there anything else I may do for you?"

She was, Abrams saw, conversant enough with the idiom to smile at the tired old double entendre. As she pushed her long, straight auburn hair back over her shoulders, he looked at her closely. "Have I seen you at the office?"

"Perhaps. I am a client."

"Where are you from?"

"From? Oh, I am Rumanian. I live here now. In this house."

"As a guest?"

"I am no one's mistress, if that's what you mean. I'm a political refugee."

"Me too. From Brooklyn."

There were a few seconds of silence in which they took stock of each other. It was, Abrams thought, unmistakably lust at first sight. He took off his jacket and tie and hung them in a wardrobe cabinet. He hesitated over his shirt buttons, then looked at Claudia, who was staring at him openly. He took off his shirt and threw it on the bed. His hand went to his belt buckle. "Are you staying?"

She smiled and left the room. Abrams finished undressing and put on the robe. He took the shaving kit and went into the hall. He found the bathroom, a small room that looked as if it had once been a large closet. He shaved and showered, then returned to his room. He opened the box of clothing and began dressing, cursing the shirt studs and the tight collar. Murray had forgotten the patent leather shoes, as Abrams knew he would, and he had to wear his street shoes, which were barely passable. He looked in the full-length mirror on the door as he struggled with the bow tie. "I hope everyone else looks like this."

Abrams went downstairs to the sitting room. Tom Grenville, a handsome man about five years younger than Abrams and about a thousand times richer, said to his wife, "Joan, Tony is studying for the bar."

George Van Dorn answered the question the wives were thinking. "Mr. Abrams was a policeman for a long time."

Kitty Van Dorn leaned forward in her chair. "That sounds so interesting. How did you happen to choose that career?"

Abrams looked at her. She was either much younger than her husband or she was heavily into vitamins, exercise, and plastic surgeons. He wondered about middle-aged women who still called themselves Kitty. "I always wanted to be a policeman."

Joan Grenville, an attractive strawberry blonde with freckles, asked, "Where do you live?"

Abrams poured himself a Scotch from the sideboard. "Brooklyn." Her voice, he noticed, was kind of breathy.

"Oh . . . so this is a convenience for you. Us too. We live in Scarsdale. That's farther than Brooklyn."

"From where?"

She smiled. "From here. The center of the universe. I want to move back to town, but Tom doesn't." She looked at her husband, but he turned away.

Abrams regarded her closely. She was wearing a simple white silk dress. He noticed she had her shoes off and that she didn't wear toenail polish, or in fact much makeup at all. Healthy and wealthy, he thought. Slim and trim, pretty and preppie, and perhaps even intelligent. The nearly final stage in the evolution of the species.

Kitty Van Dorn added, "We live out on the Island. Glen Cove. George uses this place often. Don't you, George?"

Van Dorn grunted and moved to the sideboard. Abrams could see that he'd had a few already. Van Dorn spoke as he poured a drink. "Kimberly—that is, Henry Kimberly, Senior—bought this place around the turn of the century. Paid three thousand dollars for it. Bought it from a Hamilton or a Stuyvesant...can't remember which. Anyway, Henry Junior lived here himself for a few years after he got married. When the war started, he moved his family to Washington. Then he went overseas and got killed. Damned shame." He raised his glass. "To Henry." He drank.

Abrams stood by the fireplace and watched Van Dorn drain off the bourbon. Abrams said, "Henry Kimberly was an OSS officer, wasn't he?"

"Right," answered Van Dorn. He suppressed a belch. "Me too. What room do you have, Abrams?"

"Room? Oh, second floor, second on the left."

"That was the nursery—Kate's room. Henry and I used to go in there and coo coo with her. Henry loved that kid. And her sister, Ann, too." A melancholy look passed over his ruddy face. "War is shit."

Abrams nodded. The conversation was picking up.

Grenville said, "My father was also OSS. A whole group of the firm's men and women were recruited by Bill Donovan. Donovan's critics used to say OSS stood for Oh, So Social." He smiled.

Abrams said, "Who were Donovan's critics?"

Grenville answered, "Mostly the pinkos and J—jerks who hung around Roosevelt. Jerks."

There was a long silence in the room, broken finally by Van Dorn, who was working on another drink. He looked over his shoulder at Abrams. "You might find this evening interesting."

Kitty Van Dorn made a sound that suggested it wasn't likely.

Tom Grenville stirred his drink with his finger. "You're a friend of Kate's, right? She called and said you'd be coming."

"Yes." Abrams lit a cigarette. This conversation had an unreal quality to it. Neither of these men had so much as nodded to him in the office before, yet, though both men's attitudes were slightly condescending, they were in some undefined way tentatively friendly. It reminded him of his first interview in the basement of the Bari Pork Store when he'd been dragged in for the announced purpose of having his face broken, and had emerged a Red Devil.

Joan Grenville got out of her chair and knelt on the hearth rug, a foot from where he was standing. She took up a poker and prodded the fire, then turned her head and looked up at him. "Will you be staying here tonight, Mr. Abrams?"

"Tony." He looked down and saw the smooth white curve of her breasts, ending in the soft pink of her nipples. "I don't know, Mrs. Grenville. You?"

She nodded. "Yes. Please call me Joan."

Abrams turned, avoiding Tom Grenville's eyes, and went to the sideboard although he didn't want another drink. "Anyone need anything?"

No one answered. George Van Dorn said, "You're perfectly welcome to stay."

Kitty Van Dorn added, "No one should travel on the subway to Brooklyn so late."

"I thought," said Abrams, "I might actually take a taxi."

Again there was a silence. Abrams didn't know if this was amusing or awkward, if it was democracy in action or an act of noblesse oblige. They were trying, but he was getting a bit of a headache.

George Van Dorn found his cigar butt in the ashtray and lit it. "Did Claudia get you everything you needed, Abrams?"

"Yes, thank you."

"Good." He blew a billow of gray smoke. "She's a client, you know. Not hired help or anything like that."

"So she said."

"Did she?" He settled back in his armchair. "Her grandfather was Count Lepescu—a leader of the Rumanian resistance during the German occupation. I guess that makes her a countess or something. She's staying here for a while."

Abrams glanced at Joan Grenville, who was sitting cross-legged contemplating the fire, her dress hiked back to her thighs. Abrams had a vision of a sorority-house weekend at Wellesley or Bennington, lots of beer, junk food, guitars, and chirpy voices. Strewn casually on the chairs was fifty thousand dollars' worth of ski gear, and strewn casually on the floor were the skiers. There were pert little ski-slope noses and breasts to match, and dozens of pink toes with no nail polish. There was so much straw-colored hair and so many blue eyes that it looked like a cast party for *Village of the Damned*. There would be a huge red winter sun setting below a snowy-white birch-covered hill, and the fire would crackle. He'd never seen any such thing, but neither had he ever seen his pancreas, yet he knew it was there.

"The Reds grabbed him," said Van Dorn.

Abrams looked at him. "Who...?"

"Count Lepescu, Claudia's grandfather. Didn't like his title. Shot him. Shipped the family to some sort of work camp. Most of them died. Nice reward for fighting the Nazis. War is shit. Did I say that?"

"George," reprimanded Kitty Van Dorn, "please watch your language."

"The Russians are shits too. Like to shoot people." He finished his drink. "After Stalin croaked, what was left of the Lepescus were released. Claudia's father wound up in a factory. Married a factory girl, and she gave birth to Claudia. The father was rearrested and disappeared. The mother died a few years ago. We've been trying to get Claudia out for some time."

"Who's been trying?"

"Us. We finally shipped her out last autumn. Working on a citizenship now."

"Why?"

Van Dorn looked at Abrams. "Why? We owed. We paid."

"Who owed?"

"O'Brien, Kimberly and Rose."

"I thought you meant your old intelligence service."

No one spoke. Tom Grenville walked to the window. "The car's out front. Maybe we should get moving."

Van Dorn looked at his watch. "Where the hell is Claudia, anyway? It takes that girl forever to get dressed."

Abrams put his drink on the mantel. "She's coming?"

"Yes," answered Grenville. "What table are you at?"

"I think it's table fourteen."

Tom Grenville's eyebrows rose. "That's with O'Brien and Katherine."

"Is it?"

Van Dorn flipped a cigar ash in his glass. "That's my table, too. The firm took eleven tables this year. We used to take twenty or thirty. . . ." He stubbed out his cigar. "One of you ladies should go hustle her highness along."

Claudia came into the small room wearing a black silk evening dress with silver shoes and bag. "Her highness is ready. Her highness's ladies-in-waiting are on strike. Her highness apologizes."

Kitty Van Dorn said, "You look absolutely stunning."

Abrams thought he would have bet a week's paycheck that someone was going to say that.

Claudia looked at Abrams. "Will you ride with us?"

Abrams nodded. "If there's room."

Van Dorn said, "Plenty of room. Let's go."

They put on their coats and stepped into the cool wet night. A stretch Cadillac was waiting at the curb, and a chauffeur in gray livery held open the door. Abrams climbed in last and took a jump seat facing the rear.

George Van Dorn found the bar quickly and began to make

himself a drink. "This stuff seems to taste better in a moving vehicle—boats, planes, cars..."

Kitty Van Dorn looked apprehensive. "It's going to be a long evening, George."

Joan Grenville said, "Not if he keeps drinking like that." She laughed, and Abrams saw Tom Grenville kick her ankle.

As the car moved off, Van Dorn raised his glass. "To Count Ilie Lepescu, Major Henry Kimberly, Captain John Grenville, and to all those who are not with us tonight."

They sat in silence as the limousine made its way up Park Avenue. Claudia leaned forward and rested her hand on Abrams' thigh. He sat back and regarded her. She looked vaguely Semitic in the dim light, and he thought it was his fate to become involved with women who were mirror images of himself. There were no Joan Grenvilles or Katherine Kimberlys in his life, and there were not likely to be. Which, he thought, was probably—definitely—for the best.

George Van Dorn looked as if he were going to propose another toast but instead handed Abrams his glass. "Kill it," said Van Dorn.

His wife patted his hand as though he'd done something fine and noble. Van Dorn, too, looked pleased with himself for resisting the temptation to arrive at a destination with most of his faculties impaired.

Yet there was something about Van Dorn that belied his outward self-satisfaction and shallow good fellowship. Abrams saw it in his eyes, in Van Dorn's manner when Van Dorn and O'Brien were together. Patrick O'Brien did not suffer fools, and therefore Van Dorn was no fool. He was part of that inner circle that Abrams called the Shadow Firm—the other O'Brien, Kimberly and Rose, the one that defended intelligence agents *pro bono* and sent and received encoded telex messages. George Van Dorn was one of the few people who had access to the room marked DEAD FILES.

Abrams lit a cigarette. He was, he thought, good at mysteries. That had been his job and his life. He'd never tired of the mysteries—he'd tired of the solutions, which were, in almost every case, insipid, disappointing, and commonplace.

If he'd had a flaw as a detective, it was this tendency to imagine or hope that at the end of the trail there would be something interesting or complex. But there never really was. The human drama was more often unintended comedy; the motivations for human action were depressingly trivial.

Still, he had followed the clues and had run the foxes to ground and accepted the pat on the head, while wishing the fox had been a larger beast that when cornered would fight back with the same cunning it had shown in evading him. He had always wished for a dangerous beast.

If one analyzed and thought about it—which he had been doing since the first of May—then there were logical explanations for every suspicion he had about this firm. Yet it was the sheer mass of circumstantial evidence that, in a cumulative form, refused to be explained away. He was still too much of a cop to ignore what he saw, what he felt, and what O'Brien had said to him on the observation roof.

The car slowed as it approached the mass of vehicles around the armory.

Abrams stubbed out his cigarette. Yes, tonight would be revealing. And on Monday, Memorial Day, when he entered the Russian estate in Glen Cove, he might have some answers.

The driver got out and opened the curbside door.

George Van Dorn announced, "Last stop."

Abrams got out first and walked by himself to the sidewalk. He had the gut feeling that the Carbury business was not just another of O'Brien's odd cases but was a piece in the larger puzzle. Carbury, O'Brien and Company, these people from 36th Street, the OSS, Katherine Kimberly, Glen Cove, and O'Brien's musings about Wall Street being vaporized. What a jumble of clues and pieces. But if you twisted and turned them a bit, he was certain, they would all start to fall into place.

CHAPTER FOURTEEN

Katherine put her street clothes neatly inside her suitcase. The beige guest room had a forlorn look, and for all its luxury there was something of the government facility about the entire apartment. She had a few minutes before she had to dress for dinner. She lay down, naked, on the bed, stretched, and yawned.

Peter Thorpe's adoptive father, James Allerton, actually owned the apartment and the furnishings. Peter's late adoptive mother, Betty, had decorated all the rooms sometime before the war, when it had been her home. Many of the pieces were antiques or had become so in the intervening years. There were original Turners on the walls, bought in the 1930s when Turner was out of fashion and the world was out of money. There were also sculptures by Rodin and a Gobelin tapestry. If one thought to put a price tag on the artwork here, it would exceed a million dollars. Yet, to the best of her knowledge, not so much as a towel had ever been missing despite the heavy flow of transients. This was one company from which one did not steal.

Katherine thought of the housekeeper, Eva, a Polish woman in her fifties. Katherine reflected that the housekeepers changed periodically as a direct consequence of the political or military situation's going to pieces somewhere. For the last few years there had been Polish women. For a long time before that there had been Southeast Asian women. Before her time, she imagined, there had been Hungarians, Cubans, Czechs. They were, she thought, women who had made a political and moral decision to risk their lives for an ideal. They had betrayed their country and were therefore traitors, and were traditionally treated with ambivalence and suspicion by all intelligence agencies. But Eva and the rest of them were owed something by the Company, and the Company paid.

And what these women lacked in housekeeping ability, they made up for in dedication; in any case, a day maid did the real work, and the housekeepers mostly wrote their reports or memoirs and kept an eye on the guests. This was the looking glass through which Katherine had to pass every time she stepped out of the elevator.

Katherine went to the dressing table and absently arranged her makeup, then looked into the wall mirror. Her hair was in disarray, and there was a small scratch on her neck, a result of their lovemaking.

On an emotional level she knew this place was all wrong, but on an intellectual and professional level she accepted it. What went on when she wasn't here fell into that very gray area of expedient morality, sanctioned by national security. What went on here was also none of her business. On the other hand, it might be. She thought about the third floor.

She rose and walked to the bathroom. She listened for the sound of the shower on the opposite side of the wall but heard nothing. She opened the medicine cabinet and saw a bottle of astringent, which she dabbed on her neck. "Damn."

Katherine heard a hallway door shut and walked quickly into the bedroom. She peered through a fisheye peephole and saw Peter Thorpe, dressed in his evening clothes, rapidly descending the staircase. She opened the door and stepped out. She was about to call after him but decided against it.

She began to shut the door, then paused. A few doors down was the narrow staircase that led to the third floor of the triplex. She took a robe from her closet and stepped into the hall.

Katherine climbed the narrow, unlit staircase and stood at the top landing, facing a door made of some type of synthetic material. There were two Medeco cylinder locks on the door and probably an alarm device as well. She hesitated, then turned the knob and pushed. The heavy door swung inward, and she took a step into the room.

The long garretlike room was not fully illuminated, but there were eerie blue-white fluorescents hanging above ten or twelve different machines positioned around the room. Katherine identified a telex, a shortwave radio, a stock printer, several video screens, a computer terminal, and something that could have been a polygraph. In a far corner was a table on wheels, a hospital gurney with loose straps hanging from it. She did not like the looks of that.

The other machines, large and small, she could not identify. She stepped farther into the room and let the door close quietly.

Her eyes grew accustomed to the uneven light, and she noticed, almost directly in front of her, a large electronic console of some sort. Behind the console sat a figure. The figure rose and turned toward her.

Katherine caught her breath and stepped backward toward the door.

"Yes?"

Katherine let out a long breath. It was Eva. The tall, big-boned woman with stringy gray hair moved toward her.

Katherine partially regained her composure. "I'd like a look around."

"Mr. Thorpe permits this?" Eva came closer.

"I never asked."

"I think you have no business here." She stood directly in front of Katherine.

Katherine had to look up to meet Eva's eyes. She felt exposed, defenseless, with her arms wrapped around the robe to keep it from falling open. Katherine controlled her voice. "And you do?"

"*I* work here. For Mr. Thorpe. Not the same way as you—"

"Who do you think you're talking to?"

"Pardon me...my English...that maybe sounded—"

"Good evening." Katherine summoned her courage and turned her back on the woman. She reached for the doorknob, half expecting to be restrained, but wasn't. She opened the door and stepped onto the landing.

Eva followed. She took a key from the pocket of her housecoat and quickly double-locked the door, then caught up to Katherine on the stairs. "It was not wise to enter that room."

Katherine didn't answer. She descended at a normal, carefully measured pace.

"This is secret, this room. Government secret. Mr. Thorpe has not told you?"

Again Katherine didn't answer. She reached the balcony and turned toward Eva. Eva stood a few feet away, towering a full head over her. With a barely discernible movement, Katherine assumed a guarded stance.

Eva seemed to notice, and a smile passed over her thin lips. She spoke in a tone that a teacher would use in lecturing a child. "In *my* country you would be shot for spying."

"We are not in *your* country. We are in *my* country."

Eva seemed slightly annoyed, then resumed an impassive attitude. "True. But I must make the report."

"Do what the hell you want." Katherine walked quickly past the woman and went to her bedroom. She closed the door, then looked out through the peephole and saw Eva's face very close, staring at the door. Katherine hesitated over the bolt, then angrily threw it shut. At the sound of the bolt, Eva smiled and turned away.

Katherine sat on the edge of the bed. She was upset, humiliated, furious. Never again would she make love in this apartment. In fact, she thought, she would never set foot in the place again. Her eyes rested on a bottle of chilled Principessa Gavi left on the night table. She pulled out the cork and poured the wine into a long-stem glass, then drank it.

Katherine settled herself back in a chaise longue and closed her eyes. She steadied herself and tried to clear her mind. No, she thought, it would be wrong not to come back. She owed Peter at least that degree of trust, she told herself. Also, she was curious. More than that, Patrick O'Brien had suggested in a very oblique way that he found Peter, and Peter's operation, a bit odd.

She felt herself drifting off, and her mind became confused.... There was a key somewhere; she'd always felt that. A key such as

Eva possessed, and which Arnold possessed, and it was a master key to many locks, many doors and closets and chests. And inside were secrets and ciphers, skeletons and scandals. Everyone else seemed to know this—O'Brien, Peter, James Allerton, her sister, Ann, her sister's fiancé, Nicholas West.... Her father had known it too, and Colonel Carbury knew it. It was like a great family secret that the children sensed but did not know, that the adults lived with but never mentioned.

Tonight, she thought, they would hold a family council. Tonight little Kate would be told.

CHAPTER FIFTEEN

Peter Thorpe walked into the second-floor cocktail lounge of the University Club and sidled up to the bar. "Good evening, Donald."

The bartender smiled. "Evening, Mr. Thorpe."

"Sorry about the other night."

"Hey, no problem."

"I remember looking into the bar mirror there....I saw myself leaning into a force-ten gale wind that no one else in the room seemed to feel."

The bartender laughed. "What's your pleasure?"

"Just a wimp water, please."

The bartender laughed again and poured a Perrier.

Thorpe pulled a copy of the *Times* toward him and flipped through it. "I can't believe the number of murders committed in this town. Crazy."

"Yeah, but most murders involve people who know each other. Did you know that? And not our kind of people, either. Banjos and bongos."

"Banjos and bongos?"

Donald smiled as he polished a glass. "Yeah, you know." He looked at a Hispanic busboy near the tables and lowered his voice. "Blacks and Ricans. Banjos and bongos." He winked.

Thorpe smiled back. "You have an excellent command of the

modern vernacular, Donald, and a good ear for idioms and jokes. I loved the definition of a woman. Have any more?"

"Yeah. What do you get when you cross a black with a Frenchman?"

"What?"

"Jacques Custodian." He slapped his rag against the bar and laughed.

Thorpe raised his glass of mineral water. "I salute you." He drank. "By the way, do you have any chits on a man named Carbury? Supposed to be registered here, but—"

Donald flipped through a stack of cards. "Nope."

"Englishman. Older man, tall, thin, maybe a mustache."

"Oh, Edwards. Comes in here a lot."

"He's been here since maybe Wednesday?"

"Right, Edwards." He flipped through his chits again. "Room 403. Came in maybe ten, fifteen minutes ago. Had one and left."

"Did he have a monkey suit on?"

Donald scratched his head. "No...no, he had tweeds." Donald seemed to notice Thorpe's evening clothes for the first time. "Hey, heading for a big shindig, Mr. Thorpe?"

Thorpe refolded the newspaper. "Ever hear of the OSS?"

The young bartender shook his head.

"World War Two," prompted Thorpe.

"Oh, yeah. Used to entertain the troops."

Thorpe laughed. "No, Donald, that's the USO. How about the KGB? MI6?"

"The KGB...sure—Russian spies. MI6...sounds familiar..."

"How about the SS?"

"Sure. Nazis."

Thorpe smiled. "Makes you wonder, doesn't it?"

"About what?"

"Oh, about life. About heroes and villains. About things like good and evil, about faded glory, about sacrifice, duty, honor, country...about remembering—memories. A good memory is not necessarily a good thing, Donald."

Donald didn't like the turn the conversation had taken. "Yeah—"

"The OSS Veterans dinner. Office of Strategic Services, predecessor of the CIA." He pointed to the front page of the *Times*. "That's where I'm going. They get together to remember. They remember too damned much. That's dangerous."

"Hey, you're going to hear the President speak?"

"Right." Thorpe pushed a sealed envelope across the bar. "Do me a favor, Donald. Call around the club—billiards room, library, and all—see if you can locate Edwards. Get this to him."

Donald put the envelope behind the bar. "Sure...you want me to page him, or put this in his message box?"

"No. I want you to give it to him personally, before he leaves here. You might even call up to his room. He's probably dressing for dinner. But keep my name out of it. Okay?" Thorpe winked in a conspiratorial manner.

Donald automatically winked knowingly in return, though he seemed a bit confused.

Thorpe slid a ten-dollar bill across the bar and Donald stuffed it in his pocket. Thorpe looked at his watch. "Time and wilted salad wait for no man, my friend." He slid off the barstool. "You're familiar with T. S. Eliot, of course. 'Time present and time past are both perhaps present in time future, and time future contained in time past.' Well, Donald, that future will be here soon. The tidal wave of the future, which began as a ripple forty years ago, will wash over us all. In fact, I can give you a precise time for it: Fourth of July weekend. You'll see. Remember where you heard it."

"Sure, Mr. Thorpe. Hey, have a good night."

"I'm afraid I've made other plans."

Thorpe looked out the cab window. Traffic on Park Avenue had slowed to a crawl, and ahead he could see by the illumination of floodlights that two lanes were blocked by barriers. Mounted police moved up and down the avenue in the light rain. On the left side of Park Avenue, between 66th and 67th streets, opposite the Seventh Regiment Armory, a few hundred demonstrators were chanting from behind police barriers. The cab driver said, "What the hell's going on now?"

"The President is speaking at the armory."

"Christ! You should've told me. Who's he speaking to?"

"Me. And I'm late. I'll walk." He paid the driver and began walking through the stalled traffic. Limousines were double- and triple-parked around the armory entrance, and across the street, the demonstrators were waving antinuclear placards and singing a 1960s song:

Tell me over, and over, and over again my friend,
But you don't believe we're on the eve
Of destruction....

Thorpe nodded. "You've got *that* right, bozos."

Thorpe passed through a cordon of uniformed police and approached the armory. He looked up at the hundred-year-old structure of brick and granite. These OSS functions had always been held at the Waldorf or Pierre, but in the beleaguered spirit of the times, they'd been shifted to this structure of ersatz bellicosity. Brooding towers rose into the night, topped by sinister-looking rifle ports, but the whole effect was like a Coldstream Guard's uniform: better fitted for show than for battle.

Thorpe climbed a canopied staircase past a file of tactical police and entered the armory through a pair of massive oak doors.

The lobby was paneled in heavy wood and lined with impressive portraits of the martial variety. Hung from the two-story-high ceiling were frayed and faded battle flags and regimental colors. The large chandeliers were early Tiffany, and the entire feeling was one of nineteenth-century gentility, thought Thorpe, a venerable Park Avenue gentleman's club gone slightly to seed. It had been a place where New York's upper crust played soldier on weekends, and it still had the function of providing a convivial atmosphere for East Siders who owed, or thought they owed, a modicum of national service.

Late-arriving guests scurried past Thorpe, and dozens of Secret Service men stood around in business suits or semiformal wear. A few tried to pass for waiters or busboys. The ones who wore the unfashionably long jackets, he knew, were packing Uzi submachine guns and sawed-off shotguns.

A policeman directed Thorpe to the right, and he waited his turn at a walk-through metal detector, then passed through under the scrutiny of Secret Service men.

On the far side of the detector was a broad flag-draped corridor off which wide pocket doors had been parted to reveal handsome reception rooms. Thorpe entered a room filled with coatracks and exchanged his rain-spattered cloak for a receipt. He wandered back into the corridor, crossed it, and entered a lavishly appointed reception room where predinner cocktails were being cleared. Thorpe found an untouched martini and drank it.

"Bad form to be late for the President, Peter."

Thorpe turned and saw Nicholas West approaching. Thorpe said, "It would be worse form to be early and sober."

They shook hands. West said, "Did you just arrive?"

Thorpe smiled. "I was on Company business. What's your excuse, Nicko?"

"I was stacked up over La Guardia."

Thorpe took West's arm. "Look, why don't we skip this boring reunion and go out on the town? I know a deliciously vile topless place on West Forty-sixth, with a whorehouse upstairs."

West forced a laugh, but his cheeks flushed.

Thorpe regarded West. Even in black tie he looked as if he were wearing his crumpled Harris tweeds. West was forty-one years old but looked no more than thirty, thought Thorpe. He had been an instructor of history at Washington University when, in 1967, he and several other young historians were recruited by CIA Director Richard Helms to prepare an encyclopedic history of the OSS and the CIA. That massive secret undertaking turned out to be a continuing and interminable project of which West had become the chief. Thorpe found another martini on a tray and took a swallow. "How's the book coming, Nick?"

West shrugged. "There's always newly uncovered information that makes it necessary to rewrite."

Thorpe nodded. "Newly uncovered information can be a pain in the ass. Have you found a publisher?"

West smiled. "Actually, we've got two volumes into print."

"How about sales?"

"One hundred percent. Ten copies of each volume were printed, then we destroyed the tapes."

"Who got the books?"

"Well, the Director, of course, got one set of volumes. My section got a set. . . ." He looked at Thorpe. "The other distribution is classified."

"Send me a set."

"Get a note from the Director."

"Sure. Which two volumes went to press?"

"The OSS years, 1942 through 1945, and the two years that preceded the founding of the CIA in 1947." West looked around the reception room. It was empty except for busboys. "We'd better go in."

"No rush." Thorpe finished his drink and turned to West. "I'd like to see some of that stuff. My computer can access your computer and we're in business."

West looked at him closely. "If you have a need to know and proper authorization, I'll show you what you need."

Thorpe shook his head. "These things are better done on an old-boys basis."

"I'll think it over."

"Right." Thorpe lit a cigarette and sat on a long table. West, he knew, was getting nervous about being late, which made it easier to deal with him.

Thorpe looked at the colorless man. By the nature of West's job, and because his need-to-know was boundless, he'd evolved, quite by accident, into the single most knowledgeable person in the CIA. Someone once said, "If the KGB had their choice of the man they most wanted in an interrogation cell—the President, the Director of the CIA, or Nicholas West—they would pick West." Thorpe flipped his cigarette into the fireplace. "Ever come across my name?"

West avoided Thorpe's stare and started toward the door that led to the ballroom. "Let's go, Peter."

Thorpe jumped down from the table and followed. "Does it make you nervous carrying all that sensitive stuff around in your head?"

West nodded. "I haven't had a good night's sleep in years." He slid one of the pocket doors open and passed into a curtained-off area of the ballroom. A Secret Service man asked for his invitation, and he showed it. The man checked it against a guest list and waved him through. Thorpe showed his invitation and followed.

Thorpe stopped near the curtains. "Looks like the Eastern Establishment has shown up. Last chance to split, Nicko."

West shook his head and moved toward the curtain, but Thorpe put his hand on his shoulder. "Hold up, sport. Ceremonies are beginning."

West stopped. He felt Thorpe's hand squeezing his shoulder, tighter, until finally he pulled away. Peter Thorpe made him uncomfortable. The man was a case study in excesses: too much physical strength, an overbearing personality, too good-looking, and too much money. Yet, in an odd way, West was attracted to him.

Thorpe said, "Do you have a nursemaid tonight?"

West shrugged. "I guess so."

"Can't you spot them?"

"Sometimes."

"I'll spot him. Then we'll lose him and get over to that cathouse later."

"They don't care if I go to a cathouse. They don't care what I do as long as I don't drop a briefcase off at the Soviet embassy or book myself on a Cruise to Nowhere."

Thorpe laughed. "It's encouraging to see that you can joke about it."

West looked at Thorpe. "For all I know, you're my nursemaid tonight."

"Not me, Nicko."

West smiled. "I guess not." On past occasions he had sometimes compromised himself professionally by his indiscreet talks with

Thorpe. But if there was one thing he would never do, it was compromise himself personally with Thorpe by joining him on one of his escapades. Thorpe was, in some ways, a friend, but Thorpe was also, West sensed, a seducer; a seducer of men as well as women. West felt that Thorpe wanted a piece of him, a piece of his soul, though he could not imagine why.

Thorpe said, "When you're with me, Nicholas, nothing bad will ever happen to you."

"When I'm with you, nothing good ever happens to me."

Thorpe laughed, then his expression changed. He put his arm around West's shoulder and pulled him closer in a hug that was uncomfortably intimate. He spoke softly into West's ear, "They're going to grab you, Nick. They want you in Moscow, and they're going to get you."

West craned his neck and looked up at Thorpe. "No. The Company is protecting me."

Thorpe saw the blood drain from West's face. He smiled sadly and shook his head. "They can't protect you forever, and they know it. They don't even *want* to protect you, because you know too, too much, my friend. When they terminate your employment, it will not be under the New Identity Program—the NIP—it will be under the RIP. That's how they do it. God help you, Nick, but your fate is hovering somewhere between Moscow and Arlington Cemetery."

West felt his mouth go dry. Unconsciously, he leaned closer to Thorpe.

Thorpe patted West's back. "I can help you. We have some time yet."

BOOK III

Reunion

CHAPTER SIXTEEN

Peter Thorpe and Nicholas West entered the ballroom, which was actually the regimental drill hall, a four-story-high structure slightly larger than a football field. The wide expanses were spanned by elliptically shaped wrought-iron trusses, and two tiers of arched windows were cut into the side of the sloping ceiling. The area was brilliantly lit by immense chandeliers. Galleries that could seat over a thousand people overlooked both ends of the hall. Thorpe stared into the dark upper reaches of the gallery above the dais. There were no guests up there, but every ten yards or so a Secret Service man had been posted with binoculars. The sniper rifles, Thorpe knew, were lying on the benches.

Thorpe looked out across the ballroom. The hall was hung with red, white, and blue bunting, and three huge flags—American, British, and French—were suspended above the dais, as was a large sepia-toned picture of the OSS founder, General William "Wild Bill" Donovan.

There were, Thorpe estimated, close to two hundred tables, set with silver, china, and crystal on blue tablecloths. "Where's our table?" asked Thorpe.

"Table fourteen. Near the dais."

Thorpe looked at the raised dais that ran along the north wall. He recognized Ray Cline, an ex-OSS officer and former CIA Deputy Director for Intelligence.

The Marine honor guard was trooping the colors, and the

assembled crowd stood as the colors were presented. The Army band began the national anthem, and the nearly two thousand men and women sang.

West stood at attention and joined in.

Thorpe looked back toward the dais. To Cline's left was Michael Burke, ex-OSS officer and past president of both the Yankees and Madison Square Garden Corporation. Next to Burke was Charles Collingwood, the newscaster and chronicler of OSS activities during the war, and beside Collingwood was Clare Boothe Luce. To her left was Richard Helms, ex-OSS officer, former CIA Director, and the man who had recruited West. Thorpe turned to West. "There's your old boss, Nick. Be sure to thank him for the job."

West stopped singing and mumbled something that sounded like an obscenity.

Thorpe smiled. "He got out and you're still in."

The anthem ended, and the band began playing "God Save the Queen." Thorpe said, "Hey, that reminds me—Colonel Randolph Carbury—know him?"

West stood with his hands clasped behind his back. "I've heard of him. Why?"

"He'll be here tonight. More to follow."

West nodded.

The band ended the British anthem and began *"La Marseillaise."* Thorpe looked back toward the dais. Flanking the President of the United States were Geoffrey Smythe, president of the OSS Veterans, and Thorpe's adoptive father, James Allerton, the guest of honor. Standing to Allerton's left was Bill Casey, ex-OSS officer and present CIA Director. Beside Casey was William Colby, also an ex-OSS officer and former CIA Director. "The alumni have done well," remarked Thorpe.

The French anthem was finished, and the Archbishop of New York began the invocation.

Thorpe parodied the words of the Cardinal's prayer. "Lord God, protect us from werewolves in the night." He turned to West, who was staring at him. Thorpe said, "Have you heard his howl recently?"

West didn't answer.

"More to follow."

The Cardinal finished his invocation, and everyone took their seats. Geoffrey Smythe began his welcoming remarks. Thorpe said to West, "I didn't mean to spook you before."

West almost laughed. "You scared the hell out of me." He glanced at Thorpe. "Am I in trouble?"

"Not at all. You're in great danger."

"Cut it out."

"Sorry, sport. Listen, as for the KGB, it's a matter of keeping on your toes. As for the Company, you have to buy yourself some insurance. You understand?"

West nodded. "Something like...'In the event of my untimely death or disappearance, the following documents and affidavits will go to *The New York Times* and *The Washington Post*....'"

"That's it."

West nodded again.

Thorpe said, "I'll help you with the details."

"In exchange for what?"

"Just your friendship." He smiled and took West's arm. "Let's go face the wrath of a lady kept waiting. You take the rap. I'm in enough trouble."

Katherine Kimberly looked at Thorpe approaching, an annoyed expression on her face.

Thorpe said, "Nick was stacked up over La Guardia." He gave her a peck on the cheek.

West added, "Sorry, it was my fault. Got to talking in the lounge. How are you, Kate?" He leaned over and kissed her.

She took his hand and smiled at him. "Have you heard from Ann?"

"Last night. She's well. Sends you her love."

West looked around the table. "Mr. O'Brien, good seeing you again." They shook hands.

West looked at Patrick O'Brien. He was a man in his sixties, with a full head of whitish-blond hair, a ruddy face, and dark blue penetrating eyes. West knew he kept himself in exceptional physical shape and still jumped, as he said, from perfectly sound aircraft that didn't need jumping from. The jumps were made when the spirit moved him, into the Jersey Pine Barrens, alone and at night—clear but sometimes moonless nights of the sort that one had needed to make the jumps into occupied Europe.

O'Brien nodded at the couple sitting at the table. "You both know Kitty and George Van Dorn, of course." Thorpe and West greeted them and took their seats.

Katherine motioned across the table. "And this is my friend Tony Abrams, who works at the firm."

Abrams reached across the table and shook hands with West. He leaned toward Thorpe, but Thorpe was pouring from a bottle of Stolichnaya. Thorpe looked up perfunctorily and said, "Yes, we've met." Thorpe held up a glass brimming with clear liquid. "Someone was thoughtful enough to remember my preference for Russian vodka. *Na zdorovie.*" He drained off half the glass and let out a sigh.

Thorpe addressed the table. "You may find it odd that I, a patriot and cold warrior, should drink Russian vodka." He looked directly at Abrams. "I drink Russian vodka in the same spirit that prehistoric warriors drank the blood of their enemies."

"A display of contempt?" said Abrams. "Or for courage?"

"Neither, Mr. Abrams. I like the taste." He licked his lips and laughed.

Abrams said, "Speaking of blood, you've got something on your right cuff, Mr. Thorpe."

Peter Thorpe set the glass down and looked at his French cuff. A reddish-brown stain showed on the polished cotton near the black onyx cuff link. He rubbed it between his fingers, then said, *"Looks* like blood, doesn't it?"

"Yes, it does," said Abrams.

Katherine dipped the corner of a napkin in a glass of water. "Soak it before it sets."

Thorpe smiled as he took the napkin. "There are three lines common to all the women of the world: Take out the garbage, I've got a headache, and soak it before it sets." Thorpe blotted the stain. "Decidedly blood."

Katherine spoke with a detectable coolness in her voice. "Did you cut yourself?"

"Cut myself? No, I did not cut myself."

George Van Dorn spoke from across the large table. "Then perhaps, Mr. Thorpe, considering your profession, you've cut someone else." He smiled.

Thorpe smiled back.

Kitty Van Dorn interjected, "It's probably ketchup."

Thorpe rolled his eyes in a mock gesture of disdain. "*Ketchup?* Madame, I haven't *seen* a bottle of ketchup since my school days. Now, Katherine is thinking lipstick, but I must exonerate myself and say blood. I know blood when I see blood." He looked at Abrams. "You're very observant, Mr. Abrams. You ought to be a detective."

"I was."

The West Point Cadet Glee Club had assembled near the dais and began a medley of songs.

Thorpe raised his voice above the noise and spoke to Abrams. "Weren't your parents some sort of Bolshevist agitators? Leon and Ruth Abrams? Got arrested leading a violent garment workers' strike, I think?"

Abrams stared at Thorpe. His parents had had some notoriety in their day and had been mentioned in some of the books on the subject of the American labor movement, but they weren't well enough known for Thorpe to remember them or make the connection based on a common family name. "Yes, Leon and Ruth were my parents. Are you a student of the labor movement?"

"No, sir, I am a student of Reds."

Katherine kicked Thorpe's ankle.

Thorpe said to her, "This is interesting. Colorful. Tony is the son of American folk heroes." He turned to Abrams. "Why *Tony?*"

Abrams smiled thinly. "My name is Tobias, the diminutive of which is Toby. But where I grew up everyone had names like Dino or Vito. So Toby became Tony."

"America the melting pot. And you melted right in there."

There was an embarrassed silence at the table, then Thorpe said, "Are your parents still Communists, Mr. Abrams?"

"They're dead."

"So sorry. Did they keep the faith?"

"My mother's parents returned to Russia during the Depression. They were arrested during the Stalin purges. Presumably they died in the camps."

Thorpe nodded. "That must have shaken your parents' faith in the justice and brotherhood of the Revolution."

"Most probably." Abrams lit a cigarette. "My father's family, who had never left Russia, were killed by the Germans around 1944—about the same time your natural parents were killed by the Germans. Small world."

Thorpe regarded Abrams closely. "How did you know about my parents?"

"I read it. I'm a student of the OSS."

Thorpe poured another vodka and looked at Abrams. "You know, Abrams, you might just be what that firm needs."

"I haven't been asked to join."

"Oh, you will be. What the hell do you think you're doing here? Why do you think—"

Katherine interjected, "Peter, did you happen to see Colonel Carbury on your way in? He's not at his table."

"I'd barely recognize him. All Englishmen look alike." He played with a cocktail stirrer and snapped it between his fingers. "Maybe he got stuck somewhere." Thorpe leaned back in his chair and seemed to retreat into himself.

The cadets stopped singing, and waiters brought the fish course.

West said to Abrams, "You work with Kate?"

"I'm an itinerant process server."

Katherine added, "Mr. Abrams is studying for the July bar."

"Good luck," said West. "My fiancée—Kate's sister, Ann—is an attorney also. She works for an American firm in Munich."

Thorpe came out of his reverie and sat up. "She works for the

National Security Agency, Abrams. Whole damned family is full of spooks."

Katherine said sharply, "You're in an unusually foul mood, Peter." She stood. "Excuse me. Mr. Abrams, will you walk me to the lounge?"

Abrams rose and followed her.

Thorpe seemed to pay no attention. He mumbled, "Whole damned room's full of spooks. Do you know how you can tell when a spook is present?" He held up his salad bowl. "The salad wilts. Christ, we need an exorcist."

Kitty Van Dorn announced that she and her husband were going table-hopping. George Van Dorn's alcohol-clouded eyes suddenly looked clear and he stared at Thorpe, then said, "You're here to see your father honored. See that you do." He took his wife's arm and they moved off.

Thorpe seemed to ignore the reprimand and said to Patrick O'Brien, "Pass the Stoli, please."

O'Brien looked at him sternly. "That's quite enough, Peter. We have something important to discuss later."

Thorpe's eyes met O'Brien's, and Thorpe turned away. "I guess I should eat something. . . ." He dug into his poached salmon.

O'Brien, West, and Thorpe ate without speaking. West watched Thorpe out of the corner of his eye. He was not unhappy that they might become brothers-in-law. Thorpe, though, was a strange man. His full name was Peter Jean Broulé Thorpe, after his natural parents, an American father and French mother, both OSS agents. It was, reflected West, understandable that Katherine should be drawn to him spiritually and emotionally because of their similar backgrounds, even if their personalities were quite different.

Thorpe looked up from his food. "I feel better."

O'Brien leaned toward West. "Has Peter briefed you about this Carbury business?"

"Only that Colonel Carbury is in New York—"

Thorpe said, "I'm not fully briefed either."

O'Brien gave them both an edited outline of the events of the day, and added, "Katherine and I both believe this is related to Talbot."

West nodded. "That's what Peter indicated."

O'Brien stared at Thorpe for some time. "Did Katherine tell you that?"

Thorpe shook his head. "Yes.... No... I made my own conclusions based on my reading of the Wingate letter."

"I see."

Thorpe added quickly, "The point is that Carbury should be here—in this room—to enlighten us further. I think Abrams blew it."

O'Brien said curtly, "Katherine and Abrams took good precautions." He pushed aside his plate. "Carbury may have decided to avoid a known destination. He may have slipped past our people and will send word later to meet him in a safe—"

Thorpe cut in. "This is the safest place in America tonight. And besides, on a personal level, he'd want to be here."

O'Brien nodded slowly. "Yes.... Perhaps he's still some where in the club—though we've had him paged under the name Edwards."

Thorpe smiled. "Damned if I'd answer a page call when I'm on assignment."

O'Brien nodded again. "So let's just assume he has undertaken standard precautions and will show up in his own good time, or we can assume—"

"The worst scenario," said Thorpe. "My experience has usually been that late people are dead people. But I'll allow for a kidnapping." Thorpe chewed on a stalk of celery.

Katherine approached with Abrams, and the three men stood. Katherine said, "I spoke to the Burke Agency. The detectives followed Carbury here...or thought they did. One of them was honest enough to admit that the man they were following—tall, thin, elderly mustached man in a tux, carrying a briefcase—may not have been the man who was pointed out to them by an employee of the club. When they saw this man up close in the lobby here, they suspected they were following a herring. The man, however, did present an invitation and go through the metal detectors. The detectives couldn't follow and left to make their report."

Thorpe said, "I told you all Englishmen looked alike."

Everyone took their seats. O'Brien spoke. "Carbury must have sent a look-alike out to draw off anyone who was watching him. Unfortunately, he drew off the people who were protecting him."

Abrams cleared his throat. "There is another possibility. The look-alike was not employed by Carbury, but by someone else."

Thorpe nodded. "That's a possibility. This may call for a black-bag job." He looked at Abrams. "An illegal entry."

Abrams looked at the people around him. Clearly this was an important case—and not one for which they had been retained, but a house case, a case of some personal concern for them. Clearly, too, the use of a red herring showed some planning and organization by someone and smacked of a high degree of professionalism. Yet neither O'Brien, Katherine, Thorpe, nor West seemed particularly surprised by this. No, he concluded, this was not a stock-fraud case.

O'Brien spoke. "I don't want the detectives doing it. . . . One of us." He turned to Abrams. "Do you think you could get into his room?"

Abrams shrugged. "Maybe"

O'Brien looked at Thorpe.

Thorpe smiled. "Sure. What a team. Pete and Tony out on a black bag together. Christ, how the mighty have fallen."

Katherine said, "The detectives have gone back to the club. Let's give it some time."

The main course was served, and Kitty and George Van Dorn returned. The discussion turned to the subject of the people present. Kitty Van Dorn motioned toward the dais. "The President looks well tonight."

Thorpe stared up at the nearby dais. "Yes, he looks very lifelike. It's that new embalming fluid."

Katherine leaned over and spoke softly into his ear. "If you don't behave, I'm going to have you thrown out."

Thorpe took her hand and squeezed it, then looked back at the dais and caught the eye of Bill Casey. The man looked, as usual, dour. Casey gave Thorpe a sign of recognition but not a particularly friendly one, Abrams noticed. It was, thought Abrams, more like the look a cop on the beat gives to the neighborhood juvenile delinquent.

Thorpe grinned at his boss, then spoke softly to Katherine. "If ever a man was capable of turning into a werewolf, it's Bill Casey."

Katherine fought back a smile.

Thorpe leaned closer to her ear and said earnestly, "He fits the general profile. So do Cline, Colby, and Helms.... So do a few dozen other people here, including your boss and my father. Jesus, doesn't that scare the hell out of you? It does me."

Katherine looked at Patrick O'Brien, then at James Allerton sitting beside the President, engaged in conversation with him.

Thorpe followed her gaze and said, "Yes. 'Someone who may be close to your President.'"

Katherine stared at him. "No."

Thorpe smiled. "Possible."

"No."

"Absolutely beyond the realm of the imagination?"

Katherine turned away and poured a drink.

CHAPTER SEVENTEEN

Abrams found himself standing beside Katherine at the long bar set up in a corner of the ballroom. He ordered a drink for himself, avoiding any overtures toward conversation, turned, and looked around the hall. A few men and women wore officer's dress uniforms, and there were foreign uniforms as well. Even though the invitation specified black tie, some men wore white ties and tailcoats. Abrams thought this was the kind of crowd that went home and slipped into a tuxedo to get comfortable.

Abrams brushed an imaginary speck from his shirt and checked his clothing. In some indefinable way, it *looked* rented—except for the damned shoes.

Katherine asked, "Where was the tuxedo from?"

Abrams looked up quickly. "What? Oh, Murray's, on Lexington.... Why?"

"I just wondered if he'd brought it from England."

"Oh, Carbury.... No, his was from Lawson's. Down in the Wall Street area. The ticket showed it was fitted two days ago."

She took a few steps from the bar and he followed. She asked, "What was he doing all the way down there?"

"Renting a tux, for one thing." He sipped his drink.

She looked at him closely. "Is there anything else? Any detail you may have—"

"No."

She held his eyes for a few seconds, then said, "I appreciate the risk you took. Especially considering you don't know what this is about."

"The less I know, the better."

She said, "Actually, I haven't told anyone you were in Carbury's room." She smiled. "I told you I'd protect you."

Abrams said, "I'm not overly cautious by nature, but I would like to be able to present myself to the state bar this summer without a criminal record."

"I'm quite sensitive to your position." She hesitated, then added, "I didn't tell you to break and enter . . . and I'm wondering why you did it."

He avoided the question by returning to the earlier one. "You also wondered if I found anything I'm not telling you about."

"You *did* forget to tell me where the tux was from."

He stared at her, then smiled. "Yes, I did forget." He thought, *And you forgot to tell O'Brien I broke into Carbury's room, and I think O'Brien may have forgotten to tell you he's asked me to go to Glen Cove Monday, and there will be a lot more convenient lapses of memory before this is over.*

She said thoughtfully, "I suppose Peter put you in a sour mood. I won't apologize for him. But I am sorry that happened."

"Peter Thorpe has no influence on my mood."

She didn't reply, and Abrams could see her mind was already on something else. She was carrying her program and she unexpectedly handed it to him.

Abrams took it, glanced at her, then opened it. There were three sheets of a photostated handwritten letter inside. He glanced over the first page and saw it was a personal letter to her. He looked at Katherine.

"Go on. Read it."

He began reading, and as he read, he understood that she had made an important decision about him. He finished the letter and passed it back inside the program.

She waited a few seconds for him to speak, then said, "Well?"

"No comment."

"Why not?"

"It's out of my league." He finished his drink.

"Think of it as a criminal case—a problem of police detective work."

"I've already done that. It's still out of my league."

"Well, at least give it *some* thought."

"Right." He put his glass on the bar. The letter, if genuine, partially confirmed his suspicions about the firm he was working for. He stepped back toward her and said in a quiet voice, "One question. O'Brien, Kimberly and Rose is a CIA front, right? What do you call it—a proprietary company?"

She shook her head.

Abrams was taken aback, and he knew his face showed it. "Then who the hell are you?"

She again shook her head.

Abrams rubbed his chin. "This, you'll agree, is bizarre."

"Perhaps." She reached toward the bar and picked up the guest list. She said, "First, alphabetically, James Jesus Angleton, former OSS officer, former head of CIA counterintelligence. Considered the father of American counterintelligence. As a result of his close association with the British double agent Philby, and his failure to spot Philby for what he was—and also because of some other odd occurrences—there was some suggestion that Jim himself was a Soviet agent. If true . . . well, it's too frightening to even think about. Anyway, Jim was fired by Bill Colby for reasons that remain unclear. Next possible suspect—"

"Hold on." Abrams regarded her closely. He had the impression she'd gone from low gear to second and was about to shift into high. He said, "I'm not interested in suspects. I thought I made that clear."

She looked put off. "Sorry. . . . You're right, though. I've been out of touch with . . . ordinary people." She considered a moment. "Perhaps I've misjudged you . . . and perhaps I've already said too much. Excuse me." She handed him the guest list and walked off.

Abrams went back to the bar and leafed through his guest list. There were a good number of people with French and Middle-European names, former resistance fighters, he imagined. There were

British knights and their ladies, a Romanov couple, and other titled people, including his new friend Countess Claudia. He looked over his shoulder at the Grenville table, but Claudia's back was to him. The band began playing, and he decided to ask her to dance, but she stood with Tom Grenville, and they moved to the dance floor.

Abrams ordered another drink and turned his attention to the tables around him. If there was a collective mood in the place, he thought, it could be described in one word: *proud*. There was some arrogance, to be sure, and even sentimentality, but the general feeling was one of "job well done." The years had not dimmed the memories; age and infirmity were barely noticeable in the swaggering walks or the assured, resonant voices. It didn't matter that the roll call got shorter each year or that the world was not the same as it had been in 1945. In this place, on this night, thought Abrams, it was again V-E Day.

Katherine tapped her finger against his program, startling him out of his reverie. She stood beside him and said, "Looking for someone in particular?"

"No." He added, "Want a drink?"

"No, thank you. Did I seem a bit abrupt when I left?"

"You seemed annoyed."

She forced a smile. "Our conversations often end that way, don't they?"

He seemed to hesitate and she sensed he was wavering between excusing himself and asking her to dance, so she said, "Let's adjourn to the dance floor."

The band was playing "As Time Goes By." She fit easily into his arms, and he felt her body press against his, smelled her hair, her soap, her perfume. They danced somewhat self-consciously at first, then he relaxed and she relaxed, and in stages the proximity of their bodies was not so awkward.

She said, "You've never married?"

"No...engaged once."

"May I ask what happened?"

Abrams was looking at Claudia dancing nearby with Grenville.

He looked back at Katherine. "Happened...? Oh, there was a political difference of opinion. So we separated."

"That's odd."

"She was a 1960s radical, flower child...whatever. An antiwar and civil rights activist. Then she was into whales, followed by American Indians and the environment, or the other way around. Then the ERA, then the antinuclear things. Whatever was going down, Marcy was right there with a picket sign and a T-shirt. Her life chronologically paralleled the evening news. Like artists who have blue periods, she had whale periods...Indian periods...you understand?"

"Activism and idealism don't appeal to you?"

"No 'ism' appeals to me. I saw too much of it as a child. It ruins lives."

"It sometimes helps mankind."

"It stinks. Take it from me, it stinks."

They danced in silence for a while, then she said, "So you left her? Because she was so committed—"

"She left me. Because I confessed that I was a lifelong Republican." He smiled. "The idea of sleeping with a Republican made her, as she said, nauseous." He gave a short laugh.

She thought a moment, then said, "But you loved her in spite of all that."

Abrams never imagined that the subject of love and other people's relationships could possibly interest Katherine Kimberly. "There was never a dull moment. Can you imagine coming home from work in a police uniform and finding the living room full of black revolutionaries?"

"No, not really."

"It got tense." He laughed again.

She smiled. "I'm glad you can find it amusing now."

"You don't know what amusing is until you've made love wrapped in a Cuban flag with the heat off in the dead of winter to protest oil prices, and wondering if she's going to smell the hamburger on your breath because you're supposed to be boycotting beef, and a picture of Che is staring down at you with those eyes like Christ, and two lesbian houseguests are sleeping in the living room..." He looked at Katherine quickly and saw a tight expression on her face. "I'm sorry. Am I making you uncomfortable?"

She shook her head. "No. I'm trying to keep from laughing."

They danced until the music ended. He took her arm and they walked back toward the bar. Abrams opened the guest list. "I see your sister is supposed to be the eighth person at our table."

"She couldn't make it. I was going to tell you that you could bring a guest, but it slipped my mind. If you're not looking for someone in particular, perhaps you're looking for suspects."

"I'm just interested in these names. Impressed, to be honest."

She ordered a white wine. "Anything you'd like to know?"

"Yes. Why is everyone here?"

She smiled. "It's an annual dinner. Tonight we're honoring James Allerton, Peter's father, who is the recipient of the General Donovan Medal. And, of course, we're honoring the memory of the dead and the memory of General Donovan, who is referred to in conversation simply as the General, as you may have noticed. Do you find this interesting?"

Abrams looked at her, her back against the bar, drink in one hand, cigarette in the other. Very unlike what he was used to in the office. He said, "The phrase 'old-boys network' keeps coming into my head."

She exhaled a stream of cigarette smoke. "There is no network here—this is a very mixed group. The only common denominator is a shared period of comradeship some forty years ago. The OSS ran the gamut from prostitutes to princes, from criminals to cardinals."

Abrams thought there wasn't as much in between as she might suppose. He said, "It's entertaining to think that someone here—perhaps more than one person—may be a Soviet agent." He looked out over the hall.

"Eleanor Wingate did not actually say that....Why did you say 'entertaining'?...You mean intriguing."

"I'm entertained."

She thought a moment. "You don't like us much, do you? I

suppose it would make you happy to expose someone highly placed. The police, I understand, get a good deal of satisfaction from laying low the mighty."

"Only on television. In real life you wind up testifying in court and being cross-examined by somebody from O'Brien, Kimberly and Rose who rips you to shreds." He stubbed out his cigarette. "If, as I understand it, the suspect or suspects fit a certain profile, why did you tell Mr. O'Brien?"

"I trust him."

Abrams shook his head. He said, "And I assume you've shown Thorpe the letter?"

"Yes. He doesn't qualify as a suspect, of course. Neither do you."

"I'm glad Mr. Thorpe and I have so much in common. Have you told or are you going to tell anyone else?"

"There are more people in...our circle of friends who will be told this evening."

"You're making it difficult for yourself."

"Internal investigations are always difficult. That's why I'd like your help."

"Why me?"

She leaned toward him. "You're intelligent, resourceful, an exdetective, I trust you, and I like you."

"Am I blushing?"

"No, you're pale."

"Same thing."

She waved her hand. "I rest my case. Would you like to dance?"

"We'd look silly. The band has stopped playing."

She looked around. "Oh..." She laughed.

He said, "Can I ask you an obvious question, Miss Kimberly? Why don't you turn this over to professionals?"

"That's complicated. Why don't you ask Mr. O'Brien later?... And you can call me Katherine." A half smile formed on her lips.

"Yes, we have danced. What should I call you on Tuesday in the office?"

"If we're dancing, Katherine. Otherwise, Miss Kimberly."

Abrams wasn't certain he liked her brand of humor.

CHAPTER EIGHTEEN

A brams saw Thorpe sitting by himself. He walked to the table and sat down.

Thorpe stared openly at Abrams, then commented, "Only you and me, Tony."

"You and I."

"That's what I said, only I can say it the way I want because I'm a Yale graduate, whereas you have to watch your English."

"True." Abrams began eating.

Thorpe pointed his knife in Abrams' direction. "What did Kate tell you? And don't say 'About what?'"

"About what?"

Thorpe half stood. "Listen to me, Abrams—"

"Your face is red and you've raised your voice. I've never seen a Yalie do that."

Thorpe leaned across the table and struck his knife against Abrams' glass. "Watch yourself."

Abrams went back to his food.

Thorpe sat and didn't speak for some time, then said, "Look...I really don't care that you're Jewish—"

"Then why mention it?"

Thorpe's voice took on a conciliatory tone. "I don't care about your background, your parents, the New York police force, who are not my favorite people, your humble station in life, your wanting to be a lawyer—and I don't even care about your sitting here, but—"

Abrams glanced up from his food. "How about me mentioning the blood on your cuff?"

"—but I do care that my fiancée is trying to involve you in this business. It is not your business, Mr. Abrams, and in fact it may very well be no one's business. I think it's all a crock of crap."

"So why worry about it? Have you tried this chicken?"

"Listen closely, then forget what I tell you. Katherine and O'Brien and a few others are amateur detectives—dilettantes. You know the type from your police days. They get themselves worked up over intrigue. Don't encourage them."

Abrams put down his knife and fork and placed his napkin on the table.

Thorpe went on, "If there's anything to this, it should be handled by professionals—like me—not by—"

Abrams stood. "Excuse me. I need some air." He left.

Thorpe drummed his fingers on the table. "Bastard."

After a few minutes Nicholas West returned to the table.

Thorpe glanced at him. "I still want to see those books, Nick."

West showed an uncharacteristic annoyance. "No business tonight." He mixed a drink.

Thorpe began talking, but West was paying little attention. He was thinking about Thorpe. As head of the Domestic Contact Service, Thorpe ran what amounted to the largest amateur spy ring in the world. The operation had grown so large that Thorpe, it was said, had a computer in his apartment that held the names of thousands of civilians, their overseas itineraries, occupations, capabilities, reliability, and areas of expertise. And the whole operation cost relatively little, a real plus with this administration. Everyone who volunteered to "do a little something for his country" did it without compensation, their only rewards being the thrill of it and a pat on the back from Thorpe or one of his debriefing officers.

Thorpe saw that West wasn't paying attention and poked his arm. "Okay, no business," he said. "When are you flying to Munich to see your betrothed?"

"I can't get approval for Munich. Ann is coming here in late June or early July for home leave."

"Oh, when's the big day?"

"Unscheduled."

"It must be frustrating living together in separate countries. Anyway, I'm eager to be your brother-in-law. Then you'll trust me."

"When are *you* getting married?"

"How about a Fourth of July double wedding? That would be fitting for all the patriots and spooks. Maybe we'll use the Glen Cove estate. Yes, that might be nice."

West smiled. "You mean Van Dorn's estate, don't you? Not the Soviet estate?"

Thorpe smiled in return, but didn't answer.

Waiters brought the dessert to the table, and West dug into a chocolate soufflé.

West looked up from his food. "Not to break my own no-business rule, but this Talbot thing sounds ominous. I hope it doesn't touch off one of those witch-hunting hysterias in the Company again."

Thorpe shrugged. "Christ, what would these people do without their bogeyman? Talbot. Bullshit. If there were a Talbot, he'd be about a hundred and five years old by now." Thorpe leaned toward West. "Do you know who Talbot is? I'll tell you. He's the devil in our heads. He's the fiend, the monster, the nightmare. . . ." Thorpe lowered his voice. "He doesn't exist, Nick, never did. He's what those old-timers blame for all their fuckups."

West nodded slowly. "You could be right."

Thorpe began to reply, but Katherine came back to the table and sat. She spoke in a worried tone: "We've called all over, and there's no sign of Carbury."

Thorpe did not seem particularly concerned. He said, "I'll call my people and have them contact the FBI."

Katherine replied, "I also want Tony to use his police contacts. Where is he?"

"It's Friday night, isn't it? He probably went to temple."

Katherine's voice was angry. "You've been rude all evening—to everyone. What the hell set you off?"

Thorpe looked contrite. "I guess I had a bad day. I'll apologize to everyone."

She let out an exasperated breath. "That doesn't make it right." She looked at Nicholas West, who seemed embarrassed. "Do you and Ann fight?"

West forced a smile. "Sometimes."

"Then maybe it's us—the Kimberly women. My mother is a bitch." She turned to Thorpe. "I accept your apology."

Thorpe brightened and raised his wineglass. "All for one and one for all."

They touched glasses and drank. West glanced at Katherine, then Thorpe. West was in the position of knowing more about Peter Thorpe than Thorpe's lover knew: West had read Thorpe's personnel file and his officer evaluation reports. He had done this under the excuse of historical research, but really out of a personal concern for Katherine Kimberly.

One evaluator, he remembered, had characterized Thorpe as "an enthusiastic heterosexual." Someone had scribbled in the margin, *This means he chases women.* West imagined that Katherine understood this and accepted it.

West looked at Thorpe's eyes as he spoke to Katherine. That's where the madness showed itself in brief glimpses, like the doors of a furnace that swing open, then snap shut again, leaving you with the impression of a blazing turmoil but no positive proof. West recalled something else in Thorpe's file, a CIA psychologist's report, written in the clear English favored by the Company over the psychobabble of civilian psychoanalysts. After an extensive interview—probably a drug-aided one—the analyst had written: "He at times behaves and sounds as if he's still in Skull and Bones at Yale. He enjoys clandestine assignments but approaches even the most dangerous ones as if they were fraternity pranks."

The psychiatrist had added an insight that West thought was disturbing: "Thorpe suffers greatly from ennui; he must live on the edge of an abyss in order to feel fully alive. He considers himself superior to the rest of humanity by virtue of knowing important secrets and belonging to a secret and elite organization. This is evidence of an immature personality. Further, his relationships with his peers, though good-natured, are superficial, and he forms no strong male bonds. His attitude toward women is best described as outwardly charming but inwardly disdainful."

West stared at Thorpe. It was obvious, at least to West, that Peter Thorpe was a man fighting some monumental inner struggle, a man whose mind was in a state of turmoil over some serious matter.

West had passed a casual remark to this effect to Katherine, but it hadn't gone over well and he'd dropped it. Ann, however, had been more receptive. Ann had other information—informal conversations with agents, hearsay, and the like—and though she was not specific, West could tell she was concerned.

West knew what he had to do next: request all the operation reports filed by Thorpe himself as well as the reports and analyses of all operations with which Thorpe had been associated. West had put this off, but the time had come to fully evaluate Peter Thorpe.

Thorpe suddenly turned to West. "You look pensive, Nick. Something on your mind?"

West felt his face flush, and he was unable to turn away from Thorpe's arresting stare. He had the uncomfortable impression that Peter Thorpe knew what he had been thinking. West cleared his throat and said, "I was just wondering—if Carbury was found dead, would you believe in the existence of Talbot?"

Thorpe's eyes narrowed, and he leaned very close to West and spoke softly. "If you found a sheep in the woods with its throat ripped out, Nick, would you credit it to wolves or werewolves?" Thorpe smiled, a slow smile that was itself wolflike, thought West. Thorpe said, "New York is not the most unlikely place for a man to wind up with a shiv in his heart."

West tried to stop himself, but his eyes were drawn to the spot on Thorpe's cuff.

Thorpe smiled even wider at him, a huge smile with his lips drawn back, showing a set of large white teeth. West stood and excused himself.

Thorpe turned back to Katherine, who was pouring herself coffee. He said, "That man is very high-strung. He makes me jumpy."

"I've never known you to be jumpy about anything."

"Nicholas West makes a lot of people in the Company jumpy."

"You sound as though you have a guilty conscience."

"I have no conscience, guilty or otherwise."

"Then you must be hiding something." She smiled.

Thorpe did not smile back. He said, "If I were, it wouldn't stay hidden long from that inoffensive little man—would it?"

Katherine regarded him closely. "No."

Thorpe nodded to himself as though he had made a decision about something. He said, "Actually, I'm worried about him. There are too many people who want him out of the way." Thorpe lit a cigarette and exhaled a stream of smoke. "To use a familiar analogy, Nicholas West is like a head of cattle grazing too long in the fields of intelligence archives until he's grown very fat. The farmer who owns him wants to butcher him; the wolves in the woods want him in their stomachs." He looked at Katherine. "Poor Nick."

CHAPTER NINETEEN

Patrick O'Brien's round table was assembled again. West was speaking to Katherine, O'Brien was talking to Kitty and George Van Dorn, Claudia had taken the empty seat and was speaking with Abrams. Thorpe sat silently. A few people were dancing to 1930s big-band tunes. Abrams watched Thorpe. The man had been drinking heavily all night, but was clearly sober.

Abrams looked back at Claudia and responded to a question. "No, my parents didn't teach me Russian."

"What a pity. I know Russian. We could have had secret conversations."

"About what?"

"Whatever. I'll teach you a few words and I'm sure it will start to come back to you."

Abrams didn't respond, and she changed the subject. She spoke animatedly about her life in America, touching Abrams' arm from time to time. At one point she asked, "Am I touching you too much?" To which he replied, "Not too much, but not in the right places."

She laughed.

Abrams let his mind slip back to when he had been taken by O'Brien around the great hall and introduced to some of O'Brien's friends and clients. Most of them, like John Weitz, Julia Child, and Walt Rostow, were rich, famous, powerful, or all three. Abrams did not wonder why he had been afforded this rare honor. There was a certain psychology of recruitment common to most clandestine organizations he'd been involved with, from the Mafia to the Weather Underground; you began by running errands, then advanced to committing indiscreet acts. Then you were introduced to the inner circle, followed by introductions to VIP's who may or may not be part of the group but who you are led to believe are simpatico. Then, finally, when you're psychologically ready, you're sent on a mission to prove yourself. A mission you'd been told was coming, but which you could not have conceived of participating in just a few short months or weeks before. In this case, the Glen Cove mission was how he was supposed to "make his bones," as his Italian friends would say.

Claudia broke into his thoughts. "I think you should spend the night at the town house."

Abrams looked at her. "Do you? There may not be room. I suppose the Grenvilles are staying?"

Claudia smiled at him. "Forget Joan Grenville, my friend. These Wisps are not for you."

"Wasps."

The ballroom suddenly became quiet as the president of the OSS Veterans, Geoffrey Smythe, rose and stood at the podium. Smythe welcomed everyone and introduced the dais.

When he finished his introductory remarks, he said, "It is my special honor this evening to introduce our guest speaker, who is probably the only man in America who truly needs no further introduction. Ladies and gentlemen, the President of the United States and Commander-in-Chief of the Armed Forces."

The military-oriented crowd stood and held up their glasses, making the traditional toast: "To the Commander-in-Chief!" Sustained applause followed as the President took his place at the podium.

The President spoke for some time, interrupted by much applause. He concluded, "And, finally, I've sent a presidential message to all senior personnel within the CIA expressing my desire to see revived the esprit de corps, the dedication, the flair and the daring of the old OSS. Thank you."

Abrams looked around the room. Bill Casey, whose position on the dais was close by, had a small smile on his face. Clearly, thought Abrams, the good times had returned.

William Colby, chairman of the award committee, stood at the podium and said, "The purpose of this gathering is to honor the memory of the founder of the Office of Strategic Services and to present the General Donovan Medal, which it is my honor to do at this time."

Colby referred to a written text. "The Veterans of the OSS present the Donovan Medal to an individual who has rendered distinguished service in the interests of the United States, the Free World, and the cause of freedom. This year, we are especially proud to present the Donovan Medal to a man who was present at the birth of the OSS, a man whose career in many ways paralleled that of General Donovan."

Colby glanced to his left, then said, "James Allerton is the founder of the Wall Street law firm of Allerton, Stockton, and Evans. He has been a friend and counselor to the Dulleses, to General Donovan, and to every American President from Roosevelt to our present chief of state.

"President Roosevelt commissioned James Allerton a colonel during the Second World War, and as colonel he served on General Donovan's staff. After the war, President Truman appointed him as one of the drafters of the National Security Act which gave birth to the CIA. President Eisenhower appointed him ambassador to Hungary.

"In 1961 he was appointed by President Kennedy to the Securities and Exchange Commission. But James Allerton was at heart an intelligence officer, and feeling the old pull of the shadowy world of cloak and dagger, which we all understand"—Colby waited for the slight laughter to subside—"James Allerton offered his services to Mr. Kennedy in that capacity and was appointed a presidential military intelligence advisor.

"Since that time, James Allerton's counsel has been sought by every President on matters of extreme sensitivity in the areas of intelligence and national security planning."

Colby continued, "James Allerton now serves on the staff of the

National Intelligence Officers, which as you know is a small group of senior analysts known unofficially in Washington as the Wise Men, and advises the President on matters of extreme national and world importance."

Colby's voice began building to the final introduction. "James Allerton's long career has embodied those qualities of public service and private enterprise that are stressed by the Veterans of the Office of Strategic Services in awarding the Donovan Medal. Ladies and gentlemen, may I introduce a dear personal friend, the Honorable James Prescott Allerton."

The assembly rose, and a long, sustained applause rolled through the great hall. Allerton stood and walked along the dais to the podium. The tall, gaunt figure was slightly stooped, but he carried himself with great dignity. His eighty-odd years barely showed on his ruddy face framed with thick white hair, but his deliberate movements were unmistakably those of an octogenarian.

Colby slipped the blue ribbon over Allerton's head and straightened the gold medal that rested on his chest. The two men shook hands, and Allerton stood alone at the podium.

Tears ran from his clear blue eyes, and he wiped them with a handkerchief. The applause died away and everyone sat.

James Allerton thanked Colby and the award committee, and acknowledged the President and the dais.

Abrams watched Thorpe closely as his father spoke in a voice that was strong and still carried the accents which suggested prep schools, Ivy League colleges, and the vanished world that had existed before World War II in places like Bar Harbor, Newport, Hyannis, and Southampton.

Being the son of a famous father had its well-known drawbacks, and actually following in his career footsteps was fraught with dangers, psychological and otherwise, Abrams thought.

When Allerton had been Thorpe's age, reflected Abrams, he must already have been on Donovan's staff as a colonel, helping to win a great war, changing the world, master of his fate and the fate of countless others. But those were different times, thought Abrams. Even men and women who had the potential of greatness within them were doomed to obscurity and frustration in an age that did not call for greatness. Abrams thought he had a small insight into Peter Thorpe's character, or lack of it.

Abrams returned his attention to the dais as James Allerton spoke eloquently of his years with the OSS. Abrams could see that the audience was deeply moved by his reminiscences.

Then Allerton stopped talking and bowed his head a moment. When he looked up, he slowly surveyed the assembly of veterans and guests for some time before his voice broke the stillness again. He said, "The world lost literally millions of good men and women in those awful six years of war, and we are the poorer for it. But we remember them . . . each and every one of them, in different ways, every day. We remember them tonight." James Allerton drew a long breath, then nodded, touched his medal, and said, "Thank you." He abruptly turned from the podium and took his seat. The people in the hall stood, almost in unison. There was silence for a long moment, then a burst of applause rang out.

The President stood, walked up to Allerton, and embraced him amid more ovations. Everyone on the dais was facing Allerton and applauding. Hands were being shaken all around.

Abrams had no previous experience from which to judge, but he thought this dinner must be the most successful yet. Nearly everything that anyone might want to hear was said by someone or another. He tried to empathize, to feel what they felt—triumph, vindication, rejuvenation—but he could never feel it. Either you had been there or you had not.

The closest he could come to the experience, he thought, was the twentieth-year reunion of his high school class. He had made the newspapers that day for a homicide arrest, and he'd been introduced at the reunion and given a short speech at the Italian restaurant where it had been held. Afterward, he went home with an old girl friend, recently divorced, and slept with her. He'd felt about as good then as he'd ever felt since. Nothing earthshaking, nothing of world import, but for him it was a complete experience.

Abrams sat down before the others and finished his drink. Admittedly he felt like an outsider, but was he an outsider who wanted in or an outsider who wanted to remain out? He looked at the people around him, then focused on Patrick O'Brien. Earlier, O'Brien had opened the door a crack and given him a glimpse into another world, a world of conspiracy and secrets.

It seemed to be his fate, he thought, to get involved with one netherworld or another. First it was the Red Devils; then the undercover assignments on the force.

Nearly everyone in the hall was in motion now, going from table to table, passing down the dais and shaking hands. A phalanx of Secret Service men moved the President out a side exit.

Peter Thorpe caught Abrams' eye and nodded toward the door.

Abrams stood. Time for their black-bag job.

CHAPTER TWENTY

Peter Thorpe stood at Randolph Carbury's door. He spoke softly. "You carry?"

Abrams replied, "Not tonight."

"No, even I couldn't get a piece past that crew tonight." Thorpe held the key he'd gotten from the room manager, who stood some distance away. Thorpe said, "I hear a radio. Sign says 'Do Not Disturb.'"

"Disturb."

Thorpe unlocked the door and pushed it open a few inches. "Chained."

Abrams saw the chain he'd retaped in place. He said, "Looks like he's in."

Thorpe called: "Colonel Carbury?"

Abrams said, "Shoulder it."

Thorpe shrugged, stepped back, and rammed the door with his shoulder. The taped chain flew away and Thorpe stumbled into the room, losing his balance and falling onto the floor.

Abrams smiled and stepped inside. He fingered the hanging chain. "Taped it when he left. Old trick. Are you all right?"

Thorpe's face was red as he got to his feet.

Abrams retrieved the keys and flipped them to the room manager. "Take a walk."

Thorpe looked at Abrams as though wondering if he'd been set up.

Abrams regarded Thorpe closely, wondering if Thorpe knew about the tape but was playacting his role.

They both looked around the quiet room. Thorpe said, "Well, no sign of violence here." He walked into the bathroom and called back, "No stiff here, either."

Abrams noticed an empty tuxedo bag on the bed. "Carbury dressed for dinner."

Thorpe came back into the bedroom and knelt beside the bed. "This is about the only place you could stash a stiff in this room." He peered under the bed. "Carbury? You there?" He stood. "Well, he seems to have gone out."

Abrams said to Thorpe, "Just stand there so you don't leave fingerprints, lint, and hair all over. I'll toss the room."

Thorpe smiled. "Tony in action. Don't you need a magnifying glass and deerstalker hat?"

Abrams searched the room for the second time that evening. Thorpe made a few remarks, but Abrams didn't respond. Abrams completed his search and said suddenly, "Have you been here tonight?"

"How about you?"

"I was in the club. But I couldn't get up here. Answer my question."

Thorpe walked to the window and looked out into the street. "As a matter of fact, I took out a book from the library, had a drink. Check it out."

"Coincidence?"

Thorpe turned his head and smiled at Abrams. "Neither you nor I believe in coincidence. Not in our business. I was here for the same reason you were."

Abrams seemed lost in thought.

Thorpe said, "What are you thinking, ace?"

Abrams looked at him. "You know."

"Tell me, Tony."

"It's the blood on the cuff, Pete."

"I know. I know." Thorpe shook his head as though he were considering an abstract problem that had nothing to do with him. "What can we make of that?"

"We think it's sloppy and amateurish." Abrams moved closer to Thorpe.

Thorpe said, "Keep your distance."

Abrams stopped. He smiled. "This sounds sort of silly, but I want your cuff. Rip it off."

Thorpe smiled in return. "Come and take it." He threw off his rain cloak.

Abrams shrugged. "I thought you'd say that." He also removed his raincoat and stepped closer to Thorpe, realizing he wanted not only the cuff but a piece of Thorpe as well.

Thorpe put up his fists. "Yale boxing team, Abrams. You'd better be good."

Abrams moved in, left shoulder first, a flat-footed stance, his fists protecting his face. Thorpe did the same. But Abrams did not think for one moment that Thorpe intended to box, so when Thorpe's left leg shot out, with the toe of his shoe pointed directly at Abrams' groin, Abrams was able to react. He dropped his hands and intercepted Thorpe's foot. But Thorpe's kick was so powerful that Abrams found himself lifted off the floor, still clutching Thorpe's shoe and ankle. Abrams fell back on the floor, and Thorpe pulled his foot out of his shoe, then kicked off his other shoe.

Abrams quickly got to his feet and backed off. Thorpe smiled slowly. "Smart. If I had caught you with that kick, you'd be singing falsetto for a month. Well, do you still want the cuff?"

Abrams nodded.

Thorpe feigned a look of disappointment. "How am I going to explain to Katherine what you're doing in the hospital?" He moved closer to Abrams, jabbing and feinting as he did.

Abrams backed toward the door.

Thorpe came almost within kicking distance.

Abrams' right hand was behind his back, fumbling with the doorknob. Thorpe smiled and took a quick step forward to position his kick. Suddenly, Abrams' other hand also grabbed the knob, and Thorpe saw too late what was coming. Abrams' feet left the floor, his body pivoting from the leverage of his grip on the knob. His heels caught Thorpe in the midsection and sent him sprawling backward onto the bed, then off the side to the floor.

Abrams knew the blow was not a disabling one and followed up quickly with a rush, then stopped short.

Thorpe stood with a very long and thin black knife in his hand. He spoke as he caught his breath. "This is ebony.... Passes the metal detectors and X rays.... Can puncture your heart with it. Want to see?"

Abrams' eyes darted around, and he spotted a heavy table lamp.

Thorpe shook his head. "Don't. Look." He held out his hand with the knife and pulled back the jacket sleeve. "Spot's gone. Attendant in the men's room had Carbona, God bless his Spanish soul. Military establishments are fanatical about personal appearance."

Abrams kept his eyes on the knife.

Thorpe lowered it and slid it into the seam along his trousers. "Truce?"

Abrams nodded.

Thorpe patted the seam where the knife lay. "Come on. I'll buy you a drink. We could both use one." Thorpe put his shoes on. They retrieved their raingear and left.

They waited silently in the corridor for the elevator. Thorpe lit a cigarette, then spoke as though to himself. "Cops look for things like motive, opportunity, clues...like the cuff, for instance. In my business, we have different needs. We don't care to know the actual name of the culprit. That's meaningless. We want to know the name of his employer. We do not try to perfect a case against a murderer. We always find that the motive for a murder or kidnapping is a perfectly legitimate one...from our perspective. So we don't talk about legalities. Police think in terms of crime and punishment. We think in terms of sin and retribution."

Abrams said nothing.

Thorpe went on. "The National Security Act of 1947 did not give us powers of arrest. That was supposed to keep us in line. Silly idea. What do you do with people you can't arrest and try in a special court?"

Abrams lit a cigarette.

Thorpe continued. "We're supposed to have the FBI arrest them, then watch a federal prosecutor fuck up the case. Or have a defense lawyer try to drag out all sorts of information which pertains to national security. Well, we don't go that route."

The elevator came, and Thorpe motioned Abrams inside. Abrams shook his head. Thorpe shrugged and got in alone. The doors closed. Abrams took the next elevator.

As Abrams rode down, he thought: If Thorpe did kill Carbury, why did he? Thorpe's personality, as far as Abrams could ascertain, was that of a man who would commit murder as part of his worka-day job, for reasons he himself didn't fully understand or even care about. Thorpe, though, was also the type who would kill anyone who posed even the remotest threat to the personal well-being and happiness of Peter Thorpe. Was it, then, an official sanction or a private enterprise?

Abrams joined Thorpe on the second level, and Thorpe ush-ered him into the oak-paneled lounge. Thorpe said, "Have you ever heard of the Special Homicide Squad?"

Abrams stood at the bar but didn't respond.

Thorpe stood beside him, his foot on the rail. "A handful of New York cops who come together only when it appears that a corpse met his end as a result of...official sanction. These detectives, coinciden-tally, all have special training at a farm in Virginia. You following me? So don't go beating on doors downtown with this. You may knock on the wrong door."

The bartender, Donald, approached. "Hey, Mr. Thorpe. Shindig over already?"

"Right."

"How'd the President look?"

"Terrific. Catch it on the eleven o'clock news. Donald, this group needs alcohol. Stolichnaya, and buy yourself one. My friend drinks Scotch."

Donald said to Abrams, "What do you want with that Scotch?"

"A glass."

Donald moved off.

Thorpe lit another cigarette. "My stomach is starting to ache."

"Must have been the fish."

Thorpe smiled. "You're good, Abrams. I'll give you that."

Neither spoke for some time, then Thorpe said, "So what do you think of the old boys?"

Abrams answered in measured tones. "Harmless enough old duffers. Like to talk power and politics. They're out of it, though."

"That's what I used to think. Fact is, they're not. I use them in my business."

Abrams thought that O'Brien would say he used Thorpe. "What *is* your business?"

"Something called the Domestic Contact Service....What kind of clearance do you have, Abrams?"

"Six feet two inches."

Thorpe laughed. "I like you. I'm sorry about before, at dinner."

"Thank you." Abrams regarded Thorpe closely. When Thorpe had been baiting him, Abrams knew he wasn't in any personal danger. Now he knew he was in extreme danger.

The drinks came. Thorpe held up his glass. "Death to the enemies of my country."

"Shalom."

Both men fell silent. The bartender leaned over and spoke quietly to Thorpe. "That guy got your message."

Thorpe nodded and winked.

Donald said in a normal voice, "Hey, I've been thinking...that thing you said about the Fourth of July—"

"Right. We need a good bartender. Long Island estate. Can you make it?"

Donald seemed momentarily confused. "Yeah...sure..."

Thorpe turned to Abrams. "Can you keep a secret? I'm going to ask Kate to marry me. Plan on a July Fourth wedding."

"Congratulations."

"Thanks." Thorpe absently trailed his stirrer through a puddle on the bar. Abrams looked around the room. Very clubby. Horse prints on the walls. Green-shaded lamps. A few men stood at an oyster bar in the corner. Abrams straightened up and buttoned his raincoat. "Let's go."

Thorpe held his arm. "Have you discussed any of this with anyone outside of the firm?"

Abrams thought that was the required question before the bullet in the head. He pulled away from Thorpe and walked to the door. Thorpe followed. They descended the stairs, and Abrams went into a phone booth. He came out a few minutes later.

Thorpe said, "Did you alert the police?"

Abrams nodded. "Might as well. Make O'Brien happy." They walked outside and stood under the gray awning. The rain was still falling on the dark streets. Thorpe finally spoke. "Are you staying in town tonight?"

"Maybe."

"Do you want to go back to the armory?"

"If that's where you're going."

A doorman hailed a passing taxi, and they both climbed in. Thorpe pulled two long cedar-wrapped cigars from his pocket. "Ramon Allones. Hand-rolled in old Habana. I get them from a Canadian businessman who does work for me." He passed one to Abrams. Thorpe said, "Russian vodka and Cuban cigars. What would the internal security people say to that?"

Abrams examined the cigar. "I don't know, but my Uncle Bernie would say *shtick*."

"Stick?"

"*Shtick*. That's Yiddish for affectation. Like that raincape you're wearing. Or the gold Dunhill lighter."

Thorpe looked annoyed. "No. That's panache. Flair."

"*Shtick*."

"I don't think I like Yiddish." He lit his cigar, then offered Abrams a light.

Abrams shook his head. "I'll save it for an occasion." He slipped the cigar in his coat and said, "You never suggested we look in the club safe."

"What? Oh...for the diary...Christ." He leaned toward the driver.

Abrams reached out and pulled him back in his seat. "Don't waste my time."

Thorpe smiled. "At least play the game. We have to tell O'Brien we checked the safe."

"You're sloppy, Thorpe. No attention to detail. If you want to play the game, at least remember what you're supposed to do and say."

Thorpe nodded. "I insulted your intelligence. I apologize." He flipped his ash on the floor.

Abrams said, "Was the diary worth it?"

"Worth what?" Thorpe thought a moment, then said, "Believe me when I tell you, this is a matter of extreme national security. Carbury was going to turn over a very sensitive piece of evidence to a bunch of amateurs, several of whom are high security risks, though we couldn't make him understand that."

"Is he dead?"

"No. Of course not. He'll be fine."

Abrams nodded. *Dead.*

Thorpe said, "Is this getting you dizzy, sport? Wish you'd stayed home?"

"No, it was a nice evening."

Thorpe smiled. "The night is still young and fraught with adventure."

Abrams lit a cigarette. "Is it?"

"Count on it."

Abrams sat back. A man, he thought, might be known by the company he keeps, but a woman can't always be judged by the lovers she takes.

CHAPTER TWENTY-ONE

Katherine Kimberly glanced anxiously toward the doors at the far end of the Colonel's Reception Room.

Nicholas West came across the room with two brandy glasses. "Here. Relax."

She sipped the brandy. The reception room, on the ground floor of the armory, looked out over Park Avenue. It was stuffy and noisy, filled with men, women, and tobacco smoke. An array of after-dinner cordials sat on a long sideboard. The furniture was French black walnut, the paneling oak, and the rug a pastel Oriental. A huge portrait of George Washington by Rembrandt Peale hung over the marble fireplace. On the opposite wall hung a portrait of George VI, which seemed, Katherine noticed, to have drawn the Britishers to that side of the room.

One of them, Marc Pembroke, caught her eye and approached. She hadn't seen him since the May Day party at Van Dorn's estate. There'd been some trouble, she'd heard, over Pembroke and Tom Grenville's wife, Joan. But that was probably more Joan's fault than Pembroke's.

Pembroke greeted Katherine and West. He asked, "Have you any news of Carbury?"

Katherine shook her head. She was not sure of Pembroke, but O'Brien had once indicated that it was all right to speak to him, within limits. Pembroke had access to the dead files, and he was tight with Arnold.

Pembroke also shook his head. "This is rather distressing."

Pembroke, Katherine knew, had lived and worked in New York for a very long time. He had an office in the British Building in Rockefeller Center, a short walk from Katherine's building. The sign on his door said BRITISH TECHNOLOGIES, but neither she nor anyone seemed to know for whom he worked. She remembered the shoulder holster she'd seen on the drive out to Van Dorn's.

Pembroke asked, "Where's Peter?"

Katherine replied, "He left, but he'll be back shortly."

"I'd like to speak to him later."

"I'll tell him." Marc Pembroke and Peter had a business relationship. In some ways, she thought, Pembroke reminded her of Peter, but this did not inspire confidence or closeness. Marc Pembroke was the kind of man whom women noticed and men avoided. There was something incredibly hard about him, and she had not been at all surprised at the gun holster. She would have been surprised if he didn't have one; she would have bet heavily that he'd used the gun.

Pembroke and West were speaking, and Katherine excused herself and walked over to Patrick O'Brien. He was standing by the rain-splashed window, looking out onto Park Avenue. She came up beside him. O'Brien said, "Regarding Tony Abrams, I think he'd be helpful. Did you speak to him?"

"Yes. He's reluctant. A bit confused about who we are, but we need someone with his credentials. Someone with no personal bonds to any of us, who will evaluate the evidence objectively. Someone," she added, "who could not possibly be on the other side." She smiled suddenly. "I think he'd actually enjoy exposing one of us as a traitor."

O'Brien glanced at her but said nothing.

Katherine recalled the day she had graduated from Harvard Law School, her father's alma mater. Patrick O'Brien had unexpectedly shown up and offered her a position in her father's old firm. She had accepted and moved to New York.

She had married a client, Paul Howell, and lived in his apartment on Sutton Place. Patrick O'Brien had been polite to him but did not like him. Eventually, Katherine discovered she did not like him either. He said he would fight a divorce. Patrick O'Brien spoke to him. Paul Howell became more obstinate. Subsequently, a series of misfortunes befell Howell, including an investigation by the Securities and Exchange Commission for stock fraud. Then there was a computer malfunction in his brokerage house that wiped out a day's worth of trading records. A short time later several of his best brokers left and took their accounts with them. There were other misfortunes, much like a series of divine plagues. One day Paul called her at the office and shouted, "They won't renew the lease on my apartment! Make him stop this."

"Who?" She thought he'd lost his mind.

"O'Brien! Who the hell do you think?"

She was stunned and said nothing.

He'd shouted again, "You can have your goddamned divorce!"

And within a few months she'd gotten it. Paul Howell had moved to Toronto, and she'd never heard from him again.

Katherine looked at O'Brien, who was sipping on a cup of coffee. "If Tony Abrams refuses to work with us, I don't think we should hold it against him."

O'Brien smiled in that fatherly way and patted her arm. "As long as you didn't reveal too much of the Company business to him."

"I didn't." She remembered, too, that day, nearly five years ago, when she'd walked into O'Brien's office unannounced, her heart beating and her mouth dry, and spoken the words that had led her to this time and place: "Can I belong, or do you have to be an OSS veteran?"

O'Brien had replied without hesitation, "You can belong. We need young people."

She had asked him, "Are you in charge?"

His features had remained impassive, inscrutable, very unlike his usually expressive face. "We are equals among equals."

"What are the objectives?"

"To bring the chickens home to roost. To repay the stab in the back. To avenge the dead, including your father. To find the traitors still in our midst. To find the worst traitor, a man code-named Talbot, and kill him. And ultimately to complete the larger mission we were assigned in 1942—to put an end to any power that is dedicated to our destruction."

"That assignment was terminated by Truman in 1945." She pointed to a framed document on the wall, signed by Harry S Truman.

"We don't recognize that termination order. We were born of necessity, we live of necessity, we are immortal. Not in the physical sense, of course, but in the context of the immortal corporation. We may have to reorganize from time to time, take on partners, hire and fire, but we don't go out of business. Not until we've finished what we set out to do."

Her mind had reeled under the impact of what he was saying, though she had suspected it for some years. He had let her see small glimpses of it and had waited patiently until she had made the right conclusions and the right decision. She had asked him something of the logistics, the how, why, and where of it all.

O'Brien had replied, "Do you think we couldn't see what was going to happen after the war? When they were through with us, like all governments who use people, they intended to throw us back on the scrap heap. But they miscalculated. They didn't fully understand what talent they'd assembled. The war acted as a catalyst, brought us together within one organization.

"We saw them sharpening their knives to finish us after we'd finished the Nazis. So we took precautions. We began to go underground. We kept files and records in various places. Some are right here in these offices. We formed close contacts with the British intelligence services, which, we knew, would survive into the postwar world. And we stole money. Yes, we stole. We had a section called Special Funds. We had a worldwide banking system of more than eighty different currencies. There was over seventy-five million dollars of those funds, a huge fortune in those days. Congress and the President gave us this money grudgingly, with no strings and without regard, as they said, 'to the provisions of law and regulations relating to the expenditure of government funds.' They had no choice, really. You can't run an outfit that is supposed to engage in assassinations, kidnappings, sabotage, economic warfare, and other unsavory pursuits, without unvouchered funds. Also"—a small smile broke across his face—"we actually made money on some of our operations. We were, after all, mostly businessmen and lawyers."

He had stepped closer to her and said quietly, "Over the last thirty-five years we've accomplished a good deal of what we set out to do, though I can't give you details. But I will tell you we've uncovered and eliminated a number of Americans and Britishers who were working for the other side." He had put his hand on her shoulder. "Do you still want to belong?"

"Do you know who killed my father? I mean . . . it wasn't an accident, was it?"

"It wasn't an accident. The persons who arranged his death also arranged the deaths of other good men and women, including, I believe, the parents of your new friend, Peter Thorpe. They nearly got me, too. And they nearly got the Free World after the war. Eventually, we will know all there is to know about them."

She had stood and said, "I never knew my father. . . . I always felt cheated . . . but I consoled myself with the fact that he died in the war, the way others had. But this is different. I'm not vindictive by nature, but I'd like to—"

O'Brien had nodded. "There are personal scores to settle as well as political scores. Either motivation is good. Are you with us?"

"Yes."

That night she'd called her sister, Ann, who was in Bern at the time, and asked, "Do you belong?"

After a brief hesitation, Ann replied, "Yes."

"Me too."

Katherine looked now at Patrick O'Brien standing at the window with a fixed stare on his face. There seemed to be some special quality to these men and women that had kept them mentally alert and physically sound. Yet they understood, as O'Brien said, that they were mortal, and so they'd begun to recruit. Nicholas West was one recruit. Somehow the fact that he belonged made it seem all right for her. Nick was level-headed, careful, not likely to get involved with something that was reckless or unsavory.

Katherine thought of Peter. He belonged only in a peripheral way, and that, she knew instinctively, was a good decision on O'Brien's part.

An unbidden image of Tony Abrams flashed through her mind. Abrams didn't really want in, and she liked that. O'Brien, too, preferred reluctant recruits.

She thought of the Van Dorns. George Van Dorn was in the group, though by the nature of the group one never acknowledged such a fact except in the most oblique way. Katherine did not particularly like George Van Dorn, and she sensed that O'Brien found something peculiar about him. If she had to propose a candidate for a man who could have been a traitor for over forty years, it would be George Van Dorn.

She thought of Tom Grenville, James Allerton, and all the people she'd become involved with over the years. In the conventional world, people were judged by certain accepted standards. In the shadow world, no one was who he or she seemed, and therefore no judgments could be made, except a final one.

One thing Patrick O'Brien had told her from the beginning, which she thought about now: "You understand," he'd said, "that we could not have eliminated so many of our enemies and caused them to suffer so many setbacks without incurring casualties of our own. You must be aware, Katherine, that there is an element of personal danger inherent in this game we are playing. You've attended some funerals of men and women who did not die natural deaths."

She looked at O'Brien now and spoke. "Do you think Carbury is dead?"

"Of course."

"Is this the beginning of something?"

"Yes, I believe it is. Something very terrible is in the wind. We've sensed it for some time. Actually, we have some hard information that the Russians don't expect us to be around after this summer."

She looked at him. "Don't expect... *who* not to be around...?"

"Us. America. They seem to have discovered a way to do it—with minimal or no damage to themselves. It's obviously some sort of technological breakthrough. Something so far advanced that we have no defense. It was inevitable that one side or the other should skip a few generations of technology. So far we've advanced side by side, one side or the other taking a short lead, like a long horse race. But we have reason to believe they've created a sort of time warp that will put them into the next century within a few months. It happens. History is full of such examples—the most dramatic being our atomic bombs that obliterated two great cities in a few seconds...."

She tried to formulate several questions, but no words came out.

O'Brien said, "We know their plan depends on a person or persons who will open the gates of the city in the night, a sergeant of the guard. Someone with a key."

She said, "Someone like Talbot."

He nodded.

She spoke softly, "We were so close...the diary...the papers...."

O'Brien waved his hand in a motion of dismissal. "That's not important."

"What do you mean?"

"I wrote the diary—or had it written. It's not your father's. I'm sorry. The diary was bloody red meat, and I knew if there was a beast about, he'd smell it and reveal himself. He did. Unfortunately, Randolph Carbury, who was holding the meat, got eaten too. But now we have a trail to follow, the spoor of the wolf in the wet earth."

Katherine set her brandy glass down on the windowsill. "What was in the diary?"

"I had one of our old forgers do the whole thing with different inks of the period. The blank diary was bought in a London antiques store. The dispatch case was mine. The workman who found it in Eleanor's muniment room was one of my people. She believed it was genuine. Nearly everyone who came into contact with it believed it."

"But...who did you name? Did you name Talbot...?"

O'Brien rubbed his chin. "How could I? If I could name him, I'd kill him. The diary is mostly conjecture. But if Talbot is reading the diary right now, then he is very uncomfortable. He knows that photocopies must exist, and he will reveal more of himself in his search for them."

Katherine said suddenly, "Eleanor Wingate is in danger."

A strange look passed over O'Brien's face, then he said, "She's dead. Brompton Hall has been burned."

Katherine stared at him. "You knew that was going to happen."

"I did send a friend to look after her, but apparently he's been killed with her, and her nephew. As for Carbury, he knew the material was bogus, and he made a timely visit to Brompton Hall on the day it was found. He inspired Eleanor's letter to you. He knew the danger of carrying the material but was, apparently, unable to protect himself against it."

"I tried to protect him."

"Yes. But you or Eleanor Wingate told someone about it, and that's why he's dead."

"I told Peter."

"I know."

She said nothing for a long time, then spoke. "Peter may have passed the information through normal channels."

"He may have. I suppose he did. But we have at least flushed something out of the woods."

"There are people dead."

"That lends authenticity to it." He looked at her. "I always told you this was a dangerous business. It's going to become more dangerous and very bloody very soon. I suggest you carry a pistol."

She nodded. She supposed she knew that beneath the surface of this organization, beneath the amateur spying, the old-boys network of information gathering, industrial spying, economic sabotage, or whatever game they played with the Eastern Bloc, was this potential for sudden violence. It had been part of their original mandate; the passage of forty years had not given them reason to discount violence as a legitimate option. She said to O'Brien, "I'm worried about Ann."

"Worry about yourself. Ann understands more than you the danger she's in."

"And Nick." She thought of this gentle man with the same apprehension one might feel when thinking of a child playing in traffic.

"He's in danger from several sources. I've hired private guards for him."

She looked at O'Brien. She had this comforting, childlike feeling that Patrick O'Brien could lick anyone on the block. But it followed then that the most dangerous Talbot she could imagine was Patrick O'Brien.

CHAPTER TWENTY-TWO

Abrams and Thorpe entered the Colonel's Reception Room. In an uncharacteristic display of hospitality, Thorpe went to the sideboard and brought back a cognac for Abrams. Thorpe smiled and raised his glass. "To truth."

Abrams did not drink.

Patrick O'Brien and Katherine Kimberly walked over to them. O'Brien said, "Did you find anything at the club?"

Thorpe replied, "Carbury *did* dress for dinner. We asked around but no one seems to remember him leaving. I had the manager check the safe. Nothing there. There was nothing revealing in his room."

O'Brien turned to Abrams. "Did you call your police contacts?"

"Yes. I told them it might be a matter of national security. They'll contact the FBI. They may want more information."

O'Brien nodded. "Give them what they need, within limits. Don't bring the firm into it."

Nicholas West approached and the five people spoke for a few minutes, then O'Brien caught James Allerton's eye. Allerton excused himself from a group of well-wishers and joined them. Allerton leaned over and kissed Katherine. "You look lovely as always." He turned to Thorpe. "I didn't embarrass you, did I, Peter?"

"No more than usual, James."

Allerton ignored the remark and took West's hand. "Nicholas. I'm delighted you could come. Is Ann with you? Or is she still in Bern?"

"No, sir...in Munich."

Allerton looked at O'Brien. "Good Lord, Patrick, this is like déjà vu, isn't it? The old armory, the old faces, even the old songs. *Bern.* Can't think of Bern without thinking of Allen Dulles, can we?"

West cleared his throat. "Actually, she's been transferred... Munich, I think—I mean Munich for sure."

Allerton smiled pleasantly and turned to West. "Prestigious post, Bern. Good spot. Center of things, still. It was the window on Europe in those days—"

O'Brien interjected, "James, we'd like to have a meeting—"

"No business tonight. That's the rule. It can wait until lunch tomorrow." He smiled at Katherine. "Well, when are you going to make me a grandfather, young lady?"

Katherine forced a smile. "Mr. Allerton, let me introduce—"

Allerton went on. "I should say, when is this oafish son of mine going to marry you?" He turned to West. "And *you.* What are you waiting for? Go to Bern tomorrow and marry this girl's sister."

Katherine said, "Let me introduce Tony Abrams. He's with our firm."

Allerton seemed to notice Abrams for the first time. He extended his hand, and his eyes passed over Abrams. Then he fixed him with an appraising look. "Are you having a good time?"

Abrams felt the dry, bony hand in his own. "Yes, sir." He thought it was the kind of question he'd be asked if he were a sixteen-year-old at a christening. "Congratulations on your medal. Interesting speech."

Allerton smiled politely and turned away. He seemed to notice the expressions of everyone's faces. "Is it serious?"

O'Brien nodded.

"Well, come then. There's an empty room down the hall. Excuse us, Mr. Abrams. Have a drink."

"Thank you."

Katherine touched Abrams' arm as she passed. "Don't go far."

Abrams watched Allerton, O'Brien, Thorpe, West, and Katherine wind their way through the crowd. He muttered to himself, "Yes, sir, I'm having a *good* time." He went to the sideboard, poured out the brandy Thorpe had given him into a trash can, and chose a Strega, remembering the homemade variety the Italian men used to distill. He poured the yellowish liquid into a tall, fluted glass, braced himself, and downed half of it. He felt the water forming in his eyes even before he felt the fire hit his stomach. "*Mama mia*..."

He wandered around the room, recognizing some of the faces from newspapers or television, a few from history books, some from the office. Clare Boothe Luce was holding court, seated in a small chair surrounded by mostly older men and women. Sterling Hayden, the actor, whom O'Brien had said was an OSS agent in Van Dorn's unit, was speaking with the Van Dorns and the Grenvilles. Joan Grenville noticed Abrams and smiled. Claudia was nowhere to be seen.

Abrams left the reception room and made his way to a pay phone in the lobby. The metal detector was gone, as were the Secret Service men, and people wandered about more freely, without that self-consciousness and paranoia that the presence of armed men always engenders. Abrams called the Nineteenth Precinct and got Captain Spinelli on the line. Abrams said, "Anything interesting since I spoke to you?"

Spinelli answered, "We have an all-points out. Bureau is on it. Phil told me you wanted a make on this guy Carbury this afternoon. What the hell's going down, Abrams?"

"He's missing. That's all you have to know."

"Like hell. I hear noise there. Where are you?"

"Down the block having cocktails with Arthur Goldberg, Bill Casey, and Clare Boothe Luce."

"You sound drunk...oh, you're at the armory. Is there a connection there? Is the President still there?"

"He's gone. There's no connection except that Carbury was on his way here."

"What's the national security angle here?"

Abrams noticed a man behind him who seemed to want to use the telephone. A few other people stood nearby. He spoke to Spinelli in Italian, heavily accented with the Barese dialect, filling him in on some background.

Spinelli cut in, "Your Italian stinks, Abrams. Come down here now and sign this missing person's report."

Abrams ignored him and continued in Italian, "Keep me out of it."

Spinelli in turn ignored Abrams. "Did you or that guy with you—Thorpe—touch anything in the room?"

"No, we floated around. Listen, Thorpe is Company."

"Company...? Oh, *that* Company. You sure?"

"Sure."

"What are you into?"

"Evil things. Proceed carefully with Thorpe. Check him out with whoever is the liaison these days. Watch yourself on this one, Dom."

"Okay...thanks...."

"Thank me by keeping me posted." Abrams hung up and returned to the Colonel's Reception Room.

O'Brien was there looking for him. He motioned Abrams onto a settee and sat beside him. O'Brien said, "Kate is briefing Mr. Allerton, Peter, and Nick. Let's talk for a moment."

"Okay."

"What do you think of our friends?"

"I had a good time. Thank Miss Kimberly for inviting me. Look, it's past midnight, and I think I'm going to leave."

O'Brien didn't seem to hear. He said, "She thinks very highly of you."

"Of me personally, or of my work?"

O'Brien smiled. "Your work as a process server is hardly anything to elicit admiration." O'Brien glanced around the room. "Have you had an opportunity to speak to anyone here?"

"No, but it looks like General Donovan assembled quite a group. Hitler never had a chance." Abrams lit a cigarette. "It's too bad the CIA can't get so much talent."

O'Brien nodded. "In wartime you can recruit millionaires, superachievers, geniuses in the arts and sciences...but in peacetime, what sort of man or woman do you get for a modest-paying career position in intelligence work? On the opposite side, the KGB are very well paid and enjoy privileges and prestige that exceed those of the average Soviet citizen. They get the best of the best." O'Brien shook his head. "If one could compare education and IQ levels in both organizations, the CIA would come off second best. That's a fatal fact that has to be faced."

"Like our amateur sports teams playing their so-called amateurs."

"That's a fair analogy." O'Brien glanced around the room, then said, "You haven't changed your mind about your visit to Glen Cove in light of what you've learned this evening?"

"I said I'd go."

"Fair enough. You'll meet the Edwards and Styler attorneys at their offices at four P.M., Monday, Memorial Day. You'll be briefed by a friend of mine. You'll arrive with the attorneys at the Russian estate about seven P.M. George Van Dorn's party will be in full swing by then."

"What exactly am I supposed to do once I'm in?"

"You'll be told that day."

Abrams looked at O'Brien closely.

O'Brien answered the unasked question. "Even if you're caught snooping, they're not going to murder you. It's Russian territory, but it's not Russia. But don't get caught."

"One more question—something doesn't add up here. If the Russians have something big in the works, as you obliquely suggested—something that will cancel the July bar exam and, by insinuation, will cancel all of us, then why are they bothering with a petty lawsuit?"

O'Brien replied, "You were an undercover cop. Answer your own question."

Abrams nodded. "They must appear to be going on with business as usual."

"Correct. To do nothing about Van Dorn's or Mayor Parioli's harassment would be highly suspicious. So we are presented with an opportunity, part serendipitous, part planned, to get a peek inside their command post."

"I see. And my credentials, my bona fides, are in order?"

"I have never sent a man or woman on a job unless their cover was perfect."

Abrams knew, as O'Brien knew, that the only perfect cover was the one in your bed that you pulled over your head as a child to make the bad things go away.

O'Brien, as was his habit, made one of his abrupt changes of topic. "I'd like you to stay at the town house tonight. Katherine will call on you tomorrow morning, and you'll go to the office. There's a records room there, and you can give her a hand looking for a few things. Wear your gun."

Abrams looked at him.

"She may be in danger. You'll watch after her, won't you?"

This particular shift from the prosaic to the intriguing caught him off guard. "Yes, I'll look after her."

O'Brien took two cordials from a passing waiter and handed one to Abrams. He said, "We'd like you to join the firm."

Abrams stared at him. "I'm flattered." He recalled very vividly how he felt when he'd been asked to join the Red Devils, and this was not a totally irrelevant thought. He remembered being both flattered *and* frightened.

O'Brien said, "As you must have surmised by now, the OSS has never really disbanded. And, I assure you, we are not conspiratorial paranoiacs. We don't promote secrecy for its own sake, like many clandestine societies. There are no secret handshakes, oaths, membership cards, symbols, ranks, or uniforms. It is more a feeling of the heart and mind than an actual organization."

Abrams lit a cigarette and flipped the match into an ashtray. He realized he was hearing things that, once heard, would put him in a compromising position. He considered leaving, but didn't.

For the next ten minutes O'Brien described the nature and substance of his group. When he was done, Abrams looked at O'Brien and their eyes met. Abrams said, "Why me?"

O'Brien said, "You understand crime. Find us the murderer or kidnapper of Randolph Carbury, and the things we are interested in will start to fall into place."

Abrams didn't reply.

O'Brien looked at his watch, then stood. "There would be a

good deal of personal danger. If you want to discuss this further, we can join the others in a private room at the other end of the armory. The room itself is quite interesting. May I show it to you?"

Abrams sat for a long time, then said, "Can I have more time to think about it?"

"You can go home and sleep on it. But I suspect you won't sleep very well."

Abrams took a long sip of his cordial and stood. "Let's see the room."

CHAPTER TWENTY-THREE

Abrams followed Patrick O'Brien into a huge columned chamber that was vaguely reminiscent of an Egyptian throne room. Around the upper perimeter of the walls was a running frieze depicting warriors from different periods of history. The ceiling was black, crisscrossed with beams inlaid with silver. Classical statuary stood at intervals around the dimly lit room.

Abrams' eyes adjusted to the darkness, and he saw a large fireplace made of blue cobalt-glazed tile. In the center of the room was a thick Persian rug, and sitting in the center of the rug was a large ornate table that looked somewhat like a sacrificial altar. Stained-glass windows let in a diffused light from the street.

Two red-coated busboys were in the dimly lit room, arranging chairs around the fireplace. A waiter wheeled in a coffee service. The three men left silently.

James Allerton sat facing the fireplace. Katherine sat opposite him, with Thorpe and West to her left. O'Brien waved Abrams into a chair near the hearth and took the remaining chair beside him.

Abrams was surprised that it was West who spoke first and greeted him. West said, "I'm glad you've decided to join us for coffee."

Abrams said, "I never turn down coffee." He suspected that the state of the art of saying one thing and meaning another was very high with these people.

West spoke again. "I know you were reluctant, and I was too.

But I've never regretted my decision. We're all sort of like amateur armchair detectives." He patted the arms of his chair for emphasis. "Think-tankers," he added. "Dollar-a-year volunteers, like during the war. Whatever makes you feel comfortable."

Abrams thought that West was either understating the facts or was himself not fully aware of the scope of the group. He realized then, in a moment of insight, that if he stayed with them for the rest of his life, he'd never know more than a small part of the whole. Moreover, he might never know or even feel that he belonged to anything more sinister than a coffee klatch. Unless, of course, they asked him to do something like blowing someone's brains out.

Abrams regarded James Allerton, who seemed slightly unhappy. Katherine passed him a quick smile. Abrams looked across at Thorpe, who was staring openly at him, as though trying to think of the best way to dispose of his body.

Patrick O'Brien spoke. "Let's begin. We need a bit of background. Nick?"

West tapped the Wingate letter lying on his lap. "This seems to fit the facts as we know them. First, there were three filed reports on Henry Kimberly's death, and no two of them agree."

West looked at Katherine. "I haven't ever told you all of this. Ann knows....Anyway, the last and official version is that Major Kimberly was in Berlin leading an advance party of OSS officers a day after the city had fallen to the Russians. That would be May 3, 1945."

West paused, out of the historian's habit, Abrams imagined, of ending a thought with a date. West continued, "Major Kimberly's cover was that of a quartermaster officer in search of accommodations for the coming American occupying staff. In fact, he was there to retrieve about a dozen agents he'd had parachuted into the Berlin area. He was concerned about their welfare, especially in regard to the Russians."

Patrick O'Brien nodded and added, "It was a dangerous mission. Berlin had fallen, but the surrender of Germany hadn't been signed, and there were still roaming bands of SS fanatics plying their murderous trade along the highways and among the ruins. There was also the possibility, as we were discovering, of being detained by our Red Army allies." O'Brien stared into the fire for some time, then said, "I told Henry to be careful. I mean, my God, we knew the war had less than a week to run. No one wanted the distinction of being the last casualty. I suggested the quartermaster cover. No use waving the OSS insignia in front of the Russians' noses. Henry, too, was wary of the Russians."

James Allerton spoke for the first time. "In that respect, he was not so naive as many of us in those days, myself included." He looked at Katherine. "But he felt a deep obligation to his agents... hence the fateful mission to Berlin." Allerton nodded to West.

Nicholas West continued, "There was, according to the mission report on file, one agent in particular whom Major Kimberly wanted to recover—Karl Roth, a German Jewish refugee and a Communist who was working for the OSS. Another agent had radioed that Roth had been picked up by the Russians, then released. When Roth was queried by radio, he explained his release by saying he convinced the Russians he was a Communist. Roth's radio apparently was still under his control. His message went on to say that the Russians had asked him to work for them as a double within the OSS. He agreed, he said, in order to get out of their clutches."

O'Brien interjected, "This was not the first indication we had that the Russians were trying to turn our agents who had Communist backgrounds. Henry thought this was ominous in regard to any postwar intelligence service we might establish."

West finished his coffee and said, "There is one last radio message on file from Karl Roth. In it he reports that he's sick and starving. He asks, 'When are you coming?' He gave his location—a railroad shed near Hennigsdorf. Roth had been assigned to the Alsos mission. He said he'd located two German scientists but needed help in bringing them out. Roth had two strikes against his credibility by this time: his Communist background and the fact that he had failed to report his contact with the Russians and had to be queried about it. On the other hand, he *had* reported that the Russians tried to turn him, but that's something he'd expect the OSS to assume anyway."

O'Brien interjected, "No one in OSS London felt confident in deciding Roth's fate: come to his aid or cut him loose? We radioed all the details to Henry and told him to make the decision but to proceed with caution."

Abrams listened as West and O'Brien continued the background briefing. Already he could see where it was leading. It was leading to the here and now. It was a story rooted in a turbulent past, a time when the world was in shambles, a time when forces were set in motion that would culminate in a final Armageddon that these people obviously felt was close at hand.

West said, "Karl Roth was not heard from after that message, until he surfaced again in 1948. He reported to the American occupation forces in Berlin stating he'd been rearrested by the Russians and held prisoner for three years. He claimed his back pay and benefits, but his original hiring contract with the OSS had been lost, and no one knew quite what to do with him. His bona fides were established by ex-OSS men, and he was given some money. He was never properly debriefed, however, and his three-year disappearance was never satisfactorily explained."

Abrams glanced slowly around the room again, which he had come to think of as some sort of celestial chamber. His eyes passed from Allerton to O'Brien and he was reminded of two ancient priests guarding the nearly forgotten secrets of an arcane religion.

West added, "Roth applied for intelligence work with the American and British occupation authorities in their respective zones, but was turned down. Roth then went to England, found his war bride—a girl he'd married when he lived in London running a green grocer business—and eventually was allowed to emigrate to America, again claiming this was promised to him by the OSS."

Thorpe smiled. "And now Karl Roth is assistant to the President on matters of nuclear strategy."

West look around the darkened room, then glanced at O'Brien and Allerton. He said, "As it turns out"—he looked at Thorpe—"Roth and his wife own a delicatessen on Long Island."

Thorpe smiled again. "Well, that's not exactly what I thought you were leading up to, Nick." Thorpe reflected a moment. "Maybe he would be interested in my section. Sort of a shaky and shady background, though...."

Katherine said, "This man should be debriefed."

O'Brien poured himself more coffee. "I'll see to it." He plucked absently at his black bow tie, then said, "The Alsos mission had some successes, but the Russian equivalent of Alsos was doing even better. They seemed to be one step ahead of us in locating and snatching German nuclear physicists. If you consider that most of these scientists were trying to reach us and not them, then it's odd that the Russians were doing so well. And since Alsos had the absolute highest priority and security, Henry and I, and others, concluded that someone—perhaps more than one person—very highly placed either in Eisenhower's headquarters, in Alsos itself, or in the OSS, was telling the Russians what, where, when, how, and who." O'Brien leaned forward. "Eventually we became fairly certain that the main leak was in the OSS. It was one of us. Someone we saw every day, with whom we ate and drank...."

Allerton seemed to come out of a deep reverie. "Yes... that was when we came up with the fanciful code name for this double agent: Talbot. Lawrence Talbot—you know, the fellow who turned into a werewolf by the light of the moon.... Popular movie at that time." Allerton smiled. "For the intellectuals among us, *talbot* is also the old Anglo-Saxon word for a ravaging wolf. So, then, we began an operation to expose him and... eliminate him. We called it Silver Bullet—"

O'Brien cleared his throat. "Actually, it was called Wolfbane."

"Yes, that was it, Patrick." Allerton stroked his long nose. "Time dims things that seemed so important once."

"Silver Bullet," said O'Brien, "was the joint British/American name for the termination of the operation." O'Brien took something from his pocket. "One of our more flamboyant officers had this fashioned by a London silversmith." He held up a gleaming .45-caliber silver bullet. "This was to be fired into Talbot's brain."

No one spoke for some time, then O'Brien added, "Talbot was the worst sort of traitor. He didn't confine his treachery to stealing and passing on secrets like the majority of traitors. He actively sent men and women to their deaths. I picture him sometimes on an air-strip in England, striding around the tarmac at dusk, patting agents on the back, embracing the women, adjusting parachute harnesses, wishing them luck...and all the while knowing..." O'Brien looked at Allerton.

James Allerton said softly, "You would think a man like that... a man who had lost his soul...could be easily spotted...his eyes should reveal the corruption in his heart."

Abrams listened. He had become to them as unobtrusive as a trusted servant; they knew he was listening, but they didn't expect him to talk back until they addressed him. It was, he thought, not unlike a detective's brainstorming session. He glanced at Katherine, wondering if the mention of her father was painful.

West picked up the story again. "Henry Kimberly reported in by radio twice a day for a week, then radioed what was to be his next to last encoded message, which is still in the file. It said"—West recited with no hesitation—"'Most important: Re Alsos: Have made contact with grocer'—that was Karl Roth—'Grocer has reported the location of two pixies'—that was the atomic scientists. 'Will recover same.'" West paused, then said, "Henry Kimberly's last message, a day later, reported that he'd established contact with the Russian authorities for the purpose of searching Gestapo files and interrogating captured Gestapo officers who might have information about missing OSS agents. The last lines of his message read, 'Red Army helpful. Gestapo has revealed the arrest and execution of most of our mission. Names to follow. Trace and locate bodies of them. Will continue recovery operation.'" West looked at Allerton. "Do you remember that, sir?"

Allerton nodded. "Yes. That was the last we heard of Henry. There was some suspicion, of course, that it was the Russians who got to our agents, not the Gestapo. We feared that Henry was going to suffer the same fate."

O'Brien said, "Henry signed that radio message with his code name, Diamond. If we suppose he was sending under Russian control, then he should have used the signature Blackboard, which was a distress signal meaning 'I am captured.'"

Thorpe said, "Why would you suppose he was sending under Russian control?"

O'Brien answered, "We'll get to that. But if Henry was captured and yet signed his encoded message Diamond, that told us that the Russians knew that Diamond was his code name, and therefore he could not use the distress code name Blackboard. The OSS operator who received his message recognized Henry's wrist—his style of telegraphing—so we can assume it was he who was sending, but with a gun to his head."

Allerton interjected, "It was frightening to think that the Russians knew Henry's code name, which was picked just ten minutes before he crossed the Russian lines. And that they knew code names like Grocer and Pixie."

O'Brien nodded, then added, "We thought the Russians might be persuaded to let him go. A strong note was personally delivered to Red Army headquarters in Berlin. The reply said, 'Major Kimberly unknown here.'" O'Brien spoke directly to Katherine. "I hitched a ride on one of the first American flights into Berlin. By the time I arrived, there was another message from Red Army headquarters saying that Major Kimberly and the three officers with him had been killed when their jeep hit an undiscovered German land mine—a very common accident that we and the British also used, to dispose of unwanted people. Anyway, I claimed the bodies...the ashes, I should say. The Russians cremated for reasons of expediency and sanitation...." He looked into Katherine's eyes. "I never gave you all the details...."

For the first time Katherine knew that the grave in Arlington contained an urn filled with ashes. She said, "How do you know it was my father?"

O'Brien shook his head. "We hope it was, that he didn't die in the Gulag."

She nodded. She knew that the Russians at that time usually sent healthy males to the Soviet Union to repair the devastation resulting from the war. She tried to imagine this man who was her father, young, proud, daring, reduced to a slave in a strange land, for no reason other than he'd gone on a mission of mercy. With each passing week and month he'd feel the life leaving his body. And he'd know, of course, that he'd never go home. She looked up and spoke in a barely controlled voice. "Please go on."

It was West who spoke. "Major Kimberly had undoubtedly dropped the quartermaster cover in order to inquire about his agents. But under no circumstances would he have revealed to the Russians the Alsos mission or Karl Roth's connection with it. Therefore, those last two radio messages, which were sent under duress and which mentioned these facts, were his way of saying the Russians already knew about Alsos and Roth, just as they knew our codes."

Thorpe spoke. "I think you're making too much of this high-level-mole theory. I don't have the facts you have, but it seems to me that the mission was blown by the field agents. It's fairly obvious that Karl Roth, for one, blew the whistle. That's where the leaks were. Not in London or Washington."

West looked at Thorpe closely. "Good analysis. In fact, that was the official conclusion at the time.... However, if you assume that Major Kimberly's message was sent under the direction of the help-ful Red Army, then you should look at the message more closely. He was, after all, a trained intelligence officer, and from all accounts a brave and resourceful man. So you try to read a code within the encoded ciphers—you look for non sequiturs, clumsy sentence structure, that sort of thing." West paused, then said, " 'Trace and locate bodies of them.' That's not even good radio English—"

Thorpe sat up straight. "Talbot."

West nodded. "Nowhere does the code word *Talbot* exist in my research, but it existed in the private conversations of Henry Kim-berly, Mr. O'Brien, Mr. Allerton, and a few others. Major Kimberly, in the course of his interrogation at the hands of the Russians, was told or deduced from the extensiveness of the questions that there was a highly placed traitor in the OSS. Any good agent could con-clude that. The radio message gave him one last chance to reach and to warn his friends."

Allerton rubbed his face. "I saw that radio message, and I knew of Talbot...but, by God, I never made the connection....I was a lousy spy."

Abrams wondered. His experience with codes was almost nil, but that particular line had struck him when West first read it. First-letter codes were rudimentary, the sort of thing children or lovers do in letters. It was hard to believe that neither Allerton nor O'Brien had picked it up forty years ago. Abrams concluded that they had but neither had mentioned it to the other. Interesting.

West produced a briar pipe and a pouch of tobacco. He said, "None of this is what we would call most immediate intelligence, except that"—he lit his pipe and recited from Eleanor Wingate's letter—" 'the diary, which names people who may still be with your government or who are highly placed in American society...At least one of those named is a well-known man who is close to your President.' " West looked up.

O'Brien turned to Abrams. "What do you think up to this point?"

Abrams thought the clues were old, the trail cold, the evidence circumstantial, and the theories stretched; as a criminal case, it was a bust. The culprit had escaped detection at the time and, even if he were exposed, would never be tried. But as a personal vendetta, it had possibilities, though this group would not use the word *vendetta*. That was a word whose meaning and substance he had come to appreciate in Bensonhurst and on the force. Long memories, long grudges. But O'Brien and Allerton would put it more delicately. The result, however, was the same. He remembered the silver bullet.

"Mr. Abrams?"

"I think you will find your man this time."

O'Brien leaned forward. "Why?"

"Because he knows you've picked up the scent again and he's running. He's killed Carbury. To use the favored analogy, the forest is smaller and thinner than it was forty years ago. The number of animals inhabiting it are diminished. The wolf—the werewolf—leaves a clear trail now. I think, too, he will kill again."

O'Brien stared off into the darkness of the huge room. The fire caused shadows to leap around the walls intermittently, illuminating the running frieze, giving the warriors the impression of movement. O'Brien said, "Yes, he will kill again. He has to."

CHAPTER TWENTY-FOUR

The long limousine pulled away from the darkened armory, made a U-turn, and headed south on Park Avenue. Peter Thorpe, sitting in a jump seat, lit a cigarette and said to West, "I have the impression, Nick, you've been working on this problem for some time. Long before the appearance—and disappearance—of Colonel Carbury. However, I don't recall your mentioning it in any previous conversations of our group."

West, in the second jump seat, fidgeted with his pipe. "The nature of the problem...the implications of the Talbot profile... would suggest that any of the old OSS hands, in or out of the CIA, or the government, could be...the wrong person with whom to discuss this...."

Thorpe smiled at O'Brien and Allerton sitting facing him at the left end of the long wraparound seat in the rear. He said to West, "Present company excluded, of course."

West avoided everyone's eyes. "Included, of course." He nodded toward Abrams and Katherine sitting on the right end of the wraparound seat. "Except you, Kate, and Mr. Abrams."

Thorpe smiled slowly. "Why do we always underestimate you, Nick?"

West continued, "Ann is the only one I've discussed it with. In fact...it was how we met." He relit his pipe.

Tony Abrams watched him closely. West, he thought, was a man who could easily be underestimated. His size, his manner, his whole being, judged by the primitive instincts of his fellow man, signaled a non-threat. But by the standards of late-twentieth-century cerebral man, West's mind was a danger; a danger to traitors and bullshitters, and to people with nerve and flair but with average minds, like Peter Thorpe. Intuitively, Abrams knew that Thorpe was afraid of West.

The limousine moved slowly through the Friday-night traffic. There was a silence until O'Brien said, "It's totally impossible that the American government, intelligence services, and military, which are the three highest targets of the KGB in that order, have not been penetrated. Damn it, half the people in the armory tonight, including two past CIA directors and the present director, could conceivably fit Eleanor Wingate's description." O'Brien looked around. "Do I sound paranoid?"

Katherine marveled at how O'Brien could manufacture evidence, then agonize over it as though it were real. But, she thought, though the evidence was fake, the actions and reactions of the people whom O'Brien was studying would be real. Carbury's death or disappearance was real, and the deaths at Brompton Hall were real. O'Brien was a master of illusion, and she regarded him with equal parts of admiration and anxiety.

West said, "The important questions are, how high up do these Soviet penetrations go, and what would be the *objective* of these penetrations...if they existed?"

O'Brien shook his head. "I can only tell you that something ominous is in the air. I believe the Russians have discovered a way to achieve their ultimate objective."

Thorpe said, "You mean a nuclear strike?"

"No." O'Brien waved his hand in a motion of dismissal. "That is not and never was one of their options any more than it is one of ours."

"Then what?" asked Katherine. "Biological? Chemical?"

O'Brien did not respond.

Katherine said, "How do Colonel Carbury and the Wingate letter relate to any of that?"

O'Brien replied, "As it relates at all, it would have to be that the person or persons revealed in the diary as possible moles are somehow necessary to the Soviet plan." O'Brien shrugged. "We need more facts. Let's table it for now."

Abrams could not help making the comparison between O'Brien's heavy-handed hints at Armageddon and the police game of telling a suspect they knew all about him and his accomplices, then letting the guy walk so they could see where he went. It followed that O'Brien really suspected that someone in this car was a conduit whose opening flowed into Moscow. Yet Abrams couldn't help thinking that Patrick O'Brien was a little too good to be true. Too glib. Too many answers to unasked questions. Too unruffled by the suggestion that he might be Talbot.

Incredible, Abrams thought. This was really happening. Abrams felt he'd walked into a tornado that afternoon and landed in Oz. He thought if he went home and slept, when he awoke, the tuxedo wouldn't be on the floor beside his bed. There'd be no hangover, and he'd go to work Tuesday and Katherine Kimberly would hand him a summons to serve on some poor schnook who had run afoul of an O'Brien client, and life would go on in its slightly tedious way. That's what he thought, except it wasn't true.

What was true was that he was involved in ways he could not even have imagined at lunchtime. What was also true was that the car reeked of conspiracy, suspicion, and fear. Professionally, one might speak of fear for the life of one's country, but, notwithstanding this low-key, genteel conversation, Abrams sensed the more fundamental fear these people had for their own lives.

Abrams could almost hear his father's voice. "Don't join anything. Don't carry anybody's card. It's nothing but misery. I know."

Or his mother's more basic advice. "When you see people whispering, run the other way. Only you and God should whisper to each other."

Expected advice from Communists turned Zionists, he thought. Good advice. It was too bad, he reflected, he never listened to it. He was, after all, the son of famous conspirators. They didn't take their own advice until they were in their fifties. He had some years to go. Unless O'Brien was right, in which case he and everyone might only have weeks or months.

CHAPTER TWENTY-FIVE

The limousine crept along in the heavy traffic. James Allerton was asking who knew of Carbury's mission; a good, basic question, thought Abrams.

Katherine said, "I told Mr. O'Brien. Then I told Peter." She looked around the car.

Allerton said kindly, but pointedly, "No one else?"

She hesitated. "No....Well...Arnold in archives...I mean, I asked him for Colonel Carbury's file. But I had the impression he knew Carbury was in New York."

Thorpe looked at Abrams. "How much did you know?"

"I knew I had to follow a man named Carbury."

Thorpe rubbed his chin. "All in all, Kate, you could have shown better judgment."

She flushed angrily. "Don't be absurd. I showed damned fine judgment."

"But you didn't have to tell *anyone,* including me, until after you had the diary. Now you've tainted us."

She stared at him defiantly. "Carbury himself or Lady Wingate could have been the cause of the security breach. Information progresses geometrically, and we have no way to check on who was told, here or in England. So let's keep the paranoia among us down to a minimum."

Thorpe seemed chastised. He took Katherine's hand. "I apologize."

The limousine stopped in front of the Lombardy. Thorpe raised

Katherine's hand to his lips and kissed it. He climbed out of the car and said to Allerton, "Are you staying here?"

Allerton shook his head. "You know I dislike that apartment. I've taken a room at the United Nations Plaza."

Abrams watched Katherine, but she made no move to leave with Thorpe. Thorpe turned away without a farewell and entered the Lombardy.

The limousine drove off and a few minutes later stopped at the UN Plaza Hotel. Allerton reached into his pocket and pulled out the medal he'd received. He stared at it, then looked at O'Brien. "This should have been yours."

O'Brien laid his hand on the old man's arm. "No, James, you deserve it."

Allerton smiled and his eyes became moist. "When I was young, I thought we had fought the war to end all wars. Then when I was middle-aged, there was another. And now in my final years the war drums are beating again...." He looked at Katherine, West, and Abrams. "You take all this insanity as the normal state of affairs. But I assure you there was a time when civilized men and women thought war was no longer possible."

Katherine leaned over and kissed Allerton on the cheek. "I'll see you before you return to Washington."

A doorman helped Allerton out and the limousine moved off. West directed the driver to the Princeton Club.

When the car stopped on 43rd Street, West addressed O'Brien. "Thank you for inviting me. I hope I was of some help."

"As always. Be careful...."

"I have protection."

"So did Randolph Carbury. Good night."

The car headed back east and stopped in front of a Sutton Place apartment building. O'Brien got out, then put his head back into the car. "Well, Abrams? Welcome to the firm. Watch yourself. Good night, Kate." He shut the door.

The limousine headed south again. After a long silence, Katherine said to Abrams, "I'd like you to stay at the house on Thirty-sixth Street."

"Where are you staying?"

"In my apartment in the West Village."

Abrams let the silence hang, then nodded. "Okay."

"I'll meet you at the house in the morning. We'll go to the office. The dead files."

"Fine."

The car turned into 36th Street. Katherine said, "I'm glad you're in on this."

Abrams lit a cigarette. After a while Katherine said, "Sometimes I believe we are born with an instinct for revenge. It's nearly as strong an instinct as survival or sex. Some of the people you met tonight will not be at peace until the old scores are settled. What's your motive?"

"Sex."

She looked at him dubiously, then smiled. The limousine stopped in front of the town house. Abrams opened the door.

She said, "Be careful tonight."

Abrams paused at the door. Most people, he reflected, said, "Good night"; this group was heavily into "Be careful." He said, "If there's a killer on the loose, you may be wise to stay here . . . or at the Lombardy."

"I like sleeping in my own bed. See you later. Early."

Abrams closed the door and watched the car pull away.

He lifted the brass knocker and brought it down on the strike plate. Claudia opened the door almost immediately. "You kept me up. Everyone is in already."

"Who's everyone?" He entered the foyer.

"The Grenvilles and Van Dorns. Did you have a good time?"

"No."

"I saw you outside. Why isn't she staying with that lunatic Thorpe at that horrible apartment in the Lombardy?"

"Maybe she is. What's horrible about that apartment?"

"Everything . . . when you go to the bathroom there, the toilet bowl analyzes your urine and sends the results to the CIA. I spent a week there when I came from Rumania. I was afraid to undress with the light on. Or off. They have things to see in the dark."

Abrams hung his raincoat on the foyer hook. "A CIA place?"

She didn't answer.

He said, "Same room?"

"I'll show you up."

Abrams walked by the sitting room and saw Joan Grenville curled up on the couch. She smiled as Abrams went by.

Abrams followed Claudia down the hall. It was nearly 3:00 A.M. and his body craved sleep. He watched Claudia's undulating rear as she walked. Given his choice between sleep and sex, considering his age and general health, he thought he could stay awake a bit longer.

There was a small old S-shaped telephone desk in the narrow hall, the type his parents had in their hall, a special place to hold the valuable instrument. The telephone rang and Abrams reached it before Claudia. It was O'Brien. His voice was calm and unemotional. "Telex here from England. Brompton Hall has been destroyed by fire."

"Right." Abrams had the impression that O'Brien knew this some time ago. But sometimes it was better to pretend that a source of information was still viable and record people's reactions. Then you hit them with the startling new development and do another check of reactions. Abrams said, "Bodies?"

"Three. Pending further identification."

"What time did it happen?"

"About one A.M. their time. Eight P.M. our time. About when we realized Carbury was overdue."

Abrams said, "Can you deduce anything from that?"

"Yes, I can. After Katherine first spoke to me about Carbury, I called a friend in Kent and asked him to drop by Brompton Hall and watch over things. This was about five P.M. New York time. My friend called from Brompton Hall about seven P.M. and everything was all right there. By eight P.M. it was not all right."

Abrams said, "Perhaps your friend was the reason it was not all right at Brompton Hall."

"Possible, but more likely he will be among the dead. Lady Wingate and her nephew will be the other two."

Abrams nodded. "We don't seem to have much luck covering our witnesses."

"No. Listen, Abrams, don't get a good night's sleep."

"Right."

"I have to call the others." He hung up.

Claudia said, "Bad news?"

Abrams replaced the receiver in the cradle. "As Thoreau said about news, when you've read about one train wreck, you've read about them all."

"What does that mean?"

Abrams yawned. "Ask Thoreau."

"Henry Thoreau? He's dead."

"Really? I didn't even know he was sick."

"Stupid joke."

"Right."

"Who was that?"

"It was for me."

She turned toward the stairs.

Abrams tried to fit this new information into a framework, but his mind was nearly numb. All he could make of it was that it signified a ruthlessness, and a willingness to murder, plus the wherewithal to carry out complex and daring international operations. Telexed death warrants and people in place to execute the warrants. KGB. CIA. O'Brien's network. Could be anyone, he thought. It also signified a certain desperateness on the part of the killers, and that was the only bright spot in the picture.

CHAPTER TWENTY-SIX

Abrams followed Claudia up the tilted staircase. She turned to him on the landing. "Good night." She started up the next flight of stairs.

Abrams was annoyed. He said, "I'm going downstairs to have a drink."

She smiled.

Abrams stood on the landing, then approached the door to his room. He listened, then opened it, standing off to the side. He reached in and snapped on the light. There was no place a person could hide except under the bed, and he kept his eyes fixed there as he entered and retrieved his revolver from the top drawer of the bureau. He opened the cylinder, checked the six bullets, peered down the barrel to see if it was clear, felt the hammer and firing pin to make certain no one had done any filing, then dry-fired a few times. Satisfied he still had a lethal weapon, he reloaded and snapped the cylinder in place. Abrams dropped the revolver into his side pocket.

He walked downstairs and joined the Grenvilles in the sitting room. The fire was dead and the lights were out, but several candles lit the room. Abrams looked at Joan Grenville, half reclining on the couch, a drink in her hand. She arched her eyebrows in a quizzical look, as though to ask, thought Abrams, "Why aren't you fucking Claudia?"

Abrams poured himself a glass of warm club soda. He noted that Tom Grenville was asleep in a wingback chair.

Joan Grenville said, "I love candlelight. Especially in a house built before electricity."

Abrams sat on the couch and Joan had to move her feet. Abrams said, "There's always been electricity."

"You know what I mean."

She sipped on her drink, then said, "Aren't you tired?"

"Yes."

"Did you have an enjoyable evening?"

"Relative to what?"

She looked at her husband and called out, "Tom, wake up!"

Grenville didn't stir.

Joan turned to Abrams. "He's passed out. Other people sleep, he goes into a coma."

Abrams looked at Grenville. He appeared to be really out, but his physical presence was inhibiting. Abrams said to Joan Grenville, "Are you a member of the group?"

She didn't answer for some time, then said, "No." She paused again, then said, "I'm into aerobics."

Abrams smiled.

She added. "And tennis. Things that prolong one's life-span. How about you?"

"I smoke, carry a gun, and get involved in dangerous situations."

"You'd fit right in. I could give you a warning, but it would be pointless."

"Does your husband belong?"

"I'm not at liberty to speak about any of that."

"Are you afraid?"

"You're damned right." She stretched out her legs and one foot came to rest on his thigh.

There was, thought Abrams, a certain amount of sexual tension present in any houseguest situation. He remembered when his second cousin, Letty, slept in his parents' spare room. After a week of clumsy signaling, unneeded nocturnal trips to the kitchen and bathroom, they'd finally made it on the couch at 3:00 A.M. Abrams nodded toward Grenville. "I'll help him up, if you want."

She didn't answer but placed both feet on his lap. Abrams took one foot in his hands and massaged it.

"That feels good. I hate high heels."

Abrams realized he had little physical desire for her, and what there was had to do with things far more complex than instinct.

Abrams glanced again at Tom Grenville, sprawled in the chair. It seemed, or perhaps it was a trick of the candlelight, that Grenville was awake. He considered this for a moment, then a noise brought him to full alertness and he froze.

Joan Grenville heard it too, and she looked up at the ceiling. Someone was walking in Abrams' room directly overhead.

Abrams got up from the couch and went to the stairs, taking the steps three at a time. He stood outside his door and listened. Someone was still inside. He drew his revolver, stepped to the side, and pushed open the door. He peered cautiously around the jamb.

Claudia was sitting on the bed, with her legs drawn up to her breasts, leafing through a magazine. She was wearing a loosely tied white silk robe. Abrams said softly to himself, "Jesus Christ. There's no end to the madness."

Claudia glanced at him. "Come in and close the door."

Abrams stepped into the room and drew the door shut. He slipped his .38 into his pocket. He said tersely, "What makes you think I want you here?"

She tossed aside the magazine and sat up straighter. Her robe fell open and Abrams could see her breasts, olive-colored and full. She looked serious. "I am no whore. I don't go with many men. I like you. I think you like me."

Abrams turned and slipped out the door, colliding with Joan Grenville, who had obviously been listening. Abrams said, "Sorry, Mrs. Grenville. Look, I seem to have a calendar conflict...."

Unexpectedly, she smiled. "If you can, come to me afterward. Third floor. Second on the right. I'll leave it unlocked. Wake me. Any time before dawn."

"Right." He watched her mount the stairs, then went back into his room. He walked to the dresser and pulled out a drawer. His notebook hadn't been moved, and neither had any of his other odds and ends.

Claudia was leaning forward. "Do you think I came here to steal from you?"

He walked to the bed. "I was looking for my prayer shawl." He placed his revolver on the night table. Then he ripped off his tie and shrugged out of his dinner jacket. The shirt studs gave him trouble, and he ripped the front open, then tore the cuffs loose. "Damned stupid outfit..." He finished undressing, then climbed onto the high bed and knelt beside her, drawing her robe open. Her body was full, her hips wide. He caressed her legs, arms, and buttocks, and could detect her taut muscle tone. He wondered what kind of work she'd done in Rumania. "Do you do aerobics?"

"What is that? Flying? Why do I have trouble understanding you?"

"Beats me." He leaned over and kissed her, then his mouth moved down her body.

Claudia suddenly pulled away and drew her robe around her. "Come. Follow me." She rolled out of bed and gathered a heavy comforter from the footboard, draping it around her shoulders.

Abrams watched her as she walked to the window and threw up the sash. She turned back to him. "Come. There is a fire escape. The rain has stopped, and it's a beautiful night. Have you ever made love al fresco?"

Abrams shrugged and looked around for something to wear. She called out, "Just bring the pillows. Come." She slipped through the window and stood on the fire escape. Abrams grabbed two pillows, dropped his revolver into the pillowcase of one, and joined her on the fire escape.

A front was moving through, and a warm breeze blew from the south. The sky was clearing, and a half-moon was setting in the western sky. Abrams looked around at the surrounding buildings, all of which towered over the four-story town house. A few windows were still lit.

Claudia said, "This is beautiful. I love to make love outdoors."

Abrams smiled.

"Go on. You first."

Abrams began to climb the wet ladder. He said over his shoulder, "Slippery. Be careful."

She stopped climbing at the third-floor landing. "I have brandy in my room. Go on. I'll be a minute."

Abrams continued up the ladder past the darkened fourth-floor window. He peered over the parapet. The flat roof was covered with gravel for drainage, but puddles gleamed in the low spots. There was no stairwell shed, no skylights or ducts, and he had a clear view except for a wide brick chimney in the center of the roof.

Abrams climbed over the low parapet and dropped to the roof. He walked gingerly over the rough gravel and circled the chimney, then found a relatively dry area and dropped the two pillows. He stood looking out into the backyards below, the soft wind caressing his body. *Yes*, he thought, *this will be different*. Very nice.

He heard the sound of crunching gravel and sloshing water to his left and spun around. Two rappelling lines swung from the higher roof down the wall of the adjoining building. In the dark he saw two black-clad shapes in ski masks moving quickly toward him. One held a long jimmy bar, the other a black bag, which Abrams took to be a case of burglar tools. But in an instant he knew they were anything but burglars. They were very professional killers.

Abrams was about ten feet from the fire escape ladder and an equal distance from the pillow where his revolver lay tucked inside. The men were less than fifteen feet from him. Abrams lunged in three long strides and dove for the pillow. The gravel scraped his naked body as his hand shot into the right pillowcase. He seized the revolver by the barrel. He had no time to bring it out, and he worked it around, grasping the butt, his finger slipping into the trigger guard. He prepared to squeeze off a round through the case, but the closer of the two men loosed a violent kick that caught him on the side of the head. The other man came up quickly and swung the long steel jimmy at his elbow, paralyzing his right arm. Abrams felt a flash of searing pain travel to his shoulder and almost passed out. He thought again, *Pros*.

They pinioned his arms to his sides and rolled him over on his back. One man pressed a gloved hand over Abrams' mouth. The other held up something that Abrams thought was a club. The first man knelt on his chest and pried open his jaws as he held his nostrils shut.

Abrams could see that the club was actually a bottle, and he felt the cold liquid hit his lips and splash across his face. He tried to cough it back, but it slid down his open throat. It took a few seconds before he identified the burning sensation and the faint smell that somehow reached his olfactory nerves. It wasn't poison or acid but Scotch whisky. His brand, he guessed. So it wasn't to look like murder but like a drunken tumble from the roof. He began to struggle but felt a hand clamp on to his testicles and twist. He stopped moving.

They held him pressed against the rough gravel for what seemed like a long time but was, he thought, probably a few minutes. He felt the effects of the alcohol on his brain and tried to fight it. Suddenly the two men turned him on his stomach, seized his arms and legs, and began running toward the edge of the roof.

Abrams saw the low parapet coming up quickly, and beyond the parapet the emptiness of a four-story fall.

He waited until they slowed, a few feet from the edge. He felt the imperceptible loosening of their grip as they prepared to hurl their burden out into space. At that last moment Abrams twisted violently, breaking the hold on his right arm. His shoulder dropped and collided with the brick parapet wall, causing the two men to lose their grip on him.

Abrams wrenched free and fell to the rooftop, spinning around into a crouching defensive position, his back to the brick parapet. The two men hovered over him but hesitated a split second. Abrams sprang out of his crouch, grabbing two handfuls of gravel and flinging them into the men's faces. His left foot shot out and caught the closest man in the groin. The other man lunged at him while he was off-balance and delivered a clenched fist to the side of his jaw, knocking him off his feet.

Abrams lay on his back, stunned. The man dove at him, his

hands outstretched and reaching for his throat. Abrams planted his bare feet in the man's stomach, lifting him high into the air, and the man's forward momentum catapulted him over the parapet. The quiet night was broken with a shrill, piercing scream.

Abrams sprang to his feet. The second man was already running toward the dangling rappelling lines. Abrams began to follow, but the alcohol slowed him and he felt a growing pain where his shoulder had hit the wall. His right arm was still numb from the blow on the elbow, and the sharp gravel cut into his feet.

The man was halfway up the rope as Abrams reached it. Abrams grabbed the rope and jerked it violently, but the man, wearing crepe soles and leather climbing gloves, hung on and disappeared onto the higher roof.

Abrams turned and walked unsteadily back to where the two pillows lay. He retrieved his revolver and began descending the fire escape.

Claudia was on the top landing. She looked at him in the dim light. "What happened to you? You smell of whisky...."

He stared at her. "I slipped." He took her arm and led her down the fire escape into the bedroom. He said, "You forgot the brandy."

"I couldn't find it."

Abrams pulled on his suit trousers. "Where's the comforter?"

Claudia didn't respond, but asked, "Where are you going?"

"Back to Brooklyn, where it's safe."

"But...we haven't..."

"I think I've lost the desire. Good night."

"What...?" She reached out and touched his scraped elbow. "You have cuts all over you."

"Good night." He noticed his voice was slurred.

She hesitated, then turned quickly and left.

Abrams waited, then took his revolver and went out into the hallway. He mounted the stairs and went to Joan Grenville's room. He opened the door without knocking and found her under the covers, sleeping in a sitting position, her bare breasts peeking out over the bedsheets. Her lamp was on, and a book lay on the covers. He was surprised to find she snored.

Abrams saw that she had a bolt lock on her door, and he threw it shut, then checked the window latch. He sat in an easy chair, his revolver on his lap, and closed his eyes.

His thoughts seemed a bit jumbled, but through the alcohol he concluded that if he had any doubts about the reality of what he'd heard so far, he had none now. Like a soldier new at the front or a rookie cop on a bad beat, he'd been lucky to survive his first day. Luck or chance would play no part in his future survival. He'd be harder to kill, but they wouldn't stop trying.

He had one distinct advantage over everyone now. He knew the name of one of the enemy: Countess Claudia Lepescu. But he didn't know where to turn with this interesting knowledge. In contrast to his police work, he had no brothers, no partners. He was alone. He began to appreciate the sheer terror and loneliness of intelligence work.

He looked at Joan. How, he wondered, did she fit? His instincts told him she was what she seemed to be. She might even be useful if she weren't so useless.

The obvious thing to do, he thought, was to put a lot of distance between himself and these people. But something inside him— maybe something as uncomplicated as simple patriotism—told him to see it to the end. He wondered who Talbot's next victim would be. Whoever it was, he assured himself, it wouldn't be Tony Abrams.

BOOK IV

Revelations

CHAPTER TWENTY-SEVEN

At 8:30 A.M., Katherine Kimberly entered the town house on 36th Street with her own key. She glanced into the sitting room and saw Tom Grenville sprawled on the couch, his dinner jacket and shoes lying on the floor.

She went into the small back kitchen and put on a pot of coffee.

Tony Abrams, dressed in his dark business suit, came through the rear door that led out to the courtyard. He watched her, her back to him, pouring cream into a small pitcher. She was dressed in a white sweat shirt, khaki trousers, and jogging shoes. Like most business associates one sees on a weekend for the first time, Katherine looked, he thought, not like Katherine. He said, "Good morning."

She turned and smiled at him. "You *are* awake. You look awful. Rough night?"

He looked into her eyes for any sign that she was surprised or disappointed he was still alive. He said, "I've had worse." He found two coffee mugs in a cupboard. "I was concerned about you."

She opened her handbag and extracted an automatic pistol.

Abrams looked at the piece, a Browning .45. He had expected something a bit smaller, but he could tell by the way she gripped the pistol that she was comfortable with it. He said, "You heard about Brompton Hall of course?"

She returned the automatic to her bag. "Yes. The dead have been identified. Lady Eleanor Wingate, her nephew Charles Brook, and Mr. O'Brien's friend Ronald Hollings. Autopsies are being performed."

Abrams poured two cups of coffee. He asked, "Were you alone last night?"

"That's a leading question."

Abrams stared at her, then said, "Am I on the case or not?"

She replied coolly, "I went back to my apartment on Carmine Street. I was alone. You were in the car when—"

"You may have been discreet about it. Why didn't you go back to the Lombardy?"

She seemed annoyed. "I didn't feel like staying there."

"Did Thorpe suggest you go home?"

She nodded.

Abrams sipped on his coffee. "Do you have your own room there?"

"Yes."

"And your street clothes and things were there. Then doesn't it seem odd that he should send you home, all the way down to Carmine Street? Didn't he know you had an appointment with me in midtown this morning?"

"My, you *are* a cop." She took some coffee. "No, it didn't seem odd. The apartment at the Lombardy, if you must know, is what's odd. It's a CIA safe house, or substation or something. One doesn't question the accommodations or lack of them."

Abrams nodded, then put down his cup. "How's your stomach this morning?"

"My stomach...? Fine...."

Abrams walked to the back door and motioned her to follow.

She went with him into the courtyard. Below the rear dining room window was a white wrought-iron bench with two legs broken off. On the bench was sprawled, faceup, a black-clad body. The body's back was arched over the bench to such a degree that it was obviously broken, and the head was touching the paving stones.

Katherine stared at the figure.

Abrams said, "A burglar, by the looks of the outfit."

Katherine glanced up at the top of the four-story town house, but said nothing.

Abrams bent over the body and pulled back the ski mask. The deathly white skin contrasted against the dark black stubble on the face and the dried red blood around the mouth. The face was that of a man in his mid-thirties, and the features could be described as vaguely Slavic. Abrams peered into the open, blood-caked mouth, then pulled off the mask, revealing a thick growth of swept-back black hair. "Along with the haircut, and what I can see of the dental work, I'd make an educated guess that the man is foreign. You don't recognize him, do you?"

Katherine came closer and stared into the dead man's face. "No...." She turned quickly and walked back to the kitchen.

Abrams followed. They sipped on their coffee in silence, then Katherine spoke. "What were you doing on the roof?"

"I never said I was on the roof." He picked up the telephone and dialed Captain Spinelli at home. "Abrams here."

Spinelli's voice sounded groggy. "I don't have anything new on Carbury."

"Come to 184 East Thirty-sixth Street. Corpse in the backyard."

"Oh, Christ, Abrams, what the fuck is going on with you?"

"I'll call you later."

"Where are you?"

"At said address."

"Is this related to Carbury?"

"Well, this house belongs to, or is used by, O'Brien et al., and some of those folks are sleeping here. What do you think, Sherlock?"

"I think I want to grill your ass. Stay there."

"I'll speak to you." He hung up.

Abrams and Katherine left the town house. The day was clear and mild, and smelled of the night's rain. Abrams looked at her in the full sunlight. She had probably gotten less than five hours' sleep, but showed no signs of it.

Katherine sensed he was studying her in some new way. She said, "Why don't we walk?"

Neither spoke until they reached Lexington Avenue, where they waited for a light. She said, "What do you suppose that man was after?"

"The silverware."

They crossed the avenue and turned north. Traffic was light and the city had that Saturday-morning look of sleeping off a collective hangover. They turned west into 42nd Street. Katherine said. "You'll like Arnold. He's eccentric and devious."

"What do you expect to find there?"

"You never expect to find anything in the archives. Yet, everything is there. What's missing is as important as what's on file. It's a matter of deduction, intuition, and luck. Are you good with archives?"

"No one has ever asked me that. I'll think about it."

They walked silently through the Grand Central Station area, which Abrams thought of as some sort of prewar time warp, barely changed since he was a youth—stately banks, older hotels, shoeshine stands, news vendors, tobacconists, Brooks Brothers, the Yale Club. Very masculine. Wasp Central he called it; trains from Connecticut and Westchester disgorging tons of preppies and hale-fellows-well-met. *Rus in urbe*. Scarsdale and Westport in midtown. You almost expected to see Holden Caulfield eating a chicken salad on white at the Oyster Bar. Abrams said, "I don't trust Peter Thorpe."

Katherine didn't respond immediately, but when she spoke, there was no reproach in her voice. "Of course you don't. Who does? He's an intelligence officer. He lies, cheats, and steals. But we don't speak of trust in this business. We speak of loyalty. Peter is loyal."

"To whom?"

"To his country." She looked at him. "Any suggestion to the contrary would be a very serious matter."

Abrams replied, "It would be imprudent of me to make such a suggestion." He changed the subject. "By the way, thanks for suggesting I sleep at the town house. That was convenient."

"I thought it might be. Feel free to use it any time."

They walked to Fifth Avenue and crossed to the north corner beside the Public Library. Abrams noticed black markings on the sidewalk: an arrow pointing south at a stenciled silhouette of the Empire State Building. Beside the arrow were the words GROUND ZERO, 0.4 MILES. Katherine noticed it and said, "What drivel."

He'd seen these all over the city, with arrows pointing toward the Empire State Building and the distance given. "People are afraid," said Abrams.

"There's nothing to fear," said Katherine, "except fear itself."

"Oh, I think a ten-megaton missile falling on Thirty-fourth Street would give me the jitters."

"This nuclear hysteria feeds on itself."

"Mr. O'Brien is very worried about something," he said.

"Not nuclear missiles."

"What then? Fluoride in the water?"

"Something...not biological or chemical warfare...something more lethal...I can't imagine what."

"Neither can I."

They continued up Fifth Avenue toward Rockefeller Center. He said, "What happens to Talbot if you find him?"

"What do you think?"

"And if Talbot turns out to be Patrick O'Brien, for instance?"

She answered without hesitation, "It wouldn't matter if it turned out to be my best friend. He dies. She dies. They die."

Abrams looked at her. He said, "Back in the thirties, E. M. Forster wrote, 'If I had to choose between betraying my country and betraying my friend, I hope I should have the guts to betray my country.'"

"Idiotic."

"But interesting. The whole concept of treason is interesting. Read the Declaration of Independence. It was the most treasonous document of its time. King George had every legal right to hang all fifty-six traitors who signed that document."

She stopped walking at the entrance to the Rockefeller Center promenade. "All right. What's the point? That we have no legal right to dispose of Talbot?"

"That's your problem. A moral problem. My point is a practical one. Talbot does not have corruption in his heart, or guilt in his eyes, as James Allerton suggested. He does not lose his soul when the full moon is upon him, or grow hair, or stink of blood. He wears a halo and smells of roses."

"But *you* said you could see guilt in a man's eyes—"

"But my observation was to make a contrary point. Criminals look guilty. Talbot is not a criminal, he is a patriot. Ask him."

"I see...."

"My parents...yes, they were traitors...but they were people who fed the poor when they were able, took in indigent friends and relatives, laughed, made love, and made potato pancakes. Talbot is a blue-blooded version of that. He could very well be O'Brien, Allerton, George Van Dorn, or a dozen others I met last night. His progeny could be...anyone."

She nodded. "Okay...thanks for bringing some cold, hard objectivity into this."

"That's what I was hired for." He turned into the promenade and walked toward the RCA Building. She walked beside him. Abrams said, "I don't trust you either."

She forced a smile. "Do you mean professionally or personally?"

"Both."

"How about Nick?"

"Academic background. Shaky from a security point of view. Never trust an egghead. Also, he's stayed too long on a job he doesn't seem to like. Very suspicious."

"The Grenvilles? Claudia?"

"Joan Grenville's energies are directed toward betraying Tom Grenville. Tom Grenville gives the outward impression that his idea of oral sex is talking to E. F. Hutton. But underneath, there's a quite different sexual persona, and this may be indicative of other types of impersonation. As for Claudia, never trust a foreigner."

They walked around the skating rink. Katherine stopped in front of the RCA Building. "Do you think I had something to do with that man last night?"

"The thought occurred to me."

"But I've been pushing for you to join us."

"True. But if I were under suspicion, I too would push for an outside man. Diverts suspicion. But I'd be certain he met his end if he seemed too sharp."

"You're not that sharp." She smiled.

Abrams held the door open for her and they entered the lobby of the RCA Building.

Abrams said, "But for the sake of argument, if someone *did* try to murder me, then that would prove I was real sharp, wouldn't it?"

She suppressed a laugh. "Maybe. By the way, *murder,* as you know, is a legal word connoting wrongdoing. If someone tried to *kill* you, they may be, as you suggested, just patriots doing their duty to the people."

He smiled tightly and thought, *Bitch.*

CHAPTER TWENTY-EIGHT

The main concourse level of the RCA Building was pristine Art Deco, thought Abrams, another prewar time warp but strangely modern after half a century, like a set in a Flash Gordon movie.

The lower concourse had a coffee shop where Abrams sometimes sat and watched the skaters in the sunken rink through a plate glass window. The upper mezzanine held shops, as did the main concourse. Abrams had once noticed a shop that specialized in military artifacts and Americana: pictures, statues, plaques, and such. There were bronze busts of General Donovan for sale, whose principal customers he thought must be young attorneys at Donovan Leisure, O'Brien, Kimberly, or one of the dozen or so other firms with OSS connections. Presumably these upward-bound lawyers placed the bust in a small office shrine tucked between file cabinets. Abrams smiled at the thought of a lunch-hour group of young lawyers genuflecting in front of the bust.

Katherine said, "Is that a smile I see? Did you just remember something unpleasant? Perhaps a close friend is sick?"

Abrams looked at her and let his smile widen. "God knows why, but I like you."

"Makes my day." She walked to the elevator and stopped at a small desk. She wrote their names and destination in the weekend book. They rode up and got off on the forty-fourth floor, which was wholly occupied by O'Brien's firm. A private guard in the corridor nodded to her in recognition and indicated yet another sign-in book on a rostrum. Abrams said, "I'm glad I didn't stop in to use the bathroom."

Katherine seemed not to hear as she studied the book. A few attorneys had come in, she noted, and Arnold had signed in at 8:00 A.M.

She and Abrams walked down the long, turning corridor and stopped in front of the steel door marked DEAD FILES. She knocked.

Abrams said, "Will Arnold let me in?"

She smiled. "I'll use my charm." She knocked again. From behind the door they heard the shrill whistle of a teakettle, a furiously boiling teakettle that should be taken off the burner.

Abrams reached out and turned the knob. The door opened with its familiar unoiled creak. Abrams peered inside.

Katherine brushed quickly past him and stepped into the room. Abrams pulled her back and drew his revolver. Neither spoke. The copper kettle sat on a glowing red electric ring, steam shooting from its spout.

Katherine's eyes adjusted to the uneven illumination and focused on the body lying in a pool of lamplight beside the camp table. Abram's eyes darted around the dimly lit stacks of file cabinets. They both listened, but there was no sound except the whistling kettle.

Abrams kept his revolver by his side and approached the body.

Arnold Brin, dressed in shirt sleeves and gray slacks, lay on his stomach, his head to one side and his cheek resting on a disarrayed tie. The tie, noticed Abrams, was a blue hue that closely matched the color of Arnold's face. Arnold Brin's tongue protruded from his open mouth and touched the tie. The eye that Abrams could see was wide open. Abrams knelt beside the body and touched the cheek. "Warm. About an hour, or less."

Katherine felt her legs shaking and slumped into a chair, then, realizing it was Arnold's, quickly stood and leaned back against a file cabinet. "Oh..." her voice was barely audible. "...Oh, my God..."

Abrams looked back at the camp desk. Tea things were strewn

around, and a bakery bag of tea biscuits lay on the floor beside the desk. Abrams got down on all fours, his eyes inches from the dead man's face. He reached behind, took the desk lamp and set it on the floor. He examined the open eye, then forced open Arnold's stiffening jaws, peered inside, sniffed, then stood, replacing the lamp.

Katherine still stood against the cabinet, her eyes shut, and Abrams could see moisture around her lids. He surveyed the table again, examining the kettle, the porcelain pot, and loose tea. He picked up one of the biscuits and smelled it. "It was probably suffocation, but I don't think it was brought on by poison."

Katherine opened her eyes. "What...?"

"Apparently what happened"—Abrams shut off the electric burner—"he never brewed the tea, obviously. That might have saved him."

"What are you talking about?"

"He began eating one of those large dry biscuits, without butter or jam....His mouth and perhaps throat were dry—saliva output is diminished in older persons. Perhaps his throat muscles hadn't done any food-swallowing since last night...in people his age this is not an uncommon accident."

"Accident?"

"He choked to death on a biscuit. I can see part of it lodged in his throat."

She stared at Abrams, then at Arnold. She didn't speak for some time, then said, "Do you believe that?"

"No. He was murdered. One of the best I've seen." Abrams rubbed his chin, then said, "He was held by at least two men who probably wore padded gloves so they wouldn't leave fingerprints or marks on his skin. They may have put alum in his mouth to dry him up, and maybe poured a topical anesthetic in to dull the senses in his throat. Probably, though, they just held his esophagus in a tight grip so he couldn't swallow. They rammed the biscuit down his throat and held him until he suffocated to death. Nice people."

Katherine took a deep breath.

Abrams said matter-of-factly, "The medical examiner will have a bad time with this one. But if he knows he's looking at murder, he may turn something up." Abrams lit a cigarette. "I wonder why these people are bothering with phony accidents?" He thought a moment, then said, "Probably to buy time. So all the alarms don't start going off automatically."

She nodded, "Partly true. But also, the preferred method is to make it look like an accident. There's a certain pride...in coming up with refinements.... It's standard tradecraft."

"Really? Are there awards?" He threw his cigarette down and stepped on it. "Well, this is the fourth time there's been no clear evidence of murder. Carbury vanished without a trace, Brompton Hall burned, Arnold accidentally choked. Christ, even a cop can see a pattern here."

She looked at him. "The fourth?"

"Oh...my drunken stumble from the roof."

"You *were* on the roof. That man tried to kill you."

Abrams nodded.

"What...how the hell did you get on the roof?"

"Fire escape."

"You know what I mean."

"It might be more revealing to question how I came to be at the town house in the first place."

She hesitated, then said, "Claudia suggested it to me. She likes you."

Abrams didn't answer.

Katherine added, "To be honest and more precise, Mr. O'Brien and Peter also suggested you stay there, quite independently of Claudia and each other, I presume."

Abrams again said nothing.

Katherine seemed to be coming out of the shock of seeing Arnold's body. Her tone was curt. "But what brought you to the *roof?*"

"Fate."

She said, "You know...Tony...it's not always a good policy to keep your own counsel. Sometimes people need help."

"I suppose, Kate, that anyone who deals with you people needs all the help he can get. But not from the source of the problem."

She seemed put off, but said evenly, "Why would anyone want to kill *you*?"

"I don't know, but it's always flattering." Abrams picked up the telephone on Arnold's desk and dialed the town house.

A man's voice answered, "Yeah?" which was, Abrams knew, how a detective answered the phone at the scene of the crime. Abrams said, "Captain Spinelli."

"Yeah. Who's this?"

"Abrams."

"Yeah. Hold on."

"Yeah."

Spinelli came on the line. "How'd this happen, Abrams?"

"Beats me. Listen, I hate to ruin your Saturday, but I have another corpse."

"Get off it."

"RCA Building. Firm of O'Brien, et al. Room marked 'Dead Files.' The guard will direct you. Sign in."

There was a long silence, then Spinelli said, "What the *fuck* is going on with you? What are you, Abrams, some kind of dark cloud?"

"Let's have lunch."

"My ass. You stay away from me. No...stay there."

"Sorry, have to run. Listen, it looks like an accidental food choking, but it's not. Tell the ME, okay? And remember, this is still funny stuff. Watch your ass. *Arrivederci*." He hung up and turned to Katherine. "Is it worth looking for files, or should we assume they're gone?"

She was studying the file sign-out book. "Arnold removed fourteen files"—she looked around Arnold's work area—"but they're not here."

Abrams nodded.

Katherine thought a moment. "Arnold knew at least one of the people or he wouldn't have unlocked the door."

"True."

"Someone who had access to this room."

"How many people is that?"

"Dozens. English, Americans, some French, and even a few Germans. Plus a team of Israeli Nazi-hunters."

"Do you have that list?"

She looked at Arnold. "He kept it in his mind. Every group had only their partial list."

Abrams thought a moment, then said, "He didn't know he was in danger immediately. He spoke to the person or persons he let in.... They would have exchanged words about the stack of files he was collecting. Perhaps they let him complete the task. They knew what he was doing, why he was here on a Saturday. They knew you'd be along shortly."

Her eyes suddenly darted into the dark recesses of the aisles of cabinets. She spoke in a hushed tone. "Could they still be here?"

He shook his head. "I doubt it." He thought again. "At some point, Arnold may have sensed he was in danger...and he may have—" Abrams stared at the desk a moment, then carefully moved some of the papers and tea things on the desk. "Nothing here... they would have spotted any message he tried to leave." Abrams turned over the body, quickly and expertly examining the pockets, shoes, socks, and clothing. "Nothing I can find...."

Katherine stood near him. She said, "Maybe we should...look around."

"No. Let's go before New York's finest arrive."

They left the room and walked quickly down the brightly lit corridor. At the elevator bank, Katherine approached the guard. "Did anyone other than Arnold Brin go down this corridor?"

The guard shook his head. "But then, there're fire stairs down there too."

Katherine looked at the sign-in book. Four names appeared over hers and Abrams': Arnold Brin's and the three attorneys'. "Are these men still in the office?"

"I think so. I never saw them leave."

"Thank you." She looked at Abrams as they waited for the elevator. "Arnold would not have let any of those three men in."

Abrams nodded. "It doesn't seem difficult to get past that guard. Do you know him?"

"Yes. He's been here for years...which doesn't mean very much."

"No," said Abrams, "it doesn't." He thought a moment. "Cops ask questions like that—new employees, new domestic help...prime suspects. In your game, people are planted two decades before to unlock a door or throw a light switch at a critical moment."

"That's somewhat exaggerated, but—"

"Still, Spinelli will check out the guard and the three attorneys."

The elevator came and they entered. Katherine said, "I feel terrible about Arnold. He wouldn't have been here if I hadn't asked him to come in."

"Right."

She looked at him. "You could be more sympathetic."

"It was a stupid comment. If today weren't Saturday, it would be Friday. If Hitler's father had used a condom, Arnold wouldn't be in charge of World War Two British archives in Rockefeller Center. So what?"

They rode down in silence and stepped off on the mezzanine. Abrams said, "I don't want to run into Spinelli in the lobby." They walked to the west end of the mezzanine, descended by a staircase, and exited onto Sixth Avenue. They began walking south.

The sun was warmer, and the avenue was beginning to come alive. Tourists with cameras were heading toward Radio City Music Hall and joggers jostled with pedestrians. Abrams glanced at Katherine's jogging shoes and saw they were well worn. "Do you run?"

"Yes."

"Did you ever do Brooklyn?"

"Yes. Prospect Park. Sometimes across the Brooklyn Bridge to the Heights Promenade."

Abrams said, "I can do the Prospect Park run, about twelve miles. Let's run it someday."

"How about Monday morning?"

"Am I getting Memorial Day off?"

"Sure." She smiled.

They walked in silence for a few blocks, then Katherine said, "Well, what now?"

He took a while to answer, then replied, "I have to get back to the town house, get my tux and return it to Murray's. Then I have to get back to Brooklyn, check my mail, pack a few things if I'm staying on Thirty-sixth Street, and—"

"That's so...banal...mundane."

"Most of life is like that."

"People are dead. There's a threat to national security—"

"Napoleon, on campaign in Austria, sent a long letter to his tailor in Paris complaining about the fit of his underwear. Life goes on."

"I suppose. Listen, I'm having lunch with Nick. Join us."

"Can't."

"I'd like to discuss these new developments: Brompton Hall, Arnold's death, the attempt on your life."

"We've discussed too much already. Let's wait for Spinelli's reports and whatever they've got in England. I'd rather deal in facts for a change of pace."

She nodded. "Well...can't you think of *anything* we should be doing in the meantime?"

"I have something at the dry cleaners, too. Also, we should try not to get murdered. Look over your shoulder a lot."

They stopped at 42nd Street. Abrams said, "I'm going back to the town house. Where are you heading?"

"If someone tried to kill you there, why are you going to stay there?"

"Would I be safer in my place?"

"No."

"So? Take it easy, okay? Call me about the run tomorrow."

"Wait." She took a slip of paper from her bag and handed it to him.

He looked at it. In her handwriting was written *JFE 78-2763.*

She said, "That was written in Arnold's hand in the file sign-out ledger. It is not a file number. Does it mean anything to you?"

Abrams stared at the slip of paper. "Looks like...something familiar.... I can't think of what, though."

Katherine said, "His murderers were sloppy not to read his file ledger. You were right—Arnold realized something was wrong, and tried to leave a message. There's no other reason for him to put those letters and numbers on a page that I was supposed to sign for the files."

"Sounds logical."

"You know what those letters and numbers are, Abrams. Don't bullshit me."

He smiled and handed the paper back. "Call me Tony."

"I'll call you worse than that if you start playing games with me. I'm being straight with you. Do the same with me."

He held up his hand. "Okay. Cool down. It's a library call number."

"Of course. So let's go to the library and see what book it calls."

"Which library?"

"The obvious one. Turn left. Walk."

They turned east into 42nd Street and covered the block to Fifth Avenue quickly. They mounted the steps of the main library between the reclining lions.

Once inside the towering bronze doors, they climbed up the broad staircase, past the second-floor landing, and up to the third-floor Main Reading Room. Abrams gave the librarian the call number.

They waited for their book to be pulled from the stacks. Abrams said, "Tell me about your sister Ann."

Katherine thought awhile, then replied, "She's older than me, a bit more serious and scholarly, never married—"

"I'm not looking for a date," he said brusquely. "What does she do?"

Katherine glanced at him. This reversal of the pecking order was somewhat disconcerting. She said, "Ann works for the National Security Agency. Codes, ciphers, cryptography...things like that. Electronic spying. No cloak and dagger, just radios and satellites."

Before he could reply, their number flashed in red lights on the large indicator board and they walked quickly to the desk. Katherine picked up a massive green leatherbound volume. They looked at the gold embossed letters on the cover.

Abrams said, "*Graecum est—non potest legere*. It's Greek to me."

Katherine looked at him. "Oh, I'd hoped you weren't going to say that."

"Sorry. Seemed appropriate."

"Well, you don't need Greek to read the title—*He Odysseiatou.* It's Homer's *Odyssey.*" She opened the book and flipped through the pages. The text, too, was in classical Greek, and there were numerous markings in the margins and a few odd scraps of paper that she left in place.

Abrams said, "Did Arnold read Greek?"

"I saw a Greek book on his desk once. That's one of the reasons I thought he might not be a clerk sergeant. I always suspected he was a ranking intelligence officer, which would indicate that the files had more importance than some of us thought."

Abrams watched her examining the book and said, "The clue is not that particular book. The clue, if there is one, has to be the title, *The Odyssey.* Or the author, Homer." He thought a moment. "Do those names have any significance to you? Someone's code name?"

"No..."

"How about the protagonist, Odysseus, or by his Latin name, Ulysses?"

She shook her head.

"Then," said Abrams, "perhaps the plot...the story line. Odysseus, after the fall of Troy, sets sail for home....He meets with misadventures...Circe, Sirens...and all that. He's presumed dead, but ten years later he returns. Is that about it?"

"Basically...then there's the end of the story...after ten years of war and another ten of wanderings, his wife Penelope doesn't recognize him. But he's left his bow at home and only he had the ability to draw it. He shoots an arrow through twelve axheads to prove to her it's he." She thought, then shook her head. "But I don't know what Arnold had on his mind."

"Well, you're familiar with the cast of characters. Think about it. A piece of advice—think about it alone."

She nodded, then looked at her watch. "I have about an hour before lunch. I'll go on your errands with you."

"To Brooklyn? Do you have a passport?"

"Don't let Peter's idiot jokes get to you."

Abrams returned the book to the librarian, and began walking toward the card catalog room.

Katherine fell in beside him. "You handled yourself quite well with him. Ignore him."

Abrams thought that to ignore Peter Thorpe was like ignoring a dark shadow at your window. They entered the hall and moved toward the staircase. He said, "I deduce that your things are still at the Lombardy. Why don't we go there and collect them?"

She hesitated, then said, "All right. But . . . you can't go up."

"Can you get me up?"

"No."

"Perhaps when no one is there. Do you have a key?"

"No."

"Can you try to get me in there?"

There was a long pause, long enough to indicate to Abrams that her loyalty to Thorpe was not one hundred percent. She said, "I'll think about that."

They walked through the reception area and out onto the sun-splashed library steps where people sat, read, and played radios.

Abrams said, "How important were those missing files?"

"Apparently very important or they wouldn't have murdered Arnold Brin."

Abrams lit a cigarette and stared down into Fifth Avenue. "That's a logical conclusion. But I wonder . . ."

"Wonder what?"

"They may know less than we do. They have a secret—Talbot's identity. We are trying to discover that secret. They can't know exactly how close we are to their secret. Therefore they've got to cover every angle."

"Yes . . . you did say Talbot or his friends would kill again."

"And again, and again. Half the mob murders in New York are committed to shut someone up who didn't know anything to begin with. For some organizations it's easier to blast away at all possible sources of danger, rather than approach the problem rationally. I, for instance, know very little, yet someone tried to remove me from the equation."

"You said you were flattered."

"That was glib. Motive is important. Find the motive and you'll find a suspect."

"What's the motive? Are you a possible source of danger to them?"

"I keep thinking it was more personal than political."

"Personal?"

Abrams nodded. "Just about my only contact with your friends was last night. Maybe I stepped on someone's toes at the dance."

"That's very unlikely."

"Only in theory. In practice, people who kill, kill for the most unlikely and petty of reasons. When you cross the path of a killer, and you do or say something wrong, he considers you dead meat. You breathe and walk only because he needs a little time to plan your death. He feels incredibly alive knowing he has this power of life and death."

"Were we at the same function last night?"

"As you know, some killers are outwardly charming, wear dinner jackets, and make jokes. But inwardly they are brooding individuals who are very sensitive to imagined insults or perceived threats to their existence. Then they turn psychotic, vengeful, and murderous. This is often manifested by an outward show of cordiality toward the marked victim. Did I meet anyone like that last night?"

She didn't answer.

Abrams threw down his cigarette. "You know, if I could think of someone like that—even if I wasn't certain—I might follow their rules and protect myself in the most direct manner, by eliminating that threat. I mean, why take a chance?"

"I think I'd better leave you to your errands."

"Yes, well, be careful."

She started down the steps, hesitated, then turned. Abrams saw that her face was quite pale. She said, "Look...one thing we don't do in this firm is to make unilateral decisions. Before you...take any direct action...please consult me."

He nodded.

Katherine turned and walked up Fifth Avenue.

Abrams sat on the steps beside an old drunk with a bottle of wine. The drunk asked, "Got four bits?"

Abrams put two quarters in the man's hand.

"Thanks, bub." Then with the easy social grace of derelicts he said, "Name's John. What's yours?"

"Odysseus, a.k.a. Ulysses."

"Some name. Got a cigarette?"

Abrams gave him a cigarette and lit it for him. "You know, John, the human mind is capable of some incredible things. Even your mind, John. Otherwise you wouldn't have survived so long on the streets."

The old drunk nodded. "How about a dollar?"

"Arnold Brin, I'm told, had a fine mind. I suppose he came here a lot. Like you. He, though, was not a survivor like you. He saw death approaching, but he overcame that basic instinct for survival, and instead of trying to make a break, he had the presence of mind to leave a message that might enable others to survive."

The drunk stood, swayed, and sat again. Several radios were playing loudly, each tuned to a different station. A group of students sat under the south lion and read. Abrams leaned toward the drunk. "*The Odyssey,* John. The story of Odysseus. Boiled down to one line, it's the tale of a warrior who, after the war is won, and after many years of wandering, returns home from the dead. Now what was Arnold trying to tell us, John?"

The drunk stood again, and took a tentative step. "Beats me."

"You're not trying, John."

"Beats me." The drunk navigated the steps to the sidewalk.

Abrams stood. Coming up the steps was a homicide detective whom he recognized. With him was a man who was not a cop, but might be FBI. Well, Abrams thought, the clue itself was obvious to the trained police eye, but the meaning of the clue would not be obvious to an outsider. Abrams turned away and let the two men pass, then stepped down to the sidewalk and headed south.

Arnold, he reflected, was writing to the initiated. He was writing in shorthand to people who shared common experiences and thought processes. Or who had learned enough to make all the mental leaps and inferences necessary to draw a conclusion. Abrams, too, had come to a conclusion, had deduced a possible and logical meaning to the message; though as logical as it might be, it was so unlikely, he could not bring himself to believe the answer he had arrived at.

CHAPTER TWENTY-NINE

The old twin-engine Beechcraft leveled off at 15,000 feet. The pilot, Sonny Bellman, checked his airspeed indicator: 160 knots. He spoke into the PA microphone. "Pine Barrens dead ahead. About ten minutes to jump site."

Patrick O'Brien nodded to himself. They were about thirty miles west of Toms River, New Jersey. Ten more minutes would bring them over the most desolate area of the barrens.

O'Brien looked out the fuselage window. The night was clear but not moonless. In fact, the half-moon was quite bright, he saw, lighting up the starry sky and casting a bluish luminescence across the flatlands below. This was not a night for tactical jumps, but a good night for sport. He sat cross-legged and leaned back against the fuselage.

These Sunday-evening jumps were for him a sort of religious experience, a memorial to the dead, and a cleansing ritual. He'd land in the pristine Pine Barrens, make a small fire, and spend the night thinking, talking to himself, remembering and forgetting. Before dawn he would radio his position to an old friend, a retired farmer, and the man would come out in a motor home and meet him at a designated spot on the closest road.

O'Brien would shower in the vehicle and change into a suit, having already shaved and eaten breakfast in the woods. Usually he would share a cup of coffee with the old man. By the time they reached the Holland Tunnel, O'Brien would be ready to do battle, an ironic reversal of the wartime sequence of events.

O'Brien knew in his body, mind, and heart that there would be no more jumps after this summer, and so he savored these dwindling Sunday nights the way an old man savors most everything he knows is coming to an end.

O'Brien was brought out of his reverie as he heard and felt the decrease in the engine's power. He sensed they were approaching the 120-knot jump speed.

His eyes surveyed the dark empty cabin, lit only by the red glow of the no-jump lamp. In the eerie redness he fancied he saw the fuselage walls lined with men and women, hooked to static lines, like nooses, and swathed in black shrouds. Their waxy white faces all turned slowly toward him and he saw their eyes glowing red. O'Brien shut his eyes and shook his head. After some time, he glanced up at the bulkhead that separated the cabin from the cockpit, then looked at his watch. Bellman should be giving him the green light soon.

O'Brien stood and checked his harness as he moved toward the door. The Beechcraft had been modified for sky divers and the door had been fitted with roller tracks, rather than the conventional swing-out hinges. Also, the normal eight seats had been removed to accommodate about twelve standees. The Beechcraft also had an autopilot so that the pilot could come back and shut the door after a jump, eliminating the necessity of a jumpmaster or copilot.

O'Brien stood at the door and looked out the small oval window. The craft banked to the left as a cloud passed in front of the moon, throwing a black shadow over the desolate landscape. A light twinkled here and there, and O'Brien was reminded of the signal lights from the partisans on the ground.

One never knew who was actually controlling those signal lights. Certainly, he thought, one of the most frightening experiences of modern man was taking off from a blacked-out airstrip in a plywood aircraft whose worthiness was always in question; then running a gauntlet of enemy fighters, sometimes running through anti-aircraft

fire over occupied territory; then, if you'd made it that far, jumping from the relative safety of the aircraft into a bleak, inhospita-
ble landscape and floating down, much too slowly, to an uncertain
reception.

And having survived those terrors, one had to complete the mission and get the hell out. And for secret agents, capture did not
mean POW camp. It meant a concentration camp, torture, interrogation, and nearly always a newly raked sandbox where you knelt
for the bullet in the back of the neck. There was, however, always
the L-pill.

Yet, he had survived. Others had not. There was no accounting
for it. But having survived, he felt he owed something. He owed it to
those who ended their lives in battle, in the torturer's chamber, with
cyanide, or in the sandbox, to continue the mission. Right after the
war there had been scores to settle with certain Gestapo and SS gentlemen. But within a year he and his friends had met the ultimate
enemy: the Soviet state security forces.

O'Brien looked at his watch again: ten seventeen. He wondered
why Bellman hadn't flashed the green light. O'Brien rechecked his
gear: knife, rucksack, and canteens.

How many jumps, he thought, can a man make before his luck
runs out? Every one, they said, except the last one.

Sonny Bellman turned to the man in the right-hand seat.
"Approaching jump time."

The man nodded, stood, and squeezed behind his seat to retrieve
his parachute pack.

Bellman said, "I wonder if he's going to be angry at me."

The man said, "Mr. O'Brien enjoys surprises."

"He likes to jump alone. But I suppose it's all right."

"No one will mention it to you. I promise." Peter Thorpe raised
a heavy rubber mallet and swung it down viciously at the base of the
pilot's skull. Bellman made a short sound of surprise, then slumped
forward toward the control yoke. Thorpe yanked him back, then
reached over and engaged the autopilot. The aircraft continued to
track straight ahead, holding course, speed, and altitude.

Thorpe looked at his watch and yawned. "Christ, what a weekend."

He strapped on his parachute, opened the door, and entered the cabin.

The light from the open cockpit door caught O'Brien's eyes and he turned toward it, squinting. The door closed again, throwing the cabin in near darkness except for the single red light.

Thorpe moved wordlessly toward O'Brien.

O'Brien said, "Bellman? What's wrong?"

Thorpe yawned again. "Jesus, Pat, why would you want to jump into the Pine Barrens on a Sunday night?" Thorpe stopped a few feet from O'Brien. "Most people your age are playing checkers."

O'Brien put his hand on his survival knife. "What are you doing here?"

"Everybody has a *shtick*—that means panache—mine don't always go over so well. I thought I'd cultivate yours." He chuckled softly. "Do you mind?"

"I mind that you didn't ask."

"Sorry, Pat." Thorpe peered out the side window. "Blue moon. Should be full in a few weeks. There's a shooting star. Make a wish."

O'Brien glanced at the cabin door a few feet away.

Thorpe turned quickly toward him. "Listen, Pat, this Talbot business has me worried."

O'Brien didn't reply, and the drone of the engines outside seemed to fill the cabin. The moon shone through the windows now, and Thorpe's body cast elongated shadows on the far wall.

Thorpe said, "In fact, Patrick, *you* worry me."

"You ought to be worried. We're very close."

"Are you? I wonder."

O'Brien spoke in a controlled voice. "What is your motive?"

Thorpe shrugged. "I'm not certain. Not political. I mean, who in their right mind would side with those morons? Really, did you ever meet such a drab, boring bunch of ill-bred clods? I've been to Moscow twice. Jesus, what a shithole."

"Then why?" O'Brien unclipped the strap of his knife sheath.

Thorpe saw the movement in the red light. "Forget it, Pat."

O'Brien said, "Just tell me *why*."

Thorpe scratched his head, then said, "Well, it's very complex. It has to do with danger.... Some men jump from airplanes...others race cars...I commit treason. Every day is an adventure when you commit a capital offense. When you know that each day could be your last. You remember?"

O'Brien said, "You're sick, Peter."

"Probably. So what? Insanity, like a drug addiction, has to be fed. The Company provides food, to be sure, a veritable feast for most appetites. But not for mine. I need the ultimate nourishment. I need the blood of an entire nation."

"Peter...listen, if you want to alter history—and I suppose that is your ultimate motive—you can do it by helping us foil their plans. You could become a triple. That would be the crowning act of—"

"Oh, be quiet. You're too glib. Damned lawyer. Listen, how often do you get the chance to see a nation die? Think of it, Patrick—a highly developed, complex civilization succumbing to its own advanced technology. And I can stand on a hill and watch—watch the end of one human epoch and the beginning of another. How many people throughout the ages have been in so unique a position to *cause* such a sudden and catastrophic shift in the course of this planet's history?"

O'Brien listened to the droning of the engines, then spoke in a voice that suggested he'd accepted what Thorpe said, but had a last discomforting thought.

"All right, Peter. But what kind of world will it be? Could *you* live in such a world?"

Thorpe waved his hand in a motion of dismissal. "I'm pretty adaptable." He laughed.

"And what would you do for an encore? There'd be nothing left for you. No one to betray—"

"That's enough!"

O'Brien wanted to ask how this would all come about, but as a trained intelligence officer who knew he was facing his own death, there was no reason to indulge himself by satisfying his curiosity. He was not going to be able to report or act on the information, and the more he asked Thorpe, the more Thorpe would know how little or how much O'Brien already knew.

Thorpe seemed to read O'Brien's mind. "How far along are you, Patrick?"

"I told you. Close. You won't pull it off."

"Bullshit." Thorpe rubbed his chin, then said, "Katherine once told me, and I've heard elsewhere, that you're one of the best natural intelligence men on either side. You're brave, resourceful, cunning, imaginative, and all that....So...I know you're good...but how good? I mean, if you suspected me, why didn't you act before I got to you? I should have been snatched, drugged, tortured, and interrogated at least a year ago. Are you slowing up, old-timer? Did you let Katherine's feelings for me get in the way? Or perhaps you didn't suspect me. Yes, that's it. You really don't know anything."

"I've been on to you for years, Peter."

"I don't believe—"

The Beeehcraft hit a small air pocket and bounced. Thorpe lost his balance and fell to one knee. O'Brien, who had hoped and stalled for that air pocket, immediately lunged toward the door.

Thorpe drew a gun from under his Windbreaker, aimed, and fired. A loud, deafening report filled the cabin.

O'Brien, his hand on the door lever, lurched forward, collided with the door, and careened back, toppling onto the deck. Thorpe aimed and fired again. A short, popping sound echoed in the cabin.

O'Brien lay sprawled on his back at Thorpe's feet, holding his chest. Thorpe knelt beside him, and shone a flashlight on the chest wound. Thorpe spoke softly, almost comfortingly. "Just relax, Pat. The first one was a rubber stun bullet. Probably cracked a rib. The second was a sodium pentothal capsule." Thorpe saw where the gelatin capsule had hit the thick nylon harness strap. He ran his hand under O'Brien's shirt and felt a wetness where the skin had been broken. "I think you got enough of it."

Thorpe rocked back on his haunches. "We have some talking to do, my friend, and about two hours' fuel left to do it—and about six more drugs to go through if necessary."

O'Brien felt the drug taking hold in his brain. He shook his head violently, then grabbed for his knife and brought it out in an upper-cut motion, slicing through Thorpe's left nostril.

Thorpe fell back, his hand to his face, the blood running between his fingers. "Bastard . . . you sneaky . . ."

O'Brien began to rise, then stumbled back. He sat braced against the fuselage, holding his knife to his front.

Thorpe aimed his gun again. "Would you like to find out what the third bullet is? It's not lead, but you'll wish it was."

O'Brien's arm dropped and his knife rested in his lap.

Thorpe pressed a handkerchief to his nose and waited a full minute, then said, "Feel better, Patrick? Okay, that was my fault for underestimating you. No hard feelings. Let's begin. What is your name?"

"Patrick O'Brien."

"What is your occupation?"

"Lawyer."

"Not quite, but close enough." Thorpe asked a few more warm-up questions, then said, "Do you know a man named Talbot?"

"Yes."

"What other name does he go by?"

O'Brien did not speak for some time, then answered, "I don't know."

Thorpe made a sound of annoyance, then asked, "Were you on to me?"

"Yes."

"Were you really?" He thought a moment, then removed a Syrette from his pocket. "I don't think you got enough sodium pent. Let's try something different." He moved cautiously toward O'Brien, reached out with his free hand, and pulled the knife away. With his other hand he pushed the Syrette against O'Brien's shoulder. The spring-loaded needle pumped five cc's of Surital into O'Brien's body.

Thorpe knelt a few feet from O'Brien. "Okay, we'll give that a minute or so." Thorpe found his cigarettes and put one in his mouth. The gun still trained on O'Brien, he took his Dunhill lighter and struck a flame.

O'Brien saw Thorpe's eyes close reflexively and made his move. He half stood, reached out, and pulled the door handle. The handle disengaged and the door began to slide open, letting in a powerful rush of cold air along with the rumbling sound of the two engines.

Thorpe lunged for O'Brien and caught his ankle as O'Brien back-rolled into the opening. Thorpe yanked on the man's leg, twisting as he did, and began to pull him in.

O'Brien let out a moan of pain but continued to arch back farther, getting his upper torso and arms into the powerful slipstream.

Thorpe braced his legs on either side of the open door and pulled with all his strength, swearing loudly over the din, "You old bastard! You foxy son of a—" Thorpe felt himself losing the battle against the slipstream as more of O'Brien's body was dragged out into space. O'Brien kicked at him with his free leg.

Finally, Thorpe screamed, "All right, you son of a bitch! Die!" He slid his feet away from the doorframe and felt himself yanked headlong out into the slipstream, still holding O'Brien's ankle.

Thorpe looked up instinctively and saw the Beechcraft's navigation lights disappearing into the blue moonlit night.

They both fell, at the terminal velocity of 110 miles an hour, 161 feet per second, at which rate, Thorpe knew, they had less than 80 seconds to pull the rip cords.

Thorpe clutched at O'Brien's leg and craned his head upward. He saw O'Brien's right hand going for his rip cord. Thorpe wrapped both arms around O'Brien's leg and twisted his body in a sharp torquing motion, causing them both to spin.

O'Brien's arms were outstretched now and he tried to bring them back to his body. Thorpe saw the man's fingers clawing toward the rip cord on his chest. Thorpe reached up and grabbed the cross harness running across O'Brien's abdomen and pulled himself up until they were chest-to-chest and face-to-face. Thorpe wrapped his arms around O'Brien's shoulders and drew him close into a bear hug. Thorpe stared into O'Brien's face, inches from his own. He shouted, "Do you know who Talbot is?"

O'Brien's eyes were half shut and his head began to loll sideways. He mumbled something that Thorpe thought sounded like "Yes."

Thorpe shouted again. "What is Talbot's name!" Thorpe saw O'Brien's features contort into a twisted expression of pain and his teeth sink into his lower lip, drawing a stream of blood over his face. *Heart attack.*

Thorpe looked down. They had dropped, he estimated, over ten thousand feet. They had a mile or so to go. Thorpe looked back at O'Brien's chalk-white face and was certain that Patrick O'Brien would never pull his rip cord. Thorpe shouted into O'Brien's ear. "Geronimo and all that shit! Happy landing!"

He released his grip on O'Brien and they began to drift apart. O'Brien's unrestrained arms flew up over his head. Thorpe reached out and gave him a vigorous shove, sending him tumbling away.

Thorpe looked at the ground that was coming at him very fast. "Oh, shit!" He yanked on the rip cord and looked up.

In a split second, he thought, depending on how the chute came out and opened, he might be too late. If it didn't open at all, it was much too late for the emergency chute.

The black nylon chute shot upward nicely, like a plume of smoke, then billowed as the canopy began filling with air. Thorpe forced himself to look down. About three hundred feet. Two seconds to splat. Thorpe felt an upward jerk as he heard the snap of the canopy fully spread out. He looked down to see where O'Brien would fall, but lost sight of him in the dark ground clutter of the forest below. He thought he heard the sound of snapping wood followed by a thud.

Thorpe was fully decelerated now and floated about seventy-five feet from the earth. He spotted a small sandy clearing amid the moonlit scrub pine and tugged hard on his risers, sliding toward the nearby patch of open ground.

Thorpe tucked his legs up, and hit. He shoulder-rolled, then jumped to his feet and pulled the quick-release hook. The chute drifted a few feet off in the gentle breeze. He brushed the sand from his hands and face. "Not bad." He felt that incredible high that comes after a safe landing. "Damned good."

As he gathered his parachute, he gave a passing thought to O'Brien. The man was a worthy opponent. He'd expected more trouble from the pilot and less from O'Brien, considering his age. But old foxes were tough foxes. That's how they got to be old.

He wondered what the authorities would make of an aircraft that crashed in the foothills of the Pennsylvania Alleghenies, without warning, far off-course, and with its passenger a mushy heap in New Jersey. His laughter broke the stillness of the spring night.

Thorpe stuffed his parachute into its pack and extended the aerial of a homing transmitter. He sat on a mound of sand, dabbed at his bloody nose, then broke out a bag of chocolate kisses and waited for the helicopter.

This night had two final victims to claim, and like a slaughterer in an abattoir, he had to work fast before the sheep became panicky and stampeded.

At least, he thought, *he was helping to eliminate suspects.*

CHAPTER THIRTY

The small LOH helicopter carrying Peter Thorpe landed at the West 30th Street Heliport on the Hudson River. Thorpe finished changing into sport jacket, tie, and slacks.

The pilot, under contract to Lotus Air, a CIA proprietary company, knew neither his passenger's name nor his mission. Neither had he exchanged a single word with him, nor had he even looked at him. If in a week, or a year, the news reported a body found with an unopened parachute in the Jersey Pine Barrens, the pilot would put two and two together and come up with zero.

The LOH swung out over the river and disappeared into the night. Thorpe watched, then took the pack containing his gathered parachute, clothing, and rock weights, and dropped it in the river.

He walked the dark, desolate streets by the riverfront and entered a telephone booth. He dialed the Princeton Club and was connected to West. "Nick, how are you?"

"Fine."

"Look, what are you doing now?"

"I thought I'd turn in. I have to get an early shuttle to D.C. tomorrow."

"Let me buy you a drink."

"I'm really not up for a drink."

"We'll make it an early evening. I'm really in the mood for a Negroni, and I hate to drink alone."

There was a short silence, then West's voice came back on the line. "All right...yes...where...when?"

"Meet you at my club. I'll be there in ten minutes." Thorpe hung up.

Peter Thorpe entered the Yale Club and sat on a small sofa beside West, who was staring at a martini on the coffee table. Thorpe ordered a Negroni and gave West a sidelong glance. He said, "I was afraid you wouldn't remember the code word."

West looked at Thorpe, and focused on the small butterfly bandage covering his left nostril, but didn't comment on it.

Thorpe spoke softly. "Look, Nick, this Talbot thing has really stirred up a hornet's nest. You should lay low for a while."

West nodded, then found his voice and said, "Who...them or us?"

"Our people. Langley has been on full alert all weekend. You know how it is. They start making decisions right and left, getting themselves all hyper. They made a decision about you."

"What...?"

"Well, they don't actually plan to eliminate you, but they *will* put you in the mountains...you may be there some time."

West's eyes seemed more alert. "Then maybe I should just report in and—"

"No. Don't do that."

"But...I don't mind being put on ice."

"If you knew what they do to people in the mountains, you might think differently."

West stared at Thorpe with a mixture of curiosity and dread. "What...?"

Thorpe said, "Finish your drink." The Negroni came and Thorpe tasted it. "Not bad. I've never had one. Look, Nick, for the sake of appearances can you try to smile a bit and get some color in your face?"

West sipped on his martini.

Thorpe said, "Are you carrying?"

"No."

"Vest?"

"No...I don't wear that."

"How about a signal transmitter?"

West touched his belt buckle. "Micro-miniature. I can be tracked by air, auto, or ground receiver."

"Is it activated now?"

"No. Why should it be?"

"How do you activate it?"

West licked his lips. "You just grip it, top and bottom, and squeeze. It's got spring bars, like a wristwatch."

"Are you wired for sound?"

"No."

Thorpe knew West wasn't wired, because Thorpe was carrying a bug alert and it hadn't picked up anything.

He stared at West for some time, then said, "L-pills?"

West nodded. "Always."

"Where? What form?"

West hesitated, then tapped his class ring.

Thorpe glanced at West's Princeton ring. "Pill compartment?"

"No...the stone...cyanide suspended in rock sugar, colored with dye to match onyx. Thin coat of polyurethane to keep it shiny and keep it from melting.... You bite it—"

"And death is, as they say, instantaneous." Thorpe smiled. "What will those jokers think of next? Is that the only poison?"

West shook his head. "A conventional capsule. I forgot it. It's in my room."

Thorpe smiled. "You'd forget your ass if it wasn't nailed on."

"Tell me more about the mountains," West said.

Thorpe stared straight ahead as he spoke. "You go into the mountains as Nicholas West. You come out somebody else."

"That's the New Identity Program."

"Not quite. They go a bit further than plastic surgery and a new driver's license, my friend. Electric shock treatment, drugs, and hypnosis. By the time they're through with your brain, you're neutralized."

West stared, wide-eyed.

Thorpe continued. "This is the new meaning of neutralized. No more wet stuff for our own people if you haven't committed a crime. Just a little memory alteration so you're not a walking encyclopedia anymore."

West slumped back onto the sofa. "Oh...Good Lord...they can't do that."

"Right. It's illegal, and they'd never violate your civil rights. But let's suppose they would. Then what you have to do is go underwater for a while. Keep your brain out of their hands."

West finished his martini. "When...when do I have to—"

"When? Tonight! There is no tomorrow."

West said, "My things...?"

"Things? What things?"

"You know...clothes...books..."

Thorpe laughed. "If you let them take you to the mountains, you won't even remember your name, let alone what you own. Don't worry about idiot details. On the other hand, you do need some insurance policies for yourself. If you had insurance, tucked away, spring-loaded to be released under certain circumstances, then you could call your own shots."

West rubbed his face. "I can't get any insurance now."

Thorpe considered a moment, then said, "Maybe you could get into your office early in the morning, act natural, collect some documents—maybe some computer printouts—then run."

West was quiet for a long time, then looked up. "Maybe, if I could access my department's computer from here...from your computer at the Lombardy..."

Thorpe nodded slowly, but said nothing.

West glanced at him. "I guess that's the way to do it."

"Seems like it."

"But...how could we...I...do that? The entry would leave an audit trail, leading right back to you."

Thorpe replied, "Would it?"

"Yes. It's very secure. It will record your entry, plus the information that was accessed, and identify your computer station. Langley will see it immediately."

Thorpe spoke in a casual tone. "Once I'm into your computer, I can do whatever the hell I goddamned please. If I can get in, I can erase all evidence of my penetration on my way out."

West looked at him for a long time, then said, "The computer won't allow that. It will tell them—"

Thorpe smiled. "I make buddies with computers real fast, once I shake hands with them." He lit a cigarette. "You see, it's like the difference between rape and seduction. Both involve penetration, but one is violent and clumsy, the other tender. After I fuck your computer, it won't tell the cops. Okay? Let me worry about my technique."

West nodded in acquiescence.

"Look, Nick, the only real problem we've got is if they've had the foresight to negate your access code—the modern equivalent of confiscating your key to the executive washroom."

West forced a weak smile.

Thorpe continued, "But if we act soon—tonight—I think we can reasonably assume no one has thought to tell the computer that you are persona non grata. Tomorrow it will be one of the first things they do. Step one in making you an unperson."

West nodded and brought his drink to his lips. His hand was shaking. "Just tell me," he said softly, "why are you taking this risk for me?"

Thorpe leaned over the coffee table. "I'm not a nice guy, Nick. But some of the people we work for are not nice either." He let out a deep breath. "If I let them scramble your brains and put you to work washing the windows on the farm, then I couldn't live with myself...I mean, I couldn't face Katherine, or Ann..."

West's face dropped at the mention of Ann. He ordered another martini from a passing waiter.

Thorpe continued, "Also, quite honestly, I want to pick your computer's brain. As it turns out, my wishes coincide tonight with your needs."

"Why do you want to pick my computer's brains?"

"As I told you several times, Nick, I need information on the old boys to recruit for my Domestic Contact Service."

West nodded. He'd always thought that these computerized

dossiers of amateur spies were being unreasonably withheld from Thorpe. West said, "But I would require that I be present when you access the computer."

"I wouldn't have it any other way." Thorpe stubbed out his cigarette. "I know you're loyal, Nicko. But you've read enough case histories to know that even loyalty is not insurance against some of those fucked-up paranoids in a position to do you harm. Your loyalty should end when theirs does. They're not the government or the nation. You know that, Professor."

West ran his hands over his face and finally said, "But . . . why . . . ?" His voice was filled with anguish. "What did I do?"

"Oh, Christ, Nick, we've been over this a dozen times. You didn't *do* anything. So fucking what? You *know* too much. So do a lot of other people, but in your case they get very nervous. You're not real Company. You were recruited by a fluke whim of some past director, and everyone forgot about you and your department until one day they realized you had too much on some of the bosses. That's the bottom line. The Moscow-wants-Nick shit is just a cover to justify getting rid of you."

West looked nervously around the big lounge. "Please, Peter. Lower—"

"Oh, calm down. This is the Yale Club, for Christ's sake. Half the illegal business in the nation is conducted in this lounge." Thorpe stood. "Well, think it over. I'm not pushing. It's not that important to *me*."

West grabbed Thorpe's arm. "All right. All right. Just tell me what to do. Where can I go tonight?"

Thorpe took a key from his pocket and looked around. He said, "Room 1114. That's where you can go. There's a man up there. An actor. He knows nothing. His main attribute is that he looks like you, God help him and his career. Change clothes with him. He'll leave here, pipe in mouth, and with luck he'll draw off anyone who's watching you. That probably includes a dozen CIA, KGB, and O'Brien goons. With more luck, he'll get into your room at your club undetected and no one will realize we've done a bait-and-switch until morning. Buys lots of time."

West stood, then said suddenly, "That's how Carbury disappeared."

"So what? You want originality? This works. I got suckered with it once myself. You just sit in Room 1114 until someone comes for you. There's no phone in the room, so you won't be tempted to call out. I left you a spy novel to read." Thorpe smiled.

West nodded and Thorpe dropped a key into West's jacket. Thorpe patted his shoulder. "Take it easy, Nick. See you at the Lombardy before dawn. Follow instructions."

Thorpe watched West walk forlornly to the elevator bank. The elevator came and West got on without anyone seeming to take notice.

Thorpe descended the staircase and stopped at the landing. In the lobby, he picked out a man and a woman reading. They could be working for anyone. Thorpe smiled to himself. Spies watching spies. It occurred to him, too, that the FBI and the NYPD might also be represented tonight, compliments of Tony Abrams. Undoubtedly the police were on *his* case, not West's. The thought of being followed by city detectives was distasteful. A frown passed over his face. *Abrams.* Who the hell would have figured a wild card like that? Abrams had been a soft target on Friday night. But now he was a hard target. A concrete reinforced missile silo. Yet he was vulnerable. He was vulnerable through Katherine.

Thorpe waited on the landing overlooking the lobby and surveyed the people below. By now everyone knew that he and West had had a drink together on the evening of what was to be West's disappearance. But that could not be helped.

Nicholas West was a man who was hard to get at. Thorpe was one of the few people who had access to him and to some extent had his confidence. Kidnappings of protected people were difficult, which is why it was better sometimes to let a man kidnap himself.

The man who looked like West came down the stairs wearing West's clothes and smoking a pipe. He fell in beside Thorpe without a word. They quickly descended to the lobby, Thorpe at an oblique angle in front of the man at first, then the man drawing abreast as they crossed the lobby to the doors, blocking himself from direct view. None of the people seated stared, but within a few seconds the man and the woman rose to follow.

Outside, Thorpe spotted at least two more, but in the street lighting he knew that no one doubted they were following Thorpe and West. They headed toward the Princeton Club. Thorpe felt, rather than saw, a veritable parade behind him. He hoped they didn't trip over each other. He laughed. Christ, what a circus. He said to the man next to him, "I'll get you into the room at the Princeton Club, but you've got to change your appearance and get out before dawn. Did that jerk give you his key?"

The man nodded. "Who was that other guy in the room? I didn't expect anyone else in there. He never said a word. Looked sort of tough."

"He's another actor. Actors all over the place these days."

Thorpe looked up the street. New York went about its business while he was acting out a comedy that would turn to tragedy very soon. Thorpe wondered what the city would look like after the July Fourth weekend. He was sorry he wouldn't be in town to see it.

Peter Thorpe walked into the University Club lounge. There were only two men sitting at a small table, and Thorpe recognized them as members. He sat on a barstool. "Donald, you still here?"

The bartender turned and smiled, then checked his watch. "Another five minutes. We close at midnight tonight. What's your pleasure, Mr. Thorpe?"

"Oh, just a club soda."

Donald nodded. "Good Sunday-night drink. How was your weekend?"

"It had its ups and downs."

Donald put a small bottle of Schweppes on the bar and opened it. "I think I saw you on the news. The camera did a shot of the crowd at the armory. Some party!"

"Right." Thorpe poured the club soda into an ice-filled glass.

"Listen, I'm in arrears here. Don't put that on a chit." He slid a dollar across the bar and Donald palmed it and stuffed it in his pocket.

Thorpe said, "Has anyone spoken to you about that Edwards guy?"

Donald nodded gloomily. "Cop named Spinelli. Hey, I didn't tell him about the envelope."

Thorpe said, "Oh, you could have. I have to speak to Spinelli anyway, and I'll tell him. So, if you did, no problem." Thorpe squeezed a lemon wedge in his glass.

Donald poured himself a Coke. "Well . . . I didn't know, and I figured you wanted it on the q.t. So I didn't say anything. I wanted to check with you first. Then I could say later I just forgot. You know?"

"Sure. I appreciate it." Thorpe drained off the club soda.

Donald looked around and spoke quietly. "What's with this Edwards guy? His name's Carbury, right? You knew that."

Thorpe shrugged. "I don't really know much—" Thorpe suppressed a belch. "Excuse me. That felt good. . . . No, I don't really know. They think he got mugged. Maybe stuck."

"Oh, Jesus. That don't look good. I mean a high-class Englishman and all. Gives the city a bad name." He shook his head sadly, then said, "There was nothing about it in the papers."

"Really? By the way, when did Spinelli speak to you?"

"Oh . . . Friday night. When the cops got here to look at Edwards' room. He only asked me a few questions. But then he came back Saturday afternoon, about four. When I got on duty. This time he was a little more pushy. He had a whole bunch of questions, and I got the feeling he spoke to you already. But then I thought it might've been that guy you were with Friday night. You remember?"

Thorpe nodded. "But you say you didn't mention I was looking for this guy Edwards?"

"No. Honest. Hey, fuck them. That's none of their business. Right? I figured you could tell them if you wanted them to know. Members' privacy got to be protected. Right?"

"Right. When is your appointment downtown?"

Donald looked a bit surprised and uncomfortable. "Tomorrow.

My day off. Who needs it?" Donald changed the subject. "Hey, that July Fourth thing. I'd like to work that... but, you know, we get triple time on a holiday."

"No kidding? I might do it myself." Thorpe laughed. "Well, no problem. Do you drive?"

"No, I guess I need transportation, too."

"You got it." Thorpe looked at his watch. "Well, that's it for me." He slipped Donald a twenty-dollar bill. "Thanks."

"Thank *you*."

Thorpe slid off the barstool. "Where you heading?"

The bartender shrugged. "Home, I guess. Nothing happening on a Sunday night."

"No, there isn't. Subway, cab, or bus?"

"Subway. North Bronx."

"Be careful. Banjos and bongos."

"Hey, tell me about it."

"I just did."

CHAPTER THIRTY-ONE

Katherine Kimberly sat up straight in bed, her heart beating rapidly as her hand groped for the Browning automatic on the night table. She stopped moving and remained motionless, trying to get her bearings. *Telephone. Damned telephone.* She took a long breath and picked up the receiver. "Yes?" She looked at her clock. It was a few minutes before six.

Thorpe's voice came on the line. "Good morning. Did I wake you?"

She cleared her throat. "No. I had to get up to answer the phone anyway."

Thorpe laughed. "Terrible joke. Are you running today?"

"Yes. Where were you last night? I tried to reach you until midnight."

"Ah, the wicked walk at night. Old Latin proverb."

"Latin or otherwise, it doesn't answer the question."

"The question cannot be answered over an unsecured telephone, my sweet. When are you going to learn the business?"

"Don't lecture me."

"Sorry. Listen, are you going to Van Dorn's bash?"

She sat back against the headboard and took a glass of water from the night table. She finished it, then said, "You called me at six to ask that?"

"I didn't want to miss you. I knew you'd be running. It starts at about four. Fireworks and music begin at sundown."

"Oh, God...."

"I enjoy the show. Listen, I've got my boat at the South Street Seaport. Meet me at...let's say, four."

"I guess you don't want to drive?"

"No, I want to float. Beat the holiday traffic. We can be at Glen Cove Marina in forty minutes."

She said, "Do you know if Pat O'Brien is going? I haven't heard from him."

Thorpe replied, "You know, if he wasn't an older man, and your boss, I'd be jealous of your attentions toward him."

"I'm fond of him."

"Everyone is. He's a gentleman. I try to emulate him. Anyway, I spoke to him yesterday. He can't make it."

"Oh...how about Nick? How many people will the boat hold?"

"I can get five in. But Nick had an early meeting in Washington, holiday notwithstanding. He must be on the way to the airport by now. Don't you want to ride alone with me?"

"I just think that you ought to offer someone a lift. Maybe the Grenvilles."

"They ran back to the suburbs as soon as the police got through with them Saturday morning."

"What do you think of what happened?"

Thorpe didn't speak for some time, then said, "Suspicious. We'll discuss it later. Anyway, I'll offer Claudia a lift."

Katherine looked out her bedroom window. There was a hint of dawn penetrating the alleyway outside her building. She said, "You heard about Arnold, too, of course."

"Of course. The police are looking for you."

"I'll see them in my office Tuesday."

"Real lawyer. Where are you running this morning?"

"Brooklyn."

Thorpe said, "Are you running alone?"

"Why do you ask?"

"Well, be careful of muggers."

"I haven't yet met a mugger who could keep up with me." She hesitated, then said, "Tony Abrams is running with me."

Thorpe didn't respond for a second, then said, "Ah, that's interesting."

"Why?"

"I didn't know he ran. Why him? He's not your speed, you know."

"I'm running right by his place."

She let the silence drag out, then said, "You're welcome to come along. It might do you some good."

"You're welcome to lift weights with me, practice karate, and navigate the obstacle course at the Farm."

"I'm not in the mood for one-upmanship. Also, I think your behavior Friday night was crude and uncalled-for. What's gotten into you?"

"I'm under some pressure—"

"Also, you weren't around Saturday night, and all day Sunday. And now you call me at six—where are you anyway?"

"The Lombardy. Actually, I'm in the damned garret. With the computer. I've been working all night. All weekend. I'll explain it to you later."

She drew a deep breath. "Okay . . . I'll see you at four."

"Wait. I may be able to join you. When and where do you start?"

"City Hall at about seven. Then over the Brooklyn Bridge."

"Too early. Then where?"

"I should be at Tony Abrams' place by eight. He's at 75 Henry Street. If you're going to meet me, do it there, or later." She gave him the route she expected to follow.

Thorpe said, "I thought Abrams was staying at Thirty-sixth Street."

She didn't answer for a few seconds, then said, "I think he's moving around."

"Why? Scared?"

"Cautious. You should be too."

"And you. You can stay here at the Lombardy after tonight."

"I'll think about it."

"Okay, maybe I'll run into you in Brooklyn. If not, the Seaport at four."

Katherine hung up and got out of bed. She pulled on a short

kimono and went into the small living room. She bent over the couch. "Tony." She shook him.

Abrams opened his eyes and she could tell he hadn't been asleep. She said, "I'll shower first."

"Okay." He sat up and yawned.

She said, "I'm sorry about the couch."

He stretched. "What were our options?"

"Well...I could have slept on the couch...."

"There was barely room for me. And why let a good bed go to waste?"

"You know what I mean."

He put his legs over the side of the couch, keeping the blanket partly wrapped around him. He rubbed his eyes, yawned again, and said, "Did anyone try to kill you during the night?"

She smiled. "No."

"Me neither. I would have welcomed the excitement."

"I'll be finished shortly." She turned and reentered the bedroom through a paneled door.

Abrams stood in his shorts and touched his toes a few times. He retrieved his shoulder holster and revolver from under his pillow and laid them on the end table. He walked over to the small galley kitchen and found a pitcher of orange juice in the refrigerator. He poured some into a paper cup, then surveyed the room.

It was small, but tastefully done in a few good contemporary pieces. In an alcove was a desk piled high with paperwork. It was, he realized, a transparent acrylic desk and must have cost thousands. The building, which he knew Katherine owned, was ancient, at least a hundred years old, and there was not much to recommend the neighborhood except the fact that the realtors had named it West Greenwich Village, which was, he thought, stretching the geography a bit far.

Abrams walked to the single window, a double-hung sash that looked too warped to be workable, and glazed with glass that had swirls and bubbles in it. "Jesus, this place was old when Indians lived on the next block." The room also had a tilt, like the house on 36th Street.

Abrams looked down into the narrow street. It was picturesque. He peered up and down the block. The streetlights were still on, though a thin morning sunlight provided most of the illumination. The street looked quiet enough, and no one seemed to be hanging around.

He speculated on what this place said about Katherine Kimberly. He had pictured her as an East Side bitch whose major outdoor activity was watching the displays change in Bloomingdale's windows. Then he found out she was a runner, simpatico with O'Brien, whom Abrams respected, and all sorts of other positive things. "Just goes to show you..." There was, however, still Thorpe.

He sipped his orange juice as he regarded the interesting tilt to the room. The Kimberlys must have a penchant for crooked houses, he thought. A shrink might say that was a clue to why she was here—a nostalgic reminder of a happier childhood. Perhaps, too, the Village reminded her of Georgetown, where she'd lived with her mother.

Abrams heard a noise behind him and spun around.

Katherine stood at the bedroom door. "Oh...I'm sorry..."

"That's all right. This is what I run in."

She suppressed a smile and kept her eyes on his face. *Boxer shorts. Plain white.* She thought of Peter's multicolored bikini underwear. She said, "I wanted to tell you to help yourself. I see you have. Make coffee if you want. There's...well...something in the refrigerator."

"Yes, a light bulb, and it's burned out."

She laughed. "I don't do much cooking. There *are* eggs."

Abrams looked at her. He'd had conversations like this before, but they were postcoital conversations. This was not, and so it was clumsier. He said, "I'll have something when I get home."

She hesitated, then said, "Peter may join us somewhere along the route. I hope that's all right."

"He's your fiancé, not mine."

"It won't be awkward. I mean, I run with other men." She laughed. "That didn't sound right."

Abrams finished his juice, then said, "I'll take a taxi to my place and meet you about eight."

"Fine. If you walk down to Houston and Seventh, you can get a cab at this hour."

Abrams remembered a girl who had this sort of useful information printed, with a map, for her one-night stands. "Thanks."

She began to turn away, then asked suddenly, "Would you like to go to George Van Dorn's Memorial Day party this afternoon?"

Abrams shook his head. "One O'Brien function a weekend is enough."

"Well, think it over. All right? You can go out with Peter and me—by speedboat." She shook her head. "Oh, that sounds like I'm trying to bribe a child. What I mean is, it only takes about forty minutes by boat. You can take the train home if you're bored.... There will be people you know.... Why do I sound so patronizing?"

He walked across the living room and put his paper cup on the sink. She didn't sound patronizing, he thought. She sounded flustered. He said, "Actually, I have another engagement."

"Oh...well, I'd better get moving." She went into the bedroom and closed the door behind her, then reopened it again. "Where's my head this morning? Do you need to use the bathroom?"

"No," he answered, "go ahead. I'm fine for the next fifteen minutes or so. I can warm up for the run. Uphill, downhill."

She glanced at the uneven floor, gave him a look of mock annoyance, then disappeared again into the bedroom.

Abrams heard the shower go on. He picked up the telephone and dialed. "Spinelli. Abrams."

Captain Spinelli's voice came on the line, groggy and hoarse. "Well, the Wandering Jew. Where the fuck are you, Abrams? Why weren't you at your place?"

"I slept at Thirty-sixth Street."

"Like hell you did. Where are you?"

"Down in the West Village."

"Where in the West Village?"

"Apartment 4B. Listen, what did the ME determine as Arnold Brin's cause of death?"

"Accidental choking." Spinelli cleared his throat. "No evidence of foul play."

"There were files missing."

"Impossible to prove or to tie it in. What difference does it make? We know it was murder. How come you're not murdered yet?"

"The weekend's not over. Anything on the Thirty-sixth Street jumper?"

"Yeah. There was a scuffle on the roof. Three men. But I guess you know that. We got your prints on the fire escape, fella."

"Well, I had sense enough to climb down. How about the body?"

"Foreigner. Probably East European, though the clothes were all American brands. What happened up there? Who would want to kill *you*? Except me?"

"I'll tell you about it later. Meanwhile, keep an eye on Claudia Lepescu."

"We're keeping an eye on everyone—everyone we can find. I'm trying to get a line on this Kimberly broad. Would you believe we can't even find an address for her? Even Ma Bell has nothing on her. Everybody has a phone. Right? So she's using an alias. Can you believe a classy lawyer has an alias? We tried to run down a few other characters in this script, but there's nothing on them. Everyone must have an alias. Friggin' lawyers. But it's more than that. Right? Who are these people you're working for, Abrams? Where do they live?"

"O'Brien lives on Sutton Place, but I'm not sure of the address. Van Dorn has an estate in Glen Cove. The Grenvilles mentioned Scarsdale. Thorpe is at the Lombardy. Kimberly is at 39 Carmine Street. Check the Bar Association."

"They're shut down for the weekend. But I'm going to be at O'Brien's office bright and early Tuesday morning and I want everyone there. Including you, ace."

"Listen, did you call the CIA about Thorpe?"

"Yeah. They're stonewalling. Wait until *they* need a favor. Assholes. The FBI is cooperative, but they seem a little jumpy about this. Anyway, I checked Thorpe out through normal channels on the off chance he made a police file...."

Abrams could hear the sounds of Spinelli lighting up one of his deadly black panatelas, followed by a coughing fit. "Draw deep," he said.

"Fuck you." He got the cough under control, then said, "Nassau County DA file. About seven years ago. Thorpe and his wife, Carol, boating on Long Island Sound. She was lost at sea. There was a Coast Guard report also."

"Conclusions?"

"What the hell could they conclude? Accident. Boating accidents are near-perfect murders. According to something I read, the CIA has disposed of at least three people in Chesapeake Bay that way. Christ, they've taken out a trademark, copyright, and patent on it."

"Still, it could have been an accident."

"Absolutely. Only Peter and Carol knew for sure. Peter testified at the Coast Guard hearing. Carol was never found. They had a ceremony at sea for her. The husband was visibly upset. No indictment."

Abrams stayed silent for some time, then said, "I guess you can't use that one too often."

"No. You're allowed one every seven years or so. One wife, one business partner, one brother-in-law. Law of averages. So I did check Coast Guard reports for about twenty years back. Nothing. Then I realized that not all waterways come under Coast Guard jurisdiction. So I checked with some state governments. Maryland had what I wanted. Chesapeake Bay inlet, 1971. Man overboard. Captain Peter at the helm. He comes about to rescue the unfortunate man and...oh, no, he runs over the guy's head. But all is not lost. The man is still alive. Captain Peter reverses the screws, as they say, and accidently backs into the poor bastard, giving him a shave, a haircut, and a lobotomy. Anyway, this accident looked a lot like Company business. There were no legal proceedings." Spinelli paused, then said, "This man is a cold-blooded killer."

"Don't jump to conclusions."

"Yeah. Anyway, how is James Allerton involved in this? That's one reason everyone seems so jumpy. That's *the* James Allerton, right?"

"Right. Allerton is actually Thorpe's adoptive father."

"No kidding?"

"No kidding. Allerton is also a friend of the missing Colonel Carbury. Did you find any trace of Carbury?"

"No, but I know how he disappeared. It *was* a double."

"You found the double?"

"Sure did."

"Who hired him?"

"I asked him, but he's not talking."

"Dead?"

"Bingo. Tugboat found him as a floater. Lower harbor, heading for France. It came through homicide as an apparent suicide, but I'm real sharp, Abrams. All unidentified stiffs and suspicious deaths were going through me. Long story, but the prints were on file for a cabaret license. I checked with Actors Equity, and someone who knew him came down and made a positive ID. The stiff is a guy named Larson."

"How did you connect him to Carbury?"

"Well, he's an actor, for one thing. Also, we got a wire photo of Carbury from England and a description—height, weight, age. This guy Larson could pass for him. Larson wasn't wearing Carbury's clothes, though. On the other hand, the ME feels that Larson was dressed after he was dead. He was probably drowned in a bathtub or a bucket of water, stripped, dressed in his own clothes, and tossed in the river." Spinelli paused. "We're dealing with very foxy people here. Serious people."

"Right." Yet, he thought, for all this cleverness and all this cloak-and-dagger nonsense, it all boiled down to a city homicide squad doing their job. "Nice work, Spinelli."

"Oh, thank you, Mr. Abrams. Maybe that's why I'm a captain and you're still in school."

"Maybe. Listen, did you speak to the bartender again? Donald?"

"We had an appointment for this morning at nine, but Donald came in early. Around one A.M. He's on the slab next to the actor. Mugged up in The Bronx. Pelham Bay, IRT station. Ice pick through the top of his head."

"Jesus Christ—"

"Right. Hey, the ice pick was a nice touch, though—get it? Bartender...ice pick...Well, anyway, how come you're still alive? How we gonna find you, Abrams? Crushed to death under a mountain of subpoenas?" Spinelli laughed loudly.

Abrams trailed the telephone cord to the refrigerator and poured another cup of juice. He took a long drink, then said, "Nicholas West. You watching him?"

"Yeah. Everybody's watching that sucker. Who the hell is he?"

"A man with lots of answers."

"Yeah, well, we're not even allowed to talk to him. Anyway, he's tucked in at the Princeton Club."

"Okay, how about—"

"Hold on. Now it's your turn, Abrams. Fill me in on what you know. What's this with the O'Brien firm, for instance? Why is all this shit going down on my turf? Why not Newark, or Berlin or someplace?"

"This phone may not be secure."

"Oh, cut the shit."

Abrams realized he wasn't going to tell Spinelli anything about O'Brien and the OSS Veterans, and this surprised him, but not completely. He heard the shower shut off. "I have to run—"

"Your place is staked out, you know. So is Thirty-sixth Street."

"I know. Stake out 39 Carmine, too. Thanks."

"Yeah. Thanks my ass. As soon as you go home to get your socks, I'm pulling you in. I have a warrant for your arrest. You'll be better off in the slammer anyway."

Abrams finished the orange juice. "Look, cancel the warrant and I'll be in your office at nine tomorrow morning."

"I had an appointment with the bartender at nine *this* morning. You people keep turning up early in the morgue."

"I have things to do today. I'll know more tomorrow."

Spinelli let a long time go by before responding. "Okay. Tomorrow at nine." He hesitated, then said, "Hey...Tony...watch yourself. Okay?"

"Okay." Abrams hung up and stood in the middle of the living room. He heard Katherine's hair dryer go on. He figured he should put his pants on to walk through her bedroom to the shower. On the other hand, she'd already seen him in his shorts, and he didn't want to appear unduly modest or shy. The logistics of these things got sort of muddled.

The hair dryer went off and she came to the door wearing the kimono. "Are you going to shower? I'll dry my hair in the bedroom. There are shaving things in the bathroom . . . I have disposable razors and toothbrushes."

"Does one have my name on the handle?"

"Possibly. Look under *T.*" She went back into the bedroom and he heard the dryer go on again.

Abrams hung his holster over his shoulder and went into her bedroom. She was sitting at the vanity with brush and dryer and took no notice of him. He saw the bathroom door and went in, closing it behind him. The bathroom at least was modern, which was to say circa 1955.

He slipped off his shorts and stood in front of the mirror. Neatly laid out on the sink top were the disposable razor and toothbrush along with a can of aerosol shaving cream. There was a bottle of aftershave lotion sporting a little man playing polo. A haberdasher had tried to explain to him once why the little polo player was worth about twenty to thirty dollars more than, say, an alligator or a penguin. He sniffed the bottle. It was definitely Thorpe's scent.

Abrams shaved, then showered. He dried himself, passed on the aftershave lotion in favor of some witch hazel, then wrapped himself in the bath towel. Boxer shorts in one hand, gun and holster in the other, he opened the door and stepped into the bedroom.

She was standing in front of her dresser wearing only a pair of running shorts and holding a T-shirt in her hands. They held eye contact without speaking for what seemed like a long time, then Abrams turned and walked out of the bedroom.

Abrams sat on the couch and lit a cigarette. He had, he reflected, come a long way since Friday morning when he'd arrived at work to find a small stack of terse memos and notes on his desk, all signed *Kimberly.*

There was a knock on the bedroom door and Katherine called out, "May I come in?"

"Sure."

She entered the living room, dressed in white cotton shorts and the blue T-shirt, carrying her shoes and socks. She looked him up and down, dressed in the green bath towel. "You won't get far in that." She smiled, then sat in the armchair and pulled on her sweat socks. Abrams found himself looking at her legs.

After a few seconds of silence, they both said simultaneously, "I'm sorry—" then both smiled.

Abrams said, "I should have knocked."

"Well, I should have...dressed when I heard the shower running."

"We'll get it together next time."

She tied her running shoes. "I see you hung your clothes neatly on my kitchen table. Why don't you get dressed behind me while we talk?"

"Right." Abrams walked to the small round table in the corner and began dressing.

She said, "We can't both hide out here forever."

"No, but there is a certain safety in numbers." He tucked his shirt in and slipped his shoulder holster on. "I suggest that whoever is still alive by tonight stay at the house on Thirty-sixth Street. The police are watching it."

She nodded. "That sounds sensible. Claudia will enjoy the company."

Abrams didn't respond. He walked around the armchair and sat on the couch across from her. He put on his socks and shoes.

She stood, stretched, and touched her toes. "Well, this will be a good run. I'll meet you at your place in about an hour."

"Fine." He stood and slipped on his jacket. "Is there a group that meets at City Hall?"

"Yes. People leave in groups between seven and eight. I'll be all right."

He unbolted the door and looked into the small hallway, then turned back to Katherine. "Take a taxi to City Hall."

"Of course." She stood and looked at him. "Tony...you know, I'm starting to feel guilty about dragging you into this."

He smiled. "I had no plans for the long weekend anyway."

She didn't respond.

Abrams looked at her. "Where do you think we might meet Peter Thorpe?"

She stared back at him, then replied, "Anywhere along the route."

"Well, we'll keep a sharp eye out for him."

She nodded.

Abrams pulled the door closed behind him, drew his revolver, and began walking down the four flights of stairs.

CHAPTER THIRTY-TWO

Peter Thorpe walked the length of the long, dimly lit garret and stood beside the hospital gurney. He looked down at Nicholas West, who lay naked on the table, bathed in bright light, a black strap securing his legs, another across his chest and arms.

Beside the table were two intravenous stands, a heart monitor, a rolling cabinet that held medical instruments, and two electrical consoles. There were tubes and wires running from West's body. Anyone coming onto the scene would think they were seeing a terminal patient; in fact, they were.

Thorpe put on a pair of black wraparound sunglasses and regarded West for a few seconds, then asked, "How are you, Nicko?"

West managed to nod his head as he squinted into the blinding spotlight.

"Good." Thorpe bent closer to West. "Could be worse, you know."

Thorpe's head cast a shadow over West, and West was able to open his eyes for the first time in many hours. He stared up at the face hovering over him and focused on the black, curved sunglasses, trying to recall, in his drug-clouded mind, the name of an animal, then mumbled, "A mole...you're a mole...."

Thorpe laughed, then said, "When I was a boy, Nick, I used to follow those raised mole tunnels across the lawn. Sometimes I'd be rewarded at the end of a tunnel. I would see some slight movement....I'd carry a spade with me, and I'd drive that spade into the sod where the mole was burrowed, and cut the little guy in half."

West said nothing.

Thorpe smiled. "The image of that blind, stupid mole, thinking he was safe in his pathetic tunnel, eating his grubs, but leaving an unmistakable trail, always stayed with me, Nick. And when that spade severed him in half, I wondered what passed through his feeble brain. Why did nature provide so inadequately for his survival? Is there a spade poised above *my* head? We'll discuss that."

Thorpe moved back, and the blinding spotlight fell full on West's face again, forcing him to shut his eyes. Thorpe smiled, then turned to Eva. "How are his vital signs?"

The big Polish woman nodded. "He is a healthy man. Good blood pressure, heart rate, breathing." Eva checked the catheter inserted in West's penis, then stooped down and pointed to the urine-holding bag. "His water is clear."

Thorpe glanced at the lower shelf of the gurney. There was also a jar for collecting aspirated fluids from the lungs, and a rectal tube running through a hole in the gurney. Eva said, "There is no more solid waste."

Thorpe reached up and snapped off the spotlight. West opened his eyes and the two men stared at each other for some time. Finally, Thorpe spoke. "Poor Nick. But you always knew, didn't you, that you were doomed to wind up naked on a table like this?"

West nodded. "...knew..."

Thorpe leaned closer to West. "Did you ever think it would be my table?"

West opened his mouth and his words came out in slow, labored syllables. "Peter...please...don't do this to me...."

"Why not?" snapped Thorpe. "I've done it to people who deserved it less than you." Thorpe added, "To people I've respected more than you."

"Peter...for God's sake...I'll tell you whatever you want to know...please, this is *not* necessary...."

Thorpe looked at the red digital LCD readout. "The voice-stress analyzer says that was a lie, Nick." He looked at the polygraph paper. "And the lie detector says the same thing. You *know* what happens when you fib."

West shook his head violently. "No! No! No!"

"Yes, yes yes." Thorpe nodded to Eva, who was waiting expectantly with two alligator clips in her hands. She attached the clips to West's scrotum.

Thorpe moved the dial of the direct-current transformer.

"No! No! N—" West's face suddenly contorted into an agonized grimace and he screamed as his body convulsed. "Ahhh...Ahhh!"

Thorpe turned off the transformer. He said to West, "You know, Nick, it was I who perfected this method of interrogation. It's unofficially called the Thorpe Method. I always wanted something sinister named after me. Like Monsieur Guillotine's little gadget, or Lynch's law...."

West's eyes were rolled back and saliva ran from the corners of his mouth.

Thorpe went on, "It's a combination of mild drug doses, coupled with electric shock. I combine this with physical restraint to give the subject a feeling of helplessness." He yawned, "God, I'm tired."

"...Ooooh..."

Thorpe seemed not to hear. "Also, you're given a balanced diet of sugars, vitamins, and protein so your brain won't start shorting out. Do you realize that starved prisoners can't remember things they're being asked about, even if they wanted to talk? I also use some experimental memory drugs. Very advanced technique." Thorpe put his hand in his pocket and jingled some change. "And, of course, I have the voice and polygraph analyses so that you only get a jolt when you're lying. 'The professional interrogator must suppress his natural sadistic tendencies. To inflict pain for its own sake is counterproductive. It builds resentment and resistance on the part of the prisoner.' You only get it when you deserve it." He looked at Eva, then at West. "We must be modern. Agreed?"

West tried to speak, but his tongue seemed out of control and he made unintelligible sounds.

Thorpe patted West's thigh. "There, there. Cat got your tongue? Just relax a minute."

Eva said, "He is stalling. The electric shock makes him lose his tongue, but he pretends it is for longer than it is."

"Perhaps. But within a few days I'll have my way with him. When he's broken, he'll talk and talk and even volunteer information we haven't thought to ask for." Thorpe motioned to a video camera suspended on a boom. "And it will all be recorded in color and quality sound."

Eva snorted. "Americans are too in love with their gadgets."

Thorpe laughed as he pushed the rewind button on a video recorder, then hit the play button.

Eva grabbed West's head in a powerful grip and pulled back his eyelids.

A video monitor above West's face came to life and West's voice came out of a speaker: "No! No! N—!" followed by the sound of West's piercing scream.

West stared up at the image of himself screaming and twisting in agony.

Thorpe shut off the player. "You see what I did to you, Nick? How would you like to watch hours of reruns like that? It's almost as bad as the real thing, isn't it, pal? Look at you. You're sweating like a pig."

Eva made a noise of disgust.

Thorpe grinned. "Another refinement in the Thorpe Method is the use of pleasure to reinforce truth. For instance..." He poked West in the ribs. "Pay attention. Now, answer carefully. Is anyone other than you familiar with the contents of the Talbot file?"

West blinked and shook his head, then remembered that he had to answer in complete sentences. "No...except Ann....She is familiar with the Talbot file....No one else."

Thorpe kept his eyes on the two lie-analyzers. Then nodded. "Very good, Nick. Thank you." He nodded to Eva.

Eva loosened West's chest strap a notch and West took long, deep breaths. She poured mineral oil from a bottle and massaged it into West's sweaty shoulders.

Thorpe hit a button on the console and the soft strains of Beethoven's "Moonlight Sonata" filled the room. Thorpe said, "You have such saccharine taste in music, Nick."

Thorpe turned to Eva, who was now massaging West's legs. "I

tell you, Eva, I've seen it work a dozen times. Everyone tries to avoid pain, but that does nothing to satisfy the human psyche or to get the prisoner on your side. The body and mind also need pleasure." Thorpe shut off the music. "That was torture to *me.*" He laughed.

West cleared his throat. "Monster..."

Thorpe smiled. "Another Thorpe Method, Mr. West, is to let the prisoner vilify you. In the bad old days that would have gotten you a broken jaw. But as long as the analyzers show that you really believe that, you won't receive any pain."

"I do."

Thorpe nodded. "Also, I sometimes use sex if I feel the prisoner requires it as a reward for truth." He bent over West and said in a stage whisper, "Don't worry. If I use sex, it won't be her." He laughed. "That's no treat. I know—I have to service her once a week."

Eva looked flustered, but she smiled tightly as she wiped her oily hands on a towel.

Thorpe came closer to West. "Okay, Professor, let's continue. Why did you discount O'Brien as Talbot?"

West replied, almost dreamily, "He was being set up... no real evidence...he was being maneuvered into compromising situations...by Talbot...."

"How can you be so sure?"

"They tried to kill O'Brien...after the war...real attempt...hunting accident in Utah...bullet in the stomach...almost died...."

"I never knew that."

"Secret...in the files...."

"So why can't you deduce who it was who tried to frame O'Brien during the war? Why don't you know who Talbot is?"

"Guess...guess...three people...not one...Trinity...probably unknown to each other."

Thorpe rubbed his chin, then bent closer to West. "Could one of them be my father?"

West stared at Thorpe for a long time, then closed his eyes and drifted off.

Eva passed a vial of smelling salts under West's nose. West turned his face and Eva slapped him.

Thorpe repeated the question.

West nodded. "Yes...yes...it's possible...."

"How close was O'Brien to the truth?"

"He thought he was close."

Thorpe glanced at the analyzers. "That was a tricky way to answer, Nick. Don't get tricky on me."

Eva said, "You see, these gadgets can be fooled."

Thorpe smiled. "For a while. That's how I beat the Company's yearly interrogation. But coupled with torture, time, and technique, the Thorpe Method works."

Eva picked up a surgical scalpel from the instrument table. "If I remove one testicle, he will do whatever is necessary to protect the other one."

West turned his head toward her. "No!"

Thorpe said impatiently, "I'm the interrogator, not you, Eva. Leave."

Eva threw her scalpel down and stomped off.

Thorpe glanced at West and could see the terror in his eyes. Thorpe smiled. The final refinement in the Thorpe Method was this Damocles sword, or scalpel, hanging over the prisoner.

West said softly, "Peter, please...I can't think straight with her near me...."

"Now, now." Thorpe put his hand on West's arm. "We won't give her any reason to use the scalpel."

West nodded.

Thorpe pulled up a stool and sat beside the gurney. "All right, Professor, another method of mine is to let you ask some questions. Shoot."

West stared at Thorpe for some time, then asked, "Who do you work for?"

"The KGB, of course." He smiled. "I'm actually a major. The Russians love ranks. They think I'm honored to be a major. They're more rank conscious than the Nazis were."

"If you're a KGB officer, why don't you know who Talbot is?"

"They won't tell me that. They want me to see if I can discover it. If I can, then the CIA, or you, or O'Brien, can also."

"Who do you suspect?"

Thorpe smiled. "My father, for one. But I think Pat O'Brien is—was—on to someone else, who, as farfetched as it sounds, may also be Talbot."

"O'Brien—"

"Is dead, Nick. Next question."

West stayed silent for some time, then asked, "Carbury...?"

"I confess." Thorpe lit a cigarette. "After I had the double lead off Kate's private detectives, he was vulnerable. I picked the lock in his room, and when he returned to dress for dinner, I bashed his head in with a walking stick. I stuffed him in a plastic trash bag, along with the stick and his tuxedo, and dropped him out the window into the alley. He was collected later by friends of mine. Fortunately, he had his briefcase with him. I'll show you what was in it later. Unfortunately, however, I overlooked the blood on my cuff. Mr. Abrams did not overlook it. Mr. Abrams will pay with his own blood. Next question."

"You...madman..."

"Question!"

West licked his lips, then said, "Why is Talbot so important.... Why is Moscow ordering murders on American and British soil to protect him?...Why not get him out of the country...?"

Thorpe replied, "Obviously, Nick, they need him *in* the country."

"Why?"

Thorpe shrugged. "I'm not certain. But I do know that America's days are numbered. Most probably the end will come on the July Fourth weekend. That much I had to be told so I'd be prepared...and safe."

"First strike?"

"No." Thorpe dropped his cigarette on the floor. "I thought perhaps you knew something."

"No."

Thorpe's hand was already on the dial and he gave West a massive electrical shock.

West bellowed at the top of his lungs and his body strained against the straps. He bit his tongue and blood ran over his lips.

"Oh...oh...no..." Tears formed in his eyes and Thorpe wiped them away with a handkerchief. "There, there...why do you make me do that?"

West was sobbing. "Peter...please...try to understand...I'm conditioned to respond...give me a second chance...before you do that...."

Thorpe shook his head. "I'm reconditioning you, Nick. The child psychology books and animal behavior books all say that one must be consistent with rewards and punishments. The *Torturer's Handbook*—yes, there is such a thing; I helped rewrite it—says the very same thing. Do you understand that?"

"Yes, yes."

"And I promise you, I'll stick to the book. I'll never lose my temper with you, never act out of personal motivations, whether they be evil or benign. I've had other friends on this table."

"My God..."

"Now what do you know of the Soviet plan?"

West drew a deep breath and replied, "I think...it has to do with...Peter, listen...listen to me....They're going to kill you...they won't let you live knowing...this..."

Thorpe stared at the analyzers, then said softly, "You believe that, don't you?" He looked at his watch. "I don't have any more time for you right now." He slid off the stool. "First things first, which is one of Katherine's favorite aphorisms. The first thing I have to do is finalize the plans to kidnap her."

West managed to raise his head. "Who...?"

"Katherine. While I'm at it, I'll kill Abrams."

"Tony Abrams...? Why?"

"I don't like him. But from a practical standpoint, he could become a problem. Anyway, you'll have company soon. Kate will be lying next to you by this evening. What a chorus you'll make. Stereophonic singing."

"You're sick. Everyone knows it. Ann knows it, I know it—"

Thorpe reached for the dial, but hesitated, then took a deep breath and moved his hand away. "You will not bait me, you little shit."

"Temper..."

Thorpe leaned over West so that their faces were inches apart. "Let me give you a little news about your beloved Ann—"

"Ann..."

"Is dead."

"No. No."

"Yes....And I'm going to kill you, too. And I don't care that you know, because your knowledge of Ann's death, and your own forth-coming death, will in no way alter the outcome of your debriefing."

"You...you didn't...couldn't....She is *not* dead."

"She *is*." Thorpe put his finger on West's forehead and pushed. "That's where I'm going to put the bullet in your head. Do you believe that?"

"Y-y-yes."

Thorpe looked at the polygraph and voice analyzer. "That is one of the few questions that will produce an inconclusive response." He tapped West's forehead. "Believe it. Right here. *Bang!* And that's a favor because I have nothing against you personally. For people who've crossed me, death takes two weeks."

West stared at Thorpe, then said, "How could you...to Katherine...?"

Thorpe straightened up and began moving away. "On a profes-sional level, she has information that I'd like to have. Personally, I'd like to see the arrogant bitch strapped on a table howling her guts out. What a film that would make."

"Peter...if you have any soul...any heart at all—"

"I don't. And speaking of balls, keep an eye out for Eva."

"Peter...Katherine doesn't know anything I don't know."

"We'll find out. By tonight you'll both be trying to outscream each other to get my attention."

"Ann is *not* dead!"

"Stop worrying about the Kimberly girls, West. There's nothing you can do for them. Or for anyone, including yourself."

Thorpe walked to the doors then turned back. "Within a few hours I'll have the first edited videotapes of you and Katherine deliv-ered to Glen Cove. My Russian friends will be both enlightened and amused by them. They wanted you themselves, but as with most things they do, they torture badly."

West's voice carried across the room, surprisingly strong. "They're going to *kill* you, you fool."

"Not as long as I have you. Not as long as they need me. And I'll be certain they need me until—"

"The end. Then they'll liquidate you. You have no place in their plans."

"There's always a place for a man like me, Nicko." Thorpe stayed silent for some time, then said, "Within a few weeks, based partly on what you and Katherine tell me, we will know for certain if and how we can proceed. We will know if America is to live or die. But as for you two, you can consider yourselves already dead. Speak to you later, pal."

CHAPTER THIRTY-THREE

Katherine Kimberly ran onto the Brooklyn Bridge's board-walk and began the uphill climb. The morning had dawned clear and cool, and the view was magnificent. The boards beneath her feet were resilient and, as always, she reveled in their springiness. She began the downhill portion and picked up her speed.

A few vehicles passed in either direction and she found her-self looking more at them than at the view. A brown van came up behind her and she heard it slow. She increased her stride and looked back over her shoulder. The van drew abreast of her and kept pace. She began an all-out sprint and caught up to a small group of joggers.

The van drew abreast again and a man looked out the open passenger-side window. He called out. "Hey! Want a ride?"

She glanced at him and in a split second, based on instinct and experience, knew he was harmless. She ignored him and kept run-ning. The van pulled ahead and disappeared.

Katherine stayed with the group and followed the exit ramp around Cadman Plaza, then ran south on Henry Street. A few early risers watched idly. A truck driver whistled. A small boy fell in beside her and asked in the local dialect, "Youse runnin'?"

Katherine smiled at the obvious question.

"Hey, can I run witch youse?"

"Sure...no. No, it's not safe." She put on a burst of speed and outdistanced the boy.

The few other runners she had stayed with turned into Cranberry Street and headed for the Brooklyn Heights Promenade. Katherine continued alone down Henry Street at too fast a pace, looking over her shoulder every few seconds. She was sweaty, and found her breathing to be much harder than it should have been.

She saw Abrams' building ahead, an expensive highrise set among the brownstones. She increased her stride. As the landscaped entrance to the building came up, she cut diagonally across the fore-court and pushed through the glass doors. She leaned against the foyer wall and caught her breath, then glanced at her chronograph: 4.62 miles in 39 minutes. Not bad.

Katherine pushed at the inner glass doors, but they were locked. She turned to find Abrams' buzzer, but a man inside the lobby opened the door for her. She hesitated, then slid past him and crossed the lobby quickly. She pushed the elevator button and waited. The man stood in the center of the lobby staring at her. The elevator came and she rode up to the sixth floor.

Katherine rang the bell of apartment 6C. The peephole slid back, then the door opened. "Come in."

She exhaled a long breath and stepped into a small foyer.

Abrams said, "Were you followed?"

"I don't think so . . . but there's a man in your lobby. Brown suit, tall—"

"Cop." He glanced at her. "Anything wrong?"

She forced a smile. "I got myself worked up." She realized she was glad to be there. She felt safe with him. She looked at his tattered blue sweat suit, splattered with paint stains. The sweat shirt said NYPD GYM. "Is that Brooklyn chic?"

"Right. It signals to the muggers that I'm poor but armed." He led her into the living room. She glanced around. This was not what she'd expected.

He followed her gaze but said nothing.

She turned back to him. "*Are* you armed?"

"Yes. You too. Lift your shirt."

She hesitated, then hiked her T-shirt up. Abrams took a nylon gun belt from the coffee table, wrapped it around her waist, and pressed the Velcro fastener together. "How's that feel?"

She drew a deep breath. "Fine."

He produced a holster and clipped it on the belt near the small of her back.

She pulled down her shirt.

Abrams handed her a small silver automatic. "It's a 7.65 Beretta, unloaded. Play with it."

She operated the slide, checked the safety and the trigger pull. "It's light."

"Jogger's Special. It won't bother you much."

"Will it bother anyone else?"

He smiled. "It doesn't have much stopping power, and it's pretty inaccurate, but it's otherwise reliable." He handed her two magazines of seven rounds apiece. "Aim for the midsection, and keep squeezing off rounds. It's a fast reload."

She slapped one magazine in the butt of the pistol, and put the other in her zippered pants pocket. She reached behind and slipped the gun in the holster, drawing it out to get the feel of it, then sliding it back in.

Abrams watched her, then said, "I know you're used to your own cannon, but that's the best I could do."

"It's fine. Really."

The conversation, thought Abrams, had a bizarre quality to it, as though he had given her a cheap wristwatch and she was trying to hide her disappointment. "Who taught you about guns?"

"Peter." She didn't elaborate, but said, "What are you carrying?"

Abrams tapped his chest. "My thirty-eight in a shoulder holster. Sit down a minute."

She sat on the couch, again taking in the room.

Abrams sat in a tan leather chair. "When I was on the force, I made some good investments."

She seemed embarrassed. "I'm sorry if I looked surprised."

"Well, the police internal affairs people looked even more surprised when they paid an unexpected visit. They literally took the place apart searching for bag money."

Again she seemed ill at ease. "But you were able to explain...?"

Abrams sat back. "Marcy's father was a stockbroker. She never knew I had dealings with him." He smiled.

She smiled in return.

"Anyway, the internal affairs people were satisfied, but I was pulled out of intelligence, put back into uniform, and assigned to Staten Island to watch the birds. I realized I was not going anywhere and about that time Mr. O'Brien offered to put me on full time, so I left the force."

"Yes, I remember that."

"Do you? Well, that job offer couldn't have been better timed."

There was a long silence in the room, then she said, "You aren't suggesting that Mr. O'Brien had anything to do with—"

"I'm suggesting that Mr. O'Brien could get the Pope framed on charges of heresy if it suited his purpose."

"Well..." She remembered the misfortunes that had befallen her ex-husband. "Well...he's not malicious. I mean, there's always a reason—"

"I'm sure of it. But there is no excuse. Not for manipulating people's lives. Anyway, there's no proof, is there? And no hard feelings, really."

She changed the subject. "You have good taste in decorating."

"Actually, Cousin Herbie is a decorator. Uncle Sy is in the furniture business, Aunt Ruth is in rugs.... You know how it is."

"No, I don't." She stood. "I think we'd better go."

He remained seated. "Isn't Peter going to meet us here?"

"I don't think so. Later."

He stood. "Wait." He disappeared into the kitchen and came back with two glasses of brown liquid. "My own recipe."

She held up her glass and looked at it suspiciously. "What *is* this?"

"Apples, bananas, cornflakes, and...I forget. Whatever is around goes in the blender."

"Some recipe." She sipped it. "Not too bad."

Abrams emptied his glass. "Great. Well, the facilities are down that hall."

She nodded. "I'll be a minute."

He watched her as she disappeared into the hallway. She was, he knew, in a state of turmoil. Her lover might be a traitor and a murderer. People around her were dying, and her own life was probably in danger. To add to the excitement, she truly believed the world was coming to an end. And probably, he thought, she'd already figured out that he wanted to take her to bed. This, he admitted, might not be the best possible time to broach that subject. Yet he knew he had to.

She returned. "I'm ready." She looked at him.

Abrams remembered something O'Brien had told him in a candid moment: *She's approachable. But as in warfare, you have to find a point of approach.* He considered several, remembering another martial adage: *In war, there is no room for two mistakes.* "Katherine..."

She was studying his face and said, "No, Tony. One thing at a time."

"I'm only considering one thing at this time."

"One person at a time. Okay?"

"Sounds reasonable."

She smiled slowly. "You don't sound convinced."

"Neither do you." He indicated the door.

She moved toward it, then turned suddenly.

He took her in his arms and kissed her.

After some time, she pulled gently away. "We have things to do...first things first."

"World War Three, or whatever the hell it is, can wait."

"No...come..." She smiled. "Let's go burn off some frustration."

Abrams nodded as he followed her to the door. Peter Thorpe was his major frustration at the moment, and Abrams thought that he would find some pleasure in burning him off.

CHAPTER THIRTY-FOUR

Nicholas West sensed the presence of someone near him and opened his eyes, squinting into the blinding light.

Thorpe's form hovered above him. Thorpe said, "So, how are you, buddy?"

West shook his head. "Suffering."

"It's all relative. Well, let's begin." Thorpe drew up the stool and sat.

West turned his head to both sides. "Katherine...?"

Thorpe smiled. "Not yet. But she's coming. She's coming." Thorpe lit a cigarette.

West said, "My pipe..."

"Yes, I'll get you your pipe, after we've discovered some truths." Thorpe blew smoke in West's face, then said, "What did Ann do for the National Security Agency?"

West ran his tongue over his dry cracked lips. "Water..."

"Christ, Nick, if you stall one more time..." Thorpe slid off the stool and went to a refrigerator, returning with a paper cup of ice chips. He dropped a few chips into West's open mouth, then said, "What is—was—Ann's job with the NSA?"

West mumbled something and Thorpe drew closer. "What?"

West spit in Thorpe's face.

Thorpe drew back and said, "You son of a bitch!" He wiped his face with a handkerchief.

West said, "Lies equal pain, truth equals pleasure."

Thorpe's face reddened, then he broke into a smile. "All right, you little nerd. The worm turns. Is that it, Nick?"

West replied, "Your technique is bad. I hate you, I resent you, and I will resist you."

Thorpe looked at the analyzers. "True statement. But these are early innings. Your heroics won't last very long. Now, tell me about Ann."

West hesitated, then said, "She's involved with breaking codes."

Thorpe nodded. "Russian codes. Specifically, she listens to traffic between Moscow and the Soviet diplomatic missions in New York, Washington, and Glen Cove. True?"

"True."

"About six weeks ago, Ann Kimberly's section notified the CIA and other intelligence agencies in Washington of an interesting occurrence. To wit: On the evening of April twelfth of this year, all radio traffic between Moscow and Glen Cove ceased for about six seconds, then resumed."

Thorpe studied West's face, then added, "As you probably know, radio codes between sensitive locations are continuous, even if nothing is actually being said. This is a security procedure so that people listening in will not draw any inferences from an increase or decrease in radio traffic. So, this six-second break was noteworthy, though not earthshaking. After the NSA's routine report, the FBI reported back that there was a severe electrical storm on Long Island that evening, and that the Russian house, on the highest point in the area, was struck by lightning. End of mystery."

West licked his lips, but said nothing.

Thorpe went on. "But wait. According to the NSA and others familiar with advanced electronics, something was not kosher. So, further inquiries were made. And lo and behold, a man out on his sloop, racing for the harbor during the storm, actually saw the lightning that struck the Russian house."

Thorpe leaned over and put his elbows casually on the edge of the gurney. "Only it didn't strike the *house,* Nick. It struck an *antenna* that was planted in the ground some distance from the house. The man saw this as the lightning struck and flashed. Furthermore, being familiar with that antenna as a landmark, he swears that it had a very tall extension atop it that he never saw before or since. What do you conclude, Nick?"

West said, "Lightning rod."

"Correct. They were *trying* to attract lightning to that rod. True?"

"True."

"Then why the hell did the power go out, Nick? The rod should have been grounded, not connected in some way to the house power. Even the stupid Russkies know how a lightning rod works."

West said nothing.

Thorpe continued, "Well, I told my Russian friends that this occurrence had not gone undetected, and they got pretty upset. They asked me to pursue this further. Highest priority."

West remained silent.

Thorpe flipped his cigarette on the floor, then said, "Of course, the remarkable thing was that after they attracted that huge power surge on purpose, their lights, radios, and apparently everything else were not damaged. And, in fact, everything was functioning again within *six* seconds. Conclusion: They were playing Ben Franklin, experimenting with electricity. But for what purpose? Nick?"

West said hesitantly, "The NSA...came to a private conclusion.... They told all other agencies involved to forget it.... Their conclusion was classified State Secret—"

"I know that, damn you. I never saw that conclusion. But perhaps you did. Perhaps Ann was privy to that conclusion. You had one quick meeting with her in Washington April twenty-ninth. Sometime between your passionate embraces, she told you the conclusion. What was it?"

West said nothing.

Thorpe reached for the transformer dial. "A stall equals a lie. Three seconds, two, one—"

"Wait! Wait! She said...They were testing...surge arrestors... like circuit breakers...they wanted to...to make their electrical and electronic systems invulnerable to electrical storms....So there would be no lengthy interruption of radio communication."

Thorpe was studying the analyzers. He finally spoke. "True, as far as it goes. But there's more to it, isn't there? Otherwise my friends in Glen Cove wouldn't be so nervous about it. What else did Ann say?"

"Nothing."

Thorpe twisted the dial and held it.

West's body arched off the table. His mouth opened, but no sound came out. His bladder released into the tube, and his heart rate dropped dangerously.

Thorpe shut off the current. "Well, I've been itching to give you a big blast. But now you're useless for a few minutes."

West's body settled onto the table, twitching, his muscles in spasm. His skin was pale and dry and his eyes were rolled back so that only the whites showed.

Thorpe said, "I'm fairly certain this experiment in Glen Cove had something to do with the Stroke—that's what the Russians call their plan to destroy America, or, as they put it, to bring eternal peace to the world.... Nick?"

West's face had gone ash-gray, and his breathing was irregular.

Thorpe looked at the heart monitor. "Oh, Christ." He stood quickly and took a hypodermic needle from the instrument table and plunged it into West's shoulder. "There. That ought to bring you back to the land of the living."

Thorpe waited anxiously for several minutes, watching the heart monitor. "It would be my luck that your little chicken heart would stop...and don't go into convulsions on me, you wimp...." Thorpe waited, then said, "West! Can you hear me?"

West nodded slowly.

"Good. Ready for more conversation?"

West shook his head. "You...almost...killed me...."

"Almost doesn't count. Actually, it's difficult to kill someone with the amount of volts this puts out. I tried it once. You'll get your bullet when the time comes. I promise you that."

"Now...I want...it now."

"Oh, no. You *are* a coward." Thorpe sat on the stool again. "Okay, I'll speak awhile, and you listen." Thorpe made an adjustment in the polygraph. "Think about what I'm saying. First, Moscow is concerned that parts of their plan may have been exposed. One way that could have happened is through NSA electronic snooping. So you're going to tell me what Ann has told you."

"Ann...is not...dead...you would have...kidnapped...."

"We tried. But she died. Suicide, actually. Very badly bungled. Two more for Siberia." He laughed.

"You...for Siberia..."

"Shut up. Anyway, another way this plan could be compromised is through the CIA in pursuit of its mission to uncover such nasty schemes. With the help of your high authorization code, my computer is right now scanning Langley's computer for key words and names that will let me know if there is any suspicion of Moscow's Operation Stroke." Thorpe stared at the polygraph paper and saw that West was very agitated. He said, "Will anything show up?"

West's tongue lolled in his mouth, then he said, "There's... plenty in there...about you...."

Thorpe nodded. "Rest assured, I'm scanning for that also, my friend. In fact, I may just have to go on an extended sabbatical very soon."

"You...are like me...you know too much. You have no friends... no place to hide."

"There's always China." He laughed. "But to continue—another source of trouble is O'Brien's old-boys network. They *are* on to something. But they're being led to believe that some Arab terrorist group is going to obliterate Wall Street with a small nuclear weapon. Not a bad idea, but no cigar."

Thorpe stretched his arms and legs. "I'm having sympathetic muscle cramps." He laughed, then added, "Actually, Nick, I don't think O'Brien and Company completely bought that. Neither did my people in the Company. You see, Nick, as far as I can determine, the Russians have an obsession with the concept of troika—the three-horse sleigh. They are fascinated by the trinity—three acting as one."

West stared at Thorpe and tried to think clearly. Thorpe was onto something. Just as Thorpe had always underestimated him because of his physical frailty, so, because of Thorpe's physical power, he, West, underestimated Thorpe's powers of deduction, intuition, and comprehension.

Thorpe cracked his knuckles and looked down at West. "Therefore," he continued, "they actually formulated *three* independent plans to cripple or destroy America. The first was the nuclear destruction of the financial center. The second, which I was led to believe, was the accessing of all American computers—civilian and military—and the simultaneous destruction, altering, or stealing of everything stored in the memory banks."

Thorpe rubbed his chin reflectively, then said, "And now, Nick, you and I have touched on this third plan, which I believe is the one they are going with. The other two plans seemed real to those of us who discovered them, because they were and perhaps still are real options. Nothing lies like the truth. And so all the resources of Western intelligence, including you and me, Nick, and including private analysts such as O'Brien and Company, were mobilized to uncover the details of these two plans. But somewhere along the line, O'Brien got to thinking. He realized there was a third plan. And he began operating on that premise. He received information that the Russians were acquiring certain exotic types of Western electronic technology. He alerted the government to his initial findings. And that warning leaked back to the Russians. So, we all find ourselves in a quandary. The Russians are trying to figure out how much the United States really knows and how good their defenses are. The United States is trying to figure out if the blow is going to come to the face, the stomach, or the groin, or not at all. And wondering if maybe they shouldn't strike first."

Thorpe looked down at West. "When we are through here, Nick, we will know who, how, and where. We already know when—July Fourth. We know why—because as a result of a sort of political Darwinism, the world today has been reduced to two dominant species. Only one of them can survive."

West drew a deep breath. "You're mad.... Why do you feel this need to dominate...?"

"Why do you feel the need not to?" Thorpe lit a cigarette and drew it thoughtfully, then said, "Anyway, the final problem in Moscow is this Talbot business." Thorpe reached down and picked up a leather dispatch case. "This is what Colonel Carbury was carrying." He upturned the case and dumped the contents across West's stomach and chest. "A diary and personal letters from the late Ann Kimberly to the late Major Henry Kimberly. The late Mr. O'Brien and his people would have found this diary very useful in uncovering Talbot, who was, after all, one of their own."

Thorpe lifted the diary from West's chest. "Or should I say three of their own? Yes, like you, Henry Kimberly concluded that there were perhaps three highly placed traitors. We will read this diary together and try to deduce what Major Kimberly deduced." Thorpe tapped the diary on West's forehead. "Pay attention."

"Go to hell."

Thorpe continued, "Kimberly seemed to know who these traitors were, but he never wrote the names, using only the expressions Talbot One, Two, and Three, like some ancient Hebrew who would not write or say the name of God."

Thorpe opened the diary and read an entry: "'I have narrowed down the names of OSS officers who could have been responsible for betraying us to the Russians. One of them is a close Donovan aide, and known to me. The other, a ranking officer in OSS counterintelligence, is a dear friend. The third is an OSS officer in the political section, a man who will assuredly go on to a political career after the war. Which one is Talbot? Perhaps all of them.'" Thorpe looked up. "End of entry."

Thorpe put the diary aside. "You know, Nick, if this diary had found its way into O'Brien's hands, or the hands of the CIA, it would have precipitated a massive investigation that may have led to the identity of Talbot. But once again, God was on the side of the atheists, and this message from the grave will remain undelivered." Thorpe looked down at West, then focused on the analyzers. "Did you follow what I said?"

"Yes."

"Could my adoptive father, James Allerton, be the dear friend?"

"Yes."

"Do you have any theories on the other two? Could one or both still be alive?"

"The one described as a high-ranking officer in OSS counter-intelligence."

"And the one described as a potential politician?"

"Don't know...I have no information on him."

"What is the name of the high-ranking officer?"

"I...I'm not certain...I have several names that would fit..."

"Give me the names."

West said, "Give me a treat."

Thorpe laughed, then said, "Do you want your pipe?"

"Yes."

Thorpe took West's pipe from the instrument table and packed the tobacco tightly. He put the stem in West's mouth and held a lighter to the bowl.

West drew deeply.

Thorpe said, "This is not your tobacco, of course. That was laced with nicotine alkaloid. So if you're wondering why you're not dying, that's the reason."

West squinted up at Thorpe as he continued to draw on the pipe.

Thorpe said, "You held out on me, you sneaky bastard. I *asked* you about poisons."

West suddenly bit into the stem of the pipe, crunching it between his teeth.

Thorpe pulled the pipe out of West's mouth and said, "No, no, Nick. I changed the stem, too. Do you think I'm as big an asshole as you are? I've been around the block, buddy. Now you've lost your smoking privileges." He set down the pipe.

West's body was shaking as tears rolled down his face.

Thorpe grabbed West's ear and pulled his face toward him. "Look, bozo, I'm a pro. You're an amateur. You can't beat me, so forget it. You are utterly helpless and defenseless. You are at my mercy. You will lose your soul here, and your heart. When I'm through with you, your ego will be nonexistent. You will not even have enough free will left to commit suicide. But I'll save you the trouble. Kate will not be so lucky. I'm going to let her live on, as sort of a domesticated house pet."

West raised his head and spoke softly. "You will pay for this... somehow, in some way...you will be punished...."

Thorpe smiled. "When a prisoner starts getting mystic and religious, that's a sign that he's about had it. I'll break you sooner than I thought."

West put his head back on the table and began to sob.

Thorpe gathered the contents of the dispatch case and shut off the polygraph. "I'm afraid I have to go out again. Amuse yourself. I'll be back shortly."

"Fuck you."

Thorpe reached out and held the dial of the transformer. "Not telling me that pipe smoking may be dangerous to your health was a lie of omission, which unfortunately does not always register on the analyzers. Nonetheless, it was a lie—"

"No! No! Please!" West's body began to quiver in response to a low-voltage charge passing through it. His screaming came out as a teeth-chattering stutter, as though he were freezing.

Thorpe smiled as he continued the mild shock. "That's almost comical. You should see yourself...well, you will on the reruns. Kate will see it too. And Eva. And the Russians will get a laugh out of this one. God, Nick, you look like a half-wit."

Thorpe shut off the electricity. "When I return you will tell me more about Talbot and Ann Kimberly. You will tell me what you know of O'Brien and his friends, including Katherine Kimberly, George Van Dorn, and the rest of those arrogant bastards. Also, you will tell me what you know of the Russians in Glen Cove. Your answers may determine whether or not these coming Fourth of July fireworks, picnics, and speeches will be the last."

CHAPTER THIRTY-FIVE

Abrams watched her as she ran ahead of him. She had a nice stride; long, easy, and graceful.

Abrams glanced around, but no one seemed to be following on foot, or by vehicle. They were near the southern end of Fourth Avenue, having traveled most of the distance from his apartment by subway. The route that Katherine had laid out, and had given to Thorpe, included a series of park runs, connected by subway, with little street running in between. It was, he thought, as if she'd picked dangerous territory on purpose. And, of course, she had.

The odd thing, he thought as he ran behind her, was that neither of them had openly acknowledged that what had started as a running date on Saturday had become something very like police decoy duty today.

This was partly due to the sensitive topic involved. But it was also due to this refined way of speaking, where one did not *say* things, but indicated, implied, intimated, or alluded to them. This annoying manner of communication, he observed, was common to lawyers, corporate types, and genteel people in general. He preferred the way cops spoke.

Abrams felt the blood pounding through his veins and sensed the beginning of the runner's high. He liked Brooklyn running; it was flat and laid back, unlike Manhattan running, which was flat but fanatical.

Brooklyn was brownstone running, quaint residential streets, with no skyblocking skyscrapers. Brooklyn was also the Borough of Churches, and Abrams was always able to orient himself by the dozens of familiar steeples whose clocks also gave him the time.

They turned into 67th Street and followed a strip of grassy panhandle toward Owl's Head Park, their first possible rendezvous with Peter Thorpe.

Abrams looked up. Katherine was a good hundred yards ahead of him, and he called to her, "Stay close!"

She called back, "Run faster!"

Bitch. He increased his stride.

Abrams' original intention had been to take her through the Orthodox Jewish neighborhoods where the men turned away from barelegged women runners. Why he had intended to do this, he couldn't say for sure. In any case, she'd planned the route based more on tactical considerations than sight-seeing or social studies. Still, if they ever ran together again, that's where he'd take her. Abrams closed the distance as they approached the park.

Another place he'd wanted to take her was one of the new Russian Jewish neighborhoods with their signs in Cyrillic lettering, and the combination of Yiddish and Russian spoken on the bustling streets. These, he recognized, were his real roots, and he was fascinated by the vitality of the neighborhood, the proliferation of emigré businesses and shops.

They entered the park along a path, and he followed her as she cut across the grass, and began the arduous run up the large hill that dominated the park. He felt the sweat collecting around his shoulder holster and the chafing of the holster straps against his skin. He thought of Peter Thorpe, and wondered when they would meet, and how it would happen. The preferred method seemed to be death by misadventure.

Abrams looked up. Katherine stood at the summit of the hill, silhouetted against the clear blue sky. Seagulls circled overhead, and beyond the seagulls was a gray helicopter.

Abrams sprinted up the last twenty yards and stopped on the summit. He bent over and breathed deeply, then straightened up and looked around the sweeping, grassy hill planted with well-spaced trees and bushes. "We seem to be alone."

She nodded as she caught her breath. She scanned the other slopes. "Early...we'll take ten minutes here...."

"Right." Abrams looked north at the panoramic view of New York harbor, the Statue of Liberty, and the sunlit skyscrapers of lower Manhattan seemingly rising from the water. He turned and looked at Katherine, hair disarrayed, without makeup, sweating, her mouth open, sucking in air. He said, "You're very beautiful."

She laughed and tugged on his sweaty shirt. "You look very handsome yourself."

They began walking in a circle around the crest of the hill. Katherine said, "This place is a mess."

Abrams nodded. The park was a study in urban decay and neglect. There were broken bottles everywhere, unworkable water fountains, smashed trash receptacles, dog droppings, uncared-for trees, and graffiti on every possible surface. This, he imagined, was probably what Rome's fabled parks looked like after the barbarians got the upper hand.

Katherine, who was watching him, seemed to sense what he was thinking. She said, "This park needs a good cleaning. It also needs better policing, tighter control."

Abrams looked at her. She was speaking in that obscure way again, the park being a metaphor. He replied, "Perhaps. But not too much of that. There is a vitality here of people, pursuing their own lives, unburdened by government interference. The price of nearly absolute freedom is borderline anarchy."

"A little law and order wouldn't hurt."

"Whose law? Whose order? Fascists and Communists have in common the desire to get everyone into lockstep. I don't want to get into lockstep."

She smiled. "Okay. No more politics. Ready to run?"

"No. Let's walk awhile."

She began walking down the hill. "I'll get you into shape before the summer's over."

He gave her a sidelong glance, but said nothing.

They walked in silence for a while, then she said, "The next place Peter might meet us is under the Verrazano Bridge."

Abrams didn't reply.

They walked south along a narrow asphalt path that ran parallel to the Shore Parkway. A stiff wind began blowing off the bay, churning up whitecaps. She spoke as though she were continuing a conversation, "I mean, we have no solid proof, and what we have could be explained by the fact that he *is* CIA." She waited, then added, "Your perceptions may be colored by personal considerations."

Abrams did not reply for some time, then said, "My perceptions are influenced by fifteen years of detective work." He added, "You people ask me to find the murderer or kidnapper of Randolph Carbury. I suspect I did. Now I'm just trying to stay alive."

She said nothing.

Abrams looked out in the bay. A few private boats sailed along close to the shoreline. Overhead, the helicopter made another pass. A few joggers and dog walkers appeared on the strip of park. Abrams motioned toward the rising parachute-jump tower of Coney Island in the far distance. "I used to spend hours at the shooting gallery there. These little toy ducks would move across a tank of water and I'd blast away at them."

"I'll bet the local girls fell all over you when you got those Kewpie dolls."

"I had to turn my rifle on them to keep them away. Anyway, when I grew up, I was assigned to decoy duty, dressed as an old man, trying to attract muggers. I walked through the parks around Coney Island, like a little toy duck. That's very bad duty. But rewarding. I attracted a lot of muggers, Then I'd do what the little toy ducks never did to me. I'd pull my gun."

She said, "And here you are again. That must be a lousy feeling."

"Yes, well, you can take the boy out of Brooklyn, the man out of the police force, and all that...listen to what I'm going to tell you. There are basically five ways to hunt—baiting, trapping, stakeouts, beating the bush, and decoying. It depends on the animal you're after, the season of the year, and the terrain. With the human animal, you can use all methods, or combinations of methods, in any season and terrain. Just keep in mind that when the human animal approaches, he may take any form, including the guise of a friendly animal. He may wave a cheery hello, or ask for a cigarette. But you must realize you are being attacked, and in that split second of realization you have to act, because a second later it's too late."

"But what if you do bodily harm to a man who really *is* only asking for a cigarette?"

"That's what the split second is for."

They continued along the shore for some time. Katherine said, "You're a complex man. Tough, gentle, streetwise, naive, political, apolitical, educated, anti-intellectual, committed and uncommitted."

"I've played many roles."

"So, who is Tony Abrams?"

"Beats me. What's today? Monday? I'm carrying a gun...so today...no, it's my day off...so—"

"Cut it out."

They walked awhile in silence, then Abrams said, "Do you know a bartender at the University Club named Donald?"

Katherine replied, "I'm only allowed in the ladies' lounge, so I elect not to go at all."

"Well, nevertheless, Donald was mugged and murdered early this morning."

She didn't reply.

Abrams added, "Also, a man believed to be Carbury's double was found in the lower harbor"—he pointed toward the Narrows—"about there, probably. That's where most of the floaters are found. The currents, I guess."

She said nothing, but began running again. Abrams followed, finding that his legs and lungs were in better shape than he thought.

They followed the curving shoreline as it swung south and east. Ahead, the Verrazano Bridge rose majestically, spanning the Narrows from Fort Hamilton in Brooklyn, to Fort Wadsworth on Staten Island. Abrams reflected on how simple national defense had been not so long ago: two stone forts, with artillery batteries that flung five-hundred-pound balls in a crossfire over the approaches to New

York harbor. What could be more logical than nineteenth-century military science?

Now, however, national defense began in outer space, and ended in deep missile silos. And the complexities of the system were such that if every adult human brain and hand in the nation were put to work manning that system, it would not be enough. He said suddenly, *"Computers."*

She turned her head toward him as she ran. "What?"

"That's what O'Brien may have been hinting at. They may have found a way to destroy or neutralize all the computers—military, financial, industrial...is that possible?"

She began to slow down, then returned to a walk. After a full minute she said, "Possible...yes...I've heard talk of that...the NSA, the people Ann works for, supposedly has a secret book of national access codes...not really a book, but a pulse-modulated tape...." She looked at him. "This is very sensitive—"

"Then keep it to yourself."

She went on as though he hadn't spoken. "The NSA sets security standards for military and civilian computers. Therefore, they have inside knowledge of them, and theoretically they can break any computer code in the country. Though this would be illegal."

"So of course they don't do that."

"Well, there's always been some discussion about the idea of having all computers accessible to a central command post in times of national emergency, such as war or a stock market crash. The theory is that the President could command and control better. You get the idea."

"Yes, I do. Sounds risky."

"Well, it would be if somehow all computers could be accessed simultaneously and all computer language translated into one language. Then it's at least theoretically possible that someone with evil intent could...cause complete havoc."

"Sounds pretty grim."

"It would be disastrous." She looked at him. "What made you think of that?"

Abrams shrugged. "I don't know. It must have been something

I heard, or deduced. It fits O'Brien's picture, which excluded nuclear or chemical war." He tapped his forehead. "My personal computer—sometimes it makes computations without me knowing it's even working."

She said, "It could be divine inspiration. Do you believe in God?"

"Yes. Human beings aren't capable of causing all this misery themselves."

"Cynic."

They walked silently, listening to the water washing the shore. She said, "I'll explore that further. Any other thoughts on the subject?"

"No. I'll have to wait for another divine message. I hear voices sometimes."

She smiled. "Do you? What do these voices say?"

"Lately they've been saying I should go to Miami for a month."

"Really? What language do they speak to you in?"

He smiled at the standard interrogation used by priests, rabbis, and psychiatrists on the subject of voices. "They speak a sort of English with a Brooklyn Jewish accent. Sometimes I think it's not God, but one or more of my dead relatives. That was their advice for all life's problems. Go to Miami."

"Are you going?"

"No, it's off-season. My relatives would turn in their graves. I may go to Maine. Why don't you come with me?"

She said unexpectedly, "All right."

"The catch?"

"You know."

He nodded. "First things first."

"Yes...and here comes a priority item."

Abrams looked up quickly. Under the bridge, two men on horseback had emerged from the bridge's shadow and were trotting toward them. Abrams said, "Keep walking."

The riders drew closer, and Abrams could see that they were not mounted police. He could also see that neither of them was Peter Thorpe. He had gambled that Thorpe would reveal himself personally, but now he wondered if the risk they were taking was worth it. "Damn it," he said to her. "Okay, draw your gun but keep it out of sight."

Katherine drew the small pistol as she walked and tucked her hand in her waistband.

Abrams dropped behind her so that he was blocked from view and drew his .38 revolver. He held it pressed close to his leg as he moved off to the side again. He looked around. There were a few joggers down toward the water. Some people sat on benches, a young couple walked a Great Dane, and a man was surf casting in the bay.

Katherine looked around also. She said, "Are these people all civilians?"

"We'll see soon enough."

She kept walking beside him, watching the riders closing in, glancing at the other people scattered around the shore area. She said, "How do we know when the split second has arrived?"

"It's instinct. You'll know. I never shot an innocent civilian yet. If you're not sure, follow my lead."

"Okay.... Did a mugger ever get the drop on you during that split second?"

"A few times. Sometimes you get a second chance though."

The two horsemen were less than a hundred yards distant now.

Katherine replied, "You got your second chance when you walked off that roof alive."

"Right. Sometimes you get a third chance, too."

"I hope so."

"Me too. Get ready."

CHAPTER THIRTY-SIX

The drugs seemed to have worn off, and Nicholas West lay perfectly still, able to think clearly for the first time in many hours.

He thought about secrets and how to keep them from Peter Thorpe, and from Thorpe's Soviet bosses. West wanted to believe that the mind was capable of overcoming nearly any adversity, including pain, suffering, drugs, and all the tools of the torturer's trade. He believed that given the time, he could go into a protective self-hypnosis, which would reduce the pain and confuse the polygraph and voice analyzer. He knew, too, that he was more intelligent than Peter Thorpe, that Thorpe had serious personality flaws, not to mention more fundamental problems of the mind.

On the other hand, West realized, Thorpe was, as he'd said, a professional. There was a serious question in West's mind as to whether or not he could defeat Thorpe, or at least stall him for any length of time.

West also thought about Ann, Patrick O'Brien, and Katherine. Thorpe was a one-man reign of terror, a man who had conjured up a living nightmare for those around him, and who would do the same for a nation of 240 million people.

West tried to determine what his duty and obligation were in this situation. The Company's manual on the subject was explicit: *If captured in a Communist country, stick to your cover no matter*

what. If tortured, and unable to resist, use every means available to
kill yourself.

But this wasn't a Communist country—yet. The manual went
on: *In those rare instances where an agent or other employee is held*
incommunicado by foreign and/or enemy agents in a friendly country,
he must make every effort to escape the confines of his imprisonment, or
as circumstances permit, make contact with the outside. If possible he
must kill or capture one or more of his captors. Suicide is permissible
as a last resort only if captivity will lead to the compromising of fellow
agents or the divulgence of sensitive information under torture.

West thought about that. Rational advice. But probably not written by a man who had ever been strapped to a table and attached to
electrodes. And not written for a man who was primarily a historian
and former college teacher.

"A penny's worth of electricity for your thoughts, Nicko."

West looked quickly to his right.

"The polygraph shows some deep and dark thinking." Thorpe
pulled up the stool and sat. "I spoke to my friends in Glen Cove.
They're not satisfied with the results of our preliminary discussions.
If the quality doesn't improve soon, they want you delivered to
them."

West cleared his throat. "You're lying. You're trying to frighten
me. Put the voice analyzer where I can see it, so I can tell when
you're lying to *me.*"

Thorpe laughed loudly. "Well, that's what happens when the
truth drugs wear off and you have time to think clearly. You'll need
some sodium pent to soften you up again." He reached out and
turned an adjustment key on the intravenous tube. "Nobody likes
a smartass, Nick."

West said, "Peter, the drugs aren't—"

Thorpe had his eye on the analyzers and his hand on the electrical transformer. "Aren't *what,* Nick? Aren't necessary? Go on, finish
the sentence."

"Aren't... I mean, they..."

Thorpe laughed. "You have to learn you can't make offhand,
half-assed remarks, Nicko. Now go on and finish the sentence."

"I...I meant the drugs are useful...to make me...more talkative...and to lower my resistance...."

"Right you are." Thorpe moved his hand from the transformer. "Look, I don't have the time right now to keep jolting you, so why don't you confine your remarks to truthful answers? That's a piece of good advice. Okay?"

Thorpe lit a cigarette and made some adjustments in the two analyzers. "All right....What should we talk about now? Talbot? No...that can wait for Kate. Actually, I did speak to my pals in Glen Cove. They're interested in the fact that you know something about their little electrical experiment. So why don't we talk about that? First—"

"Peter, if I told you all I knew, which is not much, and if you put that together with whatever else you discover, then you might arrive at the answer to what the Soviets have planned."

"So? That's the point. They want to know what the CIA knows."

"But they would not let you live once you knew. There probably aren't ten people in the Soviet Union who know what this is about. It's the biggest secret in the world—the ultimate plan to destroy America. You *may not* know that secret."

"Are we back to trying to scare me? You know, Nick, I thought about that. And I think that James is Talbot. And I don't think he'd let them kill his only son."

West actually smiled. "How can you be so naive? What do you mean to him? Anyone who could betray his friends and his country for nearly half a century is heartless. How many people has James Allerton killed or caused to be killed? You're a rank amateur compared to that man."

Thorpe drew thoughtfully on his cigarette. "Perhaps. I can see why the Russians might want me out of the way until July Fourth, but I'm too valuable for them to do away with me. I think I have to lay low awhile. After the Stroke I will emerge in a position of power."

"As what? Commissar of the insane asylums?"

Thorpe seemed not to hear. He said, "But thank you for thinking of me, Nick. That's what you're here for. To use your fabled brain in my service."

"I thought it was in the service of your masters."

Thorpe threw down his cigarette. "You do need to be softened up." He increased the flow of sodium pentothal. "What you really need is a good gut-wrenching, backbreaking, bladder-releasing surge of electricity. Just give me an excuse." Thorpe tugged on the clips attached to West's scrotum. "Your balls are not surge arrestors. They're conductors." He laughed. "So, tell me about surge arrestors."

West's face went pale, then he found his voice and said, "Surge arrestors...are like circuit breakers. They trip off when there's a surge in electricity...they protect electrical components....After the surge has passed...they are switched back on...."

"And the Russians have fitted out their Glen Cove house with these?"

"Apparently."

"Why? And don't say to protect against lightning."

West swallowed dryly. "Water—"

"Talk!" Thorpe reached for the transformer.

West said quickly, "EMP...Lightning reproduces the effects of EMP...lightning can be used to test EMP protective devices...."

"Hold on. What the hell is EMP?"

"Electromagnetic pulse. The Compton effect....Like an electrical storm....It would destroy every computer in the country... every microchip circuit would burn out. Wipe out all telephone communications...all radios and televisions...electronic controls in planes, cars, boats, missiles...instruments in laboratories, electronics in factories, hospitals...the entire energy grip would burn out...air traffic control...nothing left....Everything would be in shambles...every circuit in the country burnt out...the end of technology...crippled economy...crippled defense capability."

Thorpe stayed silent for several seconds, then said, "Jesus Christ." He leaned closer to West. "Are you certain?"

"Yes...it's been known for some time. The effects of electromagnetic pulse...disastrous....America is rushing to protect vital systems...but...no one can be sure the protection would work... difficult to reproduce the effects of EMP in a test situation...lightning is the closest thing...."

"But how can the Russians *produce* EMP, West? *How?*"

"Easy...but it would be risky for them...it might cause us to launch a nuclear retaliation...no choice but to retaliate...*if* the President could communicate the order to strike. EMP is the biggest threat to national security....O'Brien had a suspicion...because of Russian procurement of EMP protection technology....Fiber optics...surge arrestors...Faraday shields...cable shields...EMP filters and chokes...systems to harden all their electrical and electronics."

"Listen to me, West. How can the Russians *cause* an electromagnetic storm all over the country, simultaneously?"

"Easy..." West's voice cracked and he began coughing. "Water...for God's sake, Peter..."

Thorpe grabbed a covered container with a spout and held it to West's lips.

West sipped slowly, then looked up at Thorpe. "I can't go on. Can't think. My muscles are going into contraction...sores on my back and buttocks...painful...."

"I'll have Eva massage you with oil, front and back. Nice treat. Now go on."

"No. I have to stretch....I have to *move*, for God's sake. To scratch. The itching is driving me insane."

Thorpe replied, "I gave you Atarax—an anti-itching drug—"

"I'm *suffering*..."

Thorpe put down the water cup and glanced at the analyzers. "Where do you itch?"

West's face reddened. "My genitals...all over..."

"Oh, well, that's where I draw the line. I'll get Eva—"

"No. Please, Peter. Just let me sit up one minute....I answered your questions...."

Thorpe glanced at his watch. "All right, that will be quicker than getting her." He unfastened West's chest strap, leaving his leg strap secured.

West tried to move, but it took several tries before he could get up into a sitting position. "Oh...God...Thank you...Peter..."

"Think nothing of it. Now, how can an EMP storm be produced that would blanket the whole country?"

West was flexing his muscles, then began to scratch himself.

"West! Talk!" Thorpe reached for the transformer.

West looked at him. "You can't do that. I'm not secured to the table. My back might arch and break."

"Not if I give you a mild one. Enough to knock you back on the goddamned table. Answer my question."

West stared at the alligator clips clamped to his scrotum. "Okay... a low-yield nuclear weapon...exploded about three hundred miles above Omaha.... There would be no radiation or destructive effects on the ground.... Just a flash of light...but within milliseconds, electromagnetic pulses would begin to destroy every piece of electronics from coast to coast."

Thorpe looked at him. "Is this a theory or reality?"

"Reality. It's called the Compton effect. Gamma rays from a nuclear blast high in the atmosphere interact with Compton electrons and produce EMP.... The effect produces a hundred times more voltage than a lightning bolt—but it's invisible and silent, and it covers the entire country, from coast to coast. It happened in the Pacific during the last atmospheric testing before the test-ban treaty over twenty years ago.... But electronics in those days were primitive...mostly vacuum tubes, which are very resistant to EMP...also there was not much out there to pick up the EMP... but in Hawaii, eight hundred miles away, street lights went out... radios and televisions went out.... Today, nearly all circuitry is based on silicon chips.... These are easily destroyed by EMP...."

Thorpe said, "But I don't see how the Russians could deliver even a small warhead three hundred miles above Omaha without the President's finger pulling the nuclear trigger."

West rubbed his forehead. "They must have a way...."

"I can't imagine...." He looked at West. "But *you* know what it is. And you're going to tell me—"

West suddenly reached out and pulled the electric clips away. Thorpe lunged at him instinctively and grabbed at his hand. West, still holding the clips, clasped Thorpe's hand in his own, the two clips pressed between their joined palms. West yanked Thorpe's hand toward him, causing the gurney to roll sideways a few feet. West lunged out with his free hand and turned the transformer dial.

A surge of electricity passed through both their bodies. Both men screamed and Thorpe tried to break West's grip, but their hand muscles tightened in electrical contraction. They both shook and bounced in grotesque spasms.

Finally, Thorpe's flailing arm hit the wires and ripped the alligator clips from between their pressed palms.

West fell back on the table, his body twitching. Thorpe slumped to the floor, tried to stand, then fell on his face. Both men lay quivering and moaning.

West took several long, deep breaths, then by sheer force of will made his muscles respond to the signals from his brain. He rose into a sitting position again, slowly, like a corpse with rigor mortis. After what seemed like a long time, his arms reached out and his torso bent forward. His shaking hands rested on the buckle of his leg strap. His fingers began to respond and he worked the belt loose.

West could hear Thorpe whimpering on the floor, and every few seconds he heard a crackling electrical sound as the swinging alligator clips came into contact with each other.

West knew somewhere in his stunned mind that he had to work fast, but everything seemed to be moving in slow motion. The room looked very dim, but he knew that was a result of the shock to his optic nerves. His heart beat heavily, slowly. There seemed to be no fluids left in him; his eyes were dry, his mouth felt like paste, his skin like dust.

Slowly, West pulled his legs, then his feet, loose from the straps. He ripped out the IV tubes and pulled the polygraph electrodes from his chest and forehead. With one painful motion he slid the catheter from his penis, then reached under his buttocks, finding that the anal tube had already come lose. He heard Thorpe mumbling obscenities from the floor. West found his own voice and said, "You . . . you . . . filthy . . . you unspeakable horror."

West slowly swung his legs over the side of the gurney and looked down. Thorpe was struggling to his feet and had gotten into a kneeling position. Both men stared at each other. West could see that Thorpe's bladder had released. West said, "What you did to me..."

Thorpe made a deep animal-like sound.

West slid down from the gurney and planted his bare feet on the cold floor.

Thorpe, still kneeling, reached his shaking hand into his jacket and began drawing out his revolver.

West dropped to his knees, took hold of the swinging wires, and thrust them out, touching the two live clips to Thorpe's face.

Thorpe let out a piercing scream and toppled backward, his hands to his face, the revolver lying on the floor between him and West. West crawled toward the revolver.

Suddenly the door of the garret burst open and Eva stood silhouetted in the lighted doorway. She let out a loud bellow, like an enraged animal, and charged across the room.

West glanced up as his hand fumbled for the gun. His eyes focused on something above Eva's head. Then he recognized the blurry whirling of a whip.

CHAPTER THIRTY-SEVEN

The two horsemen were less than fifty yards off now, heading straight toward them on the path, and closing fast. Abrams said, "Spread out. Wide."

Abrams veered off to his left and moved along the rise that bordered the Shore Parkway. Katherine went to her right, almost down to the water's edge. Abrams thought that some aspects of military logic did not undergo much change, especially infantry tactics that were an extension of basic survival instincts and common sense. The horsemen would now either have to deploy and give themselves away prematurely, or keep driving straight through, putting themselves at a disadvantage in terms of who had the better field of fire.

The horsemen drew nearer and Abrams could see they were men in their early thirties, dressed in jeans and Windbreakers. They both held the reins with two hands and he watched for sudden movements that would indicate they were going for weapons or reining the horses in.

The riders were still at a full gallop as they came within ten yards. Abrams stopped and knelt on one knee. Katherine saw him and did the same.

Abrams looked at the few other people scattered around. They were either innocent bystanders or they were very good at acting the part. He kept the .38 between his thighs, both hands wrapped around the grip. The rider closest to him came abreast, let loose of the reins with one hand and raised his arm.

Abrams brought his revolver up. The rider, halfway through a wave, stared wide-eyed, his mouth open, then shouted something and both men spurred their horses.

Abrams stood and holstered his gun. He said to himself, "Another New York horror tale enters the annals." He drew a deep breath.

He walked down to the narrow path and watched Katherine approaching. He noticed she was pale and shaking, and he put his arm around her shoulder. "I think we're taking a cab back. Come on." He began leading her up the slope toward the parkway.

She pulled away. "No. We're going on. Peter may be waiting for us."

Abrams said, "This is not a good idea anymore. Too chancy. Too many people around now."

She looked at him and replied coolly, "There's a great deal at stake. We're armed, we're together, and we're expecting trouble. I don't want to get run over by a car one night . . . I want to meet this head on. Don't you?"

He nodded. "Yes . . . okay . . . I'd prefer a known rendezvous with fate."

"Let's go." She turned and began jogging. He followed. They passed under the concrete piers of the Verrazano Bridge, and continued past Fort Hamilton, around Gravesend Bay, then entered Bensonhurst Park, a distance of three miles that they covered in just under forty-five minutes. They walked through the park.

Abrams took several long breaths as he looked around. To the north there was a very reduced Manhattan skyline, to the west Staten Island, and to the south and east a great pasture of black asphalt from which rose a seaside shopping mall dominated by a discount department store. Abrams said, "Welcome to Bensonhurst."

Katherine forced a smile. "Homesick?"

"Sure." He looked at her. "Should we stay awhile?"

She nodded. "This is another rendezvous point I arranged with Peter."

They walked the paths in silence for some time. Finally, Katherine said, "I usually go into the mall and use the facilities. I'll buy you an orange juice."

"Okay. They might be having a Memorial Day sale on the large cup."

They walked across the crowded parking field toward the mall. Katherine said, "I spoke with my sister yesterday—there's a secure phone with a voice scrambler in Mr. O'Brien's office."

"Just your normal law firm voice-scrambler phone. What did she say?"

"According to Ann, there was no one code-named Odysseus, or Ulysses, who might have been involved in this business. There *was* a Homer, an Englishman, who did turn out to be a Soviet spy, but he's dead and buried. Ann tried to call Nick about this, but she couldn't get hold of him. They both have the same information anyway. I think we've reached a dead end there."

Abrams said, "I thought one of those names might have some esoteric meaning to people in the know."

"I also asked Pat O'Brien about it, but he said basically the same thing." She paused, then added, "I decided I had to trust him." She looked at Abrams, then continued, "But...he seemed very...quiet afterward. I think he knows something."

Abrams nodded, then said, "I gave it some thought...and if those names don't mean anything, then it has to be the theme of the story."

"You mean a warrior who wanders for many years after the war, then returns home after being believed dead?"

"Yes."

Katherine nodded. "Arnold was trying to give us a clue to his killer, or killers. Or a clue to Talbot himself."

"Yes. Is there any warrior—a leader, an officer who has returned from the dead? Anyone who can be generally described as an Odysseus?"

She nodded. "There *were* a number of people in the OSS who were missing in action, then turned up alive after the war. But Ann ran that through her computer and discovered that most of them are dead now. The remainder are not involved in intelligence or government work of any sort. There are four who are, but they're very unlikely candidates to be involved in this business."

Abrams did not speak.

She looked at him for some time, then said, "There's something on your mind."

He replied, "Well . . . how about a man who has not yet returned from the dead?"

She stared at Abrams, then replied, "Those who have not returned from the dead are dead."

He said, "Of course. I meant a man who was listed as missing in action but whose remains have not been found or identified. Perhaps someone who disappeared under unusual circumstances."

She stayed silent for a moment, then said, "You know, there's a scene in *The Odyssey* where Odysseus is wandering in the netherworld and sees the spirit of the hunter Orion forever pursuing the spirits of the animals he had hunted when alive. And Odysseus says of Orion, 'Himself a shadow, hunting shadows.' " She held Abrams' eyes and said, "That's how I think of Arnold sometimes. That's how I think of my father, too. Shadows forever pursuing shadows."

Abrams said nothing for some time, then decided to let this oblique response pass, to not pursue any more shadows himself.

They entered the large mall, crowded with shoppers. Katherine commented, "Do you find it odd to walk among people when you know a great secret that they don't know? Something so cataclysmic that it will put an end to this commonplace scene very soon. Do you have a sense of heightened perception?"

Abrams said, "I'm not sure we know much more than anyone in this mall. Unless, of course, Peter Thorpe is in the mall."

She looked around. "I don't see him. Do you see anyone you know?"

"No. I'm thirsty. Are you buying?"

"I don't seem to have any money with me."

"I see you've been dealing with O'Brien long enough to have picked up some of his bad habits, such as hitting me for loose change."

She smiled.

Abrams bought two orange juices from the stand and handed her one. "I don't want to miss Mr. Thorpe. What's our schedule?"

"I told him we'd be entering Prospect Park by eleven thirty. We'll take the subway up."

He glanced at his watch. "We have some time." He walked over to a game arcade and deposited a quarter into a machine. It was a space-invader game, and Katherine could see that Abrams was adept at it. She said, "I see where you spend your time."

Abrams was concentrating on the game. "These little green bastards are trying to invade the earth, Kate—take that...and that!"

She laughed. "I can't believe this."

"Eye-hand coordination...quick think...snap decisions....Watch out!...Zap!"

She looked at the video screen. "Oh...they're moving faster..."

"Have no fear...earth is safe when Tony Abrams is at the helm."

"Is it?"

"Yes." The game ended and he straightened up. "Take a shot at it."

She stood tentatively at the controls. Abrams pushed the button and the game began. She said, "I don't understand this."

"Just keep blasting away."

She moved the controls erratically. "The green aliens are winning."

"Keep blasting." Abrams had begun playing the game next to her. "This is a good one. Enemy missiles are falling on my cities."

"Sounds charming. Is there a counterespionage game?"

"No...too hard to program...oh, damn it, there goes Pittsburgh."

"No loss. How do I stop these little green men?"

"Keep blasting...." Abrams stared at his video screen and took his hands off the controls. Missile after missile arched and whistled across the screen, vaporizing the cities in video mushroom clouds accompanied by a loud audio blast. He said quietly, "You know, sometimes I think that the real world doesn't exist to any greater extent than that world exists. Human destiny may be determined by a video game tape played by colossal beings on a twenty-thousand-foot screen. The history of mankind could be a series of programmed possibilities stored in a memory chip; a few moments of idle recreation for other beings. The end of this world will come when the quarter runs out. Or perhaps the tape will break...we might see a big black rip in the sky, a short, snappy jerk. The End."

She looked at him. "You're in a philosophical mood."

He turned away from the video games. "Running excites my brain....Let's head out."

They left the mall and walked to the BMT station on Bay Parkway. Katherine said, "We'll run Prospect Park, then that's it."

"Well, I hope Thorpe can join us there."

"Yes, this is the last possible rendezvous point. He's done the park with me a few times and knows the route."

"Good. We'll keep a sharp eye out for him."

She glanced at him as they descended the stairs of the subway station.

They stood well back from the edge of the platform and waited for the train. Abrams scanned the few people on the platform. After a minute of silence he said, "There's always that one percent chance he's working solely in the interests of the United States government."

She replied in a low voice, "I give it a fifty-fifty chance."

"You're very generous. But the net result is the same—as long as I'm not a hundred percent certain, I won't summarily execute him."

She turned to him sharply. "You will not do that under any circumstances."

"Why not?"

"Because you have no proof. It's not your right—"

"Hold on. You're the one who told me you would kill your best friend if he turned out to be Talbot."

"Peter Thorpe is obviously not Talbot...he may be an accomplice....Anyway, people like Peter, if they have turned, are interrogated, not shot."

"Well, I think it should be the other way around. I'd think you'd want to talk to Talbot and find out what he's been up to for these last forty years or so. Thorpe, on the other hand, is low-level. Also, his behavior defies anything we know about human abnormality. Because he's not..."

"Not what?"

"Not abnormal. I've seen his type before. Picture a psychiatrist trying to cure a lion of his nasty habit of ripping living things apart. The lion is confused. His behavior is instinctive. The lion does not believe he is nuts. And he isn't. He's a lion, doing his thing. And if he'd been raised in a penthouse on Park Avenue, it would make no difference in his behavior. If you dropped in to chat with him when he was hungry or cross about something, he'd rip you apart and not lose any sleep over it. Lions are not guilty of murder, and some people with strong killing instincts are not guilty either. Nonetheless, a bullet in the heart is the correct way to deal with dangerous animals. The person who fires the bullet should not lose any sleep over it either."

Katherine said softly. "Do you believe that?"

"I believe I believe it. But I've never acted on it."

"Don't. Not unless your life is in danger."

"It is. That's the point."

"I mean immediate danger. Clear and imminent danger, as we say in law."

"Ah, we're back to that split second."

"It always returns to that." She glanced at her watch, then put a lighter tone in her voice. "Teach me how to play Space Invaders."

"That takes a long time."

"Good."

He nodded, then said, "First things first. Right?"

"Right."

The train pulled into the platform and they boarded.

CHAPTER THIRTY-EIGHT

West's hand found the butt of the revolver. Simultaneously, he heard the air crack around his ears and a burning pain seared his bare shoulders. West raised the pistol with one hand, but could not summon the strength to squeeze the trigger.

A second crack of the long whip raked his neck. The gun exploded in his hand and the room was filled with a deafening roar.

Behind him he heard Eva scream.

West's hand contracted again to squeeze off another round, this one aimed at Thorpe's face a few feet from his. West's fingers tightened and his trigger finger pulled back, but there was no explosion. West focused on his hand. The gun was gone and he realized it had recoiled out of his numb and nearly paralyzed hand, though he still felt its presence in his grasp.

Thorpe slid forward and retrieved the revolver. He steadied himself in a kneeling position and leveled the gun at West. "You...shit...."

West felt the room spinning as he tried to stand. He heard the whirring sound of the whip again but barely felt it as it sliced across his chest.

Eva struck again, three times in quick succession, until West dropped in a heap to the floor.

West turned his face quickly away from the smell.

Eva grabbed his ear and turned him back toward the smelling salts.

West's eyes opened and he found himself looking down at the floor. Slowly he realized he was lying on the gurney again, face-down, his head hanging over the edge. His calves were strapped, but there was no strap restraining his upper torso. Tentatively, he raised himself to his hands and knees.

He felt a ripping flash of pain across his shoulder blades, and collapsed. Another strike of the whip fell on his buttocks and he felt the warm blood trickle over his cold skin.

Thorpe's voice, shaky and tremulous, reached him through his pain. "So, Nicholas...so...you are much smarter than I thought... and braver than I imagined....Why do I always underestimate you?"

West turned his head and saw Thorpe sitting in a chair, his color ashen, and his clothes and hair disheveled. He noticed again that Thorpe's light trousers were stained with wetness. West wondered how long he had been unconscious, then the pungent smell of cordite registered, and he knew it hadn't been very long. He also noticed that there were no wires leading from his body, that all the equipment had been pushed well away from the gurney.

Thorpe said, "Eva will practice her specialty for a while." He stood. "I'll be back in a few hours with Katherine. It's been my experience that people who can endure pain and hold out under torture crack very quickly when someone they're close to is being tortured. You'll see what I mean."

West swallowed several times, then found his voice. "Be sure... be sure to clean yourself...before you go...."

Eva struck with the whip and West howled.

Thorpe smiled, then said to Eva, "I want him alive and conscious when I return."

Eva replied, "He will be a different man when you return."

Thorpe moved toward the door.

West called out, "Peter...you blew it, Peter...you're an amateur....You're not as smart as you think...."

Eva raised the whip, but Thorpe held up a hand and stared at West. There was something in West's voice that he didn't like. "What are you talking about?"

"They'll kill you for letting me die."

"You're not going to die. Yet."

"Yes. I'm going to die. Now." West suddenly yanked a small tuft of hair from the top of his head and stuffed it in his mouth.

Thorpe lunged across the room and thrust his fingers down West's throat. West bit down hard and Thorpe screamed, drawing two bloody fingers out of West's mouth.

West chewed the hair and let out a long sigh, then his body convulsed for a few seconds. He lay still, his tongue protruding and his eyes wide open. The bitter-almond smell of cyanide drifted from his mouth and nostrils, causing Thorpe to move quickly back. "Oh . . . you son of a bitch! You did it! You bastard . . . Nick . . . Nick!"

Thorpe moved cautiously closer to West and examined the small bald spot on the top of his head where the hair implant had been. "I'll be goddamned. What the hell won't they think of next?"

Eva stared at the body.

Thorpe thought a moment, then said, "Well, I won't underestimate you again, Nick." He watched Eva as she flexed the whip. He could tell she felt cheated, frustrated. He said, "Whip him."

She looked at him with wide eyes. "What?"

"Whip him. There's a drug that reproduces the effects of cyanide, but only causes a deep coma."

She nodded and raised the whip, slashing a deep wound across West's lower back.

Thorpe stepped forward and examined the wound. There was no sign of blood circulation. "Damn it!"

Eva stared at Thorpe, an accusing look in her eye, which gave way to bewilderment. "I do not understand . . . the hair . . . ?"

Thorpe gave her a sharp look. "Yes, you stupid cow. Cyanide suspended in artificial hair. Have you ever heard of that?"

"No."

Thorpe sat down and rubbed his forehead. "Oh, Christ." He glanced up at Eva. "We checked his teeth, anus . . . nostrils . . . pipe and tobacco . . . didn't you check his hair?"

She nodded. "With a comb and ultraviolet light. But I noticed nothing."

Thorpe licked his lips. "Goddamn it. We're in trouble."

"Me? You are the interrogator. *You* are the one who released his arms the first time, causing all this..." She waved her arm around.

Thorpe nodded and wiped a line of perspiration from his upper lip. He thought a moment, then said, "But *you* wanted his upper torso and arms free for the whipping. You said you liked to see them thrash around...try to cover their back and head with their arms, bite their knuckles..." He looked at her. "This was *your* show."

She swallowed. "Well...yes...but..."

Thorpe seemed deep in thought, then he looked up at her. "Actually, Eva, what happened is this—while I was gone, you released his arms and chest, turned him over, and began whipping him, against my orders. He couldn't stand the pain and committed suicide—"

"No! It was you!" She realized the danger she was in, and took a step back. She shouted, "No! Do not kill me!" She dropped her whip and put her arms out in a protective gesture.

Thorpe stood, drew his revolver, and aimed it at her face, then fired at point-blank range.

Eva's head snapped back and her arms shot out as she backpedaled, trying to regain her balance. She fell, then as Thorpe watched, incredulous, she got to her feet.

Eva stood with both hands covering her face, as though she were weeping into them, but instead of tears, blood flowed through her fingers. "Oh...oh...what has happened?"

Thorpe stepped up close to her and examined the exit wound behind her ear; a mass of blood, grayish fluid, and splintered bone and cartilage. He realized the shot had been badly placed. "Oh, shit!" He considered putting another bullet in her head, but that would look amateurish to the people who would have to dispose of the body.

Eva sank to her knees, one hand over her eye, the other now behind her ear, squeezing the entry and exit wounds in a vise. The blood was running down her neck and arms, dripping onto the floor.

Thorpe looked at the trail of blood on the floor and realized he would have to mop it up himself. "Christ, woman, die!"

"Help me. Please...who has done this? West has done this...."

Thorpe laughed. "Poor Nicko, gets the blame for everything."

Eva remained on her knees, but showed no sign of dying soon. She moaned, "West has tricked us. . . . We will tell Androv. . ."

Thorpe smiled again. "I have *my* story for Androv. You can give him yours when you meet in hell." Thorpe pulled her to her feet, and half carried her across the room. He reached out and unlatched a thick steel door, opened it, and stood her inside a butcher's freezer. He hefted her up and snagged her dress on a meat hook, then released her.

Eva hung a few inches from the floor, her legs twitching and her arms flapping. Thorpe wiped his bloody hands on the hem of her dress.

He stepped back and glanced to the right. On another hook hung the frosty-blue body of Randolph Carbury.

Thorpe said to himself, "Getting crowded in here." He turned and went back to the gurney, retrieved West's body and carried it to the freezer, dumping it on the floor.

Eva was moaning softly, "Oh, my God . . . do not leave me here with the dead. . . ."

Thorpe stepped out of the freezer and slammed the door shut. "Well, it's just one of those days. . . ."

He surveyed the dimly lit garret, then checked his watch. "Time to go jogging."

CHAPTER THIRTY-NINE

Abrams and Katherine emerged from the BMT station at Fort Hamilton Parkway and ran north, entering the five-hundred-acre Prospect Park along South Lake Drive.

Abrams breathed in the cooler, cleaner air of the heavily treed park. The terrain features had been created by the last Ice Age terminal moraine, and that, coupled with heavy plantings, offered a diversity of landscape and hiding places. But Abrams knew every inch of the park and knew where the surprises could be expected.

They turned north on East Lake Drive, ran up Breeze Hill and past the boathouse, and approached the zoo, set in an expanse of gardens. They slowed to a walk on the steep rise called Battle Pass Hill and stopped on the hill's summit.

Abrams looked west into the Long Meadow, a sweep of grassland that could pass for a rural valley. Katherine looked north and west into an open area called the Vale of Cashmere, covered with resting migratory birds. She said, "This is a good spot to take a break. Good all-around view." She sat on a patch of grass and caught her breath.

Abrams knelt beside her, wiping the perspiration from his face with his sleeve.

She said, "I think this is the spot where Washington's command post was during the Battle of Long Island."

Abrams nodded. "He picked a good place to keep an eye on the muggers."

She smiled, then looked around. "I don't see any muggers.... There's a fair-sized holiday crowd."

"Right. I don't think Thorpe likes crowds. Let's take the subway back to my place."

She thought a moment, then said, "Let's finish the park."

Abrams fell back on the grass. "The park will finish me."

"You're doing fine. You shouldn't lie down."

He didn't answer, but looked up silently and watched the sky. After a few seconds he said, "I've seen that helicopter before."

She looked up and watched a small gray helicopter disappear to the north. "Yes. I've seen it before too." She stood. "Let's go. You'll get muscle cramps."

Abrams got slowly to his feet. "I think I liked masquerading as an old man better than this."

"We'll walk awhile," Katherine said.

They began following the path down the long hill. She said, "That may have been a police helicopter."

"Possible. But I don't recognize the model. They use Bell copters. That was something else."

She gave him a sidelong glance. "*Do* you have police backup?"

"I'm not a policeman."

They walked in silence, then he said, "You realize that he could get to you anytime? On the boat out to Glen Cove, for instance. Or he could smother you with a pillow in bed."

She looked at him. "What are you getting at?"

"Actually, though, I don't think he intends to kill you. He probably wants to kidnap and interrogate you."

She thought of the garret room above the apartment, then said, "But he could have just asked me to come to the Lombardy for a drink."

Abrams replied, "'Will you walk into my parlour? said the spider to the fly; 'tis the prettiest little parlour that ever you did spy.'" Abrams added, "Would you have gone at this point in your relationship?"

"I would have gone at any point, if I thought there was something to be learned or gained."

"But you'd be covered before you went. And if you didn't come out, Thorpe would be exposed." Abrams concluded, "My theory is that Thorpe is using you to get at me. To get two birds with one stone. Time is short for him. I'm to be killed, by the way, because I'm not worth interrogating."

She replied in a slightly taunting tone of voice, "That's quite a piece of deduction, or do you hear those voices again?"

He smiled. "No, but I am getting into his head. He's clever, but predictable."

She stayed silent awhile, then nodded. "So...Peter has used me as bait to draw you out, and you've used me as a decoy to draw him out."

"Something like that."

She glared at him. "At least you're honest. Look, you don't care much about the national-security aspect of this, do you?"

He replied, "I'll give that more thought when my life is out of danger. For now the first law is not *salus populi suprema lex,* but *lex talionis*—the law of retaliation—*vendetta*." He pronounced it with an Italian accent.

She forced a smile. "Well, I'll never try to push *you* off a roof."

"I take it personally. I'm not very professional when it comes to my life."

They came to the Memorial Arch at Grand Army Plaza. She said, "I told Peter that if he hadn't joined us by this point, I'd take the subway back to Manhattan from here. Would you like to come back to my place?"

He looked at her, and her meaning was clear enough. "I would."

She nodded. "We'll wait five minutes."

Abrams waited in silence, checking his watch more often than he needed to. He looked back in the direction from which they'd come. "Well, here comes Peter Cottontail, hopping down the bunny trail."

She turned and saw Thorpe running toward them, dressed in a tan and blue jogging suit.

Abrams said, "If you normally kiss, then kiss."

"I'm not a very good actor."

Thorpe slowed and trotted up to them. "Well, the marathon man and the long-distance lady. You both look beat. Good run?"

Katherine kissed him on the cheek. "Yes. What happened to your nose?"

Thorpe touched his fingers to his bandaged nostril. "I had it where it didn't belong, as usual."

Abrams said, "What happened to your fingers?"

Thorpe glanced at his two bandaged fingers. "The same thing that happened to my nose. Why are you always so excited by the sight of my blood?"

"Blood makes me curious."

"Typical cop."

Katherine interjected, "You look pale."

"Hey, what is this? Dump-on-Peter day?" Thorpe looked around the park. "Damned awful place to run—baby strollers, little savages on bicycles, skateboard freaks, and dogs who eat joggers." He scratched his head, then said brightly, "Hey, let's run Greenwood Cemetery. I did that once. Five hundred acres of stiffs."

Abrams said, "Cemetery running is illegal."

Thorpe smiled. "Come on, Tony. I'll bet you've run cemeteries. They're great for solitude."

Katherine said, "Won't there be a lot of people there? It's Memorial Day."

Abrams replied, "It's an old cemetery. The last interment was probably sixty years ago. They don't get many visitors."

Thorpe clapped his hands and began jogging in place. "Okay, troops, follow me."

Abrams and Katherine followed. They ran down the avenue alongside the park for twenty blocks, until they came to the high wrought-iron fence of Greenwood Cemetery.

Thorpe looked up and down the block. "Okay, gang, we're in the clear." He shimmied up the fence and dropped into the cemetery. "Come on." He looked at Katherine and Abrams through the bars. "Well?"

Abrams helped Katherine up, grasping her legs, then pushing up on her rear. Thorpe said, "Watch that, Tony." As Katherine climbed down into the cemetery, Thorpe reached up and helped her, and Abrams could see he felt for and discovered the pistol.

Abrams climbed up and dropped to the other side. Thorpe reached out to steady him, but Abrams brushed him off.

They began walking through the graves until they came to a single-lane road. Abrams had run these somber acres, the final resting place of half a million souls, including such notables as Currier and Ives, Horace Greeley, Boss Tweed, Henry Ward Beecher, and Samuel F. B. Morse. And Thorpe was right about one thing: cemetery running was the best. The old graveyard was not only serene, it was a treasurehouse of Victorian Gothic Revival funerary. Statues, urns, tombstones, arches, and wrought iron crowded every acre of this place where time had stopped.

They began trotting slowly along the road lined with lonely mausoleums. There didn't seem to be anyone else in the cemetery. Thorpe recited, "Yea, though I walk through the valley of the shadow of death, I will fear no evil, for I am the meanest motherfucker *in* the valley."

"Peter," exclaimed Katherine, almost playfully, "that's vulgar."

"So is death, which is why it's second only to sex as a topic for jokes."

Abrams, running a bit behind, looked from one to another. He could see how Peter Thorpe held a perverse fascination for some women. Katherine seemed almost to enjoy his boorishness, even now. But, he reminded himself, she could feel nothing for him any longer, and was playacting, as ordered.

They came to a fork in the path and Thorpe called out, "Left one."

They ran between the black-granite and white-marble headstones for about a thousand yards, Thorpe setting the pace. Katherine fell back, and Abrams was dropping even farther behind.

Katherine called out, "Peter . . . too fast! We're pretty beat."

Thorpe shouted back, "Oh, Kate, you're fine. Tony has got to push himself a little."

After a few hundred more yards Thorpe slowed, then began walking. Katherine, then Abrams, caught up, both breathing heavily, and perspiring.

They walked in silence. Abrams tried to listen for anything out of the ordinary, but the blood was pounding in his ears. He felt very fatigued, very vulnerable here in this place of infinite ambushes.

Thorpe took up the role of guide. "This landscape architecture was very typical of the Romantic movement. Does anyone feel romantic?" He motioned toward a field of tombstones. "Tony, do all these crosses make you nervous?"

Abrams didn't reply.

Thorpe continued, "Have you ever seen so many guardian angels? Do you have a guardian angel, Tony?"

"We may soon find out."

Thorpe smiled, then looked to his left. About fifty yards in from the drive was an open grave, a fresh mound of earth beside it. Two long-handled shovels were stuck in the loose earth. Thorpe cut across the grass and stood beside the open hole. "Look at this. The stone is over a hundred years old, but the hole has just been opened." He knelt and peered into the deep grave as Abrams and Katherine approached. "Empty...I think they can disinter the bones after a certain amount of time. Sell the plot to somebody else. Not exactly a final resting place."

Katherine said, "Let's move on."

Thorpe said, "There must be a funeral today."

Abrams observed, "Then the old tombstone would be gone."

"True," replied Thorpe. He read the words carved in the black granite. " 'Quentin Mosby—born April 21, 1843, died December 6, 1879.' He was younger than us. They didn't hang around too long in those days, did they?" He stood and looked at Abrams. "Why do we expect to live so long?"

"Because we watch ourselves."

Thorpe nodded. He said, "By the way, I hope you're prepared for trouble. Things are getting a little tense this weekend."

"I hadn't noticed anything unusual."

"But you are armed?"

Abrams stared at Thorpe, and Thorpe stared back. They both understood that the time had arrived. Thorpe seemed almost to nod in acknowledgment.

Abrams looked around. Three men were approaching from

different directions, working their way between the gravestones. They were dressed in the green work clothes of gravediggers.

Katherine watched the men draw closer. She said, "Peter, who are those men?"

Thorpe shrugged, "How should I know, Kate. I guess they're who they appear to be."

Katherine said, "Let's go." She turned back toward the drive and saw three more men standing on the edge of the grass.

Thorpe said, "We seem to have gotten ourselves in the middle of a funeral."

The three men who were approaching stopped, each one less than twenty feet away, forming a half circle around the grave. Each man took up a position beside a tombstone.

Abrams saw that the three men on the drive had spread out. He also saw that Thorpe had moved beside the headstone over the open grave. Everyone was in position. Abrams could see no way out of this one.

CHAPTER FORTY

Abrams stood perfectly still. Strangely, the blood in his head stopped pounding, his heart slowed to a normal rate, and his breathing became regular. He felt the numbing fatigue of the long run lifting, and his senses became acute. He smelled the freshly dug earth, the sweaty bodies near him, and the faint fragrance of flowers. He saw clearly the fixed expressions on the faces of the six men around him, and the inscrutable expression of Peter Thorpe. The perspiration was cooling on his skin, and he was keenly aware of the shoulder holster on his chest. Somewhere, a bird sang in a distant tree. He stole a glance at Katherine and their eyes met for a brief second, just long enough to transmit assurances and confidence in each other.

Thorpe cleared his throat and said softly, "This looks a bit suspicious. If I were paranoid, I would say we were surrounded by men whose intentions are questionable."

"I would say you were right."

Katherine added, "I would say we should draw our guns."

Thorpe looked at her. "Unfortunately, I don't have a gun, but I assume Tony does." He nodded toward the grave. "Perfect fox-hole. Ready?"

Abrams took Katherine's arm in a restraining gesture, and looked down into the grave. "The law requires only six feet. This looks nearly eight. Good grave, lousy foxhole."

Thorpe shot Abrams a look of unmistakable hatred. "Well, what do you suggest?"

"It's your show, Pete. You call it."

Thorpe regarded Abrams closely, then said, "Well, let's just stay cool. They may only want to chat."

"All six of them?"

Thorpe didn't answer, but wiped his forehead with his sweatband.

The six men began moving simultaneously, as though they'd gotten a signal. They closed in around the grave, stopping only a few feet short of Abrams, Katherine, and Thorpe. They didn't speak, or make any overt threatening movement.

Abrams glanced at Katherine. She looked deathly pale, but he had to admire her composure in the face of death. He looked at Thorpe, who appeared to be lost in thought. The reason for this grotesque standoff, Abrams knew, was that Thorpe was a man who kept all his options open. He did not intend to reveal himself until he was certain that this was not a trap, that the tables could not be somehow turned.

Thorpe's eyes moved back and forth between Abrams and Katherine. He spoke curtly, "Well, Tony?"

Abrams understood the question. He took Katherine's arm and spoke directly to Thorpe. "Yes, there is a car waiting to pick us up."

Thorpe looked around. "I don't see any car. I think they forgot you."

"I think not." Abrams tapped his pants pocket. "Radio tracking transmitter." He added, "Helicopter close by."

Thorpe glanced into the sky. "I don't see a helicopter, either."

Abrams stared at the six men and caught their eyes, one at a time. "Gentlemen, I'm leaving. I suggest you do the same."

One man, who seemed to be the leader, was staring at Abrams' NYPD sweat shirt. His eyes shifted to Thorpe.

Abrams held Katherine's arm and they turned toward the drive and started walking away.

She said softly, "*Are* we covered?"

"I think so. Spinelli is probably waiting for Thorpe to make his move."

"Are we going to get away with this?"

"You have to act as though we are. Keep walking."

"Wait!" Thorpe ran up beside them as they approached the drive. He said, "There are *six* men there. I think we should cooperate with them, at least until the cavalry arrives." He said to Abrams abruptly, "May I see that transmitter?"

Abrams laughed at him. "Actually, no."

Thorpe reddened, then said, "I don't think you have one. I think you're alone."

Abrams could tell that Thorpe was torn between caution and action. Abrams realized this charade could not go on much longer without someone committing himself. Thorpe seemed on the verge of doing just that. Abrams said, "When in doubt, take the safe way out. There will be other days, Pete."

Thorpe rubbed his jaw, then nodded, as though conceding the point. "Okay...." He pulled a large bandanna from his pocket and Abrams caught a glimpse of the small flat automatic inside it.

Abrams swung, catching Thorpe off guard. He hit hard on the point of Thorpe's jaw and sent him reeling against a giant oak tree. Thorpe bounced off the tree and Abrams' fist smashed again into Thorpe's face. Thorpe fell to the ground.

Katherine already had positioned herself behind a gravestone. Abrams could hear the cap gun–like sounds of the 7.65 as she emptied its seven-round magazine in quick succession in the direction of Thorpe's men.

Abrams threw himself in a prone position on the grass a few feet from where Katherine lay, and fired twice. The reports of the gunfire reverberated through the gravestones and echoed throughout the cemetery, making the pistol fire sound like a small war.

Katherine quickly slammed the second magazine into the butt of the pistol, but before she could fire, Abrams called out, "Hold it."

They both peered up through the rows of gravestones and hedges. No one was visible, and as far as Abrams could determine, no one had returned the fire. Abrams rose to one knee, holding his revolver with both hands.

Katherine stared straight ahead, her automatic held to her front in a prone firing position. "I think they're gone."

"Could be." He rose up into a crouch and looked at the

unconscious body of Peter Thorpe lying faceup on the edge of the drive. Abrams debated with himself for a second or two, then glanced at Katherine, who was scanning the rows of tombstones. He placed the muzzle of his revolver between Thorpe's eyes and cocked the hammer.

"Don't."

Abrams turned his head, expecting to see one of Thorpe's men. Instead he looked up into a pair of cold eyes the same color as the blue-gray barrel of the Uzi submachine gun pointed at him.

Two more men appeared from behind a mausoleum, also carrying automatic weapons. All the weapons had big ugly silencers fitted to them. The men were young and hard-looking, and seemed self-assured.

"Stand up."

Abrams and Katherine stood. Abrams noticed that they wore ankle-height black basketball sneakers, and their clothing appeared to be normal casual wear, though the colors were on the dark, muted side. Abrams recognized the attire as subtly paramilitary; urban guerrillas of some sort who were dressed to mingle in the crowds or engage in a firefight.

"I'll take that."

Abrams caught the hint of an accent. He handed the man his revolver, butt first.

The man motioned with the barrel of his Uzi. Abrams and Katherine walked back toward the grave.

Abrams came through the rows of tombstones, and saw three more men, similarly dressed and also holding silenced automatic weapons, standing around the open pit. One of them cocked his finger at Abrams.

Abrams moved closer and looked down into the grave. Thorpe's six men lay at the bottom, sprawled atop each other, their bodies ripped and riddled with what could only have been bursts of automatic fire.

Katherine took a step closer. She looked into the pit, put her hand to her mouth, and turned away.

One of the men spoke. "I thought it a good idea for you to see this, so you understand we are not playing at games here."

Abrams recognized the accent as English. Simultaneously, Katherine looked at the man speaking. "Marc!" She turned to Abrams. "This is...an acquaintance of mine—Marc Pembroke."

Marc Pembroke did not acknowledge her but made a motion to his men, who began filling in the grave.

Abrams regarded the man's icy demeanor, then looked back into the pit. He thought, *With acquaintances like that, who needs strangers trying to kill you?*

Pembroke said, "You've nearly botched things up, you know. It's fortunate that Pat O'Brien asked me to keep an eye out. He said you might pursue private initiatives."

Abrams said, "We were out for a run."

Pembroke ignored him and looked at Katherine. "You ought to have known better."

"Don't lecture me. I don't even know what your role is in any of this. But I *will* ask Mr. O'Brien."

Pembroke began to reply, but then looked back at Abrams. "You have an important duty to perform this afternoon, Mr. Abrams. You had no right risking your life in this idiotic business."

Abrams replied, "Well, now I'm free to risk my life in the idiotic business of this afternoon."

Katherine looked at him quizzically.

Pembroke watched the grave fill with dirt, then without looking up said, "Why don't you just be off, then? We'll tidy things up here."

Katherine hesitated, then said, "Peter...?"

Pembroke gave her an annoyed look. "Peter Thorpe is not to be molested in any way. He's been given a little something to keep him asleep...." He looked at Abrams, then continued. "When he recovers consciousness he will find himself lying safely in a mausoleum. This grave will be covered with sod, and we will be gone. With any luck at all, Mr. Thorpe will be confused and frightened enough not to mention the incident to his controllers. It is important that Peter Thorpe maintain his Soviet contacts until *we* are ready to pull him in. Good day to you both." He turned his back on them.

Abrams took Katherine's arm. One of Pembroke's men handed them their guns and they walked down to the tree-lined drive.

Thorpe was gone. Abrams could easily believe that when he awoke in a dark vault, he would be confused. Abrams was confused himself, and he'd been awake for the whole thing.

They left the cemetery through the main gate on 25th Street. Katherine said, "What happened to your police backup?"

Abrams looked up from his thoughts. "What? Oh...I suppose your British buddy took care of them."

"I was beginning to think you were bluffing."

"So was I." He looked at her. "You understand that Pembroke would have let us die had things gone a little differently."

She nodded.

"You're all a bit strange. Do you know that? Or have you stopped noticing?"

"I know." She looked at him. "What important duty do you have this afternoon?"

"You're the last person I'd tell."

She smiled. "Well, welcome to the group, Mr. Abrams."

He grumbled something, then said, "You're a bad influence on me."

They walked slowly, absorbed in their own thoughts. Abrams took her arm, tentatively, and she drew closer to him. They covered the block to Fourth Avenue and stood at the stairs to the BMT subway station. Abrams said, "This is the line we took down to Owl's Head Park. We've come full circle."

"Yes, we have. This will get me back to Manhattan, won't it?"

"Yes, I'll ride with you as far as Borough Hall. You get off at— look, my place or yours?"

"Neither," she replied.

He looked at her.

"The house on Thirty-sixth Street," she said quickly. Her words came out in a rush. "It's safe...."

He felt his chest pounding. "Okay—"

"We'll have to sleep in separate rooms, though.... You can come to me at night...or I'll come to you...."

"We should decide so we don't wind up alone in the wrong rooms."

She laughed and threw her arms around him, burying her head in his chest. He felt her sobbing. She got her voice under control and said, "This has been one of the most awful days...one of the best days....Be careful this afternoon. Whatever it is, be careful."

Abrams saw that people were going around them to get to the subway stairs. "Maybe we should take a taxi—go to our places, pack—"

"Yes. Good idea." She straightened up and composed herself.

They stood at the curb and waited for a passing cab. Abrams said, "Thorpe?"

She replied, "I feel nothing."

"Anger? Betrayal?"

"No, nothing...foolish, perhaps. Everyone else seemed to know about him."

"Are you still going to Van Dorn's this afternoon?"

"Of course. It's business."

He nodded. "Is it possible Thorpe will actually show up?"

She considered awhile, then said, "Knowing him, it's possible. It's business for him, too."

BOOK V

The Russian Mission

CHAPTER FORTY-ONE

Tony Abrams joined the holiday crowds at Penn Station and boarded the three-twenty train for Garden City, Long Island. It was a short ride, but he had ample time to turn over in his mind the events of the morning: Carmine Street, the Brooklyn run, Thorpe, the cemetery. He thought about the Englishman, Marc Pembroke, whom Katherine had identified as another shadowy character with an office in Rockefeller Center and a door that was always locked.

He and Katherine had taken a taxi to his place and picked up a few things including the suit he was now wearing and his identification. They'd gone back to Carmine Street and gathered some of her things. Then they'd ridden up to the town house on 36th Street. During the ride, there was that awkwardness a man and a woman feel when they know they are going someplace to make love for the first time.

The town house was under discreet surveillance, and as Abrams and Katherine approached the door, they were intercepted by a plainclothesman who asked them to identify themselves and their purpose.

"Abrams," he replied. "I have no purpose."

The plainclothesman smiled and said, "Spinelli's telling everybody you're dead."

"I feel fine."

He led Katherine into the red-brick house. They expected to find

Claudia there, but the house was empty. Abrams did not construe Claudia's absence as unusual. Sometime after Van Dorn's party she would return to the town house, and Abrams meant to have a word with her. He knew she was the weakest link in this iron chain and he intended to break her before the sun rose again.

Katherine had gone to the room that had been her nursery, the room Claudia had given him the night of the OSS dinner. Abrams dropped his bag in an available bedroom across from hers, then helped her unpack. As she finished putting her things away, she said, "It's always strange returning to a childhood place."

"*Bittersweet,* I think, is the word."

She walked across the room and, as she approached, Abrams wondered how and why he had ever thought of her as the Ice Queen.

They made love in the four-poster bed, and Abrams was glad he hadn't slept with Claudia in that bed. Their lovemaking had all of the best qualities that mark a first time—passion, discovery, and a feeling of fulfillment. For Abrams, the reality had been even more satisfactory than the long-held fantasy. As Katherine had put it, "I've scratched a six-month itch."

To which he'd replied, "Six months?"

"Maybe seven. How about you?"

He'd hesitated, then said with a straightforwardness that matched her own, "From my first day at O'Brien, Kimberly."

He'd left her lying on the four-poster bed. She had wished him luck on whatever it was he was about to undertake. In the event one or the other did not return to the town house before dawn, they'd made a date to meet for coffee, before work, at the Brasserie.

Abrams' mind returned to the present as the train arrived at the suburban village. He walked from the almost empty station to the nearby law offices of Edwards and Styler, located in a Georgian-style mansion.

The building was open, but deserted. Abrams referred to the lobby register and climbed a sweeping staircase to the second floor. He drew his .38 from his pocket and held it against his side. He walked quietly across the upper foyer and found a heavy oak-paneled door marked EDWARDS AND STYLER. He stood close to the door and listened for a while. He could hear nothing on the other side of the door. He knocked hard, three times, then moved to the side.

The door opened a crack, then swung fully open. A man about his own age smiled and put out his hand. "Mr. Abrams? Mike Tanner."

Abrams transferred the pistol to his left hand and shook hands with Tanner, who was staring down at the gun. Tanner recovered his composure and escorted Abrams into a rear room, which was decorated in oak and red leather.

An older man rose to greet him. "I'm Huntington Styler."

Abrams took Styler's hand, wondering about parents who would name a baby Huntington, wondering more about the man who used the name.

Styler said, "Please have a seat."

Abrams sat and regarded Styler for a few seconds, thinking, OSS. There was something about these people that was readily identifiable. It was as though they'd all gone to the same schools, belonged to the same clubs, and used the same haberdasher.

Huntington Styler, in turn, regarded Abrams for some time, then went to a liquor cabinet. "Scotch and soda, correct?"

"Yes."

Mike Tanner said, "You've read the brief on this case?"

"Yes. I think the Soviet Mission has a good case against George Van Dorn."

"So do we," said Styler. He handed Abrams a drink. "It's not popular to represent the Soviets in a lawsuit against a well-known patriot. We've lost some clients over this."

Abrams replied, "Someone has to see that justice is done."

"True." Styler seemed deep in thought, then said, "I appreciate your misgivings about joining us, based on the fact that you've done a little work for the firm with which Mr. Van Dorn is associated. But part-time process serving does not constitute an unethical situation. It is, in fact, so minor, we didn't mention it to our Russian clients."

Abrams thought the purpose of expunging his work with O'Brien, Kimberly and Rose from his employment history had less

to do with conflict of interest than it had to do with the fact that the
Russians undoubtedly knew what O'Brien and Company was really
all about.

Mike Tanner said, "I heard on Friday from Mr. Androv. He
seemed a bit upset at your police background, but I assured him
you'd been nothing more than a traffic cop. Your police files are
sealed, I assume."

"That's what they tell me." Abrams wondered if the KGB had
ever gotten on to him when he was on the Red Squad. The more he
thought about his cover, which held closely to the truth, the more
he realized there could be problems. He had filled out a long visitors' questionnaire for the Russians, giving vital statistics and other
personal information. There were two questions he hadn't expected:
Are you now or have you ever been a member of the Communist party?
Do you have any relatives or friends who are or have been members?

The questions sounded as though they had been drawn up by
the House Un-American Activities Committee in 1948, though the
Russians were asking for different reasons. Abrams said to Tanner,
"Did Androv mention my parents' Communist party membership?"

"Yes. He wondered if we were trying to butter him up. Then he
went into a harangue about people who had been shown the light,
who were born into the faith, so to speak, and did not continue in
the faith."

Abrams nodded.

Tanner added, "He asked if you spoke any Russian. I referred
him to the visitors' questionnaire in which you said no." Tanner bit
his lip, then added, "I suppose that was a shot in the dark on his
part."

"I never listed Russian as a language skill on any form, except in
the police force."

Styler nodded. He said, "Let me give you a piece of advice from
an old play called *The Double Dealer*. 'No mask like open truth to
cover lies/As to go naked is the best disguise.' "

Abrams sipped on his drink and thought: He was going in
there under his own name and he existed in all the places where the
Russians might check; he was born, went to school, had a driver's

license, and so on. The major alteration of public and private records had been confined to obliterating his employment with O'Brien and predating his employment with Styler to fill in the gap between his resignation from the police force and the present. In all other respects his cover was solid, because it was the truth. Yet it was the truth, as he was discovering, that might be his undoing. Especially the one great truth, which he had only recently discovered, that his buddy Peter Thorpe was an agent of the KGB.

Abrams lit a cigarette and reflected on that new development. The question was: Had Thorpe filed a report to the Russians in which Abrams was mentioned by name? Abrams thought it was a sucker's bet to gamble that he had not. He knew he should abort the mission. He knew he should have killed Thorpe, if for no other reason than to try to protect himself. But it was too late for that now, and may well have been too late even as early as Saturday morning. Abrams looked at Tanner. "Have you spoken to Androv since Friday?"

"No." He looked at his watch. "But I'm to call him and confirm." He picked up the telephone, and after some time found himself speaking to Viktor Androv. Tanner confirmed the time of the meeting, then said, "Yes, sir. Mr. Styler and Mr. Abrams will be there." He listened, then replied, "Yes, they're both here now.... Yes, I will."

Tanner hung up and looked at Abrams. "He wants you to know that he looks forward to meeting the son of famous freedom fighters."

"I'm flattered," Abrams said. He turned to Styler and said abruptly, "I didn't see you at the OSS dinner Friday night."

Styler smiled slowly, "I never go. I'm out of that business."

Except today, thought Abrams. Styler was holding a one-day-only Memorial Day sale. Abrams said, "But you are acquainted with Mr. O'Brien."

Styler remained silent for some time, then a strained look passed over his face. He said softly, "I don't know how much your personal feelings for Pat O'Brien play into this.... I assume you're acting out of larger motivations... and if I were a cunning man, I wouldn't tell you this right now...."

Abrams set his drink on an end table and leaned forward.

Styler read the expression on his face and nodded. "Pat O'Brien flew out of Toms River, New Jersey, last night to make a parachute jump. The aircraft crashed in the mountains of Pennsylvania. Only the pilot's body was found on board. The authorities assume that Mr. O'Brien jumped at some earlier time. There are search parties out. But the Pine Barrens cover a large area...."

Abrams nodded.

Styler moved to the door. "I'll meet you out front later. A brown Lincoln." He left.

Tanner stood. "Please follow me."

Abrams took his drink and followed Tanner through a communicating door that led into an office space that held six cubicles. Tanner said, "There's your cubicle. A Mr. Evans will be with you shortly. He knows you as Smith. I'll see you later." He turned and left.

Abrams went inside the open cubicle that had his name on the glass partition and found a plain gray steel desk with his nameplate on it. He sat in the swivel chair and went through the desk drawers, finding them crammed with the Edwards and Styler version of the same junk he had in his desk at O'Brien, Kimberly and Rose.

On the floor was a briefcase with his initials. He opened it. Inside was the thick file marked *The Russian Mission to the U.N. vs. George Van Dorn*.

Abrams rocked back in his chair and sipped on his Scotch. Ostensibly the dozen or so employees of this law firm had been well instructed regarding his employment history with them. Still, that was another possible source of exposure.

Abrams thought also about Pat O'Brien. Was he dead? Kidnapped? If kidnapped, would he expose Abrams? Abrams hoped for both their sakes that he was alive or dead; but nothing in between.

Abrams glanced at his watch. Mr. Evans, he supposed, was his briefing officer. Jonathan Harker, he reflected, did not have a briefing officer, or mission control people. But, then again, Count Dracula did not have KGB agents in his castle.

Abrams thought of the events of the last few days, the last few months, and then of the last few years, and wondered where he had gone wrong. He consoled himself with the knowledge that even a man like Huntington Styler could get suckered into this bad business.

Abrams heard footsteps outside his cubicle and slipped his hand into the pocket that held his revolver.

A tall, lanky man in late middle age stood in a slouched posture at the cubicle opening. He had one hand in his pocket, the other held an attaché case. He looked at Abrams but said nothing.

Abrams had the impression of a rather sad traveling salesman who'd been on the road a week too long.

The man nodded, as though to himself, then said, "You know what?"

"No. What?"

"Electronics suck."

"Right. I always knew that."

The man moved in a shambling gait into the small cubicle and stood facing Abrams across the desk. "Are you Smith?"

"Right." Up close the man resembled Walter Matthau and sounded like Humphrey Bogart.

The man pulled his hand from his pocket and reached across the desk. "Evans."

Abrams released the hold on his .38, stood, and shook hands with Evans.

Evans sprawled out in a chair facing Abrams, and said, "Over ninety percent of the intelligence this country collects is through electronics. But you know what?"

Abrams sat. "No. What?"

"It doesn't take the place of eyes and ears."

"Nose and throat."

"Well, nose too. And brains. And balls. And heart. You have those?"

"I'm complete."

"Good." Evans thrust both hands in his trouser pockets and looked idly around the small room. "What a shitbox. Who could work here?"

"A guy named Abrams."

Evans looked back at Abrams. "You speak Russkie, right?"

"Right."

"Who would want to learn a shit language like that?"

"Little Russian kids."

Evans nodded absently, then said, "Look, Smith, I'm going to talk to you for an hour. I'm going to show you the architectural plans of that Russkie mansion. I'm going to teach you how to be a spy."

"Good. Do we need the whole hour?"

"Maybe. You've got some background. Right?"

"Right. Are you going to tell me what it is I'm supposed to find out in there."

"No. You wouldn't understand it anyway. Neither would I. It's electronics. But I'll tell you what you're supposed to look for."

"Okay."

"Radios and televisions."

"Radios and televisions?"

"That's what I said."

"Why?"

"How do I know? Also, look for ground-fault interrupters."

"Okay. They're easy to spot."

Evans smiled slowly. "That's those electrical outlets you see in new bathrooms and kitchens, Smith. They detect a surge of current or something, and a button pops so you don't get a short or electrocute yourself or whatever."

"Okay."

"See if they have them in place of the regular outlets in other rooms."

"Okay."

"Check the doors and windows for interlocking metal weather stripping."

"Maybe you need a building inspector instead of a spy."

"The weather stripping should be plated with a noncorrosive metal that's highly conductive of electricity—tin, silver, gold, or platinum. Scrape some off with a knife. You got a harmless little knife that they won't confiscate?"

"No."

Evans threw a small penknife across the desk, then fished around in his pockets and came up with a listless-looking cigarette that seemed to match his posture. He lit it with a bent paper match. "Also, you have to try to get up close to get a look at their antennas. Most of them are on the roof, but they've got the big one on the north lawn. At the base of that antenna you might see a surge arrestor coupled with an electrical filter. Unless they've buried them."

"I can always dig. Do you have a pocket shovel?"

Evans thought a moment, then said, "There was a tree surgeon a few months back who got too close to that antenna and they nearly took his head off. Whatever is at the base there is probably above-ground, but hidden with bushes."

"What does this thing look like?"

Evans drew a piece of paper from his inside jacket pocket and skimmed it across the desk.

Abrams opened the paper and stared at a badly done line drawing. "Looks like something I did in grade school."

"Funny you should say that. It was done by a seventeen-year-old kid, under hypnosis."

Abrams looked up at Evans.

"Memory drugs, too, if you want the whole truth."

Abrams said nothing.

Evans added, "Some local delinquent who gets his jollies fucking around on the Russian estate. He hid in the bushes around the antenna once. That's all you have to know. Except that we want a verification of what the kid saw."

"Why?"

"I don't know. But you know what?"

"No. What?"

"It's none of your business."

"Right. I thought so."

"None of my business either, Smith. So sit back, listen, and hold the questions."

Abrams lit a cigarette and sat back. Evans continued his briefing.

As he listened, Abrams realized he would have to take some risks if he was to accomplish what was being laid out.

Messrs. Styler and Edwards had wisely excused themselves from this briefing. But to be fair, they were taking a risk just by bringing him.

He looked at Evans, who was staring at him. Evans said, "That house has been subject to more electronic surveillance, low- and high-altitude picture taking, and perimeter surveillance than any spot in the country, including the Russkies' houses in Manhattan and The Bronx, and their diplomatic and trade buildings in San Francisco and Washington. But you know what?"

"No. What?"

"We've never had a pro inside before."

"Well, I'm not a pro, Evans, and I'm not inside yet."

"You will be inside. And you're more of a pro than the tree surgeon, the kid, or that stupid deli guy, or—"

"Who?"

"The deli guy. Delicatessen."

"What's his name?"

"What's it to you, Smith? What's *your* name?"

"Is his name Karl Roth?"

"Could be. Probably is. Forget that."

Abrams nodded.

Evans stared at him a few seconds, then continued. "Anyway, the Russkies have about thirty ways to detect any funny business, so I'm sending you in there clean. Are you clean?"

"All I've got is a little Smith & Wesson thirty-eight."

"You'd better leave that behind."

"I guess I better."

"Do you want poison?"

"None for me, thank you."

"Good. You wouldn't use it anyway. But I had to ask."

"Can't hurt to ask."

Evans nodded. "Are you going in there under an alias?"

"No."

"Good. If they got prints from the questionnaire, they've already got a make on you. If they get prints while you're there, the matching takes days, and you wouldn't be blown while you're there. But you wouldn't want to go back for a second visit." Evans looked at him closely. "No alias, right?"

"I said no."

"Okay. Sometimes I get clients who are being set up to be blown for some fucked-up reason. They have a cover story that wouldn't hold glue, much less water, and they have enough electronics on them to open up a Radio Shack. It's always best to be clean and to be who you say you are."

"I am."

"I don't care about you personally."

"I know."

"I don't like to lose people."

"Bad for business."

"Right." Evans lifted his attaché case onto the desk and opened it so that the inside faced Abrams. Evans said, "Do you know what that is?"

Abrams looked at the electrical components built into the case. "No."

"That's an EBI."

"EBI?"

"Electronic bullshit indicator. Sometimes called a VSA—a voice stress analyzer."

"I've heard of it."

"Good. The Russkies use this on their guests. Theirs is American-made, like this one, of course." Evans reached around and turned on the analyzer. "It doesn't have to be hooked to you. They watch this digital display as you talk. It can be hidden in their attaché case like this, so you don't see it."

"And it tells them when I'm bullshitting."

"Right. See, we establish a base number on the display for my normal voice. When I start bullshitting, the machine detects sub-audible microtremors that occur with stress and deception. If the digital readout rises fifty percent or more above my normal voice range, which is reading forty-five here, then you're listening to bullshit. Okay, watch the digital readout." Evans spoke in apparently the same tone of voice he'd been using. "Smith, I think you've got a real good chance to pull this off."

Abrams watched as the red LCD numbers rose to a hundred and six. "Bullshit."

"Right." He looked at Abrams. "Now you talk and I'll get a base number for your voice."

Abrams sipped on his Scotch, then said, "Okay, chief, I give up. How am I supposed to protect against that?"

Evans spun the attaché case around so it faced him. He played with the sensitivity dial as he replied, "Mostly keep your mouth shut in there. But what you're doing now is good too."

"What am I doing now?"

"Alcohol." Evans reached into his pocket and pulled out a small bottle. "Cough medicine for your cold. It has alcohol and some other stuff to anesthetize the vocal cords a bit. Confuses the machine." He pulled another object out of his pocket and rolled it across the desk. "Bronchial mist spray. It's spiked with helium. Don't breathe too much or you'll sound like you got your nuts caught in a revolving door. Use it only if they start asking you really direct questions, hot and heavy."

Abrams nodded.

Evans sat back, crossed his legs, and rested his hands on his stomach. "Okay, I'm a Russkie. I already fucked around with the papers in my attaché case, but what I really did was get a base number for your voice by shooting the breeze with you about the weather and your nice suit and all that. Now I'm going to pop a stressful question on you."

"And what am I supposed to do?"

"You're going to act a little slow in the head, cough, sneeze, blow your nose, clear your throat, take a swig of cough medicine, or suck up some helium."

Abrams replied, "That's going to look like a burlesque act after a while."

"You'll get real natural at it when the time comes."

"And they won't know what the cough medicine and spray are all about?"

"They probably will if you overdo it. But it's better than them knowing exactly when you're lying and when you're telling the truth. Okay, ready?"

"Sure."

Evans spoke in a mock Russian accent. "So, Mr. Smith, would you like a tour of our beautiful house?"

Abrams nodded.

Evans laughed. "Don't appear simpleminded. Answer the question."

"Yes, I would."

Evans looked at the display. "Lots of stress, but you see that can be interpreted two ways. One, you're bullshitting, and you don't want to see their fucking house, two, you want to see it so bad it's producing microtremors. No machine is perfect. Have faith."

"Right."

Evans cleared his throat and continued, "So, Mr. Smith, what do you think of our case against Van Dorn?"

Abrams replied at length.

Evans nodded, then asked, "What did you do on the police force?"

"I was a traffic cop."

Evans shook his head. "Jesus, Smith, we're talking telephone numbers here."

"Fuck you and your machine."

"But you've got to deal with it. Okay, same question, but go into your act." Evans again asked the question.

Abrams began to reply, then cleared his throat, put the mister over his nose, and sprayed. He made some heavy-breathing sounds, then said, "I was a traffic cop." The voice was a bit high-pitched, but not abnormally so.

Evans looked at the digital readout, but said nothing.

"Well?"

Evans did not reply, but asked, "So, Mr. Smith, how long have you been with Edwards and Styler?"

Abrams answered, "About two and a half hours."

Evans laughed, and peered over the top of the briefcase. "No stress. But the truth can get you into trouble too."

"It usually does."

"Right. Okay, we're going to get you good at this. Ready?"

"Ready."

Evans and Abrams spent the next half hour working with the voice analyzer. Evans abruptly shut off the machine and closed the attaché case. "Class is out."

"How did I do?"

Evans lit a cigarette. "Well, I couldn't make any final judgments about who you are and what you're up to."

"But you knew I was up to something?"

"Maybe. You see, Smith, people have stress for different reasons. Some people are nervous just being on Russian soil. Some people lie to be polite. Anyway, if I was a KGB security man operating this machine, I wouldn't feel confident about pulling my revolver and shooting you on the spot."

"That's hopeful."

Evans yawned, then said, "Electronics suck. Did I say that?"

"Yes."

"Technology sucks. Takes all the fun out of danger. Takes the soul out of this business."

"This business never had a soul, Evans."

Evans leaned forward, folded his arms on the desk, and stared at Abrams. "I used to be able to tell when a man was bullshitting me by watching his face. Now I have to look at a fucking machine instead of his eyes."

"Right."

"You know what?"

"No. What?"

"An agent on the ground is worth ten spy satellites and all the NSA's electronic junk put together."

"That's not true."

"I know." Evans slumped back in his chair. "But sometimes you need a human being. For analysis. For theory. For judgment. For instinct. For *ethics*, for Christ's sake."

"You lost me on the ethics."

Evans took a long breath. "Okay, let's finish this briefing so you won't be late for your rendezvous behind the Iron Curtain."

"In that case, take your time."

Evans smiled. "Right." For the next twenty minutes Abrams sat and listened. He asked a few questions and received a few answers. Evans showed him the old architectural plans to what had once been Killenworth.

Finally, Evans stood and said, "Listen, I know you're a little shaky. Who wouldn't be? Do you know what keeps me cool when I'm on the wrong side of the Curtain?"

"No. What?"

"Anger. I build up a hate of those sons of bitches. I keep reminding myself that the Russkies want to fuck up my kids' lives. They *like* to fuck us up. That's what they were put on this earth to do. The Russians are the most fucked-up people God ever created."

Abrams considered that a moment, then said, "Who are you working for?"

"I don't know. I'm hired through a series of blinds. I'm ex-CIA. I have a private consulting firm called Executive Information Services."

"Good meaningless name."

"Right." He handed Abrams his card. "We're a group of ex-intelligence people. Most of my clients are multinational corporations who want to know when the Yahoos are going to take over some shithole country so they can pack up their people, pesos, and property, and beat it."

"But who are your clients this time?"

"I told you, I don't know. Could be the Company. They can't operate in this country, and they don't always like to go to the FBI. So, since there's nothing that says they can't hire private people for domestic work, they do."

Abrams nodded, then said, "I've heard of a group of old boys who don't hire out their services but work only for themselves."

Evans' voice became cool. "That's not possible, Smith. Who would finance them? What would they do with their work product?"

Abrams shrugged. "Maybe I heard it wrong."

"You did." Evans moved toward the door.

Abrams stood. "Do you know a man named Peter Thorpe?"

"Why?"

"He said he had some employment opportunities for me."

Evans nodded. "That's another type of arrangement. He runs a loose group of civilians for the Company. No pay. Just trouble."

"If I lost contact with him, could you put me in touch with him at any given time?"

"I could. I might."

"How about a man named Marc Pembroke?"

Evans' normally impassive face took on an uneasy look. "You stay away from that sucker."

"Why?"

Evans stared off into space for some time, then replied, "Pembroke is a specialist. His work product is corpses. I've said enough. *Adiós,* Smith."

Abrams came around the desk. "Thanks."

"You never say thanks until you come back. I'll contact you tomorrow. Take it easy in there. It won't look good for me if they hack you up and throw your pieces into the lime pit in the basement."

"I'll make you proud of me."

"Yeah." Evans walked out, then turned back. "One more thing."

Abrams looked at Evans' face and he knew he wasn't going to like this.

Evans said, "You've heard of the Abraham Lincoln Brigade?"

"Yes. Americans who fought the Fascists in Spain back in the thirties. Hemingway types."

"Right. Most of them were pink or red. The Russkies had about twenty of these old vets out to Glen Cove for tea and borscht on May Day. One of these guys, a man named Sam Hammond, had switched sides years ago. He was working for whoever we're working for. He had the same assignment as you. I briefed him." Evans stared at Abrams.

"Sam Hammond is well, I hope."

"Sam Hammond left the Russian place that night and took the Glen Cove train back to Manhattan. Sam Hammond never arrived home."

Abrams did not respond.

Evans added, "Either Hammond blew it himself or he was blown by somebody before he even got there. I don't think he blew it himself, I think I gave him a good briefing. He was very sharp. I think there was a leak."

Abrams looked at Evans. "I'd rather believe your briefing was bad and Hammond was bad. I'd rather not believe there was a leak."

"For your sake, I hope your belief is the right one." Evans thought a moment, then looked up at Abrams. "When you were a cop, did you ever go into a dangerous situation, unarmed, with partners who would turn on you, with no radio backup, and with no one who would help you or feel responsible for your safety?"

"No. I never did that."

"Well, welcome to the great world of espionage, chump." Evans turned and left.

CHAPTER FORTY-TWO

The long Lincoln Town Car moved slowly north along Dosoris Lane. It was nearly dark and most cars had their headlights on. Up ahead Abrams could see rotating police lights reflected off the trees. Abrams said, "Is it like this for every holiday?"

Huntington Styler, sitting in the rear, answered, "Usually. Van Dorn tries to give the appearance that his spite parties have a purpose—like his Law Day party that coincided with the Russians' May Day celebration."

Mike Tanner, behind the wheel, added, "And, of course, he throws a party for every legitimate American holiday as well, because he's such a patriot."

Styler said, "As long as he continues to be careful and consistent about these occasions, he has us at a bit of a disadvantage."

Abrams flipped through the file on his lap. "I see that last November seventh, the anniversary of the Bolshevik Revolution, he came up with...what the hell is this?...National Notary Public Day?"

Tanner laughed. "He bused in about fifty notaries from the city in the middle of the week, blared his loudspeakers, and shot off fireworks again. The notaries were confused but flattered." Tanner laughed again.

Abrams suddenly looked up from the file. He turned to Tanner. "I suppose his biggest bash is the Fourth of July."

Tanner nodded. "You should have seen the one last year. He had about two hundred people and six muzzle-loading cannon manned by men in colonial uniforms. He fired those cannon toward the Russian estate until about two in the morning. Black powder only, of course."

Styler leaned over the front seat. "A few days later the Russians began looking for a lawyer. That's how we eventually became involved."

Abrams glanced at the file. The way Huntington Styler had specifically become involved was by writing an Op-Ed piece for the *Times,* roundly condemning Van Dorn for his spite parties. Abrams had no doubt the piece had been planted. He said, "Will the house be full this coming July Fourth weekend?"

Tanner hesitated, then said, "That's a good question."

Abrams looked at him. "Meaning what?"

Tanner glanced at Abrams as he negotiated through the heavy traffic. "Well, I counseled the Russians' legal advisor, a man named Alexei Kalin, whom you'll meet, that all the Russian diplomats, staff, and dependents in the New York area should make other plans—"

"To show," interrupted Abrams, "that they are discommoded by Van Dorn's harassment."

"Yes. If over a hundred men, women, and children have to change their plans and stay in Manhattan because of Van Dorn, then we've got a real strong point for our case."

"True. So what did Kalin say?"

Tanner moved the Lincoln up within sight of the Russian gates. "Kalin said he'd check; then a day later he called back and said they would cooperate with us and not come out that weekend."

Abrams asked, "Then why is there a question?"

Tanner did not reply, but glanced into the rearview mirror at Styler.

Styler spoke. "We have information that, despite their promise to stay away from the Glen Cove house, they intend to be here July Fourth weekend."

Abrams turned in his seat. "What sort of information?"

Styler said, "Well, as you know, Pat O'Brien has...had... the ability to discover these things through the most mundane ways—diplomatic staffs or their wives and children, are often sources of security breaches. Casual remarks to other diplomats, tradespeople; children saying something to their American friends. That sort of thing. Of course, that doesn't mean that the Russian staff isn't misinformed themselves, but small signs seem to point to the fact that they believe they'll all be in Glen Cove that weekend."

Abrams thought that the Russians considered this case a necessary nuisance. Necessary because they had been backed into a corner and had no choice but to proceed with it after Van Dorn's outrages. Not to proceed would look odd. And a nuisance, because they did not like these attorneys coming onto their property, or telling them to stay in Manhattan over the July Fourth weekend. This presented a dilemma. They had to cooperate on the one hand, but on the other hand they had other things on their mind; perhaps a much better way to settle their case against Van Dorn—and the rest of the country.

Styler said, "This case gives Mr. O'Brien a unique opportunity to see how the Russians react to certain stimuli. You understand what I'm saying."

"Yes."

Styler added, "Enough said."

As they edged closer to the gates, Tanner put on his left-hand turn signal. A traffic policeman approached and Tanner lowered the window. The sounds of the demonstrators filled the car. The policeman stuck his head in the window. "Where you heading?"

Tanner pointed. "There."

"What's your business *there?*"

Abrams could tell that Tanner was considering a lawyer's version of "It's none of your fucking business" but instead produced a letter written in English on Soviet UN stationery.

The policeman scanned the letter without comment.

Abrams looked out the windshield. There were over a hundred demonstrators around the gates, and the scene looked much like the one he'd viewed on the late news the night of May First, after his fateful interview with O'Brien on the roof of the RCA Building.

The policeman handed the letter back to Tanner and signaled to another officer up the road, who stopped oncoming traffic.

Tanner pulled into the opposing lane, then made his left-hand turn and headed into the gates, which had swung open.

Two burly Russian guards in brown uniforms with red trimming stood in the gravel drive. Their right arms were raised in a way that reminded Abrams of a Fascist salute. Tanner stopped.

A third man, dressed in civilian clothing, approached and spoke in good English. "What is your business, please?"

Tanner produced another letter on Soviet UN stationery, written in Russian. Abrams noticed a profusion of stamps, seals, and several signatures. There was, Abrams thought, something disturbing about a country that couldn't make do with one seal and one signature.

The Russian took the letter and went to a nearby guardhouse. Abrams could see him pick up the telephone. The two guards remained in a blocking position on the drive. Tanner snorted. "Look at those fools. Do they think we're going to try to sneak up the driveway? This is like some grade-B movie."

Styler added, "It *is* rather inane. That man knew we were coming, and has a description of us right down to our license plate."

Abrams interrupted. "I'd like to try to hear what he's saying."

The car was instantly silent. The civilian was standing at the open door of the guardhouse, speaking loudly into the telephone with all the blissful assurance of a man who believes he can't be understood.

The man hung up and returned to the car, handing Tanner the letter.

Abrams could smell cheap cologne. The shirt was dirty, the tie stained, and the suit ill-fitting. The man was a Russian icon. This *was* like a grade-B movie.

The man gave Abrams a nasty sort of look, as though he were reading his mind, then said to Tanner, "Proceed up the drive, at ten kilometers. You will see a parking yard. Go beyond this and stop at the main entrance."

Tanner mumbled a thank-you and began moving up the gravel

drive. He said to Abrams, "Could you make out what he said on the phone?"

"Just normal security chatter. He said, 'Styler, Tanner, and the Jew have arrived.'"

There was a silence in the car as it rolled up the long, S-shaped drive. The lighted house was visible now, a long, gabled structure of gray stone, multileveled to conform with the contours of the hilltop. The drive was overhung with trees, darkening it, but the borders were lit by short, squat Japanese lanterns.

Abrams reminded himself that although he was technically on Soviet soil, he was a long way from the Gulag. On the other hand, Evans' cheery remark about the lime pit in the basement had to be considered more than flippancy. More to the point, the Veterans of the Abraham Lincoln Brigade were short one member.

The car moved up the gradual incline, swinging past the north side of the house and through the parking yard. Tanner pulled into a large forecourt, brightly illuminated by modern security lighting. Abrams studied the east-facing facade. There was a half story exposed above ground level that had once been servants' quarters and that Evans had said served a similar function, though the Russians who lived there now were not called servants.

Three rising bays protruded from the stone facade, each holding long casement windows. The right-hand bay indicated the location of the dining room and above that a large bedroom. The left bay was the original study now used as the security office. Above that was another bedroom. The large middle bay was the entrance. The third floor was a gabled garret entirely devoted, according to a Soviet defector, to electronic spying.

Tanner stopped the car directly in front of the entrance and shut off the engine. Outside in the warm night the sound of insects penetrated into the plush interior, and the car's engine ticked as it cooled.

Abrams took his revolver and shoulder holster from his briefcase and stuffed them into the glove compartment.

Tanner watched him and said, "You shouldn't have brought that. Their security people will find it there."

"So what?" Abrams opened his door and stepped out into the warm, still air.

Tanner shut off the lights and he and Styler followed. Abrams walked up to the arched wooden door and pressed a buzzer. Inside the house a dog barked, followed by answering barks from around the mansion. Abrams commented, "Jonathan Harker was greeted by Dracula himself with the explanation that all the servants had retired for the evening."

Tanner laughed, somewhat nervously. Styler smiled tightly.

The door suddenly swung open, and a squat man greeted them cheerily. "Welcome, gentlemen. Welcome to our *dacha*." He laughed.

Abrams recognized the man from his Red Squad days. Viktor Androv, a.k.a. Count Dracula.

Abrams looked around the dimly lit stone foyer, larger than most living rooms. From the far side of the foyer rose a wide marble staircase.

Androv said pleasantly, "Mr. Styler, it is good to see you again— and Mr. Tanner."

Abrams thought there was something incongruous about this fat little man, dressed in baggy slacks, an open-neck flowered shirt, and sandals with socks, holding court in a great house. But he supposed since the workers' revolution it was the plight of Russians to look incongruous in elegant surroundings.

Androv turned to Abrams. "And you must be Mr. Abrams."

Abrams wanted to say, "I must be or I wouldn't have gotten past the gate." He shook hands with Androv.

Androv motioned them toward the staircase and they began climbing the half level toward an upper foyer. Androv said, by way of explaining the stillness of the house, "Most of our people have returned to Manhattan. The small permanent staff we keep here has the evening off after this long weekend. But," he added in an exasperated tone, "I doubt if any of us will get much sleep tonight when that lunatic next door begins his...his..."

"Harassment," prompted Styler.

"Yes. But another word... *capers*...yes, when he begins cutting capers. I'm surprised he hasn't begun yet. You should have been here on May Day!"

"We were available," said Styler pointedly.

"Yes, yes. But it was not convenient."

They stepped up into a square foyer, the walls and floors of which were made of a warm buff marble. The ceiling was plaster in bas-relief and badly cracked. Three arched openings gave off the foyer. The one directly ahead, Abrams saw, led into a long, low-ceilinged gallery, paneled in oak. The openings on either side led to long hallways. Androv motioned them to the left. He said as they walked, "You are late. But I am sure I know why."

Styler smiled. "Yes, we should have allowed for the traffic."

Androv nodded quickly. "I'm glad you saw what we must put up with."

Abrams had the impression of a man who was playacting without a script. He knew the Russian soul and Russian mannerisms well enough to spot bullshit.

They came to a green curtain that was drawn across the hallway. Androv pulled on a cord and the curtain parted revealing a walk-through metal detector of the type used in airports.

An attractive woman dressed in designer jeans, polo shirt, and docksiders smiled tightly. Androv said, "Gentlemen, I must ask you to step through this." He shrugged. "It is policy," he added, as though he had nothing to do with it. He turned away and lit a cigarette.

The woman held out what looked to Abrams like a cheap plastic relish tray. "Metal objects, please."

The three men put the required objects in separate compartments of the tray. Abrams tossed the penknife casually among the keys, pens, cigarette lighters, and coins.

Styler placed his briefcase on the conveyor belt and the woman pushed the start button. The briefcase rolled through the fluoroscope and the woman stared at the screen. Styler stepped through the metal-detector arch. Tanner, then Abrams, did the same.

The woman moved to the end of the stopped conveyor belt and casually opened Tanner's briefcase, rummaging through the papers. Abrams, Styler, and Tanner glanced at one another.

That one act, thought Abrams, by its total indifference to manners and custom, said more about these people and their society than anything he'd ever read or heard. *The safety of the state is the highest law.*

The woman retrieved a gold pen from Tanner's briefcase and dropped it on the tray with his other metal objects. She looked at the three men. "These items will be returned to you shortly. You may take your briefcases."

Abrams could see that Tanner was fuming, but if the woman noticed, she could not have the slightest idea what he was upset about. Outrage was a luxury item available only in the West. Abrams remembered Evans' advice. *Get mad.*

The three men retrieved their briefcases, Tanner doing so with more vigor than the act required.

Abrams glanced down at the metal detector's electric cord where it plugged into the wall receptacle, and spotted his first ground-fault interrupter.

Abrams looked back at the woman. She was carrying the tray away and disappeared through a doorway that Abrams knew led to the former study, now the security office. Each metal object would be electrically scanned and physically examined. Fingerprints would be lifted, and Tanner's car keys would be used to move the Lincoln to a vehicle inspection shop on the south side of the house. He wondered if he'd see his penknife again. Nobody trusted anyone anymore. And with good reason.

Androv approached them. "We will need a north-facing room so you can see and hear what Mr. Van Dorn visits upon us. The gallery will do. Follow me."

He led them back down the hallway to the upper foyer, then motioned them through into the gallery. It would have been a shorter walk, Abrams realized, to cut through the music room, whose door was close by the metal detector. But the music room, now a sort of commons room for the staff, was obviously off limits.

Abrams looked around the gallery, which had once been Charles Pratt's hunting-trophy room. Its ceiling beams and oak paneling still gave it the flavor of a hunting lodge, but the mounted animal heads and horns were gone, replaced by oversize canvases of proletarian art: smiling, well-muscled men and women working in fields and factories. The early capitalists, reflected Abrams, mounted animals they probably never shot, the ruling Communists displayed pictures of happy workers they probably never saw. The noble and idealized creatures of the earth were destined to wind up as wall decorations for the elite. In a just and orderly world, perhaps, capitalists would shoot, stuff, and mount Communists, and vice versa, leaving the wildlife and working people in peace.

Androv walked to a north-facing casement window. "Here you can see the lights of the madman's house." Androv looked at his watch. "Why hasn't he begun his capers yet?"

Because, Abrams thought, he is holding off on his capers to allow me at least an hour in here. Abrams went to another window and looked out from the elevated room, across the treed hollow, to the next hill, upon which sat a gleaming white house of wood. Every window was lit, as was the custom in great houses when parties were held, and soft garden lighting of various hues gave the landscape a chimerical appearance.

He could make out a few people on the lawn and terrace, and he thought of Katherine down there. He wondered what she would think if she knew where he was.

It struck him too that though he never romanticized danger, there must be some sort of potentially fatal defect in his survival instinct or he would never have taken so many jobs where people shot at you. Neither would he be here now. However, from the moment he'd walked out of Katherine's bedroom, he noticed a subtle change in his attitude and perceptions toward longevity.

He stared out the multipaned window. Beyond these hills, to the west and north, he could see the moonlit water of the Sound. Navigation lights of boats and ships blinked and moved across the calm water, and that reminded him that Peter Thorpe was still out there somewhere. He realized that Thorpe could conceivably wind up here tonight, anytime.

Androv looked at the three men, who had each picked a different window from which to look. "Well, let us sit and talk. When it begins, you will know it."

Abrams examined the copper-clad casement window. There was a screen on the inside and the window cranked out. It was tightly closed now, and he could not see the weather stripping. He looked down at the terrace below, and said, "What's that?"

Androv turned back and moved shoulder to shoulder beside Abrams. "Oh, that is a curiosity. It is what it looks like. A swastika set into the tilework."

Abrams shielded his eyes against the glare of the window. "May I open this?"

Androv hesitated a moment, then said, "Of course."

Abrams cranked. The window opened.

Androv added, "That was done, I am told, in about 1914, before the advent of the Nazis. It is the traditional gammadion—a symbol of good luck in the Orient and among American Indians. No one hates that symbol more than the Jews, except perhaps the Russians. So do not take offense."

"Of course not. It just took me by surprise." Abrams' eyes ran over the sill and jambs. The weather stripping was plated with a bright, untarnished metal of what could have been platinum or white gold. Had he had his penknife, he still would not be able to get a scraping unless the interior screen were removed and Androv were removed. He said, "Should we leave this open to hear when Van Dorn's barrage begins?"

"That's not necessary." Androv was already closing the window.

Abrams looked out across the brightly lit lawn and saw the towering antenna, held in place by guy wires. At the base of the antenna was the heavy planting of bushes that Evans had mentioned. Closer to the house and the terrace was the flagpole, surrounded by a circular hedgerow. Abrams could see the grating of the storm drain he'd been asked to verify.

At the edge of the woodline to the west, he spotted two men with a leashed dog. One man was speaking into what must have been a walkie-talkie, the other was shouldering what had to be a rifle.

There was something surreal about this whole place, he thought. The atmosphere was that of Kafka's *Castle,* in which one never knew who would answer the telephone or if it would be answered at all. A place where one had the instinctive feeling that every unseen room and corridor was filled with silently waiting men; that all the dark and dimly appreciated places held perilous shadows. A glimpse here, a sound there, a smell, a feeling, confirmed that one was not alone.

"Come," said Androv a bit impatiently, "let us be seated." He motioned them to a grouping of chairs around a coffee table and directed each of them to a seat.

Abrams sat in a club chair, Tanner and Styler on a small settee, and Androv took a large upholstered armchair, his back to the windows.

Abrams regarded Androv for a moment. According to what was known of him, he was what was called in intelligence parlance the Chief Legal Resident. Or to use Abrams' Red Squad description, Androv was the head of the KGB in New York, hiding behind a diplomatic post. This was not a great secret. What was a mystery was why he was bothering with this matter. Conclusion: He suspected a scam. Further conclusion: Whatever the Russians were up to, it was important enough to cause the KGB honcho to spend some time on it.

Androv was speaking. "I have asked Mr. Kalin, as our resident legal advisor, to join us. My function is one of community relations, so you will have to put up with me as well. Justice in this country is sometimes as much public relations as it is blind."

Androv pulled out a box of Russian cigarettes, Troika Ovals, and offered them around in a gesture that Abrams thought was very Russian. Abrams took one of the proffered cigarettes and lit the loosely packed, foul-smelling Oval. On his first draw he sucked about an inch of tobacco into his mouth and had to pick it out.

"Do you like these?" Androv asked.

"They have a distinctive taste," Abrams replied.

Tanner suppressed a smile.

Abrams marveled at the possibility that a country that couldn't make a cigarette had found a way to destroy the most technologically advanced society the world had ever seen.

Androv looked at his watch. "Mr. Kalin takes courses at Fordham and thinks he understands American law." Androv chuckled. "He is picking up all the worst habits of American lawyers. Lateness, for instance."

Styler and Tanner put on obligatory smiles, then Styler opened his briefcase and flipped through some papers. "If we can't obtain an injunction against Van Dorn for this July Fourth, then, as we told Mr. Kalin, we suggest you not come out here."

Androv replied, "We told Mr. Tanner some weeks ago that we will not come for the three-day weekend if that is what you wish."

Abrams looked closely at Androv. There was a discrepancy here between what Androv said and what O'Brien had discovered. Discrepancies were often suggestive of lies. There were two good reasons for the Russians to stay away: legal and practical. Therefore, if they intended to show up for Van Dorn's bombardment, there must be one good reason for that. Conclusion: They *had* to be out of Manhattan. They *had* to be at their estate because this place was somehow safe. Further conclusion: No place else was safe that weekend.

The conventional wisdom in defense thinking was that when the time came, it would be on a holiday. Christmas or New Year's Eve was the favored theory. But the Fourth of July was a nice, perverse symbolic possibility.

Tanner leafed through a file and said matter-of-factly, "We're thinking in terms of punitive damages in the area of five hundred thousand dollars, plus whatever costs you incur."

Androv's mind, like his eyes, seemed focused on Abrams. He looked at Tanner. "What? Oh, that can wait for Mr. Kalin." Androv rose and walked slowly across the room. He pulled a bell cord and remained standing beside it.

Presently a man in a white busboy tunic appeared at the hallway door pushing a serving cart. Androv walked beside the cart and announced, "Please help yourselves," then served himself first and sat with a glass of tea and a plate heaped with cheap, store-bought pastry.

Abrams watched him. Androv suddenly appeared to be distracted, as though he had thought of something more pressing. He noticed that Androv kept glancing at his watch.

Abrams heard Androv speak softly to the busboy in Russian. "Tell Kalin to enter."

Which to Abrams seemed more like a stage direction than an order to locate Kalin.

Styler, Tanner, and Abrams rose and walked to the cart. Beside the samovar was the relish tray with their metal items, minus, Abrams noticed, Tanner's car keys. Each man reclaimed his own things, then each took a Russian tea glass with a metal handle and drew tea from the samovar.

Androv made desultory conversation between mouthfuls of sticky pastry.

Abrams said, "Are you returning to Manhattan tonight?"

Androv glanced at him. "Yes, why do you ask?"

"I thought I could get a ride with you."

"You live in Brooklyn."

"I'm staying in Manhattan this evening."

"Are you?" Androv seemed momentarily disconcerted, then said, "I'm sorry, but we will be discussing classified matters."

"I don't speak Russian."

Androv gave him a cold stare. "The car is full."

"I'll take the train, then."

The door that led to the music room opened and a very tall and thin blond man, almost Scandinavian-looking, entered carrying an attaché case.

Androv did not rise. He said, "Gentlemen, Mr. Kalin. You know Mr. Styler and Mr. Tanner?"

Kalin nodded perfunctorily to the men present and pushed a wingback chair toward the circle of seats. Abrams noticed that he had positioned it between Androv and himself, but a few feet back from them.

Androv nodded toward Abrams. "Did I tell you, Alexei, that Mr. Abrams is the son of famous American Communists?"

"Yes." Kalin took his seat.

Abrams eyed Alexei Kalin closely. The man was hard-looking, his face the sort that one did not easily forget. In fact, Abrams did recognize him from Fordham night school. One of the things that Abrams had learned as a cop was that men who wore a gun carried themselves in a subtly different way from men who did not. And one of the things that had struck him about Kalin on the few occasions he'd seen him was the strong possibility that he wore a shoulder holster. Abrams was fairly certain he was wearing one now.

Kalin set his attaché case on his lap and opened it. He shuffled through some papers, then said, "We can begin."

Styler and Tanner opened their briefcases and brought out the ubiquitous yellow legal pads. Abrams used a small notebook that was a carry-over from his police days. Androv said, "Mr. Abrams is also a classmate of yours, Alexei."

Kalin glanced up. "Yes, I have seen him."

Androv looked at Abrams. "Yes? No?"

Abrams replied, "Yes, I recognize Mr. Kalin."

"Mr. Abrams is a former New York City policeman, Alexei." Androv spoke between bites of pastry. He turned to Abrams. "What did you say your duties were?"

Abrams replied, "I had many jobs on the force."

Kalin sat motionless, staring down into the attaché case. He took a pen and appeared to write, but Abrams was certain he was playing with the dials, which had notches so they could be adjusted with a pen.

Androv again addressed Abrams. "It is unfortunate that immigrants to this country did not teach their children their native tongue. You speak no Russian at all, Mr. Abrams?"

Abrams replied indirectly, as instructed by Evans. "My parents, like many other immigrants, wanted their children to be Americanized. They used their native language to keep secrets from their children."

Androv laughed. "What a pity."

Styler cut in. "Perhaps we should discuss the case."

Androv smiled. "Mr. Abrams is a curiosity for us. But—" He slapped his knees. "Alexei, let's see what you learned at the Catholic school."

Kalin looked up from his attaché case and addressed Styler in an unfriendly tone. "What do you intend to do about that incident of May Day?"

Styler replied, "You mean your claim that Van Dorn fired a pistol at four of your staff—"

"Yes, yes. And they harbored this boy who came on the property to steal."

Styler cleared his throat. "Van Dorn tells a different story. I'd suggest we proceed separately with that. That's a criminal matter."

Kalin's voice was impatient. "But it is important that this boy be questioned. We must serve him with a summons. Have you yet found his name and address?"

Tanner replied, "Yes."

Kalin spoke sharply. "Well, what is it?"

Tanner picked out a sheet of paper. "Kuchik. Stanley Kuchik. He lives on Woodbury Lane. He's a junior at the high school." Tanner passed the paper to Androv, who glanced at it and gave it to Kalin.

Abrams did not think it was a terrific idea to give them the boy's name and address, but they had little choice if they were to keep the Russians' confidence. Abrams' mind was working the way O'Brien's had, and he wondered if the boy had just become cheese for a rattrap. Why not? They'd hypnotized him and given him truth drugs. If they were through debriefing him, he could be recycled as bait. Abrams was having some difficulty discerning the white hats from the black hats. He had to keep reminding himself that he was on the side of truth and justice.

Androv again addressed Abrams. "How would you proceed against this young hooligan?"

Abrams looked up from his notebook. He wanted to ask how Androv would proceed. Gun or knife? He said instead, "Since I haven't passed the bar exam, I'd rather not offer a legal opinion."

Androv replied, "But you are knowledgeable, no? How long have you worked for Mr. Styler?"

Abrams thought the segue was awkwardly done. He began to reply, then sneezed into his handkerchief. He used the bronchial spray, cleared his throat, and replied in a cracking voice, "Two years."

Kalin glanced up from his attaché case.

Androv said, "Do you have a cold?"

"Allergy."

"Ah, something in this room?"

"Probably."

"It must be Mr. Kalin, then." Androv laughed.

Abrams smiled and turned to Kalin. "What is your feeling on those punitive damages?"

Kalin, without glancing up, replied, "The figure seems small compared to what one reads in the papers."

Which, Abrams thought, was interesting, considering Kalin had not been in the room when Tanner mentioned $500,000.

Kalin, realizing his mistake, glanced up at Abrams but did not look toward Androv.

Androv said, "I think we will have to send Mr. Kalin back to school."

The meeting continued for another ten minutes, during which time Androv digressed now and then to ask Abrams a few more pointed questions. Abrams either answered evasively or answered after using one of the two drugs. Abrams could not tell if Kalin was happy or disappointed with his analyzer results. He could also not determine with any assurance whether Androv or Kalin were buying any of this. Androv's manner had grown progressively preoccupied.

Finally, Androv cut off Tanner in midsentence. "What is keeping that madman from his capers?" He looked at his watch, then lifted his heavy bulk from his chair and marched to the window. He stared thoughtfully into the distance for a few seconds, then turned and faced the room. "He must know that you are here. So he won't bother us until the police report to him that your car has gone." He advanced a few steps. "You may as well leave. Park in the high school and wait for the fireworks and loudspeakers so you can satisfy yourselves. Thank you for coming on your holiday, gentlemen. Good evening."

Abrams rose and said, "I'd rather we see it from your perspective."

Androv stared at him. "I have a busy evening."

"We can wait here and entertain ourselves."

"That is against regulations."

Kalin closed his attaché case and stood. "There is nothing further to discuss or see."

Tanner said uneasily, "I guess we've got enough—"

Styler interrupted and addressed Androv. "We've gone to some trouble to get here, and we'd like to see for ourselves the exact nature of Van Dorn's harassment."

Abrams suppressed a smile. Styler had balls. Abrams glanced at his watch. Van Dorn would not begin for at least fifteen more minutes.

Androv began speaking in a voice that was not only frosty but had, Abrams thought, an edge of frenzy about it. "Gentlemen, let's be frank. This is a high-security area as you know, and I don't have the personnel to assign to keep you company this evening." He made a sweeping motion toward the door. "Good night."

Kalin began leading the way. Styler, Tanner, and Abrams began to follow, then Abrams turned back to Androv. "I'd like to use the rest room."

Androv seemed to have calmed down. "Yes, of course." He pointed to a doorway at the far end of the gallery. "Through there. You will see a door marked Powder Room." He added, "Do not get lost, please."

Kalin seemed to be on the point of accompanying Abrams, but Styler engaged him in conversation. Abrams left his briefcase on the chair and walked to the door Androv had indicated.

He passed through into a large passageway, dimly lit by wall sconces, and quickly checked his watch. He had, at best, five minutes before they sent someone to find him. He looked up at the cornices and spotted a television camera over the door through which he had just passed. He walked a few feet to the right toward the powder room door, then turned back, but the camera was not following him.

Abrams opened the powder room door, turned on the light, and looked around the small windowless enclosure, which held a single toilet, a washbasin, a vanity and chair. There seemed to be no air vent, and the place could stand a cleaning. He backed out, pulled the door closed behind him, and stood silently in the passageway.

Evans had not wanted him to take the risk of carrying the floor plans, but he remembered enough of them to know where he was. Across from the powder room was a narrow staircase, labeled on the plans *Private stairs,* which led up to the bedrooms. Beneath the staircase was a small door that led down to the basement.

Farther down the passage were two sets of double doors, directly across from each other. They were glass-paned doors, covered with sheer curtains. The doors to the right opened into the south end of the living room. The doors to the left were another entrance to the music room. At the far end of the passageway was a large set of French doors that opened onto the south terrace.

Abrams walked quickly to the French doors, unbolted them, and pushed them open. He heard no alarms, but that did not mean that a silent alarm had not gone off in the security office. Still, he hadn't committed a capital offense yet. He walked out into the clear, moonlit night. The stepped terrace dropped off to the pool below, and to the left was the stone-walled service court, used now as a parking yard. Abrams could not see over the wall even from his vantage point, but he could see the court was brightly lit, and he suspected the Lincoln had gotten a careful search there.

Abrams turned and looked up at the massive house. All the windows on the upper stories were dark, but on closer examination he could see that blackout curtains had been drawn over them. He walked back to the French doors and stared down the long, dimly lit hall. The television camera was not clearly visible, but even if it was focused on him, he hadn't committed that capital offense yet. But he was about to.

Abrams knelt and examined the weather stripping on the French doors, then drew his penknife. He scraped the metal stripping under the bottom edge of the door, letting the scrapings of bright metal plating fall into a handkerchief. He folded the handkerchief carefully and put it in his trouser pocket, then stood and closed the

French doors, rebolting them. He waited, his heart beating heavily in his chest, but nothing happened. Actually, he knew that, even if they were listening or watching, they'd let him finish—let him, as Androv would say, cut his capers. And in the process, cut his own throat.

Abrams looked at his watch. Two minutes had passed. He walked to the music room doors and stood to the side. He listened for a few seconds and heard the sound of a television. He peered through the sheer curtains into the room and saw the young security woman sitting with her back to him, smoking a cigarette and having a drink. She was watching some moronic game show on a large seven-foot screen that looked like a late-model Sony. At least, thought Abrams, she wasn't watching *him* on the screen. He began to believe he was going to pull this off.

This commons room was painted in a high-gloss enamel of avocado green, which Abrams thought would look better on a refrigerator or electric can opener. The furniture was red vinyl, split in all the right places, and the room had that special ill-used look that Abrams associated with police squad rooms and government waiting rooms. To the left he could see the door that led back to the gallery. He couldn't imagine why Androv had circumvented this rather dreary commons room, unless it was to protect his American guests' aesthetic sensibilities from severe shock. Then Abrams spotted, in the corner opposite the Sony, another television set. It was an old design with a highly polished mahogany cabinet, but Abrams instinctively recognized that it was not an old American model but what passed for a contemporary style in Russia.

His eyes began to take in the whole room through the spaces in the gauzy curtains. The wall receptacles appeared to be of the new ground-fault type. Next to the fireplace on the near right wall stood an old Philco radio console, the size of a jukebox.

Well, he thought, there's the radio and television in question. Though why there should be a primitive Russian television set in the same room as a seven-foot Sony was a bit of a mystery. And why anyone but a nostalgia buff or antiques collector would keep a monstrous vacuum-tube Philco radio was stranger still.

Abrams focused on the young woman again. As he watched, she stood, carrying her drink, walked to the television, and switched it to videotape. Presently the screen lightened to a taped version of the Bolshoi, about midway through *Giselle*. The woman turned to go back to her chair and Abrams could see she was a little unsteady on her feet. As she came toward the chair and closer to him, he began to edge away from the door, but then he noticed her face. She had, he thought, one of the saddest expressions he could imagine, and tears rolled down her face. She gulped down her drink, wiped her eyes, and sank back into the chair, covering her face with her hands. Odd, he thought.

Abrams turned, crossed the passageway, and approached the glass-paneled living room doors. He listened again but heard nothing, and the room appeared to be dark. He edged closer to the doors and looked through the glass pane and sheer curtains, shielding his eyes against the glare of the passageway's wall sconces. As he moved his other hand down to the brass doorknob, Abrams suddenly froze and held his breath. Slowly, he turned toward the narrow staircase as his right hand went into his pocket and found his penknife.

The figure coming down the dimly lit stairs stopped and stared at him.

Abrams stared back, then stepped to the foot of the stairs and looked up. He said softly, *"Zdravstvoui."*

The girl, about five or six years old, clutched at a rag doll and replied in a frightened tone, "Please, don't tell anyone."

Abrams put on a reassuring smile. "Tell anyone what?"

"That I came upstairs," she whispered.

"No, I won't tell anyone."

The girl smiled tentatively, then said, "You talk funny."

Abrams replied, "I am not from the same part of Russia as you." He looked at the doll. "How pretty. May I see it?"

The girl hesitated, then a bit nervously took another step down the stairs.

Abrams extended his arm slowly and the girl handed him the doll. Abrams examined it appreciatively. "What is your doll's name?"

"Katya."

"And what is your name?"

"Katerina." She giggled.

Abrams smiled, and still holding the doll, said, "Where are you going, Katerina?"

"Down to the basement."

"To the basement? Do you play down there?"

"No. *Everyone* is down there."

Abrams began another question, then stopped. He stayed silent for some seconds, then said in a quiet voice, "What do you mean, everyone is down there?"

"I went upstairs to get Katya. But everyone is supposed to stay in the basement."

"Why is everyone supposed to stay in the basement?"

"I don't know."

"Are your parents down there?"

"I *told* you—everyone is there."

"Are you going back to your apartment in New York tonight?"

"No. We must all sleep here tonight." She smiled. "There is no school tomorrow."

Abrams passed the doll back to the girl. "I won't tell anyone I saw you. Hurry back downstairs."

The girl pressed the doll to her chest and scurried down the remaining steps past him. She opened the small basement door and disappeared, leaving the door open.

Abrams stared down the dimly lit stone stairway, then quietly closed the door. He stood motionless for a while and thought. *Something is wrong here. Very wrong.*

Abrams hesitated, glanced at his watch, then walked quickly back to the living room door. Slowly, he pushed the door open.

The large living room sat hushed in pale moonlight, and the bulky furniture cast moon shadows over the flowered rug, some-how reminding Abrams of prehistoric animals grazing in a primeval clearing.

He took a step into the room and stopped short. Not ten feet from him was the profile of a man sitting in an upholstered chair.

The man was very still, his hands resting in his lap, and at first

Abrams thought he was asleep, then he noticed the glint of an open eye. A cigarette burned in an ashtray, a wispy stream of smoke rising silhouetted against the moonlit bay window across the room.

Abrams remained motionless and drew a silent breath through his nose, smelling now the foul acrid smoke of the Russian cigarette. It did not seem possible that the man hadn't heard him enter, but then as Abrams' eyes adjusted to the light, he noticed the earphones over the man's head. The man was listening to something, jotting notes, and Abrams intuitively knew he was monitoring the conversation in the gallery.

The man finally seemed to sense the presence of an intruder and turned his face toward Abrams, removing the earphones as he did. The two men stared silently at each other, and Abrams saw now that the man was very old. The man spoke in a peculiarly accented Russian. "Who are you?"

Abrams replied in English, "I have lost my way. Excuse me."

"Who are you looking for?"

"I have taken a wrong turn. Good night."

The man did not reply but snapped on a green-shaded reading lamp.

Abrams found that he could not turn away, but continued to stare. Even after forty years the American's Russian was not good, and that struck him, irrelevantly, as odd. Even after forty years, the face was recognizable as the one he had seen on her office wall. But even if he had never seen that photograph, he would know those large, liquid blue eyes, because they were her eyes.

Abrams understood and accepted the fact that he was looking at the face of the warrior who had returned from the dead, at the face of Henry Kimberly, at the face of Talbot.

BOOK VI

Battle Lines

CHAPTER FORTY-THREE

Marc Pembroke stood at the window, dressed only in his tan trousers. He focused his binoculars on the Russian mansion, nearly half a mile across the hollow. "This may seem a primitive way to gather intelligence, but one can learn things peeking from windows."

Joan Grenville stretched and yawned on the bed. "I'd better get downstairs before I'm missed."

"Yes," Pembroke replied. "An hour is rather a long time to be gone to the loo." He knelt in front of the open screenless window and steadied his elbows on the sill, adjusting the focus. "There's a chap in a third-floor gable. He's got a tripod-mounted telescope and he's staring back at me."

"Can I turn on the lights to get dressed?"

"Certainly not." Pembroke scanned with the binoculars. "I can see the forecourt clearly, but I don't see the Lincoln's headlight beams yet. They won't be leaving for a while, I expect."

Joan Grenville sat on the edge of the bed. "Who won't be leaving where?"

"Abrams is leaving the Russian estate. At least, I hope he is. If there's trouble, they're to flash their high beams."

Joan Grenville stood and came beside him. "What sort of trouble? What's Tony Abrams doing there?"

"It's a legal matter."

"Oh, bullshit. How many times have I heard *that* from Tom and his idiot friends?"

"You're refreshingly without depth, Mrs. Grenville. One gets tired of all these still waters that run deep. You're a frothy, fast-moving, and shallow stream. I can touch bottom with you."

She giggled. "You did. Twice."

Pembroke smiled as he refocused on his Russian counterpart. "Ivan does not believe his good luck in spying a beautiful naked woman bathed in moonlight. He's rubbing his eyes and drooling."

Joan Grenville glanced out the window. "Can he really see me?"

"Of course. Here, hold these and watch for a flash of high beams."

She took the binoculars and stood in front of the window.

Pembroke finished dressing and walked to the door.

She giggled again. "The Russian is waving at me."

"Watch for the damned headlights or I'll throw you out the window."

She nodded quickly. There was something in his voice that suggested he meant that literally. Without turning, she asked, "Where are you going?"

"As the Duke of Wellington said when asked to impart a piece of enduring military wisdom, 'Piss when you can.'" He left.

Joan Grenville shrugged and kept her eyes to the binoculars. "'Piss when you can' indeed. He probably had to use the phone more than he had to use the john. These people even lie about the weather."

Karl Roth stood at the long table in the spacious kitchen and surveyed the cellophane-covered trays of food. "There's something here for everyone."

Maggie Roth turned from the sink and glanced at the trays heaped with meats, cheeses, fruits, vegetables, nuts, and pastries. Small labels identified the special dietary items, including kosher meats. "You've gone to some trouble, Karl. Even hiring two extra serving girls. We'll not make any profit on this one."

"Van Dorn is a good customer. Sometimes you have to give a little extra. For public relations."

She laughed. "You're the best bloody Communist capitalist I know."

Karl Roth's eyes darted nervously around the busy kitchen. "Maggie, watch your tongue."

She looked at the wall clock. "We should begin serving soon." She walked to the table and peeled back a cellophane covering.

Karl Roth held up his hands. "No, Not yet."

A passing busboy reached out and deftly filched a steak tidbit, popping it in his mouth.

Roth bellowed, "Keep your filthy hands off!"

"Stay cool, pop." The boy walked off.

Maggie Roth said, "Karl, what are you so jumpy about?"

He didn't answer, but glanced at the wall clock as he hovered protectively over the food-laden table.

She said, "It's really past time. Get the girls to pull off the wrappings and let's serve."

"No." He began rubbing his hands together and Maggie could see he was very agitated. She shrugged and went back to the sink.

The swinging door opened and Claudia Lepescu entered the noisy kitchen, carrying a drink and wearing a clinging black knit dress. She looked at Karl Roth and said, "Are you the caterer?"

Roth stared at her for several seconds, then nodded quickly.

Maggie Roth turned her head and stared at Claudia, taking in the clothing, which she thought was inappropriately dressy for an outdoor party. She wondered what sort of accent that was. Like many immigrants, she didn't particularly care for foreigners. Karl, too, she reflected, was usually curt with fellow Europeans. Now, however, he was making little shufflings and scrapings of servitude toward this woman. Odd. Maggie turned back to the sink.

Claudia said, "Please leave me your card. I could use your services."

Again Roth nodded, but said nothing and averted his eyes from hers.

Claudia walked to the table and peeled back the cellophane on a tray of hors d'oeuvres, taking one and putting it in her mouth. "Very good. You should serve these before they get stale."

Roth's head bobbed up and down and he began taking off the remainder of the cellophane from the trays.

Claudia wandered aimlessly around the kitchen.

Karl Roth knelt under the table where he had stacked several boxes, found a small parcel taped closed, and ripped it open. He retrieved a plastic spray bottle and stood. He shook the bottle vigorously and began spraying the trays of food with a light misty mixture of oil and water.

Maggie looked over her shoulder and said, "That's not necessary, Karl. Everything is fresh." She shot a look at Claudia.

Roth replied in a distracted tone. "It makes everything look better. . . . You should read the trade journals instead of your stupid movie magazines."

Maggie watched him and noticed his hand shaking.

Roth finished the spraying, went to the sink, and emptied the remaining contents of the bottle down the drain. He rinsed the bottle and placed it in the trash compactor, then washed his hands with soap.

Maggie walked deliberately to the table and picked up a piece of smoked salmon, raising it to her mouth.

Roth hesitated, then came up quickly behind her and grabbed her hand. Their eyes met and she said softly, "Oh, Karl. . . you fool. . . ."

Claudia stood some distance off and watched, then began moving toward Maggie Roth.

Katherine Kimberly turned the corner of the long second-floor hallway and saw Marc Pembroke emerging from a passage that led to the back service stairs. She watched him for a moment as he approached the door to his room, then called out and walked up to him. "I've been looking for you. May I speak with you a moment?" She indicated his door.

"Actually, no. I'm rather busy."

She shot a glance at the closed door. "We can go to an empty room."

He hesitated, then followed her down the hallway and entered a storage room piled high with boxes and holiday decorations. She snapped on an overhead light and said, "Do you have Joan Grenville in your room?"

"A gentleman does not tell, and a lady should not ask."

"I ask because her husband holds a sensitive position in my firm."

"I see. Well, yes, I admit I pumped her in more ways than one. But she's rather uninformed. Tom doesn't tell her much."

Katherine said evenly, "Who exactly *do* you work for?"

Pembroke seemed a bit impatient and glanced at his watch. "Oh, different people. You, at the moment. O'Brien, to be exact."

"And what do you do for us, Marc?"

"Well, I'm not involved with intelligence gathering, analysis, or anything clever like that. I kill people."

She stared at him.

"Really. But I only kill villains. To answer your next question, I decide who are villains."

She drew a deep breath, then asked, "What do you know about these recent deaths?"

"I know I didn't do them. Except for your fiancé's friends this morning."

"Yes, I wanted to thank—"

He waved his hand. "I'm billing your firm for that. You'll see that it's paid, won't you?"

She ignored the question and asked, "And you had nothing to do with Arnold Brin's death?"

"In a way I did. I should have protected him. I wish I'd known you had him working on something—"

"Are you trying to blame me?"

"No, no, I didn't mean to—"

"And if you had the job to protect him, why didn't you?"

"Oh, it wasn't my job. I mean I wasn't *hired* to do that. I was supposed to do that. He was my father."

She drew an involuntary breath. "What? Arnold Brin...?"

"Actually Brin was his nom de guerre, but he kept it after the war. Our family name is not Pembroke, either, but that's not relevant."

She looked at him closely in the dimly lighted room, focusing on his eyes, then his mouth. "Yes...yes, you are his son."

"So I said. Archive work is dreadfully boring, and unremunerative. But it does give one some good leads to villains. I began my career bumping off old Nazis for the Israelis. Then I ran out of Nazis and I switched to Eastern Bloc targets."

"Are you working now for Mr. O'Brien? Or are you working to avenge your father's death?"

"There's no money in vengeance." Pembroke walked to a small dusty window and stared out at the distant Manhattan skyline silhouetted by the last traces of dusk in the western sky. He added, "However, as it happens, Mr. O'Brien's needs and my desires coincide. But I am a professional, and though your fiancé was the proximate cause of my father's death, I did not kill him. I'm after his bosses."

Katherine sat on a packing crate and stared at Marc Pembroke's profile. Subconsciously she had always compared him to Peter, but now the contrasts were striking and obvious. Peter was charmingly amoral. Marc was charmingly immoral. Peter, like an infant or an animal, hadn't the vaguest idea of right or wrong; Marc did, and chose to kill. By the standards of conventional theology, psychology, and jurisprudence, Peter was innocent, Marc was culpable. Yet, by those same standards, Peter was beyond help or reason, while Marc Pembroke could be saved. She thought of him standing at the gravesite and suspected she was looking at a reluctant killer, like a soldier who in times of peace would not take up arms. She said, "I like you. I wish you'd reconsider archive work. There's an opening."

She saw the trace of a smile pass over his lips. He turned to her but didn't reply. He glanced at his watch again, then said, "Well, I must run. We'll continue this another time."

She stood, blocking his way. "Wait. What do you know of Tony Abrams' mission? Where is he?"

"Close by, actually."

"Next door?"

Pembroke nodded.

"What is he doing there?"

Pembroke did not reply.

"Is he safe?"

"I rather doubt it. But if you'll step aside, I can go and try to find out."

She remained standing in front of him. "If he's not safe, will you...can you do something?"

"No. The Iron Curtain begins at the next property line."

"But—"

"Please step aside. I have pressing business to attend to." He added, as though he suddenly realized she was actually his employer, "I don't mean to be rude."

"You'll keep me informed?"

"Certainly."

She walked to the door and opened it for him. Pembroke moved toward it, then hesitated. He said, "I never ask, you know. I mean, about the larger picture. But is it true, Kate, that this is the last throw of the dice?"

She replied carefully, "That's what some people seem to think."

He nodded. "Yes, O'Brien did too."

"Yes, he—what do you mean, *did*?"

"Oh, I didn't mean to put him in the past tense. He's fine as far as I know."

They stared at each other for a few seconds. Pembroke seemed to notice her for the first time, and his distraction turned to close scrutiny. She was wearing white linen slacks and a white silk shirt with the top three buttons open. She looked sophisticated yet sensual. He said, "Look here, I don't have the time to proposition you properly now, but later...if there's any time left for any of us, I shall."

She found herself breaking eye contact with him, which was not her habit in these situations. She said, "I'm sorry, I'm already involved."

"Oh, but he'll be dead shortly."

She looked quickly at him. "What—? Who—?"

"Thorpe."

"Oh." She let out a breath. "No, I meant...someone else."

He looked surprised, then nodded. "I see...yes, of course. I'm not paying attention. Well, Abrams is a fine fellow. Do him a favor and give him the archive job." He turned and left.

Katherine watched him as he walked toward his room. Marc Pembroke, for all his guile, was not a good liar. He had some news about Pat O'Brien, and she suspected it was not good news. She was neither shocked nor stunned. She'd expected it. She'd also expected that if O'Brien was ever sick and dying, missing, or dead, the news would be held back for as long as possible, in much the same way that the death of a great general might be kept secret to avoid panicking the troops and giving comfort to the enemy.

She felt herself shaking and leaned back against the doorjamb.

No, she thought, it was no accident that the past had returned, or that there were so many coincidental relationships, personal and familial. It had been contrived by Patrick O'Brien and his friends. Marc Pembroke probably had at least a vague understanding that he had been maneuvered since childhood to perform a function. O'Brien's recruiting and manipulation had been more far-reaching than she'd imagined. His corporation had many subsidiaries. She thought of something an English jurist had written in the seventeenth century: *Corporations cannot commit treason, nor be outlawed, nor excommunicate, for they have no souls.* Also, they were ostensibly immortal. And though Patrick O'Brien might be dead, she hoped there was enough life force left in the wounded, immortal, and soulless being of his creation, so that inertia at least would carry it forward toward its last encounter with its enemy.

CHAPTER FORTY-FOUR

Mike Tanner drove the Lincoln into the dimly lit parking lot of the Glen Cove train station. The conversation had been confined to legal matters as instructed by Evans, who had warned that the Russians liked to plant bugs in their guests' cars, "just to hear them talking about what a swell time they had."

The Lincoln stopped and Abrams opened the passenger-side door. "Thanks for the ride. I'll see you in the office tomorrow." He took his briefcase and closed the door.

Styler slid out the rear. "I'll walk you." He took Abrams' arm and they stepped a few feet from the car. "What happened in there?"

"I saw a ghost." He began walking slowly toward the tracks.

"You looked it. My God, you're still pale." He added, "You're not home free yet. Are you being covered?"

Abrams turned to him as they walked, and regarded the older man closely. This was the first time Styler had actually acknowledged the fact that there was a mortal danger inherent in the situation. Abrams replied, "I imagine so."

Styler said, "I hope they saw the high beams flash."

Abrams replied, "If they were looking, they did."

Styler glanced at his watch. "You have about ten minutes until the city-bound train comes." He motioned ahead toward a flight of descending stairs. "That's the pedestrian underpass that takes you to the westbound side."

Abrams looked across the tracks at the station house, a small

Victorian-style building that was dark and closed for the evening. On the platform in front of the station house, four people stood under a lamppost: a young couple and two teen-age boys, waiting for the train to Manhattan. There was no one on the eastbound platform directly in front of him. Abrams had not realized he was on the wrong side of the tracks, and having realized it, had not fully appreciated the fact that he could not cross over them but would have to take the tunnel to the other side.

Styler peered down the dark concrete staircase. "We'll wait here until we see you board."

"No. Go on. You've been told to clear out." Abrams moved toward the stairs.

Styler nodded. "I know one shouldn't question orders, but we can take you back to Garden City and you can catch the train there."

"No, I've been instructed to take this train at this station, and if I start getting tricky I'll lose any protection that's been planned." Also, he thought, if Androv had something planned, it might be interesting to see what it was. He wondered what had happened to his resolve to be more careful.

Abrams put out his hand and Styler took it. Abrams said, "I hope I was of some help on the case."

Styler smiled. "I think you lost us that client, Abrams." His smile changed to an expression of concern. "Good luck." He walked back toward the car.

Abrams began to descend the steps. He heard the Lincoln pull away over the graveled blacktop. As he went farther down, he could smell the damp, fetid air. He reached the bottom step and looked into the underground passageway. It was about fifty yards long, and of the six or seven overhead lights, only one, in the middle, was still working, though it lit up most of the tunnel. He took the last step and waited for his eyes to become adjusted to the dim light.

Obviously the place was used by kids as a hangout. There were a few broken beer and wine bottles on the concrete floor, and Abrams spotted a flaccid rubber sheath that in his youth had been called a Coney Island whitefish. The gray concrete walls were covered with graffiti of a uniquely obscene variety, much better than the semiliterate walls of Brooklyn. Better schools in the suburbs, he thought. A cricket chirped somewhere close by.

Abrams began walking ahead, at a normal pace, through the long concrete tunnel. He was nearly halfway through it when he heard the unmistakable sound of footsteps to his front. A figure appeared out of the gloom, then another. Two men in business suits. He stopped.

Behind him he made out the soft footfalls of someone who was trying not to be heard, then a second person joined the first; then they both dropped all pretense and began advancing at a normal pace.

Abrams turned his head and saw two men coming toward him. They were in leisure suits that looked, even from this far off in the bad lighting, very unstylish. The thought would have been irrelevant except for the associated thought: *Russians.*

Abrams turned and resumed his walk toward the westbound tracks. The two men to his front moved into the brighter area nearer the single light, and Abrams could see that the man closest to him was tall and blond. At first he believed it was Pembroke. But it was Kalin.

Kalin stopped and called out. "So, there you are, Abrams." His voice boomed in the damp narrow tunnel and the cricket stopped chirping. "I was looking for you on the other side. Androv said you may ride with us back to Manhattan."

Abrams did not reply, but slowed his pace.

Kalin said, "Please hurry. The car is this way. Come."

Abrams heard the footsteps behind draw closer, probably to within forty feet. Abrams continued slowly toward Kalin. The man with him had stayed some distance back. Kalin said, "Come, come, Abrams. Don't dawdle."

Abrams picked up his pace. Kalin put his hands in his pockets. "It will be quicker this way."

Abrams replied, "I'm sure it will be." He drew his revolver as he walked.

Kalin's eyebrows rose in a look of mock surprise, then a nasty smile spread across his hard face as he went for his own pistol.

Abrams had examined his revolver in the car and it looked as if it had not been tampered with. Now he was sure that if he squeezed the trigger, it would misfire or the powder charge would have been spiked with nitroglycerin and it would blow up in his hand. He let out a blood-curdling scream and charged forward.

Kalin took a second or two to recover his composure, then raised his pistol. "Halt!"

Abrams stopped in his tracks, directly beneath the overhead light.

"Hands up!"

Abrams raised his hands and quickly thrust the barrel of his revolver up through the thick glass of the light, shattering the bulb with a dull pop. He dove for the wall and flattened himself against it.

There was no sound in the black tunnel. Abrams stood still, controlling his breathing. He reversed the revolver in his hand, making it into a bludgeon, then lowered his briefcase silently and retrieved his penknife, opening the two-inch blade. He waited.

He suspected they didn't have flashlights, or they would have used them by now. But they'd have blackjacks and perhaps knives. The KGB never left home without them.

Abrams carefully slipped his shoes off and began edging along the wall toward the westbound tracks. Darkness, he reminded himself, more than guns, was the great equalizer. He heard no movement from the Russians, not even breathing.

Abrams' left foot came down on a shard of glass and it sliced into his arch. He drew a quick breath through his nostrils and stopped moving. Carefully, he raised his foot and pulled out the glass, feeling the warm blood soaking his sock. He flung the fragment toward the eastbound exit and heard it tinkle on the concrete floor, but it produced no reaction. They were, he thought, well disciplined. But what did he expect?

Abrams' natural impulse was to make a break, but he knew that if they didn't have flashlights, he could possibly sit it out. Time was basically on his side. They couldn't stand there in a pedestrian underpass of the Long Island Rail Road forever. But he could.

Kalin must have come to the same conclusion. He called out softly to his men, and Abrams was able to understand the orders: the two men on the eastbound side—Feliks and Vasili—were to kneel in the tunnel, which was only eight feet wide, join hands, and touch the walls with their free hands, in effect blocking that side of the tunnel. Kalin and his partner, Boris, were going to move in along the walls. The space between them was going to be covered by taking Boris' suit jacket and holding the arms outstretched between them, dragging the hem along the floor. A hammer-and-anvil technique. Abrams thought that was quite clever.

He was fairly certain now that Kalin didn't know he understood Russian. But whether he did or not, Kalin had to give his men orders, and therefore give Abrams warning.

Abrams heard Kalin's and Boris' footsteps approaching and estimated they were about ten feet away. He could hear their breathing as they drew nearer, then heard the jacket dragging along the concrete floor. He thought he smelled them too: their breaths, their sweat, and a cloying lavender cologne. Abrams backtracked, edging the opposite way along the wall, toward Feliks and Vasili.

Kalin said, "How close are we to you? Say something."

Abrams assumed the question was not directed at him, but he was interested in the answer.

One of the two men replied, "You sound close. Five meters."

Kalin replied, "He's right here. Between us. Be alert now." Kalin switched to English. "Abrams, listen to me. We don't want to harm you. We want to speak to you. May we speak to you?"

Abrams thought that Kalin had picked a funny place to chat. That's what happened when you crossed a KGB man with a lawyer: you got a killer who wanted to discuss the pros and cons of slitting your throat in the dark.

He realized he had to make a move before the space between the hammer and anvil closed. He glanced toward the stairs on either side. Now that he'd been in the darkness so long, he could see something he hadn't noticed before: There was a dim light from the parking lots that could be faintly seen on the steps. If he somehow made it past the Russians and got as far as the end of the tunnel, he'd be silhouetted against the light falling on the steps—a duck in a shooting gallery.

He edged back a few more feet as Kalin and Boris approached. He estimated that he had less than three feet left in which to maneuver.

So, he thought, with nowhere to run and nowhere to hide, he had to fight. And he had to do it here and now, close in where they'd be afraid to use guns, knives, or blackjacks. His one advantage was the fact that when the fight started, he could be sure he had no friends to worry about in the dark. They did not have this assurance.

Abrams thought of his mother's advice to get an inside job and wondered if this counted. He wondered, too, what his parents would say if they knew their comrades were trying to kill their son.

Abrams took a long step away from the wall and positioned himself toward the center of the tunnel. He swung his briefcase high and flung it toward the eastbound steps. Abrams pivoted toward Kalin and Boris, dropping to one knee as the briefcase slapped heavily on the concrete floor and skidded.

Boris fired over the heads of Abrams, Feliks, and Vasili, toward the sound of the briefcase. Abrams saw the tongue of orange flame, heard the muffled cough of the silencer, and listened to the bullet whistle above and strike the steps and ricochet, causing a loud echoing. The smell of burnt cordite hung heavily in the damp, still air.

Abrams pointed his penknife three feet below the place where he'd seen the muzzle flash, and sprang forward. He felt the small knife slice into what he guessed was Boris' abdomen. Even before he heard the surprised groan, he withdrew back into a crouch.

Boris' voice sounded shaky. "I'm cut! Blood. Oh . . . I'm stabbed. Blood!"

"Shut up, Boris." Kalin's voice. "Pick up your end of the jacket."

Abrams realized he had a hole in the net and moved in a crouch between Boris and Kalin.

But Kalin had anticipated this and had dropped back, centering himself like a middle linebacker, arms outstretched, weaving left and right, a blackjack in one hand, his pistol in the other.

Abrams' forehead touched the cold steel of the gun, and Kalin sensed it and brought his blackjack down hard. Abrams felt the heavy blow on his right shoulder and let out an involuntary gasp as his penknife fell to the floor. A sharp kick caught him on his thigh as he fell back. He whispered in Russian, "No. It's me."

Kalin hesitated. Abrams stood quickly and swung the butt of his pistol at shoulder height. He felt it graze off something, and heard Kalin utter a sharp cry.

Abrams moved back against the wall, fighting back the shooting pain in his right shoulder. He knew he had to get his hands on one of their guns, but even as he thought it, he heard Kalin's voice: "Put away the pistols! Knives and blackjacks only. Move in."

Abrams thought Kalin sounded as if he was in some pain, but his voice was steady. The man was good.

Abrams listened and heard Boris a few feet away, on the floor, breathing irregularly. That was one gun that was still available. Abrams got down on all fours, fingertips and toes, to make the least amount of noise. He moved toward Boris and suddenly felt a warm wetness on his fingers, a great deal of it, pooling across the cold concrete. He must have severed the man's iliac artery.

Abrams made contact with Boris' leg, and moved his hands quickly over his body, feeling the blood-soaked abdomen, then locating his arms and hands, but he could not find the pistol. Kalin and the other two had drawn closer and were guiding themselves toward the sound Abrams was making in his frantic effort to find Boris' pistol.

Abrams braced himself on one knee, grabbed the limp body of Boris by the shoulders and, together, they rose to a standing position. Abrams shoved the dying man toward Feliks and Vasili, hearing the collision of bodies, followed by shouts, the pounding of blackjacks, and the sound of knives grating against bones. Abrams joined the melee, swinging his pistol and bringing the butt down again and again, oblivious to everything except the motion of his arm, the thud of the wooden-handled pistol—splintered now—and the confused cries of three, then two, then one man. Abrams backed off and braced himself against the wall. He assessed the damage to his own body and discovered a superficial slice on his neck and innumerable places on his body where the two blackjacks had hit him. He felt suddenly dizzy and lowered himself to one knee.

Kalin's voice came out of the darkness from some distance away. "Report."

No one answered for some seconds, then a voice, winded and in pain, replied, "Vasili."

Kalin's voice was not as steady now. "The others? The Jew?"

Vasili replied: "I don't know. I can't *see*."

Abrams heard another man—it had to be Feliks—moaning, then sobbing, then finally crying out in agony, "I'm dying!"

Vasili shouted, "Kalin, we must go. Help me with them."

Abrams felt the dizziness grow worse. He tried to stand but found himself on the floor. He realized he made some noise as he fell.

Kalin barked, "Vasili! Here!"

Abrams heard the sound of footsteps approaching cautiously. Then he heard Kalin speak. "He's lying against the wall. Don't use your gun—it's too close for a ricochet."

Kalin spoke in English. "Your last chance, Abrams. You will come with us, dead or alive."

Abrams' head was spinning. He was running out of ideas, tricks, weapons, and steam. For a fraction of a second he considered going with them. They'd rather not kill him just yet. That was obvious. Later he'd have a chance to escape. Then he remembered the basement full of Russians, waiting for something, and he doubted there would be a later. He had to get out of here—now.

The dizziness seemed to pass, but he wasn't certain he should try to stand yet. He felt the crease of a trouser leg touch his hand and didn't think the man felt it. He was aware of a fragment of glass near his fingers and picked it up. It was sharp on all sides, but he grasped the glass tightly and swung it in a slashing motion across the man's shin, feeling it slice into the flesh and scrape the bone.

The man—Vasili—bellowed, hopped back on one foot, lost his balance, and fell, still bellowing and swearing.

Abrams stood cautiously, the noise of his movement masked by the sound of Vasili whimpering.

Kalin shouted, "What happened?"

"I'm cut!"

Abrams had already stepped across to the opposite wall and was walking quickly but quietly toward the westbound tracks in his stocking feet.

Kalin shouted, "Abrams! Hands against the wall!"

Abrams could tell that Kalin had faced the opposite way when he called.

Kalin turned and called again. "Abrams! Answer me or I'll shoot!"

There was a touch of anxiety and defeat in Kalin's voice. Abrams didn't envy Kalin his next meeting with Androv. Abrams removed his belt and flung it back toward the two Russians. It hit the floor, and he could hear Vasili let out a startled shout.

Abrams reached the stairs and stopped, his back to the wall. The bluish glow of the parking lot lights fell on the concrete steps. Still, he didn't want to hang around any longer. He drew a deep breath and prepared to spring up the steps. Just before he moved, he heard a round strike a lower step, sending fragments of concrete splattering. The bullet ricocheted back and struck the wall above Abrams' head. He heard another round strike the opposite steps and echo back through the tunnel. So, they didn't know which way he'd gone, but they were letting him know that bounding up the steps was not without risk. In fact, it would be a fool's bet to gamble that he could outdistance a bullet. Yet he had to get back and make a report, and if what he suspected was true, he had to do it soon.

An unsettling thought came to him: Kalin might have backup people in cars out in the parking lots on either side of the tracks. He was not home free yet. Not even close. He waited.

CHAPTER FORTY-FIVE

Karl Roth held his wife's wrists in a tight grasp. "Get out of here," he said under his breath. "Get in the van and go home." His hands were shaking and his voice quavered.

"Like hell I will." She pulled free of him and backed away.

He took a step toward her, but she skirted across the table and said, "You stupid, you idiotic—you—you—" She stammered over her words and tears streamed down her face. A few kitchen workers turned their heads.

Karl Roth forced a tight smile and looked at the people in the kitchen. He said, "Please begin serving. Go on. This is none of your concern."

The serving girls began carrying the trays out of the kitchen.

Maggie was torn between exposing her husband and protecting him.

Roth waited until the serving girls had left, then looked back at his wife and held his hands up placatingly. "Now, now, Maggie. Calm yourself." He moved toward her, but she darted around the table, then hefted a large tray of raw cut vegetables and heaved them toward him.

The tray glanced off his upraised arm and clattered to the floor. She said, "Karl—Karl—help me throw it all out—Karl—don't let them serve—"

He nodded and made calming motions with his hands as he approached her. "Yes. Yes. Fine."

She looked into his eyes as he drew near, then she snatched a paring knife from the table. "Stay away, Karl! Stay—"

Claudia Lepescu had come up behind her. Quickly and expertly she applied a half nelson and with her other hand delivered a sharp chopping blow to Maggie's wrist, causing her to drop the knife. Maggie let out a piercing scream. Claudia brought her hand up over Maggie's mouth and nose, and Maggie smelled a strange odor, then began to feel dizzy.

Karl Roth rushed forward, and together he and Claudia propelled Maggie into the butler's pantry, a sort of auxiliary kitchen. Claudia held Maggie, whose struggling was growing weaker, then let her slip to the floor. "This is a strong old lady." Claudia went to a small copper sink and washed the chloroform off her hands. "I knew she would be trouble."

Roth looked down at his wife, whose eyes were closed now. "Will she be all right?"

Claudia dried her hands on a towel. "She will feel a great deal better than Mr. Van Dorn's guests." She smiled.

Roth was shaking so badly that he had to sit in a chair. "Why tonight? They said it would be Christmas."

She shrugged. "Christmas, July Fourth, New Year's Eve—they had many holidays to choose from." She thought a moment, then added, "I suspect the Americans are too close. Everything is happening very quickly."

Roth had his face buried in his hands and she saw that he was weeping. His words were barely intelligible. "This is terrible... terrible...."

Claudia walked up to him and slapped him sharply across his head. "Stand up!"

Roth stood and faced her, but said nothing.

"Pick her up."

Roth bent down and took his wife under her arms, and Claudia took her ankles. Together they carried her out the rear of the butler's pantry, into a small hallway and up the service stairs to the third-floor servants' quarters. They found a small maid's room and laid her on the bed.

Roth caught his breath and looked at Claudia. "What should we do now?"

She replied, "I'm going to enjoy the party. You're going to see that everyone has plenty to eat."

Roth looked nervously around the small room, as though someone might be there, then said in a low voice, "How much time do we have?"

Claudia glanced at her wristwatch. "About four hours. There won't be any effects before then."

Roth stared at her. "What did you put in the bottle? It was to put them to sleep...?"

"You know it was poison."

He began shaking his head, then nodded ruefully. His voice was barely a whisper. "What if they taste it? Or smell it? Did I put enough on...?"

Claudia looked annoyed. "It was something called ricin, which I am told is extracted from a castor oil bean. That is why it mixed well with the vegetable oil. But unlike the foul castor oil, this has no smell and no taste, and it only needed the light spray because it is so deadly. The blood begins to disintegrate. Death is by suffocation, and regardless of what Androv told you, it is very painful at the end. The KGB is very advanced on the subject of poisons. There will be no survivors."

Roth sat on the edge of the bed beside his comatose wife. "But... but... what will happen to me?"

Claudia snapped, "You fool. This is the end. Don't you understand that? At about the time these people's blood begins to disintegrate, this *country* will begin to disintegrate. No one will care about you. Just take your stupid wife and go next door. But not until you've finished here and cleaned up. Act natural. I'll be watching you."

Roth tried to stand, but slumped back on the bed. "But... what if... if this thing does not happen tonight?"

Claudia laughed. "Well, then we'll all be a little embarrassed. You will have two hundred bloated corpses ripening in the yard when the morning sun comes up, and the police will want a word with you." She laughed again, then added. "There is no antidote for ricin."

Roth stared at her in the dim light.

Claudia walked to the window and looked out onto the lawn and gardens. Over two hundred people milled about or sat at tables under the blue-and-white striped tent. Servants passed around small trays and left larger ones on the tables as instructed. Claudia said, "They are filling their faces. These pigs who have given us so much trouble all these years, they will all be dead by midnight."

Roth stood and moved to her side. He stared down onto the grounds strung with Chinese lanterns. "There are children down there."

"They are the lucky ones, Herr Roth. When you see what happens to the rest of this country later, you will not feel sorry for them."

Roth nodded his head toward the window. "Some of these people have been your friends. The Van Dorns, the Grenvilles, the Kimberly woman.... Do you not feel anything?"

"No." She added with a touch of fatalism in her voice, "What difference would it make? There is no turning back. Whatever is to happen will happen. Most of these people are enemies and would die later anyway. Androv wants them safely dead now so they will present no threat at a critical moment. Also, I think he wants some of them dead for personal reasons."

"But are *we* safe?"

She looked at him contemptuously. "Is that all that worries you? They told me you were a hero—a resistance fighter who hunted Nazis in the ruins of Berlin as the bombs were falling."

"One gets old."

"That is a paradox, is it not? The young with years to live are reckless, and the old worry about their few failing years or months." She turned and walked toward the door. "Are we safe? Who knows? When the lights go out, is anyone safe?"

Roth remembered the New York blackout of 1977, the looting, rioting, and burning.

Claudia turned back to him. "None of us wishes to be caught

in a country in its death throes. *You* remember what that was like, Herr Roth."

Roth remembered exactly what it had been like. Starvation, mass suicides, summary executions, and disease. The days were nightmares and the nights were hell.

Claudia added, "But it is our duty and our fate to witness this. If we succeed and survive, we will be rewarded."

Roth nodded. That's what they'd told him in Berlin in 1945. But this time, at least, there were no more exploiters of the people, no more enemies of the revolution. Odd, he thought, how long it had been since he had spoken or even thought of slogans or words like that. It suddenly occurred to him that he'd stopped believing in the revolution long ago.

Claudia seemed to guess his thoughts. "It's too late, Roth." She added in a whisper, "Tomorrow morning the sun will rise on a new world. The struggle will be over, and you can rest. Just survive the next twenty-four hours." She left the room.

Roth looked back at the unconscious figure of his wife. He remembered as if it were yesterday the last message he'd received from Henry Kimberly in Berlin, and it was, word for word, the whispered message he had just received from this woman.

George Van Dorn stood in his ground-floor study, his hands behind his back, and stared through the bay window. "Quite a party. I do it right."

Tom Grenville, standing in the center of the room, concurred. "Very nice, George. Should we go outside?"

"No. I hate parties."

Grenville shrugged. George Van Dorn, he reflected, was somewhat like his nearby mythical neighbor, Jay Gatsby, staging perfect parties that he never attended. "Can I get you a drink, George?"

"No. I'd like to keep a clear head tonight."

Grenville's eyebrows arched.

Van Dorn added, "You should too."

Grenville looked down at the drink in his hand, then placed the glass on an end table.

Van Dorn turned from the window and began striding around the room, hands still behind his back. Grenville watched him, juxtaposed against the walls covered with old World War II campaign maps, and a large mounted globe in the center of the room. Grenville was reminded of Napoleon brooding over the fate of the world. "Something on your mind, George?"

Van Dorn stopped pacing. "Lots of things." He looked up at the mantel clock. "I guess I should begin my assault on the enemy positions."

"Assault...? Oh, the fireworks." Grenville smiled.

Van Dorn nodded. "Sit down, Tom. I want a word with you."

Grenville sat on the edge of a straight-backed chair.

Van Dorn remained standing. He was silent for some time, then said, "Your father was a man whom I respected. His death after the war from his brutal treatment in the Jap POW camp moved me deeply. More so, I think, than if he'd died in battle."

Grenville nodded cautiously.

"Anyway, out of respect for him, I'm going to speak to you as an uncle. About your wife."

Grenville's face revealed an almost disappointed look, as though he'd expected that Van Dorn was going to confide some important business matter. "Oh..." He assumed a neutral expression.

"I want to be tactful, but at the same time direct." Van Dorn lit a cigar and exhaled a stream of smoke. "She's fucking nearly everybody. What are you going to do about it?"

"Oh..." Grenville ran his hand through his hair and lowered his head. His domestic problem had just become a professional problem. This was serious. He looked up. "I'll divorce her."

"Normally, I would concur. But I have a better idea...." He rubbed his heavy jowls, then continued, "Joan is in fine physical shape, as anyone can see." He stared at Grenville, who seemed, if not actually embarrassed, then at least ill at ease. Van Dorn went on. "You know, Tom, during the war the OSS recruited all types. A good deal of recruiting was done out of expediency. If a person had only one skill or attribute that we needed, then he—or she—was recruited on an ad hoc basis, usually for a one-time-only mission."

"George, if you're suggesting that I allow my wife to use her...
her physical attraction for some mission—"

Van Dorn cut him off with a wave of his arm. "No, Tom. I can
find fifty femmes fatales. I am interested in her body, but only in
a peripheral way. What I have in mind is a mission that requires
someone with a good deal of physical stamina, coupled with a slight
build. For all Joan's charms, she has the build of a boy." He thought
to himself, *I've seen better tits and ass on a snake.*

Grenville cleared his throat. "I don't think Joan would even
consider—"

"I have a file on her so thick you could stand on it and change
a light bulb. She will be the most impoverished divorcée in Scarsdale, or she will play ball." Van Dorn stared at the seated figure of
Grenville. "I also want you to know that there is a strong element of
danger involved in—"

The door suddenly swung open and Van Dorn turned quickly
toward it, his hand sliding inside his jacket.

Kitty Van Dorn entered, balancing a tray in one hand. "*There*
you are."

"And there *you* are."

"And Tom. Where's Joan? We haven't seen her for some time."
Kitty smiled.

Grenville stood and smiled back weakly. "She went to the
ladies'—"

Kitty said, "What *are* you both doing all alone in this stuffy,
smoky room?"

Van Dorn replied, "Tom and I are having a homosexual affair,
Kitty."

"Oh, George." She offered the tray to Grenville. "Try the pâté.
Sit down."

Grenville did as he was told, in the order he was told.

"Ginger loves the pâté."

Van Dorn commented, "I've got a wife named Kitty and a cat
named Ginger."

Kitty turned and held the tray out to her husband. "Karl really
outdid himself this time. I've never seen such variety."

Van Dorn picked up a toast point covered with pink salmon mousse in the shape of a rosebud. He noticed globules of what looked like oil or glycerin on the mousse, hesitated, then put it in his mouth and chewed. "Pussy food. Next time we'll roast a few steers and hogs."

Kitty set the tray on his desk. "George, everyone is waiting for the fireworks."

"Well, if they're paying for them, tell them to give the order to fire when ready."

A dark frown crossed her brow, as though she had just remembered something. "George, who are those pyrotechnicians? I've never seen them before. What happened to the Grinaldis?"

"They blew themselves up."

She turned to Grenville. "The Grinaldis have national reputations as pyrotechnicians. George does it right."

Grenville nodded. "Yes, he—"

Van Dorn turned abruptly to his wife. "Have you seen Pembroke?"

She thought a moment. "Pembroke..."

Van Dorn snapped, "The tall Limey with an icicle up his arse."

"Oh...yes...a friend of Tom's...and Joan's..." She glanced at Grenville, remembering there was some talk of trouble at the May Day party, then turned quickly back to her husband. "Mr. Pembroke wasn't feeling well and went to his room."

"Send someone for him."

"He's not feeling—"

Van Dorn puffed prodigiously on his cigar, a visible sign to his wife that he was about to explode.

She moved quickly toward the door. "Yes, dear." She made a quick exit.

Van Dorn shot a glance at Grenville to see if he'd learned a valuable object lesson on wives.

Grenville looked uncomfortable. He stood again and said, "I guess I'd better leave."

"I guess not."

A bell chimed and Van Dorn walked across the room and disappeared behind a Japanese silk screen that hid an alcove. He reappeared with a sheet of telex paper and went to a wall safe behind a hinged picture. He opened the safe and took out a small code book, then handed both to Grenville. "Decode this message, then we'll finish our discussion about your wife."

Grenville took the message and book and moved behind Van Dorn's desk.

George Van Dorn walked to the French doors and threw them open. The doors let out onto a small secluded garden on the side of the house, separated from the activity out back. Van Dorn walked across the flagstones and lowered himself into an old wooden deck chair. He blew smoke rings up at the moon and listened to the noise of his party.

He thought about Pat O'Brien, realizing that the shadowy mantle of leadership might settle on his shoulders, though neither he nor apparently anyone knew how these things were decided.

He thought too of Styler, Tanner, and Abrams, and wondered how they were faring. Van Dorn's opinion of Abrams had gone from bare tolerance to grudging respect after he had been briefed on the man's recent activities. O'Brien, he conceded, knew men.

But, Van Dorn concluded, there must have been one man whom O'Brien *thought* he knew well enough to let him get close to him, but not well enough for him to suspect that the man was to be his killer.

Van Dorn looked up into the clear starry night sky. Queer, he thought, that hell should lie below and the heavens above, yet the end, when it came, would come out of the heavens, just as nearly every apocalyptic writing had predicted.

And it *was* coming. That much they had discovered. Though none of them knew exactly when or how. But Van Dorn knew enough to try to stop it, and enough to know it was going to be a near thing.

Marc Pembroke returned to his room. "Have you seen any headlights?"

"Yes." Joan Grenville continued looking out the window, fearful of his reaction if she turned to him. "About two minutes ago."

"Could you see the car?"

"Yes, as it moved along the drive, I got a glimpse of it. It was sort of long and square and it had those carriage lights on the side, like a Lincoln."

Pembroke took the binoculars and focused on the Russian house. He said, "You didn't see the high beams flash, did you?"

"Well..."

He turned to her.

"Yes. I'm sure I did. Twice. I could see the trees lit up."

Pembroke threw the binoculars on the bed and moved quickly toward the door.

Joan called out, "Marc...there's something I should tell you."

He turned back and said impatiently, "What?"

"Tony Abrams...Friday night he was in my room at the town house..."

Pembroke turned his back on her and reached for the doorknob. "Who cares?"

"No...I'm not confessing—I mean we didn't make it...but he told me something I was supposed to tell—"

Pembroke removed his hand from the doorknob and turned. "Go on."

"Tony said that if he disappeared or died, I was to relay a message to Katherine Kimberly." She looked at Pembroke. "Has something happened to him?"

"Any reports of his death would be premature, but I wouldn't underwrite life insurance on him. What were you supposed to tell Katherine?"

She hesitated. Having reluctantly absorbed some rudimentary security awareness over the years, she wasn't certain Pembroke was the person who should be hearing this. But neither did she think Katherine—a woman—was the proper recipient of secrets. And Marc had been grilling her about this and that, and seemed concerned about Tony Abrams. Yet—

Pembroke crossed the room and stood in front of her. He slid his hands between her arms and the sides of her breasts and said, "Go on, Joan. It's all right."

She looked up into his eyes and saw that it was all right, if she went on; but if she didn't, it was not going to be all right. She said, "You can tell Katherine if you want to. Tony Abrams said, 'I discovered on the roof that Claudia is a friend of Talbot's.'" She shrugged. "That's it. Do you know what that means?"

Pembroke said, "Why did he confide in you?"

Joan smiled. "He said I was the least likely person to be involved in intrigue of a nonsexual nature."

Pembroke nodded. He had come to the same conclusion about Joan Grenville. Abrams judged well. It was interesting, too, that Abrams had hedged his bet regarding Katherine. He *thought* she was reliable, but was not going to bet his life on it. Best to make posthumous revelations. If you were wrong, no one could kill you. Pembroke released his grip on Joan. "Get dressed and join the party. If I'm not back within the hour, tell Katherine what Abrams told you." He turned toward the door.

"What the hell is going on now? *Marc!*"

"A legal matter." He hurried toward the door and threw it open.

Kitty Van Dorn—a firm believer in the adage that if you want something done right, do it yourself—was standing poised to knock. She smiled, "Oh, Marc, George would like to see you if you're feeling—" She spotted Joan Grenville standing naked in the room and let out a low moan, a curious mixture of disappointment and despair, as though somehow the party were irrevocably ruined by this selfish, bestial conduct under her very roof. "Ooohh..."

Pembroke excused himself formally, and brushed past her into the hallway.

Joan Grenville smiled nervously. "Oh, Kitty..."

Kitty Van Dorn put her hand to her forehead, turned, and staggered down the hall.

Stanley Kuchik sat cross-legged in a far corner of the empty swimming pool, a tray of pastry on his lap and three bottles of beer lined up against the pool wall. He wiped his mouth on the sleeve of his busboy jacket and belched.

"Hey!" called a man at the deep end of the empty pool. "Hey, aren't you supposed to be working?"

Stanley looked down at the sloping end of the Olympic-size pool, dimly illuminated by the recessed lighting in the tiled walls. "I'm on a break."

"You're jerking off."

"No, I'm on a break."

"Sure. Get your ass over here and give us a hand or I'll run you off."

"Shit." Stanley set aside the tray, grabbed a bottle of beer, and moved sulkily down to the far end of the pool. About three fourths of the pool floor was covered with boxes, wires, and clusters of small rocket launchers, loaded and ready to go.

The man who had called him said a bit more kindly, "I'm Don. This is Wally and Lou. What's your name?"

"Kuchik. Stanley."

"A Polack."

"No, Slovakian."

"Same difference."

Stanley looked at the three men. They were old. Mid-thirties, he guessed. They wore dark jeans and khaki-colored tank-top T-shirts. They were all sweating.

Don said, "We're pyrotechnicians. You know what that means?"

Stanley looked around the area and scrutinized the boxes with Chinese lettering. "I guess it means you shoot fireworks."

"Smart kid. See those barrels? When we start shooting, you take the wrappings, cardboard boxes, and all the leftover shit and stuff it in those barrels. If you do okay, you can fire a salvo."

Stanley was torn between his innate curiosity and his inherent laziness. "Okay. But I got to get back in a while."

"Right. You can start now. Get those empty cartons and crush them. But don't touch nothing else, don't push no buttons. And no smoking."

"Okay." Stanley began flattening boxes and stuffing them into the big wooden barrels.

After a while he wandered back to the center of the pool, where an old army camouflage tarp covered what appeared to be a stack of boxes. Stanley caught a glimpse of a small wooden crate peeking out from the tarp. He moved closer to the crate and stared down at the black stenciled letters: 81MM HEAT.

He continued staring at the crate for some time, thinking, *They must use these crates to store things, because that's not what's inside.*

He looked around surreptitiously, then peeled the tarp farther back. Dozens of crates were stacked to form a chest-high wall. Stanley crouched down and peered further into the tentlike enclosure. Sitting on the concrete floor of the pool was a long metal tube pointing up at a forty-five-degree angle. The tube sat on a round base plate and was supported by a bipod. It was, in fact, Stanley knew, an eighty-one-millimeter mortar, and it was pointed toward the Russian house. *"Jesus H. Christ."*

CHAPTER FORTY-SIX

Abrams crouched against the wall. The situation had not improved dramatically. Neither had it deteriorated, however. The train hadn't passed overhead; he assumed it was late. Time and space seemed frozen in this black, noiseless place, and his only awareness of movement or life was his breathing and the beating of his heart.

Abrams decided he needed help, and since none seemed to be at hand, he'd invent an imaginary friend—a dangerous one. He crouched into a tight ball and called out, "Pembroke? Is that you?" His voice echoed in the tunnel. Abrams waited, but drew no fire. He called again, "Yes, they're down here. Can you block the other exit?" He paused, then said, "Good. I'll sit tight."

Abrams listened and heard the unmistakable sounds of Kalin and Vasili beating a hasty retreat, carrying their casualties.

Abrams resisted, then gave in to a childish impulse. He called back into the tunnel in near perfect Russian, "Kalin, tell Androv the Jew sends his regards." Abrams waited a second longer, then despite his pains and light-headedness, dashed up the steps, taking them four and five at a time, until he knew he was not in view from the tunnel. He stopped near the top step and peered out onto the parking lot.

A black Ford was visible in the lot ahead, its front end facing him; it bore diplomatic license plates. Abrams assumed the car belonged to the Russians. He could see the head of the driver through the windshield and another man sitting beside him. That was the car that was going to take him for a ride if he had come along peacefully.

He rose a bit higher and scanned the hedges planted around the tracks and platform, but he didn't see anyone. He heard a sound and became rigid, listening. The Manhattan-bound train was rumbling down the tracks.

Abrams climbed the last few steps and mounted the low platform. He glanced back at the Russians in the car. They'd spotted him. One man was watching him, and Abrams could see in the dim light that the driver was holding something to his face—a radio microphone. Abrams began walking toward the darkened station house about fifty yards away. There were ten people there now, standing on the platform. Behind him the train's whistle sounded two short blasts and the track rumbled.

Across the tracks he saw another black Ford moving parallel to him through the opposite parking lot. He could make out a face in the passenger-side window staring at him and thought it might be Kalin.

Abrams stopped about five yards from the group of people and eyed them. They all looked straight. Kalin had never expected him to get this far. Several people on the platform were stealing glances at him. He realized he had blood on his face, hands, and shirt. Also, he was shoeless. He hoped that a good citizen would summon a cop.

Abrams took stock: He'd lost the briefcase, but there was nothing in it except the file on the Russian Mission versus Van Dorn. He'd lost his licensed revolver, and that would cause him some legal problems, assuming anyone would be interested after the bombs fell, or whatever was going to happen. But he hadn't lost his life, and that was a plus.

He wondered if they'd gotten Sam Hammond in the tunnel, on the train, or in Penn Station. He wondered too where the hell his backup was. Had they left him out in the cold on purpose? No, they would want him live to be debriefed. If they knew he had met Henry Kimberly, they'd have sent a limousine for him.

The train whistle blasted again and its headlight shone in a beam down the tracks. It slowed with a screech of airbrakes and came to a stop.

Abrams walked through the boarding and unboarding passengers, then stepped up to the connecting decks between the last two cars. There were two short blasts of the whistle and the train moved off, gathering speed. Abrams waited until he came abreast of the station house, which blocked the Russians' view from the parking lot. He jumped off the moving train back onto the platform, shoulder-rolled, and sprang up into a crouch. He made his way quickly to the far side of the old station house and found a parked cab at the taxi stand. The driver, a young black man, was sleeping behind the wheel. Abrams, still in a crouch, opened the rear door and slid in quickly. He lowered himself to the floor, reached up, and shook the driver's shoulder. "Let's go!"

The driver woke with a start. "What? Where?" His hand automatically went for the ignition key and he started the engine. "What? Where you goin'?" He looked in the rearview mirror. "Where you *at*?"

"Behind the preposition. Move out."

"Move out where?"

"Van Dorn's. Big place on Dosoris Lane. Let's go."

The driver put the cab in gear and began moving slowly. "You okay, man?"

"I dropped my toothbrush. Move faster."

The cab swung toward the parking lot exit. "Want a light on?"

"No. Just drive."

"Who you runnin' from, man?"

"The Russian secret police."

The driver whistled. "Whew—them dudes fuckin' with you?"

"They're always fucking with me." Abrams made himself comfortable on the floor. The cab turned north on St. Andrew's Lane.

The driver said, "Van Dorn's, you say? No sweat findin' *that* dude. Follow the fireworks."

Abrams looked up at the window and saw star clusters bursting in the northern sky. Abrams said, "Are we being followed?"

The driver checked his rearview mirror. "Headlights...don't know if he's followin' or *followin'*."

"Well, assume he's *followin'* and step on it."

The cab lurched ahead and gathered speed, swinging north on Dosoris Lane.

Abrams toyed with the idea that the driver wasn't straight, but decided he'd been unduly influenced by too many spy movies. "What's your name?"

"Wilfred."

Abrams held his wallet up over the back of the seat. "NYPD, Wilfred. Blow the stop lights and signs."

The driver glanced at the badge and ID. "Okay, man. But this is Nassau County."

"Don't sweat the geopolitics. We're all Americans."

The driver increased his speed, slowed for a red light, then went through it. He glanced in his rearview mirror and said, "They's *followin'*."

"What are they driving?"

Wilfred looked in the rearview mirror, then the sideview mirror. "Looks like a black Ford. Four men."

The cab suddenly came to a halt. Abrams said, "What's happening, Wilfred?"

"Traffic jam. Always catch it here when the fireworks start goin'."

"Is that joker still behind us?"

"Kissin' my bumper."

"Cops up ahead?"

"Way up."

Abrams rose and looked back through the rear window. A black car was, as Wilfred said, almost bumper to bumper with the cab. He could see four men silhouetted through the windshield. He turned and looked at the line of traffic. About a hundred yards ahead were police cars. Abrams gave the driver a twenty-dollar bill. "Thanks, Wilfred. You don't look Russian. I never should have doubted you."

Wilfred nodded. "You gonna 'rest them dudes?"

"Not right at this moment." Abrams opened the door and got out on the curb side. He began walking along the shoulder of the road, passing the line of stalled traffic. A few people in the cars looked at him. He heard a car door slam behind him, followed by quick footsteps in the gravel. A man came up behind him and said, "There you are."

Abrams kept walking as he replied, "If you're the cavalry, you're a little late."

Pembroke fell into step beside him. "Sorry, old man. You left Ivan's a bit earlier than we thought. Traffic to the station was dreadful. Holiday evening. No excuse, though."

Abrams didn't reply.

Pembroke continued, "Actually, I had put a chap on the train a few stations back to watch over you."

"Thoughtful of you. How about a cigarette?"

Pembroke gave him one and lit it for him, then said, "You look a bit disheveled. They went for you in the underpass, did they? I knew they wouldn't knock you off in their house, of course, but I thought they'd go for you on the train, or back in Manhattan."

"Well, they had other ideas."

Pembroke said, "I know you're annoyed, and I do apologize." He looked down and said, "You're limping. Are you going to make it without your shoes?"

"Can I get into Van Dorn's with dirty socks?"

Pembroke smiled. "I'll sneak you in the servants' entrance."

"Swell."

They walked a while longer, then Pembroke said, "Why did you decide to come back here?"

"Because I decided not to get on the train."

Pembroke nodded, then after a minute said, "Actually, you never intended to take that train, did you? You discovered something of immediate value. That's why you flashed the high beams. You thought we'd meet you at the station and take you to Van Dorn's."

"Could be."

Pembroke nodded again, then said, "Well, that's not my business unless someone makes it so. But I will get you an audience with George."

"That's all I want."

"I'm dreadfully sorry about the foul-up. Did you think I left you hanging on purpose?"

Abrams flipped his cigarette away. "While I was in the tunnel, the thought crossed my mind."

"I'm on your side, Abrams. You did me an immense favor by staying alive. My career could have been ruined."

"Mine too."

"Do you want to work for me?"

"What's your work product?"

"Corpses. I suppose you know that. The pay is excellent."

"No, thanks."

"You'd be very good. Speak Russian, ex-policeman—"

"Blue Cross, major medical?"

"Of course. I'm incorporated under the laws of New York State. British Technologies. Prestigious address in Rockefeller Center. Secretary, water cooler—"

"Gun rack. I'll think it over."

"Good."

They came within sight of the gates to the Russian estate across the road. The gates were clear of demonstrators tonight, and police vehicles were lined up on the shoulders. Pembroke said, "The police will be curious about your appearance."

Abrams took off his jacket, threw it in a clump of bushes, and rolled up his shirt sleeves. He peeled off his bloody socks, then took a handkerchief from Pembroke and wiped his hands and face. "Do I look suburban and summery?"

"Well...in the dark. Let's go, then."

They continued past the police cars, getting a few hard, appraising stares. After a few minutes they came within sight of Van Dorn's driveway and Pembroke said, "It's rather a good party, and after you're debriefed, you should stay and enjoy yourself. I'll fix you up with some clothing."

"Is Claudia there?"

Pembroke drew on his cigarette and glanced at Abrams. He replied lightly, "Yes, but Katherine is there as well. Be careful, old

man. You haven't come this far to get knifed by a jealous woman."
He laughed.

Abrams stopped to pick out a piece of gravel that had worked
itself into the wound on his foot. "Is Thorpe there?"

"No."

Abrams continued walking. "Where is he?"

"Don't know, really." Pembroke flipped away his cigarette. "You
know, Abrams, I wonder if we didn't make a mistake by not killing
him when we had the opportunity."

"When did *we* get incorporated?"

"Well, I mean—"

"Listen, Pembroke, I've never killed in cold blood, but I would
have killed Thorpe. Yet you, who've made killing a cottage industry,
did not kill the man who deserved it most."

Pembroke didn't respond immediately, then nodded. "Yes, perhaps you're right. Sometimes one can be too professional and ignore
instinct."

Abrams wiped a line of perspiration from his forehead. The night
was still, and the walk was beginning to wear on him. Days that
began at dawn never boded well for him. Days that included mayhem, lovemaking, and hard thinking left him weary. He yawned.

Pembroke said, "Joan Grenville told me about Claudia. I wish I'd
known sooner."

"Everyone wishes they'd known everything sooner," Abrams
said. "I wish I'd known this morning who won this afternoon's
Metropolitan at Belmont. So what? What are you going to do about
Claudia? Or is she already done?"

"She's among the living. It's not my business to decide what to
do about her, nor yours."

"I never thought it was mine."

Pembroke added, "I'm surprised O'Brien and Company took her
in. I've never yet had a good experience with an ex–Eastern Bloc
resident." He thought a moment, then said, "But perhaps she's been
turned, or has been a double all along. That's why you can't go
about knocking people off until you know the facts."

"Well, as of Friday night when she set me up to be pushed off the roof, she was working for them."

Pembroke nodded to himself. "I wondered who lured you up to the roof. Your story seemed to lack details. I actually thought it might have been Joan, even Katherine."

"No, it was Claudia."

"Interesting...but don't discount the possibility that she set you up in order to establish her bona fides with Thorpe and/or the Russians. Sometimes one agent has to sacrifice another to establish credibility."

"You people play a nasty game."

"Oh, don't I know it. That's why I keep out of that end of it, Abrams. Killing people is much less confusing. My father liked the intrigue. I find it too morally ambivalent for my taste."

"Your father was in intelligence?"

"Yes, recently retired."

They continued along the road, up a gentle rise. Abrams said suddenly, "Is James Allerton at Van Dorn's?"

Pembroke regarded him for some seconds, then answered, "No. He went back to Washington. Why do you ask?"

"Is he with the President this weekend?"

Pembroke considered the question, then replied, "I'm not certain. The President is at Camp David, according to the newspapers. Why is it necessary to know if Allerton is with the President?"

Abrams considered his response a moment, then said, "It may be necessary to contact the President. I thought if Allerton was with him, then Van Dorn may actually be able to get through to Allerton quickly...."

"Is it urgent?"

Abrams looked at him. "I think so. But you're not interested in that end of it."

Pembroke smiled politely. "Normally I'm not. But when people start suggesting that a working knowledge of Russian may prove useful for daily existence, then my interest is aroused."

Abrams replied, "I'll speak to Van Dorn."

They walked silently for another minute, then crossed the road between the slow-moving traffic and passed through the entrance to Van Dorn's estate. A security guard sitting in a parked car recognized Pembroke and waved them on. Abrams followed Pembroke up the rising drive and saw the big lighted house as they turned a bend. From the rear of the house another salvo of rockets rose into the clear, windless night sky and exploded in red, white, and blue showers of sparks. Abrams said, "Can I trust Van Dorn?"

Pembroke replied, "My God, I hope so." He added, "I believe he's running the show now."

"Why shouldn't I go to the FBI?"

"You may if you wish. Or the CIA. Both are very close by. If you decide to go, I'll run you over with my car—I mean, I'll *drive* you over." He laughed.

Abrams glanced at him and understood his meaning clearly. "Let's talk to Van Dorn."

CHAPTER FORTY-SEVEN

Viktor Androv stood in front of a north-facing gable window, his back to the three other men in the room. He stared toward George Van Dorn's house. Balls of fire appeared over the distant tree line and rose lazily above the horizon of Long Island Sound, then burst apart into the moonlit sky. Androv imagined that he was watching a miniature of the explosion that would soon light up most of the North American continent for a few brief but fateful seconds.

Androv said, "At least he isn't blaring his music. Well, after tonight we'll never be bothered by him again."

Androv turned from the window and faced Alexei Kalin, who stood at attention across the large darkened attic room. "So, Alexei, where did we go wrong, my friend? You had three trained men with you in the tunnel. You had two cars, each with two men, for a total of...let's see...eight men, including yourself, all of you agents of the *Komitet Gossudarstvennoy Bezopasnosti,* the most feared state security agency in the world. And you were asked to bring here, for interrogation, one Jew. Correct?"

Kalin nodded stiffly. "Correct."

"So...so it was not a particularly difficult mission, was it, Alexei?"

"No, it was not."

"But instead of delivering me one Jew, you return with one dead man, whose poor wife is downstairs waiting for you to tell her where her husband is. Also, you present me with the unfortunate Feliks, who seems to have been beaten and knifed by his comrades, and Vasili, who appears to be suffering from great mental agitation. And look at *you*. You're filthy."

Kalin stared straight ahead.

"Perhaps you can explain to me how the Jew accomplished this."

"I have no explanation."

Androv said with biting sarcasm, "No? There is no logical explanation for this deplorable failure? At least tell me that the Jew had divine intervention. Tell me that Moses descended on you swinging his staff in the dark. I would sooner believe that than believe that one Jew outwitted and outfought four men of the KGB. Please, Alexei, let me report to Moscow that there is a God and He works for the Jews."

Kalin's face was set in the immobile expression required for these dressing downs. Kalin knew that whatever Androv finally told Moscow would exonerate both him and Androv. Feliks and Vasili would not fare so well. Kalin, of course, would then be owned by Androv until the debt was repaid, or until the tables could be turned. That was the way the system worked.

Androv ended his harangue and added, "I'm only sorry that our distinguished guest had to witness this."

Henry Kimberly sat in a plastic-molded swivel chair, his legs crossed and his fingertips pressed together. He was dressed in casual slacks, blue blazer, and loafers. He said in Russian, "Please don't consider me more than a loyal party man."

Androv protested, "But you are. Before this week is out you will be the most famous man in America. Perhaps in the world. You will be the new American President."

Henry Kimberly said nothing.

Androv turned back to Kalin. "Well, Alexei, sit down. We have another bungler joining us. Your friend Thorpe." He looked again toward Kimberly. "Are you eager to meet your daughter's lover?"

Kimberly seemed somewhat surprised at the question. He replied, "Not particularly."

Androv sat heavily in another swivel chair. "If you would like, Henry, we can arrange to have her brought here tonight."

Henry Kimberly sat motionless in his chair. He thought about Katherine as he had last seen her, a little girl of two. He suddenly recalled the signed picture he had sent her, right before his "death," and he remembered that someone—Thorpe, he guessed—had told Kalin that the picture was hanging in Katherine's office. He also thought about his daughter Ann, and remembered her letters to him and his to her. He'd had to leave all his mementos behind at Brompton Hall when he left for Berlin. He'd had to leave Eleanor behind as well, and his parting had been rather temperate, his last words being, "I'll see you in about two weeks, Ellie. The war will be over by then and we'll open that bottle of 'Thirty-seven Moët."

He had put some of his affairs in order, as men do when they are going out on risky business, but had done nothing or taken nothing with him that would lead anyone to suspect that he knew he was never coming back. In fact, he remembered with a touch of amused irony, he had borrowed a hundred dollars from George Van Dorn before he left for Berlin. With interest, he owed Van Dorn about four thousand dollars.

Androv coughed pointedly, and said, "The decision regarding your daughter is entirely yours, Henry. But you should know that by now Karl Roth has poisoned everyone next door."

Kimberly did not seem moved by this news.

Androv continued, "We chose an extremely rare substance for which no antidote is known in the West. But our Technical Operations Directorate has developed such an antidote. If we get your daughter here within four hours, she can be saved." He looked at Henry Kimberly. "Please advise me."

Kimberly said, "What does her fiancé advise?"

Androv smiled slowly, then replied, "Ah, young men are fickle. He no longer loves her, but would not mind if she lived to see the wave of the future wash over her little sand castles. I believe he wants to keep her as a maidservant. He's a nasty young man."

Kimberly nodded, then replied, "If you can save her without jeopardizing the mission, or"—he nodded toward Kalin—"or any more men, then do so. But I have no desire to see her. If she is brought here, keep her away from me."

Androv said, "Yes, it might be upsetting to you if you met. And you have important work to do—"

"Please don't anticipate my psychological reaction to anything."

"Forgive me." Androv regarded Kimberly for some time. After a month under the same roof, Androv could not understand the man's motivations, much less his wants, needs, fears, or aspirations. Yet Kimberly was in many ways like other Western defectors he'd met in Moscow: strangers in a strange land, stuck in a previous time frame.

Kimberly turned from Androv and addressed Alexei Kalin. "How well do you know this Peter Thorpe?"

Kalin sat up. "I'm his control officer."

"Do you like him? Or is he, as Viktor suggested, a nasty young man?"

Kalin replied diplomatically, "He is rather...odd. But he can be charming with the ladies."

Kimberly nodded. "Takes after his natural father. James Allerton was no ladies' man." He smiled, then asked Kalin, "Is this the type of man I'd want around me as an aide?"

Kalin's eyes went to Androv, and it was Androv who answered, "This is the type of man who should be liquidated." He added quickly, "But you will want to decide for yourself, of course. Let's have him come up. I've also invited some others whom you've met only briefly." He pressed the intercom button. "Send them up."

Androv looked down the length of the long attic that lay over the central wing of the house. The sloped walls were lined with electronic consoles whose lighting provided most of the room's illumination. At the far end of the attic, nearly one hundred feet away, a lone man, the communications duty officer, sat hunched over the radio that was in continuous contact with the Kremlin.

Androv said, "Gentlemen, I do not know the precise time of the

Stroke, but I think it will be before dawn." He pointed across the room. "Do you see those two steady green lights?" The two men turned and saw two burning green lights in the distant dimness, like cats' eyes glowing in the night. Androv continued, his voice heavy, "That is the highest alert status we've ever had from Moscow—it means the Stroke is imminent. There's a third green light that will begin blinking when the final countdown begins. When all three lights are steady green, the Stroke is only minutes away."

CHAPTER FORTY-EIGHT

The heavy metal door to the attic opened, silhouetting a tall man dressed in a military uniform. He entered, followed by another Russian with swept-back hair and dark glasses, and dressed in a brown business suit. Peter Thorpe came in last. The two Russians stood aside, one of them closing the door.

Androv stood and made the introduction. "Major Henry Kimberly, please meet Major Peter Thorpe."

Kimberly stood and took Thorpe's hand. "How do you do?"

Thorpe could not hide his surprise at meeting a man he thought had been dead for forty years, then forced his features into an emotionless mask. He looked into Kimberly's clear blue eyes and replied, "It's a pleasure meeting you."

Androv said offhandedly, "That may be the last pleasure you experience, Thorpe."

Thorpe looked at Androv, a mixture of anger and apprehension in his eyes, but he said nothing.

Androv addressed Kimberly. "Henry, you may remember these two gentlemen. This is Colonel Mikhail Karpenko of the Eighth Directorate of the KGB, which, as you know, is responsible for satellite communications, ciphers, and diplomatic transmission. This room is his domain."

Karpenko, a tall, cadaverous bald-headed man with veins popping on his skull, bowed his head stiffly.

Androv continued, "And this is Valentin Metkov, of Department

Five of the First Chief Directorate, known unofficially as the Department of *Mokrie Dela*—Wet Affairs." Androv turned to Thorpe. "Coincidentally, what your CIA comrades call 'wet stuff.' Murder."

Metkov pursed his thin lips and nodded to himself, as if he were discovering this information for the first time.

Androv motioned Karpenko, Metkov, and Thorpe toward swivel chairs. He saw that Karpenko and Metkov had both glanced at the green lights on the far console. Androv said, "Yes, the time is drawing near."

Thorpe thought Alexei Kalin, who hadn't even acknowledged his presence, looked moody and sullen. Thorpe also noticed that Kalin was disheveled and there was a bruise on his cheek. At Langley, Thorpe would have concluded that the man had gotten into a scrape. Here, it was quite possible that Kalin's boss had had him beaten. These people were crude by the standards Thorpe was accustomed to. He felt an unfamiliar fear grip at his throat.

The talking stopped and Androv leaned back in his chair. He frowned at Thorpe. "Well, Peter, you were told never to come here, but here you are. Ordinarily this would be an inexcusable breach of security. However, as it turns out, tonight is the night of the Stroke, and I may consider a pardon if you can convince me that you're not an imbecile."

Thorpe's face reddened. In all his clandestine meetings with the Russians, it had been *he* who had been rude, abrasive, and arrogant. His only meeting with Androv, two years before, had ended with Thorpe lecturing Androv about the personal hygiene of one of Androv's couriers. But now he was in the wolf's lair, and apparently he'd shown up on the last night of his usefulness. Rotten luck.

Androv said, "For a man with so much to say, you're very quiet. Perhaps you *are* an imbecile."

Thorpe knew that he had to be cautious, without being apologetic. He would not, could not, grovel. He put a tone of annoyance in his voice. "I want to know why the timetable has been moved up without your informing me. I want to know what you intended to do to insure my safety."

Androv answered, "The timetable has been moved up because

of recent events, one of them being what you yourself discovered from West. If you had gone to the party next door as you were supposed to, you would have been approached by Claudia and given the instructions you needed to survive. Is that explanation satisfactory?"

Thorpe nodded.

Androv added, "I assume you would not have come here unless it was urgent. Tell us what is on your mind."

Thorpe crossed his legs and said, "Nicholas West is dead. Eva killed him. I killed her."

Androv looked around the room, his eyes passing over Kimberly; then he focused on Thorpe. "That's unfortunate but not urgent, and not crucial any longer. Tell me, where did you spend this afternoon?"

Thorpe licked his lips, then replied, "Well...that's the other thing....After West's death, I realized I had to follow up on what he'd revealed, so I decided to...to kidnap...Katherine Kimberly." He glanced at Henry Kimberly, but saw no change in his abstracted expression. Thorpe continued, "She was with Tony Abrams, so he became involved—"

Androv said, "You have a unique gift of altering the truth without altering the facts. But that is unimportant now. I assume your kidnap attempt failed, since Mr. Abrams called on us this evening. And Miss Kimberly is next door."

Thorpe found himself sweating in the air-conditioned room. He cleared his throat and addressed Henry Kimberly. "I had no idea, of course, that you—"

Androv's voice became curt. "There's a great deal you did not know, Mr. Thorpe." Androv let out a breath of exasperation, then said in a calmer tone, "You know, Peter, you have no political or personal commitment to socialism. You are an individualist in your heart. You are also an idiot, because you have helped destroy the system that spawned you and the only system under which you could survive. You will not survive long in the world you helped create."

Thorpe recalled O'Brien's warning to him before his death. And, of course, West's predictions about his future. They'd both been right, as usual.

Androv sat back, his hands resting on his stomach. "But you did kill Patrick O'Brien. That was the finest thing you ever did. If we can think of a use for you, perhaps we will let you live."

Thorpe ignored the threat and said, "Is James Allerton the second Talbot?"

Androv smiled. "Yes, he is. And lucky for you, he's fond of you, though you are not such a good son to him. He is annoyed with you at the moment. You forgot to send him a card on Father's Day." Androv laughed. "You see how these little things come back to haunt you? For the price of a greeting card, you could have laid claim to some protection."

Thorpe knew he was being played with, but he no longer was certain that he was under sentence of death. He relaxed imperceptibly, then said, "Where is my father?"

Androv answered, "At Camp David for the holiday. He will have some interesting news to deliver to the President sometime before dawn." Androv reached down under the console desk and picked up a leather dispatch case. "For now, let's proceed with the next item on my agenda." He turned the case toward Kimberly. "This, according to Mr. Thorpe, is your property."

Kimberly stared at the old scarred leather case, but said nothing.

Androv reached inside and drew out a bundled stack of papers. He handed them to Kimberly.

Henry Kimberly examined the grayish papers. They were all letters written on the V-mail stationery required during the war, flimsy paper that folded into envelopes. They were addressed to him in an adult hand, though when he turned them over, he saw Ann's childish pencil scrawl. There were drawings—hearts, flowers, stick figures, and *X's* for kisses. He read a few lines of a letter at random: *When are you going to win the war and come home? Daddy I love you. XXXX Ann.*

Henry Kimberly looked up at Androv. "Where did you get these?"

Androv handed Kimberly three folded pieces of stiff photocopy paper. "This will explain."

Kimberly unfolded the pages and saw the letterhead: Lady Eleanor Wingate, Brompton Hall, Tongate, Kent. Beneath the letterhead was written in script: *Dear Miss Kimberly. A curious and perhaps fateful incident has occurred which prompts me to write you.*

Henry Kimberly read no further, but looked off at some indeterminate point in space. He said, "They told me soon after I arrived in Moscow never to ask about anyone from the past. They said it would be easier for me...that if I was dead to them, they must be dead to me." He smiled slightly. "They did, however, give me a short yearly report on my daughters. In time, of course, I lost interest in even them...the dead soon lose interest in the affairs of the living." Kimberly looked at Androv. "This past month has awakened many memories. I didn't know, of course, that Eleanor was still alive."

Androv replied bluntly. "She's not. She lost her life in a fire at Brompton Hall."

Kimberly looked around the room at the faces of the Russians, whose eyes, mirroring his own, revealed nothing. He bent his head over the letter and read. After he had finished, he refolded it and passed it back to Androv. He said, "Where is the diary?"

Androv replied, "Here, in this dispatch case."

"May I see it?"

"Of course. But first, with your indulgence, let me ask you a question. Do you remember this English officer, Carbury?"

"Yes, Randolph Carbury was assigned to the Soviet desk. Counterintelligence. He was involved with O'Brien's Operation Wolfbane. He was, in fact, looking for me."

Androv smiled. "Well, Henry, neither Carbury nor O'Brien ever stopped looking for you. For their persistence, they suffered the same fate, and by the same hand." He cocked his head toward Thorpe.

Kimberly said, "I am, of course, relieved that these men are dead. But I'm curious to know how the rules of the game have changed so much as to allow pawns to kill kings." He stared at Thorpe.

"Yes, there are times when I wonder at that myself." Androv pulled the diary from the dispatch case and handed it to Kimberly.

Henry Kimberly examined the cover, then opened it and leafed through the cream-colored pages. A slow smile passed over his lips.

Androv said, "It's a clever forgery."

Kimberly closed the diary and said, "Whose work is this?"

Androv shrugged. "I suppose an OSS forger. Recently, I think. It smells of O'Brien." Androv added, "Did you actually keep a diary?"

"Yes, and in that muniment room—but this is not it."

Androv smiled. "It was unfortunate for O'Brien that of all the dead OSS men he could have picked to ascribe this bogus diary to, he picked Talbot himself."

Kimberly replied, "He trusted me. It was one of the few mistakes he made. I sometimes thought he had *psychic* powers, but he was human."

"And mortal," added Androv.

Kimberly nodded.

Androv said, "And after all, what did O'Brien accomplish with all his cleverness? He picked the wrong man as the author of this diary, and we did not become hysterical and expose our hand. He suffered many casualties, and lost his own life, while we have maintained the secret of the identities of the three Talbots. True, he forced us to move up our timetable, but that is for the better. Yes, these old gentlemen of the OSS have lost the last and final round to the KGB."

CHAPTER FORTY-NINE

Tony Abrams stood at the large bay window in George Van Dorn's study and looked out at the party in progress. He caught sight of Katherine on the lawn, speaking to a man, and he had the unfamiliar sensation of jealousy. Katherine and the man separated and she joined two elderly women on a bench. Abrams turned from the window.

He walked to the wall near the French doors and surveyed the rows of old framed photographs. He studied a group picture: about a dozen men in tan summer uniforms. He recognized Van Dorn's hulking frame towering over the others. Toward the right end of the group was Patrick O'Brien, appearing very boyish, his arm draped over the shoulder of Henry Kimberly.

Marc Pembroke freshened his drink and looked up from the bar. "There's nothing puts life into perspective like old photographs."

Abrams said, "A brush or two with death gives you a little perspective." He moved to another picture, a grainy enlarged snapshot of three men in battle fatigues: James Allerton, looking rather aesthetic despite the attire; beside him Kimberly again, looking more like a weary veteran than he did in the other picture; and a third man, who looked familiar. Abrams studied the face and was sure the man was a national figure but couldn't place him.

Pembroke cut into his concentration. "We were just tots when this was going on. I remember the bombs falling, though. I was evacuated from London and lived with an aunt in the country. Do you have any recollections?"

Abrams glanced over his shoulder. "A few. Nothing quite so immediate as that." Abrams scanned the other pictures. Some were captioned, and he saw Tom Grenville's father, posing with Ho Chi Minh. A few feet to the left was a photograph that appeared to be hand-colored: a short, swarthy man with deep black eyes, wearing colorful native costume. The caption identified him as Count Ilie Lepescu. Abrams saw no family resemblance, but remembered that Claudia would be this man's granddaughter.

In a grouping, there were some autographed head-and-shoulder shots of leaders of the era, including Eisenhower, Allen Dulles, and General Donovan. Below was a slightly blurry picture of a man sitting in a jeep, identified as OSS Captain John Birch, for whom, Abrams realized, the right-wing organization had been named. There were also various shots of ragtag resistance units, ranging from dark Latins posed amid classical ruins, to fair Nordic men and women against snowy backdrops. Everyone appeared somehow strangely innocent, almost naive. Or perhaps, he thought, their eyes reflected some sort of unity of purpose and purity of spirit that was not often seen any longer.

Marc Pembroke settled into a leather chair and watched Abrams. He said, "You look rather nifty in my white tropicals."

Abrams continued surveying the photographs. "Does this outfit come with a Good Humor truck?"

"That's Egyptian linen, Abrams. I had that suit made in Hong Kong—"

"By Charlie Chan's tailor."

Pembroke sounded miffed. "Well, it looks a damned sight better on me than it does on you."

Abrams looked over his shoulder. "I don't mean to sound ungrateful."

Pembroke seemed mollified. "Are those sandals all right? How's that bandage?"

"Fine." Marc Pembroke had cleaned and dressed the deep gash in Abrams' foot, and done it with the clinical detachment that one associates with doctors, soldiers, cops, and others who are not strangers to the misfortunes that befall human flesh.

Pembroke said, "Foot wounds need antibiotics. I'll see what George has available."

Abrams turned back to the pictures and said, "Only an accomplished hypochondriac could worry simultaneously about nuclear vaporization and a foot infection."

Pembroke smiled. "Still, we shave and wash on the eve of battle. We are creatures of habit and infinite optimism."

"Right." Abrams' eye was drawn to a face in one of the formally posed shots of a group of uniformed men. It was Arnold Brin, looking very much better than when Abrams had last seen him. Brin wore the uniform of an officer, not a sergeant. Interesting, but Abrams had already come to the conclusion that these people played fast and loose with names, ranks, occupations, and other vital statistics.

Abrams searched for a photo of Carbury but couldn't find one, though he saw a long shot of a manor house, captioned *Brompton Hall*. To the immediate left was a studio portrait of a lovely young woman with dark hair and dreamy eyes. "Is this Eleanor Wingate?"

Pembroke looked up from a magazine. "Oh, I believe it is. Yes, beside the Brompton Hall shot. Pity. Nice house."

"Yes." Abrams moved to his right and looked up at a long silver-framed photograph, a banquet scene that at first glance reminded him of "The Last Supper." On closer inspection he recognized the uniforms of Soviet officers, alternating with American officers. It was a victory celebration of some sort. The celebrants included George Van Dorn, whose back was being patted or slapped by a grinning Russian officer. Van Dorn did not look particularly pleased. It was odd, thought Abrams, how a picture could sometimes capture the essence of a time and place, as well as a presentiment of the future.

Pembroke put down his magazine. "Did you get to that bastard's progenitors yet? Over there. Eye level to your right. In the appropriately black frame."

Abrams spotted a slightly overexposed picture showing the fuselage of a large aircraft. Twelve parachutists, eight men and four women, stood or knelt for what could have been, and probably was for some, their penultimate photograph—the last being the one that the methodical Gestapo took of the allied agents before their execution. Among the names on the caption were Jeanne Broulé and Peter Thorpe.

Abrams looked closely at Thorpe's mother, a striking blonde, as tall as the men around her, with a figure that could not be hidden by the jump outfit. Thorpe's father, also light-haired, was a handsome man, but he looked, Abrams thought, rather supercilious. "Yes," he said, "yes, a good-looking couple."

"All the same, if they'd kept their pants on, they would have spared the world a damned lot of grief."

"Amen." Abrams quickly perused the other photographs and recognized vaguely familiar faces, perhaps men and women who had come into the office, or people from the OSS dinner. Some of them, he realized, he'd seen just a few minutes ago, much older now, wandering in the shadows outside, like premature ghosts.

Pembroke interrupted his thoughts. "How did you get involved with this group?"

"I saw an ad in the *Times*." Abrams turned from the picture. He went to the desk, where he'd set down a glass of Scotch, neat, and took a short drink, then picked up a canapé from the tray. "Chopped chicken liver."

"No. Pâté."

Abrams smiled. "To use a 1940s expression, any way you slice it it's still baloney." He ate the liver and toast.

Pembroke looked at his watch and stood. "Well, I've delivered you. Good luck, then." He put out his hand and Abrams took it firmly. Abrams said, "Will you be around tonight?"

"Should I be?"

Abrams replied, "Maybe . . . I don't make policy around here."

"I'll stay close. And please take care of that foot. You can't count on being vaporized before it gets infected."

He turned, and as he walked toward the door, it opened and Katherine Kimberly came into the study. They smiled and nodded to each other. Pembroke left, and Katherine took a few hesitant steps into the room. Abrams put down his drink and came toward her as she rushed into his arms. They embraced and she looked up at him. Her words tumbled out. "Are you all right? George just told me you were here—"

"Yes, I'm fine. Except for this suit and these sandals."

She laughed and stepped back. "That's not you."

"Neither was the tux. What's happening to me?"

She hugged him tightly, then said, "Well, you're here and that's just fine." She touched a cut on his cheek. "What happened in there?"

He stayed silent for some time, then said, "Are you going to be here when I brief Van Dorn?"

She nodded. "Would you rather talk about it then? He'll be here shortly. I'll wait."

He went to the bar. "Scotch, correct?"

"I don't want a drink."

He made her a Scotch and water and set it on the coffee table, then sat on the edge of the sofa. He took her hand and drew her down beside him.

She looked at him closely. "What is it? What's wrong, Tony? Something to do with Pat O'Brien? He's dead, isn't he? You can tell me. I'm not a child."

He could see tears forming in her eyes. He didn't know which news was worse: that Patrick O'Brien was missing, or that her father was not. He said, "O'Brien's plane crashed Sunday night. His body was not recovered. We can assume he's dead or kidnapped."

She nodded slowly, but before she could say anything, Abrams went on quickly. "While I was in the Russian house, I wandered off by myself and came face-to-face with Henry Kimberly."

Katherine was drying her eyes with a handkerchief, looking at him, and he could see she did not comprehend a word of it. He said, "I met your father. He's alive."

She still didn't seem to assimilate it. Then she suddenly shook her head and stood. He stood too and held her shoulders. They looked at each other for a long time, then she nodded.

"You understand?"

She nodded again quickly, but said nothing. She was very pale.

He eased her down onto the sofa and gave her the Scotch. She swallowed a mouthful, then took a deep breath. *"Odysseus."*

Abrams replied, "Yes, the warrior has returned." He put his hand on her cheek. "Are you all right?"

"Yes, yes." She stared into his eyes. "You knew, didn't you? You tried to tell me...and I guess I understood what you were saying... so it's not a complete shock."

"I only suspected. Now I know."

She took his hand in both of hers. "You recognized him?"

He nodded and forced a smile. "The Kimberly eyes."

She smiled faintly in return, thought a moment, and said, "My God....Oh, my God...Tony...What does this mean?"

Abrams shook his head. "I don't know, but it does not bode well, does it?"

She squeezed his hand tightly. "No. No, it is—*grave and foreboding.*"

Abrams nodded. Henry Kimberly's presence in America would have to be taken as a signal that the countdown had begun.

And if, in fact, that basement was full of people, then all systems were go.

CHAPTER FIFTY

The attic room was still, and Peter Thorpe heard the low hum of the electronic consoles, and felt the machines' vibrations in the floorboards. The big, open room reminded him of his own garret in the Lombardy, where he would have preferred to be at the moment. This place, however, was more elaborate. This was the fabled Russian spy center of North America, the subject of press editorials, congressional debates, and television documentaries. This facility also had diplomatic immunity, and his did not. Also, his attic room had to serve as both a communications center and an interrogation room, which was not always convenient. The Russians used their cellar for the messy stuff. This was the advantage of a nice big house in the suburbs over an apartment in town. He smiled grimly at his own forced humor.

Thorpe looked at his watch. The four Russians had left to put people and systems on alert status and had not yet returned. He turned from the window and saw the communications officer walking down the line of consoles, making entries into a logbook. Henry Kimberly was sitting nearby, ignoring Thorpe and reading a Russian newspaper by the light of a computer's video display screen.

Thorpe noticed that odd smell in the room that electronics emitted, and he felt the heat that was generated by the radios and computers.

Thorpe regarded Kimberly. All was obviously not well in *his* attic. Thorpe recognized that his own peculiarities of the mind were inherent and inborn. He was certain that Kimberly's strangeness was acquired. The old term *brainwashing* came to him. But it was more than that. *Forty years,* he thought. Not only was the brain washed, but so was the heart and soul.

In fact, though, they had probably done nothing more to him than they'd done to 270 million other Soviet citizens; they had made him live there.

Thorpe remembered his two brief, furtive trips to Russia. As he walked the streets of Moscow, he had had the impression that half the population was going to a funeral and the other half coming from one.

As he looked at Kimberly, he wondered how the Russians were going to present this bloodless man to the American public as their new leader; his speech, his movements, his facial expressions, his whole persona, reminded Thorpe of an alien from another world trying to pass as an earthling. Thorpe was sure the KGB had kept Kimberly abreast of the developments in American life, but the American Training School on Kutuzovsky Prospekt was a poor substitute for the real thing.

Kimberly sensed that Thorpe was staring at him and looked up from his newspaper. Thorpe hesitated, then asked, "Was it you, or James, or someone else, who sent my parents to their deaths?"

Kimberly seemed neither surprised nor put off by the question. He replied, "It was I. One of the agents on that jump was a Communist. One of my people. After he hit the ground, he tipped off the Gestapo, anonymously. The twelve people on that jump were all eventually arrested and shot. What difference does it make to you?"

"I'm not certain."

"You're hardly in a position to make a moral judgment of me, or any sort of judgment for that matter."

"I'm not making judgments. I just wanted to know." He hesitated again, then said, "James, and others, speak well of them." He looked at Kimberly.

Kimberly shrugged. "*De mortuis nil nisi bonum*—speak only good of the dead. But if it's the truth you're after, and I suppose you are, your mother was a French whore, and your father a pompous, spoiled dilettante."

Thorpe replied, "That hardly sounds like the type of people who would volunteer to parachute into enemy territory."

Kimberly replied, "Their motivations were as confused as yours. It must run in the family."

Thorpe bit back a reply and took out a cigarette.

Kimberly let the silence drag out, then said, "How is she? Does she mention me at all?"

Thorpe saw his possible salvation in these questions. He answered, "She's a bit of a bitch, actually. Takes after her mother, I understand. And, yes, she mentions her deceased war-hero father from time to time." He added, "Katherine and I had a good relationship until recently, regardless of what you may hear to the contrary."

Thorpe was amazed at the things he was thinking and saying. It must be, he thought, the shock of knowing America was finished, and that he himself might be finished. He was not contrite over what he had done, only angry at himself for playing a bad hand.

Kimberly smiled but said nothing.

Thorpe added, "I can fill you in about Ann, too. I know her. And I can answer other questions you may have about things in general over the next several months."

Again, Kimberly smiled. "Someone once wrote that the true genius is the person who can invent his own job. Well, Thorpe, I suppose you'd make a passable presidential advisor. Or perhaps a White House court jester."

Thorpe's eyelids twitched, but he kept control of himself.

Kimberly leaned back in his chair. "Before you arrived, we were discussing Katherine's fate. She's next door."

"I know that."

"Did you know that they've all been poisoned and will begin dying in a few hours?"

Thorpe's eyes widened.

"There *is* a way to save her. Do you want her?"

Thorpe had the feeling again that he was navigating a minefield. "Do you?"

Kimberly's expression took on a faraway look as he mused aloud. "There are times when I think I'd like to see a reunion of family and friends. There are other times when I want to obliterate the past...." He looked at Thorpe. "Did you know I married a Russian girl over there? She's still there, of course. Hardly a presentable first lady. I have two sons...one is a colonel in the KGB....Do you think it would be a good idea to annihilate the American Kimberly line? That would strengthen the Russian Kimberly family."

Before Thorpe could reply, the door swung open and Mikhail Karpenko strode in, followed by Androv and Valentin Metkov. Kalin was not with them, and Thorpe didn't know if that was good or bad.

Karpenko hurried to the far end of the attic room and spoke to the communications officer. He took a sheet of paper from the officer and walked quickly back to the group. He read from the paper, "Cultural affairs attaché Gordik, arriving Kennedy Airport, eight forty-eight P.M., your time. Will proceed by hired conveyance to Glen Cove. Extend usual courtesies."

Androv nodded. "That will be a verbal courier. Obviously, Moscow isn't taking a chance on transmitting any information that the National Security Agency might decode." Androv looked at his watch. "Gordik should be here shortly. He'll deliver the last direct orders we receive from Russia until immediately after the Stroke." He began moving toward the far end of the attic. "Follow me, please." Metkov, Karpenko, Kimberly, and Thorpe followed.

Androv turned into the attic of another wing of the mansion. He threw a switch and the smaller attic area burst into bright, blinding light, revealing an elegantly appointed study set in the far end of the attic. There was a walnut desk, bookshelves, a marble fireplace, and a leaded-glass window in a gabled peak. Above the fireplace hung a large American flag.

Thorpe's eyes adjusted to the light and he noticed television cameras and microphones. This study was actually a studio set.

Androv said to Kimberly, "From here, your voice and your image will go out to the world, via satellite, over all radio and television bands and frequencies." Androv motioned to the leather chair behind the desk. "Please make yourself comfortable."

Kimberly walked around the desk and sat in a high-backed chair. He surveyed the set and commented, "This does look like the type of place from which the voice of authority speaks."

Androv nodded. "The set was designed in Moscow by Special Section Four. It's supposed to convey dignity, tranquillity, authority, and control."

Kimberly noticed a clear plastic garment bag hanging on the wall to the side. "Is that what I'm to wear?"

"Yes, that's also inspired by SS Four. They decided on a blue-gray three-piece pinstripe. You'll look like one of those State Department people," Androv said.

Kimberly asked Thorpe, "What do you think, Peter?"

Thorpe replied, "Americans believe anything they see on television."

Kimberly laughed. "So I've heard." He turned to Karpenko. "How much of the population will I reach?"

Karpenko ran a handkerchief over his perspiring bald head. "We estimate that eighty percent of the population will have access to working radios or televisions. You understand, Major, that only the sets that are on at the time of the Stroke will act as lightning rods for the electromagnetic pulse and be destroyed?"

Kimberly nodded.

Karpenko continued, "But there will be no other radio or television stations operating. And switching to auxiliary power will not put them in operation, either, because these stations will not have experienced a simple power *loss* as in a blackout, but a catastrophic power *surge,* as if ten million bolts of lightning had struck all at once. The only station in America, southern Canada, or northern Mexico that will be on the air will be ours. Here in this room. The only voice anyone will hear will be the voice of Major Henry Kimberly."

Kimberly looked across his desk to where Karpenko stood. He said, "Will I begin broadcasting immediately after the EMP storm?"

Karpenko replied, "When we see the sky light up. For the first few hours you'll make periodic identification of yourself only as Major Henry Kimberly and implore the public to remain calm. Let everyone draw whatever conclusions they wish, until it's time to tell them that you're their new leader. Do you have any questions—"

Thorpe interrupted Karpenko. "Excuse me. But hasn't anyone here ever heard the term 'thermonuclear war'?"

It was Androv who answered. "To reply to your sarcasm, Thorpe, the American government will not be at all certain how this happened, but even if they do understand that it was an EMP storm, they will not be sure it was the Soviet Union that caused it." He gave a small shrug and continued, "In any event, most of the E-3I in this country—the command, control, communications, and intelligence networks—are not yet EMP-proof. America will be struck deaf, dumb, and blind."

Thorpe said, "Even a deaf, dumb, and blind man can push a launch button."

Androv said, "Yes, but keep in mind three other important factors: One, the President will be in Camp David with your father; two, the President's little black box will be useless; and, three, America has no EMP-proof missiles, bombers, warships, or fighter planes. Any American nuclear strike initiated by an automatic response would be a greatly weakened strike. Our losses would be acceptable."

Henry Kimberly spoke, "Moscow has prepared for every eventuality. So, let us not speak of war, but of victory without war."

Thorpe thought to himself, *Just like that. Two hundred years of nation-building and there won't even be a shot fired.*

Androv said, "A great deal depends on James Allerton. When he informs the President and his advisors of the helplessness of the situation, and formally requests the surrender of the United States, there may be some hysterics at Camp David. He may be shot on the spot. He is, however, an accomplished diplomat, and this will be his crowning glory if he can get cooler heads to prevail there. With luck, persuasion, and threats, he will make the President understand that capitulation is the only course of action left that will prevent nuclear destruction."

Metkov said, "The President's last duty will be to read a short prepared statement to the American people announcing...a 'peace treaty' between the Soviet Union and the United States. He'll also announce his resignation from the presidency. He will not be heard from again."

Androv walked into the studio set, past Kimberly's desk, and stopped in front of the fireplace. He stared up at the American flag, then reached out and took the corner of it, rubbing it between his fingers as though he were a rug merchant considering a purchase. There was a long silence and Androv finally said, "We could never have beaten them militarily. But as the fates would have it, there was a small gap in the complex structure of their country's armor. They recognized it, and rushed to fill the gap. We recognized it, and rushed to exploit it. We arrived first; they were too late. Space wars, indeed. Protons and neutrons, laser beams, and killer satellites. We could never have kept up. But on their way to the stars, they forgot to close their one window of vulnerability. And we jumped into it."

CHAPTER FIFTY-ONE

Katherine sat on the sofa with her legs curled up, staring at the ceiling. Abrams strode impatiently around the study, glancing at her from time to time and looking at his watch. He wondered what was keeping Van Dorn.

The telephone on the desk rang and someone in another part of the house answered it, then buzzed the study. Abrams picked it up quickly. "Tony Abrams."

"Well?"

"Spinelli? Did you get my message?"

"No, I just dialed a number at random and got you."

"Where are you?"

"Where you asked me to call from—the squad room. I drove all the fuck the way in from Jersey on my day off to call *you* from *this* phone. Now, why am I here?"

"I'll get to that. Listen, what do you see from the window?"

"Hold on."

Abrams could hear the venetian blinds rattling. He glanced at Katherine and forced a wan smile. She returned a somewhat brighter smile.

Spinelli came back on the line. "Well, I'll be damned, Abrams. Did you know that the Russian Mission to the UN was right across the street from the Nineteenth Precinct? I never knew that."

Abrams ignored the ill temper in Spinelli's voice. He said, "Are the buses out there?"

"Only the big gray bus."

"How about the minibuses?"

"They're either in the garage, or they haven't come in from Glen Cove yet."

Abrams pictured in his mind the twelve-story white brick apartment building on East 67th Street that housed the Russians' United Nations offices as well as the entire staff. He said, "Do you see anything that doesn't look kosher?"

"Look, Abrams, Russian-watching was your line, not mine."

"Well, pretend you're as sharp as me. What do you see?"

Spinelli stared down from the second-story squad room. "Okay— the street is relatively quiet. A few pedestrians. The police booth is manned. Three squad cars parked half on the sidewalk. Routine. Looks peaceful."

Abrams saw the familiar scene in his mind's eye: the partly residential street, the Russian building with the cement awning, the forbidding fence in front, and the three remote television cameras sweeping the street. Directly across the street was the firehouse and the Nineteenth Precinct, where Abrams had worked out of the Red Squad. Abrams knew every square foot of that block between Third Avenue and Lexington Avenue. He knew the street's routine better than he knew his own block in Brooklyn. He said, "How's the building look?"

Spinelli replied, "The garage door is closed, front doors are closed, first three floors are dark. Residence floors are pretty well lit, blinds drawn, but I can see some shadows passing by. Ambassador's suite on the top is lit. What's up, kid? Should I get the Bomb Squad on the horn?"

Abrams thought, *If they can defuse falling H-bombs, call them.* He said, "Where are the FBI guys tonight?"

"Not here. They may be at the firehouse. Better coffee there."

Abrams said, "Dom, can you connect me with the FBI watch? Or the CIA?" Abrams knew the CIA kept several apartments next door to the Russian building and listened through the walls. They also had a third-floor apartment in the building next to the Nineteenth, from which they videotaped the Russian building, day and night, an endless film-record of the building and sidewalk.

"No. I don't want to owe them any favors."

"Then connect me with the police booth. You can listen in."

"Oh, may I?" Spinelli grumbled a string of obscenities.

Abrams heard the phone click, then a female voice said, "Police Officer Linder speaking." Spinelli identified himself, then said, "Okay, Abrams, you're on."

Abrams introduced himself briefly, then asked, "Is this your regular duty, officer?"

"Yes, sir, on and off for about six months."

"Okay, first question—did you see the gray bus unload?"

The policewoman replied, "Yes, sir. Mostly luggage, as usual. A few men on board helped the porters carry the luggage through the service door in the right of the building. That was over an hour ago."

Abrams thought a moment, then said, "How much luggage?"

She hesitated, then said, "About the same."

Abrams did not want to lead the witness, he wanted Officer Linder to report what she'd seen, not what Abrams would have liked her to see. Abrams asked, "Can you tell me if anything struck you as unusual tonight? Anything that was not normal for the last night of a weekend?"

Officer Linder was silent for some time, then replied, "Well... no...no, sir. Could you be more specific?"

Abrams said, "Why don't you just recount to me what happened since you came on duty. That would be four P.M., correct?"

"Yes, sir." She thought, then said, "Well, it's been pretty quiet since this afternoon. About an hour ago the black Ford Fairlane arrived with the ambassador, his wife, three kids, and a driver."

"How did they look?"

She understood he was looking for her impression. She answered, "The wife and kids looked all right. The wife was smiling and nodded to the cops as she usually does. He looked a little...I can't say exactly...just not himself."

"Okay, I understand. Were there any more cars?"

"No, sir. Not tonight. Sometimes there's only one, though."

"Okay, how about the minibuses?"

Linder answered, "Yes, they arrived. Pulled into the garage."

"How many? How were they spaced?"

Linder replied, "They came in two groups, as usual. The first group arrived about forty-five minutes ago. Six or seven buses. That was the bigger group, so that would be the kids, I guess."

Abrams nodded to himself. Unless the procedure had changed, the six or seven buses would have left the Pioneers camp in Oyster Bay and made a stop at the estate in Glen Cove. The exact purpose of this stop was unknown, but it probably was an administrative routine to pick up adult monitors, or do a head count. When it came to kids, Russians were not much different from everyone else.

In any event, thought Abrams, the buses always pulled into the walled service court, where any loading and unloading could not be observed with usual snooping devices. Abrams thought that if tonight was in fact different from all other weekend nights, then the children had been unloaded from the buses at the Glen Cove estate and escorted into the basement. He spoke into the phone, "How about the buses with the adults?"

Linder said, "They arrived maybe fifteen minutes after the kids' buses. There were four buses in that group. They also pulled right into the garage."

Abrams pictured the large iron overhead garage door. As the buses drew up to the building, the door would open, and the buses would cross the sidewalk and disappear down the ramp into the underground garage. The police booth where Linder stood was less than ten feet from the garage opening. Abrams said, "Were the buses full?"

She replied, "They have one-way glass."

"I know. Listen, Officer Linder, you've been watching these buses pull in and out for a while. Now, think a moment. Were they *full*?"

Linder replied almost immediately. "No. No, they were *not* full." She added, "I think they were almost empty."

Abrams let her continue without prompting.

She said with growing certainty, "Something struck me as odd when they pulled in, and it sort of stuck in my mind. And now that you ask—when they moved across the sidewalk toward the garage..."

"Yes?"

"Well, all the buses bounced like they were pretty light. Do you know what I mean?"

"Yes."

She added, "And as they pulled into the garage, the clearance on the top was very tight." She repeated, "Tight. Close."

Abrams said nothing.

Officer Linder spoke tentatively, as though she realized she'd stuck her neck out. "Is . . . is there anything else?"

Abrams said softly, "No, no. That's fine. Thank you."

"You're welcome." The phone clicked, and Spinelli said, "Well?"

"Well, Spinelli, you heard it."

"Yeah. I heard it. So maybe the ambassador looked a little out of it. Maybe he has hemorrhoids. Maybe the buses did arrive empty. Maybe the ambassador gave them all another day out in the country."

"Could be," said Abrams. "Why should they have to work on a Tuesday after a three-day weekend? Why not just send their baggage back to town on the big gray bus, and send a dozen minibuses in empty?"

"Well, we don't *know* the buses were empty, Abrams."

"She knew."

"Yeah. . . . Okay, so maybe most of the Russkies are hiding out in Glen Cove. Okay, they want everybody to think they're all back at ground zero here. So, okay, when does *la bomba* drop, Abrams?"

Abrams remained silent for some time, then said, "Am I being paranoid?"

Spinelli, too, let some time pass before he answered in a subdued tone, "No. This stinks. I'll make a quick verbal report. Anything else new besides World War Three?"

"No, that's about it. Slow night. How about you, Dom?"

"Well, I have a few things for you . . . I don't know how important they are anymore."

Abrams could hear a definite edge of anxiety in his voice. "Go on, Dom."

Spinelli cleared his throat. "Well, this guy West did a vanish. Two-dozen fucking people watching his ass and he's gone. This guy O'Brien is still missing. Autopsy on the pilot shows the back of his skull fractured, probably with a rubber club. What else...? Oh, Arnold Brin's death. The ME says murder. And you're still alive."

"Right." Abrams looked at Katherine. She made no pretense of not listening; there was no reason to feign polite disinterest when the subject was Armageddon and the time was now.

Spinelli added, "Also, you called for a book at the main library. *The Odyssey.* I didn't know you read Greek, much less owned a library card. You want to tell me about that?"

"It's by Homer."

"Who gives a shit?" Spinelli could be heard drawing on a cigar, then said, "Look, Abrams, I can see this is out of my league. I can't get anywhere with the FBI, CIA, State Department intelligence, or even you. Everybody is asking me things, but nobody is telling me anything. So who cares?" Spinelli let out a long breath. "Look, if there's anything I can do, call me. See you later, Abrams."

"Right." He hesitated, then said, "It's not as bad as it sounds, Dom. Thanks." He hung up, then turned slowly to Katherine, who was looking at him attentively.

She said, "I caught the drift of that."

Abrams nodded.

"They're all next door."

"Most of them. A few sacrifices went back to Manhattan."

"My God...." She stood and walked quickly to him, putting her hands on his shoulders. She said softly, "I wish Pat O'Brien were here."

Abrams replied, "I think O'Brien would be the first to say we'd done all we could."

"Yes, I think we are past the time for planning, development, and intelligence gathering. We're in the operations stage, whether we're ready or not. I think perhaps it's time for Marc Pembroke. I think it's time we paid a visit next door."

CHAPTER FIFTY-TWO

A taxi from Kennedy Airport to this part of Long Island was difficult enough to find on a holiday evening, Ann Kimberly thought. And, one having been found, it was harder to believe anything more coincidental than sharing the taxi with a Russian whose destination was also Dosoris Lane, albeit the Iron Curtain end of the street.

Ann crossed her legs and openly regarded the young Russian on the far side of the seat. He was very good-looking, she thought, with curly auburn hair, long eyelashes, hazel eyes, and a cupid bow mouth.

She had noticed him on the Lufthansa flight from Frankfurt, and they had both wound up at the special passport-control desk, avoiding both the baggage claim and customs. They'd then hurried out to the taxi stand, he arriving first. She had watched him out of curiosity, professional and personal, as he approached a few cabbies. But he seemed to be having trouble finding a taker. Then he'd unluckily approached one of the Soviet Jewish emigrés who seemed to predominate in the long-haul cab business. The Jewish cabbie had seized the opportunity to vent some venom in his native tongue, and looked as if he were working himself up to striking the young Russian.

Ann had stepped in to rescue the Russian and after some conversation had discovered that they had the same destination. She had finally gotten a cab and escorted the hesitant man into it.

As she watched him now, she made some observations: Like her, he had no luggage with him, but that might not be significant—his things might have been shipped through the diplomatic pouches. He had an overnight bag of an unfortunate red vinyl, and an attaché case of good pigskin. Government issue. Her own overnight bag said Vuitton, though that meant nothing to him, and her government attaché case was not high-quality leather. He, she assumed, was going to Dosoris Lane to speak to his people; she was going to speak to hers.

They had made some perfunctory and necessary conversation at the outset of their journey, mostly regarding the necessity of sharing a taxi. Then he had retreated into a defensive sort of silence.

She said in slow but passable Russian, "Have you been to Glen Cove before?"

He looked at her, smiled nervously, and nodded.

She said, "Are you staying long in America?"

He seemed to weigh his answer carefully, as if the question were important. He finally replied in studied English, "I will work here."

"I work in Munich."

"Ah."

She wondered why he hadn't been met, though that was not too unusual. Since the Russian staff cars were almost always followed by the FBI, this was a way to get couriers in and out of the country without too much attention. The passport-control officer at Kennedy would alert the FBI to a Russian diplomatic passport, of course, but she hadn't noticed anyone following.

Ann Kimberly regarded the Russian's attaché case lying in his lap. There was no doubt in her mind that whatever was in there was very high-grade stuff. She counted it a personal victory that the Soviets did not feel they could broadcast everything over the radio. Their codes were good, but not that good. She said to the Russian, "It's very warm here."

He replied, "Very humid."

She almost laughed at the banality of the exchange. "Washington is worse. Munich is more pleasant."

"Yes."

His taciturn behavior, she decided, was a combination of traditional Russian suspicion, bureaucratic reserve, and the shyness of a young man who finds himself in the forced company of an older and more sophisticated woman.

She said, "I was in Moscow once. Leningrad twice. Where are you from?"

The young man looked unhappy at these questions. It must have occurred to him, she thought, as it had occurred to her, that this chance meeting had the look of a setup. Yet, it wasn't. At least not on her part. The Russian replied, "I am from Saratov."

She nodded. "On the Volga."

His eyes widened just a bit, she noticed, then he turned toward the window. She found she couldn't take her eyes off his attaché case, and she had noticed him glancing at her case also. She reflected that an attractive man and woman sharing a cab shouldn't keep looking at each other's attaché case. She smiled.

The Russian craned his neck to take in the passing scenery. He glanced at his watch.

Ann Kimberly looked ahead and saw the traffic beginning to slow. On the horizon she saw skyrockets arching into the air. She reached over and tapped the Russian, and he turned with a start, one hand coming down on the attaché case. She pointed out the front windshield, unable to remember the Russian word for fireworks. "A celebration. A day to honor the dead of all wars. Like your May ninth Victory Day."

He seemed distressed rather than pleased at her familiarity with his language and country. He smiled tightly. "Yes. A celebration today."

"My name is Ann Kimberly. What is your name?"

He hesitated, then replied, "Nikolai Vasilevich," giving his first and patronymic names but not his last name.

Ann said, "My fiancé is named Nikolai—Nicholas in English."

He seemed not in the mood for any more coincidences. "Yes?"

She stared into his eyes until he turned away. She wondered why he was going to the Glen Cove weekend house instead of to East 67th Street. She said, "You are with the United Nations?"

He had ceased to be surprised at her questions. He nodded. "Yes, I am with the United Nations." This time he did not look away but looked her over. He smiled, tentatively. After a few seconds, he said, "Will you be here long?"

She replied, "Perhaps." Ann Kimberly reflected that there was little she didn't know about the Soviet delegation to the UN. It was made up of about one-half legitimate foreign service people with their dependents, one-fourth foreign service people who had been co-opted by the KGB, and one-fourth hard-core KGB agents, with a smattering of GRU people—Soviet military intelligence staff.

Ann sat back in her seat and made eye contact with the young man again. He had none of the arrogance of a KGB man, nor the savoir faire of a foreign service man. She nodded to herself. He might be GRU, a military courier, strong, disciplined, wary, intelligent; he carried as much in his head as he did in the attaché case. Probably more. The paper in his case would be flash paper and would incinerate in a second, the stuff in his head could be destroyed as quickly with the cyanide pill he carried. He would be armed, but not with a conventional pistol. Some gadget out of the Fourteenth Department. She glanced at his attaché case again and thought, *Whatever he is carrying, he is prepared to protect it with his life.* She crossed her legs and put her head back.

The taxi came to a stop and the driver turned his head. "I think those fireworks drew a crowd up ahead."

Ann replied, "I'll walk from here." She looked at the Russian. "It would be better to walk, Nikolai. I'll show you the way."

He looked anxiously at his watch and seemed to vacillate.

She prompted, "It's faster. About five minutes to the Soviet delegation house. That's where you're going, isn't it?"

He nodded, but made no move.

She smiled slowly, then shrugged. She took a twenty-dollar bill from her wallet and put it on his attaché case.

He looked down at it.

Ann took her bag and attaché case and opened the curbside door, then looked back over her shoulder. She hesitated, then indulged herself in two impulses. She said, "You're very good-looking,

Nikolai Vasilevich. You should defect. The American women would faint over you." She added, "Give my regards to Viktor Androv." Ann winked at the gaping young man and left the taxi.

She moved up the line of slow-moving traffic, then crossed Dosoris Lane as a policeman held up traffic for her. Within a few minutes she came abreast of the gates to the Russian estate and peered up the drive at the guardhouse. She continued another few hundred yards and turned into the gates of Van Dorn's estate.

She walked up to the parked car and the guard turned on his interior lights. She identified herself with her passport. Though her name was not on the guest list, he dimly remembered her and knew her sister, Katherine. He said, "I'm sorry I can't drive you, Miss Kimberly. Should I radio for a car?"

"No, I'll walk." She hesitated, then said, "Has Nicholas West arrived yet?"

The guard scanned his typed list. "No, ma'am."

She nodded, then turned toward the driveway. Nicholas was not at the Princeton Club, his office, or in his apartment. A duty officer at Langley had been vague. She was suspicious, but not in the way that lovers are suspicious.

She drew in a long breath of the warm night air as she climbed the driveway. She turned a bend and saw the big white house on the crest of the hill.

She had decided to take this sudden journey for a variety of reasons: Nick, Katherine's phone calls, a Teletype message from O'Brien requesting a piece of sensitive information. But there was an element of intuition involved as well. Her job at the NSA station in Munich had been to snatch ethereal messages from the air and decipher them. Somehow, over the years, that technical skill had transcended itself to include an almost telepathic ability. She knew there was something in the air that needed deciphering now, and it wasn't going to be a routine message.

CHAPTER FIFTY-THREE

The French doors leading to the side patio swung open, and George Van Dorn entered his study. He looked at Abrams, seeming more surprised at the white linen suit and sandals than at the bandaged foot, the abrasions on Abrams' face, or the fact that he was alive.

Van Dorn nodded to Katherine, then addressed Abrams. "You wanted to see me?"

Abrams replied, "Possibly."

Van Dorn had done enough debriefing to understand the psychological state of an agent just returned from a bad assignment. The attitude was often arrogant, taciturn, and insubordinate. Van Dorn said, "Sit down, Abrams. I'll freshen your drink."

"I'll stand and I'll pass on the drink."

Van Dorn sat behind his desk. "How do you want to begin?"

"I'd like to begin by asking you if there should be anyone else present."

"There should be, but he's not available."

Katherine said, "I know about Pat O'Brien."

Van Dorn looked at her, but said nothing.

Abrams continued, "What I discovered is important. I want to be certain my report is going to reach official channels."

"You can be sure it won't unless I think it should."

Abrams replied, "How do I know you're not one of them?"

"You don't know. You do know I fit the Talbot profile, so your suspicion is justified."

Abrams considered a moment, then responded, "I didn't say you could be Talbot. I've already met Talbot."

Van Dorn smiled. "Did you?"

"Yes, I did."

Katherine interjected, "Tony, I think you can speak freely."

Abrams said, "All right, I don't have many options."

Van Dorn didn't seem particularly offended at having to be vouched for. He said to Abrams, "Pembroke filled me in about the train station. That was a desperate move on their part." He added with a slight smile, "What did you do to piss them off, Abrams?"

Abrams replied, "I only did what your friend Evans asked me to do." He took a folded handkerchief from his pocket and opened it on Van Dorn's desk. "This looks like gold."

Van Dorn picked up a pinch of the metal scrapings. "It does. Good work. Window or door?"

"French door. What does this mean?"

Van Dorn ignored the question and asked his own. "Did they see you take this scraping?"

"No."

"Then how did they get on to you? Lie detector?"

"They caught me snooping."

Van Dorn nodded. "All right, what else did you find?"

"Well, I was told to check the outlets, radio and television sets, and the outside antenna."

Van Dorn asked a few questions and made a few notes, then looked up. "Nice job, Abrams. Balls." He glanced at Katherine. "Guts." He said to Abrams, "But that's not why they decided to murder you in the railroad underpass. What did you do, or see, that got them murderous?"

Abrams walked to the side wall, took a picture off its hook, and laid it on Van Dorn's desk. He pointed to the image of Henry Kimberly as he stared at Van Dorn.

Van Dorn's gaze went between Abrams' face and the face in the picture, then back to Abrams, but he said nothing.

Abrams took his finger off the picture, then glanced at Katherine.

Van Dorn stood slowly and rubbed his heavy jowls. He looked at Katherine and saw that she knew and believed it. He turned back to Abrams and nodded several times before the words came out. "Yes.... Yes, by God." He reached out and took Abrams' Scotch from the desk and swallowed it in two gulps. He sat back in his seat.

Abrams watched Van Dorn closely as his face went from pale to its normal florid color again. Abrams said, "There's more. But I'm not going on until I get some answers."

Van Dorn stood again. "Look, Abrams, I'm most appreciative, but it's not my policy to confide in field agents."

"Well, it's not my policy to be one. I did a favor for a man I respect. I discovered something of immediate concern. I want to tell you what it is, but I want you first to tell me why I risked my life."

Van Dorn hesitated.

Katherine said, "George, *I'd* like to know what the hell is going on!" She came toward him. "My *father* is next door, for God's sake. People are dead—"

Van Dorn held up his hand and lowered his head in thought, then said, "All right, I'll tell you."

Abrams said, "Please tell it fast. I don't think there's much time left."

Van Dorn stared at him, then said, "I know. It's very close. A matter of days or weeks—"

"No. A matter of hours."

"What?"

"Is there anyone in the government or military you can call?"

Van Dorn nodded slowly. "Hours? How do you know?" He stared at Abrams, then said, "Understand, Abrams, that I can't just cry wolf—a full alert cost tens of millions of dollars.... I won't make a fool of myself. I need something other than the fact that you saw Henry Kimberly. I need something that will point to a final count-down. You tell me something like that, Abrams, and I'll call... and then I'll tell you what this is about."

Abrams replied, "Okay, here's what sounds to me like a final countdown: The basement of your neighbor's house is full of Russians, and they're not there to change the fuse."

Van Dorn shot a quick look at Katherine, then came quickly around the desk. "Are you certain? Abrams, did you see them?"

Abrams shook his head. "No, I didn't see them. A little girl told me. A big girl confirmed it." He explained briefly.

When Abrams had finished, Van Dorn stayed motionless and silent, his head bowed. Abrams could see he was shaken. *And why shouldn't he be?* thought Abrams. *He has just heard what amounts to an air raid siren.*

Van Dorn reached for the telephone on his desk and dialed. He spoke into the receiver: "This is George Van Dorn. Identification phrase, 'We went through fire and through water.' Let me speak to Pegasus, please." Van Dorn waited, then said, "Well, locate him and have him call me at home. Condition Omega. Yes." He hung up and glanced at his watch. "Pegasus will never be more than ten minutes from a message."

Abrams wondered who Pegasus was and where he was, but knew better than to ask. He said, "O'Brien once indicated to me that the threat is not nuclear war, and may not be chemical or biological either. That rules out three modern Horsemen of the Apocalypse, and ought to be a comforting thought. But knowing the capacity we have of developing new ways to destroy ourselves, somehow I'm not comforted."

Van Dorn nodded. "There *is* a fourth horseman." He took a cigar and bit off the tip. "Have either of you heard of EMP—electromagnetic pulse?"

Abrams nodded cautiously. "Some journalists call it the Doomsday Pulse."

Katherine added, "It has something to do with a nuclear explosion in space."

Van Dorn replied, "Yes, it does. But the threat itself is not nuclear. Those people hiding in the basement next door are hiding from us, not the nuclear blast. The blast, when it comes, if it comes, will be somewhere over Omaha at an HOB—height of burst—of about three hundred miles. There will be no mushroom cloud, no shock waves, no heat, no radiation, and none of the physical destruction associated with a thermonuclear detonation. There will only be a flash of light in the sky, then . . ."

"Then *what?*" asked Katherine.

"Then, to paraphrase Lord Grey, the lights will go out all over North America. And I don't think we will see them lit again in our lifetime."

No one spoke for some time, then Abrams said, "Is this some sort of electrical phenomenon? Like a lightning storm?"

Van Dorn nodded. "Yes. It's very complex; a bit of technological arcana, first discovered in the early 1960s during our last high-altitude nuclear tests. Discovered, unfortunately, by the Russians at about the same time."

Van Dorn lit his cigar, then said, "What apparently happens is this: When a nuclear device is exploded high above the atmosphere, earthbound gamma rays released from the explosion hit air molecules and create something called Compton electrons. Those electrons undergo a turning motion around the earth's magnetic field lines and emit an electromagnetic pulse. Every electrical and electronic device in the country, including that digital watch you're wearing, Abrams, will act as a lightning rod for this pulse. There will be virtually nothing left that works, including nuclear power plants, jet engines, auto and truck engines, diesels and home furnaces." Van Dorn paused, then said, "It's difficult, isn't it, to even imagine the magnitude of the catastrophe." He looked at his telephone, as though underscoring the point.

No one said anything, then Abrams spoke softly. "I assume there's some protection against this?"

Van Dorn replied, "Our friends next door apparently tested their EMP protection devices with lightning, and I suppose the bastards think they're fairly well covered. However, no one will know for sure unless there's an actual EMP storm."

Katherine asked, "What about the military?"

Van Dorn replied, "They've belatedly identified the danger, but what they've done to harden the vital systems is too little and too late. Only one of the four presidential flying command posts, for instance, is EMP-proof."

Van Dorn ran his finger through the gold scrapings on his desk. "This, by the way, conducts the EMP and keeps it from passing through the spaces around the windows and doors."

Abrams thought, *The scientific equivalent of garlic or wolfbane.* He said, "And vacuum tubes?"

Van Dorn drew on his cigar. "That's another irony. The old-type vacuum tubes are about ten million times more resistant to EMP than the fragile integrated solid state circuits that have replaced them."

Van Dorn paused thoughtfully, then said, "The Soviets may not have learned about EMP before we did, but they damned sure acted on it sooner. Do you remember the Russian Foxbat, the MiG-25 that was flown to Japan in 1976 by a Russian defector? It was thought to be the world's most advanced fighter plane. American technicians took it apart and found most of the aircraft was state-of-the-art technology. But the electronics closest to the fuselage skin were based on vacuum tubes. At first the American technicians were amazed at such primitive electronics. But as they dug deeper down into the aircraft, they discovered that the Soviets indeed possessed advanced solid-state technology. So why the vacuum tubes? Well, now we know. The electronics closest to the exterior of the aircraft that would pick up the EMP were purposely dependent on vacuum tubes. This was the first hard evidence we had that they took EMP seriously. The Israelis made similar findings on captured Russian-made equipment. We should assume that most of the Soviet arsenal is designed with EMP in mind."

Abrams said, "Apparently their house next door is designed to weather the storm as well. I suppose they'll use the place as a command and control center after the EMP attack."

Van Dorn nodded.

Katherine said, "Is this house...?"

Van Dorn shook his head. "No, and I don't have a bomb shelter, either. I don't plan for disasters, I prevent them."

Abrams thought a moment, then looked at Van Dorn. "Your close physical proximity to them must make them a little nervous.... Is it possible they have something special planned for this house?"

Van Dorn replied, "I'm fairly certain they do." He nodded to himself, then added, "I have something special planned for them, too, and it's not my usual light-and-sound show. It is instead a rather unneighborly gate-crashing." He smiled in a way that Abrams thought was both mischievous and sinister. Van Dorn added, "The larger issues of world politics pale beside the petty squabbles of feuding neighbors. If I'm to end my days on this planet, I'm going to take a good number of those bastards with me."

CHAPTER FIFTY-FOUR

V an Dorn did not expand on his views of how to deal with unfriendly neighbors, and Abrams did not probe. The study was silent enough to hear the clock ticking on the mantel. They could also hear the muffled sounds of Van Dorn's guests as they made the obligatory "oohs" and "ahhs" as the pyrotechnic display heated up. Katherine, Abrams noticed, looked sad but not dispirited, as if she'd lost a tennis set but not yet the match.

Van Dorn regarded Abrams for some time, then said, "We sent you in there only to confirm some of our suspicions. We didn't expect you to have a chat with Henry Kimberly, or to discover that their people did not take their buses back to Manhattan. Fine job."

Abrams acknowledged the compliment with a short nod, and said, "I would guess that the events of the past few days or weeks—which you and your friends precipitated—have spooked them. Perhaps pushed them into action."

Van Dorn studied the tip of his burning cigar, then said, "Yes, the final irony. We stampeded them into action. Perhaps before they were completely ready."

Abrams observed, "It doesn't appear that we're completely ready either."

"Well...we are warned."

Katherine said, "Isn't it possible, George, that this is only a drill? A test to see if they can hide their people in Glen Cove without detection?"

Van Dorn shook his head. "On the contrary. They would not normally have to hide anyone. They would simply coordinate the EMP storm with their usual weekend in Glen Cove. We've always known that the Russians would prefer to schedule a thermonuclear war or EMP attack on a holiday weekend. Their people in Washington and San Francisco would also be at country places, and American response to Red Alerts, no matter what anyone tells you, is two to three minutes slower on the weekend. For instance, Pegasus has not called back, and it's been"—he glanced at his watch—"twelve minutes." He looked at Katherine. "No, I wish I could believe it was a drill, but the fact that they've hidden those people here in Glen Cove on a night when they should all be back in Manhattan means to me that tonight is the night. Mr. Abrams is right."

Katherine nodded.

Abrams said, "I'm wondering why the Russians went to so much trouble in making their house resistant to EMP. Why not just shut off the master switch and pull all the plugs a few minutes before the EMP storm?"

Van Dorn replied, "No one is certain that cutting off the power will *completely* safeguard electrical components. But even if it were true, the Russians won't pull their main switch, because the FBI monitors their electrical usage and would be on the horn to the President within five seconds."

Abrams' eyes moved around the room, as though he were taking in all the electrical components.

Van Dorn seemed to know what he was thinking. "Yes, life would be very different. We would freeze to death in the dark." He looked at his desk. "Even my pocket calculator would give up the ghost."

Abrams said, "We seem to have no defense—but could we at least retaliate?"

Van Dorn began to reply, then the phone rang and he picked it up. "Van Dorn. Yes." He repeated his identification phrase, listened a moment, then said, "Well, where the hell is he? No, I will not give you the information. Is Unicorn there? Centaur? I repeat, this is a Condition Omega." Van Dorn nodded several times as he listened. "All right. Fine. I'm still here. Have one of them call me." He hung up and looked at Abrams and Katherine. "Pegasus is inexplicably unavailable. Unicorn or Centaur will call back soon. In the meantime, they've accepted my analysis of the situation as an Omega alert, and things are moving."

Katherine's head suddenly turned toward the bay window behind Van Dorn, and her eyes widened.

Van Dorn looked quickly over his shoulder. "What is it?"

She drew a deep breath, then spoke. "I...I thought...It must have been heat lightning."

Van Dorn licked his lips, then said, "Well, the lights are still on, so it must have been. But that's probably what it will look like.... Bad luck to have heat lightning tonight of all nights, isn't it?"

Abrams replied, "I'm not certain if it's bad luck or a cosmic joke."

Katherine added, "Whatever, it's damned unnerving."

Van Dorn cleared his throat. "There's not much more I can do right now. The question on the floor concerned retaliation, and that is a complex question. Could we? Would we? Should we?"

Katherine said, "What do you mean, *should* we?"

Van Dorn replied, "It's a moral question. The President will have to be convinced that it was the Russians who caused the EMP storm. And he will have to decide if a crippled nuclear response will serve any purpose other than inviting a massive Soviet counterstrike."

Katherine nodded slowly. "I understand...."

Abrams asked, "*How* is the nuclear device that will cause an EMP storm going to be delivered? I assume any missile trajectory out of Russia will be instantly spotted."

Van Dorn stubbed out his cigar. "That's the question. We don't know. But we do know that a Soviet submarine off the coast of California can launch a missile that will explode over the center of the United States, at the required altitude to cause an EMP storm— flight time three to four minutes. Before a submarine launch was even confirmed, it would be too late to act. The command, control, and communications network—the glue that holds our entire nuclear program together—will be gone. Once that's gone, that's it. As one Air Force general said, the winner of the next war will be the side with the last two working radios."

Abrams walked to the large bay window and gazed across the crowded lawn, past the striped tent and the tables, beyond the glare of the party lights, to where the edge of the sweeping lawn met the expanse of night sky. A sizable rocket rose from the depths of the waterless swimming pool, its fiery plume brilliant against the black sky, then exploded in a dazzling shower of golden particles. He turned from the window and said, "In effect, our own advanced technology—our microchips, computers, and transistors on which we're so dependent—leave us vulnerable. If we unleashed a retaliatory electromagnetic storm over the Soviet Union, the consequences to them would not be as cataclysmic."

"That's correct," answered Van Dorn. "This is one of those cases where primitiveness is a distinct advantage. You can't burn out a country's microchips and computers if they don't have any. And if they do but they're not dependent on them, they're not as vulnerable as we are."

Van Dorn picked up his pocket calculator and looked at it, then said, "Every civilization has its Achilles' heel. If we introduced a rice blight into China and wiped out their crop, they would suffer mass starvation. If they did the same thing to us, no one would notice much. Do you see? Do you understand why we're on the threshold of extinction?"

Abrams nodded.

Van Dorn looked at Katherine. "In mortal combat, it's not only the Achilles' heel we look for, we also need the right weapon to deal the death blow." Van Dorn walked around his desk. "Sometimes the right weapon is EMP. Sometimes it is rice blight." He opened the top drawer of his desk. "But if it's a werewolf you're after"—he set something on the desk top and took his hand away—"it's a silver bullet you need."

Katherine and Abrams stared at the gleaming .45-caliber bullet, sitting upright like a miniature missile ready for launch. Van Dorn said, "No, it's not O'Brien's. I have my own. There is one more. Because there were three Talbots."

Katherine's eyes moved from the bullet to Van Dorn's face. "Three...?"

"Yes. In fact, your father had the third bullet."

Katherine did not reply.

Van Dorn said softly, "But I think this is the one with his name on it, Kate. Would you have any objections if I used it?"

Katherine hesitated only a moment, then shook her head.

Van Dorn nodded, then scooped the bullet into his hand and dropped it in his trouser pocket. He said, "No matter what happens tonight—a national disaster or a miracle of survival—Henry Kimberly will die. We can discuss how later."

Abrams stared at Van Dorn's profile, noticing for the first time the hard angular features that were not so apparent from the front. The man may look like an old basset hound, he thought, but somewhere under the aging flesh there lurked a more ravening beast.

The silence in the room was broken by the ringing phone. Van Dorn picked it up and went through the identification procedure. He listened, nodding as he made a few notes. He said, "You must understand that one of the men with the President this weekend, James Allerton, is most probably a Soviet agent." Van Dorn listened a second, then snapped, "Yes, damn it, *the* James Allerton. How fucking many are there who would be at Camp David with the President? Yes, all right. But I still need to speak to one of the three." He listened, then replied, "All right—I have hard evidence pointing to an EMP attack—*tonight*. Get it cranked up, Colonel. Yes. Fine." He hung up and wiped his forehead with a handkerchief. "Well, now you know about Allerton if you hadn't already suspected." He glanced at Katherine.

She shook her head. "My God...this is too much...."

Abrams said, "Who is the third?"

Van Dorn shrugged and shook his head. "I don't even know if he's still alive. But if the Russians wind up in the White House, I suppose we'll find out."

Katherine looked at Van Dorn. "George...what *will* happen afterward? After the EMP attack? I mean...if there's no nuclear exchange...what happens next? Surrender? Occupation? What?"

"That's rather negative thinking, Katherine."

"Nonetheless," said Abrams, "it's a good question."

Van Dorn glanced at Abrams, then at Katherine, and saw how things stood with them. He smiled, and Katherine seemed chagrined. Abrams tried to look impassive. Van Dorn walked to the wall safe and returned with a manila file folder. He opened it and extracted a sheaf of papers, laying them on the desk facing Abrams. "Can you read that?"

Abrams looked at the typed Cyrillic letters. He read, " 'A Report on the State's Appropriation and Administration of the Garment Industry in New York.' " He looked at Van Dorn quizzically.

Van Dorn said, "Not in and of itself interesting reading. What's interesting is the fact that such a report even exists."

Katherine glanced at the thick file. "Where did you get this?"

Van Dorn allowed himself a smile. "From a local juvenile delinquent." He explained about Stanley Kuchik and added, "The kid said there were dozens of file cabinets full of papers. If he had been able to read Russian, he might have grabbed something more interesting, perhaps their plans for the court and legal system . . . not that it matters."

Abrams turned a few pages of the report. There was some element of coincidence here, he thought; his parents had been active in the garment workers' movement, and they would have approved of this expropriation.

Van Dorn slid a few photographs out of the file and pushed them across the desk. "The kid takes pictures, too. These are the electrical panels in the basement. No real surprises there. But the CIA found it fascinating that we could get in and out of Ivan's basement." Van Dorn chuckled. "I didn't tell them we came on these by pure chance." He pushed another photo toward Abrams. "Do you recognize the fat one?"

Abrams nodded. "Androv. The so-called cultural affairs attaché."

"Yes, and the man walking beside him has been identified as Valentin Metkov of the KGB's Department Five. Murder Incorporated."

Katherine stared at the faces in the photo. Androv looked so benign, and Metkov so sinister. But there seemed to be no correlation between how they looked and how they behaved.

Van Dorn continued, "Metkov is not a trigger man, he's a high-ranking officer who directs mass liquidations. He's worked in Poland, Afghanistan, the Soviet Republic of Lithuania—wherever the KGB has a free hand to deal with the enemies of the Soviet state. I never thought I'd see him in America. He is a harbinger of death."

"Who's a harbinger of death?"

Everyone turned toward the door as Ann Kimberly strode across the room. "Who's a harbinger of death, George? Not me, I hope?"

There was an astonished silence, then Van Dorn said, "One of my neighbors, Valentin Metkov of Department Five, is planning to murder us all, Ann."

"Well, George, you've been begging for it for years." She smiled, "Hello, Kate. I guess I arrived at the right time. Is this your new boyfriend, Tony? Hello. Did I miss much? Get me a drink, will you, George? I have a feeling I'm going to need it."

CHAPTER FIFTY-FIVE

Ann Kimberly sat on the edge of the coffee table with a bourbon in her hand. She said, "Do I sound like a suspicious fiancée? I feel a bit of a fool making the hop over to look for my boyfriend."

Katherine, who was standing in front of her, replied, "No, it's not foolish. Peter would disappear for weeks, but Nick's job and his...his nature argue against his dropping out of sight."

Van Dorn had little sensitivity for this female chatter. Nicholas West was among the most protected men in the nation. He said, "As a result of all that's going on, the Company probably just pulled him in for his own protection. You'll get word soon."

Ann wanted to point out that she wasn't some hysterical young girl; that she was the first person listed on Nicholas West's contact sheet, and she was in the business. But she said instead, "Let's get on to what's on your minds." She leaned forward. "Tell me all about it."

Van Dorn exchanged a quick glance with Katherine, then Katherine turned to her sister and said, "The first thing I have to tell you is that our father is alive."

Ann did not appear to react, but Abrams, standing to her side, saw her glass begin to slip from her hand before she clenched it tighter.

Katherine went on, "He's next door, Ann. He's a defector. A traitor."

Ann said, "He is Talbot."

Katherine replied, "He is Talbot."

Ann nodded to herself thoughtfully, as though storing the information for some future reference. She said, "There are two others, you know." She looked up at Van Dorn. "Did you get a telex from England a few hours ago?"

Van Dorn nodded. "From our contact in MI5." He opened the file drawer of his desk and pulled out the deciphered message. He read, "'In reply to your inquiry: Long-distance call from New York, routed through local exchange, Tongate, to Brompton Hall seven P.M. your time. Duration eight minutes. Call from Brompton Hall to New York at seven forty-three P.M. your time. Duration six minutes. Both calls, New York party at UN Plaza Hotel. Request further?'" Van Dorn looked up and said, "About fifteen minutes after the call was made from Brompton Hall, neighbors reported a fire." He turned to Abrams. "I think I know what happened, but maybe you can try to reconstruct it. I'd feel better if I heard it from a cop."

Abrams was not flattered at being asked to perform, but he said, "The person at the UN Plaza Hotel was James Allerton." He saw Van Dorn nod. "Allerton would have liked to cover traces of those calls, but time was short and he was feeling a little nervous. So he took a chance no one would check. The time of his call to Brompton Hall corresponds to the time in New York when he could have first received the news about the diary and the Wingate letter. Probably from Thorpe, who got it from Katherine." He kept his eyes fixed on Van Dorn.

Van Dorn said, "We're not certain Allerton and Thorpe knew about each other. But the news did come to Allerton somehow as a result of Thorpe's conversation with Katherine, and the timing is right. Go on."

Abrams thought a moment, then said, "Allerton spoke for eight minutes to Lady Wingate or her nephew. He was probably trying to determine if his name was mentioned in the diary in any negative context." Abrams paused, then went on, "This presupposes that Allerton believed the diary was real, though I've been told recently, it wasn't." He glanced at Katherine, then said to Van Dorn,

"Allerton never knew he and Kimberly were on the same side of the fence—which is usually how these things work."

Van Dorn nodded. "Allerton was badly frightened, which was the idea of the diary. Or, to use the other metaphor, the werewolf sensed danger, but unlike natural wolves he didn't run *from* it, he ran *at* it."

Abrams lit a cigarette and drew on it, then continued, "Allerton must have convinced Eleanor Wingate that he was working with Carbury, O'Brien, and Katherine, and that they were concerned about her safety, or something along those lines. Allerton was, of course, after the Photostat of the diary."

Abrams watched the smoke rise from his cigarette. He was aware of the absolute stillness in the room. He was aware, too, that there was a startling contrast between the gentleman he had met at the OSS dinner and seen on television, and the man he was now describing; but that was the nature of the werewolf. Abrams said, "Allerton sent someone to Brompton Hall and so did O'Brien. The timing is close and it's hard to say who got there first, but Eleanor Wingate let both of them in." Abrams remembered a line from the letter and observed, "She must have been just as confused then as she had been in 1945, when two different men showed up at Brompton Hall on the identical mission of recovering Henry Kimberly's papers."

Van Dorn nodded again, "In any event, Allerton's man murdered Eleanor Wingate, her nephew, and O'Brien's man. He may have...interrogated them first and recovered the diary Photostat. Then he called Allerton and reported. Fifteen minutes after that call, the house went up in flames." He looked at Abrams. "It's reassuring that you've come to the same conclusions." He added, "We couldn't convict James Allerton on the evidence of the phone calls, but we can kill him."

Abrams didn't reply directly to the suggestion of homicide, but said, "And James Allerton is at this moment with the President at Camp David?"

Van Dorn laughed without humor. "I'm afraid so. As if we didn't have enough to worry about."

Ann said, "What do we have to worry about, George?"

"Lots of things. The third Talbot, for one thing. But I have no evidence that he's even alive." He looked at Ann.

She replied, "I think he is. But I'd rather not comment at this time. Before you tell me what else is on your mind, let me tell you that there has been no unusual radio traffic between Moscow and Washington, Manhattan, or Glen Cove. Very banal stuff going out on the air—administrative junk. Androv's home leave has been approved, for instance. Low-level diplomatic codes, not much high-grade tricky stuff. I did a computer analysis, and it seems that whenever this phenomenon has occurred in the past—nearly every time between the Berlin blockade in 1948 and the present—it usually, but not always, means the bastards are up to something. We call it QBSHF: Quiet Before Shit Hits Fan."

Van Dorn observed, "They haven't been very quiet here."

Ann continued, "Also, I caught a break tonight and shared a cab with the sexiest Russian I've ever laid eyes on." She explained briefly, then added, "When I see an obviously high-level courier skulking around in a cab like that, his attaché case *not* handcuffed to him, trying to look unofficial, then I get a little suspicious. For two cents I would have mugged him." She smiled. "But he looked tough. And not every courier is carrying the game plan for World War Three, is he?"

Van Dorn replied, "No, but I think this one was."

"Well, had I known . . . but let's hear it, then, George."

"Right—" The phone rang and Van Dorn picked it up and listened. He gave his identification phrase, answered, and asked a few questions, then hung up shortly. He said, "Well, they wouldn't give me much over an unsecured line, but they wanted me to know the alert status has been upgraded and the President has been informed." He looked at the screen in front of the alcove. "They'll telex encoded details later." Van Dorn looked at Ann. "Well, are you in the mood for more bad news?"

"I thrive on it, George. Shoot."

Abrams watched Ann Kimberly as Van Dorn gave her a background briefing. She asked a few questions and made a few succinct comments. Abrams saw she was quick, intelligent, and knowledgeable. She was also good-looking. Her coloring was like her sister's, but her hair was shorter, and her body fuller. She was also, he knew, about three years older. Whereas Katherine radiated a sense of the outdoors, Ann looked as if she spent too much time in underground facilities, and what tan she had, he guessed, came from hickory-smoked bourbon.

As for personality, Ann Kimberly was somewhat more breezy and outgoing than her sister, and more prone to banter and profane observations. She had already told Van Dorn he'd gotten too heavy and that Kitty was looking for a lover, and suggested his parties were boring.

Also, she did not seem particularly worried as Van Dorn presented the news that America might come under attack at any moment; but Abrams could see she believed him.

He wondered how Ann Kimberly and Nicholas West ever got together and how they had stayed together. It struck him that Ann Kimberly and Peter Thorpe were more suited to each other than Thorpe and Katherine, at least on the surface.

Ann rattled the ice cubes in her glass and helped herself to the tray of hors d'oeuvres on the coffee table, as she carried on a fast dialogue with Van Dorn.

Van Dorn said, "Then the President can't order a nuclear strike?"

"That's right, George. The President would not have the ability to send out what's called an Emergency Action Message, not after we've gotten an electronic lobotomy." Ann stood and looked around the room, then said, "But I'll give you all a piece of information classified Highest State Secret. The military foresaw this EMP problem and they've convinced the President that if any such complete blackout occurs, the lack of communications will be the signal to go. It's called ALARM—Auto-Launch Response Mode. That's even a quicker response than LAW—Launch on Warning." She added, "The fucking military would have to speak English if they didn't have their acronyms." She took a deep breath and said, "To put it more poetically, the silent radios would, ironically, be the last call to arms."

She looked at the three faces that were staring at her, and added, to be sure they understood, "A communications blackout equals a launch. Boom! *Auf wiedersehen,* world, as they say in merry old Germany." She drained off her drink and held it out to Van Dorn. "A short one, George. *Danke.*"

Van Dorn took her glass and moved slowly to the bar.

Abrams looked at her, focusing on her eyes. At first he thought she was a little drunk, or mad, but then thought she just didn't give a damn. But they made eye contact, and he saw she cared very much. It must be, he thought, the way her colleagues spoke of nuclear annihilation, as though they were discussing some past war, not the next one. *Auf wiedersehen* indeed. Not if he could help it.

Van Dorn said, "I assume the Russians know this." He handed Ann her drink.

She held up her glass. "Here's to good Kentucky whisky." She tipped the glass back and took a swallow, then regarded Van Dorn. "Yes, they were told this. Otherwise what good would the threat be as a deterrent? But either they didn't believe it, or they decided to take a goddamned shot at it anyway. Our nuclear response to an EMP blackout would be weakened, but not *that* weak. We have the subs and the European nukes."

Ann walked to the French doors and looked up into the sky. The sheets of heat lightning had broken up into crackling bolts, and a wind was picking up off the sound. A distant thunder rolled into the quiet study. "God is trying to tip us off."

She turned and faced the room. "Well, that's the grim picture. You were worried about instant and total defeat, without a shot fired. Have no fear. We'll get our nuclear war." She stared down into her glass and swirled the amber liquor. "Classic case of underestimating your enemy's will to fight back. Mass delusion in Moscow. Assholes." She looked up. "So, all indications are that tomorrow's sunbeams will shine through motes of nuclear debris."

Van Dorn let out a long breath. "Maybe not. I assume the President is speaking to the Soviet Premier right now. If he lets them know that we're on to them, they may call it off."

Ann did not respond.

Van Dorn continued, "The President can inform the Soviets

that he's given all the nuclear forces the go-ahead to launch as soon as one of our missile-detecting satellites picks up a single Soviet launch."

Ann was shaking her head. "They won't see any launch, not from the Soviet Union, not from a Soviet sub, nor from anywhere."

Van Dorn took a few steps toward her. "What do you mean? How are they going to detonate that nuclear device over the center of the United States?"

Ann replied, "Satellite, of course."

Van Dorn was silent for a moment, then blurted, "Damn it! Of course—"

Ann went on, "It's simplicity itself. Tumbling now through the black voids are thousands of satellites of every sort and description, passing freely across the unprotected frontiers of space. One type of Soviet satellite is called Molniya, which aptly enough means lightning. There are dozens of these fairly innocuous Molniya communications satellites crisscrossing North America every day. One of these Molniya satellites is of particular interest to my people at the National Security Agency. Molniya Number Thirty-six."

Ann walked away from the French doors and sat on the edge of Van Dorn's desk. She continued, "Molniya Thirty-six was launched from the Soviet rocket base at Plesetsk about a year ago. It has a highly elliptical orbit with an apogee of about twenty-five thousand miles—way out there—and a perigee of only four hundred miles. The ostensible reason for this highly unusual orbit is to prolong communications sessions, which is partly true. But with an orbit like that, it is also conveniently out of range of our snooping satellites and our killer satellites for a good deal of its journey. Its twenty-five-thousand-mile apogee is somewhere over Lake Baikal in central Siberia." She added, almost offhandedly, "Its four-hundred-mile perigee is over America—around Nebraska, to be exact."

No one spoke, and Ann walked back to the coffee table, picking up the nearly empty tray of hors d'oeuvres. She said, "My people at the NSA have determined by electronic means that there is not the normal load of communication equipment on board Molniya Thirty-six. Deduction: The extra space is filled with something else.

To wit: a few pounds of enriched plutonium." She picked out a piece of smoked salmon and ate it. "Molniya Thirty-six is most probably what we call an SOB—a satellite orbital bomb. SOB's are outlawed by a 1966 UN treaty, but I guess Ivan lost his copy of it."

She searched through the tray again and found another smoked salmon. "Good food, George. Do you still have that crazy Nazi working for you?"

Van Dorn replied in a distracted tone, "He's not a Nazi. He's a German Jew."

"I thought he was an old SS man."

"No, he pretended to be one. Look, Ann, are you sure—"

Abrams interrupted. "What's the orbit time of this Molniya?" He pronounced it with the proper Russian accent and Ann glanced at him. She answered, "Well, that's the good news. The orbiting time around the earth is long—twelve hours and seventeen minutes, give or take a few minutes." She looked down into her glass and shook the ice cubes, then drank the remainder of the bourbon. "The bad news is that I don't recall offhand when it's due over Nebraska again." She handed Van Dorn her glass. "Very light this time. Mostly soda."

Van Dorn took her glass and made another trip to the bar. He said over his shoulder, "Well, we can find out, I'm sure."

"No problem. Do you have a computer terminal yet?"

"No, I never got beyond the telex."

"Oh, George." Ann picked up Van Dorn's phone as she took her drink from him with her other hand. "I think I can get through to Fort Meade." She cradled the receiver on her shoulder and hit the push buttons.

Abrams watched. He'd never seen a twenty-one-digit phone number before. Ann went through an identification procedure of some length. Abrams remembered that someone had once said the National Security Agency was so secret that congressmen said NSA stood for No Such Agency.

Ann got someone on the phone whom she seemed to know. "Yes, Bob, this is Ann Kimberly. I'm in New York, and I need some information. Do you have your little computer in front of you?"

Abrams had also been told that there were fourteen acres of

computers at the NSA facility beneath Fort Meade, so the chances of Bob having one in front of him were good.

Ann said, "No, this phone is not secure. But I only want some very low-classification stuff. Okay...?" She nodded to the people in the room, then said into the receiver, "Punch up the Molniya series." She waited, then continued, "Okay, I need Molniya Thirty-six. Got it? Now I need Molniya's perigee time and place." She listened, then said, "Okay...okay, Bob. Thanks....No, just playing trivia here. Right. See you." She hung up and looked at the three people staring at her. She said, "You don't want to know."

Van Dorn replied gruffly, "I damn sure want to know."

Ann looked at her watch, which Abrams took as a bad sign. He wondered if she was looking at the minute hand or the second hand. She raised her head and spoke. "Molniya Thirty-six is traveling in a southwesterly direction, descending now from its apogee, toward earth. Perigee time over Blair, Nebraska, a small town about twenty miles north of Omaha, is 12:06 A.M., Eastern Daylight Time, 11:06 P.M. Central Time, which is, in any case...ninety-six minutes from now." She stared out the bay window, as though, thought Abrams, she was looking for it.

Katherine said, "They may wait for the next orbit...."

"Not likely," said Van Dorn. "Even Russkies don't like to sit in the basement for twelve hours."

Abrams added, "If their mission offices don't open for business as usual, and the delegation doesn't show up at the UN tomorrow morning, it would look a little suspicious. No, they're going for it tonight. *This* orbit."

Katherine suddenly blurted, "Those bastards!" She looked at Van Dorn. "We're partly responsible for this. We should have done more, or done nothing. But we've committed ourselves, so we must see it to its end."

Van Dorn stayed motionless for some time, then said softly, "Yes, I agree. I didn't intend to let it go with a few phone calls, Kate. We'll deal directly with the situation next door." He picked up the telephone and dialed the kitchen, where one of the staff picked up. "Find Marc Pembroke and get him to my study. Immediately."

Van Dorn put down the receiver and looked at each person. "We may or may not be able to stop this ticking clock, but, by God, there's no reason why we can't indulge ourselves in some personal revenge." He cocked his head toward the window. "Tonight is their last night, too."

George Van Dorn looked at Ann Kimberly. "All right?"

She shrugged. "I don't think it matters much if one meets one's end from a small-caliber bullet or a large nuclear fireball. When you're dead, you're dead a long time anyway. If you've got a gun, I've brought my trigger finger."

Van Dorn looked at Abrams.

Abrams had a distaste for vigilantism, partly professional, partly cultural. He said, "I'm sure they're prepared to withstand one hell of an onslaught."

Van Dorn smiled grimly. "Pembroke and I have already drawn up some plans for an attack."

Abrams found that odd but not incredible. He tried another tack. "What if it *isn't* tonight? How do we explain why we attacked a diplomatic facility and shot up the Soviet Mission to the United Nations?"

Ann replied, "Look, we're proposing a preemptive strike, not an unprovoked act of aggression."

Van Dorn plucked at his heavy jowl, then said, "Abrams, if your objections are more practical than moral, please rest assured on that point. We may be amateur spies, but we're professional soldiers. In fact, I happen to have an eighty-one-millimeter mortar out back."

Abrams' eyes widened.

Van Dorn smiled almost sheepishly. "We can level that goddamned house in about ten minutes, then go in and mop up."

Abrams stared at him.

Van Dorn added, "As fate would have it, my three pyrotechnicians tonight have some mortar training."

Abrams thought fate had little to do with it. He rubbed his forehead. When this was amateur spying, it was strange enough. Now that it had turned into a discussion of infantry tactics, it had become alarming. The image formed in his mind of the little Russian girl clutching her doll. Katerina and Katya. *Where are you going, Katerina? Down to the basement.* He shook his head and looked at Van Dorn. "There are women and children in that basement."

Van Dorn let out a long breath. He spoke softly, almost gently. "There are women and children all over America. If you want to talk about women and children, try to expand your imagination to picture the results of a nuclear war."

Abrams replied somewhat irritably, "Massacring those people will not prevent any of that." He added, "If there is an EMP attack, your mortar will still work. Why don't you hold off until you see what happens at midnight?"

Van Dorn began to reply, but the phone rang and he picked it up. He listened, then said, "Yes, he's right here." He held out the receiver to Abrams. "Captain Spinelli."

Abrams looked somewhat surprised as he took the receiver. He spoke into the mouthpiece. "What's up, Dom?"

Spinelli replied, "Still partying, Abrams? Well, just a wrap-up on the evening news."

"I don't have any news."

"I do."

Abrams picked up the telephone and trailed the cord away from the desk toward the fireplace, and turned his back on the three people. He could hear them begin talking in low voices. Abrams said, "Where are you?"

"At the Nineteenth."

Abrams spoke in a soft tone. "All right, what is it?" he asked without much interest.

"I've got a follow-up on that note you left with my man at the Thirty-sixth Street town house."

Abrams replied, "Oh, right, the Lombardy. That was just a long shot. I didn't think Thorpe would leave anything lying around. It's a CIA safe house and other people use it—"

"It's not a CIA safe house, and nobody else uses it but Thorpe. Thorpe put out that CIA bullshit to cover his ass."

Abrams said to Spinelli, "So what did you find, Sherlock? Radios, ciphers, Russian tea, and a signed copy of *Das Kapital?*"

"Well, radios anyway. Listen, we couldn't get a court order so I called Henly, the CIA liaison here, and fast-talked him. We went to the Lombardy and busted the fucking door down with fire axes. Christ, what a setup this clown has. At the top of a narrow staircase, on the third floor, there was a big black door made out of some synthetic. It was resilient, like rubber. We whacked away at it for about ten minutes. Henly had a hard-on, he was so sure he was going to find something weird behind that door. But the door wouldn't give. I had to call Emergency Service, who finally blew it with a half kilo of plastic."

Abrams heard Spinelli lighting a cigar. "And...?"

Spinelli said, "There was this huge attic room that looked like a cross between the flight deck of the *Enterprise* and the Marquis de Sade's rec room. There was a trail of blood all over the white tile floor leading to a walk-in refrigerator—like they have in butcher shops. But there wasn't prosciutto hanging in there. No, sir, this sucker is running a holding morgue."

Abrams glanced back over his shoulder and saw that the three were still deep in conversation and apparently not paying attention to him. He said softly, "Who was in there?"

Spinelli drew a long breath. "Some bad stuff in there, Tony. Three—count 'em: One, the missing Randolph Carbury, skull rearranged with our old friend the blunt instrument. Two, a middleaged woman identified by the Frog concierge as the housekeeper, apparent bullet wound right eye, exit rear right ear. And number three, Nicholas West, tortured, cause of death unknown. You still there?"

Abrams nodded several times, then cleared his throat. "Yes... yes..."

"Good. Now we're looking for Mr. Peter Thorpe. Any ideas?"

"No...well, maybe. He could be next door here."

Spinelli let out a whistle. "Well, that's it for the NYPD." Spinelli paused, then said, "I think the CIA wants to take it from here anyway."

"Listen, Dom.... Good work. Thanks for calling."

"No problem, Abrams. I owe you. For what, I don't know, but I'll pay you back. What's that wine you drink?"

"Villa Banfi Brunello di Montalcino, seventy-eight vintage. Go home, Dom. Seriously. Go home." Abrams hung up and turned around.

Van Dorn looked up from the conversation. "Anything for us, Abrams?"

Abrams put the telephone back on the desk. He hesitated, then said, "The police and the CIA went into Thorpe's apartment and found Colonel Carbury's body in a food locker up in the attic."

Katherine put her hand over her mouth and sank into a chair.

Van Dorn's voice was low and angry, "That son of a bitch. Wait until I get my hands on that—"

Ann interrupted, "Oh, don't take it personally, George. Peter has nothing personal against any of us. He's just bonkers." She looked at her sister. "Sorry, Kate. I should have warned you."

"You did. I wasn't listening."

Ann turned back to Abrams. "What else did your police friend say?" She held Abrams' eyes for a few seconds and Abrams understood that she understood. Ann turned away.

Abrams said, "The police and CIA are looking for Thorpe, of course. I told them to try next door."

Van Dorn snorted, "If Thorpe is there, he's home free. All the more reason to blow the place up." Van Dorn lit a cigar stub.

Katherine stood and drew a long breath. She said, "No, George. I agree with Tony that we can't do that." She turned to Abrams. "But we absolutely must get into that house. There may be something we can do there to stop this…" She hesitated, then said, "My father is in there…Peter may be in there…I think a personal confrontation—not an artillery barrage—is more in keeping with the spirit of our group."

Van Dorn said nothing.

Ann added, "As a practical and professional matter, I'd like to get my hands on that communications equipment. That may be the key to shut down their operation." She turned to Van Dorn. "No artillery, George. We go in there *mano a mano*."

Van Dorn nodded. "All right…."

Katherine put her hand on Abrams' arm. "All right?"

Abrams didn't think a choice between a mortar barrage and a commando raid was much of a choice, but he could see the point in the latter. He said, "Look, you don't need my approval. Go ahead. Put a bullet in Androv's fat belly if you can. But for God's sake, leave Mr. Van Dorn here on the telephone to try to head off this EMP blast."

Van Dorn drew heavily on his cigar, then spoke. "I won't waste time by making a show of telling you I won't send my people where I wouldn't go myself. During the war I sent hundreds of men and women out to meet their fate without me. Everyone has a job. Mine tonight is to stay here by the phone and the telex. And to hell with anyone who thinks badly of me."

Ann put her arms around Van Dorn's huge shoulders. "Oh, George, no one will think badly of you. If we fail next door, they'll come here and shoot you anyway."

Van Dorn smiled grimly as he stepped away from Ann and patted the holster under his pocket. "In 1945 I had a shoot-out with two KGB goons in the Soviet sector of Vienna. We all missed. I won't miss this time."

Ann smiled. "Well, George, it's never too late in life to redeem yourself." She added, "I'm going next door, of course, because I can work their communications equipment." She turned to Katherine. "You're going because you must." Ann looked at Abrams.

Abrams shrugged. "I'm going because I've got a screw loose."

Katherine smiled at him. "And your Russian is good, and you know the layout."

Ann said to Van Dorn, "You ought to break up this boring party, George."

Van Dorn shook his head. "Can't. That would look suspicious. The invites said until one A.M., and my neighbors somehow have access to that sort of information." He thought a moment, then added, "I'd like to keep them all here anyway."

Van Dorn looked at Katherine. "What do you carry?"

She nodded toward her bag. "Browning automatic, forty-five caliber."

Van Dorn reached into his pocket and produced the silver-plated .45-caliber bullet. "This is melodramatic, I know...but we were young then and given to theatrics. Nevertheless, the bullet is real."

She took it without a word and held it in her clenched hand.

Ann said, "Well, George, if we're not back by the time the lights go out, I trust you won't hesitate to fire your artillery."

"If I don't see you back here, or hear from you, EMP attack or not, by midnight, I'll let loose with the mortar." He looked at the three people. "All right?"

Everyone nodded.

There was a knock on the door and it opened. Marc Pembroke walked in.

Ann smiled at him. "You're looking fit, Marc. Fit enough to do a job?"

"Oh...hello, Ann. Long time." He turned to Van Dorn. "Tonight, is it?"

"Right." Van Dorn glanced at Abrams, then said to Pembroke, "There are children in the basement. They're innocent, of course. There are also women and diplomatic staff down there. Exercise some judgment."

Pembroke nodded. "A complication but not a problem. When do we shove off?"

Van Dorn looked at his watch. "Can you get ready in thirty minutes?"

"No, but I will."

"Then gather your people and my people, and bring them here."

"I'll fetch them now." Pembroke turned.

Van Dorn called out, "One more thing. It's time to settle some old scores, right here in this house. As we discussed."

Pembroke nodded and left quickly.

Van Dorn went behind his desk and picked up the telephone. He looked at the three people in the room as he dialed, and said, "In the last war, radar gave you as much as an hour's warning. Today, they're happy with fifteen minutes. I've given them a few hours. I hope to God they've been using the time constructively." He spoke into the receiver. "Hello, Van Dorn here. We've gone through fire and through water." He began speaking to the person on the other end.

Abrams walked over to the wall where the pictures hung in neat rows, and stared at them. Katherine came up beside him. She said, "We've actually had about forty years' warning, haven't we?"

Abrams didn't reply.

She said softly, "We haven't even gotten to know each other yet."

He glanced at her. "We have a rendezvous for breakfast tomorrow. The Brasserie."

She smiled. "Don't be late." She turned and walked back to her sister.

Abrams continued looking at the pictures, but his eyes were not focused on them. He thought that in many ways events had come full circle. He remembered his parents and their friends meeting in mean rooms, plotting and planning for the day when the workers would throw off their chains. He thought of George Van Dorn exchanging gunfire with the future enemy in the streets of Vienna. He contemplated the personality of James Allerton, a half century or more in the service of a foreign power, making him perhaps the country's longest-enduring traitor. He reflected on the Kimberly diary, and Arnold Brin's message, and other dead messages, and dead files, and dead matter from the living and the dead; and he thought that somehow the dead past had returned to bury the living and the unborn.

BOOK VII

The Assault

CHAPTER FIFTY-SIX

Claudia Lepescu moved quickly down the narrow path that cut diagonally across the face of the cliff. Above, on Van Dorn's wide lawn, she heard a man shout to her in a British accent. One of Marc Pembroke's men.

She kicked off her high-heeled shoes and continued down the dark path, faster now, yet fearful she would fall off the ledge. Behind her, she heard two sets of footsteps enter the path.

Claudia reached the bottom of the incline and ran down the laurel-covered slope, picking up speed until she stumbled and fell. The pursuing men heard her cry out and headed toward her. She sprang to her feet and continued until she came to the stockade fence.

Claudia put her palms against the fence and breathed deeply as she stared up at the jagged points of the pickets, silhouetted against the sky like dragon's teeth. She turned and rested her back against the fence.

The gusting north wind rustled the branches around her, and dark feathery clouds raced across the white face of the moon. To the northeast a bolt of lightning lit up the sky and she saw the shapes of the two men standing motionless in the distance. One of them called out, "Claudia! We won't hurt you! Claudia—" A roll of thunder shook the ground beneath her feet and drowned out his words.

She turned and moved unsteadily along the wooden wall, but there seemed to be no way through it. She had been told she could climb the fence from this side because of the horizontal braces nailed to the upright pickets, but the fence was nearly twice as tall as she, and it didn't seem possible. Behind her, she heard footsteps in the loose gravelly soil.

Claudia ran on another fifty yards and stopped to catch her breath. Her feet were cut and she could feel blood oozing into her panty hose. Her black knit dress was snagged in several places, and her face and arms were scratched and bruised. She felt rivulets of warm perspiration running down her body.

Suddenly two flashlight beams sliced through the dark air.

Claudia lowered herself quickly into a crouch behind a small bush. The light beams were searching systematically over the length of the fence and through the laurel behind her. She waited until they passed by, then stood, stepped back for a running start, and ran at the fence. Her feet and hands scrambled and searched for a hold, but the first horizontal brace was too high, and she slipped down, cedar splinters sliding into her skin.

"*There* you are." The footsteps approached.

Claudia felt tears forming in her eyes and salty sweat burning her lips. She called out, "I've got a gun."

The footsteps slowed and the lights went out. One of the men said to the other, "Easy now. Circle around."

Claudia stared up at the fence again. It looked like one of those stockade walls in the cowboy movies. This brought to mind a lasso.... She quickly slipped off her panty hose and groped along the ground until she found a good-sized stone. She dropped the stone into the toe of one of the legs, knotted it so it wouldn't slip out, and clenched the other foot of the hose. She stood, twirled the panty hose above her head, then cast it up at the fence. On the second attempt the stone-weighted toe fell between two pickets and she pulled on it to wedge it tighter, then began her ascent, hand over hand up the nylon rope, her bare feet planted on the fence. The nylon stretched tauter until there was no more slack in it and she feared it would snap.

Her feet found the first cross-brace; she rested a moment, then continued and reached the second brace.

The flashlights went on again; a beam found her and rested on her face. A man shouted, "Stop, or we'll shoot." She heard that awful metallic noise of a gun cocking in the night air.

With a last burst of energy, born of fear, she hoisted herself up to the pickets, feeling them dig into her chest and abdomen.

From two different directions she heard the wheezy coughs of silenced guns, followed by the sounds of bullets smacking and splintering the wood below her. The whole fence swayed from the impact. She let out a terrified cry, then closed her eyes and rolled gently over the pickets. Before she was even aware of a sense of falling, she felt the abrupt shock of the earth slapping against her face and chest, knocking the wind from her.

She lay still for some seconds, then sucked the air back into her lungs. She heard noises on the fence and realized she hadn't pulled the panty hose over with her, and they were using it.

She jumped to her feet and began running. Across the strip of partly cleared right-of-way, a patch of moonlight illuminated the dark low outline of the stone wall that bordered the Russian property. She heard the two men behind her and tried to run faster, heedless of the pain in her feet or the aches in her legs. Her clinging knit dress constricted the movement of her legs and she slowed long enough to pull the dress up and tuck the hem in her belt, then put on a burst of speed.

Pembroke's two men were gaining, but they were not shooting, calling, or using their flashlights; nor would they, she knew, this close to the Russian property. The stone wall lay twenty feet ahead, then ten, then it was on her suddenly. She thrust her hands out to meet its capstone and vaulted over, hardly breaking stride.

Claudia plunged headlong into the bush beyond the wall. The pace of running footsteps behind her slowed, then halted at the wall. She slowed her own pace and began picking her way more carefully through the rising terrain.

Suddenly, lights blazed on all sides of her and she heard a voice bark in harshly accented English, "Stop! Stop, we shoot!"

She froze.

"Hands on head!"

She did as she was told.

"Kneel!"

She knelt, feeling her bare knees settle on the damp, rotting vegetation. The lights hurt her eyes and she shut them, thinking to herself that perhaps they had orders to shoot her on the spot.

An unnaturally long time passed, then Claudia heard the sound of a revolver cocking.

Pembroke's two men, Cameron and Davis, stood quietly at the low stone wall. Davis raised a twenty-power Starlight scope and scanned the wooden terrain to his front. The thin light of the cloud-obscured moon and stars was electronically amplified to give a green-tinted picture. Davis adjusted the resolution and focus knobs. "There. They've intercepted her...but I can't make out what's happening."

Cameron said, "Let's go back." They turned from the stone wall and made their way through the no-man's-land toward the stockade fence. About five yards from the fence, they circled around a thick stand of boxwood and knelt.

Tony Abrams, also kneeling on one knee, regarded them in the dim light. Unlike conventional soldiers, he thought, whose uniforms and equipment had to serve in many terrains and circumstances, these men were very specifically outfitted for one thing: a short, quick night raid. Their clothing and equipment were patchworked shades of black and gray, their faces dark and inscrutable.

Cameron turned toward Abrams, "Bugs?"

Abrams glanced at the microphone detector on the ground. "No indication."

Cameron nodded.

Katherine, crouched beside Abrams, whispered to Cameron, "What happened?"

Cameron shrugged. "They grabbed her."

Davis added, "I couldn't tell how she was received."

Abrams said, "I hope they don't guess we've used the chase as a cover to get into position."

Katherine asked, "When do we cross over?"

Cameron glanced at his watch. "Very soon."

Davis spoke. "I saw at least five of them. If two escort her back to the house, then we've improved our odds a bit."

Abrams thought that three Russians were three Russians more than he'd care to meet tonight. He regarded Cameron and Davis. Even this close they were nearly invisible, but they exuded menace into the night. Professionally, their equipment impressed him: black hoods and bulletproof vests, first-rate and lightweight survival gear, and everything silenced and blackened.

Abrams glanced at Katherine beside him, similarly clad and equipped, her long blond hair tucked under the raised, hooded mask. She leaned over and whispered in his ear, "I feel confident. These are good men. We'll be fine."

Abrams smiled. "I'm sure we will be."

She kissed him on the cheek.

Cameron pulled a Very flare pistol from his belt and fired into the air. The flare exploded at a hundred feet into an incandescent burst of blue-white. Cameron said to Abrams and Katherine, "That's the signal that Claudia has crossed over. Van Dorn's pyro people should acknowledge and cover that flare with more of the same." As he spoke, a salvo of Very flares burst above them.

Davis said, "Fireworks are a good cover for signal flares. The noise gives us a bit of cover as well."

Cameron added, "Communication, command, and control are a bit dicey without wireless, but Ivan has got some damned good monitoring equipment and we don't want to get his guard up."

Abrams nodded, and thought, *If you think we've got a communications problem, wait until all the radios in North America go out.*

Abrams looked at Cameron and Davis in the dying glow of the flares. When he'd met them in the locker room in Van Dorn's basement, he'd recognized them from the encounter in the cemetery. He'd been told by Pembroke that they were both former Royal Commandos, both veterans of the Falklands war, recruited by Pembroke when their enlistments ran out. Cameron was a Scotsman, Davis an Englishman. Pembroke, according to Van Dorn, hired only former British soldiers: English, Scottish, Irish, and Welshmen.

Abrams looked up at the sky. The wind was blowing steadier now; a front was passing through. The gray wispy clouds scudded at high speed across the sky, moving north to south. The air was cooling and had the smell of rain. Toward the far northeast, across the Long Island Sound, toward Connecticut, the thunder rolled, and the lightning flashed at widely spaced intervals. He remembered what Van Dorn said at the final pep talk: "If the entire sky lights up in the West, you'll know it's happened. Your mission will no longer be a preventive strike but an avenging strike. Press on. Take as many with you as you can. There's no longer any reason to come home."

It was difficult for Abrams to reconcile the genteel public image of O'Brien, Van Dorn, and their friends with their propensity to engage in political murder and commando raids.

Katherine broke into his thoughts. "Tony, look."

Abrams followed her gaze upward. A huge rocket rose slowly into the air, its fiery plume oscillating as the wind caught it. Suddenly the entire rocket erupted into a huge fireball, unlike any display rocket Abrams had ever seen. The night air was shattered with the explosion, and Abrams even felt the shock waves and saw the trees shake. Seconds later, smaller rockets began bursting with loud reverberating explosions. Van Dorn's pole-mounted loudspeakers, about two hundred yards back, crackled, then Abrams heard the opening notes of "My Country 'tis of Thee," or, as his companions would call it, "God Save the Queen." Abrams thought, *Nice touch, George.*

Cameron and Davis stood, followed by Abrams and Katherine. Cameron spoke above the noise. "Single file. Ten-foot intervals. Look sharp, now. We're crossing over."

Abrams had never heard anyone actually say that except in British war movies. He glanced at Katherine. She winked and gave him a thumbs-up, then pulled her hood over her face.

The file moved out. Objective: the communications room in the attic of the Russian mansion. The distance was about half a mile, but Abrams thought the last few yards or so up the attic stairs—if they got that far—would be, as Cameron would say, a bit dicey.

He wondered if he'd meet Androv again. He wouldn't mind

meeting Alexei Kalin. Or Peter Thorpe, for that matter. He wondered how Katherine felt about the possibility of coming face-to-face with her father.

The Fates and Furies are loose tonight, he thought, borne along on the winds of the gathering storm. And all the currents of time and history are converging on that hilltop house beyond the next tree line.

As for himself, he remembered that the Fates led the willing and dragged the unwilling.

CHAPTER FIFTY-SEVEN

Karl Roth drove southbound on Dosoris Lane for a quarter of a mile, then signaled to pull into the driveway of the Russian estate.

The traffic patrolman recognized Roth and his catering van and waved him in. Roth turned right and bumped across the sidewalk between rows of police barriers toward the guardhouse, which was about thirty feet up the drive. He approached the small lighted house, bringing the van to a halt abreast of the front door. His hands and legs were shaking badly.

Two Russian guards, wearing sidearms, appeared farther up the drive and stood in a blocking position. Roth shut off his headlights and rolled down his window. From the guardhouse door emerged a man in civilian clothes. The man stood on the stoop a few feet from the van. Roth cleared his throat and greeted the man in English. "How are you, Bunin?"

Bunin replied, also in English, "What are you doing here, Roth? They said later."

Roth stuck his head out the window. "I had to come now."

Bunin leaned forward and rested his hands on the window frame. He peered into the cab. "Where is your wife? They said she would be with you."

"She's still at Van Dorn's."

The Russian stared at Roth. "You stink of whisky, and you look terrible."

Roth didn't reply.

Bunin said in a whisper, "They have us on full alert. Do you know anything?"

Roth shrugged. "You think they tell me anything, Bunin?"

Bunin made a contemptuous sound, then said, "What do you have for us?"

Roth licked his lips and looked toward the guardhouse. Through the window was a young man in uniform sitting at the desk, writing. The two guards on the drive were a few feet from the van. He glanced in his sideview mirror and noticed that the gates and road weren't visible from this angle in the drive.

"Roth!"

Karl Roth flinched. "Yes...yes, I have blinis, caviar, and sour cream. The rear doors."

Bunin signaled the two guards and they moved quickly to the rear of the van.

Marc Pembroke crouched to the side of the left-hand door, which was locked. He held a pistol pointed at the back of Roth's head. A canvas tarp in the center of the floor covered a stack of boxes, and between the boxes lay two of Pembroke's men, Sutter and Llewelyn. In a large built-in side chest lay Ann Kimberly.

The unlocked right-hand door opened, and the two guards seized the thermal containers of food.

Pembroke glanced quickly to his right. One man's arm was less than three feet from his foot. Pembroke looked at Roth and saw he was observing the Russian guards and Pembroke through his rearview mirror. If Roth was going to betray them, it would be now. But Roth seemed paralyzed with terror.

The rear door slammed shut, and Pembroke heard the guards' footsteps retreating toward the guardhouse.

Bunin said to Roth, "Wait here. I must call the house and see if they want you so early."

Roth didn't reply.

Pembroke whispered, "Now."

Llewelyn and Sutter threw the tarp off as Ann Kimberly emerged from the chest. Pembroke threw open both rear doors and the four black-clad people jumped to the drive, tore around the side of the van, and burst into the small front room of the guardhouse.

The two Russian guards still carrying the thermal containers glanced back over their shoulders, their mouths and eyes wide open. The young uniformed man behind the desk stood and stared. Bunin, his left hand on the wall telephone, stood beside the desk. Ann shouted in Russian, "Don't move!"

Bunin's right hand shot inside his jacket.

Pembroke fired a short burst from his silenced M-16. The bullets slammed into Bunin, throwing him back against the wall. He stood for a split second, took a step forward and toppled, falling against the legs of the young man who had his hands in the air. The two guards had dropped the thermal containers and they'd burst open, scattering blinis, sour cream, and caviar over the wooden planking. Bunin seemed to be staring at the mess, watching the crimson tide of his blood creeping toward the food.

Ann gave a series of sharp orders. Within minutes the three surviving Russians were lying in a rear room, bound and gagged. Sutter stood beside the van and kept an eye on Roth and the driveway. Llewelyn checked Bunin's pulse, found there was none, and sat Bunin up behind the desk so that any official car driving by would see someone in the window.

Pembroke found the logbook in a desk drawer and took it. The four people moved quickly back to the van. Pembroke said to Roth, "That was a fine performance, Karl. I suppose the schnapps helped a bit. Headlights on. Move!"

Roth's shaking hands turned on the headlights and put the van in gear.

Ann knelt beside Pembroke and scanned the logbook with a penlight. "There's a commo check and sit rep every thirty or forty minutes. Bunin entered the last one ten minutes ago, so they may not be missed for a while."

Pembroke nodded.

No one spoke as the van moved slowly up the S-curved gravel drive. Sutter watched out the rear-door windows. Llewelyn peered over the seat and watched out the windshield. Ann flipped a few pages of the log and said, "Peter Thorpe was logged in about two hours ago. Still in there."

Pembroke nodded again.

Ann glanced at Pembroke, then said, "Orders from Androv to arrest Karl and Maggie Roth when they arrive." She winked at Pembroke and he smiled, then turned to Roth. "Did you hear that?"

Roth nodded but said nothing.

Ann turned a page. "Oh...here's something...the officer of the guard comes around at random intervals and signs the log. Last time he was at the gate was...almost an hour ago. He may come by at any—"

Roth made a sound and everyone turned. Through the windshield they saw a single headlight shining on the trees around the bend. Pembroke barked at Roth, "Keep moving until you get within ten feet, then stop." Pembroke and the other three got down behind the front seats. The interior of the van was illuminated by the oncoming headlight.

Pembroke put his pistol to the back of Roth's neck. "What is it?"

Roth's voice was quavering. "It's the guard officer. He rides in an open Lambretta...with a driver—"

Pembroke said, "Don't give him room to pass."

Roth nodded and felt the silencer rub the nape of his neck. He centered the vehicle on the narrow drive and came to a stop. The Lambretta also stopped. The driver called out in Russian.

Ann whispered to Pembroke, "He wants to know what the hell Roth thinks he's doing."

Pembroke said to Roth, "All right, back up slowly and let him pass on the right side."

Roth put the van in reverse and began edging back. The Russian driver gunned the small three-wheeled vehicle and headed toward the space on the right between the van and the stone-bordered drive.

Pembroke opened the sliding door on the right of the van as the small vehicle with the surrey top came into view. The driver sat in the single front seat holding the handlebars, the guard officer sat in the back double seat. Both men heard and saw the door slide open and turned. As the Lambretta drew abreast of the open door, the two Russians stared up into the muzzles of two automatic rifles, not three feet away. The driver let out a startled cry. Both automatic rifles spit fire and coughed. The driver was thrown out of the open vehicle, still grabbing the handlebars and taking the unbalanced Lambretta over with him. The guard officer scrambled from under the Lambretta and stood, clutching his chest. He stumbled toward the trees, staggered, and fell.

Pembroke and Llewelyn jumped down from the van, administered the coup de grace to the Russians with a single shot to their heads, then dragged them into the trees. Sutter helped them right the Lambretta and roll it through the tree line. The three men jumped back in the van. "Move out."

Roth put the van in gear and the wheels crunched slowly through the gravel.

Ann broke the silence. "I suppose we couldn't have let them go past."

Pembroke regarded her for a moment. "No, they were going right for the guardhouse."

She said, "We could have captured them."

Pembroke replied curtly, "We're running a bit late."

Llewelyn added, "That was a break to run into them. There'll be other guard posts put out of business tonight and we don't want a mobile officer of the guard running about checking his posts."

Ann didn't reply.

Pembroke said to her, "This is new to you, I know. Later, if things don't work out for us, you'll wish we'd taken a few more with us. This is a bloody awful business. But it *is* a business."

The van completed the final turn in the rising S-curved drive and the Russian mansion came into view, silhouetted against the turbulent sky. A few windows were lit on the first and second floors, and all the attic gables were lit. Pembroke remarked, "Ivan is working late tonight."

Sutter turned from the rear-door windows and said, "We'll put their lights out and lay them down to sleep."

Pembroke nodded, then said, "How are you holding up, Karl?"

Roth drew a deep breath and nodded, but said nothing. He glanced at his dashboard clock and wondered when they would begin dying of the poison. He hoped it was soon.

The van entered the long forecourt and turned toward the house.

Pembroke said, "Ladies and gentlemen, before you is Killenworth. We'll stop here awhile and stretch our legs. Don't forget to take your rifles with you."

Roth shook his head. *Madness.*

CHAPTER FIFTY-EIGHT

Tom Grenville considered himself a good company man, and he understood that in the oblique style of corporate communication, suggestions from superiors were in fact orders, much like when he was a lieutenant JG in the Navy. *The captain's wish is your command.*

So when George Van Dorn had commented that golf was not a sport he approved of, Tom Grenville had given it up, though he loved golf.

But George was not really an unfair or arbitrary person. He had a constructive alternative: Guns, not golf clubs, he declared, belonged in the hands of a man. Consequently, Grenville had taken up skeet shooting, hunting, and competition target shooting.

Then, one day at lunch about a year ago, Grenville recalled, O'Brien and Van Dorn had asked him if he had ever considered parachuting. Grenville had no more considered parachuting than he'd considered shooting Niagara Falls in a barrel, but he'd answered enthusiastically in the affirmative.

When the moment of truth had come, Grenville had some understandable reservations about his first jump. He realized, however, that almost all the old OSS crew were former paratroopers, and many, like O'Brien, still jumped. Formerly closed doors would be open to a young man who could share a jump with Patrick O'Brien and his friends.

Van Dorn had seemed pleased, and so had O'Brien and the other senior partners in the firm. Grenville now knew why.

He looked around the dimly lit cabin of the big Sikorsky amphibious rescue helicopter. The jumpmaster, Barney Farber, was an old friend of O'Brien's and Van Dorn's, and Farber's company, one of the Long Island defense-related electronics firms, actually owned the former Navy Sikorsky.

Two more old boys sat on the bench opposite him: Edgar Johnson, a recently retired paratroop general, and Roy Hallis, a semi-retired CIA agent.

This entire operation, Grenville understood, had been planned and was being controlled by the old boys. And it would not be complete without a few of them along for the actual flight. Grenville glanced at Johnson and Hallis in the weak light. They were both World War II vets, but they didn't look much past sixty. This was their last mission, their last jump, he thought. Perhaps it was the last time the OSS alumni would directly participate in an operation. Even they got too old to make combat jumps. Grenville found himself staring at them. They looked psychologically prepared for a firefight, which was more than Grenville could say for himself.

In fact, he felt queasy. The Sikorsky, sitting on its pontoons in the middle of Long Island Sound, was rocking badly. The wind had picked up and waves slapped against the hull. Grenville had never been seasick on a parachute jump before.

Next to Grenville sat two of Pembroke's people: Collins and Stewart. They looked particularly gruesome in black, he thought.

Stewart, sitting next to him, said, "Have you ever done a night jump, lad?"

Grenville had done one at O'Brien's suggestion. He answered, "A few."

Stewart said, "It's easier from a stationary helicopter."

"Yes—"

"Except in weather like this. A fixed-wing aircraft will hold fairly steady. A chopper can roll and yaw."

Grenville nodded unhappily.

Stewart went on, "It's like trying to jump off a pitching boat. Be careful you don't collide with the pontoon. Saw that happen to a lad once in the South Atlantic."

Grenville nodded again. The South Atlantic, he'd learned, meant the Falklands. Stewart seemed intimately knowledgeable about every mishap and calamity that could befall a human being.

Stewart added, "Broke his neck."

Grenville felt his stomach heave, but took comfort in the fact that the greasepaint hid the true color his face had probably turned.

Collins lit a cigar and the smoke filled the cabin. He spoke in a strong Irish brogue. "This wind'll blow yer arse all over the feckin' terrain if ye pop yer chute too soon, lad."

Grenville nodded miserably.

Collins advised, "Wait till the last second, then give it another few seconds to be sure, then say a quick Hail Mary and pull yer cord." He laughed.

The jumpmaster put his hands over his headphones, listened, then spoke into his mouthpiece. "Roger." He stood and said, "The word is go." He ducked into the cockpit, tapped the pilot, and gave a thumbs-up. The Sikorsky's idling engine revved with a deafening roar.

Grenville felt the big bird straining to break water, then the rocking stopped as the hull and pontoons cleared the turbulent sea. The rocking was replaced by a swaying motion as the Sikorsky ascended into the wind. Grenville turned his head and peered through the large square window behind him. They were already at a hundred-feet altitude, but his stomach was still at sea level.

Stewart spoke over the roar of the engine. "Damned moon's three-quarter full and the clouds are too thin to mask it. They'll spot us for sure, Tom."

Grenville pressed his fingers against his eyes.

Stewart added ominously, "I could do without the damned lightning, too. Ever seen a chutist hit by lightning, Tom?"

"Not recently."

"What's that, lad? Can't hear you!"

Grenville stared at him for a few seconds, then shouted, "I said I love to jump at night in a fucking storm! I love it!"

Collins roared with delight, "Oh, Tom, me boy, we'll make a commando of you before the night's out."

Grenville stood and moved to the door. He held on to the airframe and stared out into the night as the helicopter rose higher through the turbulence. He didn't want to be a commando. He wanted to be a senior partner in the firm, and he was willing to work hard to achieve his goal. But sometimes Van Dorn and O'Brien asked too much. A night jump into an armed enemy position was really too much.

CHAPTER FIFTY-NINE

Joan Grenville paced around the small cellar room, lit brightly with rows of fluorescent tubes. Above was an enclosed tennis court that had once been part of Killenworth but now belonged to the local YMCA. A high chain link fence, topped with barbed wire, separated the Christians from the atheists.

Joan remembered that Tom had mentioned that the FBI supposedly headquartered themselves in the Y's main building, but she'd seen no sign of anyone but the OSS.

Stanley Kuchik, sprawled on a large crate, watched her pacing. "You scared, Mrs. Grenville?"

She shot a glance at him. "For the tenth fucking time, call me Joan, and for the fifth fucking time, yes, I'm scared."

Stanley had never heard an older woman swear like this one did. In fact, there was a lot about Joan Grenville that interested him. He looked at her out of the corner of his eye. The black body-suit fitted like skin. He said, "Hey, you can stay here if you want. I can handle this."

Joan gritted her teeth. "Stanley...stop treating me like...an adolescent. I am a grown woman. I can do anything you can do, and better."

"Sure, Mrs.—okay, Joan." Stanley smiled at her. "I guess this is a two-man job."

Joan pressed her fingertips to her temples. "I'm getting a headache."

Stanley asked, "Are you one of Van Dorn's secret agents?"

She lowered herself onto a bench. "I guess I am now." She put her head in her hands, remembering Van Dorn's blackmail threats. And Tom, the jerk, had just sat there.

But then Van Dorn had come up to her and put his hands on her shoulders, and said, "Joan, we both know you wouldn't do what I'm asking because of threats. But your country is in danger. You're needed." He explained briefly, then asked, "Will you help your country?"

Stanley broke into her thoughts. "How did you get hooked up with this crazy bunch?"

She looked at him. "My country needs me."

Stanley hesitated, then said, "I do it for kicks. This is my tenth mission."

Joan looked at him dubiously, and the word *bullshit* was on her lips, but then it struck her that her life might well depend on this horny adolescent. She gave him a look that conveyed wonder and awe. "That's incredible."

Stanley flushed. "Stick close to me and I'll get you back okay."

You damned well better. She gave him a wide smile. "Okay." Joan reflected on what Van Dorn had told her, and it sounded very scary. She did not want the party to end. She was not committed to much in life, but she was deeply committed to fighting for the continuation of the party. Patriotism, she reasoned, came in many forms.

Stanley glanced at the military watch they'd given him, then tugged at the black body-suit. It was some kind of stretch material, and it looked like something a ballet dancer would wear, but the guy who outfitted him said it was a cat-burglar outfit, so maybe it was okay. Stanley felt the pistol tucked into the elastic pouch on his abdomen. He said, "Have you ever shot anyone?"

Joan came out of her thoughts. "What...? No, certainly not." She added, "But I'm capable of it." She thought she'd like to shoot Tom, George, and Marc, not necessarily in that order.

The door at the top of the stairs opened and two sets of footsteps echoed on the concrete stairs. Stanley drew his pistol. Joan snapped, "Put that away."

A man and a woman appeared, both well advanced in years, but with quick movements and alert expressions. They wore expensive warm-up suits, but Joan knew they weren't looking for tennis partners. The woman, Claire Goodwin, advanced on Joan and extended her hand. "How are you, Joan?"

Joan stood and took the older woman's hand. "Just fine, Claire."

Claire said, "I didn't see much of you at George's."

"I was lying down upstairs."

"Poor dear. Do you know Gus Bergen?"

Joan took the man's hand. "Yes, we've met." Bergen, she recalled, had been on the ill-fated Hanoi mission with Tom's father during the war.

Bergen said, "What's Tom up to these days?"

"He's taken up parachuting."

Bergen smiled and turned to Stanley, who was standing. "Hello, young man."

Stanley shook hands with Bergen and Claire. Claire said, "I've heard some good things about you."

Stanley mumbled something and glanced at Joan.

Joan had heard some good things about Claire, too, like the fact that Claire had slept with half the German diplomatic corps in Switzerland during the war. For God and country, of course. Joan thought she should have been given an assignment like that instead of this. She felt ill-used.

The four people spoke for a few minutes, then Bergen looked at his watch. He said, "Well, it's time to get moving."

The small room fell silent.

Bergen continued, "You've both been briefed on what to do inside there. Now I'm going to show you how to *get* inside."

Bergen moved to the far wall and pointed to a round hole near the top of the concrete foundation. "That's an old service conduit that runs from here to the main house. It once contained the pipe from the mansion's steam plant, water pipes, wiring, and such. Since the partition of the estate, the YMCA provides the utilities for this tennis building, of course."

Stanley stared up at the opening, which he hadn't noticed before. It looked no bigger than a pizza, large size.

Claire said, "It's free of pipes now. Gus had to use midgets to do the work." She added, "Gus is a member of the local Y board."

Stanley nodded appreciatively.

Joan thought, *Member of the YMCA. Midgets. Conduit to the Russian house. Typically bizarre.* She stared up at the opening and said, "There are still wires coming out of there."

Bergen replied, "Cables, actually. You see, it's several hundred yards to the basement of the main house, all upgrade. Nearly an impossible crawl. So I've installed an electric pulley."

Stanley smiled. These old dudes had it together.

Bergen and Claire Goodwin briefed them for a few minutes, then Bergen said, "Any questions?"

Stanley shook his head.

Joan asked, "How are you so sure it opens into an unused room?"

Bergen looked at Stanley. "You were in the boiler room once, weren't you, son?"

Stanley nodded. "Nobody there then."

Joan shrugged sulkily.

Bergen looked at her. "You don't have to go, of course."

Joan Grenville glanced at Stanley. He was frightened too, but his budding male ego would propel him into that black hole, with or without her, as surely as if he'd been forced into it at gunpoint. She said, "I do have to go, of course. So let's go."

Bergen wheeled a painter's scaffold to the foundation. "Stanley."

Stanley Kuchik pulled his black hood over his head. Bergen said, "Good luck." Stanley climbed to the top of the scaffold, where he saw two small flexible trolleys. He peered into the black, endless tube for some seconds, then lay on his back and positioned the trolley beneath his buttocks. He reached up and held the pulley cable with his gloved hands. "Okay."

He heard the motor hum and the cable began traveling, pulling him with the trolley beneath him toward the round opening. *Like a torpedo,* he thought, *being rolled into its firing tube.*

Joan Grenville said to Bergen quietly, "You must be awfully desperate or insensitive to send that kid on a mission like this."

Bergen replied coolly, "He's seventeen. I know men who saw combat at seventeen."

Joan shrugged. "Well, women and children first." She climbed up the scaffold and peered inside the small conduit opening. She called in, "Do you have room for one more?"

"Sure," Stanley's voice echoed.

Joan looked down at Claire Goodwin and Gus Bergen. She hesitated, then said, "Look, I know this is important. If anything happens to us, remember, we volunteered. So don't feel bad."

Claire replied, "We *would* feel bad if something happened, though not guilty. Good luck."

Joan looked at them. *Tough old birds.* Old OSS. They were all screwy. She took a deep breath and lay down on the trolley, then reached up and grabbed the cable with her gloved hands. "Ready."

The electric motor hummed again and the cable dragged her into the dark tube. She listened to the sounds of the rubber trolley wheels on the clay pipe, the distant hum of the motor, the creaking of the pulleys, and the rubbing of her shoulders against the sides of the pipe. She cleared her throat and called out softly, "Stanley?"

"Yeah."

"How are you doing?"

"Okay."

Joan observed, "This sucks."

Stanley laughed weakly. "Beats crawling."

Neither spoke again. The light from the opening faded and the sound of the electric motor grew fainter.

Joan knew she could let go of the cable anytime and the trolley would roll her back to the basement of the tennis building. But she knew she wouldn't.

Another few minutes, she thought, *then we'll be there.* She'd always been curious about that house anyway.

CHAPTER SIXTY

George Van Dorn stood at the bay window and watched the skyrockets rise from his empty swimming pool in the distance. He picked up one of three newly installed army field phones on the wide bay sill and cranked it.

Don LaRosa, the senior pyrotechnician, answered.

Van Dorn said, "How are we fixed for rockets, Mr. LaRosa?"

"About three hundred left, Mr. Van Dorn."

"All right, I want airbursts low over the target. I don't want the terrain lit too much, but I want noise cover."

"Okay. Hey, did you hear the motherfucker rocket blow?"

"I believe so."

"Scared the shit out of your wife's cat, Mr. Van Dorn."

Van Dorn glanced at Kitty standing across the room. "I'm happy to hear that, Don. Listen, is the tube ready?"

"Ready any time you are."

"Plan for midnight. I want a sixty-to-eighty-second time on target—no fewer than twenty rounds of high explosive. Then, when you've made kindling wood out of the target, I want about five rounds of Willy Peter to finish off whatever's left."

Don LaRosa repeated the fire mission.

Van Dorn added, "I have an amphibious chopper on station to lift your people and your tube out of here immediately. You'll land at the Atlantic City pier. All arrangements made."

"Sounds super."

"Speak to you later."

Van Dorn hung up. It *would* be super, he thought, if Mr. LaRosa and his friends could spend the night gambling and whoring until dawn. He wouldn't half mind joining them.

Kitty said, "What *is* Willy Peter, George?"

"Just a military expression, dear." He added, "Actually, it's white phosphorus. It burns."

"Oh. That's awful. Such a beautiful house."

"War is hell, Kitty."

"It's so *destructive*."

"Yes, that too." He walked to a stereo stack unit and turned up the volume. He listened to the sprightly notes of George M. Cohan's "I'm a Yankee Doodle Dandy," which was being blared out from his loudspeakers on the polo field. Van Dorn hummed along as he bobbed his head to the music.

Kitty said, "George, are you really going to blow up those awful people next door?"

Van Dorn turned off the sound. "What? Oh, only if my ground attack fails. Have you arranged things with Dr. Frank and Dr. Poulos?"

"Yes, they're in the basement aid station, setting up. Oh, Jane Atkins and Mildred Fletcher are assisting. They're so thrilled to be able to lend a hand. They were both WAC nurses."

"Well, I'll try not to disappoint them, Kitty. If there are no casualties, I'll shoot myself in the foot."

"Belle La Ponte is a psychiatrist. Should I get her?"

"Why not? We're all crazy."

"I mean, she's an MD—"

"Fine, Kitty. Are the medical supplies satisfactory?"

"I believe so. Dr. Frank seemed very impressed."

Van Dorn nodded distractedly. He tried to think of what else ought to be done. He turned to one of the other two men in his study, Colonel William Osterman, a man who had been a young lieutenant in OSS's London headquarters staff. Van Dorn said, "Phase one ought to be completed by now."

Osterman looked up from the architectural plans and aerial photos of the Russian estate spread out on Van Dorn's desk. Osterman said, "I would think so. The problem with this plan, George, is that it relies on near perfect timing without radio contact. If one group gets into a mess, the other three groups will get into a mess."

Van Dorn replied, "Pembroke and his people are very good, Bill. They're used to this sort of hit-and-run without communications. Sometimes I think they've developed telepathy."

Wallis Baker, a senior partner in the firm, appeared from behind the screened telex alcove carrying a message. "This is a rather long communication from the Joint Chiefs, George."

Van Dorn motioned him to the desk. "Get it deciphered immediately."

Baker was already behind the desk with the code book.

The telephone rang and Van Dorn saw it was his published number. He ignored it, but no one else in the house seemed to be picking it up either. Then he realized who it might be and answered it. "Van Dorn residence."

"Oh," said the voice, "Mr. Van Dorn."

Van Dorn looked at the other two men, then at Kitty, then said into the telephone, "Mr. Androv."

"Yes. I am flattered that you recognized my voice."

"I don't know many people with Russian accents. Why are you calling me at this hour, Androv? It's not polite to call people this late."

Androv said a bit sharply, "As a man trying to get some sleep, I don't care for your music or your fireworks. Do you know your rockets are exploding dangerously close to our house?"

"How close is that?"

Androv put on an aggrieved tone. "Mr. Van Dorn, as Community Relations Officer, I have attempted to maintain good relations with my neighbors—"

"No, you haven't, Androv. I have it on good authority that your people never throw the tennis balls back."

Androv made a sound of exasperation. "Oh, what does that matter now?"

Van Dorn smiled. He was mildly amused by Androv's de rigueur phone call. More importantly, the call most probably meant that neither Pembroke's team nor the team with Katherine and Abrams had been discovered. For his part, Androv had discovered that Van Dorn was definitely at home. There was intelligence to be gathered even from a banal phone conversation. Van Dorn said, "This is our holiday, Mr. Androv. Certainly the protocols of diplomacy demand some respect for the traditions of the host country, sir."

"Yes, yes. But that music—I must respectfully request of you—"

"I'm not taking requests tonight. You get what's on the tape. I am not a disc jockey, Mr. Androv."

"No, no. I mean I must request that you cease that loud music, or I must call the police."

"I think you're being unreasonable."

"I am not. My small staff here is very upset, and my dogs are extremely nervous and high-strung—"

"Then buy well-adjusted dogs, Viktor. Or get them to a shrink."

Androv ignored this and said, "At what hour may I expect the music and fireworks to cease?"

"At midnight. I promise you, you will not be bothered after midnight."

"Thank you, Mr. Van Dorn. Have a pleasant evening."

"And you, Mr. Androv." Van Dorn hung up and looked at the people in the room. "The nerve of that man calling to complain about my party when he has to stay up anyway to wait for a nuclear detonation."

Osterman and Baker smiled.

Kitty said, "You were rude to him again, George."

Van Dorn looked at his wife. "Your standards of etiquette are extravagant, Kitty." He added, "You'd have required black tie and ushers at the Crucifixion."

"Still, I think, as Mr. Churchill did, that if you're going to shoot a man, it costs nothing to be polite."

Van Dorn smiled at his wife. "You're quite right."

She announced, "I must go, but before I do, I want to tell you, George, that I absolutely will not have your Mr. Pembroke or Joan Grenville in this house again." She paused, then added, "If they are

wounded, I will make an exception. Good evening, George. Gentlemen." She turned and left.

There was a silence in the room, then Colonel Osterman looked
at his watch. "This is damned frustrating without radio contact."

Baker added, "They could all be dead or captured, and we
wouldn't know."

Van Dorn replied, "Which is the reason for the mortar. The next
call I get from Androv's telephone ought to be from one of our people. If I don't hear by midnight, then *my* automatic launch response
goes into effect. Then, as I said, Viktor Androv will be bothered by
me no more."

CHAPTER SIXTY-ONE

Viktor Androv sat at the desk in his office. The former chapel was dark, lit only by a shaded lamp whose light fell on a nearby stained-glass window.

Androv stared at the religious depiction: the inhabitants of Sodom forcing their way into Lot's house in an attempt to abduct the two beautiful angels, then the angels sending out a blinding flash of celestial light and the Sodomites turning away. He remarked, "Some say the angels were extraterrestrials, and they destroyed Sodom and Gomorrah with a nuclear device."

Henry Kimberly sat back in the green leather chair. "Four thousand years from now, who knows how tonight will be interpreted."

Androv leaned across his desk. "Tonight will be interpreted the way the party wishes it to be interpreted. Just as the events of the Bible were interpreted as the priests and rabbis wished them to be interpreted."

Kimberly said, "There will be no party four thousand years from now, Viktor, and you know that. Neither will there be priests or rabbis." Kimberly lit a cigarette. "However, as you suggest, the party *will* write world history for at least the next thousand years."

Androv shrugged. He stood and went to the side window and threw it open. The north wind entered the chapel and ruffled the papers on his desk. Van Dorn's loudspeakers could be heard in the distance, and Androv raised his voice as he spoke. "I have given the order that anyone who opens a window or door after eleven thirty will pay with his life." He fell silent a moment, then said, "It's a strange phenomenon, this EMP. Like a supernatural miasma, it can enter through keyholes and cracks, through spaces around the doors and windows. A little of it can do a great deal of damage." He added in a confident voice, "But this house has been inspected a hundred times. It's as tight as a submarine. It could float." He laughed.

Kimberly didn't reply.

Androv looked up into the northern sky. "Molniya is hurtling toward us from the dark reaches of space."

"Molniya?"

"The satellite that will deliver the nuclear blast. The courier told me. Very ingenious."

Kimberly nodded appreciatively, then said, "What time?"

Androv continued staring out the window as he replied, "It will reach its low point somewhere over Nebraska a few minutes after midnight."

Kimberly watched the smoke rise from his cigarette, then said, "What else did the courier tell you?"

Androv replied, "The Premier sends his good wishes to us and to you particularly." He added, "The Premier also informs us that news of the Stroke is being disseminated now among key people in Moscow." Androv nodded to himself and said, "Unlike the preparation for a nuclear war, this was so simple that only a few people had to be told. And only a few people had to act. Only one person has to push a nuclear detonator button, and that will be the Premier himself."

Kimberly stood and walked to Androv. He looked through the window out over the distant tree line. A faint aura of light from Van Dorn's house outlined the rolling treetops against the blackening sky. Kimberly said, "You know, Viktor, George Van Dorn and I went to the same army schools. The philosophy of the American army is aggressive, not defensive. They are great believers in the spoiling raid, the preemptive attack, the commando strike—like the British." He gave Androv a sidelong glance. "You ought to deal with Van Dorn before he deals with you."

Androv pulled the windows shut and walked to his desk. He pushed a button on a console and George Van Dorn's voice came out of the speaker.

Kimberly listened silently.

Androv said, "That is a recording of George Van Dorn calling the Pentagon. Since he has warned them of our plans, and believes the situation is under control, he is unlikely to try anything against us on his own."

Androv pushed another button and a woman's voice came on. Androv said, "That is your daughter, Ann."

Kimberly said nothing.

Androv continued, "She's speaking to the National Security Agency. About Molniya."

Kimberly listened to Ann's voice for a few seconds, then walked to the desk and pushed the stop button. He turned to Androv. "How did they find out?"

Androv shrugged. "I assume they started with the premise that we wish to destroy them and worked backward. How many solutions are there to a problem? They asked themselves, 'How would I destroy America with little or no damage to myself?' They arrived at the answer we arrived at."

Kimberly nodded slowly.

Androv continued, "So you see, Henry, I haven't underestimated Van Dorn or his organization. We know they long ago put away the dagger and use only the cloak now. Van Dorn learned something and he called his friends in the military to deal with it. He will not come here with guns blazing."

Kimberly did not reply for some time, then said, "But he *has* warned them, Androv. The Americans have an automatic launch response under certain—"

Androv held up his hand. "I know. But let me continue, please. You see, in this country almost every long-distance telephone call is relayed by microwave stations. This is very convenient for us because this house sits in the middle of what is known as 'Microwave Alley.' We intercept these microwave calls and listen to the diplomats in New York, as well as the Long Island and Connecticut defense contractors. Every call made to a government agency in Washington is monitored here. Van Dorn, of course, took precautions against this. He installed a fiber optic telephone line that runs into the main AT&T underground cables. His phone, he believes, is virtually untappable, which is why he speaks so freely over it."

Androv looked at Kimberly. "However, because these secure lines are so few, the telephone exchange has the ability to switch a call to the microwave station. Therefore, if one were to pass a sum of money to a technician at the main telephone exchange, it would be possible to have Mr. Van Dorn's calls rerouted as microwave calls without his being informed that the call was not secure. That's how we were able to listen—"

Kimberly interjected, "That won't do you much good now. The Pentagon is alerted."

Androv smiled. "It would also be possible to reroute these calls to a place other than the Pentagon, Henry. To have them rerouted here, for instance. In fact, your friend has not been speaking to the Pentagon at all, but to Nikhita Tulov in the attic, who has spent a good number of years of his young life learning how to think and talk like a Pentagon staff officer."

Kimberly's face broke into a smile in return. "*Touché,* Viktor."

Androv bowed his head in acknowledgment. "We had to let your daughter's call through because we weren't prepared to imitate anyone at the NSA. But we were able at least to listen." He added, "We've also managed to intercept Van Dorn's bothersome telex."

Androv stared down at his desk and said, "Your daughter is also quite bothersome." He glanced at Kimberly. "I don't mean to belabor this issue, but now that she is here in America, I must ask you..."

Kimberly waved his hand in a gesture of annoyance. "Oh, do what you want, Viktor. Stop bothering me with these things. If you have a personal grudge against her, act accordingly. If you don't, then let the state apparatus deal with her as if she were any one of the ten million people on the list of enemies." Kimberly walked to the door. "I'll see you upstairs later." He opened the door of the chapel.

Androv called out, "One more thing, Henry."

Kimberly turned. "Yes?"

"The courier. He said something which may interest you." Androv walked toward the door and stood close to Kimberly. He stared at him for a few seconds, then said, "Tonight...Talbot Three will be here tonight."

Kimberly nodded. "I suspected that if Talbot Three was alive and in this country, then he—or she—would be seeking sanctuary from the Stroke. I thought we might meet tonight."

Androv looked at Kimberly. "Do you have any idea who it could be?"

Kimberly shook his head, then said, "Whoever it is, it will be someone I knew then."

"Yes, I'm sure of that. One of your blue-blooded Ivy League friends. We will have a reunion in the White House. President Kimberly, Secretary of State Allerton, and Chief of American State Security—who?"

Kimberly's expression remained impassive. He said, "There's no use speculating. We'll see who shows up."

Androv nodded slowly. "Yes. And we don't even know how he, or she, will come—by land, sea, or air. But it will be interesting to see who arrives at our doorstep tonight."

"Most interesting." Kimberly turned and left.

Claudia Lepescu felt the pistol caressing the nape of her neck as she knelt in the damp earth, her head bowed. A guard pulled back on the leash of a German shepherd that was growling ominously. Another man held a radio and was making a report. The officer in charge, standing in front of her, spoke loudly in English and it startled her. "Who are you?"

She drew a short breath. "Claudia Lepescu. I work for Alexei Kalin."

The Russian officer moved his flashlight over her body, then shined it full on her face. "You are not American?"

"I am Rumanian."

"What do you want here?"

"Asylum. Sanctuary."

"Why?"

"They are after me—"

"*Who* is after you?"

Claudia said sharply in Russian, "You have all the information you need. Take me to Kalin at once, or it will go badly for you." As soon as the words were out, she realized she shouldn't have abused him in Russian so his men could understand. She waited.

The Russian did nothing for some time, then his hand flew out and struck her across the face.

Claudia cried out and put her hand to her cheek.

The Russian barked, "Stand."

She stood and the shepherd lunged at her, but was pulled up short by its handler.

Another man approached with a flashlight and searched her, passing his hands roughly over her body. She said, "Please, I *must* see Kalin. I have urgent information."

The first Russian said, "If it is urgent, you can run." He snapped an order and two of the uniformed guards fell in on either side of her, their Kalishnikov rifles held across their chests. "Quick, march! Move!"

Claudia, flanked by the two men, began moving at a near run through the trees. She stumbled once and one of the men pulled her to her feet. Stones and twigs dug into her bare feet, and branches whipped across her perspiring body. Occasionally one of the men prodded her along with a rifle jab to her buttocks.

After what seemed an interminable time, they broke out onto the floodlit north lawn, and she saw the huge stone mansion sitting majestically on the hilltop.

They made her run more quickly across the lawn to the rear of the house, then swung around on the terrace until they came to the walled service court.

The Russians slowed to a march and Claudia gasped for breath. She was nearly numb with fatigue and barely aware of being marched through the walled court filled with parked vehicles. They passed through a set of double doors, down a half flight of steps, and walked down a long, dimly lit corridor off which were small doors evenly spaced. *Servants' quarters,* she thought vaguely, but the narrow corridor and the small closed doors brought back memories of another place: The jackbooted Russians with their rifles, she dragged between them; two years of her life she wanted badly to forget. It struck her suddenly that this was what the world was coming to: dark, lonely corridors, armed guards, the sound of boots and bare feet on cold floors, and a journey to an unknown place.

The guards stopped, opened a door, and pushed her inside. She saw by the corridor's light a small unlit room, furnished with a cot and a waste bucket and nothing else. The door slammed behind her and she heard the lock turn.

She stood motionless and listened to her hard breathing, then slowly wiped her cold, clammy body with the edge of her dress. She walked carefully to the far side of the room. There was a high window and she pulled the cot to it and stood on it. The window opened onto the dimly lit service court and a weak light filtered through the dirty panes. The window was barred on the outside and she couldn't open the outward-swinging casements. The room was oppressively warm and stagnant. She stepped down from the cot and walked back to the door and felt for a light switch, but there wasn't any. It would be on the outside, she knew. This was a cell, and after two years in cells, one knew something of them.

Claudia slumped down on the cot. It was the waiting and the uncertainty that eventually destroyed the mind and the will. The interrogations and abuse were almost welcome relief—if they didn't go too far in inflicting pain. At least during the sessions you knew where you stood. Questions were asked, answers were given. Accusations were made, denials and apologies were offered. Eventually you were either freed, sentenced to a term, or shot. Sometimes, however, they did the other thing. They offered you a job. In her case they had offered her the job of impersonating Countess Claudia Lepescu, who had been arrested at the same time she had. She had accepted the job and spent a year in the same cell with the former countess, until the KGB was satisfied that Magda Creanga, which was her real name, was in every way, except by birth, Countess

Lepescu. The countess had been taken away, presumably shot to protect the secret.

Eventually the new Claudia Lepescu was allowed to emigrate to America under the sponsorship of Patrick O'Brien and his friends, who had been pressing for her visa to leave Rumania.

And she had done her duty to her Russian masters, ingratiating herself into the circles of O'Brien and his friends. She had even tempted poor Tony Abrams onto the roof. They said he was to be kidnapped, but she had known otherwise. The Russians were treacherous. And now her usefulness as a spy was over.

There was, however, a glimmer of hope. In addition to her training as an impersonator and a spy, she had received extensive training in another area: She was an accomplished and very talented seductress, a very fine harlot. Perhaps, she thought, for that reason alone, Kalin or Androv, both of whom had taken her to bed, would show mercy.

She knelt beside the cot and found the waste bucket. The water was clear and she washed herself as best she could, then finger-combed her hair and hand-brushed her dress. Russian men, she reflected, were the easiest of sexual conquests. They knew less about advanced sexual technique than a fifteen-year-old American boy. Their women knew less than that.

Claudia heard footsteps in the hall. They stopped. A key turned in the lock. The door opened, revealing the dark outline of a man. She could tell he was not uniformed, but wearing civilian clothes. The man reached out and snapped on the light switch outside her door.

"Alexei!" She came toward him.

Kalin put his hand out and pushed her away as he pulled the door closed behind him. "Why did you come here that way? They expected you at the gate."

She thought, *I came that way because Van Dorn told me to: to give his men time to get in position.* She said, "They were after me. They found out somehow—"

"The poison?"

She nodded quickly. "Yes. That's all right. Roth did as he was told. I did as I was told." She came to him again, and this time he let her put her arms around him. She said, "What is to become of me, Alexei?"

He replied coolly, "You can handle a rifle. Perhaps we will need you later."

He did not, she noted, make any long-range promises. She saw his face in the dim overhead light. "What happened to you?"

"Your friend Abrams and I had an encounter. Where is the bastard now?"

She shrugged. "I didn't see him at Van Dorn's." She buried her head in his chest and her fingers worked their way under his jacket and began pulling his shirt out of his pants.

He broke her grip and looked at his watch. "All right, but time is short."

She undressed quickly and stood in the middle of the floor, naked, her clothes piled at her feet. She smiled. "I want you, Alexei."

Kalin undressed, laying his clothes on the floor. He hung his shoulder holster on the doorknob. He said, "We don't have time for your full repertoire. Please proceed to the finale."

She crossed the small room and knelt in front of him, massaging his calves and thighs.

Kalin leaned back against the door. He said softly, "A woman like you will come in handy during a long siege...and I don't think Androv will make you carry a rifle. No, you have other talents...." He closed his eyes and let his head roll back against the door.

Claudia's hands cupped his buttocks. She felt the smooth leather of his holster brushing against her forearm.

CHAPTER SIXTY-TWO

Davis was on the point, Cameron had established a fifteen-foot interval, and Abrams followed. Abrams glanced over his shoulder at Katherine, who was close behind him. They nodded to each other encouragingly.

They approached the stone wall and Davis hopped it without hesitation, as though it were not an international barrier but just another stone sheep wall in the Falklands. Cameron followed, then Abrams, then Katherine. The patrol moved quickly into the trees of the Russian property.

Abrams held his rifle by its pistol grip, the sling across his chest, as he had been taught at the Police Academy. He knew the M-16 rifle well enough but had not fired one in some years. He kept his muzzle pointed to the left, cueing off Cameron, whose rifle pointed to the right. Davis held his M-16 under his arm pointing straight ahead. Abrams glanced back at Katherine. She had turned and was walking backward for a few steps as she'd been told, then she swung back around and scanned to her flanks.

Abrams listened to the music behind them, carried through the trees by the north wind. To the front, skyrockets traveled in a low-angle trajectory, bursting close to the horizon. Their brief glow outlined the towering tree line ahead, and in one shower of golden sparks Abrams caught a quick glimpse of the Russian mansion. They altered course slightly and moved toward the bursting rockets.

Abrams looked to the front of the file. Davis was almost no

longer visible. The night without light was disorienting, alien to civilized man, Abrams reflected, a terror from sundown to sunrise, a nightmare among nightmares. He could not conceive of a darkened continent.

Abrams heard a sound and looked up quickly. Cameron held his hand high and was clicking a tin cricket. Abrams stopped and knelt on one knee facing left. Katherine crouched and faced to the rear. Cameron and Davis walked toward each other, conferred for a moment, then Cameron came back and knelt beside Abrams. He whispered in Abrams' ear, "Davis says he sees footprints and disturbed ground. Probably the spot where they intercepted Claudia." He added, "I'd like to put away that patrol before we get much deeper."

Abrams nodded. He never ceased to marvel at the euphemisms for death and murder.

Cameron said, "We'll lure them here." He gave Abrams some brief instructions.

Abrams motioned to Katherine. She came up and knelt beside him and he put his lips to her ear, repeating the message, then added, "You look good in basic black."

Davis had climbed a huge maple tree and was scanning the terrain with his nightscope. Cameron, who had taken Claudia's panty hose with him, was dragging it along the narrow overgrown game trail that the Russians had used.

Abrams reached into his field bag and drew out a small electronic ultrasound device. He turned it on to emit a series of short sounds, inaudible to human ears. Almost immediately he heard a dog bark nearby.

Cameron doubled back along the trail until he reached a small patch of moss-covered clearing. He took the panty hose and draped it over the branch of a cedar tree.

Davis clicked his tin cricket—two short, three long, four short— enemy in sight, three spotted, forty yards' distance.

Abrams and Katherine drew closer together and knelt, positioning themselves toward the killing zone beneath the cedar less than twenty feet away. Davis climbed down to a lower branch of the maple almost directly above the small mossy clearing; he lay flat on a large forked limb. The ambush was set.

Abrams heard the sound of men moving up the narrow game trail. He heard the crackle of a radio, muted voices, and the continuous barking of a dog. He found himself holding his breath.

Suddenly the leashed dog, a big German shepherd, burst out of the trail into the clearing, pulling a uniformed man who was shouldering a rifle. Abrams quickly shut off the ultrasound device, and the dog quieted, then began to whimper and sniff the ground. The dog came to a halt beneath the cedar.

A second Russian appeared, speaking into a hand-held radio, his rifle tucked under his arm. The third Russian walked slowly into the clearing. He didn't have a rifle, but Abrams could make out a pistol in his hand and he guessed he was the boss.

The shepherd was up on his hind legs now, growling and leaping. The handler pulled him back, and the Russian in charge approached, spotted the panty hose, and pulled them out of the cedar tree. The dog handler lifted the panty hose to his nose and made an obscene joke. All three Russians laughed.

The handler knelt and let the dog sniff the hose; then, still laughing, he tied the nylon around the radio operator's neck. The shepherd seemed to be the only one still concerned; he was whining and sniffing the ground, pulling at his leash.

The radio operator spoke into his walkie-talkie. Abrams listened closely, then turned to Cameron, who was watching him. Abrams nodded, indicating what Cameron had already deduced: The radio operator had reported a false alarm. Cameron gave a hand signal to Abrams and Katherine, then rose out of the clump of bushes, put his silenced M-16 to his shoulder, and aimed.

Abrams stood also, and was vaguely aware of Katherine a few feet away standing with her rifle raised. The seconds seemed to tick by very slowly.

The three Russians turned toward the trail. The dog barked again and pulled his handler around. The handler looked up and squinted into the darkness at Cameron not twenty feet away. He let out a startled sound.

The muzzle of Cameron's rifle glowed red, and the metallic operating mechanism could be heard above the sounds of the partially silenced fire. The handler seemed to jump backward, high into the air, then fell to the ground, dragging the shepherd with him. The radio operator stood frozen, not comprehending what had happened for a split second, then dropped his walkie-talkie and raised his rifle. A burst of silenced fire from Davis ripped through the overhead branches and drove the Russian into the ground. The Russian in charge had thrown himself on the ground after the two initial bursts, and was scrambling on all fours down the trail. Katherine and Abrams fired simultaneously, their bullets a deadly hailstorm of steel. The Russian crawled a few more feet, then collapsed on his face.

No one moved for some seconds. The forest was quiet. Then the dog began to howl, accompanied by the moaning of one of the Russians. Cameron quickly stepped forward into the blood-splattered killing zone and looked down at the first two Russians. They were riddled with bullets and appeared to be dead, but Cameron shot them both in the head, then approached the wounded dog. Abrams and Katherine came quickly into the clearing and Katherine stopped short, then turned away. Cameron whispered to her, "Go thirty yards or so down the trail and keep an eye out."

Katherine stepped around the bodies without looking down, entered the trail, and stepped quickly over the Russian she had shot. Abrams saw that the shepherd had taken a bullet through its haunches and was dragging itself along the ground toward its handler. Cameron put the muzzle of his rifle to the dog's head and fired a single shot.

Davis remained in the tree, scanning the surrounding area. He signaled with his tin cricket—no enemy in sight. Abrams approached the third Russian on the trail and knelt beside him. The man had taken at least half a dozen rounds in the legs and buttocks, but was still alive. Abrams turned him over and saw that the Russian's legs were nearly severed near the hips and seemed held to his body by strips of muscle and sinew. White bone-shards and marrow covered his uniform. The man, an officer, Abrams guessed by the uniform, spoke in Russian in a pain-filled voice, "Help me, please." He repeated in English, "Please help me."

Abrams answered in Russian, "We'll send someone for you as soon as possible."

The Russian stared up into Abrams' eyes, then nodded.

Abrams leaned closer over the Russian and spoke. "What became of the woman? Claudia."

The Russian hesitated, then replied, "She's at the house."

Abrams asked, "How many other patrols are there in this area?"

The Russian seemed to be considering his answer.

Abrams prompted, "Tell me the truth and we'll send medical help."

The Russian replied, "Two other patrols...back along the wall...."

Cameron walked up to Abrams. Abrams repeated the conversation, then said, "Is there anything else?"

Cameron shrugged. "This bastard's not going to tell you the truth anyway." Cameron leaned over and shot the Russian through the forehead.

Abrams was startled, but not surprised. One never knew if a coup de grace was meant to be merciful or malicious, and he suspected that Cameron didn't know and didn't care.

Cameron took the Russians' rifles and pistols and threw them far into the bush.

Davis swung down from the maple and landed in the clearing. He looked at the three dead Russians. He said to Cameron, "Do you see the green piping on their uniforms? These chaps are from the Chief Border Guards Directorate."

Cameron nodded and explained to Abrams, "An elite KGB outfit. A bit like the Marines. Not just flunky embassy guards."

Abrams didn't know if that was supposed to make them all feel better or worse.

Cameron said, "Well, I wouldn't be keen on taking on any more of them. Let's move out, then."

Abrams got Katherine, and the patrol reformed, moving toward the exploding skyrockets. They avoided the trails and paths but made good time through the thinning woods. They reached the end of the woods and crouched near the edge of the north lawn.

Abrams looked out across the wide grassy expanse rising upward toward the great house about a hundred yards away on the crest of the hill. He stared at the fortress-like structure, black and squat against the sky, its ill-omened gables rising above its brooding windows.

Floodlights illuminated every square inch of the short grass, and spotlights shot powerful beams out into the surrounding woods. One beam fell to their right, and the blinding ray suddenly moved toward them and rested a few feet away. Cameron said, "Steady now. The lights are automatic, not manned. They'll shift at random intervals and random directions." As he spoke, the spotlight swung ten yards farther right, then shifted abruptly to the left and swept over them briefly before stopping some yards away.

Davis said, "I'm sure the bloody listening devices have us by now."

Cameron nodded and said, "Ivan does not like trespassers."

Davis retorted, "We won't be trespassers for long. We'll be in residence."

Abrams could make out three people on the raised terrace: guards with rifles walking an assigned post.

Katherine looked at her watch. "We're a few minutes late."

Cameron nodded. "It won't matter, if the others haven't achieved their objectives. We're not getting across that lawn without help."

Davis raised his binoculars and looked toward the house. "I see the walls and plantings of the forecourt....I can see the Japanese lanterns of the drive as well as where it enters the court...." His voice rose, "There's the van! Pembroke's made it past the guardhouse. The van's heading for the front door." He put down his binoculars and looked at the other three. "Damned good show."

Cameron nodded. "They've got a way to go yet. So do we." He stayed silent a moment, then said, "It's a fifteen-second run across that lawn...." He looked at Abrams and Katherine. "What you do is pick a prayer or a poem that takes fifteen seconds to recite to yourself. I've picked the 'Our Father.' When I get to 'Amen,' I expect to be on that terrace. It works every time."

Abrams thought it must have worked every time or Cameron wouldn't be here.

"All right," said Cameron, "fix bayonets."

CHAPTER SIXTY-THREE

Roth's catering van rolled slowly through the landscaped forecourt, lit bright as day with banks of floodlights. Pembroke peered cautiously over the seat. There were guards armed with automatic rifles every ten yards or so. He turned to Ann. "This doesn't look encouraging."

Roth babbled as he drove, his voice cracking with panic. "Everyone will die.... The Russians will win.... They will kill me.... Oh, my God, Pembroke... I didn't want to work for them... they blackmailed me.... I was afraid... I don't *believe* anymore—"

"Shut up, Roth."

The van swung left and drew abreast of the front door, and Roth applied the brakes. Pembroke and Ann moved to the rear of the van with Llewelyn and Sutter, who had their hands on the rear-door latches, ready to jump out and make a fight of it if necessary. All four wore black camouflage hoods.

A Russian guard approached Roth's window and spoke in English. "What are you doing here, Roth? I received no message from the gate."

Roth's mouth opened, but no words came out.

The guard snapped, "You stink of whisky. Stay here." He disappeared from the window.

Pembroke pulled back the operating rod of his M-16 and let it spring forward with a loud metallic ring. Ann and the two men did the same; each time, Roth flinched in his seat. Pembroke rose slowly and looked out the front windshield. He could see the heads of four uniformed men passing by.

The first guard returned. "Their telephone isn't working. What is your business here?"

Roth drew a deep breath. "More food. For Androv."

The guard said nothing.

Roth found his voice again. "I have something for you." He turned and fumbled with a shopping bag on the seat beside him. "Vodka and Scotch. Six bottles." He raised the bag to the window.

The guard looked around, then snatched the bag through the opening. "Get moving, Roth."

Roth nodded quickly and threw the van into gear. His foot trembled so badly on the accelerator that the van moved in short lurches. He turned left again along the south edge of the forecourt, then right into a small drive that bent around to the south side of the mansion.

Pembroke came up behind Roth. "All right, one more checkpoint. Get us through there and you've bought yourself a pardon. Easy now. You're doing just fine."

The van pulled up to the iron gates of the walled service court, and a guard shielded his eyes against the glare of the headlights. He nodded in recognition, then unlatched the gates and swung one open. Roth pulled halfway through and stopped. Pembroke sank down behind the driver's seat. The guard put his hands on the window frame. "Do you have anything extra, Roth?"

Roth nodded and took a small bag from the floor on the passenger side, and handed it to the man. The Russian peered inside the bag. "What is this shit?"

"Cordials. Sweet. For the ladies. Very expensive."

The guard snorted.

Roth said, "I'll be some time unloading and setting up a buffet. An hour."

The guard looked at him, then said, "Back up to the service doors. Don't block anyone."

Roth nodded and pulled through the gate.

Pembroke whispered to the other three, "Half the bloody Russkies must be eating and drinking on poor George."

Sutter said, "But there's no such thing as a free lunch, is there? Tonight we collect for Mr. Van Dorn."

Ann glanced at the three men. She had never seen such coolness and optimism in the face of such overwhelming odds. She supposed their past successes engendered a sense of omnipotence. They simply couldn't imagine losing.

Roth maneuvered the van through the crowded parking yard, then put it in reverse and edged it back to the service doors. He shut off the engine and headlights, then stood unsteadily and moved to the back of the van. He pushed open the van doors.

Pembroke said, "Open the service doors. Quickly."

Roth jumped down from the van and opened the large double doors, swinging them out to meet the van doors, creating a shielded passage from the van to the house.

Pembroke stared through the open doors into a large storage room. At the far end was a single closed door. No one was visible.

Pembroke jumped out of the van and prodded Roth through the doors into the storage room. Sutter, Ann, and Llewelyn grabbed a few boxes of food and carried them into the room, stacking them along the wall. Sutter went back and closed the van doors, then began pulling the service doors closed.

"Stop!" Footsteps approached.

Pembroke shoved Roth forward toward the doors. The others braced themselves along the wall near the double doors.

The guard stepped up to the doors. "Roth, I forgot to tell you. Don't leave these doors open. If they're open after eleven thirty, Androv will have you shot."

Roth nodded quickly. "I'm closing them now."

"Don't open them again."

"No, no."

The guard looked at him. "What's wrong with you, Roth?"

"I had too much to drink."

The guard stared at him, then said, "Why are you shaking? Roth? What—"

Pembroke stepped away from the wall, pushed Roth aside, and faced the Russian. The man blinked at the black-hooded apparition and his mouth dropped open. Pembroke seized the leather cross-strap of the man's gun belt and with a powerful movement pulled him in through the doors, spun him around, and sent him slamming into the wall. Sutter hit the Russian in the groin and as he doubled over, Llewelyn delivered a savage karate chop to the base of his neck. The Russian fell forward and lay motionless. Sutter rolled him over and knelt beside him, checking for vital signs. "Still alive, Lew. You're getting old."

Pembroke said, "Take him along, then."

Sutter and Llewelyn grabbed an arm each and dragged the unconscious man through the storage room, preceded by Pembroke and Roth. Ann shut and locked the double doors, then followed quickly. Pembroke slowly opened the large single door at the far end of the room and peered into an area filled with pipes and ducts. The freight elevator stood to his left. Below, he knew, was the boiler room. He passed through the cluttered area and exited through another door into a long corridor, the others behind him. He turned and moved along the narrow corridor off which were the doors to the former servants' quarters. Pembroke listened at the first door he came to, then turned the old latch handle. The door opened and he stepped inside the dark room. He motioned to the others and they followed quickly, dragging the Russian with them. Ann closed the door and knelt at the keyhole as Pembroke turned on a lamp.

The room was furnished with a single bed, a dresser, and a few chairs and a vanity. A woman's room. Pembroke opened a closet door and saw a few dresses, skirts, and tops hanging. He turned to Roth and whispered, "Get in there."

Roth moved quickly into the small closet and stood hunched between the clothes.

Pembroke said, "You've been a traitor for over forty years, Roth, but you've redeemed yourself by this single act. So you may live. Turn around."

Roth turned and faced the wall. Llewelyn bound his hands with flex cable and began to place a tape gag over his mouth.

Pembroke said, "Wait. Roth, is there anything else you wish to tell us? Anything we should know that will assist us in completing this mission? Think carefully."

Roth stayed silent for some time, then said, "No...no, nothing."

Pembroke nodded to Llewelyn, who stuck the tape over Roth's mouth.

Sutter stepped forward quickly, looped a piece of piano wire around Roth's neck, and twisted it with a gloved hand. Roth gave a convulsive jerk, then slumped to the floor.

Ann stared, wide-eyed, but said nothing as she knelt by the keyhole.

Pembroke said to Ann, "The punishment for treason in my country is death by hanging. That's the best we could do under the circumstances." He looked down at the Russian on the floor. "Take his uniform and put him to sleep."

Sutter and Llewelyn stripped the uniform, boots, and pistol belt off the Russian. Sutter produced a small Syrette and pushed it into the Russian's arm, then he and Sutter stuffed the man into the closet atop Roth's body and shut the door.

Pembroke said, "Llewelyn, you look more the chap's size. And you have sinister Slavic features." He smiled.

Llewelyn took off his gear, black camouflage fatigues and shoes, and dressed in the Russian's uniform, throwing his own clothes and equipment under the bed. He glanced in the vanity mirror as he adjusted the peaked cap on his head.

Sutter commented, "You look like a bloody concierge."

Llewelyn replied, "Fuck off." He strapped on the Russian's gun belt and holster.

Pembroke looked at his watch and said softly, "Well, people, we're in."

Sutter, too, checked his watch. "On time, more or less."

Ann snapped her fingers and everyone turned toward her. She peered out the keyhole. The sound of footsteps echoed in the hall-way. Ann held up three fingers, then pantomimed a pistol with her other hand: three armed guards. The footsteps halted and a man spoke in Russian. Another man replied, then there was laughter. The footsteps retreated down the hallway.

Ann turned and whispered, "Something to do with the Rumanian girl—Claudia. And a man named Kalin. They're in one of these
rooms. The detention room. Can we help her?"

Pembroke replied, "No, she's on her own." He added, "She volunteered to do a turn for us, and she's more useful in that capacity."
He thought a moment, then concluded, "Also, I don't completely
trust her."

Pembroke went to the door and opened it slowly when he was
certain the Russians were gone. He motioned to Llewelyn, who
walked out first. Llewelyn looked up and down the hall, then turned
back to Pembroke and nodded. Ann and Sutter went out next, followed by Pembroke, who closed the door behind them. They made
their way quickly back to the freight elevator and entered the large
wooden car. Sutter closed the doors manually, and Llewelyn pulled
the lever, sending the car creaking slowly upward. Pembroke said,
"Next stop, second floor, from whence we will take a flight of stairs
to the attic. 'Nearer my God to Thee.'"

The elevator stopped. Sutter listened at the door. Pembroke and
Ann leveled their automatic rifles. Llewelyn grabbed the door handle and slid the door back, exposing a small foyer.

The four people waited a full minute, then quickly exited into the
foyer. Llewelyn stepped out into a long hallway stretching about a hundred feet along the north-south axis of the house. Oak doors stood
at irregular intervals on both sides of the hallway. Llewelyn walked
quickly to the third door on the right. He put his back to the door
and assumed a parade-rest position. He listened, watched, and waited;
then, still standing with his back to the door, he turned the knob.
Locked. He took a spring pick out of his pocket, picked the old mor-
tise lock, and opened the door. Pembroke, Ann, and Sutter rushed
past him and slipped into the small foyer at the foot of the attic stairs.

Llewelyn began to follow, then froze. Two Russians in civilian
clothing came out of a doorway across the hall.

Llewelyn closed the door and stood again in a rigid parade-
rest position in front of it. Out of the corner of his eye he saw the
two men approach. One was a thin, bald-headed man, the other a
powerful-looking man in his twenties.

Pembroke, Ann, and Sutter waited behind the door, listening.

The older man spoke.

Llewelyn knew two words of Russian, *da* and *nyet.* Keeping his head and eyes straight ahead, he replied, *"Da!"*

The Russians looked at each other quizzically.

Ann whispered to Pembroke and Sutter, "The Russian's asking who posted him at the attic door and why. I'm afraid the answer isn't satisfactory."

Pembroke nodded and whispered, "Llewelyn's Russian *is* rather limited."

The two Russians stopped a few feet from Llewelyn and again the bald-headed man spoke insistently.

Llewelyn replied irritably, "Oh, bloody *da, nyet,* and bugger off!" He swung his big fist full in the man's face, lifting him back off his feet and sending him sprawling across the hall. The young Russian, who had not said a word so far, made an exclamation and stared at the crumpled body, then turned back to Llewelyn and found himself looking into a revolver.

The door behind Llewelyn opened and Ann stepped out. She said in Russian, "Hello, Nikolai Vasilevich." She pulled off her hood and shook her hair out. "Come in, please. I'd like a word with you."

The young man's mouth dropped open. Llewelyn gave him a shove and sent him through the attic doorway. Llewelyn carried the unconscious man in and threw him on the floor, faceup. Sutter closed and bolted the door.

Pembroke stared down at the man, his face barely recognizable with his nose broken and his jaw dislocated. Pembroke said, "I think this is Karpenko, the chief KGB communications officer here." He looked at the young Russian and said, "Karpenko?"

The man nodded hesitantly and his eyes darted to Ann.

Ann said to him, "Don't be frightened. We won't harm you." She glanced at Pembroke, then back at the young man. She said, "You will repeat, word for word, the message you delivered to Viktor Androv from Moscow."

Nikolai Vasilevich drew himself up straight and shook his head firmly. "I will not. You may as well shoot me."

Ann translated the remark.

Pembroke drew his silenced automatic pistol, cocked it, and aimed it at Karpenko's face. He said, in passable Russian, "*Smert Komitet Gossudarstvennoy Bezopasnosti*—Death to the KGB," then fired three bullets into the unconscious man's face, turning his features into an unrecognizable mass of gore.

Nikolai Vasilevich stared down at the splattered face and skull and went pale, his legs beginning to tremble.

Pembroke turned the gun on the young man and said in English, "Death to all KGB swine."

Nikolai Vasilevich shook his head quickly and spoke in English. "No. No. I am not KGB. I am a soldier. GRU—military intelligence."

Ann put her hand on his shoulder and said in Russian, "You're too young to die, Nikolai. I swear to you, you will not be harmed if you cooperate." She stared into his hazel eyes and he stared back, then nodded.

Ann said, "Word for word. I can tell when you're reciting your message and when you're deviating. Speak."

Nikolai Vasilevich stood, head and eyes fixed straight ahead, and recited in a monotone, as he'd done for Viktor Androv. When he finished, Ann summarized in English, then said to Pembroke, "So it *is* Molniya, and it is tonight. But we knew that. What we didn't know is that Talbot Three will be here—or is already here."

Pembroke nodded thoughtfully, then stared at the Russian, who was sweating now. He said, "It's no longer customary to kill the bearer of bad news, but—"

Ann put her hand on his rising pistol. "No, Marc."

He looked at her sharply.

"I promised." She added, "Besides, he's sexy."

Pembroke smiled slowly, then said to Sutter, "Stow him under this staircase."

Sutter produced a Syrette and approached the Russian. The man took a step back. Sutter said, "Sleepy time, Ivan. Let's see some skin."

Ann spoke to him soothingly in Russian and the man hesitated, then held out his arm.

Sutter rammed the Syrette in with more force than necessary, then led the Russian to the small closet beneath the staircase and stuffed him inside as he began to pass into unconsciousness.

Pembroke looked up the narrow, dimly lit staircase, which ended at a top landing. Beyond the landing was a steel door that he knew led to the south end of the main attic. There were three other attic staircases, all ending in steel doors that were cross-barred on the other side. He said softly to Ann, "The Holy Grail is beyond that door."

She smiled at him. "Keep it. I'm interested in the radios. I must speak to Washington and Moscow sometime before midnight."

Pembroke looked at his watch and replied, "We shall do our best."

Llewelyn was at the top of the stairs, fixing charges of plastic explosives around the steel casement frame.

Ann said, "You must keep the shooting to a minimum up there. Those electronics are crucial."

"I understand."

She looked at him closely. "If we succeed here, I don't want a massacre, Marc. I just want to get out."

"And if we don't succeed?"

She stared into his eyes as she spoke. "Then, as George said, we'll take as many with us as we can. There will be no reason to leave here."

Pembroke nodded. "How do you want your father? Dead or alive?"

She spoke without hesitation. "I want him put back in his grave where he belongs."

"Thorpe?"

"Alive. I want *him* alive."

"Any other instructions?"

"Yes. If Talbot Three is actually here, find him."

Pembroke nodded, then said, "Before I'm through here, this house will give up all its secrets."

CHAPTER SIXTY-FOUR

The big Sikorsky helicopter headed south toward the coastline of Long Island. The jumpmaster, Farber, called out, "Target, three miles due south!" He added, "Winds gusting from the north to nine miles an hour at sea level. Ten to fifteen miles up here. Partial cloud cover, obscuring a three-quarter moon. Rain clouds tracking this way. Target is well lit and easily identifiable. Don't land on George's property by mistake or he'll shoot you." Farber laughed, then called out, "Line up!"

Grenville stood and approached the sliding door. Behind him were Pembroke's men, Stewart and Collins. Behind them the old boys, Johnson and Hallis. Grenville knew enough about tactical parachute jumps to know that the buddy system was very important. Stewart and Collins were buddies. He guessed that Johnson and Hallis were buddies too. Only Tom Grenville seemed to be missing a buddy.

The cabin lights suddenly went out and the lights from the cockpit dimmed to near darkness. The pilots drew blackout shades around their side windows and shut off the outside navigation lights, a move that Grenville thought was highly dangerous. Farber seemed to read his thoughts and said, "Don't worry, boys, no one else is crazy enough to be flying at this altitude tonight."

The blackened helicopter stopped its forward motion and hovered nose up into the wind. The buffeting became worse and the cabin pitched steeply to port and starboard. The men held on to overhead straps. Farber called out, "Target one mile, due south."

Grenville checked his equipment and adjusted the sling of his M-16. He peered out the door window. The sky was still flashing jagged lightning, and dark clouds passed by the windows.

Farber shouted, "Altitude five thousand, five hundred feet. Target one hundred feet above sea level, give or take a chimney or two."

Grenville decided he did not like Farber's humor. He also decided in a clear flash of reason that he wasn't going to jump. He turned and found himself staring into Stewart's black eyes, which reflected the thin moonlight coming through the window.

Suddenly, Farber rolled the sliding door open and a blast of frigid air flew into the darkened cabin. The noise of the rotor blades was deafening, and Grenville couldn't hear himself speaking to Stewart, telling him to get the hell out of his way.

Stewart smiled at him. Farber gave a thumbs-up and flashed a green penlight. Stewart reached out and pushed Grenville through the open door.

Tom Grenville felt that there was no longer any floor beneath his feet, a feeling that always made him unhappy. He felt himself tumble head over heels, then righted himself and spread his arms like a bird, experiencing the exhilaration of free fall. He soared above the moonglow on the Long Island Sound, the wind carrying him toward the coastline a mile below and a mile forward. He thought, *I didn't collide with the fucking pontoon, Stewart.*

He looked back and saw that Stewart and Collins were soaring above him. Then Johnson dived out of the cabin, followed by Hallis.

In the dark cabin, Farber watched Hallis clear the helicopter, then grabbed the handle of the rolling door.

A hatch on the bulkhead of the aft stowage compartment dropped open and a man emerged. Farber sensed the movement and looked up as the shadow approached. The black-clad man in a parachute harness stood in front of Farber, who was holding the door half-open. The man said, "Hello, Barney."

Farber's eyes widened in surprise as the man reached out and seized Farber, who had no parachute, and pushed him out the open door. The man dived after him.

Tom Grenville looked down at the approaching coastline. He hoped they would spot the Russian house, though he wasn't certain he himself was going to aim for it. Like other combat parachutists who had come to their senses on the way down, he could miss his target and explain that he mistook the lights of the country club for the Russian mansion.

The air warmed as he descended, and the wind slackened. To his front he saw the village of Glen Cove and the strands of criss-crossing roads that surrounded it like a net of white blinking Christmas lights. Beyond the village were suburban housing tracts, and here and there the large houses of country estates surrounded by dark blotches of woodland and fields. Grenville spotted the Russian estate and saw that there was no mistaking anything else for it. *Scratch that idea,* he thought.

Grenville looked down. The ground was coming up fast now, as it always did at the end. He realized he could pop his chute at this moment and guide himself to a safe landing outside the enclosed thirty-seven acres of the Russian estate. A few more seconds and he wouldn't be able to move laterally far enough to do that. He put his hand on his rip cord.

But something Van Dorn had said made him hesitate. Beyond all the patriotic hoopla, and the assurances of a favorable promotion review, Van Dorn had said, "If you and Joan make it back, everything will be all right between you two for a long time to come."

Grenville knew instinctively that was true. He really did love her. They'd just gone off the track. They had to share something special to put the spark back in their relationship. Like a commando raid.

Grenville heard himself saying, "I can't let her go in there alone. I have to go too."

He looked down at the big floodlighted area around the house. It was very close now, and it was too late to avoid his rendezvous with it, his rendezvous with death or with life. "Oh, shit...."

He looked at the quickly changing red LED numbers on his altimeter: one thousand feet above sea level, nine hundred, eight hundred. He pulled his rip cord and felt the deceleration as the skydiver chute filled with air. He looked up at his chute, spread like black bat wings above his head. He felt himself drifting slowly, updrafts keeping the altimeter at five hundred feet. "Shit!" He didn't like the idea of hanging above the target. Even though the skyrockets had stopped on schedule, and he supposed no one below was looking up anymore, he felt very exposed. The altimeter read four hundred and fifty feet. Much too slow a descent. He began to guide his chute toward the house.

Grenville looked back over his shoulder. The Sikorsky wasn't visible any longer. Grenville suspected it was still there, monitoring their fall, but its gray camouflage paint and its darkened lights made it impossible to see.

The four other chutes were close behind him. They were maneuvering also, closing in on the house. Grenville turned back to his front, then his head swung around quickly. He counted: *One, two, three, four...five!* That wasn't right. He counted again and again and came up with five. "What the hell...?" He thought, *Farber?* But Farber hadn't been wearing a chute and couldn't have gotten into one quickly enough to be that close. Who the hell was that? Maybe they had a buddy for him. But Grenville could see that the other men had swiveled around also and were watching the unknown chutist above and behind them. Instinctively he knew that the sixth man was not one of them. He was no buddy.

CHAPTER SIXTY-FIVE

Stanley Kuchik held the cable tighter as the grade became steeper. He thought he should be nearing the end of the conduit by now. He called out softly to Joan, "You still there?"

"In body only. I projected my spirit to the Côte d'Azur."

"Oh . . ." Stanley said, "don't let go. If you do let go, tell me first. I'll let go too."

Joan thought the boy seemed frightened. She said, "You'll be the first to know."

Stanley was silent as the cable carried him through the conduit. He felt something brush over his helmet and face and heard the tinkling of metal chimes—the signal marker that meant he had ten seconds before his fingers reached the return pulley. He quickly released one hand from the cable and felt around the top of the conduit, finding the first of the handgrips embedded in the pipe. He released the moving cable with his other hand and reached back for the next grip, pulling himself, hand over hand, through the conduit, the trolley still beneath him.

He heard the chimes again and heard Joan feeling for the first overhead grip. Stanley said, "I'm pulling myself through."

"Me too."

Stanley felt her head come into contact with his feet. He said, "Hold it there."

Stanley heard the return pulley spinning above his face. "Christ, talk about tight. . . ." He found the next handgrip and pulled himself another foot along, feeling his helmet come into contact with the concrete plug that the Russians had poured into the conduit. He drew a deep breath. The air was foul and he felt dizzy. He whispered, "I hit the wall."

"Well, ram through it."

"Okay...." Bergen had explained that his men—the midgets— had used muriatic acid to eat away most of the concrete plug, leaving just a two-inch shell. Stanley gave a mental shrug. *Nuts.*

He began a difficult turning motion, thrusting his body around until he lay facedown on the trolley. He found a recessed handgrip in front of him, buried his gloved fingers in it, and pulled. He and the trolley traveled forward, sending his helmet into the concrete wall. The brittle acid-eaten concrete shattered immediately and fell noisily to the floor of the boiler room.

Light flooded into the conduit and Stanley was almost blinded by the sudden glare. Cool air bathed his sweaty face as he squinted into the lights. He drew his pistol and aimed it to his front.

If anyone was in the boiler room, or came in to investigate the noise, he was to call out "Red!" and they'd both push off, sending the trolleys rolling back to the basement of the tennis court.

Stanley stared at the closed door of the boiler room twenty feet away. He realized that he was the only one who would ever know whether or not that door opened. He kept staring at it, praying, but not knowing if he was praying for it to open or stay closed.

Joan whispered urgently, "Green or red?"

Stanley replied, "Yellow." He waited for some time, his eyes adjusting to the light as he stared at the door, considering his options, then suddenly blurted, "Green! Green!"

Joan replied, somewhat unhappily, he thought, "Understand. Green."

Stanley stuck his pistol into his chest pouch, then pulled the small trolley from under his body and dangled it over the edge of the conduit. He let it fall and heard a soft thud as the rubber trolley hit the floor.

Stanley knocked off a few clinging fragments of concrete, then pulled his head and torso out of the conduit. He glanced around the big boiler room, lit with naked incandescent light bulbs. He looked down. Bergen had said it would be a three- or four-foot drop, but it was at least five feet. *Shit.*

He worked his body out farther and bent at the waist, pushing his palms against the wall until his weight and gravity took over and he felt himself sliding down, face first, to the floor. He hit with his hands and somersaulted away from the wall, ending up on his feet. He drew his pistol quickly and backed up to the wall again. He called softly up to the conduit. "Okay. I'm in. Hold on a minute." He went to the boiler room door and listened. There were sounds in the distance, but he couldn't make them out. Stanley turned from the door and made his way silently around the large concrete room. He found a handmade wooden bench and carried it to the wall. He stepped up on it and peered into the conduit. He saw Joan's head and shoulders a few feet away. She was still lying on her back, the trolley beneath her. Looking at her stuffed in there, he didn't see how either of them had got through. No way, he thought, would the Russians expect this. He called out, "Okay, I'm here——"

"Get me the hell out of *here*. I can't hold on much longer."

"Okay...." Stanley reached in and worked his hands into the compressed space between her forearms and breasts.

"Watch it, Stanley."

He stammered. "This is the way Bergen——"

"Just pull."

His fingers hooked around her pectoral muscles and he pulled back. The trolley under her rolled toward him. After a good deal of twisting and pulling, she came free and dropped into his cradled arms. They stared at each other, wide-eyed, as they listened to the trolley rolling back down the conduit. Joan said, "Oh, Christ...."

Stanley looked at her. "You were supposed to secure it with a cord...."

Joan snapped, "I forgot. Put me down."

Stanley lowered her and she stood quickly, then hopped up to the bench and stared into the black conduit. "Well, the trolley left without me, Stan."

Stanley was shaking his head. "I should have reminded you."

She jumped down to the floor. "Hey, *I* forgot, not you. Don't pull your adolescent macho shit on me."

He stared at her, slightly bewildered. "Sorry...."

She drew a short breath. "Well, let's get this dog-and-pony show on the road."

He nodded, but didn't move. "How are you going to get *back?*"

"Limo. First class." She looked around. "All right, next we cover our arrival. Correct?"

Joan and Stanley quickly gathered up the thin slabs of broken concrete from the floor below and put them behind a boiler. Joan moved Stanley's trolley there as well. Stanley reached into his pouch and retrieved a round section of cloth with adhesive backing. He stood on the bench, unfolded the cloth, and stuck it over the conduit opening.

Joan looked at it from across the room. It was colored and textured like concrete and she supposed it would pass a cursory inspection of the room. "Looks terrific. We'll donate it to the Guggenheim."

Stanley hopped down from the bench and carried it back to where he had found it. Joan reached up with her gloved hand and partially unscrewed two of the four overhead light bulbs, throwing the back of the room where the conduit was into near darkness. "Much nicer. All right, let's go."

Stanley hesitated, then went toward the door. He drew his pistol again and glanced back at Joan. He saw that she had done the same. He grasped the door handle and pushed outward, peering through the crack into the large storage room that he remembered from his last visit. He motioned to Joan and they both slipped through the door.

Stanley led the way through the stacked boxes of canned food. He knew the way up to a point, but he took out a small rough diagram and stared at it. This section of the basement was a maze of wooden partitions. There were doors everywhere, some marked in Russian and a few still marked in English. He found the one he was looking for, marked in the same Russian letters as those on his diagram. He opened it slowly and began heading along a dark narrow passage, Joan behind him. They were traveling toward the west end of the house.

The passage ended and they stepped into an open area. Ten feet to his front was a wall of fairly new concrete, about fifty feet long. He approached a single massive door sheathed with lead, and he knew this was the bomb shelter.

Inside the bomb shelter, he had been told, were over a hundred Russians: men, women, and children. He and Joan had to keep them in there.

Joan came up beside him and nodded. They both pulled tubes of epoxy weld from their black stretch suits and began running a bead of the fast-drying weld around the edge of the door where it met the steel casement jamb. The Russians inside would not be able to pull it open.

Stanley looked at his diagram again. He had been told that there was a staircase that ran up to the first floor and into a hallway that lay between the living room and trophy room. He had been briefed about the little girl who had come up the staircase. Van Dorn seemed to know a lot about this place, from defectors and spies, but he didn't know if the staircase lay inside the bomb shelter or outside.

Joan was searching the dimly lit area in front of the shelter wall. She tried a few doors, but none of them led to a staircase. She whispered, "The stairs must be inside the shelter."

Stanley nodded.

Joan said, "We have to do the other thing. It's over here." She led Stanley to the south foundation wall. Standing against the wall were three steel boxes about the size and shape of large freezers. In fact, each unit was an air conditioner and air purifier for the bomb shelter. Ducts led out of the top of each unit through the wall and surfaced somewhere out in the plantings around the south terrace. Ducts also ran from each unit along the ceiling and penetrated the concrete wall of the bomb shelter.

None of the three units was running at the moment, and Stanley felt each one until he found the one that was warm with electrical heat. "This one."

He examined the steel sides. They were completely sealed, but there was a hinged access panel on the side. He turned a latch and the panel swung open. Stanley peered inside and saw the charcoal and fiber-glass filters. He pulled one out and dropped it behind the unit. Joan handed him a vacuum-sealed plastic bag and he tore it open, quickly dumping the clear crystals through the intake where the filter had been. He drew away immediately, knowing that the crystals were vaporizing into an invisible and odorless gas. He shut the access panel and stepped away from the unit.

Joan whispered, "Let's get out of here."

"I have to be sure this unit kicks on. Orders."

"I'll kick *you* in the ass, Stanley. Don't push our luck."

Stanley remained motionless, staring at the big gray steel box. After what seemed a very long time, but was less than a minute, he heard an electrical relay click and the unit vibrated, emitting a noise like a refrigerator. Stanley nodded with satisfaction. "They'll be sleeping soon. Let's—" He turned and saw that Joan was already heading back along the passage. He followed quickly.

They turned right, back toward the boiler room, but didn't enter it, continuing instead to the door of the utility room.

Stanley opened the door and stepped into the long, narrow room. He found himself standing ten feet away from a man in overalls holding a clipboard in one hand and a pencil in the other.

Joan let out a scream. The man did the same. Stanley raised his pistol instinctively and fired three times, the silencer making a noise like air rushing out of the neck of a toy balloon. *Phfft! Phftt! Phftt!*

Stanley watched the man stagger aimlessly, a surprised look on his face, his hands covering his groin and chest as though he'd been caught naked.

Stanley didn't know what to do. People were supposed to fall down dead when you shot them. He tried to fire again, but his hand was shaking so badly he couldn't have hit the wall.

Joan closed her eyes.

Finally the man fell to the floor. Stanley approached hesitantly. Blood flowed from the man's shoulder and groin, spreading over his khaki overalls and puddling on the gray floor. The man's chest heaved rapidly and his eyes stared up at Stanley.

Stanley turned away. He felt his stomach heave. Without further warning he vomited up bile, acid, and a chocolate candy bar.

Joan came up behind him and put her hand on his shoulder. "Oh...oh, my God...Stanley..."

Stanley took several deep breaths and with some effort got control of himself. "We have to...to finish him...."

Joan didn't reply.

Stanley turned and looked down at the man, hoping he was dead, but he was not. Stanley wanted the man to live, but he had his orders: no witnesses. He aimed at the man's head, closed his eyes, and fired, hearing the bullet thud against the skull and crack into the concrete floor.

Joan and Stanley stood quietly for a few seconds, then Joan said with forced calmness, "Help me hide him." They dragged the man into a corner where wooden skids were stacked and lowered a skid over his body. Joan found a rag mop and Stanley located an overhead water valve. They cleaned up the blood and hid the mop under the big electrical generator.

Joan and Stanley stared at each other for a brief second, their expressions revealing the fact that they had been intimate accomplices in something that neither of them would ever forget. Joan broke eye contact and looked quickly at her watch. "Oh, God, we're nearly four minutes late."

Stanley quickly drew a photograph from his chest pouch and compared it to the large electrical panel. The photograph was a blown-up reproduction of the shot he had taken a month before. There were grease-pencil marks next to the circuit breakers in question. One was to be shut, the other, the only circuit breaker that was in the off position, was to be turned on.

Van Dorn had explained that he wasn't to touch anything else, that it must appear that the one circuit breaker tripped off by itself because of an overload. The one to be turned on wouldn't be noticed immediately. Stanley held the photograph up to the circuit breakers, reached out, and switched the two that were marked in the picture.

Van Dorn's last instructions had been to get out fast, because there would be people racing down to the utility room. Stanley turned to Joan. "Let's go!" He dashed through the open door, Joan close behind. As they headed toward the boiler room, Stanley heard the sound of hurrying footsteps on a nearby staircase. "Oh, shit!" He picked up his pace, but he was in the area of the small compartmentalized rooms and doors and he became disoriented.

Joan said breathlessly behind him, "I think we passed it."

Suddenly a door to their right burst open and Stanley instinctively dropped into a crouch and remained frozen. Joan did the same.

Four men, two armed guards and two men in overalls, came quickly through the door, just fifteen feet away. They pivoted left on the run and ran through the passage from which Stanley and Joan had just come.

Stanley remained in his crouch, his entire body shaking and a cold sweat forming on his face. Joan rose shakily and pulled Stanley to his feet. She whispered, "Let's get the fuck *out* of here."

They moved cautiously now, finally finding the food-storage area outside the boiler room. Joan stayed in the shadow of a pile of boxes. "Go on. I'll cover."

Stanley dashed across the open space and swung the door out, slipping halfway inside. He scanned the boiler room quickly, and it appeared the same as they'd left it. He motioned to Joan and she dashed across the open area, slipping inside the boiler room behind Stanley.

Stanley wasted no time. He grabbed the bench and placed it below the conduit, then went behind the boiler and retrieved his rubber trolley. He jumped on the bench and ripped the cloth cover from the hole, raised the trolley, then stopped. His trolley was supposed to be kept from rolling down the sloped conduit by her secured trolley. But hers was gone, of course.

Stanley wondered for a second what Bergen and Claire had made of the returned empty trolley. He wondered also why they hadn't sent it back on the cable, attached by a cord or wire. Stanley took out his flashlight and shone it into the conduit. "Christ..." About two hundred feet down the conduit his beam picked out the silhouette of the trolley. It had become stuck, probably on a small ridge where the clay conduit pipes joined. "Oh . . . shit!"

Joan said, "What is it? Why aren't you going?"

He turned to her. "Your trolley's stuck in there. They don't know you lost it."

She nodded as she began to appreciate the situation. "I really fucked up. Well, go on Stanley. Here, I'll help you in." She stepped up on the bench.

"No. No, you go. I'll wait here. You tell them what happened and they'll send a trolley back. I'll be okay while—"

Joan slapped him hard across the face. "Get in that fucking hole or I'll beat the shit out of you."

He put his hand to his face as he stared at her.

She pulled the trolley out of his hand, then pushed it back to his chest, curved side toward him and the wheels facing out. "Hold that." She took a length of nylon cord from around her waist—the cord she was supposed to have used to secure her trolley to the handgrips. She passed the cord under Stanley's arms and tied the trolley to his chest. "All right, kid, you're set." She looked at him a moment, then leaned over and planted a kiss on his lips.

Stanley flushed and his eyes widened.

Joan knelt on one knee, then made a stirrup with her hands. "Come on. Move it."

Stanley stuck his foot into her hands and found himself lifted up and into the conduit opening. He felt a slap on his buttocks, and he wiggled farther in, holding his arms out to the front. He felt Joan push on the soles of his shoes and he began rolling forward, gathering momentum as the trolley began its long journey home.

His outstretched hands hit Joan's stuck trolley and set it rolling free ahead of him. Stanley closed his eyes for what seemed a long time, then opened them again and saw the light at the end of the long dark tunnel. Then the light became blurry as tears formed in his eyes.

Joan Grenville drew her pistol and walked slowly to the door of the boiler room. She knew that the shit was going to hit the fan very soon and she didn't know if the boiler room was the place to be when it hit.

Tom was out there somewhere, and so were the others. She'd just completed a very difficult task, and she was in a position to get out. The others weren't. But as Van Dorn said, no place was safe anymore. Perhaps, she thought, they could use another gun upstairs. She opened the boiler room door without fully realizing what she was doing.

She found herself wandering through the dimly lit passages of the basement, looking for a staircase that would lead upstairs. She thought that, after all, she should be with Tom.

CHAPTER SIXTY-SIX

Claudia Lepescu worked the small-caliber automatic out of Alexei Kalin's holster hanging on the doorknob. Kalin, lost in his sexual reverie, noticed nothing. She brought the pistol out, flipped off the safety, and thrust the cold steel deep between his legs to muffle the sound. She fired.

Kalin's feet left the floor from the impact and he fell back against the door, uttering only a short groan. Claudia rocked back on her haunches and stared up at him. He seemed unhurt, still standing, a puzzled expression on his face. Then she saw the blood pouring out between his spread legs like an open faucet. Kalin felt it too, and his hands shot down to the wound, the blood collecting in his cupped hands and running between his fingers.

Claudia stood and took a step back, keeping the gun trained on him, waiting for some sign that he was mortally wounded. Then she saw the color drain from his face and watched incredulously as the whiteness moved downward, like a wave of waxy death, the florid chest becoming milky, then the abdomen and pelvis, the redness pouring onto the floor, leaving his body through the hole behind his scrotum.

Kalin took a mincing step toward her and opened his mouth. *"Claudia..."*

She spit on the floor and wiped her mouth.

Kalin tried another step, but his knees buckled and he fell

forward, his hands still on his groin and his face thudding against the floorboards.

Claudia retrieved her clothes and dressed quickly. She stepped out into the hallway and began walking, Kalin's small automatic held tightly to her side. She had never been in this house before, but she had seen the floor plans in Van Dorn's study and she thought she could locate Androv's office. She had scores to settle, indignities to be redressed. She was a proud woman, and they had not broken her nor turned her into a docile, craven whore, as they'd thought. From the moment she landed in the United States, she had begun to play a cautious double game.

She passed through a door, climbed a half flight of stairs, and entered the main wing of the house. Claudia believed in preternatural evil and she possessed the superstitious tendencies of her people. She could sense Androv's evil close by and walked toward it.

Abrams, Katherine, Davis, and Cameron pulled their long black bayonets from their scabbards and snapped them onto the lugs below the silencer and flash suppressors. Abrams thought they were quite lethal-looking. He had never personally participated in a bayonet charge, but what had seemed unthinkable not so long ago seemed perfectly reasonable tonight.

Katherine looked at her watch. "What's taking them so long—"

Suddenly all the floodlights and spotlights on the north end of the house went from glaring white to dying red, then black, leaving a swatch of darkness lying over the north lawn.

Cameron stood and said simply, "Charge!"

The four people burst out of the tree line and began tearing across the hundred yards of lawn. They were all good runners and the distance closed fast. Abrams didn't think Cameron had finished his "Our Father" before they found themselves on the tiled steps leading up to the terrace.

Abrams was vaguely aware of passing over the swastika in the center of the terrace as the gray stone wall of the house loomed up, punctuated by the windows and French doors that glowed weakly from some distant interior house light. Abrams spotted a guard in the corner, silhouetted against a large window where the two wings came together. He turned and charged.

The guard heard the running footsteps and squinted into the darkness, then raised his rifle tentatively. In a split second Abrams knew he wouldn't reach him with the bayonet. Abrams fired a single shot and the man doubled over and crumpled to the terrace.

Cameron charged into two Russians who were standing together and talking excitedly. They turned toward Cameron at the last moment and Cameron buried his long bayonet into the groin of the closest one, then cut upward and opened the man's abdomen up to his breastbone. Cameron raised his leg and pushed the skewered man off his bayonet.

Simultaneously, Davis plunged his bayonet in an overhand harpooning motion through the heart of the second Russian. They both wiped their blades on their victims' uniforms.

Katherine had stopped on the steps as instructed and was scanning the windows and glass doors, rifle raised to fire, but no one seemed alerted by the sounds.

The three men quickly joined her. She said, "Let's get off this terrace before the lights come on."

They ran along the terrace, heading west to the rear of the house, and came upon a huge screened porch attached to the back of the house. Davis crashed through the screen door, followed by Cameron, Katherine, and Abrams.

They pivoted to the left and Davis ran up to a single door and pushed it open. They rushed through the doorway, into the living room, and spread out behind pieces of massive furniture.

Abrams half expected to see Henry Kimberly sitting in the chair beside the green-shaded lamp where he had last left him, but the chair was empty. The lamp was still lit, casting a small circle of light around the chair in the otherwise darkened room. Abrams noticed there were still cigarette stubs in the ashtray.

Cameron rose and looked around. He whispered, "Clear. Let's go."

They made their way across the wide room, rifles at their hips.

Cameron and Davis went to the left toward the door that led

to the gallery. Abrams and Katherine went to the door from which Abrams had spoken to Henry Kimberly. They were to make a sweep of the ground floor, from the west end of the house to the east, room by room: a search-and-destroy operation.

They were searching, Abrams thought, for Viktor Androv and his KGB pals, for Peter Thorpe, and for Henry Kimberly. They were searching in a physical way, as well as in a metaphysical sense, for the switch that would shut down the ticking clock.

Tom Grenville looked straight down. Van Dorn's house was directly below, framed nicely between his feet. He wondered how he'd gotten from there to here and if he'd ever get back there again.

He looked around and saw that the rest of his team were grouping in close around him. They had chosen the roof of the Russian mansion as their landing site, depending, as Van Dorn had said, on what was known in the military as the "pathfinder team." The pathfinder team's job was to light or mark difficult zones, and although the roof of the house covered nearly half an acre, Van Dorn had pointed out in the aerial photographs that most of the dark roof was pitched and covered with slippery slate, and where it was flat it was bristling with antennas, a satellite dish, and a microwave dish. Van Dorn had likened these to the wartime anti-parachutist protuberances that were meant to kill and maim. Grenville felt his stomach go sour again.

But the landing was possible, if the pathfinder team could get the work lights on the roof turned on. However, the pathfinder team, as Grenville knew, consisted of Joan and an acne-faced adolescent. Grenville didn't hold out much hope for those lights going on, and this brought him some modicum of comfort.

They were sailing right at the house now, the descent slow from the updrafts, but the forward movement fast because of the tail wind. Grenville knew that within the next few seconds, Stewart would have to decide if they were to land.

He looked to his left at Stewart, who was about to flash a light signal: a blinking light meant the roof, a steady light meant glide over the house and make for a clearing in the woods. As Grenville watched, Stewart's light went on, then began to blink. Grenville stared at it in amazement, then looked below.

The lights on the north lawn had gone black and the rooftop work lights glowed white. "Oh, shit. Joan...what are you *doing* to me?" But inexplicably a sense of pride swelled within Grenville, and he was relieved to discover that she was, at least at that moment, still alive.

The brightly lit roof was about two hundred feet ahead and a hundred feet below, and their angle of glide might or might not intercept it. Grenville glanced quickly back at the mysterious sixth man, who was now guiding his chute toward the illuminated forecourt that covered nearly an acre of flat grass and gravel.

Collins also watched the sixth man float farther away. Collins didn't know who the man was, only that he didn't belong there. Collins raised his rifle, put it on full automatic, and fired across the fifty yards that separated them.

The distance to the target was not far, but the relative positions of the moving chutists made it difficult to establish a point of reference.

The sixth man saw the muzzle flash and fired back. The man had the advantage of red tracer rounds, and he was able to adjust the fiery red streaks until he found his target.

Collins lurched in his harness, then dropped his rifle and hung motionless. His unguided chute floated southward with the wind toward the distant tree line.

Tom Grenville watched the exchange with a sense of incredulity. This silent death above the earth could not be happening. He caught a glimpse of the sixth chutist as he disappeared below the higher roofline to the left and dropped toward the forecourt. Grenville could see Russian guards converging toward the man.

Grenville looked down and saw the flat gray roof less than thirty feet below. He snapped out of his shock and gave a final tug on his risers to try to slow the chute from its southward drift. Stewart, Johnson, and Hallis were so close their chutes were touching his, all four of them now trying to pick out a patch of clear space amid the antennas, dishes, and guy wires below.

At ten feet it was obvious they might overshoot the house and land on the brightly lit south terrace, where the Russians below, who were in a state of alert now, could massacre them.

Grenville closed his eyes and waited.

Joan Grenville wandered around the dark basement, pistol in one hand, a diagram of the basement in the other. She had come to her senses and decided to go back to the boiler room where she belonged. Unfortunately, she was lost. She was in a section that had apparently not been seen by a defector or spy, because it was marked on her diagram *Unknown. KGB personnel only.* That sounded spooky.

She checked her compass and turned down a narrow passage until she came to an unmarked door that was painted red, the only red door she had seen so far. She passed it, hesitated, then turned and listened at the door, but heard nothing. Slowly, she twisted the white porcelain knob and pushed in on the door.

There was a black void before her as she passed through the door and stood silently in the dark. She was aware of a rank odor.

Joan pulled a small red-filtered flashlight from the elastic pouch on her stomach and switched it on. She swung the beam around the walls. *Just an empty room.* She took a step and found herself falling forward. She put out her hands to break her fall and was surprised to find herself lying in sand. "What the hell...?"

Joan got up on one knee and took the filter off the light. She played the beam around and saw that the entire floor of the small room was of white sand, newly raked. She couldn't imagine what it was for. A child's sandbox? No, absurd.

She rose to her feet and her beam caught something on the far wall. She moved toward it. It was the base of a fireplace chimney, set in the concrete foundation. There was a partly opened ash door at chest height. At least now she had a landmark. She consulted her diagram and noted the location of the fireplace chimneys. She glanced back toward the iron ash door and saw now that it was much larger than an ash door ought to be. It was also fairly new, embedded in fresh mortar around the older brick. It looked, she thought, more like an oven or kiln than an ash trap.

Joan directed the light inside the black open space and saw a charred skull, the black hollow eye sockets staring back at her. She screamed, dropped the flashlight, and stumbled backward, falling into the loose sand. "Oh...oh, my God!"

She realized, in a flash of intuition, coupled with something she had once overheard, that she was lying in the sand of an execution pit. She jumped to her feet, her hands flailing at the sand clinging to her body-suit as she made her way through the shallow pit and found the door. She ran out of the room, slamming the door behind her.

Joan leaned back against the wall and caught her breath. She had lost the flashlight, but at least the pistol was still in her shaking hand.

She began walking again, willing herself to calm down. "All right, Joan...it's all right." But the image of the skull stayed with her, and she could actually picture herself kneeling in the damp pit, a cold pistol to her neck, the cremation furnace glowing red across the white, raked sand. "Oh, dear God...what sort of people are these...?" Then, suddenly, all the cloak-and-dagger idiocy made sense in a way that Tom could never explain. Nothing she had read or heard about the KGB or the Soviets had made the slightest impression on her. But that room had burned itself into her psyche and she knew it would be part of her forever.

She walked until she realized she had come around in a circle. "Oh, shit." She glanced at the diagram under the glow of a dim light bulb, then moved to a door she hadn't noticed before. The door was solid-looking oak, set in a concrete wall, unlike the doors of thin boards that cut through the wooden partitions. This might lead to the wing of the basement from which she'd strayed.

She put her ear to the door, but heard nothing. The door was bolted on her side and she slid the iron bolt back and pushed in. The door felt as if it was on spring hinges, and she pushed harder, swinging it inward a few feet.

A blinding light hit her and she drew back, ready to run, but there were no threatening sounds. She squinted in the light that came from bright overhead fluorescent tubes and saw a room, about twenty feet square, the walls and floor entirely covered with white ceramic tile. *Like a giant bathroom.* In fact, she noticed, there was a shower head in the far wall, and close by were a white porcelain toilet and washbasin. There was a hospital gurney in the corner and leather straps hung on the right-hand wall. She thought, *A hospital operating room.* But she knew it wasn't. It was the straps, or perhaps the red stain on the floor around the shower drain, so stark against the white tile, that drew her to the obvious conclusion that she was looking at a modern torture chamber.

"Hello, Joan."

She felt her mouth go dry and almost lost control of her bladder. She swung her head to the right and stared into the corner. Her eyes widened.

"Thank God it's you," said Peter Thorpe.

She tried to speak, but couldn't. Her eyes focused on him, sitting naked with his arms wrapped around his bent knees. His face, she saw, was bruised and one eye was swollen shut. Joan felt her hand tighten around her pistol.

Thorpe stood slowly, revealing his full nakedness, and she saw his body had taken some punishment as well.

Thorpe said, "Nice outfit, Joan. Does you justice. They've attacked, haven't they? I knew they would."

Joan nodded. Nothing surprised her anymore, and she found her voice. "How did you get here?"

Thorpe ignored the question and asked, "Who's winning the war upstairs?"

Joan was wary. She answered, "We are."

Thorpe looked at her closely, then said, "Are the others close by?"

"Yes."

"Good. Well, let's go." He came closer.

"Stop there." She raised her pistol and remained standing in the open door.

Thorpe stopped, then said sharply, "Come in here and close the door before someone comes by." He added, "We'll talk."

Joan hesitated, then stepped fully into the room, and the door swung closed on its spring.

Thorpe said, "Tell me why you're pointing that at me. Certainly naked men don't make *you* nervous."

Joan snapped, "You're a Russian agent. That's what they told me when I was briefed."

Thorpe smiled and shook his head. "Would I be here in this room if I was working for them?"

She didn't reply.

"Van Dorn and his clowns think they have all the answers, but those harebrained amateurs don't know anything. I'm a triple agent, a loyal CIA operative."

Joan winced at the string of intelligence terms. "Oh, fuck this double, triple shit, Peter. You all give me a headache. They told me if I ran into you, to shoot you on the spot, and I just might do that."

Thorpe laughed, then said pleasantly, "Joan...I haven't forgotten that time we went out on my boat—"

"Go to hell."

Thorpe looked downcast. He said, "What are you going to do to me? I'd rather you shot me than leave me here to be tortured by the Russians again."

She looked at his body. They had not hurt him too badly, from what she could see. She tried to draw some conclusions. Either he was working for the CIA, or he was working for the Russians. Van Dorn could be wrong. After all, if he was working for the Russians, why did they beat him? And if he was a CIA agent, she couldn't leave him here.... She thought a moment, then said, "Look, Peter, I'm a little new at this, but I think even an old pro wouldn't know what the fuck to make of you."

Thorpe let out a long breath, then said, "Okay, but you can't in good conscience leave me here to be killed by them."

She didn't reply.

He went on imploringly, "Just let me out of here. You have the gun. I'm naked and defenseless. For God's sake, Joan, just leave the door unbolted for me." He hung his head and added, "I wouldn't *be* in this room unless I was their enemy."

Joan made a decision. She said, "I'm leaving, Peter, and I'm locking the door. But I'll be right back with a few of Pembroke's men."

She watched him carefully and thought she detected a glimmer of fear in his eyes.

He said, "They'll *kill* me."

"Why?"

"They don't know I'm a CIA triple."

"Tell them."

"They won't *believe* me."

"They won't kill you either. They'll check with your superiors in the CIA."

"No . . . don't call them. Just leave."

Joan backed toward the door, her pistol aimed at Thorpe about ten feet away. "Good-bye, Peter. I'll be back shortly." She reached behind with her free hand and grabbed the door handle, pulling it inward against its springs and working herself into the opening. She glanced quickly over her shoulder into the darkness outside—as Thorpe knew she would.

Thorpe sprang forward. Joan's reflexes were good, but playing tennis and shooting a charging man were quite different, and she froze for a fraction of a second. Thorpe's hands lunged out, one hand going for the pistol, the other for her throat. Joan fired and the bullet smashed into a far wall. The gun was suddenly on the floor, and she saw in a split second that the bullet had passed through Thorpe's palm. She felt his other hand closing around her throat, then he yanked her into the room by her neck, as though she were no heavier than a child, and threw her across the floor.

Thorpe took two long steps toward her and delivered a kick, heel first, to her groin. Joan cried out and brought her knees to her chest. Thorpe turned and bent over to retrieve the pistol.

Joan stood immediately, thinking vaguely that Thorpe had made two mistakes: kicking her in the groin as though she were a man, and turning his back on her because she was a woman. She drew her long, thin knife from an elastic pouch on her thigh and plunged it deep into Thorpe's back as he straightened up.

Thorpe took two quick steps forward, the knife still in his back, and swung around, the pistol held in his hand, pointing at her.

Joan screamed, turned, and ran to the far corner, diving behind the gurney as a bullet cracked into the tile above her head.

Thorpe stepped toward her. His punctured lung was filling with blood, and white frothy specks formed on his lips with every labored breath. He stopped, then turned in a zombielike movement and walked toward the door.

Joan watched him, and the only thing her panic-stricken mind could think of was that the black knife handle sticking out of his back looked like a movie prop.

Thorpe pulled open the door and slid through it into the corridor. The door snapped shut behind him and Joan heard him fumbling with the bolt. She got to her feet and ran to the door.

CHAPTER SIXTY-SEVEN

Tom Grenville felt the high antenna brush his foot as he drifted over the roof.

Stewart shouted, "Release!" and pulled his quick-release hook, freeing himself from the chute. He dropped straight down, nearly twenty feet, and crashed to the roof. Johnson and Hallis quickly did the same and the three chutes blew away in the wind.

Grenville hesitated a fraction of a second, then decided he'd rather break his neck on the roof than be shot on the ground. He pulled his release hook and found himself falling, feet first, onto the flat roof. He hit hard, bent his knees, and shoulder-rolled, nearly toppling off the edge of the roof where it sloped down to the south terrace below. He carefully edged back and stood unsteadily. He looked around and spotted Stewart lying near a satellite dish, and moved stiffly toward him.

Stewart sat up and glanced at Grenville. "Broke my fucking leg."

"Well, that's a hazard of jumping on a cluttered roof at night," Grenville observed.

Stewart stared at him.

Grenville added, "I'm fine."

"Fuck off, Tom." Stewart saw Johnson approaching quickly.

Johnson knelt beside him and said, "Hallis went off the south edge onto the terrace. I think he's dead."

Stewart gritted his teeth. "Shit." He looked at the old general and said, "Well, whoever that other bastard was, he's blowing the whistle on us. May as well carry on, though." As he spoke, the roof lights went off and the floodlights on the north lawn lit up again.

Grenville and Johnson carried Stewart to the north edge of the roof, then took their positions.

Grenville knelt at the low coping stone of the south edge, staring down at the terrace, pool, and teahouse below. Hallis' body was sprawled on the flagstones and Grenville could see he was dead. He could also see four Russian guards running across the lawn toward the terrace. He glanced back at Johnson, who knelt at the west end of the roof overlooking the porch. Then he looked back at Stewart covering the north. He thought, *A cripple, a seventy-year-old man, and a lame-brained attorney. An estimated twenty armed guards around the estate, an unknown number of armed civilians, plus a KGB contingent of unknown strength.* And nobody but him thought this was crazy. Ergo, *he* was crazy.

Grenville looked back at the four Russians, who were on the path beside the pool now. He moved the selector switch on his M-16 to full automatic and waited until the guards converged on Hallis' body. Two of the guards looked up and pointed their rifles at the roof.

Grenville fired a full magazine of twenty rounds, the M-16 jerking silently in his hands. He reloaded quickly, but saw there was no reason to fire again. He had killed all four men. He waited for the shock to hit him, but he felt nothing.

Stewart called to him softly, "What the hell is going on there, Grenville?"

Grenville looked over his shoulder, "I just nailed four."

"Who authorized you to fire, man? Well, never mind."

Well, fuck you. Grenville thought suddenly of Joan and looked toward the YMCA tennis building. He saw that it was partly lit. She should be back there by now, he thought. He turned and looked to the north and saw Van Dorn's house brightly lit in the far distance. The pyrotechnicians had resumed but were firing aerial torpedos now, and loud-bursting explosions rocked the night air. Grenville knew that whatever sounds of mayhem and murder emanated from these lonely acres, no one in the village or on Dosoris Lane would think anything of it. Just crazy George giving it to the Russkies again.

Claudia Lepescu opened the door of Viktor Androv's study and stepped inside, closing the door behind her. She held the pistol behind her back.

Androv looked up from the telephone, his face white in the glare of the lamp. He said into the phone, "I'll call you back." He hung up and looked at her. "Well, what an unexpected surprise. Is Kalin through with you?"

She said nothing. The room was dark except for the area around his desk, but the stained-glass window behind him glowed from the lights outside.

Androv said, "I have no time for you now."

She replied in Russian, "This won't take long."

He pursed his lips, then said, "Did you give Roth the poison?"

"No, I gave him vegetable oil."

He stared at her, then nodded. "I see."

She said, "Do you think I'm a mass murderer like you and your filthy Nazis?"

Androv said, "You're overwrought. Did Kalin abuse you?"

"Kalin is dead."

Again, Androv nodded as if to say, "I understand, I've always understood about you." He said aloud, "What's that behind your back. A pistol?"

She brought the pistol up and pointed it at him. "Stand up."

Androv stood slowly.

"I wish I had time to humiliate you the way you've humiliated me. I wish I had a whip, I wish I could have you in a torture cell—"

"Claudia."

She froze. The voice came from the dark corner of the room to her left. The voice said in English, "Claudia, put down the gun."

She kept the gun pointed at Androv, but her hands were shaking. *No,* she thought, *it can't be him. It can't be—*

She saw a flash of light out of the corner of her left eye and felt a searing pain in her side, then another. Then she felt nothing.

The man in the corner remained in the darkness.

Androv looked toward him, then said, "I certainly never thought I'd be rescued by an OSS paratrooper." He chuckled, then added, "What a game we play."

Joan Grenville rushed for the door of the torture chamber, reaching for the handle. She did not want to be locked in this room, but neither did she want to face Thorpe. She heard him fumbling with the bolt and yanked back on the handle. The door opened a few inches and she slammed it again, then repeated the motion until Thorpe understood that he was not going to be able to throw the bolt. Thorpe pushed in on the door, but she pushed it back, marveling at how much difference a pint or so of blood made even in a man that powerful. She heard the silencer wheeze and saw the door splinter, but the round, a .25-caliber, did not penetrate the oak. She kept shaking the door as she yelled, "Get out! Go!"

She heard him cough, a liquid sort of sound, then heard the sound of his bare feet slapping on the floor.

Joan waited a full minute, then peeked out the crack around the jamb. There was a trail of blood on the concrete floor of the passage leading away from the door. She was tempted to follow the trail in the hope that she could retrieve her pistol if he collapsed, but she decided she had displayed enough stupidity for one night. She slipped through the door and headed down a narrow passage that ran off to the right of the torture chamber. She intended to get out of this madhouse, fast.

The passage proved a bad choice. It ended at a door, and she had by now resolved not to open another door in this basement. She turned and began heading back, then someone spoke in a language that wasn't English. *Fuck*.

She turned and quietly went back to the door. She took a deep breath, opened the door, and slid through, standing with her back against it in total darkness, listening. Nothing. Her hands searched the wall to her right and she located an old push button–type electrical switch. She pressed it and the light went on.

Joan Grenville stared into the huge room, only slowly realizing that she was in a kitchen. But it was an incredibly ancient kitchen, the original downstairs kitchen, she realized. There were exposed pipes and antique stoves, and the walls were gray plaster. There was nothing in there that postdated the 1940s, and by the looks of the dust and cobwebs, it hadn't been cleaned since then. *The kitchen that time forgot.* She almost laughed.

Joan knew the basic attack plan well enough, and she knew that if everything had gone right, then Abrams, Katherine, and two of Marc Pembroke's people were in the house. Marc himself might be up there; yet she heard nothing above to indicate a battle. She decided to wait it out in this time capsule.

Joan looked around at the slate-topped counters, the tub sinks, the wooden cupboards. She looked for something to sit on, then noticed a dumbwaiter in the wall. She approached it curiously and saw that the cage was still there and that the cables were steel, not rope. She walked back to the light switch, shut it, then found her way in the dark to the dumbwaiter. She hesitated, then squeezed herself into the dusty dumbwaiter. "Last place they'd look." She pulled tentatively on the cable and the cage rose a few inches.

She began pulling hard and the dumbwaiter rose farther. This reminded her unhappily of the damned trolley cable. She continued her ascent. *There may be someone up there who can help me,* she thought. Certainly her luck couldn't get any worse. She felt sorry for herself but took comfort in the fact that she was alive, and would stay that way as long as she stayed in the dumbwaiter.

The cage moved surprisingly fast, with little creaking, and she saw a crack of light, then the full outline of the dumbwaiter door on the first floor. She stopped pulling, listened, but heard nothing.

Joan settled back and made herself as comfortable as possible. She closed her eyes and yawned, feeling relatively secure for the first time in hours.

She drifted off for a few moments and was awakened by a light glaring into her eyes. She turned her head and bumped her nose on the muzzle of a rifle. "Oh!" She reached for the cable but a hand grabbed her wrist. A voice said, "You snore."

She looked up into the blackened face of a very good-looking man. "I know. Everyone tells me that. You're Davis, aren't you?"

"At your service. Is the boy all right?"

"Yes, he's gone back."

Davis said, "Did you complete the other parts of your mission?"

"Yes. Sleeping gas in the bomb shelter, roof lights on—"

Cameron came running over. He glanced at Joan in the dumb-waiter but showed no particular curiosity. He said to Davis, "Paratrooper landed out there. They marched him in through the front doors."

Joan blurted, "Was it Tom? My husband?"

Cameron looked at her. "No... an older man." He shifted his attention to Davis. "I don't think it was Johnson or Hallis, either... however, the face looked familiar."

Joan said, "Listen, can I get out of here? I'm a civilian."

Davis smiled. "Not yet. You'll be safest here for a while. We'll come for you later."

Joan nodded. As Davis and Cameron started down the hallway, she called to them, "Peter... Peter Thorpe. Is he good or bad?"

"Bad," said both men simultaneously.

"Good," she replied. "Because I think I killed him."

Katherine and Abrams entered the hallway. To the right were the French doors from which Abrams had taken the metal scrapings. Across the hall were the doors to the music room, and to the left were the bathroom and the cellar stairs. Katherine dropped to one knee and scanned the doorways as Abrams moved quickly to the French doors. He peered through the panes and saw something on the north terrace that he hadn't seen on his earlier visit: four Russian guards, speaking animatedly, standing around the body of a man dressed in black. "Damn it." As he watched, two of the Russians raised their rifles. Then all four keeled over as the deadly fire from the roof cut them down.

At least some of the paratroopers had made it to the roof, Abrams thought. He hurried back into the hallway, going directly to Katherine at the cellar stairs. The door was ajar and he swung it fully open with the barrel of his rifle.

Katherine suppressed a gasp. The stairs and landing were littered with men, women, and children, sprawled over one another. Some of the men held pistols in their hands. Abrams said, "That's the bomb shelter down there."

Katherine nodded.

Abrams looked for the little girl with the doll but didn't see her. He pulled Katherine away from the door and closed it. "Still some gas...."

She nodded again and realized she was dizzy. "Let's get moving."

They approached the glass-paneled doors that led to the music room and Abrams peered through the curtains. The room was dark except for the glow of the Russian television set. The screen showed a fuzzy picture of a newscaster. Abrams opened the door slowly and they entered. Abrams walked across the frayed rug and Katherine raised her rifle.

The oak flooring creaked. A head appeared over the back of the couch. A female voice said in Russian, "Who is there?"

Abrams replied in Russian, "Me." He leaned over the couch and leveled his rifle. It was, as he suspected, the woman who had done the security check. She stared at him in the glow of the video tube. She seemed, he thought, neither surprised nor frightened. She said, "What do you want?"

"You watch too much television."

She smiled. "That's my job tonight. To watch the news. Your Russian is bad."

"You're drunk. What's your name?"

"Lara." She looked at his camouflage gear and focused on his rifle, then said in perfect English, "Are you going to kill me?"

Abrams replied in English, "Quite possibly. That's *my* job tonight."

She shrugged and reached for her drink on the end table. "We're all going to die anyway. Those asses are starting a nuclear war." She took a long drink and added, "Everyone is in the bomb shelter."

Abrams remembered the sad expression on her face when he had seen her in this room earlier. He saw the same expression now. He said, "Get up."

She stood up unsteadily.

Katherine approached and Abrams said, "This is Lara. She's a recent defector."

The woman looked at Katherine without curiosity and shrugged again.

Abrams led the two women out into the hallway where the metal detector stood. Across the hall were two impressive oak doors: one led to the security office; the other was the door to Androv's office. Abrams whispered to Lara, "Is anyone in those rooms?"

She nodded toward the security office. "At least two men at all times." She looked at the other door. "That's Androv's office. He was in a few minutes ago. He has a prisoner. An American paratrooper."

Abrams looked at the Russian woman. "Knock on the door."

Lara hesitated, then walked to Androv's door and knocked. There was no response. She knocked again. "Viktor, may I have a word with you?"

Abrams motioned with the muzzle of his rifle and Lara opened the door. She screamed.

Abrams and Katherine rushed in. The office was empty, but a cigarette still burned in the ashtray. On the floor was Claudia Lepescu. Abrams closed the door. They stared at the body a moment, but no one spoke.

Abrams looked around the office. *So,* he thought, *this is the inner sanctum of the chief KGB resident in New York, the second highest-ranking KGB man in America.* A former chapel in the former home of one of America's leading families. A preview of things to come, perhaps.

Katherine was kneeling beside Claudia's body. She saw the pistol still clutched in her hand. "Look."

Abrams knelt beside her and said, "Russian make..." He saw where she had been shot—twice in the side—and his gaze went to the wingback chair in the corner.

Katherine stood and moved to the chair. She picked up the ashtray on the end table. "American cigarettes. Camels." She saw a bottle of Scotch beside a glass. "Dewar's."

Abrams said, "By the looks of it, this American paratrooper was not a prisoner but a confederate."

A loud alarm bell suddenly began ringing somewhere in the house. Katherine, Abrams, and Lara rushed into the hall. Alarm bells were ringing everywhere now and the house was filled with the staccato noise.

The security office door burst open and a uniformed officer holding a pistol came through. Abrams' M-16 blazed and the man was thrown back into the office.

Katherine threw a concussion grenade into the office and pulled the door closed to maximize the shock waves. The grenade blew and the door fell off its hinges, followed by a billow of plaster dust.

Cameron and Davis came quickly down the hallway. They ran into the security office and began spraying the room with automatic fire. All the lights were blown out, but the windows were clear of glass and the lights from the forecourt revealed two dead men, one at the switchboard and one behind a desk. A third man was stumbling toward a small door concealed in the oak paneling. He slipped through the door and it snapped shut.

Abrams, Katherine, and Lara came into the room. Abrams and Davis ran to the door and fired through it, then pulled the splintered oak panel open. Davis burst in and a shot rang out, sending him falling back into the office, a bullet hole in the center of his forehead. Abrams dropped into a crouch and fired into the darkness. He heard a man scream, then heard retreating footsteps.

Cameron joined him and they moved cautiously through the panel door into a small, windowless room lit by a wall sconce. To the immediate left was a narrow set of service stairs, and crawling up the stairs was a man in a suit. Blood trailed from his legs onto the wooden steps. Cameron bounded up the steps as the man turned. Cameron kicked the gun out of his hand and stared down at him. The man was bleeding from the mouth and nose, a result of the concussion grenade, and his features were twisted with pain, but Cameron recognized him. "Valentin Metkov, top pig in charge of murder. Who says there's no justice in the world?"

Metkov stared at Cameron with clouded eyes. "Please...I can help you...please don't—"

"Where's Androv?"

Metkov blurted, "Upstairs. In the attic."

Cameron fired a single shot and Metkov collapsed.

The alarm bells were sounding cautiously, and the house had come alive as though awakened from an unnatural sleep. Running footsteps could be heard overhead and throughout the surrounding rooms and hallways.

Abrams heard gunfire in the security office. He rushed to the concealed doorway. Katherine was firing at the open hallway door, backing toward him as bullets ripped through the paneled walls. Abrams fired at the open door. "Quickly! Run!"

Katherine made it into the small room while Abrams looked for Lara in the dark, dust-filled room. He saw her bullet-ridden body slumped near the door. He knelt down beside Davis and felt for a heartbeat, but there was none.

Cameron shouted, "Let's go!"

Abrams took the hand grenade from Davis' belt, pulled the pin, and flung it toward the hallway door. He dived back into the small, windowless room as the grenade exploded.

Cameron and Katherine were on the first landing of the narrow service stairs and Abrams scrambled up to join them. They continued quickly up the winding staircase toward the attic.

CHAPTER SIXTY-EIGHT

Marc Pembroke heard the shooting below. In the hallway outside the attic stairs foyer, alarm bells rang and people ran. He said, "The whole bloody house is up and about. Well, another explosion won't make a difference." He nodded to Sutter.

Sutter struck a match and touched it to six twisted strands of detonator cord running up the staircase. The cords flashed and the flame ran along the staircase, split into six directions, and blew the plastic charges on the steel door.

The house shook and plaster fell from the ceiling and walls of the stairwell. Pembroke charged up the narrow stairs and dove into the room, rolling across the floor, followed by Llewelyn, Ann, and Sutter. They all began firing automatic bursts into the dimly lit attic room. Pembroke yelled, "Hold fire!"

Sutter and Ann took cover behind a wall of metal file cabinets facing toward the south end of the attic; Pembroke and Llewelyn, in an alcove formed by a gable. Pembroke peered around the corner of the alcove. "Big room. Takes up half this wing. Empty. Brick partition at the end. The communications room will be on the other side of it." He glanced back at Ann and Sutter. "Well, let's push on."

They all stood. Suddenly there was a sound on the stairs and Pembroke turned. A shot rang out and Pembroke staggered back and fell.

Llewelyn turned in time to see the head and shoulders of a uniformed Russian coming up the stairs, rifle raised. Llewelyn fired a short burst, sending the man reeling back down the stairs. He ripped a fragmentation grenade from his belt, pulled the pin, and lobbed it into the stairwell, then hit the floor.

There was a deafening explosion, followed by the sound of the old staircase collapsing.

Llewelyn slid across the floor and peered over the edge of the open stairwell. A cloud of smoke and dust filled the dark space and he could see small fires crackling below. He thought, *That protects our rear. That also cuts off our line of withdrawal.* He pivoted on the floor and crawled back to Pembroke, who was sitting up in the alcove, Sutter and Ann beside him.

Pembroke ran his hand under his bulletproof vest. "Cracked a rib."

"Don't move." Llewelyn stared at him and saw a trickle of blood running from the corner of his pale mouth. "The lung is punctured, you know."

"Yes, it's my lung and my rib, so I knew it immediately. Get moving."

"Yes. See you later." Ann and Sutter followed Llewelyn cautiously toward the partition that separated the wings. Ann noticed several canvas bags and wooden crates marked in English and French DIPLOMATIC—RUSSIAN MISSION TO THE UNITED NATIONS—NOT SUBJECT TO U.S. CUSTOMS INSPECTION.

Sutter had taken the lead, and he approached the brick wall that rose through the floorboards and ended at the sloping ceiling. A brick chimney formed part of the wall, and a sliding steel door lay to the left of the chimney.

Sutter said softly, "This is more than we expected."

Llewelyn nodded. "Nice old house. Built them like fortresses, they did. Russkies added the steel door, I should think. Well, we've a bit of plastic left."

Sutter looked at the door. The rollers were on the far side and it was probably barred with steel. "Possibly there's more door than plastic."

Ann stepped forward and the two men watched wide-eyed as she banged the butt of her rifle against the steel door. She shouted in Russian, "Androv! I want to speak to Androv."

Sutter and Llewelyn said nothing.

Ann banged again. After a full minute, a voice called back through the door in English. "Who are you?"

She replied, "I am Ann Kimberly, daughter of Henry Kimberly. Are you Androv?"

"Yes."

"Listen carefully. I know my father's in here somewhere. I know about Molniya and so does my government. They are prepared to launch a nuclear strike against your country. Van Dorn has mortars aimed at you. Do you understand?"

Androv replied, "What do you want?"

"I want you to call it off." She looked at her watch. "You have eighteen minutes before Molniya explodes. I want you to open this door and let me broadcast a message over your radio."

Androv replied, "I'll call Moscow. I'll be back to you in a few minutes."

Ann screamed, "You're lying! You're not allowed to mention this over the air. Don't bullshit me! Open this door. Now!"

Androv did not reply.

Ann shouted, "Your situation is hopeless, you fool!"

There was no reply.

Sutter said, "You can't reason with them, miss. They've gotten used to getting their own way."

Llewelyn had wedged the last of the plastic explosive in the corner where the brick wall met the chimney. He said to Sutter, "The wall is stress-bearing." He nodded up at the rafters. "If we rock it a bit, it might collapse from the weight of the roof." He looked at Ann. "But it's your show now."

Ann looked again at her watch, then said, "May as well. There's nothing left to lose."

Abrams, Katherine, and Cameron reached the top of the tightly winding staircase and stopped in a small windowless interior room about the size of a large closet. A sloping ladder with steps led to a hatch in the ceiling.

Cameron turned his attention to the overhead hatch. "Stand back." He had unslung a small cardboard tube from his back, about the size of a roll of wrapping paper. He extended the periscoping tube, which held a sixty-millimeter rocket, and placed it on his shoulder in a firing position. Cameron knelt, "Hold your ears and open your month." He squeezed the electric detonating button and a flame roared out of the rear of the tube, charring the floor as the rocket streaked up to the ceiling. The rocket hit the wooden hatch but didn't detonate against the thin wood, passing through it and streaking up to the slate-covered roof boards. The rocket exploded inside the attic, sending shrapnel spreading out across a bursting radius of fifty feet.

Abrams was already on the ladder. He pushed up on the hinged hatch, lobbed a concussion grenade through the aperture, then dropped the hatch as the grenade detonated. Sheets of plaster fell from the ceiling above them, covering them with white powder. Abrams sprang upward and knocked open the hatch, scrambling up to the attic floor and rolling away. Cameron and Katherine followed. They all lay motionless on the floor, weapons pointed outward to form a small defensive perimeter.

The pressure of the concussion grenade had blown out every light, and Abrams could see a small piece of the night sky through the hole in the roof. The floorboards were covered with hot shrapnel from the rocket. As the ringing of the explosion faded from his ears, Abrams heard the sound of dull moaning.

Cameron rose to one knee, turned on his flashlight, and rolled it across the floor. It didn't draw fire and they all stood.

They searched the large attic room and found three men and two women, all in shock from the concussion grenade and suffering from shrapnel wounds.

Cameron shot each one with his silenced pistol, not asking Abrams or Katherine to give him a hand, or commenting on the business in any way.

Katherine called out quietly, "Look at this."

Abrams and Cameron came up beside her.

She said, "It's a television studio."

Abrams stepped onto the raised set and shone his light over the desk, the fireplace, the American flag. Katherine stooped down and picked up some papers that had been blown around the set, and read the typed script. She looked at Abrams. "This is my father's speech to the American people.... He was to be the next President."

Abrams glanced at one of the sheets. "I didn't even know he was running."

Cameron directed his beam across the room and played it over a brick wall, chimney, and steel door. "If Pembroke is on the other side," he said, "then we've taken both arms of the T. The main stem is still in their hands, but Stewart ought to be on the flat roof above it. We've got them boxed in."

Katherine replied, "But we are boxed out." She looked at her watch. "We've got about sixteen minutes until the EMP detonation and less time than that before George's mortar rounds begin crashing through this roof. We've got to get in there and take control of the radios."

Cameron nodded toward the steel door. "We can blow that door."

Abrams heard sounds below. "They're coming up the stairs." He took the last hand grenade from Cameron, went to the hatch door, opened it, and threw the grenade down, then moved back. The fragmented grenade exploded, throwing the hatch door into the air and ripping apart the ladder below. Cameron pressed a kilo of the clay-like plastic around the doorframe, embedded the detonators, and ran the detonation fuse fifty feet back from the door.

Cameron looked at his watch. "Damned little time left." He looked at Katherine and Abrams. "Well, let's assume everyone is in place."

Abrams replied, "If they're not, they're dead."

Katherine nodded agreement. "We can't turn back. Go ahead and blow the door. We have people to see in there."

Abrams struck a match.

CHAPTER SIXTY-NINE

George Van Dorn looked at the partly decoded telex message on his desk, then looked at the two men standing in the room, Colonel William Osterman and Wallis Baker. He said, "Someone must have hit the wrong code key. This is completely garbled."

Baker replied, "I've sent a request for a repeat, but nothing's come through yet."

Van Dorn glanced at the mantel clock. Less than sixteen minutes remaining.

He suddenly grabbed the telephone and called the Pentagon, going through the identifying procedure, then he said, "Is Colonel Levin still on leave? I want to speak to him."

The voice answered, "He's still on leave, sir."

"Why can't I seem to be able to speak to anyone but you?"

"Because I'm the duty officer."

"Put your sergeant on."

"He's not available."

"Put anyone on. Anyone but you."

There was a pause, then the voice said, "Is there a problem, sir?"

Yes, thought Van Dorn, *there is a serious problem.* A cold chill ran down his spine. He said, "You may be dead in the next few minutes."

"Sir?"

"Tell Androv I'm going to fire the last of my fireworks. Twenty high-explosive mortar rounds. Through his fucking roof. Hold your ears."

"I'm not following you."

Van Dorn hung up the phone and looked at Osterman and Baker. "Well, I guess I've been warning the Russians that the Russians are coming."

No one spoke. Then Van Dorn said, "My fault. I never underestimate the enemy, but I sometimes overestimate our technology and the loyalty of the people who tend to it."

Osterman smiled grimly. "There's always that mortar, George. That won't let us down."

Van Dorn nodded and walked to his field phone on the sill of the bay window. He turned the crank. "Mr. LaRosa, I'm afraid we may have to proceed with the fire mission. Yes, within the next few minutes. Stand by, please. And please accept my compliments on a fine display. Everyone enjoyed it." He hung up and looked back at the two men. "No one likes to call fire in on their own people, but they understood that when they left here."

Baker said, "Give it a few more minutes, George. They may be close."

Van Dorn seemed lost in thought a moment, then looked at the clock again. "Molniya may be closer." He added, "All we know of our operation for certain is that the Kuchik kid got back and reported mission complete. We confirmed from my spotter on the pole that the lights went on and off as they were supposed to. He also tells us that the parachute drop looked bad from where he was standing. Kuchik swears he and Joan gassed the bomb shelter, but for all I know he dropped the fucking crystals in a laundry chute by mistake. Joan is missing. Also, the directional microphones are picking up what sounds like shooting above the noise of the aerial torpedos. And we also know our people haven't reached the communications room or I wouldn't be talking to that imposter." He paused a moment, then concluded, "It smells to me like a defeat." He looked at the two men.

Osterman said, "But Androv knows the jig is up for him, even if we haven't reached the Pentagon. He must also know the personal danger he and his people are in. Perhaps they'll call Moscow and abort this operation."

Van Dorn shook his head. "The Russians move like Volga barges. Slow, steady, and relentless. They can't change course so easily."

Osterman said, "Well, we've played all our cards and they've played theirs."

Van Dorn stared through the bay window at the people in his yard. He was certain that the Russians would show no mercy to him or his guests after what Pembroke's strike force had done to them. He could conceive of the Russian survivors coming to his house and slaughtering everyone, regardless of what happened in the larger sense. He turned and walked back to his desk, took a key ring out of a drawer, and handed it to Osterman. "These are for my arms room. I'd like you both to go outside, get the weak, infirm, drunk, and cowardly into the basement, and have everyone else arm themselves." He added, "Let Kitty help you. She'll be good at making sure everyone has the right gun."

The two men nodded grimly and walked to the door.

Van Dorn called after them, "If anyone feels like praying, encourage them, but don't tell them what they're praying for. Only God knows. To everyone else it's classified information."

Van Dorn walked to the coffee table and picked an hors d'oeuvre from the tray. "Tried to poison my canapés, did you, Viktor? You turkey." He popped the pâté in his mouth.

Van Dorn walked to his memento wall and stared at a picture of himself, O'Brien, Allerton, and Kimberly taken in London just a few weeks before the war ended. The last time the four musketeers were all together. *My God*, he thought, *how little we know of men's hearts and souls.*

CHAPTER SEVENTY

A brams lit the fuse and it flashed in the dark attic room. The plastic exploded and the heavy steel door leaped off its locks and hinges, crashing to the floor.

The attic wing that held the communications area was three or four steps down, and Abrams had a clear view of a large open space, about half the size of a football field, he thought, separated into work areas by half-wall partitions. The room seemed to be lit mostly by the lighting on its electronic consoles. A number of men and women dressed in brown overalls could be seen running away from the explosion.

Abrams, Katherine, and Cameron began firing from a kneeling position, single well-aimed shots, as they tried to avoid hitting the electronic units.

Llewelyn, Sutter, and Ann heard and felt the explosion at the opposite end of the attic. Sutter said, "Well, they've made it. All right, our turn." He lit the fuse on the charge and they dived for the floor behind a row of file cabinets.

The plastic exploded and the brick wall and chimney seemed to leap a few inches, lifting the roof beams. The beams resettled and the brick and mortar cracked, then bulged and crumbled, creating a large V-shaped opening in the wall.

Ann stared up through the cement dust and saw the great electronics room framed in the wide V. Even a cursory look revealed to her trained eye a very advanced multicapability array of technology.

Sutter and Llewelyn were standing behind the file cabinet, firing unsilenced single shots over the heads of the Russians, keeping them pinned down. There was little return fire from these technicians, Ann noticed. *We've cracked through the hard shell of the KGB and we are about to enter the soft nerve tissue.* She called out, "Go easy on the equipment."

Llewelyn called back, "They *know* we're after the bloody radios, and unless we keep them busy, the KGB chaps in there will destroy what you're trying to get your hands on." He fired three quick shots at a man who was swinging a metal bar at what looked to Ann like an encrypting machine. The man fell over, but the machine was hit and sparked. Llewelyn said, "Sorry. It's a trade-off."

She looked at her watch. Nearly midnight. *The very witching time of night when churchyards yawn and hell itself breathes out contagion to this world.*

Molniya was dropping rapidly toward its low orbit point, where it would consume itself in a nuclear fireball. For that half second it would light up the continent and set the world on a new and terrible course. *Where the light is the brightest,* she thought, *the shadows are the deepest.*

Tom Grenville stood at the large roof hatch, Johnson beside him. Stewart was propped up on his elbow close by. A misty wind blew across the rooftop, and Grenville could see that the threatened storm was blowing out to sea. In the far northeast, stars appeared on the horizon and Grenville looked at them as though for the last time.

Along the edge of the roof hatch sat twelve CS gas canisters in a neat row. They heard and felt the two explosions below and Grenville was startled out of his stargazing. He said, "It sounds like the time has come to chuck these canisters down there."

"Correct," said Stewart, "and you'll follow the canisters." He nodded toward two nylon rappelling lines tied to the bases of two antennas. "Ready?"

Grenville didn't think he was. He glanced at his watch. "Isn't this supposed to end soon?"

"Ready! Open it!"

Grenville opened the heavy, hinged roof hatch and heard more clearly the sound of gunfire and pandemonium below.

Johnson and Stewart began pulling the pins on the canisters and throwing them down at various angles. The CS canisters popped and disgorged billows of white nausea and tear-producing gas. Grenville threw the last two canisters down, then slammed the hatch cover closed. "We'll give that five minutes to work."

Stewart glared at him. "We'll give it sixty seconds." Stewart looked at his digital watch, then commented, "You'll be down there in less than five seconds if you do it properly, Tom. Don't panic and hang on the rope or you'll be a sitting duck. And don't let go, for God's sake, or you'll break every bone in your body. Saw that happen once."

"In the Falklands?" suggested Grenville.

"No, lad, in Glasgow. Fellow trying to get out the window of a lady's bedroom as the husband returned home." He laughed, then reached out and patted Grenville's shoulder. "You're a good lad. Steady now." He looked at Johnson. "Keep an eye on the boy, General. I'll cover as best I can up here." Stewart glanced at his watch. "Ready."

"How long were you in the Falklands?" asked Grenville.

"*Ready!* Gas masks."

Johnson and Grenville pulled their masks over their faces and adjusted the fit, then put on climbing gloves.

"Open it."

They pulled the hatch open. The nausea gas hung below, as it was made to do, a thick white blanket lying over the area like a snowdrift.

Grenville and Johnson threw their rappelling lines into the opening.

"Go!"

They each went over the edge of the square hatch, rifles nestled in their arms, and began the two-story slide to the floor of the communications room.

Abrams and Cameron slid on their gas masks and moved quickly but cautiously toward the gas-filled doorway.

Katherine stayed behind in the television studio to cover the open hatchway.

Abrams and Cameron could hear the sounds of retching and coughing coming from the room. Abrams entered first, followed by Cameron. They moved as quickly as possible through the blinding smoke. Abrams thought Cameron seemed to be passing by the incapacitated men and women very reluctantly, like an alcoholic passing a bottle. But they had matters more pressing than adding more notches to Cameron's rifle. They were looking for the main radio transmitter, and for Androv, and for Henry Kimberly—and for the third man, whoever he was.

Sutter watched as a figure appeared through the heavy-hanging gas, climbed through the break in the wall, and collapsed. He dragged the body away from the edge of the spreading gas. It was a young girl in brown overalls. Her face was blotchy and flecked with vomit.

Ann knelt beside her and slapped her. She said in Russian, "Breathe. Breathe."

The girl took a deep breath.

Ann said, "Where's the radio you use to transmit voice messages to Moscow?"

The girl squinted up at Ann through running eyes.

Ann repeated the question, adding, "You have five seconds to tell me or we'll kill you."

The girl drew another breath and said, "The radio . . . against the north wall . . ."

Ann asked her a few brief technical questions regarding frequencies, voice scramblers, and power setting, then slid on her mask and rushed toward the opening in the wall. Llewelyn and Sutter followed.

They moved quickly through the room toward the long right wall.

Many of the Russians had climbed atop the consoles to try to escape the low-clinging gas. One of them, Vasili Churnik, a survivor of the railroad tunnel incident, stood atop a computer and watched the two men and the woman walk in.

Tom Grenville's gloved hands squeaked down the rope. He felt his feet hit the floor, bent his knees, and rolled off into a kneeling position, his rifle raised to his shoulder. He peered into the dense gas, but his visibility was less than five feet. The lights on the electronic consoles glowed eerily through the opaque fog.

Johnson was back to back with him now, forming a pitiful defensive perimeter of two. Johnson's muffled voice came through the mask. "You see, Grenville, if they'd been prepared with proper chemical protective devices, we'd have been massacred. In war," said the general, quoting an old army axiom, "as in life, lack of prior planning produces a piss-poor performance."

Grenville turned his head back to Johnson. "General."

"Yes, son."

"Shut the fuck up. And don't say another word unless it has something to do with saving my life. Got it?"

Johnson replied, "All right...if that's the way—"

"Move out. You go your way, I'll go mine. See you later." Grenville made out three black-clad figures through the rolling gas, two men and a woman. He was disoriented and didn't know if that was part of Pembroke's team, including Ann, coming from the north, or Cameron's team, including Katherine, from the south. But they weren't Russians and he moved toward them.

Vasili Churnik watched as the three Americans passed by. The other Russians in the room, mostly technical people, had accepted the fact that they had been overrun by what must be a large number of commandos, and they were concerned only with gasping for air. But Churnik, by training and temperament, like Cameron, had difficulty letting a target pass. Especially after his humiliation earlier in the evening. He drew his pistol, a .38 revolver, and fired all six rounds into the backs of the three.

Grenville, who was very close, heard, then saw, the man fire from the top of the gray console. He fired a single shot and the Russian toppled over.

There was screaming in the room now and Abrams shouted, "Down! Down!" He unscrewed his silencer and fired into the walls to underscore his meaning. Men and women began diving to the floor.

Cameron rushed over to the three fallen people. Llewelyn was dead, shot in the back of the head. Sutter was stunned, but his bulletproof vest had stopped the two rounds that hit him. Ann was bleeding from the neck.

Cameron examined Ann's wound, a crease along the left side of the neck. "Well, it's not so bad as it looks, lass. Just bloody. Let's stand up, then. We ought to find that radio."

Ann stood unsteadily.

The Russian technicians were edging toward the two exits, into the short arms of the T. When they realized no one was stopping them, they stampeded out of the room.

Katherine sat on the desk in the television studio and watched silently as half a dozen people ran by her in the darkness and headed for the open trapdoor. Discovering that the ladder was gone, they stopped. Below, men shouted up at them. Guards, Katherine thought.

The Russians began jumping through the open attic hatch to the floor below. One of them, Katherine saw with horror, had separated from the rest and was heading toward her. She held her pistol tight and slipped under the desk.

The man, tall, well dressed, and distinguished-looking, came right up to the desk. The lighting was so poor, she was sure he couldn't see her crouched under it.

He opened the top drawer and she saw him remove a few items, one of them a pistol. He turned and started walking away.

Katherine rose from beneath the desk.

The man heard the noise and spun around.

Katherine said, "Hello."

The sky had cleared and the moon shone blue through the gabled window next to the fireplace. Dust motes danced in the pale moonbeams, giving them both a spectral appearance, as though they had met in a dream. A slow smile passed over Henry Kimberly's face. "That must be Kate."

"It is."

He nodded.

"Drop yours," she said.

He held one hand in his right pocket. "I don't think I will."

"Then I may shoot you if you move."

"I'll try to be still."

Katherine looked at her father in the pale light, then said, "Somehow I never accepted your death. That must be a normal reaction. When Carbury came into my office, I had the irrational thought he'd come to tell me you were waiting in the lobby."

Kimberly didn't reply.

She continued, "I always fantasized about how I might meet you, but I never thought it would be at the point of a gun."

He forced a smile. "I should think not." He stared at her and said, "Well, Kate, I thought about how we'd meet also. But that wasn't a fantasy. I knew I'd be back some day."

She glanced at the desk. "Yes, you were going to be President."

He nodded and said softly, "I was going to use the remaining years I have to try to get to know you and Ann."

"Were you? What makes you think Ann or I would want to know a traitor?"

"That's a subjective term. I acted out of conscience. I abandoned my friends, my family, and my fortune to work for something I believed in. So did a good number of men and women in those days."

She laughed derisively, "And you're going to tell me that you don't believe any longer? That you want to make amends to your family and your country?"

He shrugged. "I'd be lying if I said that. I cannot make amends and I do not intend to." His voice became distant, as though he were in another room. "You have to understand that when a person invests so much in something, it's difficult to admit even to oneself—that you may have been wrong. And once you go to Moscow, it's not easy to come home again. You deal with the devil because he has the short-cut approach to power. And when you live in Moscow, you begin to appreciate power and all that goes with it." He let out a breath and looked at her. "I don't expect you to understand. Someone of my own age who lived through those times would be more sympathetic."

"I know a lot of men from those times. They are not sympathetic." She let the silence drag out, then said, "Some men commit themselves to a cause and announce their intentions. If you were just a turncoat or defector, I could understand that. But you have lied and cheated, you betrayed everyone who put their faith and confidence in you. You've caused the deaths of friends, and you've let your children grow up without a father. You must be a very cold and heartless man, Henry Kimberly. You have no soul and no conscience. And now you tell me you were just a victim of circumstances." She paused, then said sharply, "I think all you're committed to is the act of *betrayal*. I think..." Tears ran down her face and her voice became husky. "I think... Why? Why in the name of God did you do that to... to *me*?"

Henry Kimberly hung his head thoughtfully, then his eyes met hers. He said in a voice barely above a whisper, "Sometimes I think the last time I felt any honest joy in my heart was a day on my last leave. I took you and Ann to Central Park... I carried you in my arms and Ann put her little hand in mine, and we laughed at the monkeys in the zoo—"

"Shut up! Shut up!"

Neither spoke for some time, then Kimberly said, "May I go now?"

She wiped her eyes. "Go... go where?"

"What does it matter? Not back to Moscow, I assure you. I just want to go... to walk in the village... see my country... find some peace... I'm not important any longer. No one wants me, either as a hero, or as a villain. I am not a threat... I am an old man."

Katherine cleared her throat, then said coolly, "Who is Talbot Three?"

Henry Kimberly's eyebrows arched, then he replied, "There is no Talbot Three.... Well, there was, but he died many years ago."

She looked at him closely, then said, "You're lying."

He shrugged, then said softly, "May I go? Please."

"No."

He didn't reply immediately, then spoke. "I'm afraid I must leave, Kate. And you won't shoot me, any more than I'd shoot you." He added in a tone that suggested the subject was closed, "I'm glad we met. We may meet again." He began to turn.

Katherine shouted, "No! No, you will *not* leave." She cocked the big Browning automatic.

Henry Kimberly looked back over his shoulder. He smiled, then winked at her. "*Au revoir*, little Kate." He walked into the darkness of the attic and headed toward the open hatchway.

Katherine watched him, the muzzle of the pistol following his back. Her hands shook and her eyes clouded. A stream of confused thoughts ran through her mind, then suddenly focused on Patrick O'Brien. He had been her real father for all these years, and Henry Kimberly, a man unknown to her, and his friends had murdered him. And O'Brien would not let Henry Kimberly walk away, and would not approve if she did. Henry Kimberly had to pay. She said, or thought she said, "Stop," but wasn't sure if she had actually spoken. He kept walking. She fired.

The roar of the .45-caliber silver bullet shattered the silence, then echoed off in distant places. The sound died away, though the ringing remained in her ears and the smell of burnt cordite hung in her nostrils.

She looked across the twenty feet of open space that separated them. Henry Kimberly had turned at the open hatch and stared back. He looked neither surprised that she'd fired at him, nor surprised that she'd missed. They both understood that the act was a catharsis, a symbolic gesture. Kimberly lowered himself into the open hatchway and disappeared.

Katherine found that her legs had become weak, and she sat back in the chair behind the desk; his chair—his desk. His script lay scattered before her.

Katherine put her head down on the desk and wept.

Marc Pembroke sat in the dark alcove of the gable. He heard running footsteps coming toward him and watched in the half-light as about a dozen men and women, faces pale and eyes watering, filed past, heading for the staircase opposite him. He kept his rifle in the ready position and watched. His breathing had become difficult and he knew he was drowning in his own blood, yet his mind was still clear.

The Russians were not ten feet from him and he saw that some of them carried weapons. The first to arrive were staring down at the collapsed staircase. Below, on the landing, guards shouted up at them.

Pembroke saw the top rails of a ladder rising over the edge of the stairwell. There was some heated discussion over who was going to use it first—the guards who wanted to come up, or the technicians who wanted to get down.

A man in a suit stepped forward and settled the disagreement. Looking pale and shaky, but still arrogant, Viktor Androv pushed aside the crowd and began lowering his corpulent body onto the ladder.

Pembroke unscrewed the silencer from his rifle, then shouted, "Androv! Freeze!" He fired at the ceiling and the crowd hit the floor. He and Androv stared at each other over the clear space, Androv's head and shoulders visible as he stood on the ladder, Pembroke sitting with his back to the wall in the alcove.

Pembroke said, "Did you know that Arnold Brin was my father?"

Androv's mouth opened, but before he could say anything, Pembroke fired. The rounds ripped into Androv's head and neck, and Pembroke saw the little rosettes of crimson blooming on Androv's white pudgy face like a sudden outbreak of acne. Androv waved his arms in circles, then fell and crashed to the landing below.

Pembroke thought he would rather have killed Androv in a more interesting way. But he was content that amid all this mayhem, fate had put Viktor Androv in his gunsights.

Pembroke coughed and a sharp pain racked his chest. He focused on the people at the stairwell door. They were beginning to scramble down the ladder, but he had no interest in them, nor they in him.

Face after face turned to him, then disappeared below the floor line. The already dark room seemed to be growing darker, and Pembroke's eyes were becoming unfocused. But one of the faces that sank below his line of vision was clear, and it was the face of someone who could not be there. Pembroke thought he was beginning to hallucinate.

CHAPTER SEVENTY-ONE

Ann Kimberly pressed the gauze pad on her neck as she looked over the rows of electronic consoles, noting radios of every sort and purpose, encrypting and decrypting devices, computers, microwave and satellite transmitters and receivers, as well as monitoring and jamming devices. "Diplomatic mission, my ass. Those bastards."

She sat before the big SM-35 radio and her eyes ran over the instruments. The radio didn't seem to be damaged and the power was on. A computer tape transmitted continuous encoded messages to Moscow, mostly random words to cover the real messages and to give the National Security Agency a headache. She found the tape switch and shut it off. This she knew would immediately alert the NSA.

Ann scanned a procedure booklet, written in Russian, on the console. "Damn language is difficult enough to understand when it's spoken, but these letters... What's this word, Abrams?"

"Confuser."

"They mean scrambler." She turned off the voice scrambler so that anyone tuned to the frequency could hear a voice broadcast en clair. She flipped through the booklet.

Sutter had found the switches to the big attic exhaust fans and the air was clearer now, allowing them to remove their gas masks, though everyone's eyes teared and their skin still burned from the clinging gas.

Cameron was on the telephone talking to George Van Dorn.

"Yes, it's Cameron, Mr. Van Dorn. Hold up on those mortars, if you will. We've got things pretty well in hand here. Ann Kimberly is about to begin broadcasting. Yes, sir. No, I'm not under duress. Ivan is under duress. I'm just fine. Yes, I'll stay with you and give you a running report."

Abrams looked around the huge room. Never, he realized, did he think all of this was up here, and never did he think he'd live long enough to see it. He looked at the open roof hatch and the broken gable windows, remembering the damage downstairs as well. He said to Ann, "This place doesn't look very EMP-proof to me."

She smiled as she turned a knob. "Not anymore." She leaned forward. "There, I think I've got it." She adjusted the microphone on its flexible boom, then glanced at the digital clocks on the radio. Ten minutes to midnight here and ten minutes to 8:00 A.M. in Moscow. She said to Abrams, "You stay here and help me with my Russian."

Abrams nodded. He looked out over the room. Sutter was perched on the top of the tallest console, where he had a commanding view of the entire room. Grenville and Johnson were searching the nooks and crannies and breaking all the gable windows to ventilate the gas further.

Ann began to speak in Russian. "To all stations that are listening, this is Ann Kimberly, an American citizen, speaking from the Russian Mission to the United Nations, in Glen Cove, New York. Please acknowledge, Moscow."

She turned to Abrams. "They're not going to acknowledge shit, and they know exactly where this broadcast is coming from." She added, "But now everyone who normally monitors this radio is alerted—the National Security Agency, the Defense Intelligence Agency, and the CIA. The White House, Pentagon, and Camp David will be instantly tied in. I'll wait a moment before I broadcast anything momentous." She asked, "How was my Russian?"

"Not bad...but the pronunciation is a little off."

"In other words, it stinks." She shrugged. "I listen to a lot of it, but hardly ever have an occasion to speak it." She hesitated a moment, then said, "Here, take the mike. You were supposed to fill in for me if I got killed anyway."

Abrams, too, hesitated, then adjusted the microphone to where he was standing.

Ann said, "Okay, this may be the most important radio message ever broadcast in the history of mankind. But don't be nervous. I'll coach you. You're on. Identify yourself." Ann pushed the transmit button.

Abrams spoke into the microphone. "This is Tony Abrams, an American citizen." He repeated Ann's salutation, then took a deep breath and began. "This is a direct message to the leaders in the Kremlin, the White House, the Pentagon, and everyone who is in a position to launch a nuclear weapon." As Abrams continued speaking, his eyes went to the digital clock several times, then to the adjoining electrical display panel, where he saw three steady green lights glaring in a row.

Abrams continued transmitting. "If the nuclear device aboard the Molniya satellite explodes, the United States will have no recourse but to retaliate with nuclear weapons." He didn't know if he was making up defense policy, putting the idea into the heads of the people in Washington, or trying to bluff Moscow into thinking he was speaking for the government. He broadcast for another full minute, then hit the microphone switch and said to Ann, "That's all I'm going to say."

Ann looked at him, then nodded. "I'll speak in English for a while. There are people who understand English around the radio in Moscow by now. Also, I want to address myself to Washington and the NSA at Fort Meade."

Abrams wiped a line of sweat from his forehead. "I'm going to take a walk. Good luck." He left.

Ann spoke into the microphone. "This is Ann Kimberly again, and I'm addressing my associates at the National Security Agency. Please acknowledge."

There was a long silence and Ann repeated the transmission, then a male voice came out of the speaker. "This is Chet Forbes, Ann, at Fort Meade. I read you."

"I read you, Chet. Give me a status report."

The voice still sounded hesitant, if not incredulous, but Forbes' equipment did not lie; he knew he was talking to Glen Cove, and he knew from her voiceprint that he was speaking to Ann Kimberly, an NSA employee. He said, "NORAD is on an alert status of DEFCON 5, prelaunch condition. The Polaris fleet, SAC, and the European nukes have been flashed Red Alerts. The President is at Camp David, and he is in communication with all nuclear commanders."

Ann spoke in Russian, "Moscow, did you read Fort Meade?"

Moscow did not answer.

Ann took a long breath and lit a cigarette, then said, "Chet, can you get the President to speak to those jokers directly?"

Forbes replied, "The President is attempting to contact the Premier in Moscow."

Ann said, "Tell Camp David that Presidential Assistant James Allerton is a Soviet agent."

Forbes stayed silent for a moment, then came back on the speaker. "Understand. Will do." He paused, then said, "We don't know how the hell you wound up in Green Acres," he said, using the NSA code word for the Russian station in Glen Cove, "but from what we've been hearing you broadcast to Moscow, we're glad you're there."

"I only hope they're listening. In the meantime tell every NATO ally and every Warsaw Pact country that if World War Three begins, it began in Moscow." She paused, then said in Russian, "Are you listening, Mr. Premier?"

But Moscow was still silent.

Tony Abrams walked quickly into the north wing of the attic and knelt beside Marc Pembroke in the alcove. "Pembroke?"

He opened his eyes slowly. Abrams thought he looked very pale. Abrams said, "How are you doing?"

"Relative to *what*?"

Abrams smiled. "Listen, Van Dorn's sending that Sikorsky helicopter to get us all out of here. You'll be in a hospital soon."

"Good. That's where I belong. How is the mission progressing?"

"We've won the battle, but the war is still touch-and-go. Ann is broadcasting. It's up to the Russians now."

"Too bad. They're an unpredictable lot of beggers. What time is it?"

"Approaching midnight. At least we won't have long to wait."

"No...and we've accomplished our mission, haven't we?"

"Yes."

"I lost some good people.... Don't tell me who, I'll discover that soon enough. Listen Abrams...my job offer still stands. You're very good."

"Thanks, but I'm committed."

"To what? To whom...?"

"The Red Devils."

Pembroke looked at him. "Never heard of them."

"Very secret. Okay, I just came by to check your temperature. Will you be all right alone for a while?"

"I'm always alone and I'm always all right. But thanks for dropping in."

Abrams stood.

Pembroke looked at the open stairwell door. He said, "A few Russkies beat it that way. Only technicians. I let them go—"

"Of course. Just take it easy—"

"Listen, Abrams...Androv was with them—" Pembroke coughed, and a clot of blood passed through his lips.

Abrams knelt beside him again.

Pembroke seemed to be trying to remember something, then said, "I shot the bastard. Be a good chap and go see if he's dead. Be careful, old man...guards down there...."

Abrams moved cautiously to the stairwell and peered down. An open hallway door cast a shaft of light into the small foyer below and revealed a collapsed staircase covered with rubble. A ladder extended from the floor up to the attic. There was no sign of life, or of death. Abrams said, "The guards have decamped and taken any bodies with them."

Pembroke nodded. "They've had enough of us. Wonder where they went...?" He thought a moment, then said, "I'm certain I hit the bastard in the head...."

"I'm sure you did."

Pembroke said, "Joan...Joan Grenville is down there...in the dumbwaiter....Take a few of my people..."

"Yes, she'll be fine." He didn't want to tell Pembroke that there were few people left. He'd go get her. "Stop worrying about these things. We're not helpless without you." Abrams looked at his watch. "I have to go."

"Wait...wait...Listen, I saw...I saw..."

"Yes?"

"I...I thought I was hallucinating...but I wasn't....My mind is clear...."

"Who did you see?"

"I saw Patrick O'Brien."

Abrams stood motionless, then stared at Pembroke and Pembroke stared back. Abrams said, "Where did you see him?"

Pembroke motioned with his head. "There."

Abrams shook his head. "No."

"Yes. He was dressed in black...."

Abrams stayed silent, then nodded. "Yes, you did."

"Don't humor me."

"No, I believe you."

Neither man spoke for some time, then Pembroke said, "What are you going to do about it?"

"What would you do about it? The mission is over. You earned your pay. Would you put in overtime and hope to get paid for it?"

Pembroke nodded. "Yes. If I could, I would."

Abrams drew a deep breath, glanced back at the stairwell, then checked his watch. "Down there, you say?"

"Down there. Look in Androv's office. That will be where any evidence will be, and he'd want to destroy that before he, too, begins his Odyssey to the nether regions."

Abrams walked toward the stairwell.

CHAPTER SEVENTY-TWO

Henry Kimberly walked quickly down the long, deserted first-floor corridor. The smell of burnt cordite hung in the smoke-laden air. Kimberly stopped at the bullet-marked door of Androv's office. He thought Androv might be here to recover or destroy sensitive files.

Kimberly pushed the door open and entered the dimly lit office. He heard the cocking sound of a pistol near his ear. He stood motionless.

A voice close to his ear said in English, "Henry Kimberly, I presume."

Kimberly nodded slightly. He turned his head and saw a man in a black jump suit. The two men faced each other and stared. Kimberly's voice was barely audible as he said, "Patrick..."

O'Brien nodded.

Kimberly said, "You're supposed to be dead."

O'Brien smiled. "So are you."

Kimberly's eyes went to the gun. "If you're going to kill me, do it and spare me another mawkish reunion."

O'Brien lowered the pistol and said, "I caught a glimpse of you in the attic. Androv apparently was too preoccupied with dodging bullets to tell you."

"Tell me what?"

O'Brien replied, "I'm one of you."

Kimberly stared at him, then said softly, "My God...No...you can't be..."

"Why not? I was under suspicion during the war, and for good reason. You, however, never were the subject of the great were-wolf hunt." O'Brien thought a moment, then added, "It should have been I who disappeared and went to Moscow, Henry. And you should have come home and run the firm. You had family, and you had more prestige and better contacts here...but the people in Moscow work in strange ways, don't they?"

"Yes."

"And we never question orders, do we?"

"No, we don't." Kimberly glanced around the office and his eyes fell on the body of Claudia Lepescu, then returned to O'Brien. Kimberly said, "Where's Androv?"

O'Brien shrugged. "I was waiting for him. Have you seen him?"

Kimberly replied, "He may be in the basement with the others. Let's go." He moved toward the door.

O'Brien made no move to follow. He said, "We'll wait for him here."

"Why?"

"Because, with the exception of you two, no one in America knows I'm alive, or who I really am." O'Brien paused, then said, "I think we've lost this round, and I don't want Androv to fall into the hands of our former compatriots."

Kimberly looked at him, then nodded slowly. "Yes...I see...I think Moscow would approve."

"I'm certain they would." O'Brien smiled and said, "So, you were to be the next President."

Kimberly nodded. "I may still be." He glanced out the broken stained-glass windows. "We may yet see that flash of light."

"We may. Only Moscow knows what Moscow will do." O'Brien motioned to Kimberly. "Let's wait for Androv here." He walked to the window and sat on the sill. Kimberly drew closer and remained standing. O'Brien spoke softly, "You see, Henry, while life may have been hard for you in Moscow, at least you weren't living the daily nightmare of a double agent. I've played the most dangerous and difficult game a man can play. I headed an intelligence network of extremely clever people—our old people—while at the same time I served the interests of our friends in Moscow."

Kimberly asked, "How did you do it?"

O'Brien smiled. "With mirrors. I'm a magician, an illusionist, also an acrobat, and a juggler." O'Brien continued, "It's a tough act, my friend. In the past year, for instance, I had to satisfy the OSS that I was working on what they knew to be an extremely important matter, while at the same time I had to protect Moscow's Operation Stroke, about which I knew little."

Kimberly nodded appreciatively.

O'Brien went on. "To make matters worse, Van Dorn, Arnold Brin, and a few others had zeroed in on some aspects of the Stroke, and were pushing me hard to find out more. I dragged some red herrings across their path—a nuclear explosion on Wall Street and a plot to access and erase all American computers—but it kept coming back to EMP. The old boys are good, Henry."

"Yes, they are. And the diary?"

O'Brien smiled wide. "That was both a stroke of genius and an act of lunacy. I was desperate by that time. I dropped that diary on them in the hope that the old search for Talbot would consume their energies and obsess their psyches as it did four decades ago. I knew who Talbot was. It was I. I didn't know it was you, too."

Kimberly smiled slightly. "You set off a chain reaction with that, didn't you, Patrick?"

O'Brien smiled in return.

"Yes. First that idiot Thorpe nearly killed me. Then Tony Abrams, who was pushed on me by your daughter, turned out to be cleverer than I thought. I decided to have Abrams killed rather than let him nose around. I used Claudia"—he nodded toward the body—"to set Abrams up. She thought she was working for Moscow. Abrams assumed it was Thorpe who tried to have him killed. Things are not as they appear in this wilderness of mirrors. I kept telling everyone that, and they all kept nodding, but no one seemed to understand that I was talking about myself." He laughed.

Kimberly stared at O'Brien for a moment, then spoke. "How did you get here?"

O'Brien smiled. "I jumped in from a Sikorsky helicopter."

"You *are* courageous, Patrick. But you always were."

"Yes, it's how I stayed alive when others died. I'm also ruthless." He looked at Kimberly. "And unashamedly power-hungry. I want to be king."

Kimberly stared back at him. "I am the heir apparent."

"So Androv tells me now." O'Brien shrugged, then glanced out the window. He said, "You know, Henry, if Operation Stroke succeeds, if Molniya explodes and spreads a wave of electromagnetic destruction across this continent, then, notwithstanding what's happened in this house tonight, you and I will be the most powerful men in America."

Kimberly said, "We have another compatriot who is to be rewarded with power. James Allerton. Did Androv tell you?"

O'Brien made a sound of contempt. "Androv did, but I knew long before that. Allerton is weak. Nearly senile. If it weren't for his national reputation, Moscow would have discarded him years ago."

"But they haven't. And he is to form part of our troika."

O'Brien's eyes narrowed and he shook his head. "There's a Secret Service man at Camp David whom I've spring-loaded to see that no matter what happens tonight, James Allerton will not leave there alive."

Kimberly glanced at the pistol in O'Brien's hand. He said evenly, "That leaves only you and me, and that's one too many, isn't it?"

O'Brien nodded absently, as though he'd missed the implication. He said, "You see, Henry, if the Americans win this round, then I can resurface as a hero who narrowly escaped death. But I can't do that if you or Androv fall into their hands."

"It was my misfortune to open this door."

"Fortune has little to do with it. I always suspected the existence of the third man, and I'd planned to eliminate him at the first opportunity. The fact that it's you, my old friend, makes it more difficult for me, but nonetheless, necessary."

Kimberly said, "In other words, if Moscow wins tonight, you

want to be President. If Moscow loses, you want to be head of the old boys again, until such time as Moscow does succeed."

"Correct. And you, Henry, are an obstacle in either case."

Kimberly said, "We can escape together. Go to Moscow."

"I don't want to go to Moscow. Tomorrow I want either to be in my old office at O'Brien, Kimberly and Rose, or in the Oval Office." He looked closely at Kimberly. "No senior intelligence chief worthy of the name should ever have to be a fugitive. There should always be another office from which he can practice his trade. That's the reward for living as we must."

Kimberly said, "Moscow will not reward you. They'll find out you killed me...and Androv."

O'Brien motioned toward Claudia's body. "Battle deaths cover murder well. You remember."

Kimberly's eyes fixed on the gun again. "Patrick...This is not... This is disloyal....They want me alive...Moscow wants—"

"What do I care what Moscow wants? They create traitors and they expect loyalty from us. Moscow is only a means to an end for me. The fastest, indeed the only, way to Washington for me, as for you, was via Moscow. Just as the last Roman emperors were made and unmade by the barbarians, so will the barbarians in Moscow crown me Emperor of America."

Kimberly's voice was sharp. "And depose you at their pleasure. You might be more secure if we shared power."

"Perhaps—if there were power to share. But that may not be. I may be back in Rockefeller Center tomorrow to the amazement and relief of my staff. I have to plan for all contingencies, Henry. No hard feelings, old soldier."

"No—" Kimberly reached for the pistol in his jacket. O'Brien fired his silenced automatic into Henry Kimberly's heart, and Kimberly toppled backward like a felled tree, crashing to the floor.

O'Brien looked down at his former law partner and comrade-in-arms. "And then there was one."

CHAPTER SEVENTY-THREE

Tony Abrams moved down the first-floor staircase and saw that the body of Valentin Metkov had been removed. Abrams passed cautiously through the splintered panel door into the ruined security office. Davis' body lay among the rubble, but the guards had removed Lara's body.

Abrams felt he was following the trail of death and it was leading him back to where he had begun, in Patrick O'Brien's office long ago. He could not fathom O'Brien's motives for recruiting him then, and they were even less clear now.

Abrams looked into the hallway. No one was visible, but he heard voices in the distance. He slipped into the hall, moved quickly to Androv's door, and saw that the lock was shot away. He held his rifle up and hit the door with his shoulder.

Patrick O'Brien was on his knees, rummaging through Androv's desk. He looked up quickly, then reached for the pistol on the desk top.

Abrams leveled his rifle, and O'Brien slid his hand back. O'Brien said, "I didn't think any of you would come down here again."

Abrams said nothing but just stared at the man.

O'Brien stood slowly. "Who gave me away?"

"I figured it out."

O'Brien smiled, an almost pleasant smile. "No, you didn't, Tony. At least give me the satisfaction of thinking I was the most clever double agent this country has ever seen."

Abrams nodded. "You were. Now you're not."

O'Brien nodded. "How do you feel? Angry? Betrayed? Foolish?"

"Yes. You're very convincing."

"It's a matter of believing in what you're doing and saying while you're doing and saying it. When I worked for the old boys, I did my best. When I worked for the Russians, I did my best. Don't feel too badly. I hoodwinked nearly every one of the so-called intelligence greats in this country and Britain for nearly forty years."

"Why?"

He shrugged. "At first it was young idealism. Then I wanted out, but they tried to kill me. Shot me on a hunting trip in Utah. I survived, obviously, but while I lay there in the hospital, I realized that they were ruthless, and that while we were once ruthless against the Nazis, we had gone very soft. That was the expression they used in those days. Remember that? America has gone soft. And it was true. The Russians—the Communists—were getting their way all over the world then. By 1948 it seemed just a matter of time before they took over. I joined the ruthless side." He smiled. "The tide turned the other way, but I was happy by then, or at least at peace with my double life. I have no wife or children and I devoted myself to the game. Having been the victim of an assassination attempt, I was never again under suspicion the way I'd been during the war."

Abrams glanced down at the body of Claudia, then he saw the sprawled body of Henry Kimberly partially hidden behind the desk. "Is that your work?"

"Yes."

Abrams stared at O'Brien. He said, "Killing doesn't seem to disturb you."

"All the killings in the cloak-and-dagger world since the last war don't equal the deaths in one small battle. If nations confined themselves to letting spies kill one another, we'd all be better off. This is the sacrifice we make on the altar of the god of war to keep him from killing more of us. If we'd won tonight, there would never again be the chance of war on this earth. But now, thanks to you, Van Dorn, and your friends, we're back to the nuclear brink."

"I think I'd rather live on the brink than in the hole."

"Easy to say now. Tell me that five years from now when there's another crisis."

"You won't be around five minutes from now."

O'Brien looked at him intently. "Are you going to kill me?"

"Why not?"

"Because the American intelligence establishment wants me. Every spy sings when he's in a cage. I could sing for ten years and not repeat a song."

Abrams nodded. He knew this was true. The more highly placed the criminal or the traitor, the more likely it was they'd make a deal with him.

O'Brien seemed to relax, and dropped into a conversational tone. "My one real mistake in recent years was not killing Van Dorn. But I thought he'd drink himself to death." He laughed.

"He may. But it won't do you any good."

"No." O'Brien turned and looked out the window, then said to Abrams, "We may still see that flash in the sky."

"We may. Tell me, why did you think it was necessary to fake your death? You would have been more useful to them on the scene."

O'Brien laughed. "I didn't intend to fake my death. That idiot, Thorpe, nearly killed me. What I faked was a heart attack before I opened my chute. Most parachutists whose chutes don't open suffer heart failure before they hit the ground."

"What do you plan to come up with this time?"

"Nothing...I'm ready to go with you. The CIA will make you a god, Tony. You'll never want for anything as long as you live." O'Brien stepped from behind the desk. "Here—there's a passage in this paneled wall that leads to the security office, so we don't have to go out into the hall again."

Abrams motioned with his rifle and O'Brien went to the paneled wall to the right of the fireplace. He pulled on a wall sconce and a hidden door swung open. He turned to Abrams. "You know, I often tried to imagine how it would end. But I never imagined this." He thought a moment, then said, "Do you know what I feel? I feel embarrassed. I'm not looking forward to facing Kate or Van Dorn or the others."

Abrams came closer to O'Brien. "Move."

O'Brien went through the concealed door first, followed by Abrams. They walked through the security office, passed the body of Davis, and went on through the second concealed door, stopping at the base of the stairs. O'Brien said, "If it makes any difference to you, I actually was fond of you."

Abrams thought, *That was the one thing I didn't want to hear.* He looked around the small foyer and listened. It was quiet. He said, "I've decided to save you the embarrassment; I won't drag it out and make you suffer, though you deserve to suffer."

O'Brien opened his mouth to speak.

Abrams lifted his rifle and fired. Patrick O'Brien fell back on the staircase, a surprised look on his face.

Abrams stared at him a long time, then went to find Joan Grenville, thinking, *I knew. I knew all along it was him. We all knew, but none of us can bring ourselves to believe that Daddy is a liar, or that God is a fake, or that the minister is an atheist. That was his strength. He did not have to deceive us, we deceived ourselves.*

CHAPTER SEVENTY-FOUR

Cameron and Sutter had found two bottles of vodka, and Tom Grenville had found a mobile hydraulic hoist that was used to lift repair personnel to the flat roof. They sat now on the roof, with Stewart and General Johnson, passing the bottles around, looking into the clear night sky, waiting. Pembroke was still below because they did not want to move him, and Ann was still on the radio, with Abrams assisting her. Katherine was also below tending to Pembroke.

There was a sound from the hydraulic hoist and Joan Grenville rose from the hatch like an apparition in a Greek play. She stepped off the lift's platform. "Hello, Tom."

He looked up from the bottle. "Hello, Joan." He took another swig, then said, "What are you doing here?"

"I slipped my trolley. May I have that?"

He passed her the bottle and she took a long drink and passed it back. She said, "That's awful stuff."

"Real Russian vodka. Spoils of war."

"You're drunk."

"You're beautiful," said Stewart. "I'm drunk."

Joan glanced at him appraisingly, then turned to Tom. "I told you we should have stayed home tonight."

He said, "Business is business. How many times do I have to explain to you where the money comes from?"

She sat down on the roof. "What are we waiting for?"

Sutter answered, "For the helicopter extraction. Also, we're waiting for the world to end. Look west, young lady."

Joan said, "Which way is west?"

"There," said Sutter, and pointed.

Joan looked toward the western horizon. "I can see Manhattan from here." She looked at Stewart. "May I have another?"

He replied, "Is your leg broken? Mine is. It was very painful until a little while ago." He passed her the bottle grudgingly.

Grenville said, "I lost my watch. Does anyone have the time?"

Johnson answered, "It is zero, zero, zero, five hours."

Grenville looked annoyed. "What time is that in real time?"

Sutter lay back on the roof. "Five after twelve, Tom."

"Well, why didn't he say so?"

"What time is the world going to end?" asked Joan.

Stewart replied, "In one minute, give or take an infinity."

Joan Grenville looked at her husband. "I love you."

Grenville blushed. "Please."

They passed the bottle around and waited.

Ann pushed the microphone away and shut off the transmit switch. She said, "That's all I can do. It's in the laps of the gods now."

Tony Abrams went to a gable window and stared through the broken panes, "You did a good job. If I were the Russian Premier, I'd call it off."

She looked at him. "Would you? I mean, you know them, don't you? I only know their voices and their coded messages. I've never really met one of them until tonight. I know what they say, but not how they think. I don't know their souls."

"No one does. Least of all them." He turned from the window. "They wouldn't even answer us."

She shook her head. "No...they wouldn't do that. They would be admitting to something, and they admit to nothing."

"What time is on that digital clock?"

She looked at the clock. "Twelve-zero-five, and twenty seconds. Molniya is close to its low point."

Katherine walked quickly into the room and approached them. Her face was ashen, and Ann looked at her with concern.

Abrams said, "Pembroke?"

She shook her head. "Dead."

He nodded. He knew it wasn't the time to tell them about O'Brien.

Katherine said, "Well?"

Ann motioned toward the clock. It read 12:06. Ann said, "Look," and pointed.

Abrams and Katherine looked at the three green lights on the electronic display. One by one they all went out.

The digital clock read 12:07, then 12:08. Ann said, "That's it. Molniya is streaking off into space."

Katherine went quickly to the window and stood beside Abrams. "It's a beautiful night after all."

"Yes."

Abrams said to Katherine, "Would you consider breakfast at my place instead?"

"Yes, I'd consider that."

Abrams looked out the window to the north. A golden burst of skyrockets rose over Van Dorn's property, and in the distance the green and red navigation lights of a helicopter approached. Abrams said, "Well, I feel good."

Ann replied, "It's good to be alive, isn't it?" She rubbed her forehead. "But we've lost some good friends tonight. Nick included, I'm afraid." She looked at Katherine and Abrams. "You'd make good partners. Are you joining the firm, Tony?"

He hesitated, then said, "Yes...yes, I will join the firm. There's still a lot to be done."

Abrams took Katherine's hand and looked out the window again. "The storm has passed."

Katherine said, "Yes. And we've weathered it. But this is just a reprieve. Let's use the time we've won more wisely."

John Corey is back and in the middle of a
new Cold War with a clock-ticking plot that
has Manhattan in its crosshairs.

Please turn this page
for an excerpt from

Radiant Angel

I f I wanted to see assholes all day, I would have become a proc-
tologist. Instead, I watch assholes for my country.

I was parked in a black Chevy Blazer down the street from the
Russian Federation Mission to the United Nations on East 67th
Street in Manhattan, waiting for an asshole named Vasily Petrov
to appear. Petrov is a colonel in the Russian Foreign Intelligence
Service—the SVR in Russian—which is the equivalent to our CIA,
and the successors to the Soviet KGB. Vasily—whom we have affec-
tionately code-named Vaseline—has diplomatic status as Deputy
Representative to the UN for Human Rights Issues—which is
a joke—but his real job is SVR Legal Resident in New York—the
equivalent of a CIA Station Chief. I have had Colonel Petrov under
the eye on previous occasions, and though I've never met him he's
reported to be a very dangerous man, and thus an asshole.

I'm John Corey, by the way, former NYPD homicide detective,
now working for the federal government as a contract agent. My
NYPD career was cut short by three bullets that left me seventy-five
percent disabled (twenty-five percent per bullet?) for retirement pay
purposes. In fact, there's nothing wrong with me physically, though
the mental health exam for this job was a bit of a challenge.

Anyway, sitting next to me behind the wheel was a young lady
I'd worked with before, Tess Faraday. Tess was maybe early thirties,
auburn hair, tall, trim, and attractive. Also in the SUV, looking over

my shoulder, was my wife, Kate Mayfield, who was actually in Washington, but I could feel her presence. If you know what I mean.

Tess asked me, "Do I have time to go to the john, John?" She thought that was funny.

"You have a bladder problem?"

"I shouldn't have had that coffee."

"You had two." Guys on surveillance pee in the container and throw it out the window. I said, "Okay, but be quick."

She exited the vehicle and double-timed it to a Starbucks around the corner on Third Avenue.

Meanwhile, Vasily Petrov could come out of the Mission at any time, get into his chauffeur-driven Mercedes S550, and off he goes.

But I've got three other mobile units, plus four agents on legs, so Vasily is covered while I, the team leader, am sitting here while Ms. Faraday is sitting on the potty.

And what do we think Colonel Petrov is up to? We have no idea. But he's up to *something*. That's why he's here. And that's why I'm here.

In fact, Petrov arrived only about four months ago, and it's the recent arrivals who are sometimes sent on the field with a new game play, and these guys need more watching than the SVR agents who've been stationed here awhile and who are engaged in routine espionage. Watch the new guys.

The Russian UN Mission occupies a thirteen-story brick building with a wrought-iron fence in front of it, conveniently located across the street from the 19th Precinct, whose surveillance cameras keep an eye on the Russians 24/7. The Russians don't mind being watched by the NYPD because they're also protected from pissed-off demonstrators and people who'd like to plant a bomb outside their front door. FYI, I live five blocks north of here on East 72nd, so I don't have far to walk when I get off duty at four. I could almost taste the Buds in my fridge.

So I sat there, waiting for Vasily Petrov and Tess Faraday. It was a nice day in early September: one of those beautiful, dry and sunny days you get after the dog days of August. It was a Sunday, a little after 10 A.M., so the streets and sidewalks of New York were relatively quiet. I volunteered for Sunday duty because Mrs. Corey (my wife, not my mother) was in Washington for a weekend conference, returning tonight or tomorrow morning, and I'd rather be working than trying to find something to do on a Sunday.

Also, today was September 11, a day I usually go to at least one memorial service with Kate, but it seemed more appropriate for me to mark this day by doing what I do.

There is a heightened alert every September 11 since 2001, but this year we hadn't picked up any specific intel that Abdul was up to something. And it being a Sunday, there weren't enough residents or office workers in the city for Abdul to murder. September 11, however, is September 11, and there were a lot of people working today to make sure that this was just another quiet Sunday.

Kate was in D.C. because she's an FBI special agent with the Anti-Terrorist Task Force, headquartered downtown at 26 Federal Plaza. Special Agent Mayfield was recently promoted to Supervisory Special Agent, and her new duties take her to Washington a lot. She sometimes goes with her boss, Special-Agent-in-Charge Tom Walsh, who used to be my ATTF boss, too, but I don't work for him or the ATTF any longer. And that's a good thing for both of us. We were not compatible. Walsh, however, likes Kate, and I think the feeling is mutual. I wasn't sure Walsh was with Kate on this trip because I never ask, and she rarely volunteers the information.

On a less annoying subject, I now work for the Diplomatic Surveillance Group—the DSG. The group is also headquartered at 26 Fed, but with this new job I don't need to be at headquarters much, if at all.

My years in the Mideast section of the Anti-Terrorist Task Force were interesting, but stressful. And according to Kate, I was the cause of much of that stress. Wives see things husbands don't see. Bottom line, I had some issues and run-ins with the Muslim community (and my FBI bosses) that led directly or indirectly to my being asked by my superiors if I'd like to find other employment. Walsh suggested the Diplomatic Surveillance Group, which would keep me (a) out of his sight, (b) out of his office, and (c) out of trouble.

Sounded good. Kate thought so, too. In fact, she got the promotion after I left.

Coincidence?

My Nextel phone is also a two-way radio, and it blinged. Tess's voice said, "John, do you want a doughnut or something?"

"Did you wash your hands?"

Tess laughed. She thinks I'm funny. "What do you want?"

"A chocolate chip cookie."

"Coffee?"

"No." I signed off.

Tess's career goal is to become an FBI special agent, and to do that she has to qualify for appointment under one of five entry programs—accounting, computer science, language, law, or what's called "diversified experience." Tess is an attorney and thus qualifies. Most failed lawyers become judges or politicians, but Tess tells me she wants to do something meaningful, whatever that means. Meanwhile, she's working with the Diplomatic Surveillance Group.

Most of the DSG men and women are second-career people, twenty-year retirees from various law enforcement agencies, so we have mostly experienced agents and ex-cops mixed with inexperienced young attorneys like Tess Faraday who see the Diplomatic Surveillance Group as a stepping-stone where they can get some street creds that look good on their FBI app.

Tess got back in the SUV and handed me an oversized cookie. "My treat."

She had another cup of coffee. Some people never learn.

She was wearing khaki cargo pants, a blue polo shirt, and running shoes, which are necessary if the target goes off on foot. Her pants and shirt were loose enough to hide a gun, but Tess is not authorized to carry a gun.

In fact, Diplomatic Surveillance Group agents are theoretically not authorized to carry guns. But we're not as stupid as the people who make the rules, so almost all the ex-cops carry. In situations like this, where I bend the rules, my personal motto is *Better to face twelve jurors than to be carried by six pallbearers.* Therefore, I had my

9mm Glock in a pancake holster in the small of my back, beneath my loose-fitting polo shirt.

So we waited for Vasily to show.

Colonel Petrov lives in a big high-rise in the upscale Riverdale section of the Bronx. This building, which we call the 'plex—short for complex—is owned and wholly occupied by the Russians who work at the UN, and it is a nest of spies. The building itself, located on a high hill, sprouts more antennas than a garbage can full of cockroaches.

The National Security Agency, of course, has a facility nearby where they listen to the Russians who are listening to us, and we all have fun trying to block each other's signals. And round it goes. The only thing that has changed since the days of the Cold War is the encryption codes.

On a less technological level, the game is still played on the ground as it has been forever. Follow that spy. The Diplomatic Surveillance Group also has a confidential off-site facility—what we call the Bat Cave—near the Russian apartment complex, and the DSG team who was watching the 'plex this morning reported that Vasily Petrov had left, and they followed him here to the Mission, where my team picked up the surveillance.

The Russians don't usually work in the office on Sundays, so my guess was that Vasily was in transit to someplace else—or that he was going back to the 'plex—and that he'd be coming out shortly and getting into his chauffeur-driven Benz.

Colonel Petrov, according to the intel, is married, but his wife and children have remained in Moscow. This in itself is suspicious because the families of the Russian UN delegation love to live in New York on the government ruble. Or maybe there's an innocent explanation for the husband-wife separation. Like they hate each other.

Tess informed me, "I have two tickets to the Mets doubleheader today." She further informed me, "I'd like to catch at least the last game."

"You can listen to them lose both games on the radio."

"I'll pretend you didn't say that." She reminded me, "We're supposed to be relieved at four."

"You can relieve yourself anytime you want."

She didn't reply.

A word about Tess Faraday. Did I say she was tall, slim, and attractive? She also swims and plays paddleball, whatever that is. She's fairly sharp, and intermittently enthusiastic, and I guess she's idealistic, which is why she left her Wall Street law firm to apply for the FBI, where the money is not as good.

But money is probably not an issue with Ms. Faraday. She mentioned to me that she was born and raised in Lattingtown, an upscale community on the North Shore of Long Island, also known as the Gold Coast. And by her accent and mannerisms I can deduce that she came from some money and good social standing. People like that who want to serve their country usually go to the State Department or into intelligence work, not the FBI. But I give her credit for what she's doing and I wish her luck.

Also, needless to say, Tess Faraday and John Corey have little in common, though we get along during these days and hours of forced intimacy.

One thing we do have in common is that we're both married. His name is Grant, and he's some kind of international finance guy, and he travels a lot for his work. I've never met Grant, and I probably never will, but he likes to text and call his wife a lot. I deduce, by Tess's end of the conversation, that Grant is the jealous type, and Tess seems a bit impatient with him. At least when I'm in earshot of the conversation.

Tess inquired, "If Petrov goes mobile, do we stay with him, or do we hand him over to another team?"

"Depends."

"On what?"

"No, I mean you should wear Depends."

One of us thought that was funny.

But to answer Tess's question, if Vasily went mobile, most probably my team would stay with him. He wasn't supposed to travel farther than a twenty-five-mile radius from Columbus Circle without

State Department permission, and according to my briefing he hadn't applied for a weekend travel permit. The Russians rarely did, and when they did they would apply on a Friday afternoon so that no one at State had time to approve or disapprove their travel plans. And off they'd go, in their cars or by train or bus to someplace outside their allowed radius. Usually the women were just going shopping at some discount mall in Jersey, and the men were screwing around in Atlantic City. But sometimes the SVR or the Military Intelligence guys—the GRU—were meeting people, or looking at things that they shouldn't be looking at, like nuclear reactors. That's why we follow them. But we almost never bust them. The FBI, of which the DSG is a part, is famous—or infamous—for watching people and collecting evidence for years. Cops act on evidence. The FBI waits until the suspect dies of old age.

I said to Tess, "Let me know now if you can't stay past four. I'll call for a replacement."

She replied, "I'm yours."

"Wonderful."

"But if we get off at four, I have an extra ticket."

I considered my reply, then said, perhaps unwisely, "I take it Mr. Faraday is out of town."

"He is."

"Why have we not heard from Grant this morning?"

"I told him I was on a very discreet—and quiet—surveillance."

"You're learning."

"I don't need to learn what I already know."

"Right." Escape and evasion. Perhaps Grant had reason to be jealous. *You think?*

Regarding the nature of our surveillance of Colonel Vasily Petrov, this was actually a nondiscreet surveillance—what we call a bumper lock, meaning we were going to be up Vaseline's ass all day. They always spotted a bumper-lock surveillance, and sometimes they acknowledged the DSG agents with a hard stare—or if they were pricks they gave you the Italian salute.

Vasily was particularly unfriendly, probably because he was an intel officer, a big wheel in the Motherland, and he found it galling to be on the receiving end of a surveillance. Well, fuck him. Everybody's got a job to do.

Vasily sometimes plays games with the surveillance team, and he's actually given us the slip twice in the last four months or so, which has earned him the name Vaseline. He's never given me the slip, but some other DSG teams lost him. And there's hell to pay when you lose the SVR resident. And that wasn't going to happen on my watch. I don't lose anyone. Well, I lost my wife once in Bloomingdale's. I can't figure out the logic of a woman's shopping habits. They don't think like us.

"So do you want to go to the game?"

Mrs. Faraday had already started the game. But okay, two colleagues going to a baseball game after work is innocent enough. Even when they're married and their spouses are out of town. No problem. Right? I said, "I'll take a rain check."

"Okay." She asked me, "You going to eat that cookie?"

I broke it in half and gave her the bigger half.

Surveillances can be boring, which is why some people try to make it not boring. Two guys together talk about women, and two women together probably talk about guys. A guy and a woman together either have nothing to talk about, or the long hours lead to whatever.

In the last six months, Tess Faraday has been assigned to me about a dozen times, which, with 150 DSG agents in New York, defies the odds. As the team leader, I could reassign her to another vehicle or to leg surveillance. But I haven't. Why? Because I think she's asking to work with me, and being a very sensitive man, I don't want to hurt her feelings. And why does she want to work with me? Because she wants to learn from a master. Or something else is going on.

And, by the way, I haven't mentioned Tess Faraday to Kate. Kate is not the jealous type and there's nothing to be jealous about. Also, like Kate, I keep my work problems and associations to myself. Kate doesn't talk about Tom Walsh, and I don't talk about Tess Faraday. Marital ignorance is bliss. Dumb is happy.

Meanwhile, Vasily has been inside the Mission for over an hour, but his Mercedes is still outside, so he's going someplace. Probably back to the Bronx. He sometimes runs in Central Park, which is a pain in the ass. Everyone on the team wears running shoes, of course, and I think we're all in good shape, but Vasily is in excellent shape. Older FBI agents have told me that the Soviet KGB guys were mostly lard-asses who smoked and drank too much. But these guys from the new Russia were into granola and health clubs. Their boss, bare-chested Putin, sort of set the new standard.

Vasily, being who he is, also has a girlfriend in town, a Russian lady named Svetlana who sings at a few of the Russian nightclubs in Brighton Beach. I caught a glimpse of her once, and she looks like she has good lungs.

I did a radio check with my team and everyone was awake.

A soft breeze fluttered the white, blue, and red Russian flag in front of the Mission. I remember when the Soviet hammer and sickle flew there. I kind of miss the Cold War. But I think it's back.

My team today consists of four leg agents and four vehicles—my Chevy Blazer, a Ford Explorer, and two Dodge minivans. We usually have one agent in each vehicle, but today we had two. Why? Because the Russians are particularly tricky, and sometimes they travel in groups and scatter like cockroaches, so recently we've been beefing up the surveillance teams. So today I had two DSG agents in the other three vehicles, all former NYPD. I had the only trainee, an FBI wannabe who probably thinks the DSG job sucks. Sometimes I think the same thing.

In the parlance of the FBI, the DSG is called a quiet end, which really means a dead end.

But I'm okay with this. No office, no adult supervision, and no bullshit. Just follow that asshole. And do not lose that asshole.

A quiet end. But in this business, there is no such thing.